# BIOTERROR

## TIM CURRAN

Crystal Lake Publishing
Where Stories Come Alive!

www.crystallakepub.com

First published by Bloodshot Books in 2021



Join the Crystal Lake community today
on our newsletter and Patreon!
https://linktr.ee/CrystalLakePublishing

Download our latest catalog here:
https://geni.us/CLPCatalog



ISBN: 978-1-964398-37-2

Cover Art: Wendy Saber Core | www.sabercore23art.com
Layout: Jacque Day | jacqueday.com



Follow us on Amazon:

# WELCOME
## TO ANOTHER

# CRYSTAL LAKE PUBLISHING
## CREATION

# MAY 12

# WASHINGTON D.C.

## NATIONAL MILITARY COMMAND CENTER, THE PENTAGON

**2:10 P.M.**

It was a small group, but a powerful one.

Charles VanderMissen, Director of National Intelligence, had called them together on a moment's notice to discuss a matter that was vexing the intelligence community.

"What's this all about, Chuck?" General Mason asked. "What's all the hoo-ha?"

VanderMissen and Robert Pershing, Director of the Central Intelligence Agency, exchanged a quick look. In his three-piece suit and Rolex, Pershing looked very much like the corporate CEO he in fact was. DNI VanderMissen sat down and greeted each in turn.

Lieutenant-General Walter Sleshing, Director of the DIA. Rear Admiral Colin Paulus, Director of the ONI. Brigadier General Francis K. Mason, the Chairman of the Joint Chiefs of Staff. Arlene Rabin, the Secretary of State. Roger Thorogood, Secretary of Defense. And Gus Costello, the National Security Advisor. All were high-ranking members of the National Security Council. Each man represented the real power in his respective group. There were no aides, no deputy directors, no one but those in charge.

VanderMissen sighed. "Well, by this point you're all pretty familiar with the situation in Syria, particularly in the eastern desert, and the connection between Islamic extremists and our old friend, President Ahmadinejad of Iran."

They were. It was something they'd been over again and again, but considering the touchy political situation a resolution to the problem was not forthcoming. Basically, ever since the close of the war, Iraq had been destabilized by constant acts of aggression between Sunni and Shiite radicals while the rest of the population quietly covered their heads and wondered which direction it would be coming from next. The thing was, the world intelligence community knew exactly what direction it would be coming from: Syria.

During the war, it was widely known that Syria was the main conduit for the mujahideen insurgents fighting in Iraq and when Al-Qaeda's infrastructure was decimated by coalition forces, they quickly retreated over the border into the Syrian Desert, a traditional stronghold of smugglers, outlaws, and subversives. And it was there, under the leadership of Sheikh Sa'ad al Khalafari, an Egyptian national and something of a charismatic leader in jihadi circles, that an Iranian connection was cemented solidly into place. Again, no surprise. The Iranians were the primary exporters of state-sponsored terror in the region. They had funneled cash, weapons, and foreign extremists into the Iraqi conflict. In the years since, Sheikh Sa'ad had frequently been the guest of the Pasdaran, the Iranian Revolutionary Guards Corps, at their training facilities and received logistical support from the Pasdaran Quds Force, a special operations unit that actively supported and trained members of Hezbollah, Hamas, Palestinian Islamic Jihad, and assorted Iraqi Shi'a militants.

Within the last eight months, Sheikh Sa'ad had developed something of a safe zone in the Syrian Desert, welding together his fragmentary Al-Qaeda network with Ba'athist separatists and Islamic Jund al-Sham into a formidable terror army, again with the support of Iran and the ISIS caliphate. There had been numerous clashes between Syrian security forces and Sheikh Sa'ad's somewhat disparate organization, but with the protection of the Mukhabarat, Syria's secret intelligence service, they had survived again and again.

There was no doubt in anyone's mind that the ultimate goal of Sheikh Sa'ad's group was not only the destabilization of western influence in the region, but the ultimate sacking of Israel...something many Syrians actively supported.

These things were widely known by VanderMissen and the others in the room, but now there was a new wrinkle.

"There's something going on in the desert," he said to them. "Something that Sheikh Sa'ad might be involved in...possibly coincidentally, but it may be a situation he will exploit with the help of the Islamic Revolutionary Guard."

Gus Costello raised an eyebrow. "Such as?"

"We know all about that bastard. We know where his camps are," General Mason said with his usual gruff delivery. "I was all for hitting them six months ago. One good airstrike and bye-bye one more raghead maggot."

Arlene Rabin said, "The President doesn't consider that prudent at this time."

Mason just glared at her like she was a naïve punk kid.

The Secretary of Defense sighed. "You haven't called us here for that, have you, Chuck? We've been all through this."

Admiral Paulus checked his watch. "Christ, I canceled a late lunch with the Russian Ambassador, gentlemen. I said all I had to say about those goddamn idiots the other day."

DCI Pershing held up his hands. "Let's all relax here, shall we?" He turned to VanderMissen. "You got the floor, Chuck."

The others waited.

"What we have here, gentlemen," VanderMissen continued, "may be something a helluva lot worse than some ragtag army setting off car bombs in Baghdad. You see, the area in question has been cordoned off and not even Syrian civilians are allowed in there."

"Not those ISIS fuckwits again," Mason said.

"Worse."

"Meaning?" Sleshing asked.

"Let me lay it out for you." VanderMissen got up and went to the plasma display on the wall. "This, as you know, is a map of western Iraq/Eastern Syria. The area we're concerned with is right here—" he pointed to a section just east of the Jordanian border "—the Badiyat ash Sham, the Western Desert. This area marked by the blue rectangle has been cordoned off by the military. No one's coming in or going out. About all we've been able to get from Ambassador Khassim is that they've had an outbreak of some virulent disease."

Sleshing licked his lips. "What sort of disease?"

"Again, he's not saying. He contends that his government considers it an internal problem and it will be handled internally."

"What of it?" General Mason said. "Way those people live it's no surprise. They're in the middle of a civil war for chrissake."

"Please, General," the Secretary of State said.

"Any buzz?" SecDef Thorogood asked.

"Nothing." VanderMissen tapped the plasma display and it became a grainy photographic blow-up. "However, we have some SatIntel. Not much, but enough to worry about."

Gus Costello, the National Security Advisor and the only black man in this exclusively white club, just watched and listened. Occasionally he chewed his lower lip, but nothing more. His face was tight with fear. Something was coming and he knew it.

SecState Rabin said, "That area...about how large are we talking here?"

"About fifty square miles, give or take," VanderMissen said.

Sleshing's much furrowed brow slouched, his eyes darkened.

"If memory serves me, this is the same general locality as Nkudbkah on the Iraqi side...isn't it?"

Admiral Paulus knew what he was getting at. "Oh come on, that whole business was six fucking years ago. There's no way it could be active. Right, Chuck?"

VanderMissen didn't answer him. "Nkudbkah is just east of the area mentioned."

"BioGen," Thorogood said, looking like he needed a good cry.

Costello and SecState Rabin just looked at each other. They had no idea what any of this was about.

"BioGen?" Costello said, shaking his head. "I'm not familiar with that one."

DNI VanderMissen sighed. "No, Gus, neither you or Arlene were in office back then. The rest of us, however, were in some capacity. We were involved in BioGen. All of us. The President wants you brought in now."

VanderMissen explained exactly what BioGen was and how it had been used and it wasn't long before the National Security Advisor and the Secretary of State wore the same pained expressions as the others in that room.

"What in God's name were you people thinking?" Rabin put to them.

"Maybe we weren't," Paulus admitted.

There was silence after that.

The men did not look at each other. Hands were studied, gum chewed, but eyes did not make contact. Had VanderMissen told them the President had just been assassinated, the silence could not have been more total, more complete, more tainted with dread.

Thorogood had to clutch his hands together to keep them from shaking.

"I always wondered what the fallout from that would be. Jesus Christ in Heaven," the Secretary of Defense said.

"Just keep your shirt on," General Mason said to him, lighting a cigarette even though smoking was forbidden in federal buildings. No one dared remind him of the fact. "Let's not jump to conclusions here, people, okay? Christ, you ought to see yourselves. You look like virgins on prom night about to get their tickets punched." He smoked slowly, deliberately. A veteran of the past five administrations in one capacity or another and all the shit and backhanded politics that entailed, he did not panic easily. The way he saw it, if he had kept his nerve through the past three wars and numerous minor conflicts and had not even broke a sweat for eight months as a POW in a North Vietnamese prison camp, he was not about to start pissing his pants now over something that was just a big maybe in his book.

"So... why wasn't this... situation... brought up at the Council the other day?"

Now all eyes were upon him, glaring.

"Well?" he said.

"We needed confirmation," VanderMissen explained. "This is a very classified issue. Beyond ourselves, the President, and Section 5, nobody knows about Project BioGen," VanderMissen reminded him. "Certain members of the Council are in the dark and the President wishes them to remain so."

"I wish to God I was one of them," Admiral Paulus admitted.

"You're conveniently leaving out CBT," Thorogood said.

VanderMissen sighed. "Nobody's leaving out CBT's culpability. Elizabeth Toma has been appraised of the situation."

CBT was Congdon BioTech, a multinational biotechnology firm that regularly did work for the Defense Department and intelligence communities. They handled the R & D on Project BioGenesis and were instrumental in its implementation. Toma was their CEO and had her dirty fingers in a lot of pies.

Thorogood grumbled but said no more.

DNI VanderMissen cleared his throat. "At any rate, this mysterious epidemic seems to be in the general area of the test sight, Nkudbkah...that is, just over the border into Syria. A matter of less than a mile. And that's what's worrying me. Worrying the President. He asked me to look into this personally." VanderMissen pointed to his photos. "Sat shows a locality of great military activity. You can see here what I'm told are trucks and armored vehicles, all surrounding a village called El Badji. El Badji is a small agricultural village of perhaps a hundred. Nothing there really but farmers and their families. Some Bedouin sheepherders. No industrial or military sites."

"Nothing else but a few Al-Qaeda shitheads," Mason said.

General Sleshing held up his left hand, scrutinizing it. The middle and index fingers were missing, courtesy of a Chicom landmine during the Tet Offensive of '68. "Any possibility it could be something else, Chuck? Some random infectious disease?"

"Could very well be."

"Sounds reasonable," Admiral Paulus chimed in.

"Too reasonable," Rabin said.

"But let's not depend on it," Chairman Mason said. "As usual, boys, why don't we play it safe? Worst-case scenario. What if it is fallout from BioGen? What if that's what we're talking about? Then that area needs to be sterilized immediately. I don't think I need to impress on anyone in this room the need for that."

"I don't like all that military hardware in there," Costello said. "It doesn't look like a medical response op to me. It feels wrong."

"Yes, it does," VanderMissen agreed. "Our concerns are that if this is some rogue resurgence of BioGen, that Sheikh Sa'ad and his Iranian friends might take advantage of the situation and weaponize what they find."

"And if they don't," Mason said, "the Syrian army and their Russian advisors sure as hell will."

"If they know what it is," the Secretary of Defense put in.

"Oh, they'll know. With Iranian Quds advisors with them, they'll know. Those boys are no fools," DCI Pershing pointed out. "There were a lot of questions asked about Nkudbkah—if you may remember—a lot of whispers amongst rival intelligence agencies. I wouldn't be surprised if Quds has been waiting for something like this."

Admiral Paulus sighed. "The way I understood it, that whole BioGen thing was over and done with six years ago. Isn't that what your boys assured us, Chuck? That a resurgence was impossible?"

"Improbable not impossible," VanderMissen pointed out.

"The entire area was sterilized, though," DDI Sleshing said. "At least...that's what we were told."

But nobody bit on that. They all well knew that in the world of covert ops what you were told and what really happened were often two different things.

Thorogood kept shaking his head. "Dammit. This could destroy all of us. You damn well know it."

"One step at a time, people," Mason said. "First off, what we need to do is find out what's happening before we jump the gun. Secondly, BioGen was a S5 operation—"

"Which dumps it firmly in the lap of the CIA," Thorogood pointed out, ever eyeballing his political future.

Pershing narrowed his eyes. "For God's sake, you're not going to hang me on this. Section Five had presidential clearance to test certain exotic battlefield technologies. That included biological weapons. I was not responsible for their nature."

"And you ran this particular clusterfuck past the President at the time?" Thorogood asked pointedly.

"Not...precisely," Pershing said. "It was a test. A feasibility study. Nothing more."

He didn't need to elaborate any more than that. It was common knowledge to everyone in the room that there were a great many things the acting POTUS never learned, regardless of the administration. Many gray areas that were allowed to remain gray. Essentially, anything vetted above top secret was purposely kept from the commander in chief. It was strictly need-to-know. This allowed the President a certain flexibility in denial and maintained the integrity of the office in the case of a crisis. If he or she didn't know about certain intelligence operations, no one could ever accuse them of lying to the country. In this way, POTUS saved his or her ass and the various agencies could operate freely (and often recklessly). Plausible deniability.

If the President, on the other hand, demanded information and it was withheld, that would be considered treasonous behavior. But very few of them ever wanted to know. It was easier to lie about things when you didn't in fact know you were lying.

"Okay, okay," General Mason finally said. "Quit pointing fingers already. Everyone take a deep breath."

"Exactly," DCI Pershing said.

"Right." VanderMissen drew their attention to the display again. "This photo shows what appears to be dump trucks. Dump trucks loaded with bodies. And right down here—" he indicated a large dark area "—looks very much like a pit. A mass grave, we're assuming. This truck here seems to be dumping its load into it."

"Whatever's going on," Thorogood said, "it's gotta be pretty damn bad."

VanderMissen brought up another photo on the display. "This is the last one of any real quality."

"What's that smudge?" Rabin said. "Is that—"

"Smoke," DCI Pershing said. "They're burning those bodies."

Silence again.

Sure, there was always the chance that this was some perfectly innocent outbreak of infectious disease. Such things happened. This was the hope running through everyone's mind. In fact, it was more than a hope. It was a mantra they clung to and kept repeating in the confines of their heads.

But it was so close to the original BioGen target area...

That's what bothered each and every one of them. Ever since Nkudbkah was exposed to BioGen, the U.S. intelligence community had been keeping a tight eye on that particular stretch of real estate. For six years...nothing.

But now—

"At least they moved on whatever it was quickly," Admiral Paulus said. "Maybe it's the Syrian army. Maybe it's not Sheikh Sa'ad or those Iranian assholes. Maybe."

"But if it is," DDI Sleshing said in an ominous tone, "if those ragheads have the technology to collect, proliferate, and weaponize BioGen... Jesus, our political futures are the least of our worries. And I don't think I need to elaborate on that."

VanderMissen cleared his throat. "These photos were all taken by Comm-Star One yesterday evening. Tonight we'll have others when it makes its pass...but we can't keep holding our breath and hoping for the best. The President wants some action taken. He wants confirmation or denial. And he wants it yesterday."

"We'd need some human intelligence for that," Mason said, expressing exactly what they were all thinking. "Without HUMINT, without someone on the ground..."

Costello shook his head. "Shit, Syria's a hard target. Especially these days. Do we have anyone solid?"

All eyes went to DCI Pershing, the resident spymaster. He shook his head. "No... we don't have any assets I'd trust with something of this magnitude. Everything's in disarray since the withdrawal of our forces."

Mason lit another cigarette. "Screw it. This is too big. Get some drones in there."

VanderMissen shook his head. "We've already lost two in the attempt. One had mechanical failure, the other was shot down."

Mason said, "All right, put Delta Force or some SEALs on the ground, recon the situation."

SecDef Thorogood shook his dead. "No. I wouldn't want any conventional SpecOps in on this."

"Those boys are hardly conventional," Mason pointed out.

"No, this is too...touchy."

"Well, get some spooks in there then."

VanderMissen smiled, sitting down, liking as always Mason's direct line of thinking. "Bob?"

DCI Pershing got up before the display. He went back to the map. He looked at those gathered, slowly, thoughtfully. "As of tonight, we're going to do just that. We will have someone on the ground."

Everyone looked at him.

"As we speak, a SAC/SOG team is on its way to Cypress," he explained referring to the CIA's clandestine Special Activities Center and the elite Special Operations Group, its paramilitary wing. "Tonight the SOG team will be in Kuwait. And tomorrow night—tomorrow afternoon for us—they'll parachute into the desert. We're going to get some actionable intel on this one way or another, gentlemen."

# RICHMOND, VIRGINIA

## CBT CORPORATE HEADQUARTERS

**6:10 P.M.**

*Ah,* Elizabeth Toma thought with some amusement, *the world spins, revolves, rotates, and the only constant is survival and death.* And though this might have been a chilling, helpless realization for someone else, to Elizabeth it was validation of her personal belief system. No more, no less.

Through the windows of her executive suite, she looked out over the VA Bio+Tech Park, a sprawling vertical city of glass towers and boxes, prismatic atriums, and glazed façades like greenhouses stacked one atop another. They dazzled the eye and stretched the mind with their abstract architecture. Pretty, pretty, pretty. Modern and multifunctional, the campus of Virginia Commonwealth in the distance, it was the seething lair of researchers, entrepreneurs, financiers and executives. The shining jewel of the Mid-Atlantic Biotech Corridor.

"And nothing but anthills," she said under her breath.

And that was going to become all-too apparent in the coming weeks as all that the masses had come to believe in and trust came crashing down around them. Maybe they didn't see their modern world as a house of cards waiting for a good wind to blow it all down, but that's exactly what it was.

Although on paper CBT conducted cutting-edge research into pharmaceuticals and diagnostics, nanobiotechnology and molecular biology, stem cell bio and global health and synthetics, it was also a major black biology contractor for the Defense Department. In its Level Four biosafety facilities deep underground, CBT routinely amplified hot strains of lethal bioagents, perfected delivery systems for biological weapons, and genetically engineered life forms that could not—and should not—exist under natural conditions.

Though the former activities were perfectly legitimate, the black biology was illegal as hell, yet it went on ceaselessly beneath the noses of the CDC and other regulatory agencies. With billions at stake, there was always a way.

As she waited for Bob Pershing to call, she sipped from a glass of fine Madeira that was over a hundred years old (and went for something like five thousand dollars a bottle if you could find it), a gift from a Russian colleague, and contemplated the end of the world.

She thought of money.

She thought of power.

She contemplated the enormous amount of both that she wielded, the people she had bought and sold, coerced and collected through extortion, controlled with systematic blackmailing by gathering incriminating, embarrassing, or socially damaging information about them and their families. To an outsider, she would have been seen as a corporate weasel, her activities disgusting and reprehensible, but the world of D.C. politics was social Darwinism in action. It was business as usual inside the Beltway and everybody played the game in one way or another.

She controlled an impressive network of politicians, lobbyists, and power players, many of whom opposed the policies she and her confederates pushed, but in the end they drank the Kool-Aid because it was better than being publicly humiliated and tossed out of office. This was the machine she owned and did her bidding.

It made her think of her mom and dad, humble immigrants from Yokohama that simply wanted to fit in and become part of the American dream. They never had any idea what a nightmare it indeed was once you flipped it over and studied its soft, white underbelly in any detail.

She supposed it was as an undergraduate studying biophysics at Rutgers that she first began to question the dream, noticing with rising cynicism that those with power believed they had the God-given right to impose their will upon those who had none. It was how the political structure of the university worked, from the administrative branches to the departments and committees.

Yes, on paper there was such a thing as democracy, but not in practice. Not in the real world.

It was also at Rutgers where she first read Huxley's *Brave New World*, wherein the future population was pharmaceutically drugged into loving its own servitude. It made her think of her parents and their friends, in fact, all the adults she knew. All of whom were drones that perpetually fooled themselves into believing they were free.

The very idea was ridiculous, of course. By the time your average American had graduated high school, his or her mind was already rigidly controlled and compartmentalized. Conditioned by eighteen years of schooling so they could fit seamlessly into the adult world where their fears and needs would be expertly exploited by those in power. Through spin and psychological manipulation and careful, methodical brainwashing, they would work and pay taxes and vote and even sacrifice their sons and daughters in wars, believing it was an honor to die for something that was realistically no threat to them.

It was known collectively as conformity, of course. But in reality it was a system in which the working class were bound by rules and regulations which the ruling elite were exempt from.

This was how the machine operated.

The only real threat to the machine had been the counterculture back in the 1960s. It became too powerful, too influential, and for a time it seemed the old, well-entrenched power structure might collapse under this global awakening. Such a thing was unacceptable. Which was why it could never be allowed to happen again. Wars were necessary for political maneuvering and corporate profit. Without them, the machine would stop. And it was with this in mind that the military-industrial complex had forever seized control of not only the government and corporate entities, but the media systems, thereby controlling the masses without them ever realizing they were being controlled at all.

The Internet had been a blessing for the spin doctors and social engineers. Here was a way to Big Brother your way into everyone's life at a frenetic pace, overwhelming and confusing them with data overload until they accepted things which would have been abhorrent just a few generations before. It was the perfect tool to continue the dumbing down of the populace who were now a body of non-thinkers and intellectual weaklings conditioned to accept and never question.

That was how the machine ran—fueled by taxpayer dollars, its gears well-greased by the blood of their sons and daughters which they sacrificed willingly.

Elizabeth stared at her phone. "C'mon, Bob," she said under her breath.

She controlled a lot of people, but even she had to answer to someone, and it was these individuals that she dared not disappoint.

The phone rang.

"Well?" she said, dispensing with any form of greeting.

"They reacted exactly as we planned," DCI Pershing said. "It couldn't have gone any smoother. They're afraid. They're willing to do just about anything to control it."

"Good, Bob, good. Keep me posted."

"Count on it."

There. It was beginning. It was finally beginning. Elizabeth sighed. She stared out through the windows, seeing beyond the Bio+Tech Park and into the country itself. Terror was beginning. It already had a foothold that would soon escalate out of control as an extremely unpleasant organism began its burn through the population. She thought of all the people that were going to suffer, to die as a nightmare beyond imagining took their world.

Another swallow of Madeira and she had the strength to make the call to those who stood in the shadows. Because as Bob Dylan had said, we all had to serve somebody. Dabbing sweat from her temple, she did just that.

# MAY 13

# SYRIA'S EASTERN DESERT

## EL BADJI

**12:41 A.M. SYRIAN TIME**

"All right, girls," Colonel Loomis hissed in the darkness, "drop your socks and grab your cocks, stow that gear or we'll be having breakfast in a Damascus prison."

He watched his team cut into the hard, dry earth with their shovels, digging deeper and deeper until they had a nice trench going. Quietly, carefully, the parachutes, packs, and jump helmets were placed in it. Not thrown, but placed gently like newborns into cribs.

*That's it*, Loomis thought, *bury it up real nice. Pack it down tight, spread a light layer of soil and rocks over it. The wind will do the rest. By morning, nobody will ever spot it.*

When they were done, the five of them gathered around Loomis in the murk.

"Before we go, remember this is strictly recon. I want noise discipline," he told them, even thought they were all pros and knew better. "We'll take a look, grab a few snapshots and some video, then back to the LZ for extraction. Any questions? Good. Pitts take the point. You know the way."

The Syrian desert at the Iraqi border was like the dark side of the moon.

Hundreds of desolate miles of bleak, rocky nothingness. The wind howled and carried the ugly cold bite of the winter that was to come. It was like Antarctica: endless, alien, lonely. Hot as a frying pan in the summer, colder than a meat locker in winter. May was a transitional time in the desert: cold nights and warm days. It was home to Bedouin nomads and their scraggly herds of sheep and goats. Lizards, poisonous snakes, wiry grasses, thorny bushes. Not much else but sand, rocks, and time itself. It was a place where a stranger could get lost at night mere feet from his door. Where the night and sand and blowing wind created a nightmare landscape of confusion.

On maps, trails and landmarks were easily sighted, easily followed; on the ground—particularly in the desert—they merged, moved, and vanished entirely. But Loomis wasn't worried about getting lost.

He'd been here numerous times.

Maybe not this particular stretch of real estate, but in others very similar in Iraq and Iran, Afghanistan and Yemen. He was a twenty-odd year veteran of special operations. There were few hotspots or hellholes he hadn't waded through in that time. Jungles, deserts, swamps, and frozen mountain tops were home to him. He could navigate his way through the worse terrain and often just by instinct. You got that way after a while.

If you lived long enough.

Loomis had handpicked this team on a moment's notice.

He was traveling in good company.

Dunn was second in command. An eighteen year veteran of the Navy SEALs, he was a Navy Cross winner and was literally unstoppable: nothing got between him and his target. If they did, they usually ended up with a bullet in their head or with their throats slit or necks snapped. Creech was an ex-SAS sergeant major. He'd honed his deadly skills in Northern Ireland, Oman, and Malaya. Like Dunn, absolutely lethal. Then there was Childress. A veteran of the Army Rangers and Green Berets, he lived entirely for operations like this. It was the only time he came to life. It was in his blood. Pitts, a fifteen-year veteran of Marine Corps special operations and Horse, a Delta Force vet, rounded out the team. Horse was a full-blooded Cree Indian and the best scout/sniper Loomis had ever seen. His tracking skills were almost supernatural.

They were all good.

Dressed in black fatigues with black watch caps pulled down over their ears, their faces were smeared with black camo grease. They wore fingerless black neoprene gloves and Night Vision goggles. Although they carried a lot of equipment—radios, machine pistols, knives, cameras—nothing made a sound as they stalked the desert. Everything was strapped or taped down. And anything with a shine to it was painted flat black.

They were shadows and nothing more.

They carried neutral equipment from a dozen countries, sported no vanity tattoos or piercings. If they died out there, no one would be able to tell what country they'd come from. And none of them would be taken alive. If they had to die, they'd kill as many of the enemy as possible before taking their own lives.

Each man had a cyanide tablet taped to his wrist.

Once it was bitten, death came quickly.

Loomis studied the terrain as they went—hills, rocky outcroppings, scrubby brush, and hard-packed plateau. Although it was monotonous country to the extreme, Loomis committed it to memory. He was always on the lookout for defensible perimeters, good ambush and kill zones. The NV goggles gave everything a surreal, greenish cast. He was sure they were going the right way, yet from time to time he stopped and checked GPS. ten thousand miles above, TACSAT was guiding them in the right direction, watching their every move and sending a real-time transmission of the same back to the Pentagon.

Up ahead, Pitts halted, crouching down. The others followed suit.

"What do you got?" Loomis whispered into his throat mike.

"Three camels...no, four...with riders coming over the ridge," Pitts voice said in his earphone.

"Into the rocks," Loomis said.

The six of them melted into the jagged fissures of volcanic rock. The camels, as promised, made their appearance. They and their riders halted at the top of the ridge. Bedouins, Loomis saw. Dressed in dusty robes and checkered khafias, they were armed with old WWII bolt-action rifles. They seemed to be looking for something. Their leader, an old man who sported a beard nearly to his belly, pointed off to the west and they rode away. Bedouins were not unfriendly to strangers, but neither did they trust them nor like them. They did not choose sides. They had no use for armies or governments, for terror groups or the men who hunted them; theirs was a society that predated such things.

The rocky dips and rises gave way to endless rolling sand dunes. In the emerald glow of the NVGs, they were like the crashing waves of some awesome primordial ocean frozen in time. Pitts went up the ridge, went down on his knees, looked around. He motioned to the team and they followed him into the sea of sand.

It seemed to go for days.

In reality, it was less than two hours walking time. Had it been nice, flat earth, they would've made their target in forty-five minutes or less. But with the dunes and rocks and the constant stopping to check the GPS and Pitts pausing to scan the horizon... it took time.

But that was okay.

They were all professionals and if special or irregular warfare taught you nothing else, it taught you patience. Loomis knew that well enough. Hours and hours spent lying in the jungle grass on ambush. Weeklong treks behind enemy lines on long-range reconnaissance patrols. Entire days spent hiding in trees waiting for the perfect kill shot on an enemy officer. Day after grueling day spent trailing enemy units to their base camps. The entire time you never spoke, you rarely ate or slept. Sometimes you'd creep up so close, the enemy would urinate on you as you hid in the brush but even then you wouldn't move.

You learned patience. Or you died.

Take Horse for example

When they were in Kuwait back in the '90s, Loomis remembered how Horse would go out at night alone. How he'd stalk an As Saiqa unit, Republican Guard Special Forces, taking them one by one with a silenced rifle. He'd spend hours and hours lining up a kill. And if it was somebody special, say a political officer or extremist operations chief, he'd lay in wait in the same position for days. He'd piss himself, shit himself, go crazy with the bugs biting his face, but he would not move. Not until after he'd pulled the trigger and his quarry's skull had gone to hamburger.

Patience, always patience.

Things had gone good so far, Loomis knew. They'd flown over the border in a Combat Talon cargo plane piloted by men of the Air Force's 20th Special Operations Squadron. The Talon was a souped-up C-130 Hercules loaded with sophisticated navigation and radar-evasion equipment. It could drop a team in and get out and nobody would be the wiser. The Drop Zone was a barren plain four miles south of El Badji. They'd made a quick-delivery para-insertion from six hundred feet. And the great thing was that everyone had made it down okay. No broken bones, no sprains. And that was outstanding when you considered that the DZ consisted of the hard-packed, sun-dried clay of a dry riverbed.

"We got activity ahead," Pitts said in Loomis' ear.

Everyone was already down on their bellies, lizard-crawling up the dune to join him.

They couldn't see too much out there.

Just the night pressing in from all sides, the dull gray Syrian terrain. But in the distance...lights. Flickering, flashing. A small pocket of life.

Loomis knew they'd arrived, but he checked the GPS.

Yeah, no doubt about it: this was El Badji.

"Pitts, Horse...take us in. Rest of you...spread out. Let's do this real slow."

There were great, jagged shelves of volcanic rock jutting from the dry earth. Clusters of boulders and scraggly desert bushes. Plenty of cover. As they got closer they began to hear sporadic gunfire. The staccato bursts of heavy machine guns and the hollow popping of automatic rifles. It sounded like the Fourth of July.


**3:03 A.M.**

El Badji was surrounded by flat barley fields cut by irrigation ditches. The village itself was a collection of drab, crumbling cinderblock buildings, mud huts, and raunchy trailers. A series of canvas tents had sprouted up along the perimeter like mushrooms after a heavy rain.

There were trucks, earth movers, armored personnel carriers, and reconnaissance vehicles everywhere. The entire place was lit up with lanterns and search lights that swept the depressing little village. Men were shouting and engines were revving, women screaming and guns firing.

"What the fuck is going on here?" Childress said, studying the spectacle with a spotting scope.

Loomis couldn't say. He knew no more than the others. He studied the vehicles—a lot of old Soviet war surplus—and the men—a ragtag collection at best: desert-unformed Syrian soldiers intermixed with peasants that carried AK-47s, probably Muslim extremists, a few groups of men in American-style camouflage, most likely members of the Islamic Revolutionary Guard from Iran.

He got on the encrypted net and reported what he saw.

Dunn formed up the men in a defensive perimeter along a rocky hillside overlooking the village.

Creech and Loomis gave them a thumbs up and slipped off with their video cameras. They were small handheld models that worked on the same principle as the Night Vision goggles, gathering all available light and magnifying it.

They left their submachine guns with the team. All they took were Russian Makarov 9mm pistols equipped with silencers, a few stun grenades, and a combat knife each. If the shit got deep, they could do some killing. But they couldn't hold out for long. If that happened, they were to take their own lives. Dunn would pull the team out and escape and evade to the LZ.

They didn't move straight into El Badji, they edged around it.

In ever-decreasing concentric circles, they got in closer. In this way they could see what sort of defenses—if any—or perimeter security the Syrians had set up. Loomis didn't expect much and he wasn't disappointed. From what he'd gotten at the operational briefing, it seemed unlikely the Syrians would be expecting intervention of any sort.

Within...that was a different matter.

As they got closer to the outlying trucks, they could see soldiers armed with old Soviet carbines and AK-47 assault rifles. They were keeping well away from the town. They just stood in little clusters every few hundred feet, muttering amongst themselves, their weapons held ready and high. But they were facing the town.

Loomis figured they were an outer security force. Their job, it seemed, was probably to make sure no one got out of that town that wasn't supposed to.

Most of the trucks he saw were troop carriers. But mixed in amongst them at irregular intervals were some Russian BRDM-2 reconnaissance vehicles. These were armed, he knew very well, with 14.5 and 7.62mm belt fed machine guns. But the most impressive firepower he saw were two old Soviet ZSU 23-4 mechanized antiaircraft guns. The ZSUs were pretty much tanks with the cannons replaced by four 23mm miniguns. They could be used against aircraft or ground targets. The miniguns could pump out six thousand rounds per minute with enough force to chew through a concrete wall.

The ZSUs kept circling the town, splashing search lights around in their paths.

Creech nodded.

It was time to separate.

He was taking the western side of town; Loomis the east.

As Loomis moved in, slowly, stealthily, the wind changed direction. Before it had been from the south at his back. Now it was coming from the north, carrying a nauseating stink of burning garbage and roasting human flesh. He had smelled it plenty of times; there was no mistaking it.

Licking his lips, he crawled to the edge of a little rutted mud road that looped the village. He crouched behind a mound of dirt and waited for the ZSU to pass. When it had, he scrambled across the road and slid into a ditch on the other side. Although it was dry, it smelled of piss, shit, and roadkill. The villagers must have used it to dispose of their waste, both bodily and animal. Directly ahead was a group of soldiers. The only way past them was to crawl under a pair of trucks parked side by side. On the other side, he would be safe. If he was very lucky.

*You make your own luck*, he reminded himself.

With all the commotion from the village—the screams and gunfire and shouting voices—it was easy to slip through the darkness to the trucks. The soldiers weren't looking behind them. They were probably under order to keep their eyes on business.

Loomis slipped under the first truck. The engine made ticking sounds as it cooled. A leaky manifold dripped hot oil on his face. It smelled like manure under there and he realized he was snaking his way through cow shit. No matter. Like a viper, he slithered under the next truck and peered around from behind a front tire.

The action was just ahead.

He moved on all fours before two buildings. Bathed in darkness, he had a good view of what was going on. Soldiers dressed in white NBC suits were dragging squirming, kicking bodies from huts and rickety camping trailers. The containment suits—which were designed to give limited protection from nuclear radiation, chemical agents like nerve gas and mustard gas, and biological weapons of the viral, bacterial, and fungal type—weren't even the good ones. They were old things, strictly surplus. No oxygen supply, just filtered masks. Typical Middle Eastern operation.

Loomis got it all on video.

What he assumed were officers were standing about shouting orders. Soldiers kept dragging bodies out and occasionally stopping to shoot them. What was incredible was that the bodies coming out—men, women, and children—although bleeding profusely from bullet wounds, fought and writhed like sacks of cobras.

There must have been twenty or thirty of them dumped into what looked like a village square. The officers were yelling at the soldiers. Loomis' Arabic was quite good and he knew they were being told to withdraw. And they did. As soon as they got away from the piled, tangled heaps of bodies, men with flamethrowers moved in.

Loomis stared, mouth open, videoing it.

*What in the hell is this about? What sort of goddamn infectious disease is so bad that you shoot down your own people and burn them while they're still moving?*

There was a hissing and the flames engulfed the civilians. But before they did, Loomis saw something...remarkable. A young boy, maybe seven or eight, rose up from the litter pile, his black eyes shining. His face had been blown to muscle and bone. He opened his mouth and—

Loomis wasn't sure.

A trick of light and shadow.

*Jesus, that kid should have been dead, and you know it. His face was blown off. But he stood up and you saw it. You saw that thing coming out of his mouth—*

Loomis backed out of his hidey hole and moved along the shadowy cinderblock buildings. He crept along, looking for another good vantage point.

*There was nothing in that kid's mouth, you asshole. Stop thinking crazy shit like that already. Concentrate on what you're doing. Do the job and get out. Leave the particulars to the spooks in D.C.*

That made him feel a bit better.

He spent another twenty minutes looking for somewhere to film from. But there was nowhere else safe. Too much activity. Too many lights. He pulled back the way he'd come. He hoped Creech was getting something.

As he dashed back across the road away from the soldiers, he saw Creech coming, running at a low crouch through the shadows.

"Everything okay?" Dunn's voice said in his ear.

He jumped, almost forgetting about the team in the rocks.

"So far," he said through his throat mic.

Creech fell along side of him. He was breathing hard. He slid his NVGs over his head. His eyes were wide and shining in the night.

"All right?" Loomis asked.

Creech nodded. "Yes, sir. It's...I've never seen anything like it. They're bloody shooting everyone...torching 'em. Then this big pissing front-end loader comes and dumps the bodies in a lorry, a truck."

"Where'd the truck go?"

"West. Not far, I think. I see some lights out there."

Loomis could see the lights, too.

He checked his watch. They were making good time. "Did you get it all on video?"

"Aye," Creech said. "Should be quite a show."

"I'm going out to see where those trucks are going," Loomis whispered in his ear. "You can pull back in the rocks, if you want."

"No, sir. I'm coming."

"You sure?"

Creech nodded. "Have I ever left your side before?"

Loomis smiled, patted him on the back. There was no point in answering that. Creech had once pulled his bleeding body from a burning helicopter in South Armagh, Northern Ireland. He'd carried Loomis three miles through the rain with half the Provisional IRA on his ass.

They set out together.

Away from the town, it was easier moving. They followed the road that wound west. It was pretty simple. Now and then they had to duck behind rocks as trucks sped past them. The closer they got the more they could see that it wasn't artificial lighting causing the glow ahead. It was fire. Flickering, huge fires like bonfires. But from the acrid, steaming smell in the air, they knew they were not bonfires.

They got up close and started videoing with zoom lenses.

There were more soldiers, of course. And more trucks and men in NBC suits overseeing it all. There were also bulldozers, and excavators with hydraulic booms and gigantic shovels big enough to drive a car into. The smell was overpowering. Even the regular troops were wearing gas masks.

As Loomis and Creech watched, they saw something right out of Nazi Germany.

Dump trucks unloaded great heaps of bodies. Although burned black, many of them still moved. Cried. Moaned. Screamed. The tumbled mass seemed to move in serpentine waves, as if something was in there with them—slow, crawling, undulant. Bulldozers pushed the smoldering cargo into a craterlike mass burial pit. Then men with flamethrowers hosed the living carpet of bodies down.

"They can't be alive," Creech said breathlessly. "They can't be...they can't move like that...creep like that...like they ain't got bones, like something—"

"Let's get the fuck outta here," Loomis said.

He looked back once. Great, oily plumes of smoke rose into the night from the pit. The smell was sickening. He pretended he could not hear children screaming.

They moved off into the night, both silent now. Not wanting to speak and not because they were afraid of being heard, but because they were afraid of what they might say.

The team returned their weapons and gave them canteens to suck on when they got back.

Loomis didn't want to waste time. He wanted his team at the exfil point ASAP.

"Horse," he said, "take the point."

They moved west to the LZ selected by Loomis. When they were a good two miles from El Badji and the horrors contained within, they stopped. Loomis checked the GPS and set up the SATCOM radio. It had a built-in encryption device. He spoke the words and waited for the MH-53 Pave Low helicopter that was even now coming to pluck them out.

They began moving again, heading for the LZ.

Dunn came up behind him. Put a hand on his shoulder. "What did you see there, skipper? What's got you guys so bugged?"

Loomis stared out into the blackness.

"I don't know," he said with some effort. "But I don't want to see it again.

# AUGUST 16

# MARYLAND

## BETHESDA NAVAL HOSPITAL

**9:15 A.M.**

When the Old Man arrived, they were waiting for him: Dr. Rosin and Dr. MacClure. Both were captains in the Navy. Both had spent time with the NIS and ONI. And both men had ties with S5. Hands were shaken, small talk was made. Quickly, they ushered the Old Man to the morgue.

In the office of the chief pathologist, they began.

"Lay it out for me," the Old Man said.

MacClure opened a file. "Lister, John Terry. Sergeant, First Marines. Fall 2016, Lister and his recon platoon were involved in operations in the western desert south of Ar Rutbah." MacClure paused, adjusting the spectacles on his hawkish nose. "Within the past few months, he's been in and out of the VA hospital complaining of abdominal pains. Four days ago, he was referred here. He died of sudden internal hemorrhaging two days ago. The morning before his death, an MRI found this."

He put the scans up on the illuminator.

The Old Man calmly put on his glasses and studied them intently. They showed the abdominal cavity. There was a dark, snaking mass visible from the descending colon all the way to the stomach. He nodded gravely. "No doubt about that." He turned to Rosin. "What happened between the time of the scan and his death?"

Rosin cleared his throat. "He was scheduled for an exploratory. His symptomology was confusing to say the least. Then that mass..."

"Yes. Yes, of course."

Rosin avoided his gaze, preferring to study his Naval Academy ring. "Doctor Lattiker performed the autopsy...and that's when—"

"You had Lister cremated then?"

"Yes. It was a real mess at the post, as you can imagine." Rosin shook his head, a bead of sweat appearing at his temple. "Once things were under control, the body was destroyed immediately."

"And?"

"Oh yes," Rosin said, dabbing his brow with a tissue. "Yes, the parasite was incinerated also. Along with all Lister's dressings, blood, urine samples, everything. Anything he came into contact with is gone."

The Old Man thought about it. He thought long and hard while an almost metallic silence rained in the air. "What about Lattiker? Was he assisted?"

MacClure nodded. "Yes. Lattiker died of his wounds almost immediately. His body was destroyed. His assistant was a lab tech named Cortz. He survived... but he's in shock. We have him quarantined as you asked."

"Good. Keep him there. Remember, I want scans twice a day, blood work, urine, feces—the works."

"How long should we keep him?" Rosin asked.

"Indefinitely."

"But his family. They want to know what's going on."

"That's your problem. Invent something." The Old Man withered them both with his iron stare. "How about the other one?"

"Jameson. We still have him."

The Old Man followed them through a maze of autopsy rooms. Through a heavy door that was cold to the touch. The walls were set with stainless steel compartments running from floor to ceiling. They passed through several rooms like this and stopped in the last one.

The air was brisk. MacClure rubbed his hands together. "We've moved all the other bodies from this section as you asked."

Rosin unlatched the door to a single compartment. "We've turned the temp down to twenty-five for this one."

"I hope it's enough," the Old Man said. "Gets cold in the desert, you know. And that didn't kill its spawn."

MacClure looked ill. He stepped back as the tray was pulled out.

"Christ in Heaven," Rosin said.

They all saw it.

The sheet covering the body was stained with blood and tangled around the legs of the cadaver. There was a deep, ragged chasm that ran from throat to crotch. The body had been ripped open.

The Old Man lost his composure, but only for a moment. But in that moment, he wheeled around, looking up, looking down frantically. Searching for something. "I thought this body was being watched?"

"It was," MacClure mumbled. "I was checking it myself."

"Did you check it this morning?"

"No," he admitted. "I was waiting for—"

The Old Man nodded. "Get the names of everyone who came in here last night. I need them ASAP."

Rosin hustled away, glad to be out of there.

The Old Man stared down at the cadaver. At the mutilated gorge that had once been its chest and belly. He was thinking about what could do something like that. He examined the edges of the opening. They were ragged and frayed. The abdominal and thoracic cavities were burst from the inside. Musculature and tissues were sheared, the rib cage was split. The sternum looked...chewed.

MacClure looked like he was going to be sick.

The Old Man jabbed a finger to his chest. "Do you have any idea what you've done here?" he said, his eyes wide and accusing. "Do you have any idea of what you've set loose?"

From the look in MacClure's wide, frightened eyes, he knew all right.

# WASHINGTON D.C.

## EN ROUTE

**11:51 A.M.**

The black Lincoln fought its way through morning traffic on Wisconsin Avenue and in the back sat the Old Man.

He had never been a man of great emotion.

He had learned years ago that there was no place for it in his line of work. The more human you were, the more vulnerable you became. In all his years of service, he had never broken down. He'd buried his parents, his brother, his wife, his mistress. He had never cried. Never allowed himself to. In his position, composure was everything.

*So it's happened*, he thought, trying to steel himself. *The worst case scenario has finally happened. Despite all the preparations and precautions, the worse has come to pass. Now what? Now what are you going to do?*

But he knew.

Preparations for something like this had been drafted weeks ago following what was now called the "Syrian Incident" in El Badji. Yes, one phone call would set the wheels in motion. The teams were ready to move, ready to protect the country from its own demons.

And sometimes the Old Man wondered if it was worth the bother.

If the problem couldn't be contained and eradicated, then soon enough the media would get their hooks into it and everyone would know. The flap would be unimaginable. The taxpayers would see the horrible end result of an illegal, black budget operation. And the fallout would be enough to tear the very seams of the country apart. At the very least, the current administration and all agencies concerned would be gutted. It would be a purge.

And then?

And then more men, each as equally corrupt and sinister as the ones they'd replaced, would be put into power. And the cycle would continue ad infinitum.

The Old Man knew these things because he was one of them.

He picked up his secure cell and punched in a code for the encrypted line. Waited.

"Yes?" a voice said, almost casually. "May I help you?"

"Core Seven," he said.

"Yes, sir," the voice snapped. "Whom can I connect you with?"

"VanderMissen."

A moment passed. Two. There were a series of beeps and clicks as the call was forwarded through a mazelike network.

Finally: "VanderMissen." The voice was tired, defeated.

"It's me," the Old Man said. "I've just come from Bethesda."

"And?"

"As we thought, it's begun."

# AUGUST 17

# BROOKLYN, NEW YORK

## RED HOOK

**1:10 P.M.**

In the dim confines of the Foursquare Saloon on Conover Street and Beard, Bernie Shivel calmly washed another beer mug. The lunch crowd was gone and it was just him and Lance Makowski. Sometimes Lance was quiet—good—and sometimes he just wouldn't shut up—not so good.

"Take it easy, Lance. I just asked a question is all," Bernie said.

Lance sighed. "Yeah, okay, okay. I'm upset. Can you blame me?"

"Nobody blames you, Lance."

"Sure." He pulled off his beer, wiped foam from his mustache. "Anyway, to answer your question, yes, I went to the fucking VA. You know what they told me? They told me I'd have to fill out all these goddamn forms. The forms would be processed. An appointment would be made for me. Is that bullshit or what?"

"Sounds like bullshit to me."

"Yeah, you know it. So I fill out the forms. That was three weeks ago. They haven't called, sent a letter. Nothing. It's a conspiracy. A cover-up. See, this is how it works for those Washington fuckwigs. The media is screaming and causing trouble, so the fatcat fuckwigs they smell bad publicity. So they come right out and say, yeah, Gulf War Syndrome, it happened the first time, maybe it's happening again. Maybe. We'll look into it. They don't give a shit, Bernie. They're only acting like they do to save their own careers. To save voters. Hell, you know what it's like, am I right? You were in Vietnam."

Bernie leaned on the bar. "It's only just starting for you Iraqi vets. Trust me. I've been there. You know how long it took Uncle Sam to admit to the Agent Orange mess?"

"Yeah, I was a kid. I remember. My Uncle Dick died of leukemia from that shit they were spraying. Just a grunt doing his bit for the good old US while those flyboys dumped poison on his head."

"We lost a lot of vets," Bernie said.

"By the time they do something about this...whatever in the hell it is, I'll be a dead man."

Bernie popped himself a Coke. "Maybe what you ought to do is get a lawyer."

"Wouldn't do no good."

"Oh, it might. There's a lot of publicity about shit you guys might have gotten exposed to. You might get some action."

Lance scowled, pressing his fingers to his belly. "Jesus, the pain's coming again. Feels like somebody's twisting a knife in there."

"Want an aspirin?"

Lance clenched his teeth. "No. No. I'll be okay." He grimaced. "When this first started, I was going through a bottle of Advil a day. Didn't do shit."

"Maybe you shouldn't drink."

"Helluva thing for a bartender to say."

"I'm serious. The juice is hard on your guts, take my word for it. I've got the ulcers to prove it."

Lance shook his head. "Fuck it. I'm a dead man."

The door opened with a jingle and three men wearing rubber trench coats bustled in. Bernie just stared at them. He was glad to have more customers, but what was with the rain gear? It wasn't raining outside.

"What can I get you, gentlemen?"

None of them spoke for a moment. The two younger ones—Bernie guessed them to be in their mid-twenties—had cold eyes and thick necks. They looked like they could be real trouble. They reminded him of mob enforcers, sort of guys Bernie had seen on the streets when he was a kid over in Bensonhurst. They looked around the bar as if they were sizing it up for a hit. The older one seemed to be in charge. He gave them both a curious sort of look and they sat down.

"What do you have on tap?" he asked.

He was a cruel-looking character with watery gray eyes and a short, bristly military-style haircut. He had a nasty-looking scar that circled his throat as if maybe he'd been hanged once. He looked very much like a drill sergeant, which was really funny given what Bernie and Lance were talking about when they came in.

Bernie cleared his throat. "We got Bud, Pabst, Miller, Miller Lite, Sam Adams—"

"Three Buds sound good," Crewcut said.

The two younger ones stared into space, saying nothing.

Like his associates, Crewcut seemed intent on sizing the place up. His eyes scanned the doors, behind the bar, the booths along the wall, the pool tables in the back. When the beers came, he smiled and handed Bernie a twenty-dollar bill. "Keep the change, buddy," he said.

The real crazy thing about these guys, beyond their raincoats and staring eyes, was the fact that they all wore black leather racing gloves. And what was even crazier, was that they didn't take them off as they sipped their beers. It all made Bernie real nervous. But ever since the old lady walked out on him a year before, he knew he'd been watching too much TV.

So he didn't think too much of it...or tried not to.

*These guys are a little whacked*, he told himself, *what of it? If they want to walk around on a dry, warm summer day with raincoats and hold their beers with fucking gloves on, why not? It's a free country.*

"That feels better," Crewcut said, holding up his glass and inspecting it. He looked over at Lance and then at his friends, then at Lance again. "You a vet?"

Lance was wearing a desert camouflage field jacket. It was kind of hard to miss. "Yeah," he said. "Yeah."

"Iraq?"

Lance nodded.

"We were in the Gulf, weren't we, boys?"

The young toughs nodded, but nothing more.

"Good for you," Lance said, scowling. He returned to his beer. The last thing in the world he wanted was to relive the war with a bunch of flag-waving yahoos. Their memories of the Iraq War might have been good, but his were shit. The kind of shit that just kept coming back again and again.

"Maybe you guys served together," Bernie suggested, trying to break the ice a little bit. Lance could be a little touchy on the subject of the war and with good reason, but Bernie had always thought it might do him some good to talk to other vets.

"No, I don't think we served together," Crewcut said. "We didn't serve together, did we, Lance?"

Lance swung his head around. His eyes were wide, angry. "How the hell did you know my name?" He kept staring at Crewcut, hoping maybe he'd recognize him, but he drew a blank. "Who the hell are you?"

"Maybe you guys met over there," Bernie suggested. The flesh at the back of his neck was crawling and he honestly didn't know why.

Lance eyeballed Crewcut. "I asked you who you were," he said.

The two younger guys got up and went over to the jukebox by the door. They made a big show of studying the selections there. Neither of them had yet spoken.

"Name's Cave," Crewcut said. "I was with the Army Medical Corps. I patched up a lot of you guys. I never forget a face."

Lance just kept looking at him, mentally running every face he'd seen in the war. It was obvious that Cave just didn't click. "I don't remember you."

"How you been since Saudi?" Cave asked.

"Sick. Sick as fucking dog."

"Lot of us have been that way."

Lance brightened. "You too?"

Cave finished his beer. "No, not me. But others. I think I know what you have, though. Deep pain," he said, patting his stomach, "right here in the belly?"

"Yeah! Yeah, that's it!"

"And not right away either, eh? Just in the last few months?"

Lance nodded frantically. "Yeah! Shit, I got back I felt fine… and now, five goddamn years later, I'm getting sick."

Cave nodded like he'd heard it all before.

Bernie wanted to be relieved that finally Lance had found someone who could help him, get him some treatment, but the fact was he wasn't relieved at all. He had a nasty, gnawing feeling that Cave was toying with Lance. That he was handing him a line of bullshit and that where all this was going was somewhere bad, somewhere ugly. He didn't like these men. They smelled wrong, felt wrong. He started thinking about the shotgun under the bar.

"Yeah, you've got it bad, Lance, I can see it. Problem is, there's no cure for what you've got."

"What do you mean there's no fucking cure?"

Cave sighed. "That's the sad fact of the matter, my friend. No cure. It gets worse and worse. First the pain, then the hunger…"

The younger guys moved very quickly about that time. One of them slid the deadbolt on the door. Then they stepped forward, reaching into their raincoats. They came out with twin nine-millimeter handguns, noise suppressors screwed onto the barrels.

"What the fuck is this?" Bernie asked.

He went for the shotgun under the bar and heard, from some faraway place, two muted popping sounds. The first bullet caught him in the throat, the second put a hole about the size of a quarter in his forehead. He slammed into the cash register, spilled a pyramid of beer glasses, and went down spraying blood in wild loops. He was dead before he hit the floor.

Lance just sat there, shocked, frozen, his beer glass still in his fist. It slid from his fingers and shattered at his feet. He bolted from his stool and made for the back door.

Cave shook his head and there were two more muted pops. The first bullet caught Lance in the ribs, the second hit him between the shoulder blades, directly in the spine, shattering his vertebrae into shrapnel. He collapsed like he was made of rubber, everything giving out at once. He hung onto the edge of a pool table, gasping and whimpering and shitting his pants. There was another pop and the top of his head exploded. Blood, brains, and bone chips soiled the green felt of the table. He slid down in a heap.

"All right," Cave said, "let's get to work."

**1:43 P.M.**

The bar was a hive of activity.

Through the back way, three other men came in. They were part of a Biological Containment Team, a BCT. They wore white biohazard suits with matching hoods. The dim overhead lights glared off the Plexiglas shields over their faces. They looked, if anything, like Apollo astronauts. They carried zippered body bags with them.

Cave watched them with little interest. He flipped the CLOSED sign over in the window and lit a cigarette. He did not take his gloves off. He turned to his two associates. "Okay, you guys," he said. "Make this place look lived in. Do the till."

They nodded and went about business.

Their names were McKenna and Stein. But, like Cave, these were not their real names. Just cover names. Operational names. Next week, next month, in another city, another country, they'd burn another target and would have different names. But for the time being this was who they were.

While Cave stood there smoking, the others went to work. McKenna and Stein emptied out the till, stuffed the money in a brown paper bag. They let a few bills fall to the floor. It had to look like this robbery came down in a hurry. Just another quick, drug-related crime. That's what the cops would figure, and this was encouraged. McKenna took a few bottles of booze and shattered them on the floor.

Cave nodded that it was enough.

Another man came in. He wore a black overcoat and shiny black shoes. He looked very much like a Midtown executive. His hair was neat and powder-white with a matching closely trimmed beard. His eyes were ice blue and had about as much life in them as barrels of toxic waste. McKenna and Stein fidgeted nervously in his presence. He eyed them and everything else with the same lack of compassion, the same barely concealed contempt.

"Well?" he said.

"Piece of cake," Cave told him. "Went perfectly."

"Did Makowski say anything? Anything interesting?"

Cave knew what he wanted. "Yes, sir. Said he had the pains."

The Old Man lifted an eyebrow, nothing more.

The white-suited technicians very carefully slid Makowski's corpse into a body bag and zipped it shut. They carried it outside and put it in a berth in the back of a refrigerated truck parked in the alley. The truck had CARPET KING DISCOUNT RUGS neatly stenciled on the side.

The Old Man toured the crime scene. He did not like what he saw. "This is sloppy," he said. "You've compromised our situation with your stupidity."

Cave knew it was true.

It was supposed to look like a simple murder/robbery, not a hit. Like some coked-up freak sauntered in and killed the bartender for the contents of the till. And it did look like that...except for the blood and brains spattered onto the pool table. And this would have been fine had they been able to leave Lance's body behind. As it was, they had a dead bartender, fine, and the blood of a second man who apparently had walked away, not so fine.

"This scene was to be sterile when we left," the Old Man growled.

"We'll fix it."

The Old Man did not look relieved. He glared at Cave like a bug under a scope. "See that you do and—" he touched a finger to his nose, tapping it gently "—don't screw it up this time."

Pomposity and arrogance in tow, the Old Man left.

*Asshole.*

"All right," Cave snapped at McKenna and Stein. "Let's do it and let's do it fast."

He didn't need to tell them what had to be done; they were old hands at black bag jobs like this. Experience guided them. They pulled the felt off the table and quickly rolled it up, being very careful not to get any blood or matter on the floor. Then they washed down the table, took the legs off and parked it out in the alley with the garbage, after giving it a nice used look. They washed the floor and dragged another pool table forward. This way it didn't look so bare.

It took twenty minutes.

"Next time," Cave said as they left, "we bag the guy's head, then we pop him."

**5:03 P.M.**

A light rain was beginning to fall when Gloria Makowski finished her shift at Jacklyn Machine Products. The sky was gray and the day had turned cold, wind coming in off the bay. She could feel the teeth of winter in its gust. Dressed in grubby jeans and a frayed denim shirt with too many holes in it, she felt the wind biting at her. It had been warm that morning when she'd left the apartment. She hadn't worn her coat. Now she was paying for it.

"Come on, come on," she grumbled under her breath, shivering.

She was sitting behind the wheel of her Taurus, locked in a slowly moving line with forty other cars, waiting for her chance to get out of Jacklyn's gate which was bottlenecked because of some sort of celebration going on over in Coffey Park. Traffic was thick as molasses from Verona to Sullivan, the spillover jamming up Walcott Street and Van Brunt.

Chilled as she was by the unseasonable shift in temperature, she had to crack the windows so she didn't asphyxiate. The Taurus had holes in the floorboards and the muffler was patched in too many places. The stink of exhaust was enough to make you gag if the car wasn't in motion. And how long it would be in motion was another question. The tires were nearly bald. The engine burned an easy quart of oil a week. The timing was bad. The windshield wipers didn't work. The radio was fried. And if all that wasn't bad enough, the heater did nothing but blow cold air. Except in the summer, when it blew hot air. The thermostat was gone, she knew, but there was no money to fix it.

*That's what you call living the American dream*, she thought with more than a little bitterness.

Finally, she got her chance and drove through the gate. By then she was little more than an icicle, her head pounding from the carbon monoxide she'd been inhaling.

Life was great.

It was hard enough to put food on the table let alone deal with extravagant things like getting cars fixed and buying new clothes. With Lance not working (*and drinking every goddamn penny we have*, she reminded herself), it was impossible getting by on just her pay. The Teamsters had organized Jacklyn, but you wouldn't know it from the paychecks she got.

God bless America and the working class.

The rich get richer, the fat get fatter. And all on the backs of working people. There was something very wrong about that (or so the union said as they collected their dues every month).

The rich get richer...

Everyone at the plant thought it would change when the Teamsters came in. They promised solidarity, union brothers and sisters. Better hours. Better pay. More days off. More benefits.

But did any of that happen?

Yeah, right.

The only difference was that it was nearly impossible for the company to fire anyone now. You had to be a total fuck up to lose your job. Which only meant that those who worked hard had to carry those who didn't. That's all it meant.

Everyone at the plant had their theories, of course. The execs at Jacklyn paid off the union. The union collected its dues every month and paid off the company. Conspiracies abounded. What the Teamsters local hadn't taken into consideration were the workers themselves. Solidarity was an exotic term to a pack of crawling weasels, company ass-suckers, and whining backstabbers. Not even Jesus and the Saints could bring them together.

And on and on it went and Gloria still barely made a living.

Of course, if Lance would get a job...

But no, she wasn't going to go there. Not today. She was cold. She was tired. Her back was aching. She needed a meal and a hot bath. If she got herself worked up about it, she'd just go home and start bitching at him about it all. And if Lance was drunk (not a matter of *if*, she told herself, but to what degree), there'd be a fight. An all-nighter. In the end he'd go out and get more drunk and she'd sleep on the couch.

No, she wasn't going to let that happen.

Not today.

She pulled to a stop before her building, filled with anger and self-pity despite herself. She stepped out of the car and made herself take a deep breath. Tried to purge the tension. She didn't want to fight today.

*He's probably not home anyway*, she thought dismally. *He's probably out getting wasted. It's what he does best.*

Their marriage had deteriorated significantly in the past few years. She liked to think it was Lance's fault, but maybe it was hers, too. Maybe she just didn't care anymore. Maybe she was simply out of sympathy for him. He'd had it tough, she knew that. But since he'd gotten back from Iraq... things had just gone to shit. They were both shocked when his National Guard unit was activated and sent over there. Their marriage had been so good up to that point. Just before he'd left she'd gotten pregnant. While he was in Saudi for desert training, she found out via the ultrasound that it was a boy. She'd never been so happy. Or so worried that Lance wouldn't return.

Then she'd miscarried.

A year later, Lance came home. He'd brought with him a serious drinking problem. A changed man, all he did was drink and complain and bitch about his health problems. He was certain he had a variety of undiagnosed illnesses due to his exposure to chemical weapons in Iraq. Yet, he refused to wade through the red tape at the VA that would have started a program of treatment. Instead, he drank and refused to work.

What a guy.

By the time she'd made it to the second floor and was turning the key in the lock, she was feeling very bitter. Very betrayed. By life. By fate. By Lance. Particularly by Lance.

Healthy enough to suck down a case of beer every day, but not healthy enough to work for a living.

*Goddamn you, Lance. If you were working full time, making a decent wage, we could be doing all right.*

Her face felt hot and tight. If he was home, he'd know she was pissed soon as she walked in the door. It was going to be fight night and she couldn't stop it now. She slammed the door shut and stood there, boiling.

Her voice full of acid, she cried out: "Lance? Lance?"

Her voice echoed through the apartment. He wasn't in the living room. Passed out in the bedroom? Puking in the bathroom? Drinking in the kitchen?

No, none of the above. The TV wasn't on. If he was home, the TV would be on. Even if he wasn't watching it, it was always on.

Gloria dropped her keys on the couch and kicked her shoes off. She grabbed a pair of sweats and stopped. Stopped dead. There was curious, unsettling feeling in her belly. A sense of...what? Dread? She shook her head and went into the bathroom.

What the hell was this?

The bathroom smelled like smoke. Cigarette smoke. There was a butt floating in the toilet. Ashes in the sink. Lance didn't smoke. Maybe one of his drunken buddies... except he didn't have any of those either. On the floor around the toilet and spilling down the sides of the bowl like some child's finger-painting was a viscous yellow slime. It had the consistency of vomit... but it was like no vomit she'd ever seen before. Lance must've thrown up.

She turned away, disgusted.

There was a man standing behind her.

Gloria nearly jumped out of her socks. She gripped the sink for support, a cold wave rushing through her chest.

The man was dressed in a shiny, black raincoat. His eyes were dead and gray like scum-filled pools. A scar ran down across his neck. "Quite a mess in here, eh?" he said.

Gloria stumbled past him, stepping out of the bathroom, fear like a knife in her belly. Her lips trembled. "Who...who the hell are you?"

"I'm a friend of your husband," he said, very calmly, almost emotionlessly. "He's very sick, poor guy."

"You can't be here. I could call the—"

"Police? No, you can't do that."

Two men had joined him. They must've been hiding in the bedroom closet, it occurred to Gloria in some part of her brain that wasn't screaming in raw terror.

She turned to bolt into the bathroom where, survival instinct told her, she could lock herself in. Gloved hands grabbed her and slammed her against the wall. Before she had recovered, a syringe was inserted into her neck. Her head reeling and her body gone to rubber, the two men dumped her into the tub. One of them held her up while the other slid a thick plastic bag over her head and tightened it about her throat.

She tried to scream then, but all that came out was a garbled, meaty sound. She thought madly that this couldn't be, that this wasn't right, that her life really wasn't all that bad—

Then a nine millimeter slug turned her brain to bloody mucilage.

And then there was only darkness. No worries.

**6:17 P.M.**

The Biological Containment Team came up the stairs.

They were wearing their white biosuits, but unlike before, this time there was a logo in brilliant red letters in the middle of their backs: JACK'S PRESSURE CLEANING. They carried their hoods under their arms. They passed people in the corridors, but no one paid any real attention. Just a couple of cleaners, they thought, in their starched white uniforms. The ruse worked perfectly.

The BCT was made up of three individuals.

Lieutenant Holliman, Sergeant Ramirez, and Corporal Spokes. Unlike Cave and his cleaners, these were the actual names of the team members. They were with an Army NBC unit out of Fort Detrick, Maryland, but were on permanent loan to the U.S. Army Medical Research and Development Command who jobbed them out to another agency.

When Cave or any of the others spoke to them, the three were addressed by their ranks. Nothing more. Neither Cave nor Stein nor McKenna knew their names. They were on loan to an agency that thrived on anonymity.

It was the way things worked.

When Holliman and the others reached the apartment on the second floor, Cave was waiting for them.

"She's in the bathroom," he said. "There's some weird shit on the floor. Like slime."

The lieutenant nodded. He and the others donned their hoods. Ramirez unfolded a vinyl body bag. They got right to work.

"Our plane leaves in twenty minutes," Cave said to McKenna and Stein.

He went to watch the containment team and McKenna rolled his eyes. Stein smiled but said nothing. If you wanted to survive in the business, you learned to say nothing. You did not comment on your work or the work of others. You did not ask questions. You did the job you were ordered to do and left it at that. You did not worry about how what you did might have ruined lives. You did not try to figure out the big picture. That was for guys like the Old Man. And even though you wanted to know real bad what these people were infected with, you didn't ask. And you weren't told. That's how it worked. If they told you there was no risk of infection to you, you had to believe them. If they said it wasn't contagious, then it wasn't.

And outwardly, that's just how you acted.

Like none of it bothered you one bit.

Even if, deep inside where no one could see, you were scared shitless.

Cave came back, a cigarette dangling from his lips. "Control says we're done in the Big Apple. This one makes twelve stops."

"Shit," McKenna said, "I didn't even get to Manhattan."

"Where next?" Stein asked him.

"Chicago."

McKenna wanted to say, *it's there too, then*. But he didn't dare. It was funny how something not contagious seemed to be all over the goddamn place. Boston. Atlanta. Dallas. Denver. Washington. New York. Now Chicago. Funny. He just had to remember that Cave had assured him there was no danger of contagion. Just as the Old Man had assured Cave. So there was nothing to worry about.

McKenna thought about Chicago. It made his skin go cold

# AUGUST 18

# RICHMOND, VIRGINIA

## CBT BIOSAFETY LEVEL FOUR: THE CAGE

**7:10 P.M.**

Once she was properly fitted in a one-piece positive-pressure biohazard suit with its own life support system, helmet on and air supply running, it was time to go in. Dr. Evans guided her down the dim, deadly corridor. Like him, she was dressed in a green Tyvek biosuit, rubber boots, and multilayered surgical gloves. She rarely came down here, but Evans—the biogeneticist who had done most of the groundwork for what would come to be known as Project BioGenesis—had called to tell her that he was running a hot trial on an infected host who was on the verge of biological meltdown.

"It's something you should really see," he told her, excited at the prospect. "It gives one perspective and an appreciation for the survivability of our particular GMO."

Elizabeth had very little interest in seeing any of it, but it was too late to get squeamish. This was the egg she had brooded over, the one she'd sold to the Defense Department for megabucks, and now it was hatching. Time to be a proud mother hen and see what she had wrought.

To think it had all led to this. To this unpleasant place. All the striving and hard work, scheming and duplicity of her steady crawl up the corporate ladder to the highest rung had brought her here—to a position of unprecedented power where she was about to witness something horrendous, something horrible which would haunt her nightmares for the rest of her life.

*Again, too late to be squeamish*, she told herself.

And she knew damn well that in her position at CBT, that she could never, ever afford to show any weakness. Her enemies were many. They were always looking for something to exploit. And besides, those whom she answered to expected her to oversee every facet of the project.

*No, not expected, demanded.*

Biosafety Level Four at CBT was known as The Cage to those who worked in it, but was technically referred to as the MCL, Maximum Containment Lab. By the older designation it was P-4 for the highest pathogen protection level, though that had fallen out of favor of late. It was replaced by the terminology BSL-4 (Biosafety Level 4) or BL-4 (Biological Level 4) in the industry. It was three levels below ground and very few CBT employees even knew it existed. It was a claustrophobic run of narrow corridors, airlocks, decon showers, autoclaves, and HEPA filters. The sealed modular work rooms and labs were designed to keep anything, even the minutest viral particle, from escaping.

It was, Elizabeth thought, a very oppressive sort of place. The biosuits increased that sensation, of course. Some people simply couldn't take it and began having panic attacks almost immediately. Then there were others like Evans and his staff that thrived in the secret, high-security underground lair of hot bioorganisms and lethal genetically engineered life forms.

Elizabeth was not one hundred percent comfortable down there. She was very aware of the confining suit and what a tear in the fabric might mean. In the case of an accident, the entire area would be sealed off until invasive biocontainment operations were complete.

She swallowed, listening to the hum of the blower that cycled fresh air into her helmet. Though she was not warm (The Cage was kept quite cool), sweat trickled down her temples and her faceplate fogged with her breath.

If the public ever found out about any of this, the Nuremberg Trials would be like a day in the park in comparison.

Once the decon cycle of chemical showers was complete, Evans led her through the airlock past rooms where techs labored over their scopes and slides. A maze of interconnecting corridors brought them to another airlock. Steps led below. Down here were two things: the freezers that housed the frozen zoo of deadly pathogens and experimental organisms, and the chambers where biological weapons were tested. The corridor angled off to the right, then the left.

Here it was.

Elizabeth stood there, breathing the stale air of her suit. Before her were a series of chambers much like cages in a zoo. Each were walled with one-way glass which allowed the occupants to be watched and studied. Only one was occupied and in it was a woman.

"This animal," Evans said, "has been here four days. She's at the end of her life cycle."

*Animal.* That was the word he used and it gave Elizabeth a chill. She supposed that given the nature of the work down here, it was better to refer to all test subjects, whether man, monkey, or dog, as test as animals. Psychologically, it probably made things easier.

The woman was probably in her mid-thirties. She was naked and in great distress. She stumbled back and forth, slamming her hands against the walls, crying out. Sometimes sobbing and sometimes screaming hysterically. Dark hair was webbed to her face with sweat. She was shaking, her abdomen grotesquely swollen. Blood had leaked from her nipples and was smeared over her body.

And Elizabeth thought, *I don't want to see this. I don't want to know about this part of it.*

By the end of the week, this would be happening to thousands of people across the country. The very idea sickened her and made the blood drain down into her feet. And this when she thought she was far beyond being able to feel anything as pedestrian as common human decency.

The woman dropped to her knees and vomited out a discharge of watery bile. It was hard to know at this juncture whether she was even aware of what was happening to her. Field trials had proven that the subjects were generally irrational by this point.

Now the woman stood up. She pawed the hair away from her face, revealing a pallid complexion and eyes that were red as rubies, as if every blood vessel in them had exploded. Her lips curled away from her teeth and she began making gagging, croaking noises that rose in volume and intensity. It was hard to believe human vocal cords could produce such sounds.

She went down, contorting and jerking, limbs whipsawing back and forth, head drumming against the floor. Her teeth chattered uncontrollably, blood running from her mouth and bubbling from her nostrils. Her fingers were the claws of an animal that tore frantically at her belly—there was something in her and she knew it. Something was doing this to her and she wanted it out. Her nails raked her skin, leaving red streaks across her pale abdomen.

Evans was timing it all. "And it should happen... now," he said.

The woman squirmed on the floor like a human larva, wriggling and writhing in her own waste. She made a series of hissing, slithering sounds. The popping and snapping of her joints was clearly audible. She arched her back, screaming and expelling a fine mist of blood. Every muscle and tendon was strained tight. They were like cords under her skin. Beneath the flesh of her belly something moved. The woman gyrated faster and faster and then she... exploded.

There was no other word for it as she literally burst open with a wet, tearing sound, expelling tissues and organs and steaming fluids. Blood and matter sprayed against the glass along with hundreds of marble-sized objects. Split open on the floor like a spawning fish, the eggs gushed out of her in ropy clusters. Then something else came out of her, dislocating her jaw as it fought free.

"Jesus," Elizabeth said, turning away.

"It's unpleasant the first time you see it," Evans said. Behind the plastic bubble of his helmet, his face was impassive. "All right, let's start decon. Wrap this up!"

The test chamber was sprayed with toxic chemicals. Soon everything was dead, even that which was designed to survive at all costs.

Elizabeth walked down the corridor, then she slumped against the wall, breathing heavily. This was it then. This was what BioGen had unleashed on the world.

# AUGUST 20

# CHICAGO

## PORTAGE PARK

**2:34 P.M.**

Strung out on caffeine and amphetamines, Shawna Geddes sat on a peeling bench and waited for God. Because when he showed she had a few questions to put to him. She dearly wanted to know if he was pulling the strings of her life or if she was merely fucking up all on her own. It would've been nice to believe that everything was predestined. It would have been comforting. Because if it wasn't, if it wasn't...well, then she was every bit the screwup her mother promised her she would be.

Ultimately, she knew the truth.

Just like she knew God wouldn't be showing up today. No doubt he'd long ago washed his hands of her. The thought, though not surprising, was somehow unsettling. It made her feel very alone.

*So, I've taken a few drugs,* she thought. *Ruined a few marriages. What of it? What does that make me?*

She stopped thinking about that before any answers came.

She lit a cigarette and checked her watch. No, God wasn't coming today, but the man she was waiting for was twenty minutes late. She'd checked her watch five times in as many minutes. Repeated viewing wasn't making those hands move any goddamn faster.

"C'mon, Harry," she snarled under her breath and flicked her ash into the wind.

A little league game was going on across the way and Shawna watched the proceedings with a dull gaze. The mothers and fathers cheered. Grandparents clung to the wire fence. Toddlers played in the dirt. It all seemed so foolishly, hopelessly boring and normal that she began to cry.

*Chin up,* she told herself silently. *You're okay. Too much coffee. Too many speeders. Not enough sleep and when the hell was the last time you ate?*

She honestly couldn't remember.

The last memory she had of food was two days before. Linguini with white clam sauce at Sapori Trattoria in Lincoln Park. That was it. Richard had wined and dined her...then broke off their relationship.

Oh, she'd seen it coming.

A guy like him only wanted a woman like her for one reason. Even now, she was certain, he'd picked up some other woman to take back to his upscale condo downtown to show her the stunning view of Lake Michigan...amongst other things. A woman that would be suitably impressed by his wallet, if not his sexual prowess. The thing that made Shawna really bitter was that she couldn't even make an anonymous call to his wife. A revenge call. His wife was probably carrying on with one of her lovers. No doubt in the beach house in the Canaries.

*He used me*, Shawna told herself. *And I loved every minute of it. He used me, dumped me, and the very next day... well, the very next day I lost my job.*

Richard hadn't been the first rich man she'd dallied with.

There was Jonathan. He'd taken her to nice restaurants on the Gold Coast and banged away at her in his lavish summer lake house on the tip of Michigan's thumb. Jonathan owned six factories and two investment brokerages. Eventually, he dumped her. But if Richard and Jonathan had ended somewhat peacefully, then Tom and Adam had not. Tom was a tax lawyer. Very nice. Very rich. His wife had caught on, though, and her PI had videotaped the two of them having sex. Divorce. Adam was a stockbroker. Very powerful. His wife had caught on, too. They'd been photographed as well. Out there, somewhere, there was enough tape to make a nice little porno, Shawna often thought. Adam had not only dumped her, but he'd tried to beat her up for ruining his marriage. Then he'd tried to take his life.

Suffice to say, Adam never called anymore.

Ugly, ugly, ugly.

Shawna could hear her mother's voice in her head: strident, disapproving, holier-than-thou. *God gave you the looks to go as far you wanted, too bad he'd didn't give you the brains to manage them, Shawna.*

*You're right, Mom, goddamn you.*

Well, enough of this. Harry had stood her up. He wasn't going to show and that was that. She'd been shit on by better, right? But not like this. Not when she really, truly needed someone.

"Fuck you, Harry," she muttered.

About the time she was ready to leave, a vintage luster-black 1967 GTO pulled up. The windows were tinted. It was huge, a monster. Nothing like it had prowled the streets since the early seventies.

It either belonged to Harry Niles or a pimp from 1969. In a way, she often thought, there wasn't much difference.

"Well, well, well," Harry said as she approached, "what have you gotten yourself into this time?"

**3:47 P.M.**

Harry guided the GTO effortlessly onto Long Avenue, picking up speed. A newer car would have bumped and jolted unmercifully over the numerous frost-heaved dips, but the GTO just floated over them. "I'm listening," he said. "Let the lurid confessions begin."

Shawna glared at him. Her chocolate eyes one shade darker. "I'm in trouble. Isn't it what you expected?"

He smiled. "Nothing moves me like a woman in trouble."

"You're an asshole, Harry. Do you know that?"

He shrugged. "I'll take it. Even an insult is a backhanded compliment."

Shawna lit another cigarette and brooded darkly. "Why do I bother."

"Still smoking, I see," Harry said. "Those things'll kill you. Haven't you heard?"

"Something's gotta. Haven't *you* heard?"

Harry nodded. "How true."

They drove and Shawna smoked in melancholy silence.

It was too bad, Harry often thought, that Shawna was such an unhappy girl. She had a lot going for her...save her choice in men. She was forever reaching for something she could never have. It always ended in disappointment. He had already decided that that's what this meeting was about. Whenever she was in trouble, she called him.

Harry merged with traffic on West Irving. "Well, spill it, my dear. What did you get yourself into this time?"

Her lower lip trembled. "Trouble."

She told him all about Richard. She was genuinely hurt by it all despite her claims that she'd seen it coming and that it was just a fling that meant absolutely nothing.

"Poor little thing," he said. "You fall so easily."

"I wasn't in love with him."

"No, of course not."

"I wasn't!" she snapped.

Harry lifted an eyebrow. "Are you telling me that or yourself?"

Shawna stared sullenly ahead. She was dressed in a black velour business suit, cut short to show off plenty of leg. Her glossy chestnut hair was pulled into a tight French braid. She wore no makeup. Her skin was pale and blotchy. Dark half-moons had settled beneath her eyes.

"I wasn't in love with him," she maintained. "I wasn't."

"No, and I don't want to nibble on your thighs, either."

She looked at him, lips pursed tightly. "You're a prick, Harry. You're a dirty, sexist prick of a pig."

"Are you coming on to me, Shawna?"

She growled low in her throat, staring out her window.

"Tell me what else happened," he said. "I know you're not this upset over another rich man. What else did you do?"

"Nothing. It isn't what I did... it's what was done to me."

"Tell me."

"I was fired," she said, folding her arms. "They fired me from the *Trib*."

Harry didn't say anything for a moment. It wasn't that he didn't care, because he did. It was just that he didn't regard her position at the *Chicago Tribune* with any degree of seriousness. Dead-end stuff, in his thinking. The journalistic equivalent of working the deep fryer at Burger King. No more, no less.

"Well, shit happens."

Shawna looked ready to chew glass. "Is that all you can say?"

"C'mon, my love, it wasn't much of a job anyway. It was holding you back."

"It was a good job. An important job."

He grinned. "You were an assistant to the assistant editor of gardening for chrissake."

"I wrote some good pieces!" Shawna snarled. "Some important pieces!"

Harry laughed; he couldn't help it. "Yes, you sure did. I couldn't sleep for a week after I read the one about the festive autumnal floral boxes. And that hard-hitting expose' on the cultural history of the eggplant... it was positively chilling. Good God, there's social implications in that one I'm afraid to even contemplate."

Shawna punched him in the arm. Three times. "Bastard," she said, fighting back a smile. "At least...at least I don't write about dead celebrities and Mongolian Death-Worms."

"Now wait a minute, you self-righteous little bitch. My series on the Death-Worm was provocative journalism. I write what others only dare dream."

"Yeah, my ass."

He offered her a spicy grin. "What about your ass? Does it need a good spanking?"

"Fuck you, Harry."

He sighed. "I love it when you talk like that. One of these days you'll say it and mean it and I, of course, will turn you down."

"Harry, please," Shawna said, sighing heavily. "I was fired. I have no job."

"Well, what did you do or not do?"

"I was late a few times."

"A few?"

"Fifteen times in two months." She was proud and it was hard for her to admit this. "I missed a few deadlines."

Harry had met her when he himself had worked at the *Trib*. At the time, she had been doing little more than running errands, getting sandwiches, checking copy, showing lots of leg and giving the boys on the metro desk the most sinful fantasies. Shortly after she'd started, they'd let him go for drinking. That had been six years ago. They'd stayed in touch ever since. Sometimes Harry wasn't even sure why.

*It's certainly not because she needs another lover. Your bank balance would hardly get you past first base. Father confessor? Big brother? Attentive uncle? Dear God.*

"Listen, Shawna. Don't get worked up about this. You know how many papers I've been fired from?" She didn't hazard a guess, so he told her. "I've been fired from the *Trib*. The *Times* in LA. Twice, in fact. The *Globe* in Boston. The *Times* in New York. Shit, the list goes on and on and on: Vegas, Philadelphia, Minneapolis, Washington, Milwaukee. You name the rag, they've fired me."

None of it cheered her up much. He rather doubted there was anything that could other than time. Time and a new job. A real job. He himself had rebounded each and every time after getting canned. The last time, from the *Trib*, had probably been the worst, though. His drinking had been at an all-time high and his life at an all-time low. He bottomed out. There was really nothing left and he knew it. With his track record, nobody was going to hire him. He'd barely weaseled his way into the *Trib*. He was a drunken troublemaker with absolutely no respect for authority and everyone knew it. He supposed the last straw at the *Trib* had been when he'd come back from that three-hour lunch with Jim Beam and Captain Morgan, suitably pissed to the gills, and decided to relieve himself into a potted fern on the receptionist's desk.

After that, crash and burn.

He was nearly on skid row when Gabe Hebberman had found him. Gabe had been a friend of his father's. Gabe had cleaned Harry up, dried him out, and given him a job. Gabe was the publisher of the *Weekly World Examiner*, one of those black and white rags you find so amusing in the supermarket checkout lane. ELVIS WAS ADOLF HITLER'S LOVE CHILD. RUSSIAN PRESIDENT IS ANTICHRIST. NOSTRADAMUS WAS RAISED BY WOLVES. The 1970s through the 1990s had been a boom time for the tabloids. Then around 2003, the bottom had fallen out. One after the other, they failed. Sensationalism died. For the first time in over thirty-five years, the *Weekly World Examiner* no longer appeared. Even the Internet version tanked. Then Gabe Hebberman—always smelling a buck—had brought it back to life, tapping into foreign editions and the lucrative emerging Asian and Latin-American markets. These days, the American version barely broke even, but the foreign editions brought in unbelievable profit. Along with several gossip rags, crossword and Sudoku mags, and a bevy of skin magazines, Gabe was a very wealthy man.

Harry had worked for him ever since and hadn't looked back. Yeah, so he was writing about alien abductions and vampire plagues instead of corrupt politicians and corporate sleazebags. What of it? The pay was five times as much as he'd ever earned before, so fuck legitimacy and journalistic ethics. People wanted shit so he wrote shit.

Things were okay now. He still drank, but it was under control. He had eased over the line into his forties last year and it hadn't hurt too bad. Of course, his belly was expanding and his hair line was receding. His hopes of looking like Sean Connery in his declining years weren't panning out. He worked out three times a week, but one look in the mirror told him it was a dismal failure. Yet, he was not unhappy. Things were okay.

"I just don't know what to do, Harry," Shawna said as they cruised up North Ashland Avenue past St. Boniface Cemetery and into Ravenswood. "All I've ever wanted to do was write. I always thought I was pretty good. Now...I'm just not so sure."

Harry gave her arm a squeeze. "You are good. Listen, Shawna. I'm the last person to be giving advice, but I'm going to anyway. You have to get some priorities here. Quit with the rich guys already. Concentrate on your career. Go after men because you like them, not because they're loaded. And that's all I'm going to say about that."

"Do you like what you do, Harry?"

He shrugged. "Pay's good. Hours are easy. Yeah, I guess I do. I mean, I spent years digging up the dirt on politicians and the federal government. I played my part as a good little investigative journalist. I was even pretty good at it. I know this because I still have lots of enemies." He laughed as the faces of more than a few paraded through his mind. "But I'm done with that. You might make a name for yourself being legit. You might even get the Pulitzer. But more likely than not the stress'll kill you. You'll end up with ulcers, a drinking and/or drug problem. Maybe a heart attack or a nice debilitating stroke. Beyond that, if you're really lucky, maybe a book contract. But you'll never have a family. You'll never have a real life. Take it from me, it ain't what it's cracked up to be. Nothing is."

She shook her head. "I don't know if I could write stuff like that."

"Why not?"

"I don't know."

"Well, I do. It's because you want to work for one of the majors. But listen to me for a minute. Just one minute." He cleared his throat and helped himself to one of her cigarettes. "The rag I work for has ten times the circulation of any city paper. Its writers make a helluva lot more money. And the stress level is practically nil. Think about that."

"But you make that crap up."

"No, no, no," he said, shaking a finger at her. "We make up only a small percentage. Most of that stuff is actually true. Really. True in that people report these things to the police, to their governments, to the legitimate press. We're the only ones, however, who follow it up. The cover stories are generally always bullshit. They're teasers to interest the reader, but the rest... well, we elaborate and condense and fictionalize to a certain extent, but the basic story is what someone else claims is the truth."

"Seriously?"

He nodded. "Yes. It's a weird world out there, my pet. Weirder than you can imagine. We don't have to make the shit up. Our part is basically just perception management. We steer the articles in one direction or another."

"Even the Elvis shit?"

He smiled. "All right...we do make that up. Elvis and Michael Jackson and Marie Osmond's latest diet sell tons of papers in the third world. Don't let anyone kid you."

After a moment to chew on that, Shawna said, "Do you believe any of that junk? Sasquatch? Aliens? Government cover-ups?"

Harry laughed until he coughed. "I'm as cynical as you. As skeptical as you. If I wasn't, I'd turn into Gabe, my editor. He believes in most of it. He's got a child's sense of wonderment and belief. He's also the sweetest man I've ever met. I mean, you don't want to get between him and some hard cash, but other than that...oh, absolutely fatherly."

Shawna sat there in silence.

She was thinking about the legitimate press. Its promise. Its failings. It didn't matter that it was the twenty-first century, it was still a male-dominated world. Women were generally judged by their looks rather than their credentials. It didn't matter that she'd gone to Columbia. All that mattered was that she had a nice pair of legs. And she hadn't consciously tried to play that down. And what had it ever really gotten her? Not a goddamn thing, thank you very much.

"Harry?" she said, brightening.

"Yes, my plum of delight?"

Even that didn't bother her today. "Do you think this Gabe would give me a job?"

**4:40 P.M.**

Harry dropped her back at Portage Park. They'd had a nice long chat. Very intriguing. Interesting. Informative. Harry had told her that, yes, Gabe would probably hire her. And if Harry himself put in a good word for her, it was almost a sure thing. A Columbia grad. *Trib* staff. Gabe would like that. But he told her to slow down. To take a few days and think about it. To be very sure it was what she wanted. Working for a tabloid was fun and it paid well, he told her, but... it also could seriously ruin any aspirations she might have for serious journalism. Legit editors had a habit of looking down their noses at the tabloids and anyone connected with them.

So, she was thinking about it. Hard.

At least there were options. That was good.

As fucked up as everything seemed to be, at least there was a way out. An escape route. If she chose to take it. But would she take it? She turned it over and over in her mind. Part of her said, *yes, Shawna, go for it, it's a good thing. It's stability. Income.* But, another part of her, maybe the legit part, said, *no, dammit, it's a tabloid, Shawna. Do you wanna spend the rest of your life writing about celebrities cheating on their wives and household appliances possessed by demons?* That last part left her cold.

There were big stories out there. Big, legitimate stories waiting to break. This year. Next year. Five years from now. If she joined the staff of the *Weekly World Examiner*, she'd never write them; she'd just read them. If the President was assassinated tomorrow, this Gabe would have her doing a piece on how subversive Martian elements were to blame or how the whole goddamn thing was predicted by Edgar Cayce or some other charlatan.

Then again, the *Trib* would never let her near a story like that. Not unless the President had been killed by an errant houseplant or buried in some-body's petunia bed. At least this Gabe would let her tackle it...creatively, at any rate. In her mind she just kept seeing her byline beneath those tabloid stories. I WAS ARTIFICIALLY INSEMINATED BY ALIENS. OVER-WEIGHT HOUSEWIFE DEVOURS TRIPLETS IN CANNIBAL RAGE. DEMONIC BLOOD FEASTS OF CAPITOL HILL. It all made her very ill.

"At least I have a choice," she said under her breath. "He sure as hell doesn't."

She was watching some guy meandering through the park. He was picking through garbage cans and stuffing odds and ends into the pockets of his flannel jacket. His hair looked like it had been brushed with a Braun Hand Blender, his face streaked with grime. She noticed he wore a raggedy pair of desert camouflage pants, the kind soldiers wore in Iraq and Afghanistan. That and one combat boot. His other foot was bare.

*Now why do they let someone like that wander around?* she wondered. *He needs supervision.*

But she knew the answer. America didn't have a very good track record of taking care of its vets. Federally funded programs for the mentally ill were already dangerously overloaded. They'd just closed the V.A. Hospital in Chicago Heights for God's sake.

*Thanks for serving, buddy, but now, fuck you.*

The baseball game had broken up and the guy was heading over there now. He'd found part of a sandwich and was eating it, much to Shawna's dismay. Over at the ball diamond, he looted the cans happily. A white van cruised through the park very slowly. It made its way over to the bleachers. Two men in dark rain slickers hopped out. They walked over to the bum and were apparently talking to him. It was all so far away, it was hard to say what was going on. Shawna wondered if the two men were from mental health or something.

Something about the situation got into her gut. She dug out her iPhone and put it on zoom so she could get a better look. There. Focus a bit. Tighten the field.

*Holy shit!*

One of the men hit the bum over the head with something.

He dropped motionless at their feet.

Shawna started to record it.

A third man hopped out of the van and helped the other two throw the bum in the back. Doors were shut. The van drove off, not so slowly now.

Shawna just stared, her lips moving silently.

*What the fuck just happened?*

She sat there in disbelief. Tabloids were very far from her mind now. She couldn't believe what she'd just seen. It couldn't possibly have happened and yet it did. She'd seen it. She'd videoed it.

When the van passed her, she ducked down.

It slowed and she felt her heart began to pound, then it picked up speed and drove away. She didn't dare lift her head until it was nearly out of sight.

Then she did the only thing she could.

She ran for her car and followed it.

# WASHINGTON D.C., BOLLING AFB

## DEFENSE INTELLIGENCE AGENCY

**6:02 P.M.**

Lieutenant-General Sleshing sat in his oak-paneled office and watched the El Badji video again and again. He saw the same images Colonel Loomis had on the ground, but without the horrible, sickening stink in the air.

But, then, death was nothing new to Sleshing.

When he was a young towheaded, newly promoted captain he'd been with the 1st Air Cavalry Division during Operation Rockcrusher in 1971 when U.S. forces entered Cambodia to hunt down elements of the NVA that were hiding in the remote wilderness to avoid American reprisals. A U.S. incursion into Cambodia was, through international treaty, illegal. But the NVA were doing it routinely. Attacking U.S. and South Vietnamese positions, then running across the border to hide.

No one had really warned Sleshing's unit of what they were going to find as they approached an internment camp at Doc Tho where the Cambodians had rounded up ethnic Viets and imprisoned them (they were angry over Viet incursions and had taken the law into their own hands). They were greeted at the gates by living skeletons, many too weak to even stand. The bodies were everywhere, most so rotted that they were almost unrecognizable as human beings. Men, women, children. The barracks were filled with the sick, the dead, the dying. Those in the lower bunks had drowned in rivers of excrement, urine, and filth. Those still alive were riddled with lice, scabies, gangrene, suppurating boils and lesions. Hundreds of unburied corpses were stacked like cordwood, infested with typhus. Hundreds of others smoldered in mass burning pits.

Sleshing himself had prodded something blackened with his bayonet.

As it rolled over, he saw what it was.

The skull of an infant.

One corpse causes sorrow... but hundreds, thousands, brings sheer disbelief. Sleshing and the Air Cav soldiers walked about, slack-jawed, sickened. The sheer level of death there was overwhelming. Death on an industrial level of the sort that had not been seen since Nazi Germany. A factory whose raw material were human beings.

Soldiers who were battle-hardened and toughened to the horrors of war, went mad. The remaining Cambodian guards that had not fled and their bandit underlings were shot down in cold blood.

It was a madhouse.

It took the officers and noncoms some time to restore order.

Sleshing shook his head.

He had to get those pictures out of his mind.

Over forty years later that young towheaded captain was still in him. And that stink, that hideous pervasive stink was still on him. Nothing could wash it away.

As he watched the videos of El Badji, he was reminded of that day.

The bodies.

The burning bodies.

*My Christ*, he thought, *oh my Christ.*

The Syrians weren't to be blamed, of course; they were preventing a contagion. They had little choice. That part was understandable. The scary thing was the terrorist elements and their Iranian advisors that were involved in the mess. The very frightening possibility that they would realize that what they had was a devastating biological weapon and use it as such.

*If they have the technology*, Sleshing kept reminding himself. *To cold-start BioGen will take cutting-edge biomedical technology. They may not be capable of it. But if they are, if they are—*

The door opened and Charles VanderMissen came in.

He greeted the DIA director with a limp handshake. Sleshing realized his own handshake was not much better. VanderMissen was dressed in an immaculate tailored charcoal gray suit. It hung on him like something he'd picked up at Goodwill.

"Christ, turn that off, Wally," he said in disgust.

DDI Sleshing did so. "Sorry, Chuck. I just can't stop watching it."

"Me neither," VanderMissen admitted, falling into a chair. "But I was like that as a kid, too. Never could get enough of Mighty Mouse on TV."

"God bless Mighty Mouse," Sleshing laughed. "Lord knows how we need him now."

Sleshing and VanderMissen were old friends, part of the old guard as they liked to call it. But it was only at times like this when they were alone together that they allowed themselves to relax, to unwind, to let their hair down.

"Any news?"

"Yeah, plenty. The teams have been making a good run of it." VanderMissen did not look happy about this. "They've sterilized about sixty disease vectors in the past seventy-two hours. That brings us up to a grand total of...oh, Jesus H. Christ. I can't do this anymore."

Sleshing felt for him. *Disease vectors.* Yes, U.S. servicemen and women that had fought for their country, been in the wrong part of Iraq at the wrong time, and now had to be killed, sterilized like nasty germs. It was appalling. It was unthinkable.

DDI Sleshing poured him a whiskey. It was a Bowmore single malt, twenty-five years old. The good stuff and terribly expensive. He saved it for great victories...and terrible tragedies.

"What did you get from CommStar?" he asked.

"More of the same. The Syrians are concentrating their cleanup to the north. Another little village called Mashyt. Sat photos are no different." He opened his briefcase and handed them to Sleshing. "Might as well look and have yourself a good cry."

Sleshing slipped on his glasses.

His fingers shook as he paged through them. Finally, shaking his head, he tore them up and dropped the pieces into the classified burn bag. For a long time VanderMissen and he just stared at each other, sipping their whiskey.

"Pershing's finally pitching in," Sleshing said without much enthusiasm, speaking of the Director of Central Intelligence. "Sonofabitch has had his hand in his shorts long enough. He's giving us some EDT units. Any objections?"

DNI VanderMissen shook his head. "Sounds fine. More manpower we put on this, the sooner we'll get some closure. I hope."

"I'll drink to that," Sleshing said, inhaling his whiskey.

The CIA Emergency Deployment Teams would help fill a few holes. With EDTs on the ground, it increased the chance of success and decreased the possibility that regular military or police units would become involved. The President didn't want that. Once it happened, Sleshing knew from experience, the classification of Top Secret they had slapped on this whole mess would go out the window. CNN would be crawling up the Pentagon's ass with all the newspaper and network people close behind.

"Even those dick-suckers at Fox won't be able to put a spin on this Grade-A clusterfuck," Sleshing grumbled.

"You talking to me or yourself, Wally?" VanderMissen asked.

"Both and maybe neither."

VanderMissen nodded. "I don't like how this is spilling out. Too many cooks in the kitchen. Deniability might not be an option soon. I already have a couple heavies from the NRO sniffing around my door," he said, referring to the National Reconnaissance Office, who operated America's spy satellites of which CommStar was but one.

"What's the makeup of those EDTs?"

Sleshing shrugged. "About what you figure. SAC/SOG operators, ex-Delta and DEVGRU with Blackpool thugs for muscle."

VanderMissen sighed. He didn't like that at all, more spillage, more security risks. But he knew he had no choice. He could raise some hell with Gus Costello, the National Security Advisor, who was in charge of coordinating operations but he knew in the end it was a matter of manpower. DCI Pershing, Roger Thorogood, and General Mason were all in bed with Blackpool, or XI, as it was now known. Blackpool was a private security company that provided "consultants" to the CIA who used them in counterterror operations worldwide. The Blackpool cadre were all ex-special ops soldiers under the umbrella of CIA SAC/SOG. They had been involved in a variety of bombings, assassinations, and human rights violations in Iraq and Afghanistan. XI had so many charges and lawsuits against them they had closed down their training facility in Georgia and opened up under the XI logo, Exeter International, in the UK. The name had changed but the company directive had not: they provided mercenaries and guns-for-hire. No more, no less.

VanderMissen despised everything they stood for. Under ordinary circumstances it would have been bad enough, but BioGen made it even more risky to bring in private contractors.

"I hope Pershing has control over those hoodlums," he said. "Because if he doesn't, if they leak any of this...Christ, the blowback will be like a fucking purge."

He needed to say no more.

Nobody wanted that. The country didn't need that.

"They'll be completely under S5 control, deployed where and when needed," Sleshing told him.

"Sure," VanderMissen said. "The Old Man's hungry for power and always has been. Now he has it."

"And if he has it, CBT has it," Sleshing said, referring to the fact that, technically, the Old Man was in the employ of Congdon BioTechnologies. As one of the world's largest corporate entities, their web was spun right through the fabric of the military-industrial complex. And sitting at the center like a bloated black widow spider was Elizabeth Toma.

"They've always had it," VanderMissen said. "Never doubt that."

Sleshing didn't. Through sleazy backdoor lobbying, huge bribes, and out-and-out extortion, CBT owned most of Capitol Hill. It was well known in DC that you did not fuck with Elizabeth Toma, that her network of spooks had something potentially damaging on just about everyone in power in the city.

*Wicked Witch of the East*, he thought.

BioGen had been a Section 5 project. So, technically, it was under the umbrella of the CIA as all S5 ops were, except that everyone knew that the technical and innovative muscle at S5 had come from CBT.

Years ago, when the National Security Council would meet and the topic of war in the Middle East came up, it was decided that alternative forms of warfare, if skillfully deployed, could save countless American and allied lives.

Certain groups were chosen to develop these weapons. The CIA's DS&T, Directorate of Science and Technology. The Office of Naval Research. The Army Research Office. DARPA. And they did just that. Long after the Gulf War and the terrorist attacks of 9/11, the results of these studies were looked at closely. Sleshing remembered the meeting when it all came down. It was at the White House. Those present were some of the same people present at the NMCC last May at the onset of the Syrian Incident. Sleshing was there, as was VanderMissen and Pershing. Admiral Paulus of the ONI. General Mason. A few others.

DARPA had submitted their proposals. As had the ONR and the ARO. But it was the CIA's that caught everyone's attention. Section 5 had come up with a real beauty. It was cheap, nearly impossible to trace, and controllable.

So they said.

Everyone had agreed that BioGen was a strong possibility.

And in late 2014, it was tried. Now here they were, the worst-case scenario playing out around them, things gradually spiraling out of control.

"I talked to Costello a little while ago," VanderMissen said. "He said the others will help one way or another. But we have to go through him."

"Figures. What about the Bureau?"

VanderMissen chuckled dryly. "No way. He doesn't want the FBI in on this in any way, shape, or form. Or should I say, the President doesn't."

"Ah, he's still got a bug up his ass about our G-men."

VanderMissen managed a smile. "My question is: What happens when the Bureau gets wind of this shit? Because they will. You know that."

Sleshing looked very old at that moment and felt even older. "This entire thing is going to escalate out of control. Just wait until Maddie Hughes at the DHS finds out. The reprisals are going to be bloody."

"That's for sure."

"Which brings us back to CBT again and Liz Toma. There's an unholy alliance between Langley and CBT. Pershing is a power player. He's got an agenda and we both know it. My guess is he's playing footsie with Colin Paulus and Frank Mason."

VanderMissen looked thoughtful. "Yes. Something's happening in the shadows, but I can't pinpoint it either. Whatever it is, I'm betting Bob Pershing is behind it."

"And if I know him, he's already selected his sacrificial pigs."

Sleshing nodded. "Meaning you and I?"

"You, me, possibly Gus Costello and Arlene Rabin. He's survived a lot of administrations and purges by playing the game. And we're in their sights."

"If we end up before a Senate subcommittee, I'm naming names," Sleshing said.

They both uttered dry, brittle laughs at the very idea. They could name all the names they wanted and commit professional and political suicide at the same time, but the bottom line was they'd never be able to prove it.

*Not unless we start gathering some intel of our own,* Sleshing thought. *Copying a few documents, making a few lists, duping a few CD-ROMs.*

Such a thing was technically treason and an absolute violation of the Official Secrets Act. But it was also insurance. Might not be a bad idea. If the stink were big enough, DCI Pershing's SAC boys would never dare come after them.

"We have to start thinking of ourselves, Wally. How we're going to survive this."

"You're right. Fuck the lot of em." Sleshing poured himself another. "I say we begin discussing strategy over a couple thick steaks."

"Best thing I've heard all day."

# EAST CHICAGO, INDIANA

## MARKTOWN

**6:45 P.M.**

Carolyn Argante didn't get it until it was too late.

She'd come back from the Gulf like a lot of other soldiers. A little older. A little wiser. A little more disgusted and cynical at mankind for inventing warfare in the first place. And more than a little in awe of the weapons in the Army's arsenal. Many of which hadn't even been tested under combat conditions until boots were on the ground. You could play war games with them. You could see them destroy derelict trucks and tanks at a healthy distance. You could watch endless demonstrations. Sit through Endless lectures. But until you saw them destroy enemy vehicles and turn enemy platoons into so much hamburger... you just didn't get it.

Carolyn didn't get it until Az Khubat.

Az Khubat was a desolate stretch of nothing about five miles outside of Mosul and it was where, for her, the shit truly hit the fan. Before that, Carolyn had seen more of the war on CNN than first hand. She was traveling in a convoy of six trucks. Medical supplies. Nothing exotic or exciting.

The Iraqis didn't care.

A rogue unit came barreling out of the desert in Soviet BMP-2 reconnaissance vehicles. The area was supposedly secure. The Marines had swept through there already. The dozens and dozens of destroyed tanks and trucks smoldering alongside the road had been evidence of this, as were the mangled bodies of the Republican Guard.

Yet, somehow, a few Iraqis had avoided the leathernecks and here they were.

Ready to do some damage.

The convoy came to a stop when the Iraqis opened up. The BMP-2s were equipped with 7.62mm RPK machine guns, 30mm cannons, and AT-5 Spandrel anti-tank missiles. They raked the trucks with machine gun fire. Tires popped. Radiators were ripped open. Windshields exploded. And, yes, people started dying. The transport sergeant sitting next to Carolyn—an amiable Hispanic guy from Phoenix who talked endlessly of his children back in the States—took a volley of slugs to the face. Carolyn was sprayed with his blood and brains. Bone chips had been embedded into her cheeks and chin. People were screaming and trucks were burning. Confusion. Disorientation. Blood. Bodies. Terror.

Carolyn froze in the cab of the truck as lead zinged past her, a brown bar second lieutenant ninety-day wonder and feeling every bit of it. Nothing in her training had prepared her for this. Nothing possibly could. The Iraqis (who shouldn't have been there to begin with) had surprised them, gunning out of the blowing sand like juggernauts.

"This can't be fucking happening," a voice kept saying in a shrill screech. And it took her a moment or two to realize that it was her voice and that she had most certainly peed her pants.

About that time, the door to her side was flung open and one of the senior sergeants grabbed her by the arm like an idiot schoolgirl and said, "C'mon, lieutenant! Goddammit, move!" He flung her out of the cab and into the dirt. He pushed her along and into the desert to a rock outcropping where the others were forming up a skirmish line. She noticed then that she'd forgotten her weapon.

Others were trying to make it to the rocks, too, with mixed success.

Two of her nurses made it. Three other soldiers were cut down mere feet away. The major got caught in a barrage of machine gun fire. Two of the gunners in the BMP-2s had caught him in crossfire and he was out there dancing like a puppet with clipped strings, bits of his anatomy flying this way and that. They were enjoying it. She could see them laughing as they emptied their drums of ammo. Finally the major (or what there was of him) collapsed. The Spandrel missiles had turned their trucks into burning scrap iron. Iraqi soldiers were trying to assault their position, supported by 30mm cannon fire and the ever-present popping of the RPKs. Many had died, but they had gotten no closer. The sergeant and his rifle squad were picking them off despite the incoming slugs and blowing sand and erupting real estate.

About that time, a pair of AH-64 Apache helicopters showed up.

Obviously, somebody had been smart enough to call them in.

And thank God. Because the Iraqis were tiring of the fun and games and were about to let loose a barrage of Spandrels at the recalcitrant Yankees.

The Apaches came in low and the Iraqis tried to scatter. No dice. The Apache gunners opened up with their 30mm chain guns and turned the fleeing Iraqis into dog food. They showered down salvos of Hydra-70 rockets that exploded and sent razor-sharp metal flechettes flying in every direction. What the chain guns missed, these ripped into confetti. The BMP-2s, once so deadly, seemed positively impotent. They and their crews tried to evade as well, but all they got for their trouble were TOW missiles that blew them into flaming fragments.

So as quickly as it had started, it was over.

And until she had snapped out of her shock and attended to the wounded, she just hadn't gotten it. Until she'd seen the bullet-ridden corpses torn sometimes completely in half she hadn't gotten it. But when she'd seen the seared limbs and bodies burnt black and the vehicles turned to blazing iron sculptures, then she'd gotten it.

It had put her down, vomiting, into the sand, but she'd gotten it, all right. She was a little slow sometimes, but she always figured it out in the end.

She'd been home for five years now. She'd been having pains in her belly for the past month, dropping a frightening amount of weight while her belly continued to swell like it was filled with gas...or she was pregnant. She was a trained nurse. She knew the warning signs. But she had done nothing.

Now she was pretty sure she was dying.

She was no diagnostician, but she had a good idea that whatever was eating away her guts wasn't good. The pains were unbearable now and the clinical side of her was saying that there was probably a good-sized tumor devouring her innards. It was also saying that she was a real damn idiot for not getting this taken care of in the first place. In her job, she saw people like that every day. People who just refused to go to their doctors. People who put off medical exams because they made them uncomfortable or scared them or they just couldn't spare the time in their busy lives. They put off the very things that could start the wheels of medical science spinning in their favor.

But Carolyn had never thought she would be one of them.

She hadn't been out of her apartment in three days now. She was simply too weak. Couldn't move. Could barely think. For the past twenty-four hours she'd been on the couch, near-paralysis, awash in her own filth. What sleep there was, was thin and grainy. She was not sure where reality started and dream stopped. And she was hungry. Godawful hungry. She kept dreaming of raw meat. The very idea of it made her head spin and her mouth water.

Her brain was working good enough in between the walls of gray nothingness to tell her she was hallucinating freely. For instance, right now the clammy, discolored flesh of her belly was bloated obscenely. It had become a huge, distended mound like a nightmare pregnancy coming to term. And that had to be a hallucination.

It just couldn't be.

But what was really crazy was the other thing. The tight, damp skin of her belly kept...rippling, as if some living thing were moving in there. Something muscled and thick pressing against the flesh.

This had to be a hallucination.

But, once again, Carolyn just wasn't getting it.

It was about that time that she heard a key in the door. In the back of her mind she knew it had to be Rhonda. Rhonda had been after her for weeks to go to the doctor and now, not hearing from her, she was coming to check on her. It was what significant others did.

Carolyn's head whipped back and forth. She tried to cry out, to warn Rhonda away. *Please please oh please darling get out of here get out of here.* Too late. With a gasp, Rhonda was at her side, taking hold of her.

"Carolyn!" she cried. "Carolyn! What's wrong with you?"

So Carolyn showed her—Rhonda had arrived just in time to see her give birth.

**7:33 P.M.**

Cave wasn't in the mood for it, but they gave it to him anyway.

"Listen, boss," McKenna said. "You know me. You know how I operate: I don't ask questions, I don't pass moral judgements... but this, I mean, Christ, this is just wrong. These people are vets, for godsake. This is a hell of a thing to be doing to them."

Stein nodded his head. He knew just as McKenna knew that you didn't ask questions in this game and you sure as hell didn't complain... but this, this was wrong in just about every way.

Cave said, "Just do what you're told."

"We are, boss, but this is getting weird and you know it," McKenna said with all due respect. "Usually they contract us out for one or two, sometimes a few more than that...but this...shit, what the hell is going on here?"

Cave brushed an imaginary piece of lint from his overcoat. "What's going on here is none of your concern and none of mine. We do what the Old Man says and that's that. If you two can't stomach it, transfer out."

"You know it's not that," McKenna said. "You know both of us very well, goddammit. We do our jobs, sir. We always have and we always will. But these guys in the biocon suits... what the fuck gives here?"

"He's right, sir," Stein chimed in. "We're not stupid. We know how to keep our mouths shut. Just do the job and move on. But it's different this time. I mean, what do these people have that makes them so damn dangerous? Is it a disease or something they got in the war? And if it is—"

"If it is," McKenna finished for him, "if it is, then how contagious is it? I mean, shouldn't we be wearing that HAZMAT gear, too?"

Cave nodded slowly. He wanted to tell them both that they were breaching protocol, that they were compromising a highly classified operation. That they were treading in shit so deep that they might drown at any moment.

But he didn't.

Because he knew exactly how they felt.

"Listen, boys. I don't know much more about this business than you do. But you're completely safe. You've got my word on that."

Stein and McKenna looked at each other, then at Cave. They didn't look convinced.

Cave sighed. "The Old Man assured me that if we follow proper procedure, we'd have nothing to worry about. Whatever you might think of him, I tell you that you can trust him. He might act like an uppity prick, but he's on the level." He shrugged. "Besides, do you think if there was any danger of contagion the Old Man would show up dressed in street clothes? Don't you think he'd be wearing a rubber suit too?"

They still didn't look satisfied; not really.

"Yeah, but he didn't handle those bodies, boss. We did," McKenna said.

"There's no danger," Cave affirmed. "You're just going to have to take my word for it."

"I guess we don't have a choice," Stein said hopelessly.

Cave smirked. "Oh, but you do, you do. You can get out right now, boys, if that's what you want." He looked from Stein to McKenna. "Go ahead. Don't worry, this ain't the fucking *X Files* or some such shit. Nobody's gonna kill you for what you know. Of course..."

"What?" they both said.

"If the Company doesn't think they can trust you, that you might betray your loyalty oath, that you don't deserve the security classification they stamped on your ass, they might have to tuck you away somewhere for a while." He sighed. "But it won't be too bad, boys. They'll just tuck you away in one of their mountain hideaways. There's a nice one out in Utah, I hear. They call it The Resort. Anything you want, you get. Of course...they'll have to debrief for about eighteen hours a day while you squat in a dark cell so small you can't stretch your legs or even stand up. But after a few months or a few years they'll let you out. By the time they're through with your sorry asses you won't remember any of this, let alone your own mother's fucking name or whether you're animal, vegetable, or mineral. Don't worry, though, they'll program you with a whole new personality. That's how they retire guys like you."

Stein said, "Wait a minute. Unlike you, sir, we don't work for the Company. We're private contractors, remember? We work for XI."

"That's right, boss," McKenna chipped in.

Cave lit a cigarette and laughed. "Now don't play stupid, boys. Who do you think owns XI?"

Stein said nothing. He'd suspected it as did many but here was confirmation—XI was a CIA proprietary.

"All right, all right," McKenna sighed. "Enough said."

"Stein?"

"Let's do it."

"Good. Because you've both wasted enough of my time. Let's not have this conversation again. I'm gonna let you guys get away with this and it won't go in your file. But next time..."

Stein said, "Let's get to work already."

Cave smiled, satisfied.

They made their way casually to Apartment 6. It was the residence of another Iraqi vet. Beyond that, he didn't know much. And truth be told, it was probably much better that way. When they got to the door, they all heard it—some kind of crazy howling, a loud moaning, a gobbling sound.

McKenna looked to Stein. His eyes were beady and staring. McKenna knew that look: it was fear. He knew it real well, because he was feeling it right then himself. His belly was full of cold, crawling snakes.

"The door," Cave said, an edge to his voice. "Open it."

McKenna licked his salty lips with a dry tongue. Carefully, quietly, he tried it. It was open. He pushed it in and all three men went in quickly, moving in a prearranged formation. One man slipping forward, covered by the other two. Then the next man and the next. Repeating.

The moaning sounds had stopped.

The dread silence was almost worse.

It wasn't a bad place. Nice furniture, potted plants, prints by Van Gogh and Monet on the walls. A huge oak entertainment center with a widescreen TV, Blu-ray player, a few books. The carpet was a butterscotch in color, deep and plush as summer moss. Everything looked new, expensive, and in its proper place. And that's why none of it made any goddamn sense. A person with this kind of taste, this kind of time spent decorating and arranging... they just didn't allow their place to smell like this.

And the place really stank.

It was a heavy, pungent odor, a decaying smell like a seething jungle swamp clogged with rotting vegetation.

"Jesus," McKenna said, turning away.

"Like a death camp," Cave said without a trace of humor. From the look on his face, both men were pretty sure he knew what he was talking about.

Then they heard a sound: a wet, awful slithering.

Cave nodded and Stein moved towards it, McKenna at his heels. Cave followed. All three men had their automatics out. They were all sweating, uneasy. It was hot in there...but not that hot. The rain slickers and leather driving gloves didn't help much.

On the bed they saw two bodies.

At first it looked like one... but then they separated.

"Sonofabitch," Stein gasped. "What the fuck is that?"

# LANGLEY, VIRGINIA

## CIA CRISIS CENTER

**7:46 P.M.**

The more DCI Pershing thought about it, the better it sounded.

It was the mark of a superior man that could turn an ugly, adverse situation to his advantage. And Robert Pershing was such a man. His beginnings were humble: a three-room farmhouse in northern Wisconsin. But Pershing hadn't been content to starve and struggle like his father and mother. He studied hard and was accepted to West Point. He graduated in the top ten percent of his class. In the early 1980s, he'd been a military advisor in Beirut and Honduras. Following that, he'd joined the CIA and was appointed to the Special Activities Division's Political Action Group. As a SAD/PAG paramilitary officer, he planned and executed the downfall of various enemy states and individuals (all without ever leaving his desk). He returned to Beirut in '86 as the Station Chief in the years following the abduction and murder of William Buckley. It had been a struggle from then until now. And Pershing bore the battle scars of ambition—two failed marriages, three children who wanted very little to do with him, innumerable enemies. When you had ambitions, godly aspirations, you collected enemies like a dog collects ticks.

Pershing couldn't count all the people on five hands, let alone two, that he'd shit on, coerced, and even blackmailed to get where he was today. But if it had taught him anything, it was to spot opportunity.

According to his calculations and those of his closest aides, the country was fucked.

Oh, the BioGen dilemma could be controlled... possibly... but it was seriously unlikely that that general populace wouldn't find out about it. The infestation would cause widespread panic. People would lose faith in their leaders.

They would want someone strong and capable.

In the resulting maelstrom, Pershing could be that man.

It wouldn't be easy, of course.

It would mean plot, subplot, and counterplot.

It would mean that when the country was plunged into anarchy, men in power would have to be removed by force. It would mean a military coup. A violent, revolutionary takeover of the government.

Pershing had been thinking about this for a long time.

In the coming weeks, the opportunity would be coming.

But was he up to it?

Did he have the balls, the audacity, to even consider usurping the most powerful man in the world? Did he dare to think that he could seize control via military overthrow of the United States? After all, this was the USA he was thinking of, not some Third World banana republic. America wasn't some mismanaged, backward hellhole in Central America or Africa. Had it been, the entire thing would have been fairly simple. Pershing was an old hand at such subterfuge.

In order to do what had to be done, a few things would have to happen. The first was that the current situation—the fallout from BioGen—would have to get very bad. The second was that the situation would have to deteriorate sufficiently enough to cause mass panic and confusion. When that happened, when people lost complete faith in their leader, when the country teetered on the edge of revolution, when rioting and clashes between police and civilians became commonplace and your average Joe had his civil rights violated on a daily basis... then, then there was a good chance for a coup.

Pershing had been thinking of such a coup for years.

And why not? In his job he had planned and executed many such insurrections for more than one President. What this one would need, as all usually do, would be the support of the military. Without it, it was hopeless. There was no way Pershing could take the country with the limited paramilitary resources of the Special Activities Center. Three or four hundred SAC/SOG operators bolsters by CT units could realistically seize key seats of power in the country, but they could not hold them. The moment it happened, the Joint Chiefs of Staff and CENTCOM would qualify the SOG teams as saboteurs and enemy combatants and they'd be put down by the military and police.

No, if that's all Pershing had, his revolution would die quickly. The regular military would crush them. Counterterrorist teams like Delta Force and SEAL Team Six would be mobilized instantly. Although such groups were prevented by the constitution from being deployed domestically, the President or his replacement would find a way. A simple slash of the pen.

No, he had to have support.

There were plenty of old hard-liners in the military's command structure who despised the country's half-assed leadership. They would be the ones to work on when the time came, as well as their counterparts in the police and intelligence communities. And by that time, the seat of power would already be seized.

The bottom line was this. Once the President and his cabinet were eliminated, the power vacuum would be filled by Pershing and his associates. They would cut off the head of one snake and graft another onto its writhing body and the vacuum would be sealed.

Pershing smiled.

It was possible. It certainly was. He would support VanderMissen and Sleshing for the moment. He would turn over some Emergency Response Teams. And they would play along...until he gave the order for things to begin. And then everyone involved with BioGen (save himself) would be the first to go.

The time was coming.

He began looking over his list of names.

# EAST CHICAGO, INDIANA

## MARKTOWN

**7:56 P.M.**

Stein, like McKenna, had been through the shit.

He'd been playing the game for twenty-odd years, first in the Army, then for the DEA, and now with Blackpool/XI. He'd seen dead men before. He'd seen them blown piecemeal by grenades, artillery, airstrikes. Seen them ripped in half by machine gun fire. Seen guys get their throats slit, their heads cut off by machetes. He'd seen men beaten to death with baseball bats, tortured, skinned, turned to blackened husks by napalm. He'd seen mutilations of every possible kind. He'd seen human wave attacks reduced to human pulp by heavy machine guns and airburst shells.

In his way of thinking, you could not truly understand the human condition until you saw the wreckage of war firsthand, until you'd smelled death and tasted its blackness in your mouth. Until you looked down the smoking barrel of failed diplomacy and saw death staring lividly back at you. Then, and only then, would you know the sort of hell on earth men had made of their Eden.

And having seen it, he was perfectly fatalistic in every way.

Just like every other man or woman who'd been in combat.

No flag-waving, no patriotism, no political agendas, just death laid raw. That's what life was, he knew: a hand reaching towards the grave.

He knew it as McKenna knew it and Cave knew it.

McKenna had spent three years in Afghanistan with MARSOC and four more with Blackpool as a private operator. Cave was a twenty-five-year veteran of Army Special Forces, raising hell everywhere from Africa to Central America. And since, with the Company, he'd seen more human wreckage and destruction save anyone but God himself.

But this...this was insanity.

This was beyond death.

The bed was a bog of blood and noxious slime and mucus. They originally thought there was one body, but then they saw two. Two women, bloated and naked, wet with a yellowish jelly. They were connected at the mouth by something that looked very much like a huge, pale segmented worm. As it convulsed, their bodies rose up, expanding as if they were filled with gas, limbs trembling and eyes rolling like mad marbles...and the worm itself—if worm it was—grew pink and swollen as if it were drawing blood from its hosts with slow deliberate sips.

Tingling waves went up and down Stein's spine, spreading out over his forearms. *Alive*, he thought. *Those people are alive.*

And by the looks of unparalleled horror in their eyes, they were not only alive but aware of what was happening to them, what had burrowed deep inside them.

"Oh shit, oh shit," McKenna whimpered.

"Keep back, gentlemen," Cave said, his normal baritone gone to a shrill, dry scraping. "Don't get any closer."

Neither man had any intention of doing that.

Cave whipped out an encrypted secure cell with a trembling hand. He nearly dropped it. His breath coming in short, sharp gasps, he punched in a number very quickly. "Get that team up here for fuck's sake... we got a couple live ones! You hear me? I need a BCT stat! We got fucking adult forms in this room..."

Stein just kept staring.

There were some things in life you just couldn't look away from. And the worm was one of them. It just kept doing its thing, expanding and deflating with an absolutely horrid rubbery squeaking sound like an over-inflated balloon. As if air was being pumped into it, then bled off. But it wasn't air, of course, it was blood. The thing was about as big around as a man's forearm, but each time it deflated it went nearly flat like the peel of onion. Each segment had little glistening hooks set on either side.

The woman on the left opened her eyes completely and looked at them, gagging and gasping as the worm moved in her throat. Neither Cave, McKenna, or Stein had ever seen anything so absolutely repulsive. Or pathetic, for they could see she wanted help.

"Jesus fucking Christ, she's alive," McKenna blubbered. "She's alive! She's fucking alive!"

"Knock it off," Cave said. "There's nothing we can do for her."

"We can put her out of her misery," Stein suggested.

"No firing," Cave said, "unless we have to."

McKenna didn't see it that way, though.

Something had been boiling in him for days and this... this obscenity was just about what it took to set it free.

"Fuck that," he said.

He started shooting on full auto. Stein followed suit. Before Cave could do a damn thing to intercede, bullets were slamming into the parasite and the two bodies it fed off of. Blood and flesh and worm-matter splattered against the walls. It didn't take very long. Within what seemed seconds both men had emptied their clips.

"GODDAMMIT!" Cave shrieked. "WHAT THE FUCK DID I JUST SAY?"

McKenna and Stein didn't really care what he'd just said or what he was saying now. Mechanically, they ejected the old magazines and inserted fresh ones.

But Cave got in front of them. "No," he said. "Either of you start shooting and I grease both of you." He had his Steyr nine-millimeter pointed at McKenna's face. The big, barrel-like silencer was inches from the man's nose. "Swear to God," he murmured.

And then behind him... a sound.

The bodies on the bed were so full of holes they reminded Stein of death photos of Bonnie and Clyde he'd once seen. They were bulging and jutting, the skin stretched taut in some places, sagging in others. Like maybe bones and organs and tissues had ruptured inside, exploding beneath the flesh. But they were dead, they could feel no pain.

But the worm... it wasn't dead.

Punched with bullet holes, it was very much alive.

It slithered out of the woman on the right, sliding free of her mouth with a wet, slippery sound, segment by hideous segment, a good three feet of it if not four. Its flesh was a bleached, glistening white, nearly translucent where the segments joined. A white like bacon lard. When it was free of its host, the corpse slid off the bed, a tangled loose-limbed torso that hit the floor with a meaty, sprawling thud, jaws springing open with the impact and a slush of black fluid draining into the carpet.

"Where the hell are they?" Cave asked in an airless voice. "Where the fuck is that containment team?"

Slowly, he backed up, forcing Stein and McKenna back with him.

The worm squirmed on the bed sluggishly, twisting and writhing, seeming to pulsate thickly as if it were breathing. Then, straight as an arrow, it shot up into the air, its hooks digging into the stucco ceiling. It pulled the other woman up with it. She hung there momentarily like a corpse-puppet, swaying back and forth with the motion of the worm, then its posterior end slid from her mouth and she dropped to the bed.

It dangled from the ceiling like an inchworm from a milkweed leaf, moving with a slick serpentine motion. It was eyeless, featureless save for an X-shaped slit at its bulbous snout. As they watched, mesmerized by the sheer malignant beauty of the thing, the slit opened up, the flesh seeming to retract from it. There were four undulating snakelike things that might have been tongues, wriggling like night crawlers on a hook.

"WHERE THE FUCK IS THAT TEAM?" Cave shouted.

The worm let out a perfectly hideous mewling sound and that was pretty much all it took. Stein and McKenna snapped. They knocked Cave out of the way and drew their guns. It was either that or run. Inaction was impossible; you couldn't let a thing like that live.

They started shooting and as the first bullets hit it, the worm contracted to half its length and vomited a stream of black bile at Stein. It missed by scant inches, striking the wallpaper in a wet spray.

"Fuck this," Stein said and kept firing.

The slugs shattered the thing into a million flabby fragments, worm blood and worm tissue splattered everywhere. This time Cave made no attempt to stop them. When they were finished, there was worm meat everywhere...on the walls, dripping in vile gouts from the ceiling. There was a stink of cordite and a sharp, agonizing stench of ammonia. There were shell casings gleaming everywhere.

And eggs...a spreading pool of snotty, glistening eggs.

About that time, the containment team showed up.

**8:41 P.M.**

Shawna Geddes was parked about half a block away.

She'd followed the van—a white Ford Econoline with HAPPY VALLEY MEATS stenciled on the side—from Portage Park to what looked like an old disused warehouse in one of the River North neighborhoods in the Furniture District. The place was enclosed by a chain-link fence with dogs and a couple guys with crewcuts watching the gate. They admitted the van, then quickly locked the gate with chains and padlocks. She drove by the place twice, but saw nothing. No signs or indications of any sort as to what was going on there.

But she knew one thing.

Whatever was going on at that place wasn't good, wasn't normal. HAPPY VALLEY MEATS or not, it sure as hell wasn't a meat processing plant. And if it was, the security was awfully tight. On her second pass, she saw that there were men walking the fence all over the place. And what did that imply?

She'd heard that some of these old warehouses were sometimes used by the Chicago Outfit for whacking enemies and disposing of the remains. As chop shops for stripping and repainting stolen vehicles. Or even as factories to process heroin and cocaine. If that was the case, then she wasn't too sure if she wanted to look into this any deeper.

She parked at a convenience store about a block away and just kept watch.

The minutes turned to hours. She dozed off more than once. Then, around 7:30, the van took off again. It went on a long drive and she followed at a very discreet distance, sometimes with her lights off. The van went south on

I-94, out of the city and across the Indiana border into the tri-city area of Gary, Hammond, and East Chicago. Finally, settling on the latter, it went to an apartment complex over in Marktown at Prospect Street and Pine where they had all those historical buildings, the white stucco rowhouses that looked like they'd been plucked from Victorian slums.

And that's where she was now, waiting and waiting, and not really even knowing why she was doing any of this. Maybe it was boredom. Maybe it was diversion. But, deep inside, she knew it was something more.

Curiosity.

*Maybe this is none of your business,* she kept telling herself. *Maybe this is Mob business. Something to do with drugs or a turf war or something equally unpleasant. If that's the case, Shawna, they won't appreciate you nosing around.*

Yet...yet something told her it wasn't that simple.

Using her little binoculars from the glove compartment (the previous owner had left them and she'd never found a use for them—until now), she tried to keep an eye on what was going down at the apartment house. But it was no easy trick; it was too damn dark out. The front of the building was illuminated well enough, but the streets were murky. She saw three men go into the building, but nothing more. She couldn't really tell if they were the same guys from the park or not.

There was nothing more to do but get in closer.

On foot, she slipped up the opposite side of the street until she found a darkened house nearly across from the building. Squatting behind a row of wild rose bushes, she kept watch.

About a minute after she got there another van pulled up.

It was also stenciled with the same logo, but it was much larger with a humming refrigeration unit hanging over the cab. That fit in with the meat thing, but still it didn't make a hell of a lot of sense when you came right down to it.

*Oh shit... oh shit... what is this all about?*

With a shaking hand, she took out her iPhone and zoomed on the vans, videoing them. Sneaking forward carefully, ducking behind parked cars, then trees and shrubs, she got in close enough to get some good shots.

Three more men dressed in what looked like white rubber suits hopped out of the back of the refrigerated van. They carried matching hoods with glass face masks. They also carried—and very carefully—silver tanks with sprayer attachments. Like the sort exterminators might have. Quickly, they went in. She kept the video rolling, getting as much as she could. Two other men hopped out of the cab of the other van and just stood there, scanning the street and nearby houses.

Like a security detail.

Shawna was scared shitless by that point.

This entire thing was weird beyond weird. Whatever HAPPY VALLEY MEATS was a cover for, it had to be real bad news.

The big question, of course, was: Why the hell wasn't anybody noticing any of this? It was low-key, yes, but it was still damned weird. Somebody had to notice guys in white radiation suits, you'd think.

Somewhere in these tightly pressed blocks of houses there had to be at least one grumpy old man or crotchety old lady with nothing better to do than stare out their windows. People like that called the cops every time a car backfired for chrissake.

But not now?

Shawna began to get very suspicious when five, then ten, and finally fifteen minutes passed and the police did not show. It was unnerving and somewhat creepy.

What if you called them and they didn't come because they weren't SUP-POSED to come?

Paranoia. She had to take it down a notch.

With those guys watching the street, she didn't dare move. She crouched in the bushes until her feet and calves were numb, her face beaded with sweat. Once she tipped forward and grabbed a rose stem for support. The thorns sank into her thumb and forefinger. She wanted very badly to cry out, but didn't dare. She chewed her lip and waited, stock still.

*What the fuck have you gotten yourself into now?* a little pissed-off voice in her head asked. *Isn't it enough to ruin marriages and lose jobs, now you have to lose your life as well?*

But maybe she was being paranoid.

Maybe there was a perfectly innocent explanation for all this, though she seriously doubted it. Call it woman's intuition or journalistic instinct, but something was really rotten here. Rotten and deadly and bizarre and it stank like shit. Something that was apparently above and beyond the law.

And Shawna Geddes was stuck right in the middle.

And for the time being, that's exactly where she was staying.

**9:03 P.M.**

After they'd put the worm out of its misery, the hit team climbed back into their van without saying a word. By that time, a BCT had arrived and taken over. The bedroom of Carolyn Argante, deceased, had to be cleaned and sterilized before anyone called it a night. And that included digging bullets from the walls.

*We make the mess,* McKenna thought, *and they vacuum it up.*

Cave drove about three blocks and then pulled to the curb, just down from a saloon called Happy Hannigan's. He dug out his gun and handed it to Stein. "All weapons in the bag."

They each put their handguns and remaining magazines in a plastic bag for disposal. They had been used and were now traceable. They had to be destroyed.

When Stein zipped the bag shut, he said, "Thank God for silencers or we'd have had cops crawling up our ass."

"The containment team knew," McKenna said. "They knew exactly what they were coming into."

Cave lit a cigarette in the darkness, sighing. Finally, he shook his head and said, "Boys, I had no idea—"

"You knew," McKenna said, his face screwed up into a sour mask. "You knew all about those...things."

Cave looked to Stein, but he wouldn't meet his gaze.

"I had some indication that—"

"Fuck you!" McKenna snapped. "And don't you dare look at me like that, goddammit! I don't give a healthy shit how you outrank me or how fucking long you been in! You knew. You fucking knew, boss! You knew what kind of risk we were running and you never warned us."

"Take it easy," Cave said, more of a request than an order. "Yeah, I knew some. More than you guys did. But you couldn't be told. The Old Man wouldn't allow it. Can't you see that? The security classification on this whole operation is right through the roof. I've never seen anything like it."

McKenna just shook his head and kept shaking it. His hands were balled into fists and they were trembling badly. His whole body was jittering, shuddering, his mind bugging out.

"Maybe I wanna transfer out, boss," he said. "Maybe I don't give a shit if they send me to your Resort and pick my brains clean. Maybe I just don't give a shit. Because with what I saw in there, I don't want to remember anymore."

Cave pulled a pint of Jim Beam out from under the seat. He cracked it and drank long and hard off it. He handed it to McKenna who did the same, spilling a great deal down his chin.

Stein declined; whiskey wasn't going to solve this mess.

He'd sat there quietly and listened to Cave and McKenna go at it and he hadn't said a thing. Now he changed that.

"Sir," he said, quietly, respectfully. "We had a right to know about what we were up against. We didn't need to know everything, just the basics. It's a soldier's right, I think. I mean, if I was still in the Army and we dropped in to snatch some ratbag terrorist, then we'd have the right to know if said ratbag had two bodyguards with AKs in the room with him. Not telling us that could compromise the entire mission." He let that sink in for a few seconds. "And you not telling us just what kind of shit we were wading into compromises this mission. Do you see that?"

Cave exhaled a cloud of smoke. "Yes, I see that," he said. "And if it was up to me, you would have known. But the Old Man calls the shots."

"It's bullshit, sir."

"I know it is."

Stein sighed. "Maybe McKenna's right. Maybe we should get out."

"That's your choice."

Cave started up the van and let both of them think it over.

He drove slowly, heading out of East Chicago and getting back on the freeway. He did not speak and neither did the others. All the way back across the Illinois state line and into Chi, they did not speak. Cave let the silence lay so his men could sort it out in their own brains. Once at the Operations Center down by the river, they would have to make a choice. He dearly hoped it was the right one. They apparently didn't comprehend the gravity of this whole thing. All across the country, there were other teams doing what they were doing. For once it wasn't blind killing. For once what they were doing had a reason beyond politics. Beyond security leaks. This time they were attempting to protect the entire country.

When they got back to the warehouse, they would have to be sterilized, all three of them. They had come into close proximity with the nasty end result of what had once been called Project BioGen. Their clothing would have to be burned. They would have to be showered and scrubbed with special chemical soaps that would kill any egg casings they may have come into contact with.

The thought of one of those things growing in his belly made Cave break out in an icy sweat.

"Make the right decision, boys," he said as he drove up I-94 into the depths of the city, purposely not looking at either of them. "Because if you don't... God help you."

**9:29 P.M.**

About the time the white van pulled away, Shawna made her move.

An awful knot in her guts, she crawled across the side yard of the house and made it to the alley. Luckily, there were no dogs around. Coming face to face with somebody's Doberman would have been bad...but not as bad as coming face to face with the men across the street.

The alley was fairly dark and she made good time.

She carried her heels and went as fast as she could, ruining a good pair of nylons, but for once not really giving a shit. She was almost to the end when some old guy—dressed in sagging underwear and nothing else—decided it was time to take the garbage out. Under any other circumstances, it would have been hilarious. He stood there, Hefty bag swinging in his fist, underwear drooping down his ass, staring. It probably wasn't every day he met some leggy brunette in an Anne Klein business suit cut to mid-thigh jogging up his alley.

Shawna muttered "Hello," and kept going.

She saw her little Nissan waiting for her.

She took a few minutes and just watched, satisfying herself that there were no heavies hanging around waiting to grab her.

When she was behind the wheel, she had a cigarette and allowed herself to breathe.

"You're going to walk away from this," she said under her breath. "You're going to walk away from whatever this mess is and you're not going to look back. If you do that, you'll live."

It was the thing to do.

The only sane thing to do.

And it really was her intention until the patrol car pulled up next to her.

"Problems?" the cop said through his unrolled window. His white teeth gleamed like the grille of a Pontiac.

"No. Just leaving... something wrong?"

He shook his head. "Nothing at all. Have a good night."

That was fucking weird.

The knot was back in her belly again as she drove away. She sensed, rather than knew, that that cop just hadn't casually stopped by. Maybe he'd been sent. Regardless, he probably jotted down her license number.

*Don't be paranoid.*

But was she being paranoid? Is that all it was? What she'd seen today and tonight would give anybody a healthy sense of paranoia. But she didn't really believe that was it. There was an unfathomable gnawing dread in her belly and try as she might she just couldn't dismiss it.

She didn't want to know any more about this.

But she had a terrible feeling it wouldn't be that easy.

# CHICAGO, RIVER NORTH

## THE WAREHOUSE

**11:17 P.M.**

The warehouse proved to be a perfect location for the Operations Center. There were general, low-containment areas such as living quarters for the teams, logistics and control, and computer sciences which allowed the teams to be linked up with other operational teams as well as the Defense Department, and the data base at the Army's bio-research center at Fort Detrick, Maryland. There were high containment laboratories, operating theaters, and dissection rooms. All of which were at P-4 containment status, the most physically secure available. It was the status at which deadly bioengineered pathogens were manipulated and studied. The Op Center was also equipped with state-of-the-art medical incinerators to dispose of contaminated and/or hazardous biological materials.

It was assembled from prefab materials in under eight hours.

After Cave, Stein, and McKenna had been thoroughly sterilized, they were assembled in a small, makeshift office with the Old Man. The atmosphere was tense, deadly with implication.

"Colonel Cave has told me that you men are unhappy in your work," the Old Man said. "And I really can't adequately tell you how that troubles me."

Stein just sat there, studying his hands.

McKenna shrugged. "We weren't briefed properly, sir. We went blindly into a situation. We could have all been killed by that thing."

The Old Man rubbed his manicured fingers together. "Yes. Yes, that was an unfortunate situation." He stared at McKenna, his icy blue eyes withering the other man until he looked away. "But now you know. You know what we're dealing with here."

"Not really, sir. We're as confused as ever."

And he was.

All he really knew was that they were assigned to remove certain members of the armed forces that had served in the Iraq War. That's how it had started. They were told it was a matter of national security and nothing more. And now they were dealing with what appeared to be some sort of parasitic worm of all things.

When they got back from East Chi, they were stripped and showered and scrubbed with chemicals. Then there were blood samples, urine, feces, MRI scans. Their clothes went into biohazard bags for disposal. The bodies and assorted biological waste were taken from the refrigerated BCT van and put directly into the incinerator.

McKenna was at a loss. A total loss. "I feel like I'm living some nightmare. I wish somebody would wake me."

Stein nodded to that. "Sir...what the hell is this about?"

"I'm afraid I can't tell you that...being that you both wish to terminate your employ."

McKenna was starting to sweat now.

He didn't like the way the Old Man said that. In fact, he didn't like any of this at all. But when you came right down to it, he wasn't sure who scared him more—the worms or the Old Man. That something like the worms existed at all was beyond the realm of what he'd always considered reality. Things like that couldn't be. But they were. Regardless, they were still just animals, creatures of an extremely disgusting variety, but just animals. The Old Man, on the other hand, was perhaps worse. McKenna truly wished he'd kept his mouth shut. He knew the Old Man too well to want to fuck with him. He ordered the deaths of others the way other men ordered shrimp as an appetizer.

That was the real scary part.

McKenna was no stranger to death and killing. But there was always a certain code, very ambiguous at times, but still a code. You killed the bad guys, you killed the targets which were assigned to you. Targets which generally were terrorists, enemy operatives, security risks within the establishment. But through all of it, you knew (or hoped) that you could trust those you worked for.

It was different with the Old Man.

He saw his people, all people for that matter, as tools. Mechanical con-trivances performing a required task. And when they ceased to be useful...w ell, McKenna had a pretty good idea what happened then.

And that's why he was scared shitless.

"Yes," the Old Man went on, "this is a most unfortunate time for you gentlemen to be retired from service, now as we stand at the threshold of the ultimate evil. What we're dealing with here is perhaps the most deadly threat this country has ever known. In fact, it goes beyond the perimeters of this country. The entire world, gentlemen, may be at risk."

"Is it that bad?" Stein wanted to know.

"Yes, I'm afraid so."

Cave paced nervously back and forth. "What we dealt with tonight, guys, is bad. I agree. It was ugly and horrible. But now you know. So, if you don't want to continue on through loyalty to me or the Company, then how about just for the country itself?"

"The world," the Old Man added. "The future of mankind. Surely, gentlemen, you owe some loyalty to that?"

Stein said, "All right, I'll stay."

They all looked at McKenna now.

"What the hell."

"Excellent." The Old Man looked pleased. For, after all, if your screwdrivers or hammers didn't work right anymore, you had to throw them away and get others.

Cave patted them both on the back. "You made the right choice, guys. For yourselves, for the country. You'll both be taken care of very well after this."

The Old Man attempted a smile. It was a dismal failure. "Oh, I can guarantee you of that."

McKenna didn't want any of this, but what choice did he have?

If Stein went for it, then he had to, too. That's the way it worked. Even the worms were better than cyanide in his coffee or a bullet to the head or brain-scrubbing at The Resort. At least for now. This was all madness. He'd never thought anything like this could possibly happen, let alone to him. Sometimes, when other operatives had a pretty good load on, they'd tell stories out of class. Horror stories about things they claimed to have witnessed or taken part in. McKenna always dismissed them. He never bought any of that crazy bullshit about mind control and alien bodies and genetically engineered fungi that could swallow a man whole. Fantasy.

Now he wasn't so sure.

He was starting to get a good look at the black belly of his country and he didn't like what he saw. He didn't like it at all. Political subversion, assassination, money laundering, mercenary armies—these were one thing and every civilized country played the game, good or bad. A way of life McKenna had long ago become accustomed to... but this...

The Old Man ordered sandwiches and coffee.

"Now, gentlemen," he said carefully, "I'm going to tell you a tale you may wish you'd never had to hear. I'm going to tell you about Project BioGen..."

# AUGUST 23

# ST. LOUIS, MISSOURI

## CORTEX DISTRICT, EN ROUTE

**12:05 A.M.**

Usually, the humming of the train and the muted click-clack of the trails was soporific to Miles Singer, an escape from the drudgery and long hours of selling office space to bioscience and tech startups. He rode the MetroLink home every night to his building in the Central West End and some nights were much later than others. There'd been a real hoo-hah at SLU to celebrate the merging of two biotech conglomerates that would easily funnel ten thousand jobs into the technology hub. It was all good and it was going to pay out in a big way.

It should have been one of the greatest days in his life, had Miles not felt like shit. He didn't know what it was—the flu, a good cold—but it was coming on strong and had been for days, if not weeks. Problem was, with everything on the table, he just didn't have the time to be sick and he certainly didn't have the time to be sitting around in a doctor's office. So he pushed forward even though it was hell just getting out of bed the last few mornings.

But tonight it caught up with him.

The drinks at SLU made him feel woozy, the appetizers turned his stomach, and the people, all those goddamn people, made him want to scream. So he bugged out early, walked the streets trying to clear his head, and now here he was two hours later feeling like he was going to die.

Everywhere, it seemed, crowds, crowds, crowds. There was some kind of street festival going on—Miles figured he should've known what it was, but his mind was too loopy—and people were spilled out on the sidewalks, drinking and eating and listening to bands. Christ, it was all too much.

He rode the train every night to prove it was safe, that there was nothing to be afraid of despite rumors to the contrary. MetroLink was an important part of the hub and he did everything he could to promote it when he could have easily taken a cab or his own car for that matter.

There were only about fifteen people in the car. No one was getting out of hand, being loud or rude, or paying the slightest attention to him. That was good. That was fine. Because tonight, he could barely stay upright in his seat.

For the past four days there'd been some awful stabbing pains in his guts and now he was suffering a headache that just wouldn't quit. Every roll, thump, and lurch of the train made his skull feel like it was going to split open. Even his eyes hurt. He had thrown up three times today, suffering from a randomly spiking fever, hands that shook uncontrollably, and odd little hallucinations. He hadn't felt this bad since he sampled some of the local cuisine in Iraq, five years previous.

The MetroLink trains had large windows on either side so riders could enjoy the view, but all Miles could see in the night was his own reflection. It was very clear, very detailed. Had he been in the right state of mind, he would have been frightened by the visage that looked back in him. But his mind, like his body, was undergoing extreme decline. Something in him had accepted it. It no longer fought. So the frozen, grotesque face that looked very much like the face he knew, did not scare him—not the yellow, mottled skin, the brilliantly red pinprick sores on his cheeks, nor the eyes which had gone the color of fresh blood.

But the others on the train were more than aware of the corpse-like man in the next section and they kept their distance. And when he bent over, face contorting in a primeval mask, body jerking, teeth chattering, and limbs shaking, they pulled that much farther away. But it wasn't until he began making gurgling, grunting noises that they became really afraid and it wasn't until his vomit splattered the floor that they began to get really alarmed.

The vomit came out of him like water from a high-pressure hose, practically gushing from his mouth and spreading out in a hot, sickening pool at his feet. It was not ordinary vomit by any means—it was red with blood and purple with chunks of sloughed tissue. Black tarry globs floated in it and something else, something like fish roe that was netted together by fibrous tendrils like pearls on a string. Several people swore later that things were moving in the viscous discharge, wriggling in it. One woman claimed they looked like tadpoles.

With a great bubbling cry, he fell from his seat, splashing into the pool of his own waste. Though his brain was still operating at a basal level, his mind was gone. He no longer knew who he was, what he was, or why he was. Everything inside him was dissolving with a morbid liquefaction—muscles and organs and connective tissue—as his primary function as a host reached its climax. Blood and bile and eggs poured out of every available orifice as he shuddered and kicked, his brain firing with rampant seizures. He writhed, spitting out teeth, eyes rolled back like juicy red cherries. His body drummed against the steel-plated flooring, thrashing and gyrating with amazing violence. Then there was a wet, tearing sound from inside him as what had come to term forced itself from his mouth along with great sections of rubbery, macerated intestine.

By then, the other riders were out of their minds as they pounded on the windows, screaming and crying for help and frantically pounding on the emergency call button.

The bloated, horridly pregnant thing was among them, seeking them out.

# CHICAGO, WEST MONTROSE AVENUE

## RAVENSWOOD

**12:35 A.M.**

Harry Niles did his best work at night.

Always had. For whatever reason, his creative juices really started to flow after midnight. He was drinking a Coke (but wanting a Vodka gimlet very badly) as he sat before his laptop trying to figure out whether a human being could really swallow live rats. And, if so, how many.

There was a sudden buzzing which meant somebody wanted to come up. No, he would ignore it. It was probably Arby Alheim from below. He often came home stewed to the gills—lucky boy—having forgotten his key and randomly thumbed buttons trying to find his own so his wife would let him come in. Which she often wouldn't. Which meant he would keep thumbing buttons until the entire building was awake.

Harry cleared his throat. "If the average diameter of the human esophagus is one inch and your average sewer-dwelling Norway rat can squeeze his execrable bulk through a drainage pipe some one-and-a-half to two inches, is it feasible that—"

But it came again.

Shit.

The buzzing. If it was Arby, he was getting his ass kicked. Harry stepped away from his desk and thumbed the intercom. "Who in the fuck is it and what in the fuck do you want?"

Heavy breathing.

Intriguing.

"Harry," said a voice. "It's me. It's Shawna."

"Are you naked or would you like to become so?"

"Please, Harry." Desperate. "Please let me in. I'm in trouble."

Now there was a surprise.

"All right, my fine little minx," he said, opening the door for her.

Not a full minute later: a knocking that became a pounding and then a hammering.

"I knew you'd stop by some night," he said, opening the door, "but I was expecting you to be naked. That was our agreement."

Shawna shoved by him and he could see she was in no mood for jokes.

Her hair was hanging over her face in wild loops. There was dirt streaked on her cheeks and hands. Her nylons were torn and there were leaves clinging to her skirt and blazer.

"What the hell happened to you?" he asked. "Who did this to you?"

She found his sofa and collapsed onto it. Immediately, she began to cry. She fought the tears as best she could, but they came regardless. And they kept coming as she trembled and shook. Harry went to her, holding her in his arms, realizing for maybe the first time that underneath it all she was very human, very vulnerable. And as he held her and soothed her, his mind filled with ugly images. Shawna being beaten. Shawna being robbed. Shawna being raped.

As it turned out, it was none of those.

When she'd gotten control of herself and Harry had made her a strong whiskey sour which she nearly inhaled, she told her tale.

"... and when I got to my place, I don't know, I just knew something was wrong. I didn't recognize those cars parked out front," she told him, drained of emotion. "So, I parked up the street and waited. After a while, I drove to a phone booth and called my landlady, Jill. I was afraid to use my cell. They can track you with your cell. Jill...Jill said two men had been looking for me. She said they wore dark suits...said they were very nice, but she thought they were Feds. Jesus H. Christ, Harry, what the hell is going on here?"

Harry stroked his thinning hair as he always did when there was trouble. "I don't know. I just don't know."

He knew Shawna.

Knew her as well as anyone probably. She didn't run around making up crazy stories about conspiracies and strange men lurking about assaulting screwed-up war vets. He didn't really know what to think. HAPPY VALLEY MEATS? Refrigerated trucks? Kidnappings? Men in what sounded like protective suits? Well, it was all way out there, wasn't it? He wanted to tell her she had made some mistake, blown fairly innocent, unrelated circumstances out of proportion and strung them together on a string of coincidence.

But he couldn't do that.

Cynical as he was, skeptical as he was, suspicious as he was about the human condition and its innate ability to spin lies, he believed her. And when was the last time he'd really, honestly believed in anything or anyone?

If cops and reporters really had what was called a gut instinct (and Harry believed that some of them did even if his own was more often than not gas), then his was telling him something unusual was going on. Very unusual. That combined with the fact that Shawna, a pretty normal girl, was terrified, made him very uneasy.

He refreshed her drink and poured one himself.

One wouldn't hurt, would it?

"So, let's think about this," he told her. "I drop you off at Portage. You brood a bit about the horrible wreck you've made of your life and—"

"Harry, please!"

"I'm only setting the scene in my mind, pet." He took a pull of his drink. *Mmm. Now isn't that nice? Like a blowjob from an old lover.* "Now. You're at the park. You see some guy, some emotionally disturbed person, EDP, dressed like a Gulf War vet digging in the cans. A white van pulls up, a couple guys conk him on the head and throw him in the back."

She nodded, pressing her glass to her lips. Not drinking, just wetting them as if they were so hot they might melt.

"About how far away were you from them?"

"I don't know. Less than half a city block, I'd say. I saw them clearly. I used the zoom on my cell, but I could have watched the whole thing without it."

"And the guys were wearing trench coats—"

"Yes. Black ones. Like rain slickers."

"—and they drove off with that guy, our EDP. You followed them to an old warehouse down by the river—"

"Yes, over on North La Salle Boulevard. You know, the Furniture District."

"—un-huh, and the place had more security than Fort Knox. You later followed them across the state line to some place in East Chi, historic little Marktown. Again, the HAPPY VALLEY van and a refrigerated truck. And later another truck came?"

"Yeah. I couldn't read what it said very good. It was too dark. I thought it was Something or Other Pressure Cleaning. But I can't be sure."

"Perplexing. Weird shit. Now these guys at your apartment looking for you. You sure you didn't stiff a date with a couple FBI boys?"

She glared at him. "Don't, Harry. Not now."

"Okay, I'm just kidding."

"Do you think it's...it's the Mob?"

Harry shook his head. "I doubt it. The thing that bothers me are those guys in the white rubber suits. Sounds like protective gear of some kind."

"They reminded me of those suits people wear when there's a radiation leak at a nuke plant. You remember those pictures from Chernobyl and Japan?"

"Only too clearly. But this can't be a radiation leak and if it was, why the ruse with a meat truck? If something like that happened, they'd evacuate for blocks. And whoever heard of a radiation leak at an apartment building?"

"That cop must've given 'em my plate number."

"Probably."

"Harry, what can we do?"

He sat down by her and put his arm around her, kissed her forehead. "There's only one thing we can do. We have to go to your apartment and see what there is to see."

91

# DETROIT

## RIVERFRONT

**12:58 A.M.**

Johnny Kopok made his way along Jefferson Avenue East, cutting into the park until he got so close to the Detroit River that he could smell it. It didn't have the same stench it had back in the good old days, but on a warm night like this, yes sir, she still didn't smell too good.

He could see Belle Isle Park out there and Canada on the other side. He'd heard or read once how when you went through the Windsor Tunnel into Canada the crime rate dropped like sixty percent. And that was something to think about when you came right down to it.

Johnny supposed by that they meant Detroit was a real hellhole. And Canada was some kind of fucking paradise.

He had to laugh at that. He'd been to Canada once. Him and a few of the old gang (all dead now, of course) had gone over there after someone told them the booze was cheaper. It wasn't. In fact, it was a lot more expensive. Johnny had ended up in bar fight with a trio of Canucks and what had he gotten for his trouble?

A month in the can.

And not a real jail like they had in Detroit or Bay City. But one of those Canadian joints that was full of Canadians. All them Canadians thought they was better than real Americans. But if that was so, how come Johnny had laid out three of them without working up a sweat?

The trouble had been when Johnny took on them Mounties.

Now those guys, hell, they could fight pretty good. And to prove it, they'd kicked the shit out of him. Ah, now those were the days. Good memories and good times.

Johnny couldn't remember what year that was.

Sometimes he had trouble remembering what year this was.

It had been like that since Hue. He'd taken some shrapnel in the head and after that, well things got a little fuzzy sometimes. That's what had started him drinking. Before then, he'd been okay. His old man had always told him he didn't have the brain power to light a frigging candle, but Johnny had shown him when he passed that exam and made it into the Marines in '67.

Or was that '68?

Not that it mattered.

Before that shrapnel things had been good. Johnny had been a boxer. He'd been pretty good. A light heavyweight. He'd been ranked at number four in the Marine Corps. After the shrapnel, well, he just couldn't think straight enough to fight anymore. Sometimes things got real hazy. That one match—the last match—he'd kind of went berserk. Accidentally, of course. He'd knocked down that big guy...what was his name? Earl Freed? Eric Freed? Laid him out like the fucking weeks' wash. And then...well, hell, things got funny then. He could've sworn that Earl had gotten up again... so Johnny pounded on him until he went down again. Next thing he knew, the Shore Patrol was all over his ass like flies on a juicy shit roast. Seems that big fellah...God, now what was his name?...had never gotten up at all.

Johnny had been knocking around the ref.

No more fights after that. And no more Marines.

Like yesterday, Johnny found himself thinking. Seems like that might've happened yesterday or the day before.

He had a pint of Ten High. There was one good swig left. He downed it and smashed it on the fancy-dancy cobblestone riverwalk. Then people started shouting at him, saying some terrible things.

"Dirty cocksucking stoolies," Johnny said back to them. "Bastards! Fucking shitters! Yeah, you, buddy!"

Some guy was walking up the cobbles, looked like Earl Freed. He was staring at Johnny.

"You got something to say to me, bozo? Huh?" Johnny stood his ground ready to do some swinging. Nope, it wasn't Earl. Some other guy. Big, looked like he wanted to go a few rounds. "Go ahead, punk! Run! Run home to mama and suck her tit!"

Johnny kept arguing and gesticulating. The only problem was that he was quite alone.

"Bastards. All of ya."

Johnny kept moving. Wasn't a good idea to hang around like that. Metro cops sometimes cruised the park and those sonsabitches would throw you in the clink for next to nothing. Once they'd thrown Johnny in citing he was a public nuisance. But that was a load of shit. They claimed he was standing out front the Renaissance Center saluting cars as they went by. Johnny knew they were lying because he didn't remember doing none of that. But that was cops for you. Made up stuff. They'd harassed Johnny plenty. That one time they said he'd peed right out in the middle of Ford Freeway. Another time they said he'd been walking up Gratiot without his pants on, his Johnson hanging in the breeze. And that bit about him taking a dump in the parking lot of Tiger Stadium with all the kiddies watching now that was ridiculous.

Sometimes things got a little fuzzy, but he wasn't that bad.

"You know how it works," Johnny had told Lou Priam one night as they sprawled out front the Greyhound depo in Royal Oak. "You give a guy, some ordinary Joe Jackshit Nobody a badge, and all of a sudden...all of a sudden, well he's a god. He runs the show. He owns the world. He can just shit on anybody and everybody he goddamn well pleases. That's what. Bastards. Gimme a hit of that, Lou. Better. Now what was I saying?"

But Lou couldn't remember either.

Those damn cops. They had thrown Johnny in dry-out half a dozen times. Like it was any of their business. That last time in the hospital, that Pakistani know-nothing doctor told Johnny he was a dead man if he didn't quit with the hootch. Said his organs and whatnot were all swollen up. But that had been a year ago or a month ago or something and old Johnny was still ticking like the gold watch on some rich man's arm.

He stumbled along through the park.

It was a shame what they'd done to Jefferson. Used to be lots of warehouses and breweries and factories there and now all the rich uppity little suits from Seventh Avenue had turned them into trendy hotels, ritzy apartment buildings, and high-end restaurants.

It was disgusting.

They called it urban renewal or reclamation but what it really was, was a damn shame. Lots of people had been employed in those places. A shame.

Johnny sometimes forgot that those places had been empty and rotting for years. A hangout for rats and drug addicts and cheap criminals. And guys like him that weren't real particular as to where they stretched out for the night.

He always had to be careful, he knew that much. Cops were everywhere, looking to roust guys like him. In the past month, he'd been driven out of his corner over in Roosevelt Park, chased from beneath the overpass near Joe Louis Arena, and run out of Hart Plaza along with a dozen others. Only safe place was getting to be the Rescue Mission on Third, but all that preaching over there...gah.

Remembering all that, or trying to, he started getting scared.

It came on him like that sometime.

The shakes. That's what he called it. The fuzz in his brain got so bad it was like spun cotton. His heart began to pound, his temples throbbed. He had trouble catching a breath and everything started hurting real bad. Sometimes he fell right down. It was like that now. He couldn't remember where he was or where he'd come from.

Down in the grass, leaves stuck to his face, Johnny pissed himself. "HEY! HEY! OVER HERE GODDAMMIT! GOTTA MAN DOWN NEED A MEDIC! MEDIC!"

A couple of teenage youths who'd been lounging nearby smoking some weed came over.

"Pete? That you?" Johnny asked. "Fucking slopes! Goddamn, Pete, they tried to run the perimeter again! Crazy fucks! VC hardcore for sure... oh, God, Pete... I hurt... I hurt. I must've cut a dozen in half with the fifty! Kansas City kept poppin' the recoilless... zipperheads were coming apart like water balloons! Jesus, Pete, is it bad... is it bad... WHERE'S THAT FUCKING MEDIC?"

"What the fuck's matter wit you?" one of the boys said.

"Old Johnny," said the second one. "Don't you know Johnny? Still in the war, man. Insane in da membrane."

"No shit? Zat right, Johnny?" He prodded him with the toe of his Nike. Then he kicked him. "Get the smell of that motherfucker. Shit his pants. Damn."

Johnny's natural bouquet acted like a repellent and the boys took off, wanting to be anywhere but with him.

"Hey!" Johnny called after them. "You're not Pete. I know. I know."

"Why don't you dry yer white ass out!" one of them called.

"No, no, boys. I'm okay. But you gotta help me. What...what city is this? Am I still in Detroit?" Johnny rubbed his face in hands. "MEDIC! I NEED A MEDIC OVER HERE!"

The duo, only shadows now, disappeared into the night laughing.

"Fucking bastards," Johnny said, dragging himself to his feet. "No good mouthy brat shitters. That's all."

Two minutes later, Johnny had forgotten all about them.

He had more pressing business. Whistling a tune he thought was from "The Sound of Music" but was actually the theme for "Green Acres", Johnny scoped out the park. He was looking for Lou Priam. Lou was the closest thing Johnny had to a friend these days. It was too bad about Lou, though. Lou had developed a real problem with the hootch, the old Sweet Lucy. Other than that Lou was one hell of a stand-up guy.

The park was big and Johnny looked and looked for over an hour before he came upon a dark shape collapsed in some bushes by a bench.

"That you, Lou?"

"Who dat?"

"Johnny. You know Johnny, eh, Lou?"

"Yessir, I do. C'mon in," Lou said as if he was indoors.

Johnny dug in his pocket for the half-smoked cigar some rich SOB had dropped outside Joe Louis. Lou just loved cigars and Johnny always brought him one. It was what friends were for.

"How are ya, Lou?" he asked.

"Not...not so good, Johnny. Not so good."

Johnny plugged the cigar between his lips and lit it up. In the glow of the flame, he could see that it was true: Lou looked like hell. His black face was beaded with sweat and his eyes were bulging from their sockets like runny fried egg yolks.

*He's bad*, Johnny started thinking. *Real bad. Guy's got to cut down on the sauce or he's gonna damn well kill hisself.*

He handed the cigar off to Lou.

"Good old Johnny bringing me cigars," Lou said, his voice raspy and dry. "Good friend Johnny. You a saint, my friend. You a saint."

"Got anything to wet the whistle, old friend?"

Lou giggled then started coughing with a deep, phlegmy rattle. "Sure as shit." He handed Johnny a bottle. There was no label on it. It could've been drain cleaner or goat piss; neither man would've probably known the difference. "See how this sets ya."

Johnny raised it to his lips. "Goddamn. This Don Q?"

"Yeah, yeah," Lou laughed. "Yes sir."

"Where'd ya get it?"

"Couple kids left it yonder. Out sparkin' they was. Did their business and left—not that I watched. Bottle stayed. Yessir."

Johnny gulped off it. It was fire in his belly, bringing parts of his anatomy to life he'd pretty much forgotten about. It made his head tingle with a nice buzz. He was a happy man. Content and relaxed like a tomcat sprawled in the sunshine.

"I was going to suggest we leg it over to Moxie's, but this is better," Johnny said, grinning wide and proud. He stood up uneasily, swaying like a sapling in a December blow. He began urinating on the bench nearby. "Fucking town's going to shit, Lou. Lookit this fountain. Used to be lit up and pretty and now look at it. I'll just pee in it then."

"Ain't no fountain, Johnny. It be a bench."

Johnny's vision swam in and out of focus. "Well, I'll be go to hell," he said. "It does look like a bench."

He sat down by Lou and they passed the bottle back and forth, just as happy as happy could get.

"Iss bad, Johnny. Iss real bad," Lou began. "Did I tell you... did I tell you or not?"

# FORT MEADE, MARYLAND

## NATIONAL SECURITY AGENCY

**1:26 A.M.**

It was a perpetual flood, all days, all hours—millions upon millions of snippets of data, everything from solid leads to dry holes, gossip and rumor, images and text, classified briefings and leaked high-profile conversations, encrypted fragments and private transmissions. It was sifted and mined all courtesy of NSA computers which scanned billions of channels per minute, storing vast amounts of information that might be pertinent to national defense and dispensing with that which was trivial in nature.

In the wake of 9/11, the search had been broadened to glean anything that might be considered a security threat to the United States or its allies. Much of the technology used was exposed in the Snowden disclosures, but there was plenty of exotic, classified tech that could not even be guessed at.

Following the Syrian Incident, a great deal of the NSA's resources were directed towards the outbreak and overspill of Project BioGenesis. Everything from emails to cell conversations to medical records and VA files were filtered and scrutinized, anything of value passed on to the office of DCI VanderMissen and then to the ERTs of S5.

NSA Director Gordon Parks, sat in his lavish yet functional office, fully aware that he was without doubt the most powerful man in the country. And if not that, then certainly he chaired the most important intelligence position in not only the country but quite possibly the world. In an arena of interagency squabbling, he sat above it all, a spider in its web, connected to every strand, feeling every tug of silk, every nuance regardless how slight, of every friend and enemy and potential prey.

It was late now, and all the administrators and civil servants had gone home. Those left—intelligence analysts, security people, hackers and techs—were mostly locked away in their private domains.

"I appreciate you coming out here at such a ridiculous hour," Parks said to his guest, Elizabeth Toma.

"Well, there are certain things more important than sleep."

"It's coming in from every corner of the country now, Liz. Everything is proceeding right down to the letter. What has been sown will now be reaped. Countless tiny details, a million things that could have gone wrong, but due to our foresight and diligence and, yes, imagination, it's happening. It's really happening. Within a week at the very outside, there will be no hiding the outbreak. It will reach epic proportions and with the future of our great union at stake, the President will call martial law."

Elizabeth did not smile at this, she just studied him with her dark, simmering eyes. She was hard to read, hard to know. An attractive woman, she had been courted by men (and women) of great power and learning, but the only ones who were invited into her private world—and bedroom—were those who had something she wanted. She was a venomous snake and Parks knew it. He was always very careful around her because she was notorious for her shifting loyalties. And a wise man never turned his back on a viper.

"You and I and a few select others are in the rare, godlike position of engineering not only our destiny but that of the world. Did you ever stop and consider that?"

Elizabeth sipped her coffee. "Sometimes."

She was uncomfortable with it and he knew it. He didn't like that. She should have been overjoyed. She should have been embracing the brave new world that she had no small part in crafting. He didn't like that and those he worked for would like it even less when he reported it to them, which, of course, he would. That was how the game was played. If you wanted power, real power, then you had to play the game.

*Be careful*, he warned himself. *She's an old puzzle player. Don't pretend to know her or understand her. And, dear God, don't underestimate her. Don't think for one moment that she's not reporting you as you report her. The Collective considers her a valuable asset and you don't want to cross them or her.*

"You're bothered about something," he said. "I can see it."

She didn't smile and that reassured him somewhat, because when this lady smiled it meant she had you by the balls.

"I'm not comfortable discussing particulars out loud," she said.

"It's perfectly safe, Liz."

She uttered a cool laugh. "Here? In this place? Nothing's safe here."

"Really, Liz. This office is swept a dozen times a day for bugs."

"And you're certain you can trust the people doing the sweeping?"

"Yes."

It was obvious she didn't. Then again, she hadn't gotten where she was today by being reckless. Parks believed he was well-informed as to the various technologies used to eavesdrop, so he tried to reassure her as to their complete safety.

"There's no more secure location in the world," he said.

"The onion, Gordon, never forget it's all a big onion."

He knew the analogy. Like an onion, the dark world of espionage had many, many layers. It was the people you trusted that you had to watch out for. Still, he was satisfied they were alone, that the walls did not have ears.

*It's more than that. Much more. She doesn't trust you and she never has.*

Parks suspected that was true. Nobody in the game trusted anyone else and particularly not at the level they played ball. There was just too much at stake. Every admission, confession, or offhand comment could and would be used against you for leverage. She was being exceptionally careful because there was more on the line here than ever before. She was afraid of being recorded, of saying something that could hang her later.

He understood that perfectly. No one really knew what limits there were to the power of The Collective or what exotic listening and interception technology they might be employing. He'd heard rumors that were too fantastic to believe.

As he thought this, a fly landed on his desk. He immediately swatted it. You could never be too sure these days.

He finished his drink and handed a yellow envelope to her. "This is a list of cities that will fall first, the beginning of the chain reaction. According to the latest research, it's quite accurate."

She nodded, opening the envelope and scanning its contents. "Amazingly detailed."

He took that as a compliment. "Sorry to have to call you out here for this, but you have to understand I just didn't trust a courier."

"Not a problem, Gordon. Always nice to see you."

He sat back down, giggling.

"Am I missing something?"

Parks shook his head. "I just keep thinking about Bob Pershing and his power plays."

"The less said about that the better."

"I suppose."

Still, he thought about who was playing and who was being played. Layers upon layers. The outbreak of BioGenesis was just the beginning and he knew it. It was a tool of terror. A country wide, worldwide trauma was necessary to impose control over the masses. By the time the dust had settled, they wouldn't know what had hit them.

"Is there anything else, Gordon?"

"No, that should do it. I don't have to tell you to be very discreet with what's in that envelope."

Her dark eyes drilled into him. "No, you don't."

He smiled. It was getting so close now, so very close. He thought about the detailed dossier he had on her and wondered what she had on him. Hopefully, neither of them would have to play that hand. Then again, if the Collective deemed it prudent to expose her, he would not hesitate.

A good marionette had to respect the hands that controlled it.

After she had gone, he got on his sat phone and called the boys upstairs, as he often referred to the heavy players of The Collective.

"Yes?" a voice said. "Tell us."

Parks swallowed. "She's evasive. She refuses to speak directly about anything concerning the project. That could be just playing it smart or—"

"She could be thinking of betraying us."

"Yes."

"Keep an eye on her. We can't have any problems at this juncture. Understood?"

"Yes."

"Excellent."

The connection was broken. Parks sat back in his chair, mopping sweat from his forehead. Yes, he would watch her, of course, but his greatest fear was that he, too, was being watched.

# CHICAGO, NORTH SHORE

## EVANSTON

**1:45 A.M.**

"You don't have to do this."

Shawna looked at him and rolled her eyes. "I'm not some little cringing violet, Harry. I can take care of myself."

"Good, glad to hear it. But who's going to take care of me?"

"My hero."

They took Harry's GTO over to Shawna's building off Ridge Avenue. They drove by once, casually scoping it all out. There were no cars she didn't recognize. Everything looked terribly normal, terribly mundane. And it was this, more than anything, that made Shawna start to wonder if somehow she'd imagined it all. If she was in reality living some crazy paranoid fantasy brought on by all the shit in her life of late.

Harry parked a block away, an old hand at nosing into places he wasn't wanted. He sat behind the wheel, lost in thought for a few minutes.

"I don't suppose you have a gun?"

Shawna sighed heavily. "No, I don't have a gun." She tried to dismiss it as one his jokes, but she could see he was dead serious. "Do you really think we'll need one?"

He shrugged. "Who knows?"

They moved up the sidewalk, trying to stay in the shadows and at the same time trying to appear nonchalant in case anyone was watching them. It was not very easy: one pretty much canceling out the other.

There were ten units in Shawna's building, all run by a widower named Jill Morell. She was the kindly, motherly type, Shawna told Harry, until it came time for the rent. Then she was a cutthroat mercenary. She took no prisoners where money was concerned.

There was no one loitering out front. No shadowy figures waiting in a parked car. But to be on the safe side, they went in the back way. Shawna was so nervous she dropped her key three times. Harry was better; he only dropped it twice.

They went in and all was quiet.

The beige corridors were empty. They could hear TVs in a few of the units. Everything appeared quite sane and commonplace. Amongst the potted ferns and deep-pile carpeting it was hard to imagine underworld types skulking about. If, indeed, that's what all this was about.

Harry seemed to have a few ideas, Shawna knew, but he wasn't saying.

They came to the elevator and Harry shook his head. "Stairs," he said under his breath.

He was very good at this, Shawna found herself thinking. Maybe too good. It made her wonder exactly what sort of life he'd lived as a professional journalist. He often joked about the enemies he'd made. How certain politicians and corporate figures would have liked him dead. But she'd always thought they were just that: jokes. It was hard to tell with him when he was serious. He seemed to think just about everything was humorous.

But now Shawna wondered.

The stairs were carpeted and they made no noise whatsoever. She'd been edgy coming back here, but Harry's uncharacteristic solemnity positively unnerved her now. Her entire body was packed down tight like a spring waiting to pop. Her arms trembled, her legs trembled, even her lips trembled. There was an unpleasant, infuriating little tic in the corner of her eye. And she hadn't experienced that since she'd been busted with a joint in gym class, her junior year of high school.

She was thinking about those old movies where the young couple always seem to be investigating some abandoned, decaying house looking for clues. The ones where they get separated and the hero always sneaks up behind the heroine and places his hand on her shoulder, scaring the living shit out of her.

*If somebody put their hand on my shoulder right now*, she thought, *I'd scream bloody murder, piss my pants, and then I'd gouge out their eyes.*

There was something about fear, she realized. Although every heart-pounding, gut-twisting second of it was like dying one gasping breath at a time, it sure kept you alert. It sure gave you an edge. She was ready to pounce, hiss, scratch and claw with the slightest provocation.

At her apartment all looked well.

Shawna handed Harry the keys (noticing with some terror just how incredibly loud they jingled), but he was already trying the knob.

"Did you lock this before you left?" he asked.

She nodded soberly. "Yes. It locks automatically."

"It's not locked now."

She tried the knob herself. It wasn't catching at all as if the mechanism in there had been damaged...forced. Filled with some bizarre emotion between terror and curiosity, she tried it again and again. The tongue was jammed, it wouldn't catch.

"Harry, let's get the fuck out—"

But he'd already opened the door.

Everything seemed to be the way she'd left it. The place wasn't torn apart like in the movies. Nothing seemed to have been touched. They went from room to room to room. They even looked in closets. Harry found a Harold Robbins paperback she used as a doorstop in her bedroom.

"Just what I always expected: dirty sex books," he said in a conspiratorial voice. "Naughty thing that you are, tsk, tsk."

"Fuck you, Harry."

"We'd better wait till later."

Nothing was out of place. She was fastidious about her digs. She liked them very orderly and organized. It was one of the things she relished about living alone. Things were always where you left them.

She looked around. "What do you think?" she whispered.

"I think those drapes are hideous," he said.

She kept looking around. Yes, everything appeared to be fine, except—

Standing in the living room on the pretense that he was looking for her hardcore sex videos, Harry found a leather glove poking from beneath a cushion. "Always hide your gloves there, dear?" he said.

"I didn't put that there. That's not my glove."

"Placed quite strategically, one would think," he said, trying to remain calm and failing. He reached into his coat and took out a pair of rubber surgical gloves and put them on.

"Do you always carry rubber gloves?"

"Actually, yes. You'd be surprised at the disgusting things I've had to touch in my job."

Shawna stared wide-eyed as he took hold of the glove under the cushion and gently pulled it free.

It was wet with something.

Harry's gloved fingers were stained red. "Not ketchup," he reported.

"Blood?" Shawna moaned. "Blood?"

"Afraid so."

He pulled off the rest of the cushions.

There was something wrapped in what looked like a dishtowel. A dishtowel soaked with blood. Harry unwrapped it carefully. It was a knife, also bloody. The kind used to carve a roast.

Shawna stood there, disgusted, but also very confused. "Harry? What the hell is this? What the hell gives here? That's not mine! I didn't put that there."

"I know that. You know that."

He went to the kitchen and found a plastic garbage bag. He dropped the glove, towel, and knife in there.

"Somebody's playing a twisted fucking game here," he said loudly as if he hoped someone was listening. "Obviously planted to incriminate you...but, dear God, how amateurish. How obvious. Whoever we're dealing with isn't exactly the imaginative sort."

Shawna was breathing heavily. "Let's get out of here before we find out who that is."

They left the place as they'd found it save for the unusual items from beneath the sofa. They slipped down the stairs. Harry had to practically drag Shawna with him. Her dander was up and she wanted answers. It was one thing to fuck with her, but you never touched her stuff, her place.

"Where's that landlady at?" Harry asked when they got downstairs again.

"This way," Shawna said, motioning down the corridor. "Why?"

"I think we better have a talk with her."

"It's pretty late, Harry."

"Then we'll be rude."

At Jill Morell's apartment, they knocked and knocked.

Harry tried the door and it was open.

"It's never unlocked," Shawna informed him, her voice dry as dust. "Jill's got this thing about burglars. She was robbed once...at gunpoint...years ago. She'd never leave her door open..."

Harry stared into Shawna's eyes. For the first time she saw real concern in them. It had been there, of course, when they found the knife, but it was really starting to blossom now.

"This is starting to smell bad, Shawna."

He went in and right away they smelled it.

A pungent, cloying odor of piss, shit, and something wet, metallic almost. Harry had smelled it many times before poking about crime scenes.

In the kitchen, they found Jill.

She was on the floor, cut and stabbed so viciously her head was nearly coming off. There was blood everywhere. Pooled on the floor, spattered on the walls, running down the refrigerator. All of it fresh, very fresh.

"Oh my God," Shawna said, turning away, nearly losing her lunch.

Harry said nothing.

There was money on the table, scattered on the floor.

"Rent money, I'll bet," Harry said. "Was the rent due?"

"Yesterday," Shawna managed, trembling like an autumn leaf.

"And if we go back to your place and look around, Shawna, I'm betting in some of your drawers we'd find more money. And maybe a little coke for good measure."

"I'm being set up." It wasn't a question.

In the distance they could hear sirens. They were getting closer all the time. They looked at each other. They knew the sirens, like the rest of this carefully plotted nightmare, was no coincidence.

"Let's get the hell out of here," Harry said.

They went out the front and hit the sidewalk running. And they kept running until they made it to Harry's car.

"What is this about?" Shawna demanded. "What the hell did I do?"

"It's not what you did. It's what you saw."

She only wished she knew what that was.

# WASHINGTON D.C., BOLLING AFB

## DEFENSE INTELLIGENCE AGENCY

**2:00 A.M.**

Things weren't going too well for Charles VanderMissen.

He was sixty-six years old. He had four children, seven grandchildren, and was on his second wife. He owned a colonial in McLean worth nearly seven million dollars (if not more), a summer home on Cape Cod, and a winter retreat in St. Thomas. At one time he had been a Navy Rear Admiral with Naval Intelligence. He'd also been deputy director of the Central Intelligence Agency for five years. There was an ugly patch of old scar tissue on his neck he'd received after bailing out of a burning helicopter on the Laotian border in the waning days of the war in Southeast Asia. He was a thin, lanky man who perpetually looked exhausted and old beyond his years.

And he was also one of the few men who knew about S5.

Section Five had originally been called SIG, the Scientific Intelligence Group, back in the early days of the Cold War. Or just "the Group", to those in the know. Some still called it that. Beyond himself, there were only a few select high-ranking individuals in the military establishment and intelligence bureaucracies who knew of Five's existence or the shadowy rumors of the same. But within the country's political structure, S5 did not exist. You would not find it in the Congressional Registry. It operated as a shadow agency under the umbrella of the CIA, but few in the CIA had heard of it. Unlike the NSA, FBI, DIA, or the military intelligence complex itself, it was kept from the public for reasons of security. S5 did, in effect, serve the public (though their methods would have been frowned upon by the general taxpayer), but their real loyalty was to national security. A vague term if ever there was one. Even the industrial scientific sector, which carried out research for them via CBT, did not know whom it was they really worked for.

Five was a bureaucratic tangle that no Senate Select Committee or Congressional investigation would ever penetrate. S5's payroll was handled by the Defense Department. There was no readily accessible paper trail. They existed within the cracks between the other intelligence organizations and had, in one form or another, since the early days of the Cold War.

And it was S5 that was keeping VanderMissen up late these days.

In fact, it was aging him well beyond his years.

He was one of the nation's secret keepers, you see.

He could tell you the truth behind the Iran–Contra affair, the Kennedy assassination, the Philadelphia Experiment, Watergate, Area 51, the Clinton sex scandal, why we really invaded Iraq, and even what America's true role was in the fall of the Soviet Union. He could tell you how high-ranking Nazi war criminals were protected by the United States after World War II via Operation Paperclip and in what capacity they then served the country. He could turn your hair white with tales of MK-ULTRA, the CIA's mind control program of the 1960s. He could go on for hours about numerous black budget operations worldwide. He could even tell you why British MI5 had Princess Diana killed or how America really battled Islamic extremism with an ongoing policy of state-sponsored terror and even why President George W. Bush did not look at all surprised when he was told about the terrorist attacks of 9/11.

But one thing he didn't like to talk about was Section 5 or the things they'd done in Vietnam, Beirut, Central America, Africa, the Gulf, and numerous other places. He denied, even to himself, that he knew anything of Project Coldfire, Project Razortooth, Project Spearhead, or even Project Lazarus or Nightshade or Laughing Man.

And Project BioGen itself simply made him ill and always had.

"I hate it," he told Brigadier General Walter Sleshing earlier that night. "I hate this entire thing."

DDI Sleshing, like VanderMissen himself, was one of country's truly informed men. "It seemed necessary at the time, Chuck. You know that. If it had worked...shit, those ragheads would have beaten themselves."

VanderMissen knew that.

But what he'd always disliked about biological operations was that the weapons themselves were unpredictable, they did not respect territorial boundaries. And they sure as hell didn't care what uniform a man was wearing or if he was wearing one at all.

VanderMissen and Sleshing had gone out to dinner and then they'd tried—ineffectively—to get drunk. But it just wouldn't work. There was too much cooking on the back burner and it was getting harder and harder day by day to contain the stink. Their dinner turned into a skull session about how to protect their own asses now that it seemed they were being hung over the fire for a slow, even roasting.

Now they were back at Bolling and still no closer to a resolution to the country's problems and the shadows they felt moving around them.

"I never liked S5, but it wasn't my decision," VanderMissen admitted. "When they threw BioGen on the table it made me sick, the very idea of it. I knew it was coming from CBT. I just knew it. If it's dirty, that goddamn bitch Liz Toma usually has her hand in on it. But I supported it, didn't I? Because politically and professionally I had little choice. I was the DNI and I would remain so as long as I played ball. I knew it was wrong, but I played ball anyway. But I never foresaw something...something like this."

Sleshing nodded. "We knew the risks. We had the statistics for an outbreak. We knew there was a chance...but nothing to this extent."

Sleshing rubbed his red-rimmed eyes. Like VanderMissen, he was beginning to look very much like an Egyptian mummy—all wrinkles, worry lines, and seamed flesh.

"Listen, Chuck," he said. "There's no point in going over this. The shit, as they say, has hit the fan. We'll handle it."

VanderMissen just stared at him. "Do you really think so?"

Sleshing simply sighed. Too many people and too many agencies in the labyrinthine network of the federal government and military were getting involved now. The outbreak—and the blowback from it—simply wasn't containable. He'd gotten word that the FBI were arranging a call-down, which was a meeting of experts and feds, everybody from the Bureau's NSD (National Security Division) to the CDC's EIS (Epidemic Intelligence Service) to the Navy's BDRP (Biological Defense Research Program) to biohazard specialists from USAMARIID and suits from the Public Health Service, as well as leading civilian specialists in biotechnology, medical pathology, and weaponized biological agents. The meeting was to be held at the FBI Command Center. And when it was, the shit would really hit the fan.

"What are you getting from the teams?" Sleshing asked, ignoring the question.

"Only a few casualties. Things are going well. So far we haven't had any episodes in the civilian sector. If one of those things pops out of someone in a hospital, I don't think our shovel will be big enough to clean up the mess." Then he uttered a weak laugh that was the clear despondent sound of defeat. "You know, I almost hope one will. I almost hope this mess gets blown up right in everyone's faces. God knows we'd deserve it."

Sleshing looked at him for a time, then said, "Chuck, if this thing gets out of hand we'll be offered up as sacrifice. You know it and I know it. The writing's already on the wall. If it comes down to it, if they try to take a bite of my ass, those bastards are gonna find me tough and stringy."

Over dinner they had developed a strategy of sorts. If they were offered up, they were going to bring enough dirty secrets to the table that no one would escape unscathed. From the CIA to the Joint Chiefs of Staff to the upper echelons of the Pentagon and the White House itself, they'd all be wearing the same pie on their faces. VanderMissen fully realized that if and when that happened that their enemies would be extremely dangerous. The power they wielded and the resources at their disposal were awesome and more than a little frightening. They were not the sort of people you crossed in Washington and lived to tell the tale...but public outrage would be such by that point that the power brokers would find themselves quite neatly emasculated.

VanderMissen hoped it would not come to that.

But he had his doubts. For already some questions were being asked—under the table and behind closed doors as yet—but the smell was definitely in the air. Sleshing had told him that General Holzencamp, the CENTCOM J-2, Chief of Intelligence, and Vice Admiral Dahn of SOCOM, the Special Operations Command, were already sniffing around. The ERTs themselves were activated by DCI Pershing's direct order...but the CIA was notorious for its inability to keep a secret and with that many ERT operators mobilized at once, well, it was bound to leave ripples in the special ops community.

VanderMissen shook his head. "Thing is, Walt. I don't trust Bob Pershing and I never have. Same goes for Colin Paulus. I see those two together in bed over this."

"Add General Mason to the list. Every time I'm in the same room with those three I get the damnedest feeling they're up to something, that they know something I don't."

"We need some assets of our own."

"It can be arranged if it comes to that," Sleshing told him. "But we have to move carefully. We already have too many damn teams in the field."

VanderMissen nodded. "Pershing's got something going on under the table. I know it. You know it. And if you need more evidence, I just got word through my contacts that he's calling in another asset."

"Who?"

"Tommy Quillan," VanderMissen said, chewing the words slowly.

There was silence after that. For a moment.

"He's turning that psychopath loose domestically?"

VanderMissen nodded. "Quillan's in Afghanistan right now," he said. "He's been on the trail since the Syrian Incident."

Sheikh Sa'ad's trail went cold in Syria. Quillan, through his numerous contacts, had traced Sheikh Sa'ad's movements to Afghanistan. It was now believed in the upper echelon of the American intelligence community that there had been a splintering between Sheikh Sa'ad's Al-Qaeda and his Iranian Pasdaran advisors. It was also believed that Project BioGen's technology had been spirited away by Sheikh Sa'ad to Afghanistan, perhaps to keep it out of the hands of the Pasdaran. Something which was both good and bad for in this case it was truly hard to say who was the lesser evil of the two.

"Quillan'll get him, if it's not a ruse," DDI Sleshing said. "That slimy bastard might be slithering towards the Pak-Iranian border as we speak."

"We've got pretty good HUMINT on this," VanderMissen said. "I'm confident. But Quillan…it bothers me…why would Pershing bring him in out of the cold?"

Pause. "I suppose the hunt for Sheikh Sa'ad could be carried out by his confederates. That part I understand. But if Pershing's bringing Quillan over here, it means he's expecting some heavy wet work."

VanderMissen looked pained. "That's what scares me."

# NORTH CHICAGO

## VA HOSPITAL

**2:44 A.M.**

"Tell me something, Stein."

McKenna and he were sitting in a van in the parking lot, waiting. They had chosen a nice little corner, well shadowed by the overhanging branches of several giant spruces. It gave them a good view of Marcus Grimes' Toyota truck.

"Tell me why you decided to continue with this nightmare," Mckenna said to him. "Was it the Old Man? Afraid of a trip to The Resort?"

Stein smiled. "It was the right choice for the time being. I'd rather be hunting worms than be fed to them."

"And you think the Old Man would do that?"

Stein just looked at him and he knew the answer. Of course, he would do it. This was a man who was ordering the deaths of veterans nationwide because they may or may not have come into contact with the parasites. What were a couple ERT Blackpool operators? Just more meat to be splashed about to cover the trail that started in Iraq and, no doubt, led straight to highest positions of power in the land.

"The Old Man is a sadist and we both know it," Stein said. "I don't pretend to be a Boy Scout. Obviously. But next to him, I'm a virgin. So are you. He's the asshole who oversaw the BioGen Project and that's something else that scares me."

McKenna looked at him.

"That he admitted to us the entire thing. When's the last time you received background like that? I've been all over the world on dozens and dozens of ops and mostly I never had a clue why I was doing anything...now the Old Man trots out all the dirty secrets and admits his complicity in the entire thing."

"And?"

"And I think when this is wrapped up, we're going to be a security risk. I think we'll be taken care of."

McKenna had actually been thinking along the same lines, but he was glad Stein had voiced it. As he had learned from his years with the Company, there was no such thing as paranoia in clandestine operations. Your worst fears were often true. They would be killed. Some cleaners would get the job and it wouldn't be something messy like a gun, but something much more subtle...cyanide in their coffee, arsenic trioxide in a donut. Suicide in a motel room. There were limitless ways.

McKenna's pained sigh answered that. "I want out."

"So do I. And when the time's right, we'll get out."

"And when will that be?"

"You'll know. And so will I. Right now, we'll do what we're told and act like good little soldiers. It's the only thing to do," Stein explained. "Haven't you ever heard the saying that in times of trouble a wise man holds his tongue?"

"No. But I like it." McKenna repeated it to himself. "Makes sense. Who said that? William Shakespeare?"

"William Shatner for all I know."

McKenna and he got a good laugh out of that one. It felt good to laugh.

"Tell me, though, Stein. Level with me."

"About what?"

"About all of this crap. What you think."

Stein held his head back and stared at the ceiling of the cab. "What I think? What I think is that this entire affair really broke my faith in the people we work for. I guess I never trusted the Company. And I sure as hell never trusted this S5 bullshit. Any organization this secretive has to be up to no good. And, lo and behold, I was right." He laughed dryly, angrily. "And now this shit. A covert op that went sour. And we have to clean up the mess before there's a goddamn worm in every man, woman, and child in the good old US of A. I think it's a fucking atrocity. It makes me sick, that's what."

McKenna nodded. "How could they fuck up like this? I just don't get it."

"Because they're too ambitious, my friend. Too fucking ambitious. Those bastards are developing evil technologies that they're not smart enough to handle."

"I suppose you're right."

"Unless," Stein said, "we only have half the story."

"Meaning?"

"Suppose what's happening is no accident."

McKenna sighed. "Yeah, it did occur to me." He shook his head. "It's getting too complicated, too dirty. When this op is done, we walk. No better, we run."

Stein laughed cynically. "You know, I've seen some insane shit, took part in some real dirty games in the name of security. But this...this is like nothing I've ever seen before. This is big. This is huge. XI isn't going to just pat us on the back if and when this ends."

"What are you saying?"

"I'm saying the Company can't afford security leaks here. Do you have any idea what the taxpayers would say about all this? It would be the mother of all shitstorms. Something like this would be enough to pull the government right down. No, when this is done, we'll be retired. And not to some brainwashing clinic."

McKenna just sat there in stony, prolonged silence.

"Besides," Stein pointed out, "I don't think this is going to end. You saw that fucking worm? Did it look like something that's just going to lay down and take it? Hell no. It looked like what it was: A creature mean enough and smart enough to survive. To breed. To overcome. They designed it to be like that."

"It wasn't supposed to breed," McKenna said weakly.

"But it did and I don't think we can stop it. If there's as many out there as they're saying, this country, this world's in some very deep shit."

McKenna couldn't or didn't want to understand what he was thinking. Worms. They were just worms. They really couldn't spread that fast. There was no way. Stein was just being a fatalist. That's what.

"There," Stein said. "There's our boy."

They got out of the van and made a big show of hurrying towards the hospital entrance. Then they slowed, looking confused.

"Excuse me, buddy," McKenna said to the hunched-over black man getting into the Toyota. "Could you tell me where the front desk is?"

Grimes coughed sickly. They both knew he had it.

"Yeah... yes... you go into that door there..." he began. "Right over there by the sign..."

The man was so weak and disoriented Stein could hardly believe they let him walk right out the door. But that's what they were doing. Apparently, Grimes had been bitching for the past two days about getting released, despite his ill health. The Old Man had made a phone call and Grimes got his wish. And in the middle of the night yet. But it had to be that way.

It wasn't safe to snatch people in broad daylight.

Particularly in a hospital parking lot.

It was much simpler to do it by night. To slip up behind your target and give them a shot of gas in the face. And that's exactly what they did with Grimes. A taste of the gas and off to la-la land he went, slumping right into Stein's arms.

"Easy as pie," Mckenna said.

Then the woman on the passenger side—the woman they had not known was even there—started screaming.

Then it got ugly.

# CHICAGO, NORTH SHORE

## EN ROUTE

**4:45 A.M.**

Harry and Shawna were driving to Gabe Hebberman's house in Kenilworth. After the events at Shawna's building, they'd driven around in confused circles for some time, the both of them absolutely silent, brooding and worrying.

"Why are they setting me up, Harry?"

"I just don't know."

She chewed her lip. "But, Harry...God... these things don't happen... they don't happen to normal people." She hugged herself, still shaking a bit. "I don't even know what I saw for chrissake! Why the hell don't they leave me alone?"

"I hate to say it...sounds like an old movie...but you know too much."

"I don't know anything!"

"They think you do." He shrugged. "Listen, I'll tell you what I think happened. They saw you nosing around, they ran your plate. They found out you work for the *Trib*...or did...and they started to sweat. Whatever it is they're up to, obviously they don't want the press involved."

"I don't work for the paper anymore. Have you forgotten?"

"I know that. They probably ran your plate like I said, got your social security number and ran you through the database at the IRS or something. As far as last years' tax returns go, you work at the *Trib*."

"Shit," she said. "I don't believe this."

Harry was watching her in the glow of the dashboard. Her face had that sallow, wasted, empty-eyed look green soldiers got on their first patrol when they finally saw some real killing and realized it was no game. Harry knew that look very well. He'd covered plenty of wars. He'd seen that look on his own face for the first time in 1992 when he'd witnessed the aftermath of an IRA car bomb attack on a Protestant pub in Londonderry. He remembered the rubble, the smoke…the bodies. The police pulling out human remains from the wreckage, some of whom were children who'd been sleeping in an upstairs flat. Burned beyond recognition, their tiny bodies were curled in obscene fetal positions from the inferno. He'd vomited all over himself and hadn't been able to sleep for three days. But in the mirror… yes, in the mirror that night, his face had had the look: skeletal, wizened. After that when someone asked him when he'd lost his virginity he told them he'd lost it in Londonderry.

Shawna had the look about her now. She'd probably never seen a butchered corpse before. Particularly of someone she knew. Once the look settled in, it never really left. Your eyes were forever glazed.

He supposed it was probably even worse for her.

Not only had she seen a hacked body, but some very, very bad people were going out of their way to make it look like she was a killer. And the really sad, twisted thing about it all was Jill Morell had meant nothing to them. She was just a convenient piece of meat to be slit and chopped to further their deranged ends. And who would do such a thing? The mob? The police? Some maniacal secret sect? No. None of the above.

These were the sort of acts people with absolute power committed.

People who didn't have to worry about being brought to trial.

Harry knew these people. They carried a smell of corruption about them. The higher up the ladder of power they went, the stronger the smell.

"Who, Harry?" Shawna wanted to know. "Who would be this fucking low?"

"Our own government, I would guess."

"No."

"Yes. Certain segments of it at any rate. Trust me, Shawna, unless I'm totally confused here, that's who these people are." He thought it over, narrowed his eyes. "I keep thinking about those white rubber suits they wore. They don't have to be for nuclear contamination, you know. They're called NBC suits—nuclear, biological, chemical."

Shawna didn't buy it. "C'mon, Harry. Listen to yourself, will you? Someone spilled some nerve gas or dropped a vial of cholera or something and now they're going around murdering people to cover it up? Is that what you're thinking?"

"Vaguely, darling, vaguely."

"It can't be."

"And why not?"

"Well, that's…that's like a conspiracy, Harry. That doesn't really happen."

"Doesn't it?" His face was green in the dashboard lights. "Well, I beg to differ, sweetheart. I've seen half a dozen of these things in operation. I know the feel and I know the stink of absolute power. Do you really think underworld heavies snatch people in the middle of the day? That they walk around in protective suits and sterilize their enemies? C'mon, Shawna."

"I don't know, Harry."

"Listen, you little idiot. You're into shit up to your pretty little ass and the men who are dumping on you are above the law. Maybe I'm wrong. But if I'm not—and I'm damn sure I'm not—then you are in trouble. If they'd kill your landlady just to set you up, you can bet they'll do the same to you."

Shawna wasn't saying much now.

"But if you need proof, I think we're about to get it."

Shawna looked behind them.

A police car was coming up fast with its lights blazing.

# DETROIT

## RIVERFRONT

**4:59 A.M.**

Johnny Kopok must've passed out because the next thing he knew he could hear voices. He pulled himself up on one elbow and rubbed the sleep from his eyes.

"No, no," he could hear Lou saying. "Oh please motherfucker, no..."

He thought maybe Lou was having a nightmare or something. But as he looked closer, he could see there were three guys there with him. The moonlight wasn't too bright, but bright enough to see some things. The guys with Lou looked like those skinheads that had been showing up around the city more and more of late. The kind with the bald heads and the tattoos. They'd been breeding like rats in a sewer.

"What—" Johnny started to say but stopped.

The words caught in his throat as he saw two of them hold old Lou down while the third did something horrible. Johnny saw it and couldn't believe what he was seeing. But he knew what he was smelling—something rank and damp like the water in a clogged drainage ditch. That, but worse. An awful black, almost evil stink.

He wanted to be sick, but he didn't dare look away.

*Oh my Christ.*

Something was coming out of the guy's mouth. The one that was sitting on Lou's chest. Something glistening white. As Johnny watched, it slid right down Lou's throat.

Johnny wanted to puke right then.

But he couldn't. He had to sit there and ride it out, chewing his fist like a baby until those freaks were done.

Johnny's head filled with fuzz and he was lost in the war again.

When he woke, the skinheads were gone. He steeled himself, not remembering the last time he'd been so godawful scared. He crawled as silently as possible over to Lou. Lou's face was dappled with moonlight, his jaws sprung wide.

"Lou? Lou?" he gasped. "You okay?"

Lou's skin was like ice.

Johnny was hoping it was all some crazy, boozy nightmare, but the fear, the raw ugly terror, just wouldn't go away. It wasn't until something moved in Lou's belly, right beneath Johnny's hand that he screamed.

Then he ran until he dropped.

# CHICAGO SOUTH SIDE, HYDE PARK

## UNIVERSITY OF CHICAGO MEDICAL CENTER

**5:17 A.M.**

In the morgue, Bridey O'Donnel did what she did best.

She'd examined three bodies since coming in at midnight, but those cadavers had been simple; any third year med student could've arrived at the same results as she. The first was a heart attack, the other two gang members shot at close range. One of them, a young man of twenty, had been executed in classic gangland style: three bullets to the head—*nine millimeter*, she thought—at close range. The other, and messier of the two, was barely sixteen. He'd taken a load of buckshot to the chest. He was nearly torn in half.

The first boy was black and the second was Hispanic. The Hispanic boy—Ramon Alverez—had been wearing a crucifix, but as Bridey well knew, there was no God in Southside Chicago.

After she finished the endless reams of paperwork that accompanied any cadaver, she started on the next one.

This one, she knew, wouldn't be so simple.

Snapping on her latex gloves, Bridey sighed, and began to speak. The red light on the voice-activated recorded blinked on.

"Subject is a white John Doe," she said, cutting his clothes away with scissors and dropping them into an evidence box. "Approximately forty years of age. Cause of death unknown, though emaciation is apparent. No external signs of trauma. A tattoo on his right forearm reads J.J.K. with a heart speared by a knife."

The recorder clicked off.

She gave the body a thorough external exam. There were no entry wounds or exit wounds. An appendix scar on his lower abdomen, something that might have been an old knife wound on his chest. Beyond that, nothing seemed out of order. What did puzzle her, though, was the swelling of the abdominal cavity. The man was horribly shrunken as if from some wasting disease, but his belly was full and round. It was more than normal distention due to collection of gases. Strange.

Where the hell was Frank with those X-rays?

She sighed, shaking her head. If she waited for him it could be an hour, maybe two. Radiology tended to give priority to the living.

Bridey wasn't a large woman. At five-foot-eight, she barely weighed a hundred twenty pounds. So it was no easy task for her to lift and shift her John Doe for the external. Thin as he was, he still made an ungainly corpse to lug about. She did it, but it took time and a lot of straining.

When she was done, her face was beaded with sweat.

"Didn't miss any meals did you, buddy boy?" she said.

The red light of the recorder was on, she noticed. It was like being watched by Big Brother with that damn thing. If you sneezed or coughed it came on.

"Got a present for you," a voice said, startling her.

It was Frank with the X-rays.

"Great. Just in time. Set 'em up for me, will ya?"

"Will do," Frank said. He clipped them to the screen. "I think you're going to like these. Or not like them, depending on your mood."

Bridey sighed. Whenever he said something like that it meant there was going to be trouble. It had been a long night. She did not want anything that challenged her fuzzy brain at this hour of the morning.

Frank was a radiological technician. He'd actually finished pre-med before he decided he didn't care for cutting up dead bodies. It wasn't uncommon.

"Just check out these scans, Doc. Unreal."

Bridey did, studying them so closely her nose nearly brushed against the abdominal series. "My...God."

Frank bit his lip. "What did I tell you? It looks like this guy swallowed a hose."

Bridey stared and kept staring.

There was a dark, snaking mass that looked very much like a hose winding its way through the intestines.

"Look at the dilation of those bowels, Frank."

Frank nodded. "Tell me about it. That colon must be big around as a Coke can."

"Bigger," Bridey said. "Much bigger. More like a quart of Coke."

"Is that even possible?"

Bridey just lifted an eyebrow. "Why not?"

"What could cause that?"

"I've got a few ideas," she said, "but there's only one way to find out."

"This is where I check out." He looked a little pale.

"C'mon, Frank where's your sense of adventure? Besides, Rick's on break and Sheila called in sick. I need some help. You're not afraid are you?"

Frank glanced around the room. The sickly green tiles that climbed half way up the walls. The stainless steel tables. The refrigerators. The sinks. The scales. The racks of specimen jars and chemicals. The instruments gleaming dully in the fluorescent overheads.

It was too much like the dissection room in anatomy class.

"I...I don't think so." He rubbed his belly gently. "This place gives me gas."

Bridey scowled at him. "You *are* afraid."

"Oh, don't start with that business. I'm squeamish. What of it? I bet if I dropped a nice fat spider down your cleavage you'd be a little green, too."

"Well met, Frank."

"And well played." He made a disgusted face. "If Iversen finds out I'm helping you instead of doing my own job... oh shit, all right. I'm not touching anything, though."

"Thanks, Frank. All you'll have to do is help me move him. That's all."

"That's all, she says."

Inside, Bridey was grinning broadly. Poor old Frank. He was so easy to manipulate she just couldn't help herself.

No matter. The cadaver was what really interested her.

She'd went through med school on a government grant. A federal program where Uncle Sam would finance your education with the proviso that after you'd been certified, you'd practice for slave wages in a free clinic on an Indian reservation or some such similarly depressed area. At the Hopi Reservation outside Flagstaff, Bridey did her time. One of the most interesting and unusual things that happened there was an outbreak of human tapeworms caused by poor sanitation. It was practically unheard of outside the third world.

And that's what she was thinking now: tapeworm. Parasitic worm infection.

It looked much like one, save it was much larger.

Selecting a scalpel, she intended to find out. She made the standard Y-incision for investigation of the thoraco-abdominal cavity. The incision began at each armpit and ran beneath both breasts to the bottom of the sternum where the incisions joined and proceeded down the center of the abdomen to the pubis. It didn't take long.

"What an expert you are," Frank said, disgusted. "I'll bet you're a real demon with a rump roast."

She ignored him. The world around her was gone, there was only the anatomy before her and the impossibility it suggested.

Using an oscillating saw, Bridey cut through the sternum and the front of the ribs. She then removed this section in one piece. Everything was pretty much laid open now. She ignored the pleura, the serous membrane which covers the lungs and lines the chest cavity. Her interest was solely in the peritoneal membrane and the viscera beneath.

She cut through it, exposing the bowels.

*Jesus H. Christ... look at the size...the size...*

The duodenum and colon were swollen to the size of a man's forearm, if not much larger. And the really strange, really impossible thing was that though they were cold and lifeless, they were throbbing, moving of their own volition.

*This is no tapeworm*, she decided then and there. *No tapeworm ever got that big, moved like that...*

"I don't like this," Frank said and Bridey could hear the tension in his voice.

Her mouth felt like it was full of beach sand. She tried to swallow, but there was no spit.

The scalpel poised above the transverse colon, she looked at Frank and he looked at her and she wondered if she was sweating like him. If her lower lip was trembling like his. If her eyes were bulging like those of a decompressing fish.

*You don't have to do this*, a voice told her. You can stop right now and get this guy in the freezer. *Wait till Dr. Conniker gets here at eight. He's been at it thirty odd years. He knows his shit even if he is an arrogant, racist bastard. You can do that and nobody would blame you because this whole thing is bad and it's going to take you somewhere you just don't want to go...*

*Can't you see that?*

She could, but she wasn't going to stop.

Deftly, carefully, she made a horizontal slit about six inches along the colon, her heart pounding in her ears, her lungs barely able to draw a breath.

An odor rose from the incision. One that was beyond the smell of death, of waste. It was an awful salty rottenness like marshes and fetid swamps.

"Holy shit," Frank murmured, his voice puny and weak.

"Can't be...can't..."

The words trembled on Bridey's lips. She felt helpless and small. Then something happened which could never adequately be envisioned—the bowels seemed to split with a rubbery shriek and a huge segmented white worm erupted from the belly of the dead man. It snaked and coiled obscenely in the air like a python considering a new branch to climb. By the time Bridey and Frank accepted what they were seeing, the thing—eyeless and glistening like wet plastic—surged at Bridey's face. Her jaws sprung open with the impact and the thing pushed down her throat, moving with a repulsive juicy sound that Frank would never forget.

He started screaming as she fell into him and spilled the both of them to the cool, tiled floor. The scream kept coming as he crawled frantically away from her, backpedaling on elbows and heels, the scream steadily becoming an insane, mindless sound.

Bridey flopped around with boneless, spasmodic gyrations, about three feet of the worm hanging from her open mouth, twisting and hissing in the air with a stink of hot blood and steam.

Frank collapsed against an instrument caddy, pissing himself and vomiting down his scrubs.

Bridey's body continued to writhe and contort, the worm wrapping its slimed length around her head. Something like a mouth opened. It made a squealing, mewling sound and disgorged a stream of black fluid into Frank's face.

His mind, which had clung to sanity by a tenuous thread, plummeted into blackness as the juice burned his flesh and blinded him. He clawed and tore at his eyes which swelled shut behind heavy meat-red sockets, a yellow mucus running from them like tears.

He hit the floor, his scream now a high, screeching laughter that echoed in the confines of his skull, a dirge.

In time, there was silence.

Broken only by a pathetic sobbing and the wet, horrible feeding sounds of the worm.

# CHICAGO, NORTH SHORE

## EN ROUTE

**5:36 A.M.**

As Harry Niles stumbled out of his GTO, he fell to his knees.

"You been drinking, sir?" the cop asked.

He was a Metro cop and although he looked completely normal, Shawna had to wonder if he were somehow mixed up in this...this conspiracy.

"I had two beers," Harry slurred. "No more. No less. What I do, officer? Run a stop sign or something?"

Harry knew how it was done.

He'd been pulled over enough times to know what cops expected of a drunk and he was giving it his all. Maybe when this was over he'd get an Academy Award. Probably just a jail cell, though, if he were lucky. Real lucky.

Shawna came around the side of the car. "He's drunk all right," she said, trying desperately to sound trashy and cheap. "Drunk and behind the wheel. That's his way, officer. Ain't it yer way, Harry? Ain't it?"

The cop looked stressed. Maybe because he saw he was in for a real treat here. "Ma'am," he said, speaking slowly. "Ma'am, please get back in the car."

Shawna pushed right past him. "Why don't you tell him what you got in the trunk, you goddamn drunk?"

"Ma'am, will you please—"

"Tell him, dammit." She moved in quick and gave Harry a little kick in the side. It landed a little harder than she'd meant it to. Harry grunted and started swearing. The cop was on her before she could do any more damage.

"Ma'am, please," he said, pulling her back, "that's enough."

And then Harry was on his feet. "No good tramp, that's all she is."

"Fuck you," she said, really warming up to this now. "Fuck you, you cheap sonofabitch! You goddamn drunk!"

The cop had his hands full now, keeping them separated. "Knock this off or I'll take you both in!" he snarled. But his heart clearly wasn't in it.

Harry made like he was going to hit Shawna and when the cop inserted himself conveniently between them. Harry fought in his grip, being very sloppy and uncoordinated. The cop spent most of his energy keeping Harry on his feet.

"Fucking slut!" Harry spat, falling.

Shawna nodded and brought out the slim little can of Mace. Before the cop knew which end was up, she gave him a full shot in the face. He went down, hollering and cursing, rubbing at his eyes.

"Sorry about that," Shawna said and gave him another blast for good measure.

Then they were in Harry's GTO, tooling down the highway.

Harry drove another mile or so and then exited off Sheridan into Kenilworth where Gabe Hebberman lived. What he thought Gabe could do about any of this Shawna had no idea. But she supposed they needed somewhere to hide out.

Especially now.

*God, do you realize what you've just done? Assaulting a police officer? Fleeing and eluding? Just great. Just fucking great.*

Already the cop was on his radio alerting half the state about the black GTO. They'd been lucky in many ways, though. First, that the cop was out alone. Second, that no other cops had stopped by to assist. And third that they had managed to pull off that crazy stunt in the first place.

"Why do you keep Mace, Harry?" she asked.

"I'm afraid of date rape," he told her. "And who can blame me with the company I keep?"

Shawna shook her head. "You never quit, do you?"

"Not so far. It all depends on what you just got me into."

"What did I get you into?" It was a rhetorical question. She sighed deeply. "That cop'll have everyone in the state looking for us and this car now."

"Or maybe not."

She looked at him. "How do you figure?"

"It all depends on what's going on here."

They drove in silence after that.

Shawna sat there, arms folded, feeling quite hopeless and helpless. She wondered if this conspiracy or whatever the hell you wanted to call it could possibly go this deep. She supposed it was possible. Maybe if those were government men and they had the cops working with them, maybe none of this would be handled in the usual way. Maybe a typical manhunt would not ensue.

But she couldn't believe that.

They had just assaulted a police officer. There was no way they could let that lay. It would have to be handled through normal channels.

*Yes, it sure as hell would*, she thought nervously. If these guys were government types—CIA, FBI, whatever—and they were involved in some bizarre, hush-hush operation, then it would be unlikely they would have the local John Laws working with them. They might have them pick someone up for questioning or throw someone in the can overnight, but that would be the extent of it. The cops wouldn't be involved in the conspiracy any further than that.

"Do you think the cops are in on this, Harry?"

He shrugged with a slow roll of his shoulders. "Not to any extent. I think the feds, or whoever these guys are, murdered your landlady and set you up with the knife. That's obvious. Then maybe they called the cops with an anonymous tip. The cops are just doing what cops do."

She had to agree with him.

If this was a secret operation, then involving Chicago's finest would not only be sloppy but make the entire thing very public in short order. Somehow, knowing the police weren't involved in this nightmare restored her faith in humanity. It calmed her, lessened the paranoia that had been eating at her. There was nothing worse than thinking the entire world was ganging up on you.

"Do you think they could've really pinned Jill's murder on me? I mean, it's all kind of circumstantial isn't it?"

"Sure it is. It's an old trick with outfits like the one after you. If they'd have really wanted you out of the way they'd have killed you. This was just a ploy to buy them time. You would have been kept overnight, maybe a few days. In the end you would have been released." He drove slowly through Kenilworth so as not to arouse any suspicion. Most of the houses were dark, but it was still a very exclusive sort of place and he knew from experience that some of the neighborhoods had their own security goons. "When you got out of jail, Shawna," he continued, "the people who are doing this would be long gone and no trace would remain. The cops would have a lot of questions and so would you. But nothing else. A game, just a game."

"A game in which innocent people are murdered," Shawna said. "That's some game."

Harry slowed and turned into a private drive. He stopped before a gate set into a stone wall. There was a camera mounted there. Harry grinned into it. "Gabe! Open the hell up! I've got some hot women with me!"

Shawna thought it would never work. Good God, it was five in the morning. Gabe Hebberman, the publishing magnate, would be sleeping. But a voice said, "All right, but don't steal anything."

Harry drove slowly down a winding drive flanked by huge birch trees as the gate slid close behind them.

The grounds of Gabe Hebberman's estate were impressive. Shawna couldn't see much of it in the dark, but what she could see—sprawling gardens, tennis courts, and what looked to be a riding stable in the distance—made her envious.

She wondered if this Gabe was single.

"He's a widower," Harry said, reading her mind. "And he's still faithful to the memory of his wife."

"I wasn't—"

"Like hell you weren't, Shawna. I could hear the gears turning over here."

She said nothing. Harry was way too intuitive for his own good. She would definitely have to watch herself around him. Already she owed him a lot and by the time this was over? She didn't even want to think about it.

# CHICAGO SOUTH SIDE, HYDE PARK

## UNIVERSITY OF CHICAGO MEDICAL CENTER

**5:44 A.M.**

When Rick Perreau got back from break, he made for the lab to hurry along the blood toxicology on those gangbangers they'd brought in. It came back about how he'd figured—both of them were coked to the gills. It was a pretty common finding. Some people just thought they were ten feet tall and bulletproof after a few rocks.

When he got to the morgue, it seemed awfully quiet.

It wasn't exactly a lively place (no pun intended) on the best of days and at night it was downright...dare he think it...*dead*. But, still it had its own feel, its own sounds of occupancy: the noises of instruments being clattered into stainless steel pans, the buzz of saws, the clicking of computer keys as things were filed and processed.

He heard none of these.

"Wake up in there, Bridey," he called out. "Not you, pal."

The body on the gurney slept quietly in its body bag. It paid the lab tech no mind.

"Where'd you come from?" Rick asked.

There was a large yellow envelope hooked to the foot of the gurney. Rick opened it and scanned the contents, shaking his head. He hated when they did this. The nurses would wheel a body in here and just leave it. No word, nothing. Just push it through the doors. Not their problem.

The death certificate said the guy was eighty-eight years old. Heart disease.

Rick set the toxicology reports on the gurney and pushed their newest occupant towards the freezer. "We'll find a place for you, chum."

He had to go through the interconnecting autopsy rooms to do so. He looked around for Bridey in the first two and saw nothing. Maybe she'd slipped out for a sandwich or something. No biggie. He made it into the third room when he stopped cold.

He looked around quickly, suspecting a joke.

"What the hell is this?" he said under his breath.

There was a body on the table. It had been opened up... in fact, it had been sheared open. It didn't look like the work of a scalpel as much as that of a chainsaw. But as he looked around, he saw the sternum sitting in a stainless steel specimen tray. The air was pungent with an acrid, burnt smell.

*What in the Christ?*

There was blood and slime greased over the floor. But no bodies. Instruments were scattered about. A cart was knocked over. There was a shoe laying in a puddle of blood. A man's loafer. Bloody footprints led away into the freezer. There was a smeared trail following in their wake...as if something large had been dragged away.

Rick stood there. A clot of grease had formed in his throat.

*You better get security. That's what you should do.*

He turned and paused...waiting.

He could hear something from the freezer. A wet, flabby sound. A sucking sound. Like a dry vac hose working a bucket of chum. He licked his lips and found himself staring at the shoe, the blood. Somehow, some way, they seemed to be the answer to everything. But he wasn't sure he wanted an answer.

"Bridey?" he said, very softly. "Dr. O'Donnel? Is that you?"

Chewing his lip in indecision, he knew he had to go in there. If he went and got security, they'd wonder why he hadn't followed the trail. Someone could've been dying in there. With the amount of blood, it would be the natural conclusion.

All right, all right.

He pushed through the door and had a look.

Someone in an ensanguined lab coat was bending over a body. Despite the ruined, flayed features, he could see that it was Frank. And bending over him, Bridey. She was making a horrible sucking, gasping sound, her entire body shuddering with slow, rolling spasms.

His stomach in his throat, Rick just stared.

"Bridey," he said in a controlled, monotone voice. "Bridey... are you..."

She fell back against him and he had to hold her trembling weight in his arms. He liked the woman. He respected her. He looked forward to seeing her. To chatting and joking... but at that particular moment, he wanted to push her aside. She was cold in his arms. And wet. Her body had been slimed with some sticky, gelatinous ichor. The stink was unbearable. It reminded him of a beach strewn with rotting fish. It was that sort of smell: cold, brackish, decayed.

"Bridey..."

She brought her head up with a jerking motion. Her hair hung over her face in moist, knotted tendrils. It was clotted with blood and something oily and black. She brushed her hair aside. Her eyes were filled with blood, her cheeks painted with lurid streaks of red mucus.

A bloated, blackened tongue rasped over her craggy lips.

"NO! GET OFF ME! GET OFF ME!" Rick screamed madly, shrilly, his voice echoing in the confines of the freezer. His eyes darted wildly, swimming in his sockets. "GET THE FUCK AWAY FROM ME GODDAMMIT DON'T YOU TOUCH ME—"

He tried to pull away, to fight, kick, claw, but she overwhelmed him with a savage, brutal strength, slamming him to the floor.

Screaming and gagging, warm bile squirting into his mouth, he thrashed his head violently side to side. But it was no good. Bridey moved up and over him with a fluid, boneless grace, pinning him. Inches from his shrieking face, she opened her mouth wide and wider still. Her breath was like hot brine. Her tongue came out—at least what he thought was her tongue—licking and twisting in the air, impossibly white and glistening. It went into his mouth and down his throat, deeper, deeper, until he thought he'd burst.

And the pain. Christ in Heaven, the pain.

It radiated in white-hot waves from his belly, up, up into his head where it gathered in an explosion of agony that became a sweet, warm numbness. He drifted off with no worries.

When he awoke, he would have a new set of priorities.

# MCLEAN, VIRGINIA

## PARKVIEW HILLS

**6:25 A.M.**

When you were the Director of National Intelligence and the phone started ringing off the hook before six, you knew you were in for another long day. Charles VanderMissen had slept little more than two hours when a call came through his secure line. He'd just gotten off the phone with the President and now here was more good news.

"Yes?" he said, still wiping sleep from his eyes.

"Chuck. It's me."

It was Walter Sleshing, still in his office at the DIA keeping watch. He probably hadn't slept more than a few hours since this entire ugly mess began. The old, tireless watchdog.

"Tell me."

"We've had a confirmed incident in St. Louis. Dozens of witnesses. The lid's off this damn thing," Sleshing said in a pained voice as he reeled off the details of the St. Louis MetroLink train incident. "People are going to be asking a lot of uncomfortable questions. The media are already nosing around."

"It was only a matter of time."

In a way, VanderMissen was relieved. Questions would be asked, answers would have to be supplied. The blowback from this could be potentially damning. Now it would land squarely in the President's lap. His advisors and cabinet—which included VanderMissen—would be expected to come up with something to either whitewash this or some creative misdirection to mislead the public. Deniability was a mantra when you were deep in the hotbed of DC politics.

"Okay, Wally, send what you have into me and I'll let the President know at the Daily Brief."

"Hang on, Chuck. Something just came in."

*Oh, Christ.*

"Another possible in Chicago. U of C Medical Center. Not confirmed yet. Sounds probable, though."

"Shit. Okay."

When he got off the line, he checked the call logs of his secure sat phone and his personal cell. He had calls from Gus Costello and Arlene Rabin, the Secretaries of Defense and State respectively, but he'd already returned those. There was one from Admiral Paulus, the ONI director, another from Bob Pershing, and a raft of others ranging from Gordon Parks of the NSA to Charlie Goade of the FBI and even Colonel Donnelly from INSCOM, the Army's Intelligence and Security Command. The latter was a nosy, jittery, downright paranoid career spook who spent a great deal of his resources spying on the CIA, DIA, Homeland Security, and any other intelligence and security services that crossed his radar.

VanderMissen knew it was just the beginning. Calls and cables and emails would be flying in from every corner of the country and the world. And as Director of National Intelligence, it would be his job to answer them.

All right then. Time to get the stove hot and see what they could cook up this time.

# RICHMOND, VIRGINIA

## CBT BIOSAFETY LEVEL THREE, THE MIRROR MAZE

**7:35 A.M.**

"As you can see," Dr. Evans said, peering out at Elizabeth Toma from the plastic bubble of his hood, "the behavior of the host is obvious if you know what to look for. What we have here are mice, but, behaviorally, there's little difference between them and humans. Once parasitized, the host no longer exists as an independent entity. It is a slave of the parasite and lives only to propagate it and its spawn."

Standing there in her green biosuit, listening to the suction of filtered air and Evans' droning voice, Elizabeth felt a curious combination of fatigue and claustrophobia. How Evans and his people spent hours upon hours in these confining suits and never went out of their minds was beyond her. Level Three wasn't as bad as The Cage, Level Four, but it was hardly comforting. The corridors and rooms were made of special reflective glass, hence it was called The Mirror Maze.

As Evans droned on, she watched the techs bustling about to and fro in their suits. Most of them were coming from the autopsy room carrying sample jars of blood and bile and spinal fluid, sectioned brainstems, intestines, and lymphatics. The parasites were amazingly prodigious, in that they mothered their eggs and hid them in the most unlikely places. Tissues would be cultured and sliced micron-thin for the electron microscope.

"The eggs have a tendency to migrate," Evans explained. "Which we find absolutely amazing. The survivability of these creatures is beyond anything we could have hoped for."

In one of the biology labs, he performed a simple experiment. It was meant, of course, to fill her with shock and awe and it did just that. He had two clear plastic biocontainment vessels that looked like small fish aquariums or the old glove box isolators they had used years before. In one, were six healthy white mice. They were confused, obviously, as to where they were. This was not their normal environment and they clustered together in fear. They would overcome it in time. If they lived that long which, of course, they wouldn't.

In the other plastic vessel were two mice that did not look healthy at all. Their eyes were dull, their bodies swollen, fur discolored with gray streaks. They laid on the bottom, twitching and trembling.

"These are our vectors," Evans explained, though that was obvious. "What I want to illustrate to you is how quickly the infected hosts will sense healthy animals."

Using remote manipulators, he prodded the infected mice. They barely responded. They looked, if anything, as if they were dead or near to it.

"See how sick they are? One wouldn't expect much of them. Even rising up and moving an inch or two would seem far beyond them...but watch as I introduce Group A to Group B."

Using the manipulators, he transferred the infected mice into the vessel with the healthy ones. The healthy group initially stayed away from them, cowering together in the corner. They were more agitated than they had been a few moments before. They sensed something was amiss. The infected mice were on the other side of the vessel. They merely trembled a bit.

"Keep watching," Evans told her, as if she was going to turn away.

Approximately four minutes after Group A was placed in the vessel, the two infected mice began to thrash uncontrollably. They spit out blood as they writhed and squeaked. Then they were up. Slowly, painfully, they moved in the direction of the healthy mice who began to squeal and run about in circles. Their terror was obvious. One of the infected individuals leaped on a healthy mouse with startling speed. It pressed the healthy animal down, holding it, as it disgorged a larval worm from its mouth. The healthy animal fought, refusing to accept the parasite. Then something happened. It went limp. It became pacific, soporific even. It no longer moved. It acted as if it was drugged.

"See? See?" Evans said, clearly excited. "The infected mouse has overcome the healthy specimen by secreting biochemically specific pheromones which have triggered its brain to release a cocktail of endorphins. The healthy animal is quite literally stoned. Now it happily accepts parasitization."

A worm crawled into its mouth and the mouse seemed unaware of the fact. Now it was inside. The worm would not only use the host's own body to protect it and nourish it, but it would appropriate the host's genetic machinery to produce a comfortable ecosystem with the necessary proteins and chemicals that would help it grow as its host mothered it and quite literally destroyed itself in the process. Which it would do quite happily, stewed to the gills on the pharmacy of drugs its parasite forced it to manufacture. The host would become a zombie more or less with a single relentless drive: to not only protect its parasite but to become an incubator for thousands of eggs, to seed them to the world and infect thousands of new hosts.

"A perfect lifeform," Evans said, still clearly excited.

Elizabeth figured it was about as close to an orgasm as the man got. Any normal person would find it sickening; he was thrilled, exhilarated, breathless over it.

*And what about you?*

This *was* what she kept asking herself. She had recognized something inside her that was completely alien—sympathy and a rising moral indignation that was not part and parcel of who and what she was. She did not like it. Such things could make you weak and she could not afford to be weak. Not now. Not at this stage. Not when ultimate, omnipotent power was within her grasp. She was surrounded by countless enemies. One sign of weakness would be her undoing. The Collective would not allow it; they would crush her.

Evans kept talking and she nodded behind the plastic bubble of her helmet. She had known him for years. He was a brilliantly gifted molecular biologist and a darling of S5 (and as such, a protégé of the Old Man's). But when this was done, he was going to be removed as were the entire staff that had worked on BioGenesis. All trails would end here.

The demonstration at an end, Elizabeth went through decon, then back up to her office. After a time, she picked up her sat phone and rang up The Collective. This was a call she had to make and one she was putting off.

"Well? We've been waiting to hear from you," the voice on the other end said. "We were beginning to worry. We don't like to worry."

"No, of course not. I apologize."

"And how is our good friend at the NSA?"

They wanted to know about her meeting with Gordon Parks last night. She would tell them what they wanted to hear, just as he had. It was part of the game.

"He's committed."

"But?"

She sighed. "He seems too eager to discuss things that are sensitive by nature."

"I see. Is there a question of his loyalty?"

"No, I don't think so. He just has a big mouth."

"I see. And you're uncomfortable with that?"

"Aren't you?" she asked.

"I'll ask the questions, Elizabeth."

"Yes. Sorry."

There was an uncomfortable silence from the other end that made her sweat. She was dealing with one of the most powerful individuals in the world. A word from him and she disappeared. He had started civil wars, eliminated political rivals, sacked economies, and destroyed nations at a whim. You didn't fuck with power like that.

"It's his loyalty that concerns me."

"He's loyal. I'm sure of it."

"Would you stake your life on that?"

"I'm as sure as I can be without climbing inside his head and reading his mind."

"Well, hopefully, that won't be necessary. Good day, Elizabeth."

She set the phone on her desk and only then did she begin to shake with fear.

# AFGHANISTAN

## NANGARHAR PROVINCE

**4:22 P.M. KABUL TIME**

Dead men.

Dead men all in a row.

Tommy Quillan stood there smoking an American cigarette, wearing French DPM camouflage, holding a British commando knife, and drinking Austrian beer. And all this in some stinking, bombed-out town in a hell zone that had once been part of Jalalabad.

He laughed under his breath. *Don't tell me the world isn't coming together into one seamless global fucking community.*

He was standing in a rubble-strewn building with a trio of Northern Alliance intelligence specialists, all CIA-trained, who were led by a Pashai commander named Colonel Abu Rashid. Crowding outside was Quillan's bloodthirsty garrison of Uzbek mercenaries. Before them, tied securely to the legs of a stout table were two Al-Qaeda fighters. Beaten, bloody, mumbling incessantly to their god, they were dressed in the typical hodgepodge uniform of the Middle Eastern Islamic extremist: worn fatigues, faces covered in red-checked shemaghs. Their beards were long and filthy, matted with leaves and sticks. Neither man had probably seen running water in many weeks and smelled like it.

The two fighters had been captured during a series of raids on Al-Qaeda safe houses in Jalalabad that Quillan himself had directed after receiving a tip from his underground network via MI6. Some sixty extremists were killed in a pitched battle that lasted two hours

His raiders discovered a great cache of documents on U.S. military weapons, tactics, and strengths. Many of them were directly from the U.S. Printing Office. All that was to be expected, but what made him particularly curious were the documents related to biochemistry, microbiology, and biological warfare that contained detailed information on the various types of available bioagents, the vectors used to spread them, and the estimated casualty numbers to a large urban population center. There was also a DVD in the cache that looked to have been shot at Darunta, the former Al-Qaeda training camp outside Jalalabad. It showed men in containment suits performing experiments on laboratory animals.

Quillan believed these to be Iranian videos and it only further hinted at something nobody wanted to discuss: Al-Qaeda's increasing interest in germ warfare.

All of this was relayed back to the CIA's Counterterrorism Center and from the CTC to the Defense Department, DIA, DHS, and all the other alphabet soup agencies of the United States security services. Supposedly.

Colonel Rashid wanted to kill their prisoners outright. He'd already consulted his blue prayer beads and knew it was what Allah wished.

His junior officer, Captain Aget, wanted to let the Uzbeks mutilate them.

Quillan appreciated the zeal of both men, but he was in charge and until that changed, he would decide who was killed or mutilated. There were things he wanted to learn from these two, even if they were only rumors. For in any war, even a rumor contained a seed of truth.

"They are infidels," Colonel Rashid said as if that explained it all. "To let them live would be a crime."

"Of course."

"We should kill them now," Captain Aget concurred. "Outside, there are dozens of men who would be honored to slit the throats of these animals. I myself would gladly do it."

Quillan grinned.

He looked down at the Al-Qaeda fighters. They were known for their brutality. With this in mind, there was no need of a trial here. That they had to die and painfully was a foregone conclusion. They would respect nothing less and Quillan would not disappoint them. He knew if he didn't waste these two, the Uzbeks would waste him. The fever of revenge ran very deep here. And Quillan didn't blame them a bit. The Al-Qaeda extremists were monsters. He himself had seen what they did to women and children, to infants, even. They had no respect for human life and Quillan could appreciate that because he had none himself.

But he needed information.

It was why he was there.

He was a contract mercenary specialist currently under the employ of the CIA. He had worked for no one else in the past twelve years and as long as the checks were deposited in a timely manner in his offshore account, he never would. Having honed his skills with the British 22 SAS Regiment in places like Oman, Central America, Iraq, and Northern Ireland, he came at a high price but he guaranteed results. And, thus far, the Company had been pleased with his work. Ever since taking up his rather peculiar profession, he had lived entirely in the shadows, completely off the grid: he owned no property, paid no taxes, had no checks or credit cards in his name, no cellphones registered to him. He was in no database—save his file with the Regiment which was a dozen years out of date now—and had no family.

Men like him did not exist. They were summoned like demons out of the cold and darkness for particularly delicate assignments, wet work, and various clandestine ops that were easily deniable.

He had originally been sent to Afghanistan to train and equip counterterrorist pursuit teams that would hunt down and kill remaining Al-Qaeda cells in the area that had not fled south. Flush them out, put them down. Standard CT ops.

Now the Company wanted him to track down Sheikh Sa'ad who supposedly was in possession of some sort of bioweapon.

Quillan was very familiar with Sheikh Sa'ad and looked forward to disrupting his network and interrogating him if they could take him alive. They had pretty good intel that Sheikh Sa'ad was in Nangahar province. He had been seen by many witnesses traveling in a small convoy of olive-drab military-style trucks, surrounded by soldiers in fatigues who were all armed with AKs and SKS rifles, just begging for a drone strike. He was seen in Jalalabad outside a mosque, then addressing a small gathering outside the Institute for Islamic Studies. The soldiers were hardcore Al-Qaeda.

He was here...or had been.

He was very close, Quillan knew, so close he could smell the dogshit kebabs on his breath.

The problem, as always, was interrogation. It took forever. Quillan's Farsi and Pashai were weak and he had to rely on Colonel Rashid to translate and quite often the meaning of things were lost because Rahid's English skills were rudimentary at best. He spoke his native Pashai and Pashtun rapid-fire, but his Farsi and English came unbelievably, almost tortuously, slow. Captain Aget, on the other hand, spoke excellent English, Farsi, Arabic, and Dari, as well as Pashai. But Rashid would not let him translate; Rashid himself was in command and to let a junior officer take charge would have been an insult to him. When one was in the Pashtun heartland, one had to play by the rules...as much as that pissed Quillan off.

He stripped the shemaghs off the prisoner's faces, then turned to the colonel. "Ask them where the Al-Qaeda base camp is in Logar Province and who is commanding it."

Rashid did so. Both men just stared blankly at him.

Quillan expected as much. You could say what you wanted about these boys, but they sure as hell knew how to keep a secret. He flicked his cigarette out the door. Half-smoked, two Uzbeks dove for it, fighting over it like starving dogs over a joint of meat. They were a rugged lot, but fiercely loyal. They wore no true uniforms, just whatever they found lying about or what they could strip off the bodies of dead soldiers. Both wore sneakers and camo pants stained with blood and dirt. One wore a MOLSON sweatshirt, the other a Russian tunic with the previous owner's bloodstains prominently displayed.

"Tell them I have no interest in them," Quillan said. "I seek Sheikh Sa'ad al Khalafari, the Egyptian. If they tell me where to find him, they'll live to praise Allah another day."

Colonel Rashid tried again and got the same blank, stony stare.

Quillan laughed. *You stupid fucking ragheads. I can make this quick or it can take all day.*

He lit another cigarette to calm himself. He looked around, knowing that the ancient dark stains on the walls were the blood of Spanish journalists who had been captured by the Taliban and executed in this very room. The men with them—progressive Afghans—had shaved off their beards in violation of Taliban law so their ears and noses were cut off as punishment.

Both of the terrorists were injured. One had been kneecapped by shrapnel, the other took a volley of slugs to the belly. The one with the gut wound was bleeding badly. He wouldn't make it much longer.

The one on the left with the mangled leg began to squirm.

Rashid cleared his throat. "He wish a doctor."

"Tell him I wish to know where Sheikh Sa'ad is," Quillan said.

Rashid did, but the man kept shaking his head.

Quillan sighed, wondering why everything had to be done the hard way, and pulled a bayonet out of his pack. Without a word he went over to the one that was gutshot and slid the bayonet into the wound. The man came alive, twisting and writhing and screaming. Quillan twisted the bayonet back and forth until more and more blood gushed forth.

"Ask him!" he snapped.

Rashid did, but the fighter had passed out.

Quillan left the bayonet in his belly. He pressed the muzzle of a nickel-plated Colt .38 automatic to the man's head and pulled the trigger. The gun barked three times and the extremist's head exploded, spraying gore over the walls.

He turned to Rashid. "Tell him he will die next," he said, indicating the other prisoner with the mangled leg. "But not so quickly."

The other man still shook his head, though tears ran down his face as he prayed to a god that had now abandoned him.

Quillan pulled out his knife and cut the man's pant leg away from the gaping wound. He inserted the tip of the blade into the gash and drew it back at an arc, freeing a four-inch strip of skin in the process.

The prisoner screamed and Quillan punched him in the face.

"Tell him I'll skin him like a fucking rabbit if he doesn't talk."

The man shook his head, spitting in Quillan's face and screaming insults at him.

The Uzbek mercenaries were pressing in the doorway now.

They had seen Quillan work before and they didn't want to miss out.

Quillan didn't let them down. He cut the prisoner's clothes off and sheared a flap of skin from his belly. He took off his left nipple, then his right. Within a few minutes, the man's torso was raw, bleeding, and skinless.

He was also beyond speech.

He cried and moaned and trembled.

The knife moved in Quillan's practiced grip, the blade flashed dirty light.

"I'm gonna skin your manhood off, son. What do you think of that?"

The prisoner continued babbling prayers.

In Quillan's experienced hands, it took over two hours for him to die.

# CHICAGO, RIVER NORTH

## THE WAREHOUSE

**8:05 A.M.**

Well over three hours after they'd made the snatch at the VA hospital, Cave was still pissed off. "You're both pretty fucking pathetic, you know that? With your histories, your experience, I can't believe you let something like this happen." He paced up and down like a drill instructor. "Two freaking hours of surveillance and you didn't notice the woman in the truck? Jesus H. Lovely Christ. You two are really something. Where was your OpSec?"

Neither of them could answer because their operational security was shit and they knew it.

"She must have been slumped over, dozing or something," McKenna said.

"Uh-huh. It didn't occur to you that a sick man might have someone waiting for him?"

Cave stared them both down, his face livid, his hands balled into fists. Finally, he exhaled and dug a cigarette out of his shirt pocket. He lit it with a stick match struck off his boot.

"We fucked up," Stein told him. "What more can we say, sir? We simply fucked up and that's it."

"And do you know why?" Cave asked him.

Stein nodded slowly. "Yes, I do."

"Great. I can't wait to hear your assessment."

Stein ignored the sarcasm. "We've gotten...complacent. We've gotten lazy. I mean, that bit with the parasite aside, this entire thing has been pretty dull by our usual standards," he explained, choosing his words carefully, enunciating "parasite" like a child pronouncing a new word. "Let's face reality, sir, we're killing innocent people here—"

"Infected hosts," Cave corrected.

"—not armed enemy combatants. We've run up against no opposition. Any dipshit with a gun could do what we're doing. It's child's play. We're being used as fucking hitmen. So, if we're starting to make mistakes, I think it's understandable, don't you? There's nothing in this to keep our edge, to challenge us. It only makes us sick to our stomachs."

"Point taken, Stein," Cave said. "But hear me now, gentlemen, and hear me good: this is heavy shit here and if you make mistakes you're not only putting yourself at risk, you're putting the whole city, the whole damn country at risk. Do you follow me?"

McKenna nodded, saying, "If we botch a hit here, a snatch, whatever, then we stand a chance of spreading this shit farther than it already is?"

"Bingo, McKenna. Right on the money." He looked at Stein. "Not bad for a guy who looks like he just went ten rounds with a pepper shaker."

Stein chortled.

"With all due respect, fuck the both of you," McKenna said. How the hell was he to know the woman had pepper spray?

Cave laughed himself now. "You guys get a few hours' sleep. Then we have to go back out again." The smile faded from his face. "I spent an hour with the Old Man straightening out your mess. I'm not going to go through that again. Do you understand?"

They nodded.

"Sir?" Stein said.

"Yeah?"

"Tell me the truth. Are we winning this war or are the worms?"

Cave left without answering.

"There's your answer," McKenna said, rolling over in his bunk and covering his head with a pillow. In a few minutes, he was snoring.

Sleep didn't come so easy for Stein.

He'd never been in a situation like this before. Never been a player in a game that just might spell the end of the human race. He was starting to seriously think about bailing out of this one. Even if they wasted all those fucking worms, he didn't see his chances of survival as good. This project was just too big. He had a nasty feeling that McKenna and he were going to get whacked when this was done or not done.

He didn't like the look in the Old Man's eyes.

There was something very fatal about it.

Under the Old Man's directive, the worms were to be referred to as *parasites*. People infected with them were now *hosts*. Killing them was known as *eradicating diseased vectors*. And the job the teams were doing was to be called *contagion control*.

It was all a load of bullshit.

Politically correct psychobabble. Perception management taken to the extreme. There wasn't much Stein liked about the Old Man. In fact, there wasn't a damn thing. And especially his cold gray eyes. They were dead, clinical. He looked at everyone like a new species of bug he wanted to dissect.

Stein just wondered when McKenna and he would become vectors that needed eradication.

# CHICAGO, NORTH SHORE

## KENILWORTH

**8:17 A.M.**

Gabe Hebberman was slicing smoked ham and arranging the deli-thin slices on a platter atop the butcher block table that ran through the middle of his vault-like kitchen. He'd already sliced pastrami, hard salami, Swiss and Muenster cheeses. There were jars of pickles, olives, relishes, peppers, mayo and hot mustard. A loaf of bread sat nearby awaiting his attention.

Although it was breakfast time, Gabe preferred a good sandwich.

He snatched a slice of ham and chewed it up. "You know," he said, "it's a helluva thing for a Jew to say, but I love a good ham sandwich."

Harry looked at Shawna and grimaced. "Gabe has a way of speaking about food metaphorically."

Shawna just sat there, looking tired, vulnerable.

"Such a face," Gabe said. "You'd think this was Shiva here or something. Where's the casket?"

"Shiva?" Shawna said.

Harry chuckled. "Shiva. The Jewish mourning period."

"So tell me," Gabe said, slicing olives lengthwise, "who came up with the bit about Macing the cop? Surely not you, Shawna. You seem too levelheaded for such theatrics. This has Harry Niles written all over it." He shook his head. "What I wouldn't give for some really good kippers. You know how hard it is to find good kippers?"

"Gabe is addressing our problem," Harry said.

Gabe shrugged. "Or maybe I'm just hungry."

"Enough," Shawna said. "I don't have time for this crap. Right now, somebody might be writing out a contract on my life."

"This is true, if what you tell me is correct." Gabe started cutting the bread in flawless rectangles. "If it's not... who can say? All I know is that I'll not let them take you on an empty stomach. Did I ever tell you, Harry, that my mother's people—Kladovic was her maiden name—were Polish Jews? No?

"Well. Her mother and father, my grandparents, were deported from their farm to the Lodz ghetto. My mother, thank God, was not with them. She'd been hidden by relatives in Warsaw. Her parents both died later at Treblinka, God rest their souls. But my mother always said that when the Gestapo were rounding up Jews, there was little that could be done, so everyone would take a last meal together so as not to go away hungry. Sometimes the belly is more important than the life."

Harry nodded. "Sure, great. But we're in trouble, Gabe."

"Yes, apparently. So, being in trouble, you came to me. You came to my house and now I, too, am in trouble. Does this bother me? No, I think not. Does it trouble me? Yes, oh yes it does."

He made sandwiches for each of them and put potato salad on the side. Then he poured them coffee.

Harry and Shawna just sat there.

"Well? Eat. Fill your bellies while we sort this out. Then you can both rest. You're safe here. Who would suspect me of harboring criminals?"

They both ate, surprised at how good it all tasted. The sandwiches were hearty and hot with peppers and mustard. The potato salad creamy and cool. The coffee flavored with a delicious dash of almond.

"See? You were hungry. Like my grandparents, it's easier to face the unknown with a full belly." He looked at his own plate. Shook his head. "If it weren't for these ulcers, I'd eat, too. Ah, well."

Shawna chewed slowly, watching Gabe. He was a round, pleasant man. Although he was bald on top, the sides of his head were bushy with gray hair like wild tufts of crabgrass that made her think of Larry from The Three Stooges. He looked very much like someone's grandfather with those kind brown eyes and laugh lines around his mouth. And, she supposed, he probably was.

"Can you help us?" Shawna said, wanting to waste no more time.

"I'll try, pretty girl," he said, patting her hand. "And if I can't, I'll at least keep you safe. Those stormtroopers won't get you here. If you're not safe with a Jew, who are you safe with?"

"Goddammit, Gabe. Would you quit kibbitzing us to death already," Harry said.

"I'll remind you, Harry, that I'm not only your host but your employer." He turned back to Shawna. "Don't you pay any attention to him, dear. He has a poor temperament and a lousy disposition. If they come for him, we'll just throw up our hands and say, who knew? But we won't let those fascists get you. Never you. Harry is expendable. Men named Harry are always expendable, am I right?"

"Shut up, Gabe."

Gabe smiled, then frowned. "So, tell me one more time. Run it by me again."

They did for the fourth time. With retelling it became easier. What had once been gangly and stuttering, lacking cohesion and synchronicity, devoid of narrative flow, now had become tight and direct through repetition.

Gabe chuckled low in this throat. "Imagine this, will you? For nearly thirty years I've been writing and editing a tabloid rag that concerns itself with the unusual, the bizarre, the paranormal, the impossible. And now, here I am, thrust into what surely seems like one of my own teasers: YOUNG WOMAN HUNTED BY FACELESS ASSASSINS. SHE INCURRED THE WRATH OF A SINISTER GOVERNMENT AGENCY. THE CONSPIRACY THAT KILLS. I like it, don't you, Harry?" Harry did not answer. "No? Maybe you're right. I don't like it either. This is like...what? *The Twilight Zone?* Yes, and I am trapped in my own headlines. Is this Karma, Harry?"

Again, Harry did not answer.

Like Shawna, Gabe had never known him to be without a comeback, a one-liner, a salty bit of sarcasm. Harry always had an answer for everything and everyone. But right now he had nothing.

This was what deeply bothered Gabe.

"Later in the morning I'll run down some sources and do some checking. Discreetly, of course. See if anything smells bad. Until then, the both of you need rest."

There was no argument on that.

Gabe, who lived alone in this rambling Tudor house, gave them both rooms and showed them where they could both clean up. They both showered, but had nothing clean to wear, just the flowing terrycloth robes from Gabe's own collection which were soft and luxurious, pure comfort.

"Do you think we're going to make it, Harry?" Shawna asked, in the corridor outside their respective rooms. She looked tired, drawn, yet her eyes sparkled.

"We'll get by. One way or another. Gabe'll help us."

"Do you really think he can?"

"He'll try," Harry said. "He really will."

Shawna slumped against the wall. "I've been thinking. As much as this sucks, it is without a doubt the most interesting thing that's ever happened to me." She waited for him to interrupt, but he didn't. "I keep thinking about how dangerous this is. I keep playing it over and over in my mind. But at the same time, I keep thinking that for us, as journalists—"

He laughed. "You're the journalist, remember? All I care about are alien abductions and household pets that devour their owners. Did you ever read my series about the demonic cannibal kitties of Newark?"

"Shut up, Harry. I'm serious. You said it yourself: this is big. And you're right. This entire thing could be colossal. It could be bigger than Watergate or Iran–Contra combined." That gleam was in her eyes again, burning brighter than ever. Harry knew what it was now: opportunity.

"Yes. Yes, it very well could. This could be a Pulitzer or a shallow grave. Take your pick. Maybe both. Sometimes you have to skirt the second to get the first. This could very well be the sort of thing that could make your name very big."

"Our names, Harry," she reminded him.

"I've already had my run, dear. Give me sasquatch babies and kitchen appliances possessed by demons."

She cocked her head to the side. "You're telling me you're not interested? Not curious?"

"Sure I am. There's no one nosier than me. There's no one who likes to be a thorn in the side of the fat cats more than Harry Niles. Hell, when I was in Washington, you know what I did? I wined and dined congressional pages, press agents, chauffeurs, cooks, domestics—anybody who might know anything dirty about the men they worked for." The memory of it all filled his eyes, stayed there, finally faded, replaced by something like bitterness. "In Detroit, at the dear old *Free Press*, I did the same damn thing. But it was the auto execs I was after. In Atlantic City it was the mob, the casino owners. In LA, the entertainment moguls...and the mob. You see, I had a mantra: Rich and powerful men became rich and powerful by playing dirty games and I thought the public had a right to know just what those games were. I rattled so many skeletons out of so many dusty closets I had more old bones piled around me than the vaults of the Smithsonian.

"And where did it get me? I got fired in one place after another. Oh, the drinking helped, of course, and sometimes it was the cause. But that's the price you pay. If you want answers, you can get them, but you won't have a life in the process. Powerful men—and women—might get ruined by what you do and what you print, darling, but they always have friends. Always. And those friends, they get you a little at a time. Trust me."

"Are you afraid, Harry?"

He shrugged. "Yes. I don't want my life ruined. This may be hard for you to understand, but I like my life. For the first time, I really do. I don't want to lose any of this."

"So what, Harry? Are you backing out of this?"

"Really, ducky. If I wanted to back out I think I might have done it before I assaulted a Metro police officer. There's no backing out so I might as well make a crusade of it," he told her. "It might cost me my way of life, my freedom, and maybe even my life itself, but I'll do it. I'll probably think differently next month when I'm in the Cook County slammer in the arms of my outlaw biker lover, but I won't let this go. I'll hound those bastards until the truth comes out. I'll do it for you. And I'll do it for your landlady and all the other innocents they kill. And—" he said pointedly, planting an index finger to her chest which was still wet from her shower "—I'll also do it for myself. When we find out—if we find out—you write it. It's your baby, your ticket. I'll help you and I'll even take a cut, but I don't want a byline. I don't care about that shit anymore. The thrill for me is in the hunt, in the kill, not in the aftermath, not in the warm amber glow of success."

"You just want to take them down, don't you?"

"You're goddamn right I do."

She smiled, beaming. "I didn't know you had such a big heart."

"Oh no? Is that why you always come to me when you're in trouble?"

"I guess it is."

Her robe came open a bit and Harry caught a glimpse of one high, jutting breast. He did not look away and she did not cover it up.

She stared at him for a long time, then leaned up against the wall covering her chest with folded arms. "You're really something, Harry. You really are. Beneath all the cynicism and sexism, you honestly believe good must triumph over evil. And you're willing to take up any cause—even one as crazy as mine—just to see that it does. Harry the white knight. Who would have thought?"

He shrugged. "Yeah, whatever. Now are we gonna stand here jawing all day or are you gonna come into my room and do me?"

She licked her lips. "It's under consideration."

Then she shut the door in his face.

# CHICAGO, RIVER NORTH

## THE WAREHOUSE

**10:02 A.M.**

The Old Man contemplated the end of the world.

It hadn't been the first time he'd wondered about the end (of human civilization really, because the actual world would not end with the extinction of the human race). He'd thought about it many times, in many places. And always, always, he'd wondered and not needlessly if he'd have a hand in it.

In the BSL-4 containment area where only those with the highest possible security clearance were allowed, he thought about these things. He watched the scientists and technicians mull about in their rubberized hot suits. They all did their jobs efficiently, professionally. All of them were either Section 5 employees or on loan from CBT.

Watching them, the Old Man wondered if they blamed him.

He could not know their thoughts or what they spoke of to each other in private. Cave had suggested that the entire warehouse be threaded with listening devices.

But the Old Man refused.

He already knew what they thought of him, at least some of them. They thought he was forged from iron, sculpted from ice. A dutiful mannequin, emotionless, inhuman. An alien entity who thought only of national security.

And it was true, but not entirely.

*I'm not so one-dimensional,* he thought, the words echoing through his skull like pennies dropped in a metal drum. *Don't you think I'm scared, too? I have children out there. Grandchildren. Friends. And all of them are at grave risk. What I do to contain this...this horror, I do for them. I do it for all the mothers and fathers out there.*

Of course, they would never believe that. Very few of them knew that he was deeply involved in the CBT team that had bio-engineered the parasites and the others wouldn't have been surprised if that knowledge was leaked to them. It was what they would expect. As far as they were concerned, he was a mad scientist who looked at people no differently than he looked at lab rats.

What they didn't know, was that he was afraid of the outbreak and what it might mean for the human race if it continued unchecked.

Computer models predicted that even with swift and decisive action, only about sixty percent of those infected could be tracked down and disposed of in time. Another thirty percent would already have infected others before they were found. And ten percent would never be located at all. Given this in combination with the behavioral patterns of the parasites and their newly acquired mutative reproductive capabilities, 53 percent of the Earth's population would be infected within one week of first contact. Within a month, 86.5 percent.

The computer freely admitted error of plus or minus five percent.

Project BioGenesis.

It had been a major breakthrough in transgenics and molecular biology. Science had finally achieved the point where it could not only alter living organisms but create entirely new species. It only followed, of course, that eventually this revolutionary and highly coveted biotechnology would be applied as a weapons system. Bioweapons were all the rage. Entire enemy populations could be decimated without the loss of a single soldier.

What more could be asked for?

Biological warfare had finally reached its full potential.

And it had... except that the problems with GMOs was that they did not respect borders or boundaries. They did not differentiate between friendly and hostile forces. It had always been the problem with bioweapons. BioGen had been tested originally on Iraqi forces in Badiyat ash Sham, the great western desert which made up much of western Iraq and eastern Jordan, bordering Syria. Near a small village called Nkudbkah there was a small Republican Guard mechanized infantry unit. Sat intel had confirmed their position, their relation to the village. How both were not within fifty miles of any real population center. An Army Special Forces recon team had watched them for a week; they were staying put.

It was the perfect target.

A desolate area. Easily containable.

It was begging for a feasibility study. S5 got the go-ahead and the parasite eggs were disseminated via aerosol from low-flying Blackhawk helicopters at night. The entire area was sprayed. Especially high concentrations were dusted on irrigation ditches and water holes from which the small goat and cattle herds drank. This was how the parasites worked: livestock were contaminated first and the eggs passed to the human population through flesh or milk. Within a week, the recon team reported that the majority of the village and soldiers were ill.

Ten days later, there was no activity whatsoever.

The recon team was exfiltrated immediately.

Within hours, a containment team was brought in. Most of the population, they reported, was either dead or dying. Both human and animal were infested. The team, using the greatest precautions, performed hasty autopsies on the dead. Everything had worked as they'd planned.

And then something went terribly wrong.

The team, out there in the stifling desert heat in their biosuits, made a mistake. The suits were sometimes called hot suits because although they carried a self-contained oxygen supply, there was no provision to cool the wearer. Several men passed out. Others, driven hysterical by the heat, removed their helmets to cool themselves.

No one was certain what happened then.

The team were infected by the parasites. While they called for medical evacuation for their heat-prostrated comrades, the infected villagers and soldiers attacked them. The team managed to kill them, but not before the parasites had infected their ranks. Once this had happened, there was no choice; the entire area was blanketed with napalm and phosphorus. American, Iraqi, anything that lived, was burned to ash in the resulting inferno. The Air Force pilots, thinking they were hitting an enemy target, poured it on for hours.

Nkudbkah no longer existed.

And it should've ended there.

The parasite eggs were only designed to remain active for seventy-two hours without a host. And although each segment of the parasites contained hundreds of eggs, as did the parasitic flatworms they were developed from, all the eggs were incapable of independent fertilization via radiation saturation.

After the Nkudbkah episode, the entire Project BioGen scenario was scrapped, tucked away in the vaults of the DoD.

And now, some six years after the controlled experiment at Nkudbkah, the parasites had returned, this time just over the border in Syria at El Badji. No one knew how or why. But environmental factors had long made biological dispersion less than an exact science. They had designed the creatures to survive, to be extremely aggressive, but not to go dormant for years and years, then mutate and begin to reproduce on their own.

Yet, that was exactly what had happened.

Somehow, some way, a few of the eggs must've survived in the desert. Survived and mutated into an even more hideous, virulent form.

Unless...unless there were things he did not know. There was always the possibility that the parasites had been engineered with this ability at a different facility. It wasn't impossible...not when you were dealing with S5 and CBT and the multiple layers of subterfuge they hid behind.

Anything was possible.

*Liz Toma would know*, he thought. *She's an expert at hiding deception within deception within deception. Who can say what she's capable of?*

The Old Man didn't want to think about it or the possibility that what was happening had been made to happen, part of some larger, shadowy agenda, some sickening power play.

The parasites were developed from the parasitic flatworm known as Cestoda, the tapeworm. It was known that Cestoda, in its earliest prehistoric incarnation, was a free-living predatory marine worm that developed parasitism via a variety of factors. And it was this proto-worm—still locked up in the tapeworms genes—that was the template for the parasite. Once the worm's genome sequence was mapped, cutting edge biotechnology came into play. By using DNA sequencing, a sort of molecular biology cut-and-paste, the worm was reverse engineered to its primal form. Using transgenics, attributes of the parasitic modern form were introduced into the genome along with certain desirable characteristics of hookworms and roundworms as well as a few other exotic transplanted genes. After much trial and error, what was eventually brought forth was the parasite itself: a hideous flatworm with an almost inconceivable survival instinct.

And now, for lack of a better term, it was on the loose stalking its chosen prey: the human race.

Another area of concern was that sooner or later, one of the worms would be studied by people who knew what they were looking for. That they would spot the engineered genes carefully placed in its genetic code.

"Then the shit will most certainly hit the fan," the Old Man whispered.

He ran it through his head again and again. Sterile organisms which could not survive without a host for more than three days had slept for six years and began reproducing. As yet, there had been no repercussions from the Syrians. No hint that they suspected the Americans of unleashing a plague upon them. As far as intelligence could discern, the Syrians were not discussing the recent outbreak in the desert. They had reacted swiftly and decisively in exterminating the infected populations.

Still, the Old Man worried.

Not so much about the American outbreak, but that the Syrians and their Islamic extremist colleagues had gathered specimens of the parasite and would one day use them as a weapon. Perhaps against Israel or even the US or its allies. If that happened, if a plague of parasites was allowed to spread, there would be no earthly way to contain it.

*And that may happen anyway*, he thought, *if we don't stop them here and now.*

With that in mind, he went to the cubicles and watched.

One of the hit teams had snatched two living subjects for further study. Actually, they'd only been sent to grab the man, one Marcus Grimes, but through unforeseen circumstances they'd had to take his wife as well. Which was probably for the best. Grimes had been one of the unlucky Gulf vets who had tromped through the vicinity of Nkudbkah some months after the destruction of said village.

No one at the time, of course, thought there could possibly be a danger in troops moving through the area. But they were wrong. And Grimes, like hundreds of others, had picked up a little passenger in his belly that had waited six years before making its terrible appearance.

Behind the reinforced Plexiglas, Marcus and Teresa Grimes were a pathetic and frightening sight. They both had parasites in them. Marcus had infected his wife within hours after arriving. As the research teams watched, the drama unfolded. Marcus slipped into a coma. Teresa was nearly mad with rage, screaming at the team outside the cubicle, pounding her fists on the Plexiglas shell. She wanted to know why they'd been arrested. Why they were being kept in a cage. Why they wouldn't help her husband who was obviously very ill. And why everyone was dressed in those goddamn space suits.

The medical staff did not respond, they merely observed.

Within a few hours of slipping into his coma, Marcus began to stir.

The team watching and making copious notes (as well as digital video recordings), Marcus sat up. Teresa told him he should lie down, rest, conserve his strength until these CIA honky motherfuckers let them out.

But Marcus didn't want to rest.

Or maybe what was inside him didn't want to.

He shambled after his wife, his flesh like old candle wax, his eyes glassy and wet. And it was about that time that Teresa finally saw the light. Finally got a firsthand taste of what had been causing her husband's medical problems. Marcus launched himself at her, forcing her down. She screamed...oh God, how she screamed...then she became almost docile, accepting. Then Marcus let go of her. He didn't have to hold her down because what he had she wanted. She clung to him, wrapping herself around him... then he opened his mouth.

*Yawned wide*, one of the technicians said later, *like an open manhole*.

The worm came out, segment by segment, shiny white and eyeless. It went right down Teresa's throat like a snake into a mouse hole. And for a time, it stayed like that. The two were connected by the thing. Marcus' eyes rolled back into his head and something like slime ran from his mouth in sparkling loops. After about twenty minutes, the worm slithered back into Marcus, leaving a segment of itself in his wife's belly.

Like the flatworms they were engineered from, each segment, or proglottid, was a sexually complete hermaphroditic unit in which sperm and ova were produced. When the ova were mature and fertilized, the parent worm would break off a segment into another host organism. And each segment contained hundreds of eggs and each egg, an embryonic worm. Thereby, propagating itself and its species.

And when you considered that the worms were basically made up of segment after segment of fertilized eggs, the potential for proliferation was awesome. The threat to any population was staggering.

Left unchecked, these creatures could decimate a city in weeks.

The Old Man chuckled dryly in his throat. *And wasn't that exactly what we'd designed them for?*

They were much nastier than anyone imagined or could imagine.

And what it came down to—and what should serve as a benchmark for further weaponized organisms—was that never, never should a life form's inherent desire for survival be overlooked or underestimated.

The two in the cubicle proved that.

They sat next to each other now, two dead-eyed zombies clutching each other while parasitic guests cowered in their bellies. Teresa was comatose for the most part. From time to time, the head, or scolex, of a worm would emerge from Marcus' mouth and coil in the air. But never for long. Slowly, slowly they drained their hosts of life, wanting only to breed and infest.

"We could starve them to death eventually," one of the parasitologists told the Old Man. "Eventually, if the original project research was correct, the worms will begin to cannibalize their hosts."

The scientists often argued the finer points of parasitization, but one thing they did agree on was that by the time the worms were sexually mature (and that seemed to be when they were four or five feet in length) their hosts were no longer capable of independent reasoning or action. They were merely vessels for the worms, zombies as it were. No one was sure how they managed neurological control of their hosts, but the facts remained. There was one theory, of course. That somehow, the creatures managed to tap into the cerebral cortex of their hosts. Once this was done, their hosts would be incapable of independent actions.

At least that's what the medical staff were thinking.

Further study was needed.

But it raised frightening possibilities.

The Old Man was beginning to sweat profusely standing there in his hot suit watching the hosts.

There was only one lucky thing in all of this, he knew.

That Marine in Bethesda. If it hadn't been for him dying mysteriously and the autopsy revealing the parasite inside him, the outbreak might have gone on unchecked for many weeks more than it already had. They'd gotten lucky with that. After the Syrian outbreak, the DoD had put a plan into action. They formed a database with the names, addresses, and medical histories of all servicemen and women who had passed through the Nkudbkah area. They monitored these vets for any medical problems and particularly anything related to "Gulf War Syndrome" which was a blanket term if ever there was one. If it hadn't been for that...well, things might have been over for the country before action could have even been initiated.

And as it was, the Old Man knew, things were bad enough. The very idea of the parasite biomass out there right now scared the hell out of him. Because he knew one thing—it was spreading. Fast.

# AUGUST 23

# OUTBREAK

## NATIONWIDE

It was everywhere.

In every state, in every population center, in bustling crowded cities and small towns alike. And although a few remote rural hamlets had avoided the contagion thus far, it wouldn't last. Statistically speaking, it was near on impossible. The country was filled with walking vectors and transmission was a certainty. Like germs spreading through contact, hand to mouth and body to body, the infestation spread and became something of a silent epidemic. Though wild stories of giant worms and frightening conspiracies were thick on the Internet, as usual no one paid attention. And those in power, the very people—or some of them—that had started this particularly ugly ball rolling, hid away, covering their heads and cowering, praying for it to end as suddenly as it had started, while damage control was still possible.

But they were deluding themselves.

Though they continued to press on, fighting a covert war against carriers and disease vectors, the enemy was thoroughly entrenched and the infestation was quickly reaching epidemic proportions. The parasites, as hideous and horrible as they might be, were only doing what they had been programmed to do.

Hour by hour and day by day, the plague sunk its claws that much deeper into the red meat of the human population.

Critical mass had nearly been reached and as the country took one shambling step closer to the graveyard, no one was the wiser.

# BALTIMORE, MARYLAND

## FEDERAL HILL

**10:27 A.M.**

They were after him and Craig Gooding knew it. He saw them in every crowd, peering from every alley, every nook and doorway and cul-de-sac. Cops. Had to be cops, in his way of thinking. Maybe they'd seen him snatch that purse over in Harborplace—goddamn tourists were such easy marks—but if they had his number, then why weren't they putting the arm on him?

Crazy.

It was just crazy.

He told the bartender to give him another shot of Jim Beam and his hands were shaking so badly, he could barely get it to his lips. Of course, the bartender noticed. He was keeping his eye on Craig and Craig didn't like that.

*Asshole. I'm a vet. I fought for this country. Don't you look down your nose at me.*

He went back out onto the streets.

Where to now? He'd snatched three purses in the last twenty-four hours and there hadn't been shit in them. Twenty bucks. That was it. Everyone was using fucking debit cards now and he needed the green. Just a month ago things had been good and he'd been riding high and proud, good booze, good hookers, a crib over at the St. Charles, dig it...now, just the streets. Sleeping in parks and alleys. Panhandling for dimes. And now a goddamn purse-snatcher.

Wait.

*There. See 'em over there? Don't look. Pretend you don't see.*

Yup. They were there, all right. Those same two dudes that had been following him all morning. Crewcuts. Thick necks. Looked like a couple jarheads. Had to be narcs. They were sitting on a bench down the way, pretending they were reading newspapers.

Shit.

Craig couldn't shake them.

That was because they knew. They knew.

For nearly a year he had a good thing going. He did his bit in Iraq so he got free medical at the VA. There was a Pakistani doc over there, fucker barely had a green card, that was giving Craig pretty much all the Oxycontin and Dilaudid he wanted. Like four hundred pills a month. Even Craig's addiction wasn't that hungry. He sold most of it to Biscuit over in Cherry Hill. The living was easy and the cotton (as in Oxy) was high. Then that Paki doc got busted for trafficking prescription drugs and the narcs raided Biscuit and put her black ass behind bars. Now they were looking for Craig because Biscuit might have been all that but she was terrified of doing time, so she sang like a tweeting yellow bird and now the narcs wanted the conduit: Craig himself.

He stepped into the flow of the crowd.

Lots of tourists. Easy to lose himself in their masses. Sure. Just slip into the crowd, become one of the many. Down past the park he went, making for Cross Street. They had something going on down there. It was worth checking out. Steel drum bands playing and tourists everywhere, standing in the street, hanging out in the beer garden. He moved faster now, caught in the surge of bodies, but being careful because he knew those two had him in their sights and were going to run him to ground. They probably wouldn't do it around all the tourists, though. Gentrification and all that, look how pretty our inner city is, no crime, no bullshit, just easy living and colonial beauty, keep spending those dollars, keep on—.

Oh Jesus.

There it came again, right down in his belly like a knife scraping along his stomach.

Fuck, fuck, fuck. Burning, digging, white pain in his guts. Crackling, sizzling, snapping like a whip in there.

People were looking at him, staring at him, hands reaching towards him and others wanting no part of him. *You all right? You okay, buddy? You don't look so good... Get away, get away.* Christ, if they only knew what it was like inside when you felt the pain and had the need. Nothing could touch it. Craig had eaten his last two Oxy this morning and now every nerve ending in his body was tightening, tightening, twisting like screws.

He plowed through the crowd, doubled over, the agony kicking him in the stomach again and again, and everyone was staring and pointing and shouting at him as he knocked them aside, running, stumbling, going back the way he came, making for the park where the crowds wouldn't be so thick, pushing in from all sides, their eyeballs all over him.

He made it up the park steps, then he was crawling through the grass on his hands and knees. Into the bushes now, his face bleached white, mottled red, cold/hot sweat flooding down it. He threw up bile into the grass because there was nothing else inside him... *gah*... everything went loose, his body no longer his own, breath wheezing from his lungs in a dry ragged gasping, hot shit leaking from his ass, his bladder voiding itself. His muscles were flab, nothing connected, blood roaring in his head, fever sweat filling his eyes, and inside him that pain moving and coiling, sharp and cutting... like needles piercing and puncturing, a horsehair rope snapping taut in his bowels...

He was rolling on the ground now, contorting and jerking while pink saliva flew from his mouth in slimy tangles and inside his belly...pressure building, bloating, distending...and then, oh dear God, release, release as it all came up out of him, filling his throat and his mouth with an awful sewer-black taste, a convulsive white rope of jelly pushing from his lips in the form of a contracting, pulsing white worm thick around as his arm.

By then, Craig's mind was no longer his own.

He lay there, shuddering in his own waste, as the worm slid back into his mouth, down, down into the coveting blackness. It had wants and it had needs. It telegraphed them to its host with hunger pangs that were so severe that Craig cried out with a lunatic shrieking.

Then he was on his feet, staggering, stumbling, his eyes the color of fresh blood, shining and wet. The hunger pains ratcheted up in his belly—drilling, cutting, punching deeper and deeper. What he did then was purely automatic: he ate. He ate anything that was available, biting into his own tongue again and again until his mouth filled with blood. There should have been pain but the worm had neutralized his neuroreceptors and kicked the hunger drives of his hypothalamus into hyperdrive.

He was quite literally an eating machine.

All else was suspended. He chewed away at chunks of his own tongue, licking blood from his lips. It ran down his chin in great gouts. He bit into his lower lip, tearing and ripping at it until a great bleeding section of it came loose that he could mash between his teeth.

But it was hardly enough.

The hunger pains hit him again and again like a buzzard striking at a carcass. He was in starvation mode. He needed fuel. He needed lots of it. He spotted a hot dog vendor on the sidewalk and made for him. Said vendor had his back turned as he chatted with a young woman.

Craig knocked a man out of his way in his frantic flight to the hot dog cart. "HUNGREEEEEE!" he cried out in a weird, childlike voice. "I'M SO HUNGREEEEEE!"

He began grabbing handfuls of cooked franks from the cart and shoving them in his mouth, gnawing them greedily into strands of pink meat. He went through them like a buzzsaw. He was insatiable.

"Hey!" the vendor shouted. "What the hell are you doing?"

He grabbed Craig by the arm and spun him around. It was then that he knew he had made a terrible error. Craig was drooling and chewing, blood running from his nostrils, his face a waxy blotched yellow.

Craig leaped on him.

He knocked the vendor down and pounded his head against the sidewalk until there was an audible cracking. People were shouting, screaming, crying out for help. But nobody dared get anywhere near Craig. Not that he cared. The world no longer existed. There was only the hunger. He bit into the vendor's throat, tearing open his rubbery carotid until a hot—and satisfy-ing—gush of blood sprayed into his face. And still he bit, he chewed, and tore like an animal. He gouged out the vendors eyeballs and savaged his cheeks and nose, pulling his tongue from his mouth and biting into its warm, wet, beefy goodness, salivating and moaning.

Though he was violently cannibalizing the vendor—and in full view of a dozen shocked and horrified witnesses—in his mind, what was left of it, he was no monster but a starving little boy glutting himself on sour cherry balls and crunchy jawbreakers, sucking nougat from chocolate wafers and lapping up chewy ribbons of caramel. He ate and ate and ate.

He did not see the two men that had been following him pull out 9mm handguns and pop about eight rounds into him or hear their voices on cells: "We got one here... adult form... we need cleaners..."

# RICHMOND, VIRGINIA

## SWIFT CREEK

**11:45 A.M.**

Kitty McKee—a.k.a. Little Kit—had a gopher snake in a jelly jar and she was hunting flies for its lunch. It was a baby gopher snake, and it was good-tempered and did not bite. Sometimes when they got older and bigger, they would hiss or snap, but not the babies and Kitty's snake was only five inches long. She had named it Lady. She loved how sleek and smooth Lady was. People thought snakes were slimy, but that was only people who had never held one. Because in truth they were smooth like glass.

"I'm gonna find you big fat flies for your eating," Kitty promised her new friend who was extremely bored in the jelly jar, beneath the shade of an old termite-pitted gum tree.

Through the field and into the stand of woods that bordered it, Kitty and her jar went. If Mama caught her out of the yard there would be trouble, but Kitty would be quick. The first thing she saw was the clubhouse. It was where Logan Peets and the Chumbly brothers hung out. A BOYS ONLY sort of place and that ruffled Kitty's feathers because she figured she could go anywhere she pleased, eight years old or not.

Funny, though. As she stood there, she couldn't seem to remember the last time she'd seen Logan or the "Dumbly" brothers (as they were known to children far and wide).

Hmm. Curious.

A mischievous grin on her face, Kitty went down on all fours, stalking through the grass like a bobcat closing in on a quail. Quiet. Easy. The wings of cabbage moths in the heather made more noise than she. Within minutes, she had closed in on the shack. Because that's what it was: a SHACK, not a clubhouse. Sort of place some boozer might live, Kitty's dad once said. And it did look the part: tin roof, tar paper stapled to the bowing walls. Probably full of rattlesnakes and black widows, not to mention stinking, stupid boys.

Kitty paused at the door. "Ssshh!" she told Lady.

Usually, by now, the boys would come out and chase her off, call her a little runny-nosed shitcrawler or something. *Shitcrawler* was Logan's favorite word for everything. Kitty knew it was a bad word, but boys were bad, so she was not surprised.

Wiping sweat from her brow because this was serious, dangerous business being in enemy territory, she took hold of the door and opened it a crack and the stink that came rolling out...whew! It was a fusty, noisome odor, dark and secret. She could hear flies buzzing in there. Something telling her she should run away as fast she could, Kitty threw the door open and stuck her head inside and—

And two hands that were moist and feverish took hold of her and yanked her inside. The three boys were in there and they threw her to the dirt floor and held her down while she fought and cried out. But it was dark, and she could not see as tears rolled down her cheeks and those shadowy, rot-smelling forms held her down and dropped something into her mouth...something small and squirming that she first thought was Lady as it looped thickly over her tongue and slid down her throat.

She smelled a sudden overpowering sweetness.

Gagging and crying, Kitty stumbled from the shack, feeling a greasy sickness in her belly. On her mad flight home she dropped the jelly jar and it shattered against a rock.

As it turned out, Lady was the only one who truly escaped that day for by the time Kitty got home, she didn't have a care in the world.

# MILWAUKEE, WISCONSIN

## ARLINGTON HEIGHTS

**1:33 P.M.**

Just off West Keefe Avenue, Dicko the Ratman ducked into the alley where all the boys slept it off during the daytime. Brick walls to either side were painted up with gang graffiti, lots of spilled garage and rats in the shadows, blown leaves everywhere else. Dicko moved down there very carefully until he came to the L at the end and rounded it, finding all the old boys curled up beyond the dumpster where it was cool and shady. They had their cardboard boxes and newspapers.

They were all sleeping off a good one.

Perfect time.

Dicko had gotten real good at scavenging and that's why they called him the Ratman. While the boys were off in la-la land, he'd grab anything they had found during the night. That was their way: find something good and pass out, leaving their wares unattended.

Now Dicko didn't smell real good himself—his bed out back of the lard bins at Ruby's Rib Shack didn't scent a man too well—but even he could smell the stink coming off the boys which was pungent and ripe and just damn unnatural. None of them even moved as he crept about amongst them.

He saw the bottle right away: leave it to the Sterno King to find himself a taste of the old juice and forget to drink it.

Dicko smiled. Well, didn't that beat all.

It was some of that fancy south-of-the-border swill with the worm in the bottom. Almost looked for one crazy moment like the worm was moving.

No matter.

Dicko brought the bottle to his lips and began to drink.

# SPRINGFIELD, MISSOURI

## GRANT BEACH

**6:58 P.M.**

There was a time when Macie Godfrey made a good living turning tricks in the park. Sex to her was no big thrill being that she was raped by her stepfather when she was twelve. Just business. Nothing more. Economy could be up or down and still she was busy. Then those do-gooders over in Robberson and West Central brought the police into the whole thing and business dried up overnight.

Insult to injury.

Just like the time she'd been six months along and her pimp, Bobby Priest, had tossed her down the stairs and she'd lost the baby. Life had a way of insulting you like that, stretching the seams, pulling you in every direction to see just how much you could take before you snapped.

That was life.

And this was death...

For the past two weeks, Macie had been shut up in her room. She had no friends. She had no lovers. And once her customers dried up, she didn't even have them. The only one that came to see her was Diggs. Diggs always had money and when he drank he wanted a quick one, cash on delivery, thank-you-very-much.

But Diggs had given her something and she had it bad.

She lay on her bed which was a steaming miasmic lagoon of fevers and drainage, feeling movement within her that was far different than the kick of a baby. It was slow, thick, nearly gelatinous somehow. Sometimes in the mush of her brain, she thought it felt good, pleasurable even. Then other times...no, like scratching fingers in her bowels and sharp-toothed little mouths in her stomach.

It had been like that for many days now.

A rational thought, fleeting but there: *He did something to you, Macie, that last time he came, he did something to you...holding you down, pressing your head against the mattress, forcing that throbbing thing between your lips that slid in deeper and deeper.*

Her eyes snapped open, bleary and red-rimmed, unfocused. Her fingers slid over the trembling mound of her belly, the flesh white and soft, fever-hot and moist with a slime of scum almost like jelly.

"Diggs," she said. "Oh God, Diggs..."

Where did he go? Was he still there, still grinning at her in the darkness, his blotched face dripping with sour-stinking sweat? No, she was alone. She had to remember that she was alone and Diggs had not come back. Did they send him back to Iraq or one of those places? No, no, no, Diggs wasn't in the Army anymore.

Now inside her as her belly continued to expand as if it was slowly being inflated, she could hear...sounds. Sucking, slurping sounds, the noise of tiny hungry mouths leeching soft meat.

A wave of agony: spiking, knife-sharp.

Another.

Dear God, another.

Unbelievable pain broke loose inside her now in jagged, cutting pulsations that made her twist and flop on the bed. Fluids and bile ran from her in warm, yellow rivers, her head thrashing from side to side, teeth sinking into her tongue and drawing freshets of hot blood that filled her mouth and stained her teeth pink.

*No, no, no oh Jesus oh Mary I can't take it I can't take it—*

She uttered one last hysterical scream before her belly, that great shining mound, sheared open with a gushing necrotic flood of milky ooze and pink blood that was threaded with webby strings of glistening pearl-eggs. Clusters of them like roe and spider-spawn, more pushing out and out like she was bursting with bubbles, a thousand-million glossy bubbles that overflowed her and sank her in pulpous afterbirth and juicy ova. And amongst them, the slimed white looping worms, thick and undulant, raising hooked sucker-mouths in the air and making serous mewling sounds as they tended the eggs.

And Macie—a shuddering flesh-waste, a parasitized meat river—was gone, her mind stripped away like bark from a jack pine, nothing left but a smooth and soulless void. For she was only a host now, a hothouse incubator, the mother of worm generations. And was content to be so.

# ATLANTA, GEORGIA

## OAKHURST

**7:25 P.M.**

The screams still ringing in his ears, Perry stumbled from the black Lexus at the intersection of Oakview and East Lake Avenue. He went down to his knees on the sidewalk and vomited while people stood and stared. He crawled forward on his hands and knees, pulling himself to his feet and all the shocked onlookers scattered when they saw the webwork of blood on his face, his torn shirt, and the bluesteel Beretta nine in his hand.

Perry wanted to tell them that his name wasn't really Perry and that the team was dead, the neighborhood—not two blocks away—absolutely infested. But they ran, bumping into one another, crying out, scared little rabbits sensing the hawk circling overhead. He wanted to tell them about the Old Man and S5 and CBT and Project BioGen and how the team was dead and how he wished to God he was dead because the world was about to go belly up.

He wanted to tell them about the houses. Those trim neat houses. And in them...cannibal faces and fish-white eyes, little boys and girls and mommies and daddies with worms sliding out of them like maggots from green roadkill.

Shaking and gibbering, his mind gone to a cool gray sauce, he tried to tell them but they ran so he went into the first place he saw which was the Burrito Cantina and he saw, he saw—

People eating. Sitting at tables. But they were not people but worm zombies, all of them infested and rotting black inside. *Hey, how's the sour cream quesadilla and the black beans and the chipotle Maduro, you fucking monsters, YOU GODDAMN FUCKING MONSTERS...*

He started shooting and they were screaming, but he was an exterminator and it was his job, didn't they see that? Kill 'em all, kill 'em all. Make sure you pop them in the heads, that puts 'em down, head-shots, brain ooze spilling onto the tables and the floors, blasted red-gray skullmeat spraying everywhere.

Oh Jesus, none of them were human, not anymore. Just worm gardens, smoke-glass eyes and shadow faces and reaching white fingers, nesting with worms, so many worms.

Then his weapon was empty and Perry knew it was done.

Because behind him they were shouting and shouting. "DROP THAT WEAPON! DROP THAT FUCKING WEAPON!" And he turned and saw badges and let loose with a demented braying as blood ran down his face from a scalp wound and tears squeezed from his eyes.

Then a volley of bullets slammed into him and he dropped, dying, going cold on the tile floor while inside him, something lived, burrowing deep and biding its time.

# OMAHA, NEBRASKA

## THE CATHEDRAL DISTRICT

**10:44 P.M.**

Bella had fallen asleep again, sinking into her bed of fevers, and the only thing that brought her out of it was the perfectly hideous gobbling/shrieking voice that was the sound of pure insanity. It raged. It screamed. It echoed off the walls. It took her some time to realize that it was her own voice.

*The fever, the fever...oh God, it's tearing my mind apart.*

As she thought this, a breeze blew in through the window and she began to shake uncontrollably. The shivers moved up and down her body in frigid waves.

*Get that window closed! It's bad for you and if it's bad for you, it's worse for the baby!*

The baby.

The baby.

The baby.

Everything was for the baby. Everything she did and didn't do was for the health of the baby. She placed her hands on her belly, feeling it moving in there with a slow, terrible rolling that made sweat run down her face.

*Where? Where is Michael?*

But she remembered. Michael had flown to Kansas City on business and she was alone. When was the last time she had talked to him? Was it yesterday? The day before? She couldn't be sure. It was getting hard to differentiate between dream and reality these days. Pregnancy really took it out of you.

The last time Michael called, he hadn't sounded good at all. "How's the baby?" he asked, sounding breathless and tired.

"Good. The baby is good. And you?"

He sighed. "Getting those goddamned pains in my gut again…they're—"
And here he broke off, gasping. "God, that was a good one. I better get in and
see someone."

"You better. Baby needs you healthy."

Bella couldn't remember if there was more to the conversation or not.
Things were so muddled these days. She wiped sweat off her face. Her memory
was so bad. Nothing seemed to make sense. Often, the harder she tried to
remember, the less she could.

She let out a cry as an awful pain ripped through her belly, making tears run
from her eyes as she contorted with the agony of it.

*Baby's coming.*

No! It couldn't be. Not yet. Not for another month. Knives of agony cut
through her, one after the other, filling her mind with blinding white flashes.
She fell out of bed and crashed to the floor and by then she was twisting and
writhing. It felt as if something inside her—*the baby, the baby, it had to be the
baby*—was turning around and around, spiraling faster and faster, knotting
up her guts and twisting her spine like a rubber band.

Somewhere during the process as her mind blanked and the pain punched
holes in her consciousness, the baby came. Her water broke followed by a
perfectly horrible gushing of blood and slime and glistening blobby matter.
The fetus was expelled, tearing free of the amniotic sack.

It was alive.

Bloody and dripping with clots of birth jelly, it was alive. It crawled up her
legs, dragging its umbilical after it, a grotesque, malformed monstrosity with
glittering black eyes and a bulbous head threaded with black veins. It was hot
against her bare legs.

Bleeding out, Bella slowly slipped into unconsciousness, but not before she
saw a dozen coiling white worms slide out of the baby's mouth.

# AUGUST 25

# CHICAGO, NORTH SHORE

## EVANSTON

**1:51 P.M.**

After several days of laying low, letting things cool off, Harry drove Shawna to the First Chicago branch on Skokie Boulevard in one of Gabe's cars, a Chrysler LeBaron, since his own car was probably hot. If Shawna had to hide out for God knows how long, then the first thing was to at least empty her savings. She wasn't about to spend days, weeks, or (God forbid) months sponging off Gabe Hebberman.

"We'll look into this slowly, carefully," Gabe told them. "If there's real danger here, real trouble—and I'm not saying there isn't—then we'll err on the side of caution. Agreed?"

Everyone did.

While they hid out at his estate, he did the looking, the digging. It was much safer that way. If some faceless agency was really after Shawna and Harry, then they would be waiting for them to make a move. So they wouldn't make it. They kept that promise while Gabe sent out feelers.

After four days of it, the two of them decided it would be safe enough to make a quick run to the bank. First Chicago had branches everywhere and if they found out she banked there, then they'd need quite a few men to stake it out. In essence, it was an acid test.

"Maybe we should slip down to Joliet or Calumet City or somewhere equally as distant to do this," Harry suggested. "One of those banks in a strip mall. If they're monitoring our accounts, at least they won't be looking in Gabe's neighborhood."

"I doubt they'll watch my savings account, Harry."

"Oh really? And why is that?"

She shrugged. "It just seems..."

"What?" he interjected. "A little excessive?"

"Yeah, I guess."

Harry shook his head.

He liked the old paranoid Shawna better. This new Shawna was a little too dangerous, a little too reckless. Oh, he knew what it was. He knew what it felt like when you thought you were poised to pounce on the biggest story of the year. He hadn't felt that special all-consuming buzz in years. It was addictive. Even after your big story and your juicy national byline dissolved into so much journalistic suet, you kept looking and digging and sifting. Certain there was another one out there just as big.

He didn't think this one was going to fade away (it was big and he knew it, he could feel that in every fiber of his being), but the sheer intoxication of it was destructive. You got careless. You started taking crazy chances. Like maybe the story wasn't quite big enough so you gave it the opportunity to swell a little more.

He knew that's what Shawna was thinking.

Maybe not consciously, but deep down it was there, that manic drive.

"I think, Mister Grinch, that your balls have grown two sizes since yesterday," he told her. "You've got it, don't you?"

"What?"

"The fever. You're different today and you know it. You're like a lioness stalking a wildebeest," he said. "You smell the blood. You smell that big, meaty story and damn anyone or anything that gets in your way."

"Amusing analogy, Harry."

"Is that all it is?" He waited for her reply and got none. He pulled into the asphalt lot of the bank in Gabe's Chrysler. "Last chance, sweet thing."

She crossed her legs, pretending to be smooth and unworried. "I told you it's under consideration."

He forced a laugh. "Believe it or not, getting you naked is not foremost on my mind right now, Miss Cheeky Von Glib."

"Am I insulted?"

"You should be."

She gave him a challenging look and stepped from the car. She waltzed right over to the ATM machine and pulled out her debit card. He went with her after a quick reconnaissance of the area. He didn't see anyone that seemed to be watching. She moved the way he had instructed her: very casual. No looking around. No hurried movements or nervous mannerisms.

"Just like any other tourist," he told her. "Like we belong."

Shawna fed her card into the little slot and punched in her pin number. The computer screen wanted to know how much and from what account. She chose savings and punched in nine hundred dollars, which left her with like twenty dollars in her account, enough to keep it open.

Harry stood behind her, keeping an eye on the traffic. But no one seemed to be paying any attention.

The ATM machine beeped and said: INVALID ACCOUNT.

"Maybe you put in the wrong pin," Harry suggested.

She tried again. Same thing. She let Harry do it on the third try and again it was invalid. The machine promptly sucked her card in.

"Shit," she said. "I hate when that happens."

Harry was starting to feel a little nervous.

Sure, it could've been a mistake... but what if it wasn't?

"It's happened to me a bunch of times," she reassured him. "It's nothing."

"All right. But why don't you just fill out a withdrawal slip inside and do it the old-fashioned way?"

She chewed her lip indecisively. "Okay."

Her confidence was rattled a little now. Harry felt the same. But he was going in there with her. She seemed to think the people they were dealing with here didn't have an extremely long reach. But she was wrong. He knew she was wrong. There wasn't anything they couldn't do.

"Hello," a woman with a CATHY name tag said. She was pleasant, perky, efficient.

"I want to make a withdrawal," Shawna told her, handing her the slip.

"Certainly." She started punching her keyboard.

Harry looked around. He was as nervous as a kitten and he didn't mind admitting it. Everyone he saw was one of them.

"I'm sorry, ma'am," Cathy said, "but I can't find a record of this account number."

Harry was starting to sweat now.

"Try again," Shawna snapped loud enough that people started looking.

"Yes," Cathy said. She punched her keyboard. "Sorry. Nothing."

Shawna shook her head. "This is crazy." She gave the teller her checking account number.

"Nothing on that either," Cathy said. "I...I don't know what to tell you. Did you recently close your accounts or transfer funds or—"

"What do you think I am?" Shawna said. "A goddamn idiot?"

"Easy," Harry told her.

"All right, all right. Then just look it up by my name. Can you do that?"

"Yes, ma'am," Cathy said, trying hard to keep that helpful, friendly smile on her face.

"Geddes, Shawna Geddes. G-E-D-D-E-S."

One of the managers was keeping an eye on them now. Pretending not to and doing a very poor job of it.

"Sorry, ma'am. Nothing on Shawna Geddes. I'm sorry. I—"

Shawna sighed. "I've had accounts here since I was sixteen for chrissake. What the hell's going on?"

The manager started threading his way over.

"Just a simple mistake, I'm sure," Harry said, grabbing Shawna by the arm and dragging her to the door like a kid from a candy store.

He shoved Shawna into the car.

"Nice," he said. "They'll remember you for sure."

"When I start to freak out, Harry, I get pissy. I can't help it."

He squealed out of the parking lot and merged in traffic. "I hate to say it, Shawna, but I think you've been erased."

175

# LOUISVILLE, KENTUCKY

## SHAWNEE PARK

**4:13 P.M.**

About three hundred of them had gathered: a large, angry cluster of young men and women dressed in combat fatigues, leather vests, black jeans and T-shirts. Some proudly wore the black parade helmets of the German SS and others sported Waffen SS field caps. Gestating a thick, savage odor of hate and intolerance which was mother's milk to them, they displayed their ultra-right wing philosophies on their skins: Swastikas. SS runes. HITLER WAS GOD, proclaimed biceps. HIMMLER FOREVER, said a heavily tattooed back. Etched into flesh were remarkable, artistic likenesses of the Fuhrer himself, Reichsfuhrer SS Himmler, Eva Braun. The skull and crossbones of the SS Totenkopf Division, the raised Z of the Polizei Division. The anarchic symbols of WAR (White Aryan Revolution), the Aryan Brotherhood, and the Nationalist Front. They marched in rowdy, bustling columns waving flags with the stars-and-stripes or the good old Union Jack formed into swastikas, hoisting banners proclaiming **JESUS WAS WHITE, WHITE IS RIGHT, THE HOLOCAUST IS A MYTH**, and **ARBEIT MACHT FREI**.

As they marched and thronged, the anthems of the movement sung by such punk and metal bands as Belzec, Blitzkrieg, and Das Reich blasted away. Groups of skinheads looking for a good fight chanted the words of "Aryan Exterminator" as performed by Stormtrooper:

"THIS IS HOW IT GOES!
THIS IS HOW IT ENDS!
STAND UP MY ARYAN BROTHER!
STAND UP FOR YOUR PURE-BLOODED MOTHER!
THE NIGGERS ARE GONNA DIE!
IMMIGRANTS ARE GONNA FRY!
IS THERE ANYONE FUCKING CRAZY ENOUGH

TO BELIEVE THE JEWISH LIE?
SEIG HEIL WHITE BROTHER SEIG HEIL!"
If there was anyone of non-white, non-European, non-Christian lineage in the park that morning, they were keeping a low profile. And that was probably for the best.

On a raised platform, one man rose above the rest. He gave the crowd the stiff-armed Nazi salute and it was returned with a deafening chant of "SEIG HEIL! SEIG HEIL!" The man addressing the faithful was Robert Schlising, a computer programmer of German-American heritage from Trenton, New Jersey. He was something of a prophet to his people. His father had served in the German Army in World War II. Two of his uncles had fought with the Waffen SS on the Eastern Front against the Bolsheviks. And his Great Uncle Heinz had been the chauffeur of Gestapo chief Heinrich Muller for a short time. Later, Uncle Heinz had achieved a certain notoriety by proving himself quite efficient in bayoneting Jewish children during the Warsaw Ghetto uprising. But his true claim to fame was as an SS guard at the Chelmo extermination camp.

Uncle Heinz was hanged at Nuremberg in 1946 for war crimes.

Schlising held his hands high. "JEWISH LIES! COMMUNIST CON-SPIRACIES! DEMOCRATIC IMPOTENCE! LIMP-WRISTED LIBER-AL AGENDAS! WHERE WILL IT END?" he cried out. "MY FRIENDS, MY DEAR, DEAR BROTHERS AND SISTERS, I ASK YOU: WHERE WILL IT END? AS BLOOD CALLS TO BLOOD, I SAY TO YOU NOW—IT COULD HAVE BEEN AVOIDED! THE NEGROS COULD STILL BE SERVING THE WHITE MAN AS IS THEIR DESTINY! THE HISPANICS COULD STILL BE SQUATTING IN THE MEXICAN DESERT! THE JEWS COULD HAVE BEEN BUT A MEMORY! WE WERE WARNED BY A GREAT MAN THAT IF THESE SUBHUMAN ELEMENTS WERE NOT PURGED AND PURGED COMPLETELY THEY WOULD RISE UP AND BITE THE HAND OF THEIR WHITE MASTERS! HE WARNED US! ADOLF HITLER WARNED US THAT THE WHITE RACE WOULD BECOME A MINORITY! OVERRUN BY SUBHUMAN RACES THAT WOULD POLLUTE OUR BLOOD!"

The crowd was driven into a near-religious fury.

"WILL WE ALLOW IT? I SAY AGAIN: WILL WE ALLOW IT?"

Schlising fanned the flames of hatred; something he was an expert at. He told the faithful to grind every non-white, every Jew, every immigrant under his or her heel for it was the right of the Aryan race to subjugate the "turd-skinned races."

The faithful, many with children learning the message, watched Schlising with wide eyes. They did not turn away. So they did not notice the other Skinheads who infiltrated their ranks. Did not see them slip in, insinuate themselves so easily, so effortlessly.

Though they dressed the same, sported the same buttons and badges and tattoos and hairless skulls, they were very different. The advance guard of a truly new order. And they had come in force. Twenty men and woman all with that horrible dead look about them.

They came on, their skins baggy like old suits, their faces waxen and sallow. They wore sunglasses as if the afternoon sun was too bright for them. They moved mechanically, lacking that certain muscular fluidity that defines human grace. They jerked. They twitched. They shambled. Insane marionettes controlled by the trembling fingers of puppet masters wired out on amphetamines.

No one noticed anything unusual.

Save for the smell.

A mephitic bouquet of sewers and backed-up drain pipes. Heavy, raw, almost sulfurous.

"What the fuck is that stink?" Heddy Lister said to her sister Anna and her boyfriend Max. She wrinkled her nose, forgetting about Schlising and Hitler and the thousand-year reich. "Do you smell that?"

Anna paid no attention, neither did Max.

They'd both been drinking and coking for almost sixteen hours now. They saw nothing but Schlising and smelled nothing but the spilled blood of dark-skinned races.

But somebody behind her said: "Fucking roadkill, man."

One of the new arrivals threaded through the crowd, bumping into people and leaving that awful stench in his wake. His face was beaded with sweat, his teeth chattering. He slammed into a woman who fell into Anna and Heddy dropped her beer.

"Fucking prick," the woman's boyfriend snarled. "Do you want my boot upside your fucking head?"

The skinhead laughed dryly and punched him in the face.

And it wasn't just here; the entire crowd was suddenly in disruption. The newcomer skinheads were hitting people, knocking people over, stomping them when they were down, spitting in people's faces, and all in all spreading a wave of unrest, violence, and the ever-present odor of bad meat.

"PLEASE! PLEASE! BROTHERS AND SISTERS, PLEASE!" Schlising shouted over the cacophony of angry, screaming voices. "WE MUST NOT FIGHT AMONGST OURSELVES! WE HAVE A COMMON ENEMY! A COMMON—"

But he didn't finish that as a beer bottle caught him in the head. He looked out at his flock, a thin trickle of blood coming from his cut ear. Though sixty years old, Schlising was a thick-necked bull of a man with a flashpoint temper that burned hotter than a firebrand. Clenching his teeth, he charged into the fray, fists lashing.

Whatever unity had existed amongst this new, dangerous master race, had evaporated like dew under the glare of hate.

Heddy pulled herself up and kicked some guy in the ribs until a fist crashed into her mouth. Her sister went down next to her, catching a knee in the face. Max punched, kicked, and head-butted anyone within range. Bodies were tumbling and falling, voices shouting and cursing and screaming. The very rage that was like a bond to these people exploded in shockwaves.

And through it all, Heddy, blood running down her chin, saw what was really going on.

Stoned, drunk, raging, she still saw it.

She saw one skinhead grab a woman by the face and smash his forehead into hers continually until she went limp. And then...

And then it came out of his mouth in a nightmarish, undulating ribbon: a worm as big around as a man's arm. It whipped and coiled in the air, leaving an awful smear of gray slime on the woman's face right before it dove between her lips.

Heddy just sat there, staring, staring.

*What the fuck?*

She could see heaps of tangled bodies.

And worms. Worms slithering amongst the thrashing limbs. Some were no bigger than grass snakes, others like bloated garden hoses whipping and winding and making a hideous mewing sound.

She saw them slide down throats. Emerge from throats. Wind themselves around writhing victims like constrictors. Burst open with clotty torrents of pearl-white eggs. She saw one huge worm—too large for her enfeebled brain to accept—explode out of a man's throat in a spray of blood and tissue (that neatly severed his head) and slam into another man, burrowing through his chest with the spinning motion of a drill bit, each bloated ropy segment quivering with life.

And suddenly...silence.

Yes, complete silence. Oh, in the distance she could hear the wail of police sirens. She knew that would happen. But all the combatants were quiet. Eerily so. Some were sprawled on their backs, others sitting up, still others on knees and elbows. But all of them—even those bleeding and broken—were absolutely quiet.

For one rambling mad moment, there were the sounds of normalcy.

Birds sang. Leaves fluttered in the breeze. A dog barked. A car squealed its tires. Heddy found herself pressing her eyelids shut. Finally, she had to open them.

And madness, it seemed, bred madness.

For the spirit of brotherly love had descended on this gathering. It was more than the fact that everyone was sitting around with that stupid, almost bovine look of absolute peace and serenity on their faces. It was a physical thing she could feel. Where the atmosphere moments before (and in fact ever since the unofficial gathering had taken place) had been charged with electric negativity...now it seemed harmonious.

Everyone had been tranquilized. Pacified. Injected with a serenity that was somehow frightening.

But it wasn't brotherly love, she knew.

It was the worms.

Because now…Jesus Christ…now people were stroking the worms that fed from their mouths. They were waiting with their jaws open to accept them. Many were picking them up and feeding them between their lips. Some were dropping them into the mouths of lovers and friends in glistening loops.

Heddy felt an odd fuzzy grayness wash over her mind like a storm cloud.

She knew she had gone insane. Maybe it was all the acid. The mushrooms. Who could say? Too many years of purposely distorting reality and now it was permanently fucked-up. A hallucinogenic canvas of running colors and distorted imagery.

And what really nailed that home was when she saw a little girl pick up a worm. The thing had to be four or five feet if it was an inch. It squirmed and pulsed in her hands, a ghastly, violent white, segmented like a bendy straw. The little girl just smiled at it and pressed it to her mother's lips as if she were giving her a flower to kiss or a sweet to relish.

Heddy didn't buy it.

She didn't buy any of it.

*You got hit in the head too fucking hard,* she thought. *Your brains are scrambled and poached and fried and seasoned in too much fucking acid. Hah, hah, hah! My God, look at it! Look at them!*

But she wouldn't.

She pressed her face down between her trembling knees and vomited, trying to void all the black, twisting dementia.

"Fucking bullshit," she sobbed. "All bullshit…"

She didn't believe any of it until her sister brought the worm to her. Anna was smiling and her eyes were misty like exploded stars. Heddy looked down the undulating black sucking maw of the worm and a split second before she would have screamed… she felt better as waves of a sweet, debilitating scent flooded through her, making her feel calm and relaxed, plugged into something much bigger than herself, her eyes looking beyond the here and the now and into the forever after.

She understood, knew the thing was in her brain, already had her wound up tight and happily so.

She grinned and took the worm between her lips like a lover, sucking its phallic mass deep into her throat.

# CAMP PEARY, WILLIAMSBURG, VIRGINIA

## THE FARM

**6:09 P.M.**

DCI Robert Pershing rarely visited The Farm. Now and again, he would drop by, often unannounced, to get a look at the caliber of training going on. Located within the Camp Peary Military Reservation, The Farm was the home of the CIA's elite Junior Officer Training Program. It was here that agents learned the basics of running clandestine operations in a twenty-week paramilitary course.

It was also a place the CIA SOG teams could practice their craft.

SOG had originated in the Vietnam War where they operated under the whitewashed, politically correct name Studies and Observation Group. To outsiders, at any rate. To those inside or in the know, SOG meant Special Operations Group. SOG teams ran long-range reconnaissance missions deep into North Vietnam, as well as Cambodia, Laos, Thailand, and even into mainland China. They executed quick commando-type raids in enemy territory such as the liberation of POW camps and the destruction of enemy base camps. They were also involved in sabotage, guerrilla operations, agent insertions, abductions, and the assassination of enemy officers and intelligence personnel. On more than one occasion, SOG teams had been formed into four-man hunter/killer squads who were tasked with the elimination of American deserters and traitors. Such activities were illegal, of course. But then no one suspected a harmless organization like the Studies and Observation Group.

Pershing liked the SOG teams and the fact that they answered to no one but the Company itself. When he became Director of the CIA, he took it upon himself to expand SOG from a paramilitary force of few hundred men and women to a secret strike force of nearly a thousand.

His own army of sorts.

He could deploy SOG teams anywhere in the world within a few hours.

It gave him a tremendous feeling of power.

And the great thing about SOG operatives was that they did their jobs without question. If Pershing were to, say, order them to kill certain powerful political figures, they would.

Today was a special day.

Pershing had invited General Francis K. Mason, the Chairman of the Joint Chiefs of Staff, as his guest.

After a gourmet meal prepared by Pershing's own staff, he took the General on a tour of the facilities. They watched the SOG operators conduct combat drills with live ammo. Watched them on the shooting range. Watched them stage kidnappings and assassinations, counterterrorist operations, and even take down an enemy camp.

Mason was impressed. SOG did very well.

"But how are they with the real thing?" he wanted to know.

Pershing filled him in on classified details of operations in Africa, the Middle East, and Latin America.

"They cut their teeth in Vietnam," Pershing told him. "They had an unprecedented kill ratio of a hundred fifty to one. And they haven't lost their edge since. We give them the best of everything. We expect results and they deliver."

Mason nodded his thinning crop of white hair. He was watching troopers in black fatigues orchestrate a fast-rope helicopter assault on a two-story building. The helicopters—Blackhawks—came screaming over the horizon and hovered thirty or forty feet above the rooftop. Ropes were dropped and troopers slid down them and entered the building by crashing through skylights and blowing doors with small charges. The whole thing came down in just a few minutes.

"Impressive, Bob. Very impressive," Mason said, sucking on his pipe.

In the back of Pershing's car, they had some eighty-year-old cognac and some pre-Castro Havanas.

Mason studied his cigar. "I appreciate you having me out here, Bob. A lot of us wonder what your SOG teams are up to." He exhaled slowly. "But, I guess there's more to this than a pleasant afternoon of war gaming."

Pershing smiled. "I thought we might have a little chat about this and that."

"All right. Tell me."

"BioGen, General. It's a fucking mess and we both know it. It's raged out of control. It's simply not containable, neither politically nor realistically. The President has Costello trying to clean it up through VanderMissen and Sleshing but, let's face the facts, it simply can't be done. This country is in grave peril."

"Yes, it is." Mason looked grim. "Biggest mistake any of us made was giving the go ahead on that one. It felt wrong then, it feels worse now."

"And the entire thing is being helmed by a President who's fighting a losing battle with the tabloids. A man like that...a man so concerned with self-image...so morally and ethically bankrupt... how can he lead this country in the trying times ahead? He's turned our beloved Union into an idiocracy."

Mason smoked and thought. His features were set, dire. "What are you saying, Bob? Lay it out for me."

Pershing did. "This BioGen business is getting bad, General. You know that. I know that. And it's going to get a helluva lot worse before it gets better. And, frankly, a few weeks from now—maybe even a few days from now for all we know—this country is going to go through hell, through turmoil like it's never seen before. This country is going to hit the skids unless it gets the proper leadership and right now."

Mason stared at him with a look of cold iron. "Are you saying what I think you're saying?"

Pershing nodded. "Yes, I am. Of everyone involved in this BioGen mess, only you and I and maybe, maybe Admiral Paulus have their head screwed on right. We're the only ones who can fix what's broken."

The silence that reigned in the car was absolute. It went on for seconds, minutes.

Mason sighed finally. "Tell me more," he said.

# CHICAGO, NORTH SHORE

## KENILWORTH

**6:31 P.M.**

They spent the rest of the afternoon visiting various state, county, and federal offices. It took time as such things often do. In the process, Shawna's confidence slowly and inexorably disintegrated. The idea of some big, career-making story was the last thing on her mind now. When they were finished checking into things, she fell into a black mood, saying nothing, just staring off into space. Nothing Harry said or did could lift her out of it.

But it was understandable.

It was tough realizing you just didn't exist.

At the Social Security Administration, Shawna told them she'd lost her card and couldn't remember her number. They went through the computers and could find no record of a Shawna Geddes. Harry called a friend of his at the DMV and had him trace Shawna's license number. Nothing. No license. No registration. Neither applied for recently or in the past. Not even a voter's registration card. Their last stop was the Hall of Records. And what they found there was the worst of all possible things: Shawna Geddes had not been born. There was no birth certificate on file for her. Her parents' records were there, all right, but not hers.

Officially, Shawna Geddes did not exist.

Even on the Internet... her Yahoo and Facebook accounts were wiped out.

By the time they got back to Gabe's, she started talking again. But the old Shawna was gone. The person who'd replaced her might as well have not existed.

"What does it mean, Harry?" she asked. "What does it mean when you don't exist? When there's no record of your birth, your life?"

"It could mean a lot of things, I guess."

She gave him a death stare. "Tell me, Harry. Or should I tell you?"

He sighed. "It means that you nosed into something they can't afford having you or anyone else know about. Something so incredibly secretive that they're willing to kill for it. They're wiping you out, figuratively," he told her, pulling into Gabe's driveway. "They hacked into the system and destroyed you. Your history, your credit, your finances. They don't want you to exist on paper at all."

"It's more than that, isn't it?" She laughed bitterly. "When the cops find my body in some ditch with my throat slit, there'll be no way to tell who I am. I'll be some Jane Doe buried at the city's expense."

Harry wanted to disagree, tell her she was wrong, but he didn't have the heart to lie to her. "Have you ever been fingerprinted?"

"No."

"Regardless, there's still got to be something on you somewhere."

Harry had heard of things like this before, of course, but it was usually in connection with old movies or espionage novels. There had been a few occasions—in Washington—where he'd heard State Department employees start rambling after six or seven vodka martinis. They told him about people being groomed for murder. About them being given non-person status. Once the paper trail was eliminated, they told him, the rest was easy. No body to extract DNA from, no nothing. The people who did these things had never been specifically named or to what branch of the federal government they belonged.

Harry had listened, but never truly believed.

Not until now.

"Let's go inside," he told Shawna, helping her from the car.

"And do what?"

"Call your mother," he said. "She knows you exist."

# CHICAGO, RIVER NORTH

## THE WAREHOUSE

**7:13 P.M.**

The Old Man was thinking about Shawna Geddes.

He didn't like this business of killing innocent civilians. It made S5 dirty. The Gulf War vets were innocent, too, he knew and knew very well, but that was an entirely different scenario. That was a matter of cutting off the thumb to save the hand. The alternative was unthinkable: an entire country infested.

But Shawna Geddes.

He didn't like the idea of having her killed. But if he didn't, he wouldn't be doing his job and he had to answer to superiors like everyone else. And the way his superiors were thinking was quite simple: anyone or anything that stood in the way of eradicating the parasites and their hosts was to be removed. His superiors were of the mind that this entire thing could be contained. That it could be halted and hushed up before the public was any the wiser. The Old Man was not so sure of that. They had been lucky so far, but how long could that luck hold?

Something had to slip between their fingers.

Statistically, it just had to happen.

A hundred men could stick their fingers in a dike and still a few drops of water had to escape. It was the law of probability.

He thought about Shawna Geddes.

*If you don't have her removed,* he thought, *someone else will. If she breathes any of this to the legitimate press and someone starts digging...well, it'll be you that's removed in her place. Think about that.*

He had a sister in Virginia. His only family. She had a daughter about Shawna's age. Like Shawna she was pretty, bright, and ambitious. But if it came down to it...if his niece was a threat to national security...

*Yes,* he thought, *yes, I would have her removed.*

Long ago the Old Man had dispensed with such things as guilt or morality or self-loathing. Such pristine, unrealistic virtues could hamper a man's career and the man himself. They had to be discarded. Particularly in the business of security. There were no real friends in his game, no lovers or confidants he could really trust. There was only the state itself and his unwavering loyalty to it. It had to be this way. Cut off the thumb to save the hand? God yes. He'd done it, he'd personally cut the order a hundred times. And would a hundred more times if necessary. The lives of a few were meaningless. Just a few less ants crawling about on the sidewalk. When you started thinking of them as human beings with lives and loves and families...then you became impotent, ineffective. The few would have to be sacrificed to save the many. It was the way things had always worked. And sometimes only a patriot could see that.

But the Old Man, blinded by loyalty and duty as he was, could not entirely dismiss the poor young woman. He was not a monster. Not an Adolf Eichmann sending thousands to their deaths with the sweep of a pen.

If there had been any other way...

Had there been more time he could've dealt with her less harshly. He would have had a string of red herrings planted. A trail she would follow to Philadelphia or LA for that matter. Once there, she would be arrested on some minor drug offense, held over. Cocaine in her glove compartment. Crack under the seat. Heroin in the trunk. It had been done countless times before. By the time she'd extricated herself from the whole mess, the operation would have been over with.

But there was no time.

Already he had given the order. No one was to go out of their way to apprehend her, it was an unnecessary drain on manpower, but if she was seen...if a clear opportunity was presented...no witnesses...well...then so be it. Her body was to be disposed of. There would be no physical evidence. Even now the computer hacks at the NSA were wiping her life from existence.

Maybe if she was smart, she'd just run away. No one would interfere.

If she didn't...and she started talking...well, there was always her mother. Good bait to draw her in with.

*Quit pretending, you old fool. You hate this. You hate all of it. You hate what you are, what you've done, what you've allowed your life to become. Other people celebrate life and you specialize in death. That's exactly what you've been thinking. All the blood on your hands, the lives on your conscience, the people you've played with like toys...it's rotted you black inside. And now, in your twilight years, you've become soft... sentimental... you feel guilty.*

*Yes, yes, yes! I do. God knows I do. All these killings to protect the secret machinery of a corrupt democracy. Was it worth it? Was it really worth it? Wouldn't it be better if it was laid out at the feet of the taxpayers and all the scheming, meat-hungry maggots they'd put into office were exposed? Finally, ultimately?*

No, no, no, he could not think that way...

What really bothered him was Shawna's association with Harry Niles.

A file had been assembled and faxed to the Old Man at the warehouse. He didn't know Niles personally, but apparently there were still many in Washington who didn't care for him. He had made a major nuisance of himself stepping on important toes and nosing into everything from the House Intelligence Committee to the State Department. He'd gotten close too many times and so his termination from the Washington *Post* had been covertly arranged.

And now Niles worked for some foolish tabloid writing stories about the conspiracy to kill Kennedy and crashed UFOs.

*How close you'd been back then, Niles,* the Old Man thought with some mirth. *How close you'd been to the very things you invent now. How close to those monumental truths only a few are privileged to know.*

No matter. If he showed up with the Geddes woman, he would be removed as well. The Old Man knew there'd be no tears in Washington.

Cave came bounding in, shattering the Old Man's train of thought.

"We got trouble," he said. "Real trouble."

The Old Man touched the tips of his index fingers to his nose. "Tell me."

"We've had another major incident. It's a real mess..."

# RICHMOND, VIRGINIA

## CBT CORPORATE HEADQUARTERS

**8:02 P.M.**

The voice on the phone was cultured and silky, smooth as glass and just as slippery. As to who it really belonged to, that was a mystery. And maybe it was better that way.

"Tell me things I don't know. Tell me about loyalty and disloyalty," it said.

Elizabeth figured that was a loaded question because she did not honestly believe there was anything The Collective did not know. They kept secrets. Secrets were not kept from them.

"You're referring to Bob Pershing?"

"Am I?" the voice asked.

She had just finished listening to the recording of Pershing's conversation with General Mason. As one of the conspirators, nearly all his communications were intercepted and delivered to her and Gordon Parks at the NSA. "He's doing exactly what we thought he would do. Mason's in bed with him now and my assets tell me that Admiral Paulus is practically a certainty. It couldn't really be going better. Everything is proceeding according to plan."

"That's very good to know."

"I thought you'd like it."

"We're all very happy that things are following the scenario. Nothing is more important than that. I don't need to tell you why."

"No, of course not."

"Keep us advised, Elizabeth."

She set her cell on the desk. It was always a relief to get off the phone with that man. There was always an undercurrent of menace to his voice. She had spent many, many years accruing the power she now wielded, but next to her caller—and The Collective in general—she was weak and impotent. They were the ones that wrote history and steered world politics. They were the makers and unmakers. She was always careful in what she said, whether that was here in her office or the boardroom, her car, her apartment, her house in the country, even out for a casual dinner. Didn't matter. She was certain she was being listened to, that The Collective and their confederates studied her every move and listened to her every word.

A few years before, she'd been carrying on an illicit, torrid affair with Astrid Austin, an attractive—and married—CDC epidemic intelligence officer. She held a position of some influence at the CDC's Epidemic Intelligence Service, the EIS. Astrid's husband had no idea she was bisexual and she had been quite successful in keeping her secret secret. Elizabeth met her at a DC party and afterwards they engaged in a very discreet, very careful, yet very passionate relationship. They covered their tracks expertly. When they passed on the street, they did not acknowledge one another. When they encountered each other at social and political functions, their conversations were short and trivial.

Then one day, Elizabeth discovered a flash drive on her desk when she came back from a meeting. On it was a video of Astrid and she making love in a hot tub at Elizabeth's house in Brookhaven. It was not only shocking but invasive, disgusting that her most private moments were fodder for the camera.

Not two minutes after she'd finished watching it, as if on cue, her contact from The Collective called.

"Quite steamy and entertaining, Elizabeth," the predatory voice said. "But also quite compromising. Someone in your position needs to be very careful of the company she keeps. A scornful jilted lover could prove embarrassing and we don't like embarrassing situations. Are you understanding me on this? Need I go into detail of what the cost of exposure might be?"

She wanted to scream and shout about the invasion of her privacy, but she didn't dare. "No," she said, a shy well-trained squeaking mouse.

"Very good. You will, of course, break off your entanglement with Dr. Austin."

"Yes."

"Excellent, excellent." There was a pause, the sound of him breathing on the other end. "And in the future, choose lovers with less credentials. The easily disposable kind. We really don't want the CDC sniffing around CBT."

"I'll need time to do it properly," she said, already hurting inside.

"And that is the one thing you don't have, I'm afraid," the voice informed her. "Just step away from the relationship. That's all you have to do. We'll take care of the details."

A week later, after trying to contact Elizabeth again and again with no success, Astrid committed suicide. She was found in her car over in Dupont Circle with her wrists slashed open. She was parked just up the street from Sushi Taro, one of their favorite meeting places. The irony of that was not lost on Elizabeth. Astrid's car was placed there for a reason by the people who killed her.

Elizabeth tried not to think about it because when she did, she hated and she craved revenge. She knew enough to take down the dirty machine at the heart of DC politics. There was enough in her head and in her hidden files to destroy dozens of dirty politicians, corrupt military leaders, and countless lobbyists, to sink them all in the same foul swill barrel. But so far she had resisted the urge.

So far.

*You should be careful of even thinking such things,* she told herself. *As fantastic as it sounds, there's always the possibility that your thoughts are being listened to as well.*

The ultimate in paranoia. Maybe. But that was her existence—she could trust no one and nothing. She was not ignorant of the puppet masters that manipulated world events behind the scenes like ninety-nine percent of the country. She was the CEO of a powerful corporation that employed thousands worldwide. People kissed her ass and courted her favors. And each and every one of them from the lowliest janitor to the highest section head to her personal secretary, could not be trusted. Any one of them could have been reporting to The Collective and others to the CIA, DIA, NSA...the list went on and on.

Astrid had been her only real friend. Then and now.

Sometimes Elizabeth enjoyed the fantasy of quitting, of walking away and leaving the entire sordid mess behind her, but she knew that wasn't an option. The Collective would tell her when it was time to step back. But it would be on their terms, not hers. If she tried to get away sooner, they'd find her in a car like Astrid or floating in the Potomac if she was found at all.

Like it or not, she was a slave to the system, married to it. A player in the game. And the game had many layers and few had navigated them as carefully as she.

Which made her think of Project Biogenesis.

She wondered how far The Collective would go to sanitize knowledge of it and how many people would have to die. Right from the very beginning, they had orchestrated the entire thing.

It had begun with a phone call from her puppet masters. "The Defense Department is seeking exotic technologies to be employed in the Middle East. They'll want something inexpensive and nearly impossible to trace. DARPA, ARO, the NSA, the ONR...all of them will be submitting their proposals. As will CBT. You will find research on a project called BioGenesis in the S5 files. You will pitch it to the DoD and win the contract."

That's how it began. Project BioGenesis was born. Once the final stages of R & D were complete, it was field tested in Iraq at a small agricultural village called Nkudbkah. The results were nearly instantaneous and devastating. Within three days of aerosol dispersal, ninety-eight percent of the village was infected. BioGenesis was effective and field-tested. It was not used again. At least, that's what the word was.

But that wasn't exactly true.

Elizabeth hadn't understood completely at the time what was going on. It was only now that it made sense. The Collective used the DoD to create a situation they could later exploit. Even the Old Man, who supervised the research on BioGenesis, wasn't privy to the big picture. He didn't know that a new generation of parasites had been engineered from the ones he and his team had created. The original breed had wiped out Nkudbkah, but weeks later a new and improved strain was sprayed over the area to test its survivability and adaptability.

And through this zone of contamination—which had absolutely no strategic value—a variety of U.S. troops were marched. Once again, The Collective had manipulated things. Marine and Army units passed through the area, many of them sent far afield from their theater of operations. And nearly all of them were infected by a particularly nasty parasite which was designed to go dormant inside them for several years. As far as anyone was concerned, BioGenesis was over with. Meanwhile, The Collective sat back and bided their time, watching for a sign of resurgence.

And now that had happened.

Now the parasites were active and spreading across the nation and soon, the globe.

But that had been The Collective's intention from the very beginning. It was part of their overall plan. They had used the war in Iraq and the Department of Defense to create a situation that would seed a greater, more ambitious scenario.

Other such scenarios had been played out in the country more than once.

To meet the objectives of certain clandestine agendas which would be in direct conflict with the needs and lives of the general population, a conflict was created. The ruling class—The Collective—engineered an artificial crisis that both enraged and numbed the public, who would then throw their civil rights and common sense to the wind and beg the powers that be to intercede on their behalf. The ruling class was then given a free hand to manipulate events and crush personal freedoms with absolutely no fear of repercussion. The public became dazed, wide-eyed children triggered by fear and uncertainty, begging adults for intervention—help us please, do what you need to do but save us from our enemies.

Herd instinct was a simple animal stimulus response and humans were hardly exempt. The Collective was so good at such things that they regularly influenced the public's perception. They knew their patsies and how to play them. The public's Pavlovian response was typically simple-minded and predictable to the extreme.

This scenario had been historically very effective. It had been used at Pearl Harbor to draw the country into World War II, in the Gulf of Tonkin to escalate U.S. involvement in Vietnam, and, more recently, on 9/11 to throw the military-industrial might of the country into the so-called War on Terror.

And the one that was going on now would be the biggest, most ambitious scenario ever attempted. BioGen would weaken the country and horrify the populace. The Collective would use this to advance their agenda of full spectrum dominance via a military coup played out by puppets like Bob Pershing at the CIA, General Mason at the JCS, and Admiral Paulus at ONI.

What came after that was the question that Elizabeth could not answer. She only knew one thing—BioGen and the resulting coup would only be the first phase of something much larger, something that was closely guarded by The Collective. What that was, she did not know. But as Pershing and his crew of traitors were being played, she was certain that she was, too. Another puppet dangling on strings held tightly by the shadowy fingers of the masters of this world.

Whatever it was, it was beginning to take shape and that's what really scared her.

# LOUISVILLE, KENTUCKY

## SHAWNEE PARK

**8:49 P.M.**

"That's it," McKenna said. "Down there."

The pilot took them closer, flying directly over the park and the hive of activity below. As far as the police and emergency crews below were concerned, they were just another TV news chopper.

"Cave said we got at least two- or three-hundred down there," McKenna told Stein over the headset. "This is a farce. There's no way to contain this now. Just no way. I don't know why we're bothering."

Stein sat in the rear cabin with McKenna, staring down on the mess below. He said nothing. A few hours before, Cave had gotten the both of them on a Learjet 85 to Fort Knox where they hopped on a chopper for air surveillance of the scene. They'd been buzzing it for the past ten minutes.

"It was bound to happen," he said over the set, dejected and spent. "And now it has. So the shit hits the fan."

Stein grunted. "It's hitting everywhere. Don't you read the papers? Surf the net?"

"Nah. I don't like to have opinions. It gets in the way."

The pilot made pass after pass with the chopper. It was a Gazelle, a stripped-down civilian version of the military helicopter. It was fast, dependable, and could carry a good load.

"Cave's contact on the Metro Police says they're skinheads or neo-Nazis or some shit," McKenna explained. "Cops were called in and this is what they found. A couple hundred people, totally comatose. Spooky."

"In more ways than one."

McKenna nodded. His mouth was dry.

"Oh boy," Stein said. "They're loading them all up, taking them to the hospital. You know what's going to happen then?"

McKenna did.

"The whole place'll be infested by tomorrow or the next day. I want to see the Old Man cover this one up."

The chopper flew off and brought them back to Knox. There was very little they could do. The skinheads were in the hands of the local authorities now and things were about to go raging out of control.

After they touched down, they stood around on the tarmac and brooded. They did not speak for some time. They avoided looking at each other.

Finally, McKenna said, "What now?"

"Maybe it's time we bail," Stein told him. "Remember what I said? That we'd know when the time was right? Well, it's getting real close."

"Where would we go?" McKenna asked. "I mean, we'd have to go somewhere, right?"

"We'll worry about that when we get there. Just to be out of this mess will be enough for the time being."

"What about Cave? The Old Man?"

"What about them?"

"I don't know. I feel like I'm letting 'em down."

"Fuck them all. Fuck the Section. Fuck the Agency. Fuck Blackpool. Don't go getting all patriotic on me, McKenna. That flag waving business has a time and a place. And, believe me, this isn't it."

"Yeah, I guess you're right."

"Of course I am."

McKenna lit a cigarette. "You've got it all figured out, don't you, Stein?"

"No, I don't. I'm going purely on instinct here. You with me?"

"I'm with you. You know that."

Stein watched him very closely for a time like he wasn't so sure he believed that at all. McKenna could not meet his gaze and he wondered if Stein was aware of that.

"I'll go see about our flight back to Chi," Stein said. "We're out of options here."

McKenna nodded, watched him walk away. When he was gone he sighed deeply. He just hoped the wire had picked up all that.

After this, there'd be no question of his loyalty.

# CHICAGO, NORTH SHORE

## KENILWORTH

**9:51 P.M.**

Shawna was alone at Gabe's house.

Harry was off doing a little legwork, as he'd called it, and Gabe had a late dinner engagement. The staff were gone. Gabe thought that wise for the time being. So it was just Shawna in that big, rambling Tudor with too much time on her hands. There was a pool. Horses. Footpaths through the woods. A trout pond. An immense library. Plenty of ways to pass time.

But when you didn't exist...it just wasn't fun anymore.

And why start reading a book or watching an old movie when there was the nasty possibility you might not live to finish it?

*Why didn't you just look the other way, Shawna?*

*Because I couldn't. Maybe some people could, but there was no way I could do that. I had to find out. I had to know. I had to see what the hell they were doing with that poor guy in the park.*

*So, why didn't you call the cops and let it go at that?*

Good questions. No good answers. She'd put her life on the line now and what had she gotten for any of it? More questions. Many more questions. That and a mystery she probably wouldn't live to solve. But if she had to die, was it too much to ask that she be told the truth before they pulled the trigger?

She went into the kitchen. She made herself a sandwich, a bowl of ice cream. Then thought: *What the hell? Putting on weight isn't much of a worry any longer.* She raided the refrigerator, eating everything from pickles to pecan pie, smoked trout to frozen lasagna.

One thing that all of this had accomplished for her was that she'd finally called her mother.

It was Harry's idea.

She used her cell and when the conversation was completed, she tossed the phone into a dumpster. Harry's idea, again. Cell phones were not much different than the electronic security bracelets or tethers that convicts wore: each had a beacon that constantly transmitted the wearer/user's exact GPS coordinates. In the case of a cell, even when they were off or the battery was removed, the signal was there. It was simple enough to triangulate someone's exact position in that way if you had the technology. And their perceived enemies had all kinds of toys.

Shawna's mother wasn't unkind. No more so than any other time. She knew something was bothering her daughter, but Shawna wouldn't tell her what it was. Her mother started telling her how she should find a man and settle down and how her father would have wanted it that way and did she go to church and why not because accepting Jesus into her life was just what she needed.

Shawna had grinned through the entire monologue.

Good old Mom. Same as always, only now she was incapable of getting under her skin. It was all hopelessly amusing and there were times as they chatted when Shawna wanted to laugh out loud and still others when she wanted to break down and cry. In the end, she promised her that she would be coming to visit her soon. Her mother made her swear on the Bible. *And don't you dare take that lightly, Shawny.*

It was, in retrospect, the best thing that had happened in days.

Shawna wanted to go home... but if she did, would she be endangering her mother?

# CHICAGO, NORTH SHORE

## EVANSTON

**10:15 P.M.**

Harry studied the building real close as he approached.

There were lots of cars on the streets, but none that looked overly suspicious. But he supposed if he was hoping to see a couple guys with silenced machine guns, he would be sadly disappointed. It would be nothing so obvious, he knew. He pulled the FedEx truck to a stop before the main entrance, right in the NO PARKING zone. But it was okay; he was delivering a package.

He'd borrowed the truck from Dwayne Brown, his first wife's brother.

Unlike the rest of the family, Harry had kept in close contact with Dwayne. Dwayne was the kind of guy who could get you a ticket to any pro game in town. Bears were playing the Packers and the box office was sold out? No problem. Dwayne could fix you up. Same went for the Cubbies, White Sox, and Bulls. Oh, it would cost you, but he always had some. Dwayne also managed some very lucrative and very illegal sports lotteries and pools. When it came to pro sports and betting, he was the only guy to trust.

Harry had borrowed his FedEx truck, jacket, and cap. And it had only cost him a hundred bucks. And this for an hour.

"I'm making a run over to Rockford at four in the a.m., Harry," Dwayne had said. "That truck better be in my driveway by then, you dig? And don't go getting into trouble and having the cops run my plates. That's a corporate vehicle and I ain't gonna lose my job for this shit."

"No problem."

"Got a nice spread on the Lions/Bears game at the dome Sunday. You interested?"

"How much?"

"Hundred. Pays ten to one."

"Count me in."

Dwayne would bleed you dry, but what could you do?

Harry needed to get into Shawna's building and for that he needed a good cover. What better than a FedEx guy? Even if it was a little late for deliveries.

He sat in the truck, his belly filled with tiny wings.

This was the real thing here. No bullshit about it. The individuals they were dealing with killed people for a living. They arranged suicides. They swept nosy bastards under the carpet like dust bunnies. They buried them so deep the fucking worms couldn't find them. That's the kind of people these were.

And this was why Harry was trembling.

Maybe they weren't watching Shawna's place. And maybe they weren't necessarily interested in him. But he didn't believe that. These people were thorough.

*Damn right they're thorough. You think they haven't made the connection between you and Shawna yet?*

Maybe. Maybe not. Depended on how desperate they were.

Taking a deep breath, he hopped out of the truck and waltzed right into the building like he belonged there. Under his arm was tucked a package and a clipboard. It didn't matter that the package was for some guy in Hickory Hills. Nobody had to know that. He had the brim of his FedEx cap pulled down low so it would obscure his face a bit. He went up the stairs to Shawna's apartment. He walked right by it like it didn't mean anything to him. At the end of the corridor, he paused. He looked around and found he was quite alone.

*Get it over with, dipshit.*

He went back to Shawna's door.

It was locked.

His heart pounding, his palms sweaty, he slid the key in the lock. It opened and he stepped in, closing the door quietly behind him.

The apartment was empty.

His skin feeling prickly and hot, he went from room to room. Everything had been methodically stripped and carted away. Even the furniture was gone. There wasn't so much as a spoon or a slice of bread. No glasses in the cupboard. No food in the fridge.

Somehow, it was worse than finding a couple thugs with guns waiting for him.

His blood running cold, he left.

# AUGUST 26

# DETROIT

## EAST DEARBORN

**12:44 A.M.**

While counterterrorist units hunted the wastelands of Afghanistan for Sheikh Sa'ad al Khalafari, he sat in a small cramped apartment above a furniture store on Warren Avenue drinking Shaymenno feeh, a light tea with milk.

Sheikh Sa'ad had entered the U.S. illegally aboard a Lebanese tanker, disembarking by the light of the moon in Cleveland before making his way north to Detroit where he was warmly welcomed by Al-Qaeda sleeper agents, who, for many years, had been prosperous Dearborn merchants.

They did not question why it was he had come.

They did not ask what was in the crates he carried.

He had come highly recommended and his business was that of God, so why dare question?

The ten crates Sheikh Sa'ad traveled with each contained three aluminum-shelled biological containment vessels that looked much like briefcases. And in them was the very thing that would bring the United States and Israel to their knees. The technology had been harvested by the Iranian Pasdaran and then stolen by Sheikh Sa'ad and his confederates of Palestinian Islamic Jihad. Something the Iranians were very angry about.

That the technology was horrendous beyond belief, Sheikh Sa'ad did not doubt. But in the war against infidels, one often had use such deplorable means. Besides, the technology had been invented by the Americans so why should they not inherit their own horrors and reap what they had sown?

While his brothers played with incendiary agents and roadside bombs, loaded trucks or vans with fuel oil and fertilizer wired to acetylene tanks, vainly sought radioactive wastes...only Sheikh Sa'ad held the weapon which was the finger of God.

There was a slight knock at the door and a woman stepped in.

She did not greet Sheikh Sa'ad and he did not greet her.

She stood there like some positively striking automaton in her skirted business suit which showed plenty of leg. She was a lovely woman, breathtaking really, with long, lustrous black braids sweeping over one shoulder, her cheekbones high, her face angular, her eyes a slow simmering green. Such a clean, pure, olive-skinned beauty Sheikh Sa'ad had never seen before and he knew, at that moment, that he viewed one of Allah's finest creations.

The woman looked very much like the high-priced personal secretary of an auto magnate that she indeed was. Though she had no accent and her English was flawless, she was of Iraqi Shia birth and was a member of Hezbollah. Her people had strong contacts with the Iranian Pasdaran and he wondered if one like her would be the instrument with which they would enact their revenge upon him and his network.

Yes, she was clean and pure like the room itself. The wudu, the ritual ablution, had already been performed. Sheikh Sa'ad could feel the comforting presence of God and knew that what he would now do was sanctioned by Allah. It was holy work.

The woman covered her body and head with a dark Hijab, which was draped loosely, leaving only her face uncovered. Standing with her hands at her sides, she faced Mecca and recited the Iqama, the private call to prayer. When she was done, she went down to her knees on a prayer mat and, squeezing her eyes shut, turned her face upward. *"Allaahu Akbar! Allaahu Akbar!"* she repeated again and again with something quite close to frenzy...and fear. *"Ashhadu Allah ilaaha illa-lah!"*

Kneeling before her, Sheikh Sa'ad opened one of the specimen vessels. Within were six Lucite vacuum jars of fluid. He removed one as the woman prayed and set it before him, asking Allah for guidance in this great battle against the westerners who had usurped the holy lands and enslaved the chosen people of God.

He licked his lips.

His limbs trembled.

The woman was shuddering with something quite near religious ecstasy.

When Sheikh Sa'ad had come to this country there had been ten crates, each holding three biological containment vessels which in turn held six specimen jars. This was the only vessel left in his charge. The others had been sent to the faithful in New York, Atlanta, Los Angeles, Dallas, San Francisco, and various other cities for dispersal.

He looked down at the jar and what floated in the liquid.

Pulling on a pair of rubber gloves, he took up a forceps and unscrewed the lid on the jar.

*"Ash Hadu anna Muhamadar rasuulullah,"* the woman cried, her voice wavering and choked with emotion as tears broke from her eyes. *"Ash Hadu anna Muhamadar rasuulullah..."*

Sheikh Sa'ad dipped his forceps carefully into the brine and seized the pale larval worm within. It began to writhe, twisting from side to side as he removed it and held it up before his eyes.

"God is good," he said. "God is great."

The woman's prayers were incomprehensible now as she shook and sobbed and plainly begged for mercy. Sheikh Sa'ad told her that she was the divine vessel of God and all would remember her sacrifice to martyrdom.

Nearly out of her mind, she opened her mouth.

Sheikh Sa'ad brought the worm to her, gripping it firmly with the forceps so that it did not escape. He held the squirming maggot-like creature an inch from her yawning mouth. A clear slime dripped from it.

"*Allaahu Akbar!*" he said with great reverence. "*Laa ilaaha illa-Lah...*"

He dropped the worm into the woman's open mouth.

Immediately she shuddered and cried out with a choking, gurgling sound as the worm gripped her tongue with appendages like fishhooks, digging in deep before sliding down her throat like a snake, its acidic secretions burning her throat and making her cry out in agony and then... something in her melted, her personality became a river of nothingness flowing into a calm gray sea. Inside, she felt warm, soft, oddly pliable in every way. No hate, no love, just a wondrous liberating neutrality which was seamless and whole.

For twenty, thirty minutes, there was nothing. She was blanked, motionless, harmless in every conceivable way.

Then she began to shudder. Fever sweat boiled from her face. Drool hung from the corners of her mouth. Her body twitched with pinpoint seizures and her beautiful green eyes went a glistening pink like fresh mincemeat.

"God is good," Sheikh Sa'ad said to her, wanting to embrace her but secretly repulsed by the thing she now was. "Seek the world of infidels and be fruitful, let what is within multiply..."

The woman did not speak.

She stood up, tearing off her Hijab frantically like a moth escaping a cocoon. She turned and went through the door without a word.

There were five jars left.

And in the corridor outside, five martyrs waiting.

Waiting to be embraced by God.

# DETROIT

## HOLY CROSS HOSPITAL DETOX WARD

**6:31 A.M.**

Johnny Kopok couldn't believe the system.

Couldn't believe what kind of Nazi shitfuck bureaucrats ran things. Now, he wasn't the sharpest knife in the drawer (he would have been the first to admit his brain cut about as good as your average spoon), but even he knew what he'd seen. Knew that something not so wholesome was coming down in this city.

Of course, nobody believed him.

Or so they said.

He didn't give a good goddamn how many times he'd been in this place or what sort of crazy things he'd ranted about those other times, this time it was no hallucination. He wasn't talking about the bugs crawling under his skin (the red spiders were the worst, those bastards really liked to bite) this time. And he wasn't talking about the little men in the stocking caps crawling up the walls. And he sure as hell wasn't talking about the snakes that liked to crawl up his nose sometimes. This was the real thing.

Goddammit, why wouldn't they listen?

*Conspiracy,* Johnny thought. *Conspiracy of silence. I know the truth, so they're locking me down here with all the drunks. Jesus H. Christ.*

They'd picked him up a few days before—even Johnny couldn't be entirely sure when it had been—over near Ford Field maybe. He'd wandered out into traffic. Nearly got run down. Cops picked him up, said he was a menace. Bastards. All he was trying to do was warn people about them worms. He even warned the cops. But they wouldn't listen either.

*Worms, is that it? That's a new one.*

Now he was a prisoner.

God, but a drink would've went down good about now. Not that he needed it, you understand, he wasn't no rummy like the rest of these stoolies. Just a little something to calm his nerves. Some good bourbon, maybe. Or some not-so-good bourbon. Just a taste of medicine, you see. And not that dream juice they'd put him on last night. Christ, he was only just now coming out of it.

They had him in a hospital bed, strapped down, IVs stuck in him every goddamn place. He thought he looked like the inside of a freaking radio.

"Hey, Johnny. How ya feeling?"

Johnny looked up. It was Jimbo, the orderly. Jimbo was ape-ugly, but he was okay. He didn't treat you like a fucking lab animal. That was something.

"Oh, I'm doing," Johnny told him. "When the hell can I get out of here?"

"Up to the doc. You know that."

Jimbo set down a tray of food. "Doc says you can eat, though. They're gonna pull those IVs later today."

"What the hell did I need IVs for?"

Jimbo smiled. Jimbo always smiled. "Your blood chem wasn't too good, Johnny. Doc said your blood cells were having a bit of trouble swimming upstream against the alcohol."

Johnny shook his head. "Prick don't know his own dick from a doorstop."

"How about something to eat, Johnny?" Jimbo said, pulling the lid off the plate. "Scrambled eggs? Bacon? Toast?"

"Suppose you gotta feed me, too?"

"You know the rules."

"How about one hand, Jimbo? Just one hand? I'll clean that plate off, then you can tie me back up. I do anything smart, you got my permission to belt me a good one."

Jimbo shook his head. "Sorry, Johnny. No dice."

"Fuck ya then. I don't want any. My gut's turned to jelly anyway from that shit you been pumping in me."

"Johnny," Jimbo said. "You've been here before. You know how things work, am I right? You don't eat, you'll never leave."

"But I gotta get out of here. I gotta warn people."

"Warn them about what?"

"About the worms."

Jimbo sighed, clasped his hands on his lap. "Johnny. C'mon now. You have to realize that was just a delusion. There were no worms. It was the booze. You got to come up for air every now and then. There are no giant worms in people's mouths. A delusion."

"Delusion my hairy ass, Jimbo. Just remember what you're saying when they stick one down your throat."

"I've got some rounds to make, Johnny. I'm going to leave this food here. I want you to look at it while I'm gone. I want you to keep in mind that unless you eat it you're not going anywhere."

Johnny watched him leave.

They were all the same, these medical types. He'd hoped Jimbo'd be different. He had been last time… or was it the time before? No matter. One way or another, Johnny had to get out of here. If it meant eating that food, then so be it. He'd eat it and keep the worm business to himself. Then they'd let him go. That was the ticket. Because he didn't want to be strapped down when those worms showed up. When they tried to stick one down his throat, he was going to pound their teeth out their assholes.

He looked over at the food. Steam was coming off the eggs. It made him alternately hungry and nauseous. He couldn't remember the last time he'd had a sit-down like that. Usually, he'd grab a sandwich or some crackers. Very often he fished this or that out of a restaurant dumpster. But a meal…Jesus. Most mornings, his breakfast consisted of a soup bowl of whiskey. He had to take it in a bowl because his fingers shook so damn bad first thing in the morning. After that, maybe some dry Corn Flakes. He had to have a little sauce in his belly to hold things down. Lunch and supper weren't much better.

But a meal?

Well, if he wanted out, there really was no choice.

"Hey, Jimbo!" he called out. "Hurry up, will ya? I'm gettin hungry in here! I'm so hungry I could eat the asshole out of a skunk."

# THE COLLECTIVE

## LOCATION UNKNOWN

**10:05 A.M.**

While Mr. Brown waited for the others to arrive, he sipped his tea and thought about the decline of western civilization and his own part in the same. And as he thought about that, he pondered the corridors of power of this great country and how very intricate it all was. If his mind had been any less disciplined, he would have long ago gotten lost in them.

But that wouldn't happen—an architect could always find his way through a house he had built.

*And it is my house,* he thought with some delight. *I stand with the others, but in the end, it is my hand that rocks the cradle of this nation, this very world.*

He finished his tea and picked up his sat phone. So many calls, so many briefings and emails and texts, snippets of intelligence, hearsay and rumor, wiretapping transcripts and video. So much information constantly pouring in. Keeping a steady hand on those that served The Collective directly and a constant eye out for traitors and those that might threaten it.

It was really a matter of control. And one of the most effective—and simplest—methods of control was the management of information. Creating it, exploiting it, withholding it, disseminating it. Creative misdirection was a powerful tool, as were spin and perception management and complete deception. The common man could easily be manipulated like a hungry rat in a box if you gave him too many choices and assailed him with a constant flood of conflicting information—newspapers and magazines, movies and TV, radio and particularly the Internet. Inundate him and he'll beg for someone to sort it out for him, make sense of it, streamline it. Sell him your agenda properly and he'll buy it if for no other reason than to save his sanity.

Basically, that's what politics were—the hard sell, the packaging and presentation. Marketing. It was all a matter of careful social engineering and experimental psychology. Make sure the masses had their bread and circuses and they would give you all the power you desired, they would slave their lives away to support you, defend you even as you stepped on them, and gladly sacrifice their children in wars you created (as long as they were offered in a pretty box of patriotism). You could kick them like dogs and they'd keep coming back for more. That was the idiot beauty of the system and the ma-and-pa drones that supported it.

Mr. Brown called his friend at the NSA. "Hello, Gordon," he said. "And how are things proceeding from your end?"

"Very well. Everything is proceeding according to the scenario. It's moving like clockwork."

"No problems? No troubles? No minor inconveniences?"

"None. The BioGen incident is keeping the country quite busy and we've been disseminating a steady stream of half-truths and utter fiction to our journalistic friends...so the media is doing a lot of our work for us."

Mr. Brown smiled. Of course they were and they always had. Gordon knew many things, but like so many in the military-industrial complex and security services, he did not understand the bigger picture. He did not know that there was no such thing as an independent press in the United States any longer. Ninety-eight percent of the newspapers, magazines, and media outlets were owned by corporations, gigantic monopolistic entities which themselves fawned at the feet of The Collective, whose elite membership included representatives of the Trilateral Commission and the Bilderbergers. And all of whom were disciples of the Skull and Bones society.

"And the installations?" Mr. Brown asked.

"They're online," Parks said, a bit of nervous tension under his words. "We'll begin testing at the end of the week, but I don't foresee any problems."

"That's what we like to hear, Gordon. That's why we selected you to be our friend. You realize the importance of the scenario and that nothing can stand in its way."

As Parks rambled on, again nervously, concerning classified psychotronics and biocybernetics, bioelectromagnetic experimentation and psychotropic weapons, Mr. Brown grinned broadly. Elizabeth Toma was right—he did have a big mouth. But he would serve his purpose as did all. Later, he would be dispensed with.

"All very interesting," Mr. Brown said. "Unfortunately, I must break off this conversation. My granddaughter has a dance recital I don't dare miss."

*He does go on.*

Mr. Brown set the phone down on the conference room table. It was amazing that after so many years now, what The Collective sought was only days away from fruition. This made him grin again. Out there in the streets and cities and towns, tucked away in houses and offices and sweating away in mills and factories, were all the mindless white mice seeking their cheese, following their inborn animal instincts to feed and procreate. And all of them completely ignorant that they were manipulated every day of their pathetic little lives. That their unseen masters created the reality they held so dear. That as they toiled about in their pitiful existences, events were orchestrated, conflicts created, wars engineered, economies destroyed and politicians mass-produced. And all to have the very effect it did have—minds molded, insecurities exploited, tastes and intolerances generated.

*And that is our job*, Mr. Brown thought. *To pull the wires and make the puppets dance in a way that we find both pleasing and constructive. We guide them by harnessing their minds and subverting their intellects. Chaos brings terror and through terror there is control.*

As the philosopher Hegel had said, the State is the absolute reality and man is subordinate to it, finding fulfillment only by serving it and offering his obedience.

Mr. Brown could not have agreed more.

*Reality is what we make it.*

Conflicts were created every day and all of them with predetermined outcomes. If the proper bell was rung, the masses would always salivate. It was known as operant conditioning. Reinforcement of negative stimulus and punishment, must be followed by positive stimulus and reward. In other words, with controlled chaos society can be rendered to a blank slate where it will not only willingly, but *gladly* submit to greater control by its masters. The Freemasons had a legend for it, *"Ordo Ab Chao."* Order out of chaos. With proper technique, desired beliefs can easily be implanted in the common man or woman. Once they are sufficiently disturbed or disassociated by fear or anger or excitement, they're easy to control. They become frightened children begging to be led.

Such a mindset followed the bombing of Pearl Harbor and 9/11. And it would follow BioGenesis as well, in a much more enhanced manner. Exactly as it had been planned, right down to the smallest detail.

For BioGenesis was only the first stage of something much larger known as MINDWORM. The world was about to change for the better.

# CHICAGO, RIVER NORTH

## THE WAREHOUSE

**12:05 P.M.**

They were beautiful.

You had to give them that much. Maybe not beautiful the way a fine horse or a sleek greyhound was beautiful, but aesthetically pleasing on some primitive level. The worms were unmistakably hideous as all huge invertebrates were, but handsome in their very deadly design. Perfect machines of dread.

The Old Man stood there in his biosuit looking down at the thing.

And what did he feel? Was it awe? Was it fear? Was it maybe even something akin to pride? Was he proud that his team had created a creature that was far worse than their wildest expectations? A biologically engineered flatworm that even now was threatening the future of the human race?

Was he proud of that?

No, it was far from pride.

They had set out to create a biological weapon. A parasite that could seriously weaken an enemy and their will to wage war. The weapon would first infest livestock and ultimately the enemy himself. Such a weapon would be the prelude to an invasion. By the time the attacking force was on the ground, the enemy would be weakened beyond even simple resistance. It was a good idea. A sound scenario: it could and would save lives.

And this was what the Old Man told himself.

This was what he had to believe... for if he didn't, then he would have to start thinking about all the blood on his hands. And guilt would do the rest. That simplest of human emotions would destroy him day by day, piece by piece.

And there wasn't time for that.

*Maybe I am proud. I headed a team that created the perfect weapon. So goddamn good even we can't stop it.*

He moved slowly through the laboratory. Everything was sterile, white, utilitarian. BSL-4 Containment was like that. Not so much as a crust of bread or a dust bunny got into this area. Negative air pressure kept anything within from getting out. The Old Man wound his way past the electron microscope and the spotless, gleaming shelves of instruments and chemicals.

The specimen had to go back in the freezer.

It probably wasn't a good idea to leave it out in the warmth too long. No one knew for sure if the worms could survive freezing and no one wanted to find out. Not now, anyway. Maybe later when there was time for such trivialities.

*So, put it back then.*

But he couldn't. Like a collector with a new, rare coin, he just wanted to look at it.

He set the container on the table.

It was a Lucite specimen jar with a pressurized lid. Even if the worm did wake up, it wasn't going anywhere. The Old Man knew he was violating the protocol that he himself had drafted. But there was no one around. And, if there was, they wouldn't question him.

The worm was coiled up like a snake in the jar, floating sluggishly in a brine of preservative. Bloated, white as cream, it didn't look like much. Stretched end to end, it might've been four feet. Much smaller than some. Sexually mature. It was sectioned like a slice of onion, each section possessing a set of curled hooks that it clung to the intestinal walls of its host with.

Fascinating.

It was the only word that seemed to fit the things.

*Fascinating.*

The Old Man stood there, staring through the Plexiglas faceplate of his hood. He thought for a moment the thing had moved. But it had to be dead. It was stored at below freezing. The only reason it didn't freeze solid was because of the alcohol-based solution in the jar. And there was no way it could survive that sort of toxic immersion.

Wait.

He'd seen it again. One of the segments had...shuddered. He supposed it was possible there was still some low-grade neurological activity in it. The idea seemed unlikely, but it was possible with a flatworm. They didn't have brains as such, but collections of nerve cells that evolutionary biologists thought were the forerunners of brains.

It moved again.

Not just a segment this time, but the entire worm.

It turned in the fluid, uncoiled, its tail end brushing the glass. The Old Man could see its head now. Eyeless, colorless, like some ghastly flower bulb. It had two bisecting slits for a mouth.

*It can't possibly be alive.*

The very idea was insane, of course. But he could almost feel the life in the thing—an appalling, primeval vitality that was unnamable, unbelievable, and maybe even unholy. He brought his face closer to the jar, staring, connecting with the thing like he was part of it, part of its life cycle. A warm, dull sensation settled into the back of his brain. It was not unpleasant. Calming, gentle...like soft stroking fingers. Something a baby might feel as it was held by its mother. He wondered what it would be like to feel the worm his hands, coiling in his palm, sliding through his fingers, caressing his cheek as it moved towards his mouth. The very idea gave him a weird, exotic, erotic sort of thrill. *The worm...dear God, the worm in my hands...touching it, feeling it.* It really wasn't ugly when you got to know it. It was beautiful. Slender, smooth, almost poetic in its convolutions. Something that demanded to be touched, felt, handled. The tactile attraction was almost addictive in its pull.

*I want to feel it...to slide my fingers along its pale obscene length—*

"No, damn you," the Old Man said suddenly, startling even himself. "It won't be that easy, you sonofabitch."

He put it back in the freezer. Put it back to sleep.

So, that was how it worked.

The thing had mutated beyond anything they could have imagined. It had developed some bastard form of mesmerism. Not unknown in the animal world, but unprecedented in the lower invertebrates. By God, was such a thing possible? He thought of those skinheads in Louisville. Gentle as lambs to a man and woman, the reports were saying. And was that it? Was that what mankind was to become? Host organisms devoid of free thought and independent action?

That's what the worms had mutated into: puppet masters.

It put a new and deadly spin on everything.

They had to work faster now.

*Dear Lord, what have I set loose upon the face of your creation?*

# DETROIT, 6 MILE ROAD

## WOODWARD AND CASS

**6:40 P.M.**

Her name was Dee Dee Rubelle.

That was not her real name, of course, but when you were firmly ensconced in the entertainment world as she was, you had to have a stage name. Dee Dee was pushing forty and getting that wizened, alley cat shuffle to her prostitutes often got after too many lean years in the dirty streets. Dee Dee had seen some good times, but not in the past ten years. She'd started hooking to support her junk habit and the more junk she did, the more hooking she had to do. The more you did, the more you had to do.

Once upon a time she'd been an attractive young woman. Her Johns used to tell her she looked just like Pam Grier. They used to ask for her by name. But the years had passed and now she was looking less like Pam Grier and more like an emaciated Rosie Greer. Starting out, she'd told herself it was just for a time, that when her manager got her some good-paying singing gigs, the whoring was done.

But that time had never come.

Oh, her manager had once set her up with some record execs... but they were more interested in what they could put into her mouth rather than what came out of it. She guessed her manager—Joey Lips—was nothing but a pimp like everyone said.

But at least then she'd had a pimp.

Now even those shitballs wouldn't touch her. She was on her own and had been for six years. Tonight, she was working a stretch of sidewalk with a few other independents. Sometimes, it was a good place.

Sometimes it wasn't.

One by one the other girls had been picked up and now it was just Dee Dee.

She could've moved, maybe. But she knew better than that. The prime areas were worked by hookers who belonged to some pimp's stable. If she were to try and muscle into any of those areas, she'd probably get beat-up. If not something worse.

But she had to do something soon; the pain was getting bad. She needed a taste. Her head was starting to ache something awful, like a vise was turning just behind her eyes, squeezing, squeezing. And the cramps...oh Christ...she could feel them starting to work at her insides, pulling, chewing, tearing. She wiped a dew of sweat from her face, flashing plenty of leg and ass at every car that passed.

Bastards would slow, but then move on.

*They want the young stuff down there,* Dee Dee told herself. *All that luscious sweet and sassy pussy that hadn't yet seen twenty. You work it, girls, you just work it. Give you ten years or fifteen, you'll know the taste of pain and desperation once your looks are gone and the tracks are etched into your arms and you've been pumped so full of cream your brain ain't much but sponge cake.*

Shit.

She turned just as someone came walking up the sidewalk. It was Squabs. Squabs was her man. Only Squabs was kind of hunched over, walking like some old man.

"Squabs?" Dee Dee said. "That you?"

"Yeah," he grunted and fell against the building next to her. "How...how you doin', baby? How...oh shit...motherfucker..."

"You don't look so good, Squabs."

"Feel like shit, girl." He was clutching his belly, his black face contorted in a mask of agony. "Got a bug or somethin'...last couple days...my guts hurt... fuck..."

"You need some rest, baby," Dee Dee told him, keeping her distance. There was something about him she just didn't like. He smelled... funny. A strange sort of hot, yeasty smell was wafting off him in feverish waves. It was gagging. "You look like I feel."

"I ain't...got none, girl, if that's what yer thinking."

"Just a little...maybe a little?"

Squabs was doubled over now, shaking his head. "Nothin'. Tripper, man, Tripper got busted. Gonna be dry for a while."

Dee Dee hugged herself with trembling fingers. "Shit, baby, I need a taste. I'm feelin' real bad, you know? I'm hurtin' real bad..."

"You and me both...oh shit, shit," Squabs groaned, going down on his knees. His body shook with dry heaves for a moment, then it abated, leaving him crouching there, his teeth chattering violently, saliva dangling from his lips. "Somethin' goin' around... somethin'...some bug... lots of motherfuckers got it... hope you don't get it..."

Dee Dee helped him shakily to his feet. His flesh was hot and damp. She felt bad for him, real bad. The human part of her that wasn't completely dead felt pity. But that part was minute, overshadowed by the need which was huge and glaring and sharp-tooth hungry.

"Better get yourself to bed, baby," she told him. "You know anywhere I can get somethin'? A name, somewhere. I don't care. I gotta have somethin'."

But Squabs had found his feet and staggered off, his sickness in tow.

Oh, shit, oh fuck.

The pain was rising up now, burning fire-hot in her veins. It was like every cell in her body was crying out, needing, wanting. She had to get something, some way, somehow...

A black Chevy van rolled to a stop at the curb.

The window unrolled. Some bald white guy was staring at her. Dee Dee didn't like him right away. Something just plain wrong about him. His eyes were black and empty. They gleamed like glass.

"Get in," he said. No emotion. No attempt at it.

Dee Dee looked up and down the street. "It'll cost you."

"Yes," he said. "Get in."

Knowing somehow she was making a big mistake, Dee Dee got into the back. There was another guy back there. Another dude with skin that was fish-belly white...pasty, dry as death.

The van rolled down the street, found an alley, turned in.

"What you boys like tonight? You want everything? You want..."

Her old spiel evaporated on her lips. The car smelled like Squabs had, only worse, a hundred times worse. It was like a burning, gaseous envelope in the car.

"I want you to put something in your mouth," the guy next to her said.

His friend in the front seat just sat there quietly, motionless as a dime store dummy.

"Is that what you want, baby? You want something sucked?" Dee Dee managed, though her heart was not in it. But the money. If she got the money...maybe, somewhere, somehow she could get a taste. "I'll suck you so good, baby, you'll die and go to heaven. Show me that cock. Show me what I love."

It was dark in the back of the van, Dee Dee couldn't see a thing. Then again, she didn't need to.

She reached for the man's crotch, but he batted her hand away. Instead, he grabbed a handful of hair and led her down to it. And that was okay. Lots of guys liked it that way. Dee Dee had done it more times than maybe she'd ever breathed.

She could see something glistening.

His cock? Why was it so wet?

And that smell...that dirty, dank smell was gone, replaced by something sweet like the juicy pulp of peaches and fresh-running sap, a cloying odor that filled her mouth with water and made her ache inside with something like a cellular hunger.

Then her head was pressed down, and she felt something cold, wet, and rubbery pressed to her lips and then it was in her mouth, gagging her, sliding down her throat, too thick, too long...

She started to fight, to squirm, but hands held her in place. Her fingers found the guy's balls. And that's when she realized it wasn't his cock suffocating her at all. What was in her mouth and feeding down her throat was coming out of a ragged hole in the guy's belly.

But by then, she was no longer fighting.

She opened her mouth as wide as it would go, feeling the worm filling her with sinuous, flexing contractions that brought a shuddering erotic pleasure.

And then...and then, like being in a dream. Like finding a cloud and drifting on it, hitching a ride into distant candy cane fields, nothing but sweetness in her mouth and up her nose, oozing in through her pores, owning her and becoming her. One minute she was on those cold, barren streets hungering for the needle and the next, she was out of her skin. She shed it like a snake, left her bones behind and rose up higher and higher like petals on the wind, ascending into a stream of gushing pheromonal warmth where she was not only safe, but belonged.

And this was how, as her sanity, life, and self-respect dangled by a dirty thread, Dee Dee Rubelle finally realized her purpose on the planet.

# CHICAGO

## THE LOOP

**7:12 P.M.**

Gabe Hebberman sat in his office in the Theater District, the wheels of his mind spinning in a dozen unpleasant directions. On his desk before him was a blank pad of paper, the top sheet nearly filled with doodling and scratchings. The name Shawna was written a dozen times. Underlined. Circled. Followed by countless question marks and exclamation points. He'd been at it for several days now and still, he was no closer.

No closer at all.

It was a busy day. Writer's meetings. Meetings with the circulation manager, the foreign distribution manager, art directors, design people, the production director. It went on and on. The problem of Shawna Geddes had arrived at a most inopportune time: the weekly deadline.

After a drawn-out lunch with the controller and the accounting manager, Gabe told his secretary to cancel everything. A woman's life was possibly at stake and there were other people who could do what needed to be done. It was what he paid them for.

He resumed his search for Shawna Geddes.

He started with the Hall of Records, the local hospitals, and the Social Security Administration. Nothing. He moved on to the DMV, his contacts at the IRS and the IDES. Still nothing. He called Columbia University, talked with their alumni director. There was no record of a Shawna Geddes. He double checked that on their web site. More nothing. Finally, he called the Chicago *Tribune*. He gave the personnel director a line about hiring a Shawna Geddes, a former employee of theirs. There was no record of her. And that was funny, the director said, because she knew Shawna. Odd. Gabe's parting shot was to call the Metro Police. He had a contact there. A good one. There were no outstanding warrants on a Shawna Geddes. Gabe even had his contact search the police database at a state, municipal, and even federal level. No good. Beginning to feel more than a little paranoid himself, Gabe inquired into Shawna's landlady. Yes, the woman had been murdered. An investigation had begun. And Harry Niles? Anything on him? Yes, he was wanted for eluding police on a standard traffic stop. No assault involved.

So Harry still existed, but not Harry's friend.

On a hunch, Gabe called a friend at the FBI. He searched their database. Nope, nada on old Shawny. That girl just did not exist. Not anywhere. Non-person from the word go.

It was scary.

Unless she was using an alias or was just plain bullshitting him about who and what she was, they had a real problem here. Whoever was after her was goddamn thorough. So thorough it was scary.

Gabe mulled it over in his mind for the thousandth time.

Harry was right about it not being any organized crime family or upper echelon drug gang. Even they couldn't pull off something like this. This took real power, complete and omnipotent power. The people behind this had resources that were positively staggering.

Unless, of course, this was all a load of shit.

But Gabe didn't believe that. Not for a minute.

Unless Shawna Geddes was the greatest actress since Meryl Streep and Harry was in on it, too, then this was a major conspiracy. Something so black and ugly it literally defied the imagination.

But who had such power?

The clue, as Harry had indicated, were the men in the protective suits. They had to be feds or military. Shawna had seen something so secretive they were willing to kill to keep it that way.

But what?

What was happening here?

# RICHMOND, VIRGINIA

## CBT CORPORATE HEADQUARTERS

**7:17 P.M.**

What bothered Elizabeth was that there were things going on that she could not adequately fathom. She did not like not knowing. Good intelligence had served her well for many years and without it, she felt blind. It was like being in a pitch black room, fumbling about for the light switch or the door that would lead out. It made her nervous. It made her angry. It made her want to lash out and mainly because she was afraid.

On the desk before her was a classified intelligence briefing from 3Eye, or Third Eye technically, which was the security arm of CBT. They spent the majority of their time and resources spying on those who spied on CBT—everyone from the FBI to the CIA to the DoD—and conducting multileveled corporate espionage, particularly against other biotech companies, here and abroad.

The document was brief, simply a detailed log of the movements of Gordon Parks of the NSA. He was in bed with The Collective, too. As far as Elizabeth knew, he was the only one beside herself (and The Collective) that knew that the BioGenesis outbreak in the U.S. had been carefully planned. Forget DCI Pershing and the rest of the conspirators, they were being played by expert hands, reaching for some Machiavellian dream of power that would be snatched from them in the eleventh hour.

They had no idea of the bigger picture.

Elizabeth herself knew about the BioGenesis end of things and Pershing's upcoming coup, but not what happened beyond that. What bothered her was the fear that she was out in the cold, no longer a player but another hand puppet being carefully worked.

What if Gordon Parks knew? What if The Collective had brought him in? What if he knew the big picture?

*That would mean I'm not to be trusted. That would mean that I will be cast aside or disposed with completely once I've served my purpose.*

In the intelligence world, she knew, very few ever knew what was REALLY going on. The majority of agents, operatives, bureaucrats, and players were in the dark. Things were compartmentalized. Everyone had a piece of the pie. They knew a little about what was going on, but only enough so that they could do their jobs properly. Only the elite received full disclosure and saw the big picture.

For a long time now, Elizabeth had been one of them. Many years before, she had been a biophysicist at CBT who had ruthlessly clawed her way to the upper echelon of the synthetics division. Her ambition was legendary. As a scientist, she was competent; as a player, a major contender with godlike ambitions. She had risen to the top of the division via subterfuge and blackmail, by taking credit for work that wasn't her own and hacking her way into the computers of more brilliant biologists and stealing their work. And when that didn't work, she seduced them, both male and female, using her looks when all else failed. But certainly never above such a thing.

*You would have crawled through shit for a bump in pay and prestige*, she later chastised herself.

And it was in this way that she had become CEO of Congdon BioTech, climbing over the warm bodies of friends and trusted associates in her ascent. Sooner or later, she would have been forced out. But fate interceded. One day she got a phone call from a man she would come to know as Mr. Brown.

"We've been watching your every move with breathless excitement," he told her.

"And who is we?"

"We are your friends. You must never forget that. We've been very impressed with your activities. Rarely do we find someone with such innate predatory skills. You, my dear, are immoral, unethical, and wholly unscrupulous," said Mr. Brown. "You are a rare beast. One with looks, brains, and very sharp teeth. You are exactly what we look for in an executive."

"Okay, that's enough. I'm hanging up now."

Mr. Brown tittered. "Oh really, Elizabeth, enough pretense. Your skin is hardly that thin. You've been called everything from a Judas to a thief to a whore to a fanged cunt by those you've used and abused. You would drink my urine if it would better your position and we both know it."

That made her grit her teeth, but she dispensed with that because she sensed...opportunity. "What do you want?"

"I want you. *We* want you. If you hang up on me, I won't call back. But if you stay on the line and do exactly as I say, within one year you'll be CEO of Congdon." He was silent for a few moments. "I don't jest, my dear. We've been grooming you for the position. You're a marvelously oily, unprincipled little minx. The sort of cunning alley cat we can use. Do as I say and you will rise effortlessly to the top. Refuse me, and you'll be facing charges of extortion, illegal wiretapping, money laundering, and industrial espionage. You will spend a minimum of thirty years in prison and everything that you've worked for will be taken from you and your personal assets will become property of the federal government."

Mr. Brown had her and she knew it. Even without seeing the evidence of her guilt or the file that they had no doubt compiled on her, she knew she was busted. There was something omnipotent in his voice that you didn't dare argue or barter with.

"What do I have to do?"

He told her in some detail. She didn't pretend to be offended by the devious, cold-blooded details of it or his assessment of her humanity (or lack of the same). She was more than capable of doing what he suggested. In fact, she would have no doubt followed much of the same path he laid out.

"Are you with us then?" he asked.

She sighed. "Yes. Though I can't help thinking I just sold my soul."

He tittered again. "Really, Elizabeth. You can't sell something you never had."

Now here she was these many years later, worrying, wondering from her throne of power if she was indeed a player or just another pawn in motion. If BioGenesis and the coup was just part of something much more insidious and terrible, then what was the big picture? Where was it all heading and what would it mean for her and CBT? And, more importantly, the country itself?

# CHICAGO, NORTH SHORE

## KENILWORTH

**7:31 P.M.**

After he got off the phone with Gabe, Harry felt a sickness within him spread until it filled his belly. Gabe had pretty much gone through the same steps that Shawna and he had, save with a bit more subtlety and the added advantage of contacts with Metro Police and the FBI. But in the end it all came down to the same thing: Shawna Geddes had been erased and she would be physically removed when the opportunity presented itself. She had two choices, the way Harry saw it. She could let them get her or she could go underground like some 1960s radical.

Neither of which was remotely palatable.

As for himself, the future was not much brighter. There was a warrant on him for fleeing and eluding. No mention of assault. What it came down to was that they were waiting for him. When he showed at his apartment or work or any other place he frequented, they would arrest him. And through him, they would get to Shawna.

Staying here put Gabe in incredible danger. It was only a matter of time before they put two and two together and realized he was hiding out at his employer's house.

It was time to run.

Shawna was sitting in the den on a recliner, legs pulled up, arms encircling them.

"Well?" she said.

He shook his head. "You're gone. I'm wanted." He paused, sat down beside her. "It's only a matter of time before they erase me, too. It's inevitable."

Shawna lit a cigarette, her haunted eyes staring out at him from clouds of blue-white smoke that rose lazily into the air. "I guess I'm all done. There's no way out of this. I should simply let them find me and get it over with. How fast and how far can I hope to run?"

And it was in her eyes as she spoke: her life. It danced there uneasily for a moment or two—music and laughter, desperation and misery, dating rich men in hopes of an easy, fat future and every time watching it all crash down around her and she would pick up the pieces, start again, fight and scramble and scavenge, looking for a fat vein to leech onto that would give her the sort of life she thought she deserved but was never hers in the first place. He saw that and then he saw the absence of the same: an ugliness, a dark despair, a waiting silence winding out into shadow.

"No," he said to her, rising to her pain like a fish coming up at night to feed. "No, you silly twit. That's exactly what you don't do. You don't give in and you don't give up."

"But—"

"But nothing. We hide out, we wait for our time because it's coming. And when it comes, we pounce. We spill this story and when we do, when our names are linked, they won't dare lay a hand on us."

"And until then?"

"We go underground and we watch from the shadows," he told her. "Get your things. We're getting the hell out of here soon as it's dark."

# LOUISVILLE, KENTUCKY

## UNIVERSITY HOSPITAL

**7:42 P.M.**

When Rachel Lofquist came back to the ward after her lunch break, it was filled with mulling bodies: men in black nylon jackets, granite-faced, eyes like cold mud. She guessed there were thirty or forty of them. Amongst them were her nurses, Dr. Conlay and Dr. Rich, a few security guards.

"What exactly is going on here?" she asked.

Dr. Conlay opened his mouth to speak and one of the men stepped in front of him. "We're here for the individuals from the Shawnee Park location," he told her in the typical dull monotone favored by cops and federal agents. "They will be taken to an alternate location for treatment."

Rachel felt her blood rise. "First off there is protocol. You do not come barging in on my ward—"

"We have the authority, ma'am."

He and two other men standing at her side flashed laminated IDs at her: the Department of Homeland Security and the Center for Disease Control. That stopped her. She was about to read him out and let him know goddamn well that here in the quarantine ward, she was the nurse practitioner and she was lord and commander of all who passed through her realm...but the CDC? Homeland Security? What the hell did they want with those skinhead turd monkeys?

"Somebody should call Dr. Towers," she said then, referring to the chief of staff.

But the CDC man handed her a court order signed by not only Towers, but Henley, the chief administrator, and the governor of Kentucky of all things. The documentation was there and even Rachel knew she couldn't stand up against it. Lord and commander had now been quite thoroughly emasculated.

She was reduced to a wallflower like the others, just looking for a yellow sunny patch to melt into.

"Can you just tell me what this is about?" she finally asked.

"It's about moving these contaminated individuals to an alternate medical facility, ma'am."

Rachel swallowed. "No shit. I got that part. And where might that be?"

"I am not authorized to divulge that. Sorry."

Which was about all she was going to get and she knew it. The men went to work immediately. They wore plastic gloves and face shields. They moved into the rooms and when Rachel went in there to supervise she was ushered with the rest of the staff into the waiting room. A thick-necked goon with the noticeable bulge of a firearm beneath his coat stood in the door so they could not leave.

"This won't take long," he promised her.

One of her nurses—Jenny Johnson—took out her cell and the goon shook his head. "No cell phones, please. If you do not comply I will be forced to take it from you."

"You can't do that!" Jenny said. "I'm an American citizen! I have rights!"

Rachel almost laughed. Wasn't that the last pathetic gasp of all Americans who suddenly realized that those they put into power with a simple mindless pull of a voting machine lever had now pissed all over those aforementioned rights they were deputized to protect? Poor Jenny. She was good-hearted, simple-minded, had about as much working gray matter as a Hostess cupcake. Life was a romantic comedy to her, some vacuous Oprah-approved shitboiler of mediocrity starring Julia Roberts. The government will never violate my civil rights and there's a silver lining behind every cloud, an angel sitting on every shoulder and a chicken in every pot. Hopelessly naïve, she just couldn't accept any of it, her brain a stew of mush jumping from one weak Hollywood-inspired pop culture reference to the next.

"I have complete authorization under the Homeland Security Act," the goon informed her. "If you resist, you can be detained for an indefinite period of time and prosecuted."

Jenny made a sobbing sound. Today just wasn't puppy dogs and butterflies and Rom-coms, that was for sure.

Rachel sat there by Dr. Rich, astonished, shocked, dismayed...too many emotions to properly categorize. It was like some scene out of a movie only no one had given her a script. So this was Homeland Security in action, eh? Nice. Like Berlin in 1938.

"They just came charging in and took over the place," Rich said. "I don't know what the hell this is about and they won't say."

"Why the skinheads?"

That was the question, of course. Nobody knew for sure what the nature of their condition was. Their white cell counts were through the roof and they were comatose. There was no indication of anything else.

"They must have some sort of infectious disease," Jenny said.

"Do you think?" someone else said.

As they bickered and the goon at the door looked noncommittal in all aspects, Dr. Rich whispered, "We just got the first series of scans back on them."

"And?" Rachel said.

Rich wiped a few lone beads of sweat from his brow. "They all have what appears to be some sort of parasite in them. I can't—"

"What the hell are they doing?" Dr. Conlay said, standing up and pointing beyond the goon at the door. "Those men and women are alive!"

But that didn't seem to matter. The CDC/DHS team was sliding them into rubberized body bags and zipping them shut. One after the other, the bags were carried down the corridor, some wheeled on gurneys.

Now everyone in the waiting room was on their feet and the goon looked seriously outnumbered. His hand crept to the gun under his coat with a subtle easy motion and removed it. "Please, everyone, remained seated. Those individuals are infected and must be removed," he explained. "We'll detain you no longer than necessary."

"Infected with what?" Jenny wanted to know.

And Rachel thought: *Yes, that was a good one: infected with WHAT? What sort of infection would bring these greasy shadow warriors out of their reptilian nests? Probably something more than the common cold. And what did that say? Were they talking PLAGUE here? Some new bug? Bioterrorism? Fucking Ebola?*

She was probably the only one not demanding answers.

She was watching the skinheads being removed, the CDC/DHS teams moving very quickly, very efficiently, without a word. And no doubt so they could accomplish this little atrocity before the media arrived and this horror show was on every cable news network in the land (sandwiched conveniently between corporate propaganda for Geico and the latest superhero tripe from Hollywood as the dumbing down of the country rolled on and on).

"This is outrageous!" Rachel finally cried out. "Those people will suffocate in those damn things! DO YOU HEAR ME? DO YOU HEAR WHAT I'M SAYING, YOU FUCKING APE?"

"Ma'am, I—"

But he never quite finished that for from the ward came the sound of first one scream and then another.

Things were starting to happen.

# WASHINGTON D.C.

## THE WHITE HOUSE

**8:35 P.M.**

Charles VanderMissen was fingering the burn scars on his neck and thinking about his family. Whenever he was nervous, upset, or stressed (something commonplace in his position, particularly of late), his fingers sought the old scar tissue. Some people stroked their chins, others fooled with their hair, still others drummed their fingers. VanderMissen went after the scars. Rubbed them, traced them with his fingertips, kneaded them. Their intricate convolutions pleased his sense of touch. Soothed him somehow.

For he was a very nervous man.

He'd been in the frying pan many times. Been in the shit so deep he'd had to tread it just to keep breathing. But never, never, had he known anything like this. He thought of other problems the country had waded through. Some of these shitstorms had names familiar to all—Watergate, Blackwater, Iran–Contra—but still more had no names at all save ambiguous operational titles and case numbers—assassinations, bombings, kidnappings, military coups, conspiracies ranging from the complex to the childishly simple. Many of which, in his position or former positions, he'd been involved in or knew about.

But always under the table.

Always black bag jobs.

Whether it was political subversion or a black budget genetics program, it was always handled under the table. Safer that way. Politically, morally. The American public and its media watchdogs were very carefully controlled. Their consumption of the truth was strictly monitored. Entire fictional scenarios were developed to divert attention from sensitive issues. They were knitted together from truth and lie, loaded with red herrings in order to direct prying eyes in other, less compromising directions. The puppet masters were the military/industrial/intelligence complexes of the United States and a host of other nations. The media and the public's hunger for conspiracy in all forms led to the creation of countless imaginary subversions. These elaborate lies were spoon-fed to the curious, the nosy. Very often, the people involved actually thought they were reporting the truth, thought they were caught in some vortex of governmental intrigue. But it was all engineered. And only those at the very top knew what was real and what was not. Sometimes unfortunate situations were exploited for the press: Navy ships were bombed; Presidents had sex with pages in the Oval Office; terrorists kidnapped civilians. And, although there was a basis of truth to most of these, they were blown completely out of proportion by a media starving for news. These were the best kind, because, once begun, they gained momentum, fed by half-truths, public imagination, and ruthless competition between the networks that necessitated elaboration of facts to hold viewers, to capture markets and percentiles.

And at the top, as always, the surface-feeders, the apex predators, the puppet master executives like VanderMissen himself and their fanatical need for perception management.

VanderMissen knew a lot.

He could have told you that very often volatile political situations were orchestrated in certain directions. The Vietnam War, for instance, on the surface appeared to have been waged to halt the spread of communism and had, as its foundation the so-called Domino Theory in which if one Southeastern Asian country fell, the others wouldn't be far behind. But that was bullshit. Posturing. Double-talk. The real reason America (and other NATO countries) were involved in Vietnam was to test and deploy new weapons systems and combat strategies in real world scenarios. A preparation for the Soviet Bloc/NATO war which never came to be. The Gulf War had very little to do with the military incursion of Iraq into Kuwait. The bottom line was oil. Oil reserves had to protected and the Middle East as a whole had to be shown the overwhelming devastation that NATO (and particularly America) could rain down on them. Two important goals were reached simultaneously. The Iraq War came down to the same thing: America selling its soul for crude oil.

And behind it all, once again as always, the military/industrial/intelligence complex and its web of deceit, half-truths, and out and out lies.

The mega-corporations, the multinationals, each with staggering financial resources, controlled the politicians who controlled the military and intelligence agencies. Behind it all, was money. Or usually. If, say, a certain African country had a wealth of titanium, nickel, or uranium ores, but said country, due to an unstable political environment, refused to do business with an excessively powerful multinational, then action was taken. With billions of dollars in the balance, nothing was seen as too excessive. The CIA, for example, bowing to pressure from certain politicians (themselves owned by said corporation), would hire a mercenary army usually through a second or third party to invade and usurp the countries' leaders and military. The mercs themselves never know whom it was they really worked for. And they were not supposed to. If, by some crazy coincidence they did find out, then maybe the planes or helicopters extricating them from the warzone would mysteriously explode in transit.

Because cleanup and damage control is a major factor in any clandestine operation.

That's why very few involved ever knew who it was they really worked for.

And if they found out... they had to be removed, silenced. Their names would appear on the Disposition Matrix, the kill list of enemies of the United States.

When a project like BioGen, successful or unsuccessful, is completed, all loose ends have to be tied up. And in BioGen's case where it was necessary to launch a major cleanup—the eradication of disease vectors to avoid a major infestation—then the cleaners themselves had to be sterilized at operations' end.

There were special men for such tasks.

Spread on VanderMissen's desk was the file of one such man.

Thomas Malcolm Quillan.

Tommy Quillan was an ex-British SAS terrorist hunter and contract mercenary recruited by CIA/SAC for their own wet work programs following 9/11. Though his specialty was bagging Middle Eastern extremists and disrupting their networks via assassination, sabotage, and ruthless subterfuge, the Company had sent him after enemy agents, drug kingpins, traitors, politicians and industrialists. He was a professional, an expert that left no loose ends dangling.

But VanderMissen did not like him.

Nobody really did.

Men like him were necessary, but no one wanted to admit that they paid the salary of psychotics like Tommy Quillan. Other cleaners, other assassins, very often had tenuous moral codes they would cling to like refusing to kill children, but not Quillan.

His motto was simple: Anyone, Anytime, Anywhere.

Though DCI Pershing would never admit it, Quillan was being brought in for a very select purpose: to sterilize the ERT cleanup crews following the eradication of disease vectors. When Quillan was finished, BioGen and everything to do with it would be a secret even the men in power would only whisper amongst themselves. Because if they started whispering it other places, then Tommy Quillan would find them. Somehow. Someway. He always did.

Tommy Quillan loved to kill.

Even when he wasn't being paid, he was still killing, torturing and murdering for the love of it. He could have been arrested in two dozen countries for unsolved serial murders. None of which had anything to with politics or military intelligence. You might send him into country A to liquidate a terrorist cell, but chances were he'd do a few civilians out of amusement. That's why, between important missions, he was kept in third world hellholes where he could kill at will.

And now, he was coming to the States.

There was no doubt in VanderMissen's mind that Pershing would be using him for damage control, to eliminate any tongues that might wag, but did it end there? He wasn't so sure. He had the most awful feeling that Pershing was up to something, taking advantage of an ugly situation, and to those ends he was unleashing a monster.

# LOUISVILLE, KENTUCKY

## UNIVERSITY HOSPITAL

**9:19 P.M.**

The Biological Containment Team came through the fire door into the quarantine ward and it was worse than they thought. One of the infected was waiting for them, a bald dude whose face was so white that his pink-hued eyes looked like blazing rubies in comparison. Compton thought he had vomited out his intestines because there was a slimy white cord hanging from his mouth only it was a worm and it was twitching, coiling obscenely. The guy held its segmented length in his hands like a pet snake.

He was petting it.

"Do it!" came a voice over Compton's helmet intercom. "Burn him! C'MON, COMPTON! DO IT!"

Compton stood there as the guy, quite casually, walked over to him. The other members of the BCT—Tanney, Barks, Quinn—bunched together nervously while Captain McCardle screamed at Compton.

Shit.

"BURN HIM!"

Swallowing, Compton squeezed the trigger on his flamethrower and a tongue of fire shot out, engulfing the man and his parasite. He thrashed around, slammed into the wall, and hit the floor with very little ceremony where he continued to burn and pop, letting off acrid plumes of black smoke.

There were bodies everywhere: the skinheads, the CDC/DHS team that had come to take them away, hospital workers. They were piled together in the corridor, all tangled together in a loose-limbed heap like mating spiders. Some of them were dead, torn wide open by their parasites, others were not—eyes glazed, faces bleached, but moving...sliding around in a great fleshy reptilian mass, the dead ones carried along with them.

"What the hell are they doing?" Quinn asked.

Good question, but nobody wanted to field it.

Nobody except old hard-ass Captain McCardle. He waltzed right over there, absolutely fearless, grabbed some woman by the ankle and dragged her from the heap. She separated from the others with a loud, wet smacking sort of sound as if she was suctioned to them. And maybe she was at that because long snotty streamers of some transparent material attached her to the mass.

McCardle dragged her about four feet.

She did not fight against him or even seem to know that he was there. When he released her, she crawled right back, making some weird sort of cooing sound that went right up Compton's spine.

"Clusterfuck," McCardle said.

Compton and the others kept their distance.

Even with his protective helmet on, the assorted air filters that kept out the bad stuff, he could still smell the burning body. Worse than that, he could smell those tangling, writhing bodies that stank of piss and shit, blood and vomit, and something worse like grapes fermented not to wine but a rotten, sharp-smelling mush.

"Let's get this done," McCardle said.

The BCT inched forward.

They hadn't made it ten feet into the corridor, carefully edging towards the bodies, when something came looping down at them from above. It made a wet rubbery sound and slapped against Tanney's helmet...its hooks scraping against the face shield. He let out a choking, guttural bark and went on his ass.

Barks knocked the questing worm aside and promptly tripped over Tanney, something which would have been most comical at any other time and in any other situation.

"GET THE FUCK OUT OF THE WAY!" McCardle snapped, elbowing Compton aside.

Quinn opened up, casting fire in every which direction. It hit the walls, the floor, rose up in billowing flames and churning clouds of smoke. Whether he got the worm or not was anyone's guess and it didn't honestly matter because at that very moment the worms were everywhere—they were hanging from the ceiling like gauzy ribbons of mist, erupting from the bodies like missiles from silos, squirming on the floor in tangled networks like tree roots.

Suddenly, they were everywhere.

Massing.

Slithering.

Compton heard a voice in his head say, *this is where things go from bad to worse,* as he backpedaled, trying to avoid the flames, the mass of bodies that were moving with rhythmic pulsations, the reaching convolutions of parasitic worms. Many were small, no more than a few feet in length, and some considerably smaller, but others were gargantuan—eight, ten, and fifteen feet at least—inching forward like caterpillars, a clear slime draining from their pulsing white segments, hooks scraping on the tiles. They had head-like bulbs ringed by trembling stinging spines the size of pencils. The bulbs opened to reveal candy-pink mouthparts and great hooklike teeth that were meant to grab and never let go.

One of them dropped from the ceiling, winding itself around Quinn's helmet like some massive undulating earthworm, its mouth fixing itself to his face shield, suckering itself there with a moist sound like a slobbering kiss. He tried to knock it free but it clung tenaciously as he stumbled around. It kept searching for a point of entry, detaching its mouth and suckering to new spots on the face shield. Over the helmet intercoms, they could all hear him screaming, crying out for help.

McCardle torched three or four worms crawling in his direction and then took hold of the pulsating worm on Quinn's helmet with his gloved hands. Its flesh was unbelievably slippery like petroleum jelly and he couldn't seem to get a grip. When he succeeded in seizing on a segment and began pulling on it, its hooks tore great gaping holes in Quinn's biohazard suit. The segments bulged, swelling like straining musculature...and then the thing burst, literally exploding with a great gush of slime and gray ooze, hundreds of glistening pearl-white orbs that must have been eggs.

Another worm made a mewling sort of cry that was dry and screeching and enraged-sounding.

Compton burned five or six of them moving in his direction and then a shadow fell across his face shield as one of them dropped on him. He fought wildly with it, gripping its looping form in his gloved fists as it squealed and whipped, a boneless slithery thing that was almost impossible to get a hold of.

Its smell came through his air filter—hot and feverish like green meat and spilled blood, sharp and evil. As he wrestled with it, that stench seem to fill his head, making his stomach roll, making him gag...and then, it shifted. It was not rot and soft decaying things, but a cloying sweetness that nearly drove him to his knees. For one insane moment it reminded him of Halloween...of buckets of candy corn and caramel apples cooling on wax paper.

Then something hit him.

Knocked him into the wall and the worm hit the floor.

It was Tanney fighting with a parasite that had wound him up like a python with its prey.

Compton saw his own worm attempting to investigate his boot and he stomped on it, smashed it to steaming eggs and pulp as it squirmed at his feet.

It was absolute pandemonium now.

Tanney was losing the battle against the worm that was constricting him and Quinn was on the floor, his entire body shuddering as a worm slipped through the rents in his suit like a snaking white cable and disappeared inside him. Blood blossomed from the entry wound, bubbling from a tear in the suit...and then Quinn was no longer fighting.

Not that McCardle saw any of that.

He was too busy torching the body heap. He had turned it into a great blazing pyre whose flames licked the walls and ceiling. The bodies—those still living—rose up in the bonfire, swaying and screaming, jumping and contorting as if they were being electrocuted.

Barks torched Quinn, then fried a few worms on the ceiling as the sprinkler system rained down water on them.

"BACKUP!" McCardle was shouting into his headset. "WE NEED FUCKING BACKUP IN HERE!"

Compton tried to assist Tanney, but one good sweep of the worm's body—or tail—and he was knocked away, right into the fire. He threw himself free, his suit scorched, crawling on his hands and knees. He looked up just in time to see a worm swinging above him like a rope on a gallows.

He rolled to the side as it dropped.

When it tried to strike at him, he kicked it into the fire where it twisted and flopped, snapping like a bullwhip.

"GET IT OFF ME!" Tanney was crying over the headset. "SOMEBODY GET THIS FUCKING THING OFF ME!"

Which McCardle was trying to do…but then the mother of all worms came slithering out of the smoke and haze and spraying water. It was white and segmented like the others, but it had to have been bigger around than a man's thigh, not flattened like the others, but swollen, distended, each segment fat and heaving and perfectly round. It was thick-bodied and slug-like as it bore down on him, the spines on its bulb head twitching like fingers. It struck him and he hit the wall, then the floor. He let out a weird, almost babyish squeak as the thing covered him in its bulk, its mouth opening wider and wider as it struck, the hook teeth seizing his helmet.

But he fought.

Nobody could take that away from him.

Right to the end, he fought and clawed and snarled like a tomcat as the thing flattened him with its weight and its mouth began to crush his helmet. The hissing/sucking sounds it made were hideous. And that's when Compton knew that it wasn't crushing the helmet—it was putting out an almost unbelievable vacuuming suction that was causing the helmet to collapse, to implode, to smash McCardle's head to sauce.

And just before that happened, McCardle got his knife off his belt and slit the worm open until it buried him alive in a surging river of gray jelly.

And about then, the helmet collapsed, spewing out pink and red goo.

In the meantime, Barks' own suit was ripped open by the hooking appendages of a great worm as it encircled him in its fifteen foot length of throbbing segments. In his mind, his broken raging mind, it was not a worm that he fought with but some monstrous jungle serpent like the kind that always showed up in those comic books he read as a kid. He did not see the suckering invertebrate mouth of a worm suctioned to his face shield, but the fanged jaws and forking tongue of a snake. It wanted to break through the

Plexiglas bubble, it wanted to spit poison in his eyes and sink its fangs into his cheeks, injecting venom that would turn his face to a suppurating mush that would be as soft and rancid as a brown apple.

But like McCardle, he did not give in.

He gripped the worm, fighting against its natural oily secretions of slime and digging his fingers into it until he felt them pierce its shivering, globby flesh, sinking deeper and deeper until the thing came apart in a slushy discharge, but still its mouth would not release the face shield.

Covered in slime, burnt, three or four worms hanging off him, Compton crawled to the fire door in time to greet the backup team...who put him down with a volley of bullets.

# CHICAGO, NORTH SHORE

## KENILWORTH

**10:14 P.M.**

Dark. It was time to move. As Harry stood outside by the rental car Gabe had gotten them, waiting for Shawna, he felt like dozens of eyes were upon him, watching him, studying him, plotting out his every move. It was paranoia and he knew it, but he'd been in situations like this before where he'd made enemies of powerful people that wanted him to disappear. Although it was not a particularly warm night, he was sweating. He could feel the wetness in his armpits and up his spine. His stomach was rolling over itself, the back of his neck prickling. Fear. The fear of the hunted and he'd felt it before, but this time it was somewhat elevated.

Shawna came out of the house. Her eyes shined brightly in the darkness. She had said little after he explained earlier how it worked, that they were dead now, that Harry and Shawna as such no longer existed. It was the only way they could stay alive, by forgetting who they were and who they had been. At least, for the time.

"Are you ready?"

Her eyes did not blink. "Are you going to tell me where we're going?"

"No, I'm not. And you know the reason for that, don't you?"

She did. It seemed like excessive cloak-and-dagger to her, but Harry had instructed her that starting right now, until they were in an absolutely safe location, they would never mention where they were going or who they were going to see in case they were being eavesdropped on by listening devices.

"Bugs, Harry?" she had said. "Oh, really. Isn't that a little dramatic?"

"You are now in the game, my dear. A wanted person. Welcome to the world of high drama."

They got in the car and Gabe did not see them off. He had given them money and everything they'd need to go underground for a while. He would continue nosing about unofficially using his contacts, but they would prob-ably never come face to face with him again until this blew over.

As he sat behind the wheel of the little nondescript Toyota Camry, Harry felt himself tense up. He remembered a skinny kid named Harold in baggy pants and a threadbare shirt with moist dishrags for hands that had won an essay contest in the fifth grade—*America and What it Means to Me*—and had to stand on the stage at St. Katherine's beneath the lights while the award was handed to him. That kid had been filled with butterflies and hope. The nuns had beamed down at him. Father McKay kept patting Harold on the back. And out in the audience, Harold's peers, all the other scruffy Catholic school kids he had beaten out for the hundred-dollar prize were eyeing him with contempt. Not all of them. Most would take it with grace, Harold had known, but others would hate. And some—the older kids, the dirt mean ones—would see it as a good reason to torment him on a daily basis. They didn't realize that he'd never see a red cent of that hundred dollars. That Harold's old man would drink and gamble most of it away and if his mother intervened she'd get the strap. They didn't know that he lived not only in fear of the strap and his old man's violent outbursts, but of the rats that came out of the walls at nights and bit his toes. And as Harry remembered all that, he was amazed that as kid, writing had gotten him in nearly as much trouble as it did when he was an adult.

"Harry," Shawna said. "Are we going to sit here all night?"

"Of course not."

He pulled away and down the long drive, feeling her eyes on him all the while. He couldn't meet them. He did not want to accept the bright fear in them because he knew it was in his own eyes as well. Shawna was terrified and he could not let her know he was, too.

"When will I find out where we're going?"

"When we get there, my love."

She sighed. He could feel her in the seat next to him—tense, trembling, gnawing on a knuckle. As they passed through the gates he reached over and grabbed her by the neck and, before she could stop him, he forced her face down in his lap.

"What the hell are you doing?" she said, fighting to pull her head away.

"Just relax. It's better if only one person is seen driving away," he told her.

"It's dark out," she said and he could feel her hot breath at his groin and forced himself not to let it arouse him.

"The people were dealing with have night vision devices, dear," he ex-plained to her. "Now stay down there for a while."

She sighed again.

"Don't worry. If you get bored down there, I'll find something for you to do."

Shawna bit him in the leg none too lightly.

# CHICAGO

## EN ROUTE

**10:34 P.M.**

"Kansas City, Kansas City, this is Romeo-Three. Do you copy?"
"Five-by-five, Romeo. We have you on the grid."
"Subject Hotel November is leaving the residence."
"Roger that, Romeo."
"Hotel moving south on Green Bay. I'll keep you advised."
"Do that, Romeo. Maintain current. Over."

# WASHINGTON D.C.

## GEORGETOWN

**10:56 P.M.**

In the rear of the parking garage, the limo idled as it had been idling for the past twenty minutes. Gus Costello, the National Security Advisor, rubbed his temples and listened to Maddie Hughes, the Secretary of Homeland Security, go on one of her rants as she often did when she did not get what she wanted or was left out of the loop.

"Maddie," Gus said, swallowing a couple aspirins and washing them down with a bottle of mineral water from the limo's minibar, "there was never any attempt to delude you or your office. Please understand that. The President decided to keep DHS out of this until the time came when they needed to be activated on the issue."

Maddie shook his head. "This is a domestic threat, Gus."

"Yes, it is. If it was up to me, you'd have been brought in. But I'm not in a position to supersede a presidential directive and I think you know that."

Maddie sighed, trying to control herself. The fact that her office had only been brought in on this three days ago irked her. The parasites were an obvious threat to the domestic security of the nation and yet she'd been left out of the loop.

"What were you people thinking?" she finally asked. "Toying with a nightmare like this?"

"Please leave 'we' out of the equation, Maddie. I was not in office then. My job, all of our jobs now, is clean up."

"Creating something like that, allocating the funds, then turning it loose in a warzone," she said, her face twisted into a mask of disgust. "Now...now it's been tracked back to this country. Jesus Christ. Jesus H. Christ."

Costello let her stew a few moments until the piss and vinegar ran out of her as he knew it would. Maddie had quite a temper, but it blew itself out very quickly.

"It seems to me," she said, "that my office should have been put in charge of this from the start. We're in a unique position to coordinate—"

"Again, not my decision, Maddie. I follow orders like you do."

She helped herself to the minibar. She skipped the mineral water and went straight for three fingers of Grey Goose. She sighed. "Every time there's something rotten in the wind you can trace the smell back to CBT and Elizabeth Toma. Why doesn't somebody clip her fucking wings already?"

"You know why."

"They're that afraid of her?"

Gus shrugged. "Of her and maybe who stands behind her. I don't recommend taking a stab at her. She's ruined careers and destroyed lives. In fact, it's a specialty of hers."

Maddie contemplated that. "You think it's real? All those whispers about The Collective?"

"Maybe. If there is such an organization, you can bet she's hooked up with them."

"I've heard rumors about Gordon Parks and the NSA more than once," Maddie said, lowering her voice as if she feared someone might hear. "I know one thing, Gus, the both of them are behind that business in Alaska. They're in bed with the Navy and DARPA on that one and I don't like it one bit."

He didn't either. She was referring to the ECHO ionospheric array in Alaska. The entire thing was passed off as an atmospheric communications facility, but popular conspiracy claimed its aims were much darker—weather control, an EMP weapon, or even mass mind control. He had never taken any of that seriously until a "T"-secret communication had crossed his desk concerning an identical facility hidden in the mountains of Mexico. Something the conspiracists hadn't found out about as yet. When he asked questions, he was told to back off. Something was afoot there, but just what no one would say. But one thing was for sure, the NSA was involved and CBT was one of their research contractors.

Feeling uncomfortable, Maddie decided to change the subject. "You're never going to contain something like this, Gus. Not if it's spreading the way you say."

"Which is why the President wants you on board."

"Damage control? Spin? Perception management?"

"You got it."

Costello explained to her that a directive had been assembled. It would be known as Yankee Alert. If and when the news of the parasitic infection broke to the general public, Yankee Alert would go live. It was, essentially, a false flag attack, a beautiful piece of fiction in which foreign extremists would be blamed for engineering an insidious biological warfare attack against the continental United States. It would be supported by intelligence and documentation so cleverly created and aligned that even the world security community could not disprove its validity. Such a directive went into effect following 9/11 and the public swallowed it wholesale.

It was a wonderful, creative pile of bullshit, but it wasn't complete fabrication, he explained to her. There *were* extremists seeding the worms in the country, all associates of Sheikh Sa'ad al Khalafari and his well-entrenched terror network.

"Who've, no doubt, been allowed to make matters worse so that their guilt in this matter is beyond question," Maddie pointed out.

"Yes. Again, not my call."

Maddie swallowed more vodka. Damn, if she didn't need it. "And what's my part in this horror story?"

"Yankee Alert will now be the responsibility of your office."

Maddie liked the idea. It meant power. Reams of it. "All right. We can handle it."

"As of now, it's yours. You'll be meeting in the morning with the architects of the directive."

"Excellent."

Costello thumbed the intercom. "Drive on," he said into it.

"I have one more question, Gus."

"Yes?"

"Why couldn't we meet in your office over this?"

Costello did not smile. "Because I can't be certain that my office has not been breached by listening devices."

She just stared at him. "That's insane. Your office is swept daily. Three times daily if I recall."

"Trust me on this one, Maddie," he said. "There are people involved in this situation who may be nameless, but their intentions are deadly. They're just waiting for the right moment."

Maddie caught his drift. "But that's treason."

"Yes, that's exactly what it is."

# CHICAGO

## BELMONT CRAGIN

**11:14 P.M.**

Tommy Quillan watched the stripper work the pole and he was greatly impressed with not only her liquid grace but the size of her breasts. After months in Afghanistan, it was easy enough to forget what a western woman looked like let alone what the right one could do with an oiled pole and an equally oiled body.

He ordered another bottle of Newcastle Brown and sipped it slowly, catching the stripper's almond Asian eyes as she caught his. His table was at the edge of the stage and she belly-crawled to within feet of him, rising up and thrusting her pelvis at him. Quillan smiled and slid a fifty dollar bill into her G-string. She grinned salaciously at him and licked her lips, letting him know that for the right price what she was doing with the pole she could do with other poles.

*It's so easy with American women*, he thought. *It's always about money. You can be the ugliest heap of shit that ever crawled out of the loo and if your wallet's fat enough, they'll ride your leg like a cat.*

Money.

Always money.

It was different with the Afghanis. The Pushtun and Uzbeki men might have been notoriously corrupt, but their women lived by a rigid moral code you could not subvert with money. At least, most of them did.

Quillan sipped his beer.

He knew at that very moment that certain individuals within the Washington intelligence community were going out of their minds wondering where he was and exactly what he was doing. He had flown like any other civilian into O'Hare where he knew there would be a couple Agency boys waiting for him to brief him on ops and direct him to a safe house. But, more for his own amusement than any other reason, he'd given them the slip. Using a fake I.D. that identified him as a member of the U.S. Marshals Service, he did not disembark with the other passengers. The I.D. bought him a quick route through security to a rental car that was waiting for him...leaving the Agency boys empty-handed and no doubt in disfavor with their employer.

*When I'm ready, I'll show.*

But not until.

The dance finished and the rowdy blue collar element of Pinkie's exploded with raucous applause. The dancer disappeared as another took the stage. Quillan abandoned his table and it was quickly taken by a couple drunken laborers. He threaded his way through the noise and bustling bodies. There was an open table in the back, out of view of the stage.

He sat alone.

And waited.

About fifteen minutes later, the dancer appeared as he knew she would. Seeing no reason to stun him with her body since he had already seen every inch of it, she dressed casually in cargo shorts and a loose yellow tee. She approached his table cautiously as he knew she would. Years upon years of counterterrorism and intelligence work had made him an excellent judge of character. While the other rowdies were tossing dollars at the girls on stage, Quillan had sought out this woman, giving her first a twenty and then a fifty, making her think that the gifts would keep going up and up.

"Mind if I sit down?" she said.

"I was hoping you would," Quillan said without a trace of his British accent. He spoke with a perfect Midwestern twang.

She smelled of baby oil and green apple body wash. It was delicious. She sat down, sweeping her long auburn hair over one shoulder and crossing her long legs.

"Would you like a drink?"

He ordered her a Bacardi and Coke and watched her drink it with those luscious lips. Her eyes were upturned, Asian, and it only magnified her allure. There was a scar tracery that ran from her right earlobe to the jawline. Barely noticeable except to a trained observer like Quillan, who surmised from her eyes and the scar that she had lived a rough life. That and the trembling of her fingers from a drug habit told him all he needed to know about her.

He set five one-hundred-dollar bills on the table.

"Do you have a room?" he asked her.

She finished her drink, her eyes filled with lust for the cash. She stood up and he followed. It wasn't until the door was locked and she was naked and gagged on the bed that he let her see the knife.

The smell of fear coming off her by then was absolutely mouthwatering.

# CHICAGO

## DOWNTOWN

**11:34 P.M.**

"Romeo, how do you copy?"

"Subject Hotel November is heading south on Wabash. Traffic heavy."

"Hang tight, Romeo. Eye in the sky has him tagged."

"Kansas City...Hotel has cut onto East Randolph...getting evasive. Driving erratically. Request back-up."

"Backup confirmed, Romeo. Tango at your location, ETA of three minutes. Eye in the sky reports Hotel now cutting in behind you. Watch it!"

"Kansas City, Hotel is spooked...we're losing him."

"All units, this is Kansas City, move in and restrict Hotel. Repeat: move in and restrict Hotel..."

**11:37 P.M.**

"Are you trying to fucking kill us or what?" Shawna asked as Harry squeezed the Toyota between a bus and two taxis and then merged in front of a public works truck.

"Just cleaning our tail, pet," he explained, slowing down, then speeding up, overtaking a minivan, cutting off into the slow lane and firing down an alley. "We've had a black SUV on our ass for two miles, making every turn we make. Not getting any closer, but not getting any farther away either."

"We're being followed?"

"Yes."

Harry performed some more death-defying maneuvers, easing them up North Garland. The SUV was nowhere in sight but he knew that really meant nothing. They would be using a tag-team of chase cars probably directed by aerial surveillance if they wanted him bad enough.

He slipped in between Garland and Wabash, flooring the Toyota, overtaking another bus and cutting off yet another taxi to the scream of horns and then slowing down and turning into a parking garage. He slid the card Gabe had given him into the slot and drove up to the third tier, backing in next to a Hummer.

Shawna fumbled a cigarette into her mouth. "I want to get away from them, Harry, but I don't want to die."

"Death is what I'm keeping you away from, dear."

"Can I ask what we're doing here?"

He pulled her over to him and whispered in her ear so she understood. He was taking no chances with bugs. "Now we wait twenty minutes while our trail cools off. Then..."

They waited and neither of them spoke.

Harry watched the garage very carefully. He figured if their tail had followed them here, then they would stake out the street, wait for them. Probably bring in plenty of backup, but if things went well that would do them no good at all.

At 11:47, he said, "All right, now."

Gathering their things, they stepped out of the Toyota and crossed the lot to where a Maroon Chevy Tahoe awaited them. They climbed in and waited again.

"All right," Shawna said. "Who does this belong to?"

"It's a rental. A friend left it here for us."

"My how resourceful we are."

At midnight, the elevators opened and about twenty people from a software support firm came bustling out, all jumping into their respective vehicles, anxious that the day was in and the evening shift was done. Harry merged the Tahoe in with them. The queue moved down the ramp and to the exit, their cards opening the gate. One by one they sped out into traffic.

"And that's how it's done," he told Shawna as they moved south, just another anonymous vehicle.

# AUGUST 27

# SUITLAND, MARYLAND

## NATIONAL MARITIME INTELLIGENCE CENTER

**12:14 A.M.**

Admiral Paulus stared down at the pile of intel reports, briefings, and national security assessments on his desk. The entire BioGenesis affair was supposed to exist in the shadows. There should have been no paper trail, but his desk begged to differ.

*I should sweep it all in the trash where it belongs and go spend a few days on my boat,* he told himself.

The very idea cheered him even though it was wholly unpractical. Not now. Not at this stage of the game. Bob Pershing wanted his confederates (*traitors, you mean*) close at hand and available for immediate consultation now that zero hour was quickly approaching.

*You can get out of this anytime you want,* Paulus told himself as he sipped his bourbon, the glass trembling in his hand. *One phone call and your car and driver will whisk you away to Emerald City for an audience with the great Oz.*

He wondered if the President would believe him. It wasn't every day that the most powerful man in the world (supposedly) was dragged out of bed and told that his country was about to be overthrown by some of the men he trusted the most.

*You even try that and you're a dead man.*

He finished his whiskey in one swallow.

Yes, that's what it came down to. He was being watched and he knew it. Watched, listened to, his every move plotted and graphed. Pershing's spooks were everywhere. There was no way in hell he would allow Paulus or any of the other conspirators to squirm out of this now and live to testify against him. It was too late. Far, far too late.

Every time the ONI Director walked out of a building he could feel eyes on him, feel the crosshairs on his back. But if he betrayed Pershing it would be nothing so melodramatic—or obvious—as a bullet. It would be something more subtle. He knew that Pershing had a certain love for binary poisons. That's how it would be done. One day at lunch, a certain chemical would be introduced into Paulus' lobster bisque where it would sit inert in his system. Three days later, he would swallow another with his salad dressing. The two chemicals were harmless alone, but together they would combine to form a deadly, untraceable poison that would kill him in minutes, mimicking a stroke or a major coronary event.

That's how it would happen.

*You've probably already swallowed the first dose.*

Paulus sighed. What a mess, what a mess. That morning he had been involved in a closed-door call-down of experts at the FBI Command Center. It was an absolute, rowdy zoo of biomedical specialists, spooks, civilian techs, and security people. The purpose was to examine the outbreak and how it could be contained. If at all. There was no focus, no agreement, no cooperation, only chaos as the NSA and CIA, FBI and DIA spooks pointed fingers at each other, at the Army and Navy, everyone panicking and brooding over their political futures and pretty much ignoring what the scientists and medical people had to say. Typical. A hotheaded State Department DSS agent took a poke at a suit from the National Security Council and a high-ranking agent from Homeland Security's Science & Technology Directorate called a FEMA administrator a "dumb cunt" and it just got worse from there.

If the situation hadn't been so grave, it might have been comical. Most meetings of that sort were a bit more civilized, but the worse the situation the farther down the evolutionary level people tended to slide.

As Bob Pershing later put it, "Like a bunch of apes throwing shit at each other." And that pretty much summed it up.

Pershing, Paulus knew, was secretly pleased with the chaos because one federal agency turning on another created an atmosphere of not only mutual suspicion but of pandemonium. And this was exactly what he wanted. It was fertile grounds for what came next.

Paulus rubbed his tired eyes. The ball was rolling now and the inevitable was but days away. Pershing was excited. General Mason of the JCS was exhilarated at the power coming his way. And Paulus himself was scared. These were dangerous times, and he was playing with dangerous men.

*God help me if I've made a big mistake here*, he thought.

# CHICAGO, RIVER NORTH

## THE WAREHOUSE

**12:33 A.M.**

*Poor Mr. Smith, I knew him well.*

McKenna and Stein stood there watching the techs strap Smith down to a gurney. He had lost it. Flipped right out during a containment op in Forest Park. He and his partner, Mr. Coombs, had slipped into the house of a Sgt. Donahue, retired, and when the worms started coming out of him, Smith had lost it. He drilled not only Donahue but two members of the biocontainment team.

It was a mess cleaning that one up.

Now poor Mr. Smith, heavily sedated, was off to points unknown for a good long rest.

*They're sending that poor shit to the Resort*, McKenna knew. *They're going to pick his brain apart. Reconditioning, they call it. But brainwashing is brainwashing.*

It was another busy day for Stein and McKenna, who, along with two other teams, were sweeping the greater Chicago area. The Old Man had decided he did not like them using 9mm weapons—too messy, slugs flying about drilled into walls and might be found—so they were equipped with .50 cal smoothbore tranquilizer pistols with Ketamine darts. All the ERT cleaners were armed with them. Their 9mm silenced pistols were only for emergencies.

The Warehouse had two incinerators operating now and they had personally watched the containment boys feed a dozen disease vectors (bodies) into the flames.

McKenna was tapped.

Down in Jackson Park not three hours ago, they'd entered a building on a tip and found a dozen infected ones. It was a little dicey there for a bit as the hosts, drooling and delusional, became violent and came at them with everything from kitchen knives to hammers. Maybe the worms were giving their hosts some survival instincts in order to protect themselves. Regardless, the hosts had been foaming at the mouth like they had rabies.

They all went into the incinerators after the containment team sterilized the area.

The real disturbing part was that Cave told them later that none of them were Iraqi vets. However they were infected, it must have happened here and probably within the past week.

Afterwards, McKenna sat alone with Stein and tried to get him to talk about running so he could get some more evidence on him over the wire, but Stein wouldn't utter a word.

As they watched the techs wheel Mr. Smith away, McKenna said, "I wonder where they're taking him?"

"You know damn well where they're taking him," Stein said. "Same place we're going when this is done."

"Maybe you, but not me. They have faith in me. I'm good."

"Don't you wish."

McKenna smiled...then frowned.

# DETROIT

## 8 MILE AND JOHN R

**12:53 A.M.**

*The infestation spread...*

"Now that you paid, baby, you can play," the girl said.

Charles Kingle couldn't believe his luck. It had been months since he'd dared show his face on 8 Mile ever since those two undercover cops had set him up on that soliciting charge. And it had been a setup, make no mistake of that. A few phone calls and his lawyer had dispensed with the entire thing (along with a warning, of course, for Kingle to stay off 8 Mile after dark, to not even show his face around there in the light of day—a Lexus in that area marked him as a target for hoodlums and cheap cops). So for many months, Kingle had taken his business elsewhere, noticeably Jefferson Ave and Woodward, but it was never as exciting.

Now he was back.

It didn't take long to pick up some street goodies. A little trolling and the girls were ringing your car in, sniffing, horny, and hungry for green. That was a turn-on, especially when they started getting territorial fighting for the right to be used.

*Nothing sweeter than that*, Kingle thought.

Except for maybe when he got one of them in the backseat of his high-dollar ride.

This girl, certified street goodies, just wanted to please. She didn't seem to mind when he was rough with her, when he put his hands on her and hurt her. She liked that and she told him so, staring up at him with those glassy drugged-out eyes. He got on top of her first, pumping her savagely until she started making those fine squeaking sounds he liked. She was thin and long-limbed, a delicious brown with heavy round breasts. And she was pregnant, judging from the tight mound of her belly. Kingle didn't know why, but he really liked that and he always had.

Then she got on top of him because that's how he liked to finish off and seal the deal.

The heat coming off her young body was intoxicating. She was like a furnace going from hot to molten and he was melting underneath her as he gripped her ass and she pumped away. She kept at it, pushing her breasts into his face and he was licking them, squeezing them, biting into them until he tasted blood which was a sweet dark wine on his tongue and she didn't scream or fight or cry out like the others. That was exciting, too, so he bit harder, knowing he'd never reach climax until he she screamed in pain because that's really what it was all about and it was only at moments like this when it was getting close that he allowed himself to admit it.

He bit into her nipple and her entire body shuddered.

A slick, sweet-smelling sweat that was cool-warm covered her naked body and...dear God, it had never been like that before. Not sweat, but nectar and honey, cloying and thick. He lost his head as he plummeted into exotic realms of ecstasy.

And it was then, as he came, that she gripped his face in her hands and brought her mouth closer to his own, opening it, letting her tongue slide slick and greasy into his mouth...only that tongue, which tasted like sugar, was filling his mouth, wriggling and crawling, and then it was down his throat, pushing deeper and deeper.

By then it wasn't pleasure but horror.

A horror mixed with pleasure.

The worm in his throat detached a single segment of itself which was basically an egg case, and then...

*Oh God, oh God, that feels so good...so good...*

And then if there truly had been pain or discomfort, he forgot about it all as the larval worms inside him, sensing a warm and hospitable environment, allowed digestive juices to dissolve their individual egg capsules which set them free. They parasitized him immediately. Each worm, taking advantage of the fact that Charles Kingle was still reeling from the endorphins flooding his system—chemically triggered by the mother worm's sweet scent—got down to work as he lay there in a mindless euphoric state. They burrowed into his abdominal walls and, within minutes, they had appropriated their host's chromosomes. Hijacking genetic codes in his DNA, they directed the formation of viruses which invaded healthy cells, using the genetic machinery of each cell to reproduce themselves millions of times. When the nucleus of each cell was leeched and crowding with viral bodies, the cell burst, releasing the viruses. The purpose of the viruses was not to make Kingle ill, but to force his cells to create new proteins which would effectively cripple his immune system. Once that was done, the larval worms could control the host without interference.

And once that was accomplished, and it took only mere hours, the worms fought for complete dominance of the host, knowing only one could succeed.

By then, Kingle would be tamed.

Enslaved.

He would be a biological vessel which existed only to cultivate and propagate the worm within and to infest others with its spawn. Stuffing himself primarily with well-marbled juicy red meat, the worm itself would grow at an unprecedented five hundred percent each day, its self-fertilized eggs filling each proglottid to the bursting point. Kingle would not know he had been parasitized. He would be rewarded for the proper behavior—the getting of food and the protection, the mothering of the worm within—and punished for anything that deviated from it. The worm would do this by mastering him as a drug masters an addict. When he was good he would be rewarded with chemical neurotransmitters released from his endocrine glands which would mimic the effects of heroin and cocaine; when he was not, these secretions would be withheld and he would know a punishing agony.

Within fifteen minutes after initial infestation, the organism once known as Charles Kingle ceased to exist.


**1:16 A.M.**

*And spread...*

After Kingle, the woman once known as Shara Pontre was picked-up by three white men in a van who were drunk and looking for a little fun with the same girl. Parked in an alley, she stripped for them, watching their eyes as they drooled over her large, firm breasts. They giggled. She performed oral sex on each in turn until they were all wonderfully hard and ready. Then she took them all at the same time. She mounted one, while a second penetrated her roughly from behind and she slid her lips over the penis of the third.

She brought them all near-simultaneously to orgasm like they'd never known before, and by then it was too late.

The after-euphoria of cheap, emotionless sex usually faded within minutes, she knew, replaced by guilt and anxiety. But not this time. The worm within her, using her own altered biochemistry, made her sweat out chemicals that were sweet and intoxicating, causing the midbrain neuroreceptors of all three of her johns to produce euphoric levels of dopamine and norepinephrine, making them feel more relaxed and easy than they had ever felt before in their lives.

Then she had them.

They were helpless.

She was a blazing sun and they were caught in her gravity sink. As she hovered over each of them, whispering things to them, they experienced something quite like a near-death experience. As her worm slid into each of their mouths slowly and lovingly, sacrificing a segment in each, they knew a sharp, uneasy sensation of fear…then a chemically induced calmness and tranquility as if the light at the end of a tunnel, a warm and comforting light, was reaching out for them, enveloping them, filling them with a sense of well-being unlike anything they had known before, fusing them with something larger and grander than their individual petty lives.

Shara watched as the larva took possession of them.

She felt absolutely nothing, only a vague interest which was not her own but that of the parasite within her. Now and again, something like dread or horror would spike within her but her worm would block it instantly.

She watched the bodies of her johns squirm as their eyes remained glassy and unfocused.

It had been that way for her and millions of others by that point.

After fifteen or twenty minutes, she went outside and sought new hosts. She had very little trouble in finding them. By the time the night was over she would have infected twenty-three more individuals who themselves would do much the same. Up and down 8 Mile, Shara Pontre and the other worm hookers spread the seed that would be carried from one end of the city to the other.

**1:38 A.M.**

*And spread…*

When Buchmiller finally got him in the patrol car, Pulson was an absolute mess. He was ranting and raving and when he got that out of his system, he just sat there, breathing, making a choking, sobbing sound deep in his throat like he had seen something that had completely stripped his gears.

Buchmiller figured he had. "I want you to relax," he told him. "It's out of our hands now. The feds are taking over the scene and we're nothing but bystanders. Ronny? Look at me. Goddammit, I want you to look at me."

Pulson's black face was beaded with sweat, his eyes huge and staring. "You don't know what I saw in there, Sarge."

"You already told me."

He just kept shaking his head. "I…I…I…"

"Easy now."

Pulson swallowed. "Davy's dead. Davy's fucking dead and I couldn't do a goddamn thing about it."

"Sometimes you can't. That's the awful part of this job: sometimes you just can't."

Buchmiller stuck a cigarette in his mouth, figuring Pulson was about as close to shock as anyone he'd ever seen. He lit it for him and Pulson pulled hard off it, coughed out a cloud of smoke. He hadn't smoked in four years but at that moment he couldn't seem to remember the fact.

"They were everywhere, Sarge. Everywhere. It was like...it was like a fucking nest in there. A nest."

Buchmiller listened while Pulson went through it one more time, squeezing the poison out of his soul. They'd received a call. Screams from inside an empty building. A crack house, that's what they figured. Maybe someone in there was getting beaten or murdered, you could never tell on 8 Mile. You always expected the worse. They went in and the place was full of derelicts and junkies. Except they weren't the usual sort. They took down his partner, a dozen or more of them falling on him. Pulson emptied his 9mm into them. He kept shooting but more kept coming.

"I killed four or five of them."

"Okay."

"I thought they were dead."

"Right."

Pulson took a drag from the cigarette, caught somewhere between hysterical laughter and tears. "They went down. I saw them go down. Then... they were *moving*. Moving, Sarge, they were fucking moving. Except... except it wasn't them. It was what was inside them. Worms, Sarge, big white worms... I saw one crawl out of guy's mouth. It was big... like a fucking snake."

Buchmiller nodded. "Okay. Now forget it."

"What?"

"You heard me. Forget it. When we get back to the station and you get your feet under you, you're gonna write this up. But you won't say shit about worms. You read me on this?"

"But—"

"But nothing, Ronny. You got a kid, don't you?"

"Yeah, but—"

"How old?"

"Eight, but—"

"You wanna be around when he's ten? When he graduates from high school?"

Pulson nodded slowly, still confused.

"Then you write it up like I say. Got it? No fucking worms. Nothing. Just a crack house with a crowd of whacked-out homeless people. They attacked. They overwhelmed you and your partner. You shot out of self-defense. Then you ran out and called it in. Okay?"

Pulson was staring at him.

Buchmiller licked his lips. "Listen to me, kid, and hear me good. You think it's strange that the feds arrived before our own backup units? This city is all of a sudden thick with feds. They're monitoring our radio calls. They have jurisdiction."

Pulson stared out the window. There were dozens of men in black wind-breakers and others in white spacesuits dragging bodies out of the building. They were being bagged and loaded up into a white delivery truck.

Buchmiller wiped sweat from his brow. "Those people are Department of Homeland Security, Ronny. At least, some of them are. The others...I don't know. But they've all got the same spooky eyes. They think there's some kind of outbreak in there. I told them you never went inside the building. That Davy did and when you went to his assistance a bunch of crazies poured out after you and you drove them back inside. They're gonna question you, son. You better stick to my story or they'll take you with them. They have the authority. And if they take you with, you won't be coming back."

Pulson was looking really scared now. "How do you know that?"

"Call it a gut feeling."

"But I was just doing my job. This is a free country for chrissake."

Buchmiller barked a cynical laugh. "Yeah, you tell yourself that on the Fourth of July when you wave your flag. Until then, don't be so fucking naïve."

"Okay."

Two men in windbreakers approached the car. They looked dangerous.

"It's all or nothing right now, Ronny," Buchmiller said.

"Okay."

Buchmiller unrolled his window.

"We need to speak with Officer Pulson," one of the DHS thugs said.

"Sure," Pulson said, feeling the bullshit inside him rising to the occasion. "Not much I can tell you. I lost my partner. He went inside and they came out, crazy and shouting. I opened up..."

Within forty-eight hours, fifty-two percent of Metro Detroit was infected.

# CLEVELAND, OHIO

## ST. CLAIR AVE, CHINATOWN

**2:16 A.M.**

How he slipped in unnoticed, Raymond Ho did not know. Only that suddenly, it seemed, he was there and everyone seemed to see him at precisely the same moment: a tall, reed-thin man with a bald head, wild eyes, and a three-piece suit that was ragged and filthy with dried vomit and bloodstains. It was all bad enough, but those eyes—glossy black, wide and unblinking—were what put a chill up Ray's back. Running the Peking Buffet until three in the morning, of course, they often got some strange types in there. But this guy...damn...now he was something.

He stumbled forward, an awful sickening stench wafting off him that was equal parts body odor, medical waste, and a sickening sweet odor that was pungent enough to curl eyebrows.

*Aw, Christ*, Ray thought, *and it was looking like an easy night tonight. Now here comes trouble.*

There were about fifteen people in the buffet and the crazy man (which was how Ray began to think of him) moved right past them, knocking two drunken women out of his path, moving straight past the steam tables of General Tso's chicken and Crab Rangoon and making for the Mongolian Barbecue in the back.

"Hey!" Ray told him, coming up behind him. "You can't be in here. You get out of here or I call the police."

But the crazy man kept going and Ray grabbed him by the shoulder, and he spun around and smashed Ray right in the face. It was no gentle love tap either. It knocked Ray to the floor, several of his teeth feeling very loose, blood trickling from his mouth from a split lip.

Several patrons, bless them, went to Ray's aid. A couple burly college-age kids went at the crazy man, taking hold of him but he was out of his head and tossed them around like they weighed about as much as feather pillows. By then, people were vacating the premises.

That's when Bobby Tran got in the act.

Bobby was a security guard, a former Golden Gloves boxer with a second-degree black belt in a Korean martial art called Hapkido who spent his weekends as a competitive kickboxer. Ray had seen him put some pretty big boys to the canvas. Six-foot-three inches and two hundred thirty pounds of sculpted muscle, he could intimidate the best.

Bobby grabbed the crazy man around the throat, pivoted quick, and flipped him up and down.

The crazy man was very crazy because he got right back up with that lunatic shine in his eyes.

Ray got on his cell and called 911 after dropping it like four times. "YES! YES, THIS IS GODDAMN EMERGENCY! CRAZY MAN TEARING MY PLACE APART! COME QUICK! THIRTY-NINTH AND ST. CLAIR! PEKING BUFFET! YES! YES! YES! HURRY! THIS SONOFABITCH CRAZY!"

By the time he broke the connection, the crazy guy went right at Bobby.

Bobby hit him in the solar plexus and chopped him across the temple with no effect. He drilled him in the face four or five times and the guy bled, but he did not go down. Bobby kicked him twice...and then the guy grabbed him. Grabbed him and lifted him up over his head, shaking him and screaming out a warning to the others that were making for the door in a rush.

Then, howling like an animal, he threw Bobby.

Bobby flew about twelve feet, landing right on top of the sizzling surface of the Mongolian barbecue grill. Bobby hit it, his flesh searing, and rolled off of it screaming. The stink of burned flesh was nauseating.

Then the crazy man went right over to the Mongolian buffet station where the raw meat, noodles, and uncooked vegetables were kept in refrigerator compartments. Completely oblivious to the agony of Bobby Tran—several pieces of his skin were still on the grill, bubbling and blackened—he went over to the raw meat and stood there, stuffing himself with beef, pork, and chicken. Just shoving it in his mouth and making the most obscene slobbering sounds.

He was still at it when the police arrived.

Ray waited behind the counter.

The cops called out to the crazy man and he turned, meat falling from his mouth, a slick of yellow slime at his chin. He said something unintelligible, sensed the threat, and grabbed a butcher's knife from the cook's station and came right at them.

"DROP IT!" one of the cops called out to him. "DROP THAT GODDAMN KNIFE! THIS IS YOUR ONLY WARNING!"

The crazy man came on.

The cops opened up with their 9mm handguns. They put a total of six rounds into the crazy man and he kept coming. Ray actually saw meat and flesh-shrapnel and gouts of blood blasted free but it never even slowed the guy.

And by then, the cops aimed for his head.

Two in the skull and the crazy man went down face-first, convulsing, then going limp.

And it was then, as they stood there with Raymond Ho, that they saw the most appalling thing come sliding out of his mouth to make itself known to the world.

# CHICAGO

## BELMONT CRAGIN

**2:47 A.M.**

Again, Tommy Quillan was amazed and possibly even disgusted by American women. Everything was for sale. Everything could be bought. Morals were a matter of convenience. Ethics were dispensable. All it took was a fat wallet. You had the green, you laid on the honey, they'd come in droves. After spending so much time in the Middle East he was truly intrigued by the synthetic culture of America.

He laid next to the dead stripper, smoking a cigarette.

Sometimes he would think about ghosts. His experience in death—which was quite extensive by that point—told him that there was no such thing as an afterlife. He'd seen many die and in the end it was never beautiful nor inspirational, no morphing to a higher state of spiritual being but an ugly, messy affair. When humans died they died like crazed, angry animals. Nothing more. Nothing less.

Still...the ghosts.

He had to wonder sometimes if the dead didn't leave bits of themselves behind, psychic footprints. Right then for example, he could have almost sworn that it was not just him and the appalling butchered shank of meat next to him that had once been a very alluring and attractive female. He could almost feel an unseen other in that room with him. Nothing dangerous, of course, like in some bad movie, but just a reflection, a ghostly trace that could not be erased with a knife.

Something almost permanent.

That made him chuckle.

Of all things and of all people to think it.

He had taken his time with the woman, enjoying her in the flesh and post mortem. He wasn't quite sure which he enjoyed best. Both had their advantages and disadvantages. It was like trying to decide which was tastier, a hot flame-broiled steak or a cold leg of Southern fried chicken.

He prodded the torso next to him. "Have an opinion then, love?"

She remained silent and Quillan pulled off his cigarette, sighing. He looked over at her and was somewhat aghast at the unsightly mess which was the end result of his passions. She looked like a fish that had been crudely filleted. Her legs were splayed wide and what was between them was no longer recognizable as part of the female anatomy. Her breasts had been severed. She had been gutted, quite neatly, what was in her belly now on the bedside table. Her face—once so captivating—had been peeled like an apple. But unlike a freshly carved fruit, it was hardly appetizing.

The knife.

It was the knife that had done it.

*Funny how it's gotten with you, old son. Once you had but one penis. That simple, quite average shaft of flesh and you were quite good with it when properly aroused. Then you found the knife, the razor-edged steel phallus. And with it, you became an artist. A sculptor that found realism in his subject and hacked at it until it was purely abstract.*

*Dear God, the ugliness of it.*

The obscenity.

He had to turn away from the dead woman as some nearly submerged sense of right and wrong bobbed to the surface and made him aware of what he had done. But he sent it back to the bottom and looked at the woman. *See the beauty in death?* es, yes. In fact, it aroused him again to a nearly painful degree. He stood up on the bed, hard as a tent stake and masturbated until he spilled his seed over the disemboweled corpse.

Immediately he was guilty.

Then pleased.

Then guilty.

Then both at the same time until he screamed and then he felt better. Just because he tortured women, raped them, carved them with a knife, violated their corpses and then despoiled them with his semen... that hardly meant he was some kind of deviant.

It was simply how he got his kicks.

And, by God, with the state of the world these days you had to get them where you could. One shouldn't be too dainty about expressing the inner man (or woman) and satisfying base urges.

With that in mind, Quillan felt much better about who and what he was. Because truly, his private life aside, he was a professional and very good at his chosen profession. His bank account stood testament to that.

Relaxed, almost giddy, he took a leisurely shower and washed the blood off himself. Once he was finished and dressed, he left the stripper's room and faded into the night. One phone call and a car came to get him to bring him to the safe house. Now that the fun and games were done, it was time to get to work.

# MANHATTAN, 50TH AND BROADWAY

## THE THEATER DISTRICT

**2:59 A.M.**

Robin Hewitt saw the whole thing and moments after it had transpired, she was still standing there, slack-jawed, wide-eyed, listening to the woman in the I LUV NY hoodie screaming her tourist brains out. It happened fast, of course, like all truly weird and wild things. It came and went with such rapidity that she questioned exactly what she had seen.

Robin and her three associates—Kim, Cherise, and Tony R—had watched *Wicked* at the Gershwin, did a little clubbing and bar-hopping, and by the time they were standing on the downtown platform of the 50th IRT Broadway, waiting for the A train, they were feeling no pain. The dozen or so people standing around with them were mostly theater people coming back from late-night parties. They gathered in little groups, laughing and chatting and then—

"Hey!" said the lady in the I LUV NY hoodie. "Hey! Lookit! There's a lady on the tracks!"

Robin hadn't actually heard what she said, but she'd noted the volume.

Kim said, "No shit! Check it out!"

And by then Robin was looking. In fact, they'd all inched closer to the edge of the platform to see something down on the tracks which was not rats like usual. As Robin stared, a voice in her skull was saying, *what's that crazy bitch doing? Doesn't she know the A is coming any second now?*

Maybe she was expecting some crazy old bag lady or homeless person with a paper bag of empties because no one in their right minds got down on the tracks...but what she saw was a young woman. And although she was dirty, her face streaked with grit, her dishwater blonde hair hanging over her face in a greasy tangle, one look and Robin knew she was no street person.

It was the way she was dressed more than anything.

Robin was a buyer for Macy's and she knew money when she saw it. The wool crepe executive jacket, finely tailored...the matching pencil skirt...there was no doubt in Robin's mind that the woman was wearing at least two thousand dollars and that didn't take in the torn hose, the jewelry, or the single black pump she wore. And it was more than the money because this lady knew how to wear that suit. There was something very elegant about her.

And that made it all that much more insane.

"Ma'am!" Cherise called to her. "There's a train coming! You have to get out of there!"

Already, two or three people were down on their knees reaching out helping hands.

The woman just stood there, staring at them.

There was something devastated about her. Like she was a vessel that had been poured out and filled with something poisonous. She stared up at them through strands of hair, her mouth moving but no words coming out. Her skirt was slit up one side, revealing more leg than the designer had intended. One spidery white hand was pressed to her belly and everyone saw the curious mound beneath it.

*Pregnant?*

*This woman's pregnant and wandering around on the fucking tracks at three in the morning in a high-dollar business ensemble?*

These were the words Robin heard in her head and she was about to speak them when I LUV NY said in a clear Midwestern twang, "She's... she's gonna have a baby! Would you look? She's gonna have a baby! She's carrying a baby for the love of Mike!"

Now everyone was calling to her, doing everything they could to entice her to edge towards the platform so she could be plucked free and she was shaking her head violently from side-to-side. And the really disturbing thing—if it could get more disturbing, that was—was that she would move a step closer to them, then physically, violently throw herself backwards as if something inside her was fighting against her and she was fighting against it.

"Somebody should go down there!" I LUV NY was saying. She was looking around at the men on the platform. "What the hell's wrong with you guys? There's a pregnant woman down there! There's a train coming! DON'T THEY GOT ANY FUCKING MEN IN THIS CITY?"

"She's right," Kim said. "Somebody better get her out of there before that train gets here."

And then Cherise, Robin, and Kim were staring at Tony R, of course, who sighed and said, "Okay, okay. Shit."

He made his way to the edge of the platform, looking down at the oily tracks, the garbage, the rats scurrying into darkness, and trembling at it all. He swung his legs over the edge and instantly felt the rumble.

"The train," someone said. "It's coming."

"Oh dear Jesus," said I LUV NY.

"Tony! No!" Charise said.

Tony R nearly hopped down, then thought better of it. With all the others calling out to the woman, his own voice cut through them all—a dramatic tenor, Julliard-trained, thank you very much—and was even more desperate than theirs. "Lady, please! Just three, four more steps and you can grab my hand! We'll pull you out! We'll be careful of the baby...but please, please, take my hand! C'mon!"

Now they could see the train's lights coming through the tunnel and it was mere seconds away, the din it created getting so loud that they could not hear what each other were shouting and they certainly could not hear what the woman said as she chose that moment to speak.

She backed away.

"THE TRAIN!" I LUV NY shouted now. "THE TRAIN IS COMING!"

Tony R was suddenly possessed by a madness of heroism and valor. He would jump down there, pull the woman away from the tracks and save her life and the baby's life and he'd be a hero, by God. But as he made to do so, the train like rolling thunder in the tunnel now, hands grabbed him and pulled him back.

And then he saw why.

With the train bearing down on her, the woman sank to her knees right in its path, convulsing, shaking, her entire body whiplashing like it was plugged into a 440 line...and then, just as the train's shadow reached out for her and I LUV NY screamed with primal terror...she vomited out a pink/yellow slime of bile and they all saw what came out with it...the squirming white worms, immature and writhing, each no longer than a pencil...then five or six larger ones like living hoses. They hung from her mouth like white lace, each of them segmented and hideously squirming.

Then the train took her.

There was a meaty thud, a spray of blood, and it was all over with, except for the continual blaring screams of I LUV NY and the sound of someone vomiting. It didn't take long before Robin joined in and all that rich food and good wine came pouring out.

# CHICAGO, SOUTH DEARBORN

## PRINTER'S ROW

**3:41 A.M.**

It was a hell of a hunt to find a pay phone in these enlightened days of cells but Harry Niles found one near Dearborn Station. He had Shawna hid out down in Chinatown which he figured would be the last place their enemies would be looking for them. He dialed Gabe Hebberman right away and was surprised when it was answered on the second ring.

"Harry? Glad to hear it's you. I was worried. Where are you?"

"Probably better if I don't tell you."

"Understood."

"What's going on? Did you find out anything?"

"Same, same."

Harry had a bad feeling it would work out that way. These people were desperate and they had resources. They'd already scratched Shawna out and he figured they'd do the same to him if they couldn't bring him in within the next day or so. They wouldn't fuck around. He wondered if Gabe's phone was tapped yet or they had a line on his cell. It was probably only a matter of time. They'd make the connection between Harry and Gabe quick enough and then Gabe would be in danger, too.

"There are things happening, Harry. Just murmurs so far but I think things are going to break come morning."

"What sort of things?"

"Whatever Shawna saw, I'm guessing, it's connected with some sort of outbreak. There's rumors coming into my office of Homeland Security running biological containment operations. It's quite possibly an outbreak of contagious disease."

"Jesus."

"Yes, I think we'll begin hearing things later today."

Gabe went on to tell him that there were several hospitals under quarantine as they spoke. He didn't know what it was or where it was coming from, but it was big. This wasn't a state or local matter. It was federal and even his staunchest contacts were getting jittery about it all.

"Jittery?" Harry asked.

"Yes. To put it in plain King's English they're scared shitless."

"Because of the possible outbreak?"

"No, Harry," Gabe said. "Because of the people who are trying to contain it."

Harry knew it was big the moment Shawna laid it out for him. He played Devil's Advocate more to reassure her and calm her down than for any other reason. But he'd known. He'd felt it in his guts: something rotten was beginning to stink and somebody was trying damn hard to keep that particularly foul odor away from the American taxpayers.

"Harry?" Gabe said, sounding very old and worn suddenly. "You know me. You know how I work. You know I don't run scared. But I'm getting a bad feeling here and when an old Jew gets a bad feeling, you'd better walk softly. I don't know where you are and I don't want to know, but you better stay there and keep your head down."

"Okay, Gabe. If you hear from me, it'll be normal channels," he told him, which meant Harry would call him at the office during regular business hours or get a message to him. It would be low-key whatever it was.

"I gotta go, Gabe. Watch yourself."

"God bless, Harry. Give my love to your lady."

The connection was broken.

# CHICAGO, 77TH AND LOOMIS

## AUBURN GRESHAM

**4:17 A.M.**

When Stein and McKenna arrived, there were four tactical vans on site, the area cordoned off by a combination of Homeland Security goons and Chicago Metro cops. And when Stein saw that, first thing he thought was, *this is out of control now, way out of fucking control, we'll never contain this situation*. But he didn't say a word and part of that was because he knew better and another part was the fact that he was not so sure of McKenna anymore.

There was something going on with him.

He was certain of it.

Once Cave got them within the defensive perimeter which kept the locals at bay, he pulled them into the back of a tac van and said, "We have what looks like a major infestation. We have four BCTs standing by. The three of us will be Green Team. We're going in the front. Orange Team will take the back. Blue Team is on standby. We're going in heavy."

And that was another indication to Stein that this had gone way beyond putting down a few infected veterans. This was no longer a black bag job, a covert op, this was a major cleanup.

McKenna and he outfitted themselves in black Kevlar vests and black fatigues, combat boots, and ballistic helmets with night-vision goggles attached. They weren't bothering with the .50 cal dart guns this time. They were issued H & K MP5 submachine guns and 12-gauge Remington tactical pump-action shot guns. This time, when they put one of the worm boys to sleep, they'd stay asleep.

Stein noticed with some amusement that they had U.S. MARSHALS SERVICE printed on the back of their fatigues. Apparently perception management had not been completely abandoned. This one couldn't be swept under the carpet so they'd tell the media it was an assault against armed criminals. The BCTs were strapping on flamethrowers of all things.

"All right," Cave said. "Let's go in."

"That's it?" Stein said. "That's our briefing?"

"You got it," Cave told him. "We have an unknown number of vectors in that structure. All are contaminated. All have to be put down. When we finish, the BCTs will mop up."

Stein got it. Maybe McKenna was still scratching his head but Stein got it loud and clear: they'd waste everyone in the building and the BCTs would torch everything after making sure there was nothing living. The story that would reach the media would be fairly sterile: a tactical unit went up against armed combatants and the building burned to the ground with no survivors. All the coroner's people would find would be charred bones. The worms were invertebrates, no skeletons, they'd melt away.

*Ah, the architects of bullshit have already plugged up the loose holes in this one*, he thought.

They went through the front door of the tenement, smelling cat piss and human excrement, garbage and something much worse, something sweet and foul at the same time and Stein knew it was the stench of the worms themselves. He'd smelled it before. It was positively nauseating.

They were here in numbers.

Within minutes they'd located Orange Team and coordinated the cleanup. Orange would take the first floor and cellar. Green Team would take the second and third floor. They'd all keep in constant communication via TacSat radio and with command outside. Blue Team would monitor communications and stage if necessary.

"Let's make this short and sweet," Cave said as they went up the stairs.

When they reached the top, the lights went out. Tactical flashlights bolted to the MP5s were clicked on.

"Where's those lights?" Cave said into his headset.

Power failure, he was told. They moved out slowly, playing their lights around, making sure there were no ugly surprises waiting for them. McKenna was on point, moving forward, sweeping his light back and forth across the corridor that in the blackness looked like a subterranean tunnel.

"Look," he said, crouching down.

Cave and Stein were at his side. They saw it. It was hard to miss: a trail of blood droplets that moved up the corridor until they weren't droplets anymore but puddles and then an unbroken river that led to one of the doorways at the end.

"Where's those lights?" Cave said over the headset.

The voice from the tac van told him that some whacko—probably infected—had gone at the old fuse box out back with a sledge hammer. He'd smashed the shit out of it. There'd be no lights. Not for a while.

Stein and McKenna just looked at Cave, knowing it was his call.

They waited in the dark and the stink.

*The sensible thing to do is pull back*, Stein thought, *until we get those lights on. But he won't. I know he won't. This entire op is timed and they want it cleaned up right now.*

"Let's go," Cave said, true to form, leading them down the hallway, following the blood trail.

McKenna gave Stein a desperate look in the glare of their lights but Stein ignored it. He should have known better. A bullet-eater like Cave would not be deterred by lights or lack of them.

Cave crept up to the doorway. He tried the doorknob but it was locked. He slapped a shaped charge of C-4 on it and set it. They pulled back and the charge went off with an echoing concussion and a brilliant flash of orange-yellow light.

Cave charged in, kicking the door open and McKenna and Stein came in after him, the three of them spreading out and maintaining low firing positions as they swept the room with their lights. It was a living room apparently and it looked like a hurricane had whipped through there, furniture cast around and broken, holes punched in the walls, everything shattered underfoot. And the smell...hot bacterial decay tainted with that sick/sweet smell of rank fungal rot.

Some chatter came over the headset and they heard the sounds of weapons being discharged below. Orange Team had made contact.

"They got it under control," Cave said.

*Yeah, I'll bet they do*, Stein thought.

Playing their lights about, Green Team moved forward, shadows jumping and crawling up the walls, broken pipes hanging from the ceiling and dripping dank-smelling water. There was an archway leading into a hallway and this was where they went. Their lights showed them walls stained with runny red blotches and strings of tissue. On the floor, midway down the hallway, there was what looked to be the remains of a woman...or something like a woman.

"Shit," McKenna said which was a pretty apt observation.

Stein studied the remains in his light and decided they were what a human being might look like if it was shaken around in a bottle of acid and then poured back out. He saw four splayed limbs—arms, legs—that appeared to be intact, but everything else had gone to a liquid slushy seepage of blood, flesh, and hair melting down into a bubbling swamp of biological refuse. In his light he saw red-slicked bones and floating teeth and a single bobbing eyeball.

He wondered then if this was what happened to a human host when a worm was done with it. After it had been used and abused, leeched and drained and was of no further use.

Then one of the legs moved.

It was impossible, but he saw it.

"Moved," McKenna said, breathing hard. "It fucking moved."

"It can't move."

"It did," Stein said. "I saw it."

Cave moved in closer, keeping his light on the runny mess but there was nothing, no movement, nothing more than a few bubbles of blood popping on the surface of that grisly sea.

"C'mon," he said.

Stein and McKenna stepped to either side, trying to avoid the human compost on the floor and that's when McKenna cried out. One of the arms reached out and gripped his ankle. He tried to kick it free, but it hung on tenaciously, connected to the remains by strings of tissue and nerve and ligament. Finally, his face wild and beaded with sweat, he kicked it loose. It hit the wall and slapped to the floor, the fingers drumming the bloody tiles like it was bored or impatient.

They heard a giggling from one of the rooms farther down.

All four of the limbs were moving now, thumping and splatting in that sea of flesh-humus.

Stein and McKenna almost collided with each other trying to get away from that...that horror.

But the laughing...

Cave followed it and stepped into a room and here was the epicenter of the evil and infection: an ugly, deranged man with a face that looked pitted as if by thousands of hornet stings. He crouched in the corner, a fat white worm coiling in his hands. It was two or three feet long and as they put the lights on it, he made a snarling sound and opened his mouth, the worm sliding back down his throat.

Cave swore under his breath and shot him point-blank with two three-round bursts that blew him apart and sprayed him up the walls, releasing his parasite which crawled through an aperture in his torn-open abdomen and rose up like a rattlesnake ready to strike. Cave shot it, too, blasting it into gray drainage and white pulp. It seemed to dissolve into itself, becoming a snotty discharge of webby eggs.

Stein turned away and that's when he saw that they were not alone.

There were people chained to the walls.

"Jesus," he said.

**4:39 A.M.**

On the first floor, Orange Team—commanded by Captain Smith—had eradicated no less than eight infected vectors and it went well. It got a little hairy for a few moments there, but his boys held tight and maintained their killing positions. As the BCT moved in to assess the dead vectors and what had crawled out of them, Orange Team went to the cellar for phase two of their cleanup op. The first thing they saw was the cat.

At least, it looked sort of like a cat.

Johnson saw it and White did, too.

Smith brought his light around and looked right at the thing, its jade-green eyes glistening and wet with running puss.

It waited atop a stack of water-stained boxes, its hair standing on end like it was filled with voltage. It was a swollen, ulcerated thing. There was something hanging between its legs like a clown-white penis: a worm dangling from a hole in its belly. The cat yawned its jaws wide and made a croaking/mewing sort of sound that was equal parts torment and agony. Worms burst from its eyes and ass and pushed out of its mouth like white fingers.

And it leaped.

Maybe Smith and the others should have expected it and maybe they were just too shocked by what they were seeing.

It made it about three feet into the air, fanning its flesh out as if it was some kind of mutant flying squirrel, and they opened up, rounds busting everywhere. Eight or ten of them drilled into the cat and it literally exploded in mid-flight, spraying them down with blood and fluid and cat-meat...and worms.

"Get 'em off me!" White cried. "Oh, God, get these fucking things off me!"

Whilst Johnson and Smith himself were struck mostly by tissue and fluids—save one looping worm that Johnson crushed to paste—the spray pattern had tossed half a dozen worms right at White. They were on his Kevlar vest. One was wrapped around his wrist. Another trying to find a way into his fatigues and two more going for his face, climbing up him with amazing speed.

That's when Johnson lost it.

That's when whatever glue that held him together ran like warm sap and he stumbled back, shouting, "NO! NO! NO! NO, THIS AIN'T FUCKING HAPPENING! I AIN'T SEEING THIS!" Smith barked orders at him, but Johnson was no longer listening. In fact, he had torn off his headset and dropped his weapon, clapped hands over his ears and sank to his knees, making a high wailing that was the sound of a human mind that was literally emptying itself.

Smith, swearing a blue streak, grabbed hold of White and threw him up against the boxes and stripped worms from him and White, of course, was so out of his mind by that point that he threw two punches into Smith's face. Once the worms were clear, Smith slapped him three times until he got himself under control.

Two things happened then.

A worm dropped from somewhere overhead and draped itself over Johnson's face. It was a big one, thick and writhing, and it wound itself around his throat while Johnson's clawing fingers dug at it, fingers piercing the white greasy flesh, segments erupting with gushing gray drainage and pearly clusters of eggs.

None of which seemed to bother the worm.

It went right for Johnson's left eye.

In his light, Smith saw it happen.

The worm had a head or something like a head that was sort of an elongated globular bulb with a slit-like X-shaped mouth surrounded by wiry spines that it jabbed right into Johnson's face...and almost immediately he went limp, head lolling on his shoulders like he'd been spiked with Seconal. Then the worm opened its mouth and it was perfectly round and pink inside, filled with three or four slender appendages that were pulsing, extending from the mouth, then retracting.

Before Smith could do a damn thing, that bulb-head reared back, hooked protrusions like teeth slid from the mouth, and those slender appendages seized Johnson's eyeball and the teeth sank into his face.

Johnson screamed... drugged or desensitized, he still screamed.

The worm yanked its bulb-head back and pulled the eye out by its bleeding stalk. The sound of that was sickening: like someone tonguing a juicy cherry from its sheath of chocolate.

Smith had his MP5 in his hands and he pulled the trigger.

The clip was empty.

The worm ripped Johnson's eye out and tossed it aside, forcing itself into the bleeding socket with a moist, slithery sort of sound. By the time it had penetrated four or five inches, Smith had his pistol-gripped Remington tactical shotgun in his hands. He put the bracketed light right on the worm and blew Johnson's head apart in a raw splash of skull matter and pink tissue.

Johnson slumped over dead.

Smith, seeing the worm pulling itself back out, racked the pump and blew it to fragments. He racked it again and pulverized anything that was left.

That was the first thing that happened.

The second happened at nearly the same time. As Smith saw the worm fall on Johnson, White heard a voice. Despite everything going on, he heard a slight whispering voice. Turning, he grabbed up his dropped weapon and put the light on the source.

*A girl...is that a girl?*

It was.

Just a little slip of a thing in a bloodstained nightgown, her dark eyes huge and pathetic and very glassy. But he did not notice this or the yellow cast to her face. He only heard the voice that came from her lips— "Help me, mister, oh won't you please help me?" —and was blissfully unaware that her eyes were fixed, unseeing glass balls and that her mouth was opening and closing like a fish gulping air, but her lips were not truly forming words.

He went over to her and picked her up. She was amazingly light, a sweet stink coming off her that made his head reel. But in his state of mind, he was not truly cognizant of this because his common sense had already jumped its rails and was wildly careening this way and that.

"WHITE! WHAT THE FUCK ARE YOU DOING?" Smith shouted at him.

But White was oblivious.

He held the poor little girl to him.

Smith moved forward towards White, his flashlight beam jiggling and tossing shadows around. He saw the girl and knew she was no girl. She was a puppet and her master was a worm. When White had picked her up he thought her remarkably weightless and there was a good reason for that: for the biggest worm Smith had yet seen, thick as a man's leg, was behind the girl. It had impaled her, burrowing into her back, lifting her up like a hand puppet and drawing White in. White was ignorant of the fact in his childlike stupor...at least until the worm's bulbous head drilled out of the girl's chest in a spray of gore and opened its jaws, spitting a stream of black bile into his face.

Then he noticed.

His face hung in ribbons and strings of flesh as the acidic juice burned into it. He screamed, hands wrapped around the worm whose thick pulsating body was greasy and stinging with secretions. He tried to keep its mouth away from him as he stared down the black tunnel of its gullet, smelling the hot sweet stink of its digestive tract blowing out at him. He saw the teeth-like projections that looked very much like shards of glass. Then the stinging spines at its mouth injected their venom and he flopped forward.

"WHITE!" Smith cried out but it was hopeless, and he knew it.

The worm forced itself into his mouth, breaking his jaws in the process, and pushed down his throat. Smith jumped forward with the shotgun and by then the worm had both the little yellow-faced girl and White threaded onto its length. It lifted them in the air, making them dance and flop about with loose limbs.

Enough.

Smith fired two times at it and turned, running. He clambered up the steps as dozens of worms slid out of the warm darkness to claim him.

**4:47 A.M.**

The people chained to the walls weren't chained exactly.

They wore dog collars like precious pets. Collars attached to dog chains that were nailed to the plasterboard behind them. It was insane and more than a little disturbing.

As he put his light on them, a single thought came veering white-hot into Stein's mind: *They were brought here. That crazy man with the holes in his face, he brought them here one by one, chained them up and let the worms have them. Probably his own worms.*

They were mostly women and children, about seven or eight of them, horribly emaciated with pipe cleaner limbs and bellies rounded like root beer barrels, their flesh scaly like the leprous skin of rats. They were making wet smacking sounds with their lips, eyes rolling in their heads, tongues thick in their mouths like pink slugs. Their heads were moving side-to-side, not whipping exactly, but with a sort of rhythmic motion like they were hearing some distant music.

When the lights had been trained on them maybe ten seconds, they each disgorged worms that came gliding wetly from their mouths with succulent noises that went right up the spines of Green Team.

"What..." McKenna began to ask.

Cave shook his head. "All vectors. Waste 'em."

"Sir?"

"WASTE 'EM!"

McKenna and Stein didn't need to be told twice. They opened up and perforated the worm-carriers with slugs until their magazines were empty and the people were slumped over, held upright only by their chains.

That was it. This room was done. And there were God only knew how many more apartments to go through and at that particular moment, each man wondered if he'd have the strength for it. That's what Stein was thinking. Could they and would they? Why not torch the place? Just burn it and be done with it.

"Back away slow," Cave said then. "Real...slow."

Stein had no idea what he was talking about, then he turned and put his light over in the direction of the deranged man's corpse. He saw it. Just as Cave and McKenna had. A worm. Probably the biggest worm yet seen by the teams. It was rising up from a pocket of shadows behind a broken sofa the way a spitting cobra will rise up in a defensive posture before it strikes. It reared up and seemed to be looking right at them. Each glistening white segment was round and tinged with pink as if the worm had glutted itself on blood. Its bulb-head opened and its mouth yawned wide, lined with hook-like teeth and whipping pink tendrils. The stinging spines around the mouth were trembling, the color of fresh blood.

Mouth wide, it made a hissing *thh-thh-thh-thh-thh* sort of sound and launched itself at them in a hot wave of honeyed stench.

Green Team did not hesitate.

They opened up and blew it into strings of pulp and worm-meat and then got the hell out of there. It wasn't until they reached the corridor that they saw there were worms everywhere, slithering across the floor and inching down the walls and hanging from the ceiling, all of them hissing and shrilling.

**4:53 A.M.**

Captain Smith, the last survivor of Orange Team, came vaulting up the steps from the cellar screaming over his headset for reinforcements. He was told to link up with Green Team on the second floor and even though he knew somehow it was a horrendous mistake, he had been following orders for too long to disobey now. Sometimes orders could be a comfort, he knew, another brain making the decisions that you had lost the ability to make yourself.

He called out to Green Team and they told him they were coming down. It was time to evacuate, the entire building was infested. It was a nest.

Smith made it to the stairs when he saw, in his light, that a half-dozen people were coming down to greet him and none of them were with Green Team.

What he saw stopped him.

It not only made him hesitate but it made a stream of hot urine run down his leg because there were things you could look at that could strip your mind bare and this was one of them. Those people...not truly people any longer...were parasitized by an immense worm, threaded on its length like pearls. The worm had slid up the ass of the first man in that hideous rumba line, through his body, and out his mouth only to loop down and enter the ass of the woman in front of him, through her, and out her mouth, and to the next and next and next and next. It was so long that six feet of it trailed behind the last man in the line. The worm had them. Their arms flopped limply at their sides, their legs shuddering with each step down the stairs, heads thrown back and mouths wide. They were dark with blood and slime and what might have been feces. The lead woman of the line opened her mouth and the parasite showed itself.

Smith brought up his gun.

But not quite fast enough.

The worm spat a stream of ink-black juice into his face and he was blinded instantly. He shrieked, dropping his pump-shotgun and falling against the banister, fingers going to his face that now had the consistency of jelly.

Then the worm jabbed its spines into his back, and he went to his knees, drugged and boneless. He was barely even aware of it when the worm sheared through his fatigue pants and violated him with immense force, running through him and out his mouth, threading another mad-eyed pearl onto its pulsating, flexuous length.

It was only seconds later when the BCT showed.

They opened up with their flame throwers and torched what they saw until it dropped down the stairs in a writhing, convulsing, many-limbed heap, burning and putting out a black, vile-smelling smoke.

By the time Green Team arrived on the scene, the BCT was lighting up the building. When Cave and his men were clear, they tossed white phosphorus grenades about so it would all burn that much hotter.

# CHICAGO, CERMAK ROAD

## CHINATOWN

**5:28 A.M.**

Harry Niles couldn't sleep and he honestly wondered if he'd ever feel safe enough to close his eyes again. Surely not this night—or morning—or tomorrow night either for that matter. Although he surely was not old, he certainly did not feel so young anymore. And the game Shawna and he were playing was most definitely a game for the young—hiding out, living on the lam.

*You haven't done this in years*, he told himself. *You're rusty as hell and that could be very dangerous for the both of you. One mistake is all it takes, and you know it.*

Oh yes.

God, how he knew that.

There had been times in his checkered past as an investigative journalist where he had seriously pissed-off powerful people—politicians, industrialists, members of various federal agencies—and had to lay low and go undercover for a time. And, back then, he had discovered that he was practically a natural at hiding out, erasing his trail, living the life of a gypsy...or a criminal. But he hadn't done anything like that in many years now and it was not, he feared, second nature any longer. He had grown soft and weak, a middle-aged guy who liked his comforts: good food, a nice apartment, a comfy bed. He wasn't the same guy he was at twenty-five or thirty. The guy who would have happily lived on bread and water for a year and slept under a table if it meant he could nail someone, expose some fat cat or political puppet master.

Back then, the hunt, the stalking, then the kill itself were everything.

Now, it all seemed to mean very little.

He was no longer a predator biding his time before striking, now he was prey. Maybe what was really bothering him this time around was that, yes, he was a little out of practice at this sort of subterfuge and that it was more than just himself on the line here. Shawna, he knew, was depending on him to keep her safe and that's what scared him the most: that he would let her down.

For the time being he figured they were safe.

They were hid out in a little furnished room above Fong's Gourmet Noodle House. Chinatown was always a good place to hide out, he knew. The proprietor, Kathy Ling, was a friend of his from the old days. Not only did she supply the room, but the Chevy Tahoe Shawna and he made their escape in. His relationship with Kathy was tenuous and pretty impossible to trace. She had given him sanctuary before. Many years ago when Harry had worked for the *Trib*, he had gotten evidence that overturned the murder conviction of her younger brother. She had never forgotten that. Though he had seldom asked a favor from her, the invitation was always open.

Feeling like a cheap hood in an old film noir, he got out of bed and crept to the window, pulling the shade aside just enough so he could see the dark streets below. There was nothing out there. *What did you expect? A couple guys sitting in a black sedan smoking cigarettes? A mysterious figure reading a newspaper under the streetlight at the corner?* The streets were relatively empty save for a few early morning delivery vans making the rounds. He could see the Chinatown gate over Wentworth Avenue and not much else of interest.

He got back into bed—a rollaway provided by Kathy, Shawna had the real bed—and laid there, thinking, thinking. According to Gabe, Shawna was erased completely and probably by now, Harry himself was as well. It all was linked (Gabe thought) to some sort of outbreak of infectious disease, a containment operation being run, at least in part, by the Department of Homeland Security. Which, of course, meant the feds were behind it. And if the feds were behind it, the odds of evading were very slim. The federal government had a very long arm. But, on the other hand, Gabe said that there were hospitals under quarantine and that meant the whole thing would go public soon. Whatever sort of black budget op this had been would become general knowledge...at least the outbreak part of it.

But Harry was not reassured.

Because Gabe also said that his contacts were afraid of the people behind it.

Not good.

Shawna sat up in bed and stumbled over to the rollaway. She pulled aside the covers and got in next him, pressing her back up against him and pulling one of his arms around her.

"Don't get any ideas," she said. "I'm just scared."

"I wouldn't get any ideas. It's not the sort of person I am," he said. "There's nothing I detest more than sex with attractive young women."

"Ha," she said. Then after a time: "What are we going to do, Harry?"

"We're going to live like rats until it's safe to come out of our hole."

"I'm serious."

"So am I. We have to wait this out. From what Gabe said, it's all going to break soon and when that happens I imagine we'll be of little interest to the powers that be."

"Except that my life has been wiped out."

"It wasn't much of a life anyway."

She elbowed him. "You know what I mean. You might be erased by now, too."

"For the time being, only for the time being," he assured her. "You see, I live in a state of readiness...or paranoia, if you prefer. They can wipe me out of computers, but I have the paperwork: bank statements, social security card, stock certificates, bonds."

"If they clean out your place, they'll get all that."

"They would, except I keep it all in a safe deposit box under an assumed name."

"And the key to it?"

"Kathy Ling has one. The other is in my wallet as we speak."

He explained that they could wipe him out all they wanted, but the paperwork with account numbers would raise an immediate red flag. Accounts don't just disappear. Numbers can be traced.

"What is it with you and Kathy?"

"Jealous?"

"Hardly."

He shrugged and gave her the gist of the story. "We keep in contact but our relationship is very discreet. No one can trace it or even prove that it exists."

"So we're safe?"

"For the time being."

"That doesn't make me feel reassured."

"Sorry, Shawna. But we'll take it one hour, one day at a time. If what Gabe says is true, this whole thing is about to blow wide open."

# DETROIT

## EAST DEARBORN

**6:41 A.M.**

Down in the sewers like a rat. Listening to the rumble of cars and trucks and buses. Staring up at the world through a rusting sewer grating.

There were many in this world, infidels all, that would have been quite pleased with Sheikh Sa'ad al Khalafari's new accommodations: rats belong in holes. But he knew that in war there was suffering and the physical plane was a plane of suffering and only through God was there grace.

There had been a raid by the FBI on the furniture store where he had been living and hiding. It had been but one of a dozen such raids across the country by the U.S. government. Some thirty people had been taken into custody and nearly half of them were illegals which would either be deported or imprisoned permanently.

Sheikh Sa'ad had been tipped off.

He went into hiding.

In the sewers.

There would come a time when he would re-emerge and by that time the American dogs and oppressors would be brought to their knees by the most humble of Allah's creations: the worm.

Sheikh Sa'ad smiled.

God had given him a duty, a blessed mission, and that was to bring America, the great evil, to its knees. And had it not been so then God would not have delivered the very weapon of extermination into his hands: the lowly worm. Sheikh Sa'ad knew that the worm was an American invention. The technology had been harvested by agents of the Iranian Pasdaran from which he had liberated it. That was the beauty of it truly: the irony of America being destroyed by its own inhumanity and ruthless hunger for domination.

*The worm*, Sheikh Sa'ad thought not without amusement, *has certainly turned.*

It was Allah's plan, of course, that it be so. Sheikh Sa'ad firmly believed this. He would not entertain doubt for doubt was the kingdom of the fallen and he would rise to glory as the spiritual leader of the Islamic uprising. In his mind he could hear the voices of his advisors, all of them dead now, the seeds of doubt and uncertainty they had tried to place in his mind, how they had tried to tell him that the worm would spread—and quickly—beyond the borders of America. That it would take the world country by country and within weeks, if not days, the Middle East would be infested as well.

He purged those voices from his head.

God was the great architect and God would destroy the infidels and send the worms into their graves with them. The true believers of Islam would not be harmed. As prayers fell from his lips, Sheikh Sa'ad truly believed this.

And never had he been so very wrong.

# CHICAGO

**7:00 A.M.**

When the morning editions of the *Sun-Times* and the *Tribune* hit the streets, they both carried extensive coverage of the raid on the tenement in Auburn Gresham by members of the U.S. Marshals Service. The story each told was much the same: on a tip, the Marshals went into the building in force to capture members of a fanatical Black Muslim sect that were stockpiling weapons for a violent overthrow of the city. Six of the men killed were on the FBI's Most Wanted list. Following a desperate gun battle, the building had caught fire by the use of incendiaries by the Marshals and burnt to the ground.

The people of Chicago were either publicly outraged or secretly pleased that this homegrown terrorist sect had been eliminated. Questions abounded, of course, and all were answered quite neatly by a statement given by the Department of Homeland Security. A press conference was scheduled for ten a.m.

The newspaper coverage featured images of the blackened ruins of the building and various quotes by locals who claimed they were glad the rat-infested tenement had been burned, although many said that to their knowledge the old "rat trap" was a crack house and nothing more. Several said they didn't like it, that there was something fishy about it all and they frowned upon such stormtrooper tactics.

In Chicago and other cities, the debate would go on throughout the day, thereby distracting inquiring minds from other and more disturbing events that were breaking out in every quarter of the city as they were in cities nationwide. The story created great buzz on the Internet and extensive coverage by CNN and the other news networks. Papers from Boston to LA covered the story.

But not one of them made mention of parasitic worms.

# DETROIT

## HOLY CROSS HOSPITAL DETOX WARD

**7:17 A.M.**

Maybe the rest of the country was a little slow catching onto the conspiracy in their midst, but there was one guy who had it pegged and that was Johnny Kopok. He would have been the first to admit he had a little problem with the sauce—he and old Sweet Lucy were fast friends—and sometimes he saw a few things that weren't there and maybe he didn't always know what year it was, but he knew a big juicy shit-smelling cover-up and conspiracy when he saw one.

"Wait a minute now," he said to the nurse. "I been a good boy and did what you told me and ate my grub like a good soldier. Now I wanna get out and you're telling me I can't go?"

"I'm sorry, sir, but this hospital is currently under quarantine. Everyone will be processed out, but it will take time. We appreciate your patience."

Jesus, this broad talked like a U.S. government flyer, kind of thing you found tacked to the wall at the Social Security office. Johnny figured he didn't care for her much. He got the feeling she thought pretty highly of herself. She stood there, holding her clipboard in black rubber gloves, decked out in a white plastic suit and green rubber HAZMAT boots, that crazy hood over her head with the plastic bubble and twin air filters. Damn, like something out of the trenches of the First World War. Maybe one of those space shows Johnny had seen when he was a kid.

"You don't need that space suit around me," he told her. "I ain't got the worms, least none that I didn't have before."

"We're under quarantine," she said.

"Yeah, but you're giving me the creeps, you know? Every time I see you I think we're being invaded. Take me to your leader." Johnny laughed because he thought that was funny but the nurse maintained her mannequin demeanor. "You remind me of that one picture. The one with the Martian guy in the spacesuit, wandering around causing trouble. Then he gets out of the suit and he's invisible. When he dies he glows in the dark. You ever seen that one?"

"I'm sure I haven't."

"Where's Jimbo?" he asked her.

"Jimbo?"

"The orderly. He's always here."

"I'm sure I don't know. Some of the staff are going through DECON procedures and will return at a later time."

Boy, this lady had personality. Real personality. Talked like a fucking answering machine. "Okay. Then where's the doc? Dr. Claddahfadda or whatever his fucking name is. Short fellah. Foreigner."

"I'm sure he'll be in later."

Johnny had half a mind to jump out of bed, strip off her mask, and give her a big wet kiss. That ought to just about make her piss her pants. Least she might act human then, angry but human. He didn't mind them drying him out for a few days, absence made the heart grow fonder and all that, but this business...Jesus, what was this about? Not that they would tell him. Some kind of infectious disease they were saying which was gamey bullshit and he knew it. Worms. It was about them goddamn worms.

"You think I got 'em, don't you?" he said.

The nurse just stared at him through her plastic bubble. "Them, sir?"

"Yeah, the fucking worms. Don't play dumb, sister, you're no good at it."

"We currently have an outbreak of H1N1 and are following standard quarantine procedures."

"H one N one...now what the fuck is that?"

"A form of viral flu, sir."

"Flu? Oh my Christ. This ain't about flu, it's about fucking worms. I saw 'em. They come out of people's mouths. But they never got me. No sir. Now why don't you go tell your boss that and turn me loose. I'm starting to get awful thirsty."

"I'll report it, sir."

"And send Jimbo in here, will ya?"

"I'll look into it, sir."

She left and Johnny laid there on the bed, trying to wrap his brain around this Grade-A clusterfuck. That woman was in the Army or something. You could always tell by the way they talked like they had a size-ten bug up their asses. Johnny knew all about that because he'd been in the Marines and he could smell a jarhead a mile away. Just like he could smell a good conspiracy cooking and this one was really starting to stink.

With that in mind, he began to plot his escape.

# TEL AVIV

## BEN GURION AIRPORT



Nobody noticed the small, swarthy man reading the newspaper near the British Airways terminal. He blended in perfectly. Chameleonic, one might say. He paged through his newspaper, now and again making eye contact with another man sitting in the lounge. They did not smile or even nod. The swarthy man watched the security queue as passengers were questioned. Most were desensitized to Israeli methods and answered the questions without hesitation in bored voices. Others—foreigners—objected.

The swarthy man smiled.

He knew the questions quite well. Why did you visit Israel? What did you do while in the country? Who did you stay with? Are you a Jew? How long have your friends lived in the country? Are they Jews? On and on and on. Foreigners could become quite angry with the barrage of intrusive questions. If they raised too much of a fuss, security would take them aside and if they were not satisfied, flights would be missed.

The swarthy man's name was Isser Shabbat and he was a twenty-seven-year veteran of Mossad, Israeli intelligence, and currently a member of the elite and shadowy Kidon, an ultra-secret arm of the Mossad which handled its most delicate and dangerous tasks: assassination, abduction, sabotage, and infiltration of high-security installations. That he killed for his country using everything from silenced weapons to knives, car bombs to injected nerve agents was a fact. He routinely and quite ruthlessly hunted down Palestinian terrorists and Hamas insurgents and agents of Islamic Jihad.

But you would not have suspected it.

With his twinkling blue eyes, round face, and easy smile he was someone's favored and kindly uncle. He was harmless. And he had spent many years cultivating this persona that made him the perfect chameleon that immediately adapted to its environment and became part of it.

Today, Shabbat was waiting for someone.

So far, he had not shown.

But it was early. The flight to Heathrow in London would not leave for another hour or more and there was plenty of time. And if Shabbat had learned anything in these past twenty-seven years it was patience.

He looked over at the man in the lounge. The man caught his eye but no more.

Back to his newspaper. Back to waiting.

The man Shabbat was waiting for was a very dangerous fellow. Though his true name was Abu Zakari, he would be traveling with an expertly forged set of documents that would identify him as Saul Lavonik, an Israeli national and software designer. He would pass through security quite easily just as he had been trained to.

But Shabbat would not let him get that far.

For Mossad knew who and what he was. Abu Zakari was a confederate of Mahmoud Al-Kassin, an Islamic militant and the number three man in Hamas. He lived secretly on the West Bank, running a fanatical underground terror network and overseeing a factory that produced car bombs and IEDs. Al-Kassin's activities were largely supported by the extremist Iranian Pasdaran Quds Force, though, of late, Al-Kassin had broken off with them and taken up with Sheikh Sa'ad al Khalafari's organization which promised to bring down the west in a most peculiar and novel fashion.

And it was to this end that Abu Zakari would depart to London.

Shabbat kept watch as he always kept watch. He was the eagle in its high nest and hawk of the desert. When he woke each day, he accepted that it might be his last. But if he died, he knew, he would die knowing satisfaction that he had been a constant irritant to the mujahideen in their campaign for innocent blood.

A group of girls passed by him, all teenagers fulfilling their compulsory National Service obligations. They spread out and began to ask impatient people in the queues a barrage of silly questions, the answers to which they had little interest in.

The man in the lounge looked over at him.

He blinked twice.

It was enough.

Shabbat saw Zakari and continued to read his newspaper. Zakari would walk right past him and that would work fine. Shabbat waited, humming beneath his breath. Out of the corner of his eye he saw his target getting closer and closer. Mere feet away, Shabbat could see the arrogance and absolute confidence of the Hamas killer. He carried death with him and was only too happy to release it upon the unsuspecting.

When Zakari made to pass by him, Shabbat stuck out his foot and tripped him. Zakari went down and came up quickly, shrieking curses in Arabic. Shabbat hit him twice and he did not get up again. By then a crowd began to gather and airport security rushed in. A look at the ID cards of Shabbat and his Mossad partner made them realize this was none of their concern.

By then Zakari had been handcuffed and dragged to his feet. *"Au'dhu Billahi Min ash-Shaitan Ar-Rajeem!"* he cried as he was dragged from the terminal and Shabbat smiled thinly, gripping his elbow all that much harder. "Yes, my friend, ask your god for protection. Where you are going, you will need it."

# LOUISVILLE, KENTUCKY

## UNIVERSITY HOSPITAL

**8:02 A.M.**

When Dr. Gilbeki returned after a refreshing two-week vacation in his native Calcutta—always glad to visit, thankful he did not have to stay—he was whistling. A happy, contented man, he was anxious to get up to Pediatrics and see how a few of his patients were doing. Although his wife told him to leave his work behind, he had thought of little else while he was gone.

Then he saw the police cars, ambulances, and unmarked gray vans parked out front of the hospital. Wooden barriers had been erected at every drive that said POLICE LINE—DO NOT CROSS. There were lots of TV vans around with aerials and the cops were keeping them at bay. What intrigued Gilbeki the most were the men in black windbreaker jackets and sunglasses...and the others in white plastic biohazard suits.

It didn't look good at all.

As Gilbeki tried to pull into the physician's parking lot, one of the men in the windbreakers stopped him. "Sir, this hospital is under quarantine. You need to leave."

"I work here," Gilbeki told him.

"Can I see some ID, sir?"

Gilbeki, not unused to such things in his native country, silently complied.

"Okay, Doctor. Pull into the lot."

After he had parked, the man in the windbreaker came over to him, identifying himself as a member of Homeland Security. "You'll need to talk with Mr. Swenson." He pointed to one of the drab unmarked vans. "He'll answer all your questions."

"Why is the hospital under quarantine?"

"An infectious outbreak, sir."

"Of what?"

"I'm not at liberty to say."

"Well...really," Gilbeki said to him. "Is it a virus?"

"I'm not at liberty to say. I can only tell you that the hospital is currently under a decon operation."

Gilbeki shrugged and made his way over to the van, moving along the police barriers where other men in windbreakers kept a close eye on him. He was nearly there when a young, attractive woman in a skirt leaned over the barrier.

"Excuse me...are you hospital staff?"

"Um...yes...I'm Dr. Gilbeki, pediatrics."

"Could you tell us what's going on?" she asked. "A lot of us have family members in there and these Nazis won't let us in to see them."

Gilbeki shook his head. "I don't know what's going on, miss. I have only arrived just now and am told the hospital is under quarantine."

"Quarantine for what?"

"That I do not know and no one is telling me."

"But—"

"All right," one of DHS men said. "I warned you before about approaching the barriers. Now back away."

"You can't—"

"Back away, ma'am."

She did, calling him a few unsavory names in the process and returning to the others as a cop came and ordered her to stay back or he would put her under arrest for inciting a riot.

The DHS man led Gilbeki over to the van. "That woman is a newspaper reporter, sir, and I'm going to have to ask you not to talk with any of them."

He was brought to the van and taken inside. There was a command-and-control station set up in the back. Two or three DHS agents were tapping away on laptops.

"Dr. Gilbeki?" said a man with a white crewcut. "We have a situation here and I'm sure you've heard a few things by this point."

"I have patients on fifth floor," he said.

"And we're going to make sure you see them. Right now the hospital is being decontaminated. We're getting patients out as fast as we can and moving them to other facilities. We definitely need your help."

"I'm ready to go in."

"First you'll need Level D Personal Protection Equipment, PPE Four."

"Yes, fine. I've had HAZMAT training."

"Excellent. Now all you have to do is sign this release."

Gilbeki looked at the form on the clipboard. It was a copy of the Official Secrets Act.

# CHICAGO, RIVER NORTH

## THE WAREHOUSE

**8:29 A.M.**

"It's going to start coming apart now," Stein said as he sat in the little makeshift lounge, his eyes crusty from lack of sleep, his nerves still jangled from the operation at the tenement.

"What do you mean?" McKenna said.

"You know what I mean."

McKenna stared blankly at the TV screen. The volume was off. They had CNN on and things were happening. Hospitals were under quarantine. People were missing. The National Guard was on the move. Federal agents were arresting people and SWAT biocon teams were raiding houses and apartment complexes. Rioting had broken out in a few cities with more expected. People were afraid. They knew something was going on but they weren't being told what. By tomorrow, both Stein and McKenna knew, things would reach crisis stage. It was not good.

"The lid's about to blow off this whole mess."

"You think so?" McKenna said.

"You don't have eyes?"

McKenna said nothing for a time, then: "What do you think about all this? I mean, honestly?"

"I think it's dirty and ugly. That's what I think."

"What do you think we should do?"

"Do?"

"Yeah. I mean, you and me. What should we do?"

*Why the hell is he asking me that again?* Stein wondered. Day by day he was getting a real bad feeling about McKenna. He couldn't exactly put a finger on what it was but the guy was bugging him. He kept asking the same questions.

That's what bugged Stein. He had been playing this game too long not to recognize when he was being played.

But McKenna?

Would McKenna be up to something? Trying to test his loyalty? To what end?

But that was obvious. Stein had told him more than once how they should just get out while they still could. If McKenna had mentioned any of that to Cave then...then the both of them might be up to something. Something like amassing a file on him and that would mean a trip to The Resort for brain-scrubbing.

Stein was not naïve by any means.

He knew the sort of cutthroat pond he swam in. There were sharks everywhere and no one was to be trusted. That was intelligence work, the nature of the game. And the kind of thing they were doing now—cleaners, assassins—and the people they were hooked up with—the Old Man and S5—made things even more sketchy and dangerous than usual. He honestly didn't believe that any of the team members would walk away from this, not knowing what they knew. Even if the worms were contained there was still the fact that they had been terminating infected veterans, killing on order.

That was politically volatile stuff.

And it wouldn't be the first time that cleaners were cleaned.

Stein let himself relax. He lit a cigarette and tried to be nonchalant as possible. McKenna was essentially a hothead. People like that were easy to play. Time to bait him.

He pulled off his cigarette. "What do you think about all this?" he said.

"I think like you. It's a mess and I'll be glad when it's done."

"What if it's not done?"

"What do you mean?"

"I mean, what if it keeps getting worse and worse and the worms are everywhere. What will you do?"

McKenna shifted, but gave nothing away. "What will you do?"

"I like your idea."

"My idea?"

"Sure. About saying fuck the Company and S-Five and XI and just running."

"That wasn't my idea!" McKenna said. "That was yours! You're the one who keeps talking about it!"

"Sure. But it was your idea in the first place."

"Bullshit."

Stein shrugged. "That's what I remember."

McKenna was breathing hard. "Are you questioning my loyalty?"

"No, I'd never do that. But if we're being listening to—and we probably are—then I'll bet somebody is."

# LANGLEY, VIRGINIA

## CIA CRISIS CENTER

**8:51 A.M.**

*It was all coming into focus now*, DCI Pershing thought. Just as he'd always planned and perhaps even fantasized for many years. Not that he would ever admit to such. Even to himself. He was simply a man in a position of power that knew how to play the game and exploit his resources. The country was edging closer to chaos day by day and when critical mass was reached, he would play his card and seize control.

He sipped his coffee, the caffeine making him alert and clear-headed, a predator preparing to leap.

But not yet.

Not just yet.

The worms were everywhere now and that was a scary thought. He believed they could be contained but not by running covert ops. This was far too big. This would require a nontraditional approach, his advisors told him. Something overt and aggressive, a nationwide op run with the coordination of the intelligence and security services, military and police. And sitting atop that nest of vipers could only be one man.

It would take a man with vision.

A man with courage.

A man who wasn't afraid to bury his opponents.

Such a man was Robert Pershing, the Director of the Central Intelligence Agency.

As things stood now, DCI Pershing already had Rear Admiral Paulus of the ONI in his corner as well as Francis Mason, Chairman of the JCS. Both were men with balls, with connections, with immense power within their circles and theaters of operation and whose orbits included a veritable who's-who of the military/industrial complex. But Pershing wasn't satisfied with that. He wanted more. He had a good feeling about Charlie Goade, the Director of the FBI and an old friend. But there were others he needed on his team—men like Roger Thorogood, the Secretary of Defense, and Arlene Rabin, the Secretary of State. Unfortunately, he knew they were both fiercely loyal to the President as was Gus Costello, the National Security Advisor.

So that was trouble.

If Costello wouldn't come on board—and Pershing knew he wouldn't—that meant Maddie Hughes, the DHS Secretary wouldn't either.

Trouble, trouble, trouble.

Pershing would have to be patient and he knew it. Gordon Parks of the NSA made him nervous because he was a veteran game player and mix-master who was in deep with Liz Toma of CBT. Though he had no intel to support it, he suspected both of them of the worst possible subterfuge. He would watch them as, he knew, they watched him.

As things stood, he knew he'd never get DNI Chuck VanderMissen or Walt Sleshing of the DIA in his corner. But then, he didn't really want them. He had already identified them as scapegoats. When the dust settled, the evidence would point to the both of them.

Pershing's plan was simple.

He would let the chaos run rampant. When it reached critical mass, he would bring in an X-RAY team to take out the President right on down to Costello and everyone in-between, including the Vice President. It would be a strike carried out with mathematical efficiency. The assassinations would be blamed on domestic terror units in collusion with Sleshing, VanderMissen, and Costello. The country would be, essentially, stripped of leadership and Pershing himself and his confederates would fill that void. Martial law would be enacted and a nationwide bio-containment op would be initiated. Along the way, certain civil liberties and constitutional rights would be stripped away as they had been with the Patriot Act of the Bush Administration and never, ever would they be returned.

Chaos would become domestic strife and then...a land controlled by one man. A man who was particularly ambitious and assertive. A leader.

Until then, let chaos reign.

The time would come.

Already, Pershing was assembling his assets on the ground and one of them was Tommy Quillan who would serve his purpose by eliminating the members of the Emergency Response Teams S5 was using. And when he was done, he would himself become a corpse. All loose ends would be tied up.

Pershing sighed, feeling destiny within his grasp.

He looked at a report on his desk. Three names had gone into the system: Harold Niles, Shawna Geddes, and Gabe Hebberman. They were considered security risks. They had been seen nosing around by some of S5's people. The Old Man wanted them contained and a kill order was put out.

Pershing didn't see why they mattered now.

What could they tell of...still, if the Old Man and S5 wanted it, why not? As long as VanderMissen didn't find out it would be just fine. And, really, it was only a matter of time before an X-RAY was ordered on VanderMissen and all the others.

The future was beckoning.

# RICHMOND, VIRGINIA

## CBT CORPORATE HEADQUARTERS

**9:03 A.M.**

As a veteran of executive-branch politics and corporate subterfuge, Elizabeth Toma had learned to trust her instincts. Sometimes it was the only thing that saved your neck. Reams of metadata crossed her desk every day and dozens of employees, politicians, aides, and professional spooks walked through her door, flooding her with more intel, more info, some of it thinly sourced and some of it actionable. And nearly all of it conflicting in one way or another.

She trusted no one because she could not afford to open herself up to some of the meat-eaters she dealt with and she didn't dare turn her back on them. Loyalty was an abstract concept from where she sat and everyone, everyone, had an agenda.

In general, when she spoke to The Collective, she held her tongue and played the game, kept everything dry and official and never, ever exposed her true feelings. But today, she was done with that. Her back was up and when she got that way, she had no true fear.

"The problem being, Mr. Brown, that I have the worst feeling based on information that's been coming my way that you're being less than forthcoming on certain matters," she said over the phone. "I don't care for that. I've been very helpful and very cooperative. I don't care to be left out of the loop."

There was silence for a few moments and she knew without a doubt that she had just displeased The Collective. Good, dammit. She had reached the point where she didn't give a good goddamn how powerful they were—she was done being an obedient, fawning follower.

"Would you care to share that information, Elizabeth?"

"No, I would not. What I would like to know is what happens next. BioGen is active and Pershing is unleashing his beast...but there's another stage, another level. I want to know what that is. I cannot align my resources until I know what the endgame is."

More silence. Mr. Brown was either carefully considering what she said, pros and cons, tactical advantages and political blowback...or he was about to clip her wings and leave her out in the cold.

"And what makes you certain there is another level?" he wanted to know.

Elizabeth's turn for silence. Well, she started this. If she backed down now, she would appear weak, conflicted, insecure. A captain who was no longer steering her own ship. And before The Collective, she could not be those things. She knew she must always be confident, almost supernaturally so. But on the other hand, if she pushed too hard and too far...well, she wouldn't live to regret it.

Before answering, she studied a report on her desk. It had come from 3Eye. Mostly speculation, fanciful projection. But buried in there somewhere was a grain of truth.

"I'm confident there is another level," she said. "And I believe that our friend at the NSA knows what it is. I've made myself clear on this in the past—he likes to talk, he likes to brag, he likes to overinflate his place in the scheme of things."

"And?"

"And word has it that he's been hinting around about a certain classified project up in Alaska. Do I need to mention it by name?"

"No, I'd rather you didn't."

"Word reaches me that it's about to go live."

"And that...eh...comes from our NSA friend?"

"Indirectly."

She could hear him breathing on the other end. The sense she got was not that he was going to clip her wings, but that he was nervous, possibly even scared.

"And you think we're leaving you out of it?"

"Yes, obviously."

"And we should be more forthcoming?"

"I trust you. I've done everything I could to further our cause. I have the distinct feeling you don't trust me," she said. "I don't like that. Not after what I've sacrificed."

She expected more dramatic silence, but she got none. "Perhaps you're right. Perhaps we've underestimated your usefulness. Let me speak to my associates. If they agree, there will be full disclosure."

"Thank you."

"Yes, well. It's high time we met face to face. I'll be in contact."

She sat there for some time, thinking, wondering. Professionally, she was excited at the idea of advancing beyond her present station. But her instincts—well-sharpened and sensitive from years upon years of survival—were warning her.

*Be careful.*
*Full disclosure can be a very dangerous thing.*
*It's not always good to know too much.*

But she couldn't back down. Again, it would make her look weak. She had to go through with this even if her nerves were on edge, her stomach turning, and her instincts screaming at her.

*If they bring you in, it means immense power.*
Or—
*It means you'll be killed.*

# CHICAGO, WEST ROOSEVELT:

## FBI FIELD DIVISION

**9:20 A.M.**

In retrospect, Danny Pasquel did not see where he was doing anything wrong. It wasn't like he was selling state secrets or had become a mole for organized crime. Gabe Hebberman was an old friend. He was basically a sleaze publisher and would be the first to admit as such...but he was handy and had infinite resources and contacts. Pasquel had found Gabe handy in more than one investigation. Sometimes you had to repay favors, give a little to get a little. That's how things worked.

Pasquel was an FBI Assistant Special-Agent-in-Charge with a good clean record and he was being groomed for bigger and better things. So when Pohlman came up to his desk and said, "Hey, Danny. Let's take a walk," right away he expected trouble.

When Special Agent-in-Charge Pohlman took you for a walk it usually meant you fucked up something and Pasquel honestly could not think of a thing. He had just been appointed to the Chicago Joint Terrorism Task Force for his work busting up an Islamic extremist group that had plans to detonate bombs in the Sears Tower. He was well liked and respected.

Then Pohlman took him for a walk.

When they got outside, casually walking side-by-side up the sidewalk, SAC Polhlman said, "I need to talk to you about a phone call you took."

"Sir?"

"Gabe Hebberman."

"Gabe? What about it?"

Pohlman told him that Hebberman's name was on a watch list and when somebody at the Chicago Division took a call for him...then later called him back...it sent up red flags all over the system.

"I got three calls from Washington, Danny," Pohlman said. "Friendly calls...but stern."

"Sir...are you telling me my phone is tapped?"

Pohlman sighed. "Danny, this whole goddamn building is tapped. The NSA is listening in on everything. When you got a call from Hebberman, their computers immediately ID'd it because he's on a list."

"Gabe? Christ, he's harmless."

"What did he want, Danny? The NSA knows what you guys talked about, but I'd like to know."

"Sir, it was hardly anything. You know Gabe. He's a contact. One hand washes the other. He wanted me to run a couple names through the system...let's see..." he dug out a notebook from the inside pocket of his suit coat "...Shawna Geddes and Harold Niles. He wasn't specific about what he wanted with them, just that they were connected with something he was running down." Pasquel shrugged. "I suppose, sir, you're going to tell me I can't be using Bureau resources on things like this."

SAC Pohlman smiled. "No, Danny. I know how it works. I played the game for years. Assets are assets. You have an impressive record and don't think they're not aware of it in Washington. A favor for a favor, like you say. It just so happens that this time, your friend's name got the NSA and the Department of Homeland Security all worked up. He's being watched in connection with a possible terror cell."

"That's ridiculous."

Pohlman arched his eyebrow and no more. "That's not for us to decide. We have to play ball. So do me a favor and break off contact with Hebberman. He calls, you're not in. It's the right thing to do. The people who called me can make trouble, Danny. A lot of trouble. And we don't want that, do we?"

Pasquel sighed. "Of course not."

"Good."

"I suppose this is going in my file?"

"Of course not."

*Like hell it won't*, Pasquel thought.

# NEGEV DESERT, SOUTHERN ISRAEL

## BIR SHIVA DETAINMENT CAMP

**4:14 P.M. ISRAEL TIME**

The Israelis took no chances with Wing #6, for it was here in this pale two-story building that some of the nation's greatest enemies were housed: Fatah dissidents, Hamas terrorists, and Palestinian Islamic Jihad militants. The building was circled by razor wire and an electrified fence. Guards with automatic weapons patrolled the perimeter.

Isser Shabbat was waved through and into the building where he was greeted by a guard in a pale blue uniform. The guard looked very beleaguered, telling Shabbat that they had a Hamas hunger strike going on and about a dozen appeals from the Palestinian National Authority to deal with. Not a good day. Though, Shabbat figured, there was probably no such thing as a good day in this place.

He was led down a concrete walkway to an interrogation room. Inside, Abu Zakari was tied to a chair. His legs were shackled. He was bloodied, beaten, mumbling prayers beneath his breath. The confidence that Shabbat had seen in him at Ben Gurion had evaporated. It had been drained off as if someone had opened an artery and maybe they had at that.

When he saw Shabbat, simmering black hate filled his eyes.

"And how are we faring?" Shabbat put to him, grinning broadly. "I'm told you do not wish to speak to us?"

Zakari kept staring at him. "Ah..ila jaheem ma'ik," he said in Arabic, telling Shabbat to go to hell.

"You can do better than that," Shabbat said. "Come now. Talk to me. Your Hebrew is perfect and I know it. Probably much better than my Arabic. Let us talk. You're going nowhere. You will be in this place for many years. You might as well tell us why you were going to England."

Zakari just stared.

"You have a wife and two sons. Shall I have them brought here for the amusement of the other inmates?" Shabbat asked him. "Or does such a thing mean nothing to you animals of the West Bank?"

Zakari swallowed. In perfect Hebrew, he said, "I am a man of God. I am a man of peace."

"As am I. Ask any of the Islamic trash I have killed. They will concur that I am a man of peace."

Zakari began to pray again.

"If you are a man of peace, please explain this to me." Shabbat set a tiny vial on the table before Zakari. "We found this inserted into the handle of a disposable razor. It was ingeniously hidden and x-rays would not have picked it up. But we of the Mossad have more intensive methods." He picked the vial up. It was made of plastic. Inside was a tiny, fleshy object curled like a grub. "This is very interesting. The x-rays would not harm this little horror, eh? Which means by the time you arrived in London, the little beast would still be quite active...yes?"

Zakari continued to pray.

"Come now, my friend. Please do not make me get unpleasant. I've been told that I get carried away. I become excessive in my attention to a man's genitals." Shabbat shrugged. "But, no matter, perhaps there is a better way, hmm? British MI6 will be very interested in what we found in this vial. Unfortunately, we cannot share it with them."

Zakari looked up.

Shabbat motioned with his head. Two Mossad operatives took hold of Zakari. They wrapped a leather strap around his forehead, yanking his head back as far it would go. Another such strap was placed in his mouth, forcing his lower jaw down so that his mouth was open.

Still smiling, kindly, compassionate, yet most pitiless, Shabbat donned a pair of rubber surgical gloves, ensuring that they fit snugly. From a small case he removed a forceps. He began to unscrew the small lid of the vial. He grasped the dormant larval worm with the forceps and brought it within inches of Zakari's open mouth.

No longer smiling, he said, "You have five seconds to tell me what I want to know before this little horror infests you."

Zakari thrashed but could go nowhere.

He tried to close his mouth. Impossible.

He tried to turn his head. Unattainable.

Shabbat brought the worm closer. "Yes?"

Zakari began to sob and plead so Shabbat placed the worm back in its vial, screwing the lid shut. "Good. Now...understand me: if I have to open that vial again, I will drop the worm down your throat. Do you understand that?"

Zakari nodded, tears running down his cheeks.

"Tell me," Shabbat said.

Knowing that he was not just betraying his Muslim brothers but Allah himself, Zakari sobbed and whined, but when Shabbat reached for the vial, he shook his head, saying in Hebrew: "It is too late! It is far too late... don't you see? It is much later than you think..."

# WASHINGTON D.C.

## WHITE HOUSE SITUATION ROOM

**11:07 A.M.**

DNI VanderMissen had watched it go from bad to worse so by this point, nothing was really surprising him. God knows he loved his country and the ideals it stood for…it was just the men that ran it that sometimes gave him pause (and the idiots who voted them into office). The President, he knew, was a good man, a compassionate man, a man of integrity and conscience. He could not be blamed for the scourge that was taking the country. At least not directly. That fault lay solely with the various agencies and executives who'd green-lighted this mess (and VanderMissen himself was one of them, may God help him). Regardless, POTUS was tasked with cleaning up the mess.

If such a thing were even possible.

And Charles VanderMissen was beginning to have his doubts.

The men and women gathered in the Situation Room were the muscle behind the National Security Council Intelligence Committee: the secretaries of state and defense, the directors of the CIA, DIA, ONI, members of the Joint Chiefs of Staff, the President's military and intelligence advisors, a few high-ranking medical and scientific specialists, the President and Vice President. All of them presided over by Gus Costello, the National Security Advisor.

"Ladies and gentlemen," Costello said. "I want to thank each and every one of you for coming. I honestly can't think of a more dire set of circumstances than the ones we face now."

Everyone quietly picked up their NSC estimates and briefs. All of which were well-thumbed by that point, but they looked anyway, more than a few a little pale at the predictions within.

"The question is, as always, how are we going to handle it?" Admiral Paulus, the Director of Naval Intelligence asked.

"We want to proceed with the least amount of collateral damage to this country, this office, and the people who've put their trust in us," Arlene Rabin, the Secretary of State said.

There were a few murmurs to that.

General Mason, the JCS Chairman, cleared his throat. "You all know me. You know I don't dick the dog. I come right out and say what's on my mind. So...the sooner we declare martial law the better. I want congressional power to deploy our combined forces domestically. We need more than the National Guard and reserves here. And we need to move on this goddamn yesterday."

"Hold on," Robert Pershing, the DCI said. "Let's not be hasty."

"We could always try a full confession," Charles Goade, the FBI Director said. "Spill the beans. Tell the public that it was a horrendous error in judgment that set this monster loose and now it's in the hands of foreign extremists."

"Now wait a minute," the Secretary of Defense said. "Quite a few of us were involved. Personally, people, I don't like the idea of being offered up as a sacrificial lamb."

"He's right," Costello said. "I wasn't involved then, but do we really want the public to find out about this... this atrocity? Do we want the dirty laundry of Section Five made public? The repercussions could be devastating."

"Maybe it's high time," Pershing said.

They all looked at him. It was totally out of character, for nobody swept more dirt under the carpet or covered his ass as expertly as did the Director of the CIA. He wouldn't have gotten where he currently was if he was a man of truth and they all knew it.

Admiral Paulus and General Mason were staring at him.

"What I mean is, maybe the time has come for full disclosure," he said, knowing and knowing full well that everything that was being said was recorded and his position would be a matter of record.

"I don't see that helping matters," the Vice President said.

But the President was considering it; they could all see that.

Gus Costello stood up. "This is more than just a matter of national security," he told them. "From all indications the outbreak is poised to become global. We need to carefully consider this and assess the possible damage to this country and our international position."

"Meaning," General Mason said, "if we want any friends when this is done, we better cover our asses with both hands."

"Agreed," said the Secretary of State.

Costello looked down the long table at all the expectant faces. "We've just gotten word from Israeli Mossad that Abu Zakari, a known Hamas agent, was attempting to smuggle worm larva out of Tel Aviv and into London."

"Jesus," DDI General Sleshing said. "That's all we need."

"The point being, gentlemen," VanderMissen piped in, "is that this might have started with a colossal fuck-up on the part of those involved in the ground level development and deployment of BioGen, but it's beyond that now. Maybe we could have contained this had it only been our own soldiers and Marines infected. Maybe. But, as I said, it's beyond all that now. The cat, so to speak, is out of the bag. Iranian Pasdaran somehow, some way, managed to harvest the technology. And now that technology has been stolen from them by Sheikh Sa'ad al Khalafari. I imagine the Iranians are pissed...no matter. BioGen will not recognize borders and if what we suspect is true, the Iranians will soon get all the firsthand knowledge of the parasites they want.

"Regardless, the worms will soon be everywhere. Our own forces brought BioGen back with them where it cooked for a number of years before becoming active. And now Sheikh Sa'ad has worsened the matter by spreading BioGen to a variety of terrorist organizations. Hamas is a fact. Al-Qaeda is a near certainty. Hezbollah and Palestinian Islamic Jihad are probable as well as every extremist Shi'a group you can think of. These are facts. And now we have reason to believe that a variety of hardcore Islamic militants have entered this country illegally and are, and have been, spreading BioGen in nearly every major city in conjunction with terror sleeper cells. The same goes for Canada, South America, the UK, Europe, Russia, Asia...dear God, this is out of control."

"You're absolutely right on every count, Chuck," Costello said. "So let's not worry about explaining the origins of this mess. In light of an absolute global pandemic, they really don't matter. As far as we're concerned, it was started by terrorists and that's where we'll leave it."

"So where does that leave us?" the Secretary of Defense said.

"Straight in the shitter," Mason grumbled.

"And to think," General Sleshing said, "I thought things we're going to get better after SEAL Team Six popped fucking Bin Laden."

"It's your call, Mr. President," Arlene Rabin said.

The President was deeply pained by it all. Sickened, worried, frustrated, and most of all angry about what he considered to be an absolute lack of ethics by S5, lack of judgment by his own administration, and reckless ambition by many of those at the table. "Yes," he said, "it is my call and it's a call, by God, I don't want to make. But I don't honestly see where I have a choice. We need perception management here or this entire country is going to come down around us with the rest of the world following in short order. We'll have to give the terror threat—which is real anyway—the hard sell. The origins no longer matter. We need to get this under control right now."

DCI Pershing said, "If we can. We've got riots out there, Mr. President. We have quarantined hospitals. We have a populace gripped by fear and a lack of faith in their leaders."

The last was a cheap shot, but the President lifted his hand when several at the table rose to his defense. He'd had Pershing's number from day one. Like he often told Gus Costello, "Bob Pershing is strictly a front-and-back man. If he's not trying to suck my dick he's trying to stab me in the back.

"Gus," the President said. "Get Homeland Security on the phone."

Costello picked up his encrypted sat phone and called Maddie Hughes. "It's time," he said. "Initiate Yankee Alert. Repeat: Initiate Yankee Alert..."

# CHICAGO, CERMAK ROAD:

## CHINATOWN

**11:44 A.M.**

Harry Niles decided it was time to play a little game and test the level of his paranoia (which was deepening by the hour). He had left the Chevy Tahoe parked well away from Fong's on Cermak where they were hiding out in an upstairs room, courtesy of the always exotic and mysterious Kathy Ling. It was parked out front of an acupuncture shop and herbal remedy hut on South China Place. It would have been easy enough to walk a few blocks over there and pick it up...but Harry was not quite that naïve. He was not about to underestimate those who were hunting him.

What he needed was an acid test.

But he wasn't about to use himself as bait.

*Just do it the way you did it in the old days,* he told himself. *Find some perfectly innocent bystander and let them take the heat for you.*

"Good idea," he said under his breath.

It was a matter of simply choosing the appropriate sucker. What he needed was somebody a little down on their luck...yet, someone fairly trustworthy. The sort of person who would not scam him while he was scamming them.

He cruised West 22nd and Archer, searching high and low.

When he found the mark, he'd know it. Unless his instincts were totally dead after all these years, when he saw the right person the old light bulb would go on in his head. But it took patience so he bided his time, merging with the crowds on the sidewalk, trying to look like another tourist peeking into Chinese bakeries and gift shops, doing plenty of window shopping. He edged his way north up towards South China, lingering on Princeton Avenue which was the cross street. The Tahoe was only about a block or so away from him.

That's when he spotted the grungy dude playing guitar and panhandling for money. Just a kid with dirty feet and probably a habit judging by his eyes.

Harry dropped some coins in his can. "How's it going, man?"

The dude shrugged. "Not my best day. Not yet. You wanna hear something?"

"No. I want to hire you."

"Cool. What kind of gig is it?"

Harry smiled. "It's the kind of gig that pays forty bucks. Twenty now and twenty when it's done, and it only takes you ten minutes."

"Hell, I'm up for that."

Harry explained that his Tahoe was parked up the street and his leg was bad; he'd never make it that far. "Here's the keys and a twenty." He handed them to the kid. "I can trust you... can't I? You won't steal my ride?"

"It's cool, man. I'll have it back here in a couple minutes."

The dude took his guitar, blanket, and coin can with him. Obviously, Harry was supposed to trust him, but that didn't go both ways. Harry waited until he had faded into the light traffic on the walk. Then he went after him. He got within half a block of the Tahoe and watched his test subject waltz right over there. With the guitar and blanket over his shoulder, he looked like he should be hanging out in a Mexican cantina.

Harry secreted himself at a newsstand. He paid for a Hong Kong newspaper which he could not read and was probably three or four days out of date. He lingered about and read it.

The kid went up to the Tahoe.

He opened the door.

And the trap was sprung. Four guys in dark suits came out of a waiting van and seized him, throwing him up against the Tahoe and handcuffing him while he shouted out his innocence.

*I knew it, I fucking knew it.*

Harry got out while the getting was good.

# ARKANSAS

## BALD CAW

**12:33 P.M.**

When the kids started disappearing, everyone pointed their fingers at Iver Coxswell. Everyone but Willis, that was. Willis was the county sheriff and he wasn't about to instigate some godawful Medieval witch hunt or old-fashioned lynching party. Besides, Willis was the guy who found Massy McQueel hanging from the light fixture with the belt around her throat, face green as moss on a well-rope, that can of Raid still clutched in her stiff, dead hand. The Raid was the kind that killed hornets and wasps only Massy had used it to kill what was lying on the floor—a worm. It was one hell of a worm, too. About four-feet long, the size of a big copperhead, and corpse-white...although, by the time Willis found it, it was getting a little gray and slimy.

The county coroner—that asshole Steebs—said it looked to be some type of Trematoda, or flat worm, but he had no idea how it got so damn big. But he did know what killed it: Raid. That worm was saturated with Permethrin, which was a neurotoxin and the active ingredient in many household bug killers. Steebs sent the worm carcass away yesterday to the state lab.

Probably be weeks before they heard anything.

But people in Bald Caw didn't care about Massy McQueel because she was a crazy old whore and they figured that worm had crawled out of her privates and they would have been surprised if it was living up there alone.

*Goddamn people here in the Caw sure are a sympathetic lot,* Willis got to thinking as he drove out to Iver Coxswell's place. No, they surely didn't give a damn about Massy McQueel and her worm. All they cared about was Iver Coxswell. There were three kids missing and that was enough to incense anyone, Willis figured, but the fact that Coxswell was A), black, and B), had a criminal record that included statutory rape and child endangerment, was the deciding factor. Willis told them that Coxswell's conviction was a gross miscarriage of justice (he enjoyed saying that). When he was seventeen, he knocked up his sixteen-year-old girlfriend. There had been no rape or endangerment involved and it had all been purely consensual, but the fact that Coxswell was black and the girl was white made her daddy pressure the D.A. who put Coxswell away for five years (of course, Willis' predecessor, Luke Kingly, had admitted to Willis that the girl's daddy was not only a bigot but a hypocrite because it was common knowledge that he was banging his pretty eighteen-year-old black housekeeper that he had imported from Botswana and that girl was so black, coal-black, that she made Coxswell look Norwegian).

But people in the Caw were not interested in that.

They wanted Iver Coxswell investigated.

That they hadn't put on the white sheets and gone after him with shotguns and a good stout length of horse-rope was testament to the fact that those of the Caw were either more tolerant than anyone suspected or just too damn lazy to go to the trouble.

Willis found Coxswell's house out on Point Sipp Road easily enough being that it was pretty much the only one out there. It was tall and ramshackle, upstairs windows boarded over and the downstairs mostly broken from local kids pegging rocks at them on dares. It looked pretty much like a traditional haunted house and driving past it, Willis couldn't help but feel a cheap illicit thrill much like the rock-throwing kids themselves must have experienced.

He pulled the cruiser into the yard by the big sweetgum tree and stepped out, listening to the drone of August and feeling that wet-dog heat falling over him now that he was out of the air-conditioning.

Shit and shit. Sweat stains had already blossomed under the arms of his uniform shirt after he had knocked for a good two or three minutes.

"Mr. Coxswell?" he kept calling out. "I got a warrant and I'm coming in."

The door was open so Willis stepped inside, wondering if he shouldn't have brought Barnes and Mirce with him after all. He hadn't only because they were both such insufferable bigots and he didn't want to elevate this beyond where it currently stood...which was nowhere, the way Willis was thinking. The judge had issued the search warrant pretty much on hearsay and Coxswell's criminal record. Willis really had no choice but to execute it.

The stink that blew out of the opened door was black and hot and rancid. It near brought tears to his eyes. He knew something was dead in there, it was only a matter of finding it. Lights didn't work so he had to go back out to the cruiser for a flashlight.

Then he began his search.

The light beam was filled with dust motes like bubbles in champagne as he moved around in that dirty old house. Rugs on the floor were filthy with boot-tracks, grimy handprints on the walls. The ceilings were water-stained and drooping, the furniture well-nibbled by mice. Yes, a real pearl of a haunted house. No wonder it drew kids like flies to a cow-flop. He checked the living room, the kitchen, a bedroom piled with newspapers and cardboard boxes.

He examined holes in the walls and rat droppings in the corners, the smashed mason jars on the floor in the kitchen.

"Mr. Coxswell?" he said, knowing he had to. "You here? It's me. Sheriff Willis. Got some questions for you and I gotta search the place."

There was nothing but his own voice echoing out in the stillness, nothing alive in the house. In fact, he was so certain of it that had a voice answered him back he would have jumped clear of his skivvies. He paused at the stairwell. The smell was stronger up there and he could feel it coming down at him in a black, festering pall that stirred his stomach up.

Up there then. That's where the goodies would be.

Willis hesitated, then forced himself up the narrow stairwell. He felt like a kid on a dare himself. No cop in his right mind liked poking around houses for corpses, and this house and being alone didn't help matters much. The stairs were old like they had been in the house in Little Rock where he grew up. And like those stairs, these creaked behind you like someone or something was following you.

*Quit that shit, you idiot. Jesus, you're fifty-years old.*

Right. Act like a cop.

The heat up there made the water run from him. His uniform shirt was sodden, sweat beaded his face.

He stepped into a dusty hallway and in the first room he checked, he found a corpse. It was pushed up in the corner between the bed and the chest of drawers. It was blackened near down to a skeleton, the walls to either side dark with soot and smudged with smoke, the bed half-burned up. It was hard to tell whether the corpse was male or female with that degree of oxidation, but Willis figured it was Iver Coxswell himself. It was lucky the house hadn't burned to the ground. Though he would never know the chain of events, it looked like Coxswell had sat in the corner, emptied the metal can of gas over himself, then lit a match. The can was still there, black as coal, but a gas can, all right. The corpse's jaws were sprung like it had died screaming, eyes boiled right out of its skull. The little nodules on the floor must have been teeth. Sometimes when a body cooked real hot, he knew, the teeth would pop like corn kernels.

Enough of that.

Willis checked the other rooms and saw no evidence of kidnapped children so he went back downstairs. He was smelling that rotten stink again. His nose led him into the kitchen. It was thick as lace in there. The refrigerator. Sure. Using a hankie, he opened it and the smell almost put him on his knees. Milk that had gone solid. Meat and cheese that were furred green. The only other thing in there was a mason jar like the ones smashed on the floor. Funny, that. Putting his flashlight on it, he saw that there was a label on it: DO NOT OPEN, it said. Oh boy. That was the problem with being a cop: you went in places you'd rather not go and looked into dark corners where there were things you'd rather not see.

He found a hand towel and lifted out the jar and put it on the counter. He wiped perspiration from his face with his arm. It felt like his skin had been sprayed with cooking oil. It took some doing, but he got the lid off the jar. The liquid in it was murky. It smelled like vegetable rot. There was something in there, though. Using a carving knife he gripped with the hankie, he dug around in there.

*Dear God, please tell me there's nothing in here that's gonna give me nightmares. I don't want to find some kid's heart in here.*

He kept digging with the knife, trying to get the mysterious object up and out of there but it was like trying to dig a pickle from a jar with a butter knife.

*Hell is that?*

*There. Got it.*

He brought it up into the flashlight beam. It was white and segmented. Just like that worm Massy McQueel killed with the Raid. Except...except this one was alive. It moved and the bulb on the end opened and a sweet stink filled Willis' brain. After that, he wasn't aware of much. Surely not putting the jar away and shutting the refrigerator. And certainly not that sweet smell like golden honey flooding his brain and his hand gripping that pale white worm and feeling its grasping hooks digging into his palm or the warm, sour taste of it as it slid between his lips and moved thickly down his throat, gagging him.

There was some pain.

But it didn't last.

# CHICAGO, CERMAK ROAD

## CHINATOWN

**1:17 P.M.**

When Harry got back, Shawna was sipping tea and watching the little TV Kathy Ling had brought for them. "Hurry up," she said. "There's about to be an emergency presidential address."

Harry stumbled past her, grabbed her cigarettes and lit one. He sank on the bed next to her. His face was pinched, eyes squeezed shut. It looked like someone had just given him a good shot to the kidneys and he was gritting his teeth against the pain.

"Harry... are you all right."

"No... not really."

"What happened?"

So he told her his merry little cat-and-mouse tale and while he told it, he would not look at her. He told her about getting the kid to fetch his car on South China and the suits that moved in on him. About his run, hiding out in junk shops and Chinese emporiums, laying low in a Malaysian restaurant eating fish head soup and shrimp paste on noodles. And as hideous as it sounded, it was quite tasty, he admitted, even though his appetite wasn't much. The men in suits were everywhere suddenly. And after a while, it was like something out of Hitchcock: surreal, claustrophobic, and paranoid. He had never noticed before how many men dressed in suits there were in Chinatown.

"It seemed that they were all watching me," he told her.

"There couldn't have been that many."

"No, but after a while my common sense abandoned me."

He looked quite near tears and that's what made Shawna shrivel white inside. He was scared. Really fucking scared. And though part of her wanted to, needed to, fly into hysterics, she knew that now was not the time. She held onto him because never had he looked like he needed her as much as he did then. It was gone. All of it: his smug, arrogant, breezy façade. It had been stripped free like a mask and he was shivering. Actually shivering.

"I think I fucked up," he said.

"How?"

He shook his head. "With all this. Christ, Shawna, I'm too old for this. That's the problem with this game. You keep getting older but those bastards always seem to get younger."

"I think you've done a good job taking care of us."

"I've tried. But, hell, these guys...whoever they are...they must have unbelievable resources."

Shawna sighed. "How could they have found the SUV? I don't get it. Unless your friend..."

"No, Kathy wouldn't do that. Besides, she didn't rent the Tahoe under her name. She had some third cousin or something rent it and leave it in the garage. They'd have a hell of a time tracking it back to her. Her family tree is an absolute maze."

"Maybe the cousin talked."

"No, it's nothing that simple."

"Then what?"

"I don't know...maybe some sort of targeting system. Maybe they marked every vehicle that came out of the garage that night. Something that could be tracked."

"Is that possible?"

"Of course it's possible."

On the TV screen, the President stepped up to the podium in the East Room of the White House. He was markedly grim. "Good afternoon. Today I stand before you and ask for your help. I ask for the help, the resolve, the bravery of every American. The time has come, once again, for us to stand together as one, hand-in-hand and shoulder-to-shoulder. The time has come to put aside religious and ethnic disparity, to breech party lines and become one people united against a common enemy. For, my friends, that enemy is here and now."

Shawna felt a chill run up her arms. This was like 9/11 again but without the pyrotechnics.

"It can come as no surprise to any American that events are occurring in this country that are seemingly beyond our control. There is rioting and civil unrest, spiking incidences of violent crime. Quarantine procedures have been enacted at many of our hospitals. Yes, this great nation is under attack from within."

Harry and Shawna looked at each other.

"For many years now we have been warned by our own security forces and intelligence networks—and most particularly by the Department of Homeland Security itself—that there still exists the threat of domestic terrorism.

9/11 was the most heinous and cowardly attack this great nation has ever witnessed, but I now say to you it is not the last. Nor did we expect it to be. Even the death of Osama Bin Laden was no guarantee that our enemies would not mount a second and deadlier attempt to bring down this great nation. And now that has happened. Foreign subversives and terror agents have let loose a parasitic infection amongst us that is communicable and deadly."

Shawna held her breath and she could almost feel the rest of the country doing the same.

"Who these people are is not important right now. They will be hunted down and destroyed. You have my word on that. What is important is that we must not let this evil attack of bioterrorism break our unity, our resolve, our national integrity. The entire country has been put on a state of emergency and all state and municipal agencies are currently being briefed and called to action with the full resources of the federal government behind them. And it is with regret that I announce that martial law will be enacted as of midnight tonight, nationwide. And beginning tomorrow, a curfew from midnight to dawn will be in effect excepting only those who must work in the night. The police and National Guard will have full authority to enforce this and so I must ask for your help. I ask you to cooperate freely. To help, aid, and assist law enforcement in the execution of their duties which will be immense in scope."

"Holy shit," Harry said. "We've just lost our civil rights."

"It can't be that bad," Shawna said, knowing that she was speaking just to be heard, to reassure herself like whistling down a dark street and this street was certainly dark.

"It *is* that bad, Shawna. This is America for chrissake. Land of the so-called free. When you transform a Democracy into a police state overnight there's going to be trouble. Big trouble. You can forget about civil liberties. Welcome to Nazi Germany."

"But they can't do that."

"Yes, they can."

The President went on, "The most important thing at this juncture is not to panic. The situation is containable. We will restore order and eradicate the threat amongst us. But until that time we must stand strong and resilient, we must remain on guard. Your local TV and radio stations will be issuing further instructions over the next forty-eight hours. Understand that the search for the individuals responsible is ongoing and we will not tire or hesitate in our mission. We are a people resolved to justice and peace and we will not waver in our commitments to each other and to our nation. So let our enemies be warned: we will and shall defeat them regardless of the cost as we have in the past. May God bless each and every one of us and all that we stand for and uphold. Thank you and good day."

After that, Shawna and Harry just sat there, holding onto one another.

"A parasitic infection?" she said.

"Yes, nice and sterile and unbelievably vague."

"That's what I must have seen: some kind of containment operation in its earliest stages. Now it's out of control and they have to admit to it," she said. "And that's why we're being hunted down."

"I imagine."

"But we don't know anything."

"They must think we do."

"I don't suppose it would help to turn ourselves in?"

He laughed bitterly. "With martial law about to be enacted? Don't be so naïve, dear. Our lives will be worth that much less."

Shawna felt deflated. "Now what?" she said. "Now what are we going to do?"

"We're going to hang on tight, that's what."

# DETROIT

## HOLY CROSS HOSPITAL DETOX WARD

**1:47 P.M.**

Johnny Kopok tried to keep down the swill they offered him, but without some good—or bad—booze to cement it in place, it all came rushing back in a foamy mess of bland scrambled eggs that tasted no worse coming up than it had going down. He set the bedpan aside and wiped his mouth. God, but his guts were in a state. One little taste was what he needed. His hands were shaking, his guts twisting up on themselves.

*Oh boy, here comes trouble.*

The nurse in the white plastic suit came through the door and looked at what he produced. "You'll never get out of here if you don't eat.

"Then get somebody in here that can cook for chrissake. Coffee tastes like it was strained through somebody's bladder and green eggs and ham is supposed to be a fucking kid's story not something you put on a plate."

The nurse-cum-spaceman just stared at him like he was some new, potentially hostile life form.

"I can't keep it down," he told her.

"Are you trying?"

"Trying? Jesus H. Christ, of course I'm trying. I need a taste, you know? Just a taste to sort out my insides. When you're a drunk like me it's like glue: without booze, nothing sticks."

"I'm afraid that's against regulations."

"Fuck regulations. Why don't you let me out?" he asked her. "I watch the TV same as anyone else. Ain't you Nazis got enough to worry about without babying an old drunk like me?"

"Regulations," she said again.

Johnny had to hold himself back at that point. He wanted to jump up and snatch that mask off, get a good look at this one.

"Where the hell's Jimbo?"

"I already told you, Mr. Kopok. He's no longer at this location."

"Then where is he?"

"I don't have that information."

"What the fuck good are you?"

But the faceless nurse was very much used to Johnny's outbursts by this time and she completely ignored him. As he insulted her, she took his vitals and by the time she was done he had calmed.

"Jimbo get the worms?"

"I don't know what you mean."

"The parasites, you airhead. Like the President was saying."

"I don't know anything about that."

"Oh, you don't? Then why are they moving people out of here? I can see it right out my window."

"The hospital is being evacuated as part of a containment operation."

"So evacuate me."

"The most critical patients are being evacuated first."

He started laughing and the laughing became a coughing fit. "Critical? I haven't had booze in weeks."

"You've only been here a few days."

"Ah, you're out of your cunting mind."

"I don't have time for this, Mr. Kopok."

The nurse turned and left with the swish-swish of her HAZMAT suit. Then Johnny was alone with nothing but the goddamn TV for company, his guts complaining, his nerves shot, every inch of him begging for a taste. And all the medications in the world couldn't touch it.

He laid there, feeling the need like needles in his belly. What goddamn right did they have to hold him? With everything else going on, you would have thought they'd boot him right out the door. Just another drunk. God, he was going to go out of his mind like this. On the TV, the mayor was being assailed by reporters and she was doing her usual shuffle trying to keep ahead of them. They wanted answers. In fact, they were demanding them. They wanted to know exactly what sort of parasitic infection was plaguing the country.

"Tell 'em," Johnny grumbled. "Worms, goddamned worms."

There were shots of the National Guard rolling through the streets voiced over by a proclamation from the mayor's office that looters and rioters would be put down by deadly force as per federal mandates. Then there were shots of some kids running up the streets with stolen TVs and DVD players and one shot of a kid eluding police with a shiny brass tuba of all things.

*Damn*, Johnny thought, *now that's where the action is.*

He turned from the TV because suddenly there was action in the hospital. He could hear people shouting, screaming, running feet, then the unmistakable sound of gunfire. Full-auto, too, by the sound of it. Some explosions. More gunfire.

Johnny got out of bed and dug his clothes out of the closet.

Hospital was under goddamn attack. It was like the Battle for Hue City during the Tet of '68 all over again. Jesus Christ. Fighting house-to-house through the rubble. Kick in the doors, toss a few grenades, some frags and WPs, spray down anything that was left with your Sixteen. Where was the rest of his unit? He'd lost his weapon, his pack. He heard more gunfire and figured the gooks were closing in, trying to constrict the platoon. Lieutenant Guiterrez was shouting out, "Goddamn slopes are trying to flank us! Get some CS out there! Now! Now!" Damn straight. Johnny grabbed a canister of CS tear gas and tossed it with the rest of the boys. Let Uncle Ho's shiteaters have a taste of that. Goddamn zipperheads.

Johnny moved forward.

He opened the door, then kicked it and dove out into the hallway. Goddamn, where was his weapon? Platoon leader was going to chew his ass over that. A Marine without a weapon? In goddamn Hue during the Tet? Lot of commotion. Oh Jesus, Gutierrez was down. Filthy gooks stitched him with an AK.

"MEDIC!" Johnny cried out. "WE NEED A FUCKING MEDIC! LIEUTENANT'S DOWN!"

That was about the time that Johnny realized he wasn't in the 'Nam. Hue was fifty years before. Gutierrez was dead. He'd died in Johnny's arms, his guts hanging out, blood rushing out of him. No, no, no. This wasn't Hue. This was the detox ward and there was shit going down and worms and crazy people in spacesuits that claimed to be doctors and nurses. And, oh, just one good taste of the Sweet Lucy was what he needed to get his act together.

But oh my Christ, would you look at that.

Bodies.

Bodies all over the place. Bullet holes in the walls. No, this wasn't Hue but it sure looked like Hue. It was enough to make you sick. But...listen. Footsteps coming. Running steps. Johnny was caught out in the open so he played dead. He laid down by the other ones and troopers came in with those white plastic suits on. Except these guys had guns.

"All clear," one of them said. "Let's get 'em down to the morgue. They're all going into the incinerator."

"Check," somebody said.

Johnny just laid there. They came and grabbed him by the ankles and dragged him off. He was going down to the morgue and he was okay with that. Nobody would suspect a corpse of trying to escape so he acted like a corpse.

# FAIRFAX COUNTY, VIRGINIA

## CIA COUNTERTERRORISM CENTER

**2:12 P.M.**

Just as he'd suspected, the country was going to shit and that made DCI Pershing smile as he sat there behind his desk at the CTC because it was all playing out the way he wanted. Now with the press screaming about an "unknown parasite", the specter of martial law looming and the suspension of civil liberties that it would entail, the natives were growing restless. They were taking to the streets. There was looting and riots, clashes between police and protestors, politicians howling from atop their soap boxes and ministers prophesying the end of civilization as we knew it. Good and good. It was working out perfectly.

Let chaos run rampant.

Let the blood run in the streets.

Let civil rights be violated.

Let the natives get desperate, oh so very desperate.

Because when they do, Pershing knew, when all seemed hopeless and there was darkness at every quarter and despair knocking at the door, they would seek a messiah, a savior that could lead them into the future and out of the eternal night. They would seek a candle burning bright and Robert Pershing would be that candle.

"I will lead them," he said.

"Sir?"

DCI Pershing looked up and Matt Connelly was standing there. Connelly was the DD/CIA, the Deputy Director of the CIA and the number two man within the Company.

"Sorry, Matt," Pershing said, recovering from delusions of grandeur quite quickly, "I was gathering wool."

Connelly, ever the good little politico, did not comment upon it. "Sir, our field operators in Chicago's Chinatown are about ninety percent certain that they're closing in on Harry Niles and Shawna Geddes. They're obviously hiding out there somewhere."

Connelly explained what happened with the stakeout of Niles' Chevy Tahoe on South China Place. How Niles had sent that street kid in and he had been grabbed and interrogated. The man who paid him to move the SUV was Harry Niles without a doubt.

DCI Pershing chuckled. "Our friend Mr. Niles hasn't lost his talent for subterfuge, I see."

"With any luck, we might have him and the girl by tomorrow," Connelly said. "Our Asian assets are making some discreet inquiries in Chinatown and we're fairly certain they'll bear fruit."

Of course they will, Pershing knew. Because greed was the language of the streets and those without always wanted their share and they would sell anyone or anything if the price was right.

"When you find him, I want no contact with him."

"No contact, sir?"

"None. Not yet. I want him followed. I want to know everywhere he goes and everyone he sees. Mr. Niles will prove indispensable if he's played the right way."

"I'm not following you, sir."

"And for right now, you don't need to. When the time comes I'll fill you in completely. Just find him. Watch him."

"Yes, sir." Connelly hesitated. "One more thing. We're fairly certain that the Old Man is trying to track down Niles, too. He's using S5 assets if what I'm hearing is correct."

Which meant he was using XI/Blackpool mercenaries to do his dirty work. No surprise there. They always performed S5's heavy lifting. And therein lie the problem with the Old Man—as head of Section 5, his business was strictly R&D, but through the years he had become so powerful that he was something of an entity unto himself. Now he was acting like the Blackpool heavies were his own private army. That was not good and Pershing knew that, sooner rather later, the Old Man would have to be put out of business.

"Let's try and get to Niles before S5 does."

"Yes, sir."

"Keep your ears open. If S5 gets him, I want to know about it yesterday."

As Connelly left the office, Pershing contemplated the sacking of the world's most powerful democracy. And as he contemplated this, he knew that his people needed to get to Niles first. It was paramount. If the Old Man and S5 got their hands on him he'd end up getting a complete personality reassignment and Pershing couldn't have that. He needed Niles' mind intact. Niles was to be his own personal propaganda tool and he didn't want anything interfering with that.

# DETROIT

## EAST DEARBORN

**2:29 P.M.**

On the floor....
*Creeping...*
*Creeping like a slug...*
She could no longer remember her name and wondered if she really ever had one. When she tried to think, tried to remember, what was inside her showed her the price of defiance: agony. Unbelievable red-hot agony like cutting blades and slicing razors opening her from the inside out. When she stopped trying to think and cause trouble, she was rewarded with a sweet chemical transmission of endorphins.

She lay there on the floor, no longer creeping, staring at her hands. At the blood that bubbled from her pores. Each bubble popped as it exited her skin. Webbed with blood and fouled with slime and piss and excreta, she began to creep along the floor again in imitation of that which lived inside her, growing fat and bursting with eggs.

The idea of standing no longer appealed to her.

It was better to creep.

To crawl.

To wriggle along the floor.

Breathing hard and coughing out tangles of bile and clotted curds of tissue, memories paraded through her brain. She was seeing a man. He held a worm...a tiny writhing white worm...with forceps and as she cried out non-sensical entreaties to a God who had turned his back upon her, the worm went down her throat.

And then a name: *Sheikh Sa'ad. It was Sheikh Sa'ad who did this to you.*

And then...sweet merciful Allah, the pain came. It flooded through her in burning white waves that were blades that scraped her nerves raw and needles that worried her organs and a million-billion separate pinpoint agonies that made her shudder and convulse and heave out snotty ribbons of bile...and worms. Immature worms, eight and ten inches in length, that hung twisting from her mouth.

Gagging, she pulled the worms from her throat and threw them to the floor where she pounded them to pulp with her fists and the mature worm within her, the mother worm, flooded her with endorphins for what she did was good and right. *They are infidels and I am God*, the mother worm told her without actually telling her. *Seek only me and have audience only with me, for I am good and I am great, I am deliverance and purity; know only me.*

The woman laid there, wiping bile from her lips with shaking fingers. She looked around with eyes that were no longer the translucent green of an Egyptian twilight, but a dull inflamed red. They cried tears of serous fluid.

*I have been hijacked.*

*This body is no longer mine.*

*The worm is not good it is the great Satan. It is the destroyer and unmaker, not the finger of God but the claw of the Evil One—*

More agony that was intense and blinding, a thermonuclear destruction laying waste to her insides and making her vomit and convulse upon the floor, pounding her head until it faded.

She started creeping again.

She crept into the bathroom.

She did not think of what she was doing so the worm could not punish her. She could feel it sliding through her, feel it swelling and thickening, gestating with millions of juicy ova that existed only to drain the world dry and she would no longer be host to them.

Long before she had agreed to be a vessel for Sheikh Sa'ad's worm, she had made arrangements of her own. Though it was forbidden by her religion, she had procured a release if things became unmanageable: a syringe of strychnine. Simple. Effective. A horrible death, all things considered, but minor in comparison to parasitization.

*Do it.*

*Take your life.*

Now the mother worm knew. The mother worm would not tolerate such defiance or the idea of the host animal destroying itself. It sent out waves of pain that were bright/hot/crackling and the woman screamed as she pulled herself up by gripping the sink. The worm was attacking her. Having mastered her neurochemistry, it now used all the weapons in its arsenal, doing everything short of permanent damage to bring the host under control. The woman stood uneasily as her nerves fired and her eardrums popped, as her teeth chattered and her brain was bisected by white-hot knives, as bile gushed up her throat and a hot flow of diseased menstrual sewage flooded between her legs. Her left arm went numb, her right leg shook with spasms.

*Do it! Do not hesitate!*

*Rabbanā Aṣrif ʿAnnā ʿAdhāba Jahannama ʿInna ʿAdhābahā Kāna Gharāmāan!*

Her mouth filling with hematoseptic drainage, the world around her spinning, every cell in her body seeming to implode in a blazing death fury, she reached into the medicine cabinet as the mother worm tried to kick her legs out from beneath her. It constricted her throat, it sealed off her lungs, it forced her mind into the darkness. But battle was joined for possession of the husk the woman knew as her body and the worm knew merely as a vessel. NO!NO!NO!NO!NO!IWILLNOT RELENT I I I I WILL NOT!

Then it robbed her of her sight, but it was too late because her fingers held the syringe and she cried out through a mouth filled with blood, "God is good... God is great..." And she jabbed the syringe into her throat and pushed the plunger. Death came and she welcomed it, together they became one as she fell to the floor, gagging out a pink-yellow foam. The strychnine tore through her insides like a buzzsaw and her head fell against the toilet as gouts of blackening blood poured from her mouth and nostrils.

The host was dead.

The worm knew it could not repair it, so it forced itself from the woman's mouth, all four feet of it, with a surging undulation, sliding right into the toilet. It slid down deep into the bowels of the building's wastewater system where it bathed itself in filth and excrement, an environment it could thrive in. Then it began to explore this new system, looking for a host.

# CHICAGO, CERMAK ROAD

## CHINATOWN

**2:45 P.M.**

Sprawled on the bed, Harry Niles rolled his eyes back in his head as Shawna rode him at first softly and delicately, then picking up the rhythm, pumping her thighs and forcing him deeper and deeper inside her as her breath came in short, sharp gasps and he could feel the tension in his groin mounting, thickening, reaching for release... then she slowed it down again, toying, teasing, playing with him. Her hair hanging in her face, her breasts beaded with a dew of sweet sweat, she lowered herself down on him with easy, relaxed thrusts, riding his inches with a hot-breathed, barely concealed hunger.

She knew he was close, just as she was close.

But she would not allow it.

Not yet.

She pushed herself down on him slowly, barely even moving, letting gravity pull her down bit by bit. She was shaking, shuddering, feeling the heat in her loins spreading up into her belly and then into her chest.

She grasped his head and pulled his mouth to her breasts. "Please, Harry," she said. "Oh God...please..."

He mouthed her nipples, licking them, sucking them between his lips, then releasing them, sucking them and releasing them, until they stood hard as they pressed into his face. He toyed with her like she toyed with him until she was shaking and gasping anew, then he took one pert breast into his mouth, then another. Shawna could stand it no longer, crying out, she pressed him down on the bed and pumped at him savagely, her thighs slapping against his own and she let out an exhilarated moaning as she found her orgasm and rode its wave, her body jerking and shuddering with release.

And Harry did the same, gripping the cheeks of her ass in his hands and forcing her down, burying himself in her until he came. And when it was over, they collapsed into a womb of heat and exhaustion.

"Don't think... don't think," Shawna gasped, barely able to catch her breath, "that... it'll happen...again..."

"Of course not," he sighed. "Just because I let you use me once... doesn't mean you can have your way twice."

She uttered a low laugh and rested her head on his chest, her hair splayed over him. He held her to him, skin against skin, and wondered where it had all come from. They were on the bed talking, then she kissed him. Then... well, things had escalated. As he held her, running a hand down her smooth back, he knew he couldn't let himself feel too deeply for her. She was a friend and he'd always felt protective of her, but he had to keep in mind who she was.

At least, that's what he told himself.

But in reality, he'd already fallen from his lofty perch and belonged to her and he only prayed that she would not hurt him in the end.

"I want to see my mother," she suddenly said. "If something happens, I want to see her one last time."

"Nothing's going to happen. Not if we're careful."

"I need to see her."

Knowing it was an absolutely dangerous idea, he said, "If you want to see her then we'll make sure you do."

She hesitated a moment, then said, "You mean that?"

"Yes."

"But the danger... what if they're watching..."

"You let me worry about that," he told her. "Now shut your mouth and press yourself against me. I need to enjoy this, my little dumpling."

"Oh, shut up, asshole," she said, pressing herself against him with a giggle.

# HAMMOND, INDIANA

## FOREST-IVANHOE

**3:22 P.M.**

It had been eating away at her all day and by late afternoon, Claire just couldn't take it anymore. She was not only ready to come out of her skin, she wanted to hang it on the wall and call it a day. It wasn't bad enough what was going on in the country with all this crazy talk about martial law and Army troops in the streets, some kind of awful terrorist attack involving parasites, but then there was George. George was off from the university with his bad knee and all he did all day was sit in the chair (which was fine, rest up) and watch the news, hour after hour (which was not so fine.) Never had Claire known him to take such an interest in current events.

"But it's different now," he told her for maybe the second, third, or fourth time. "It's all different now."

"Yes, I know that, George. I'm not stupid. Everything's changed."

After that, of course, he went right back to his brooding—something he was getting very practiced at by that point. And what could Claire really say? Was there any point in telling him that she was terrified? That the country was coming apart at the seams? That everything she'd ever known or cared for seemed like it was about to split the seams of its proverbial pants?

No, there was no point. Absolutely no point.

He had always been very, very stoic about things. Even the worst situations he took in stride...but this was eating at him in ways that simply seemed out of character. So finally, after he'd brooded all day, pretending he was worried like everyone else, she sat down by him and waited.

Finally, he looked away from CNN and said, "What?"

"Tell me," she said. "Tell me what's bothering you."

"You know what's bothering me. Same thing that's bothering everyone else."

But her intuition told her differently. "It's something else. Something about all this you're taking very personally. Now I want to know what."

It looked like he was going to dismiss it all, but he didn't. He swallowed. His eyes got very wet. His lower lip trembled. "We started this," he said.

"Who?"

"We did. The parasite. I know what it is, you see, and I know where it came from."

He told her when he'd worked for the government it wasn't just for the FDA like he'd always said. Sure, maybe his checks came from the FDA but he actually worked for the CIA's Directorate of Science and Technology in R and D. "I was part of a shadow group called S5. We developed biological weapons, Claire. And the team I was on, we developed a particular type of bioweapon by genetically enhancing the human tapeworm. It was called Project Biogenesis."

She wanted to laugh at him. *You, George Canning, worked in a top secret CIA lab?* The idea seemed preposterous. It was far too James Bond for her husband who was a sweet, kind little man. A biology professor at Purdue University. Yes, he had been involved in research for many years when they lived out east, but he'd always told her it had something to do with diseases of livestock. It was very boring. And now he was saying it was biological weapons? Tapeworms?

"George, really..."

"I'm serious, Claire. It was classified research. I had to sign the Official Secrets Act. I had to tell you I worked for the FDA. That was the front. We all worked for the FDA."

It made Claire feel very dirty somehow. Like the man she'd shared a bed with all these years was a stranger that had been playing around behind her back. It wasn't anything like that, of course, and national security was national security...but bioweapons?

George?

It was devastating. Like learning that Bozo the Clown was a pedophile or Mister Rogers was a serial rapist. But she knew she couldn't look at it that way even if it did feel like their husband-wife trust had been somehow violated. "And... and what you created, those awful worms... they're loose?"

"Yes."

"You can't know for sure."

"Yes, I can. This morning before you were awake, I got a call from Charles Durlain."

"Charlie... you worked with him at the...the FDA."

"He was a senior biogeneticist on the project."

"He said these things are loose?"

George nodded. "You see, we developed them and afterwards the rest of us were shuttled off to other projects. But Charlie was involved from beginning to end. He told me what I never knew: they tested the weapon in Iraq five years ago. Somehow, he figures, our troops got infected. They brought it back with them."

"Good Lord, George, that's...that's—"

Then the doorbell rang. Claire was glad of the interruption. Glad she didn't have the time to speak her mind because it would have been ugly and hurtful. She had a very clear opinion on things like germ warfare and the like. The development of weapons that could not be contained and caused unbelievable suffering.

She answered the door and found a man in a NIPSCO uniform standing there. He tipped his hat to her. "Afternoon, ma'am," he said in a fine Midwestern accent that was as pure as Indiana wheat under a high sun. "I've been going up and down the street checking natural gas lines. We're trying to trace the source of a leak." He flipped a few pages on his clipboard. "We show you as having a gas water heater. I need to check the feed. Won't take but a minute."

Claire sighed. Now? She wasn't in the mood for it.

"It could be serious, ma'am," he said, smiling brightly.

And for a moment there, Claire nearly stepped back and away. There was something about that smile and his flat dark eyes that did not belong. She shrugged it off and said, "Come in."

He followed her, a stocky man with a hard jaw and a flattened nose like an old-time fighter.

"George... the natural gas people have come to check the lines."

George mumbled something, fixated on CNN and the rioting in Los Angeles.

Claire led the gas guy down into the basement, over into the corner where the water heater was. He examined the feed line coming in, scribbled stuff on his clipboard. He pulled a wrench out of his bag and checked the fittings. With his sleeves rolled up, Claire saw that he had tattoos. On his left forearm there was a dragon and on the right some sort of bird of prey.

He took a meter from his bag. "Ma'am, would you mind turning off that valve down by the floor."

He pointed to a line leading into the water heater. She crouched down, switched it off. She thought it was a water line, but then what did she know about these things?

"Just wait a sec there, ma'am," the gas guy said. "Keep it off. I don't want to get a false positive. Gotta make sure everything's on the up-and-up."

Crouched down, Claire waited, her back to him.

She heard him dig in his bag. "Okay," he said. "That's lovely."

Claire felt a chill go right up her spine. His accent wasn't Midwestern USA now... it was English. She turned and looked at him. He had a gun in his hand. There was a long black silencer threaded onto the end of it.

"No, wait..."

But he didn't wait. He put two in her head, spraying blood and brain matter over the white face of the water heater. She laid there, dark fluid seeping from her ruined skull.

The gas man went upstairs.

He was whistling.

He walked up behind George's chair.

George turned and looked at him.

"We might not have found you if Charles Durlain hadn't rung you up," said the gasman.

"BioGenesis," George said, a whimpering breaking loose in his throat.

"That's right, mate. Nothing personal."

Two more in the head for George and that was it.

Tommy Quillan broke down his weapon and tucked it safely in his bag. When he got out to the van, he scratched another name off his list.

# NEW YORK CITY, EAST BRONX

## PELHAM PARKWAY

**3:47 P.M.**

Virginia Astato got a front-row view of the action down on the street from her third-floor apartment window and it was better than anything on TV. You couldn't get this kind of action on *Dancing with the Stars* or *16 and Pregnant*. This was the real juice, man, this was the shit, and it was free, honest-to-God free.

"Hey, Virge," Joey said, "maybe you ought to get away from there, eh? All it takes is one stray bullet and I'll be vacuuming your teeth out of the rug."

"Don't worry about it. Go back to your fights."

"Don't worry about it, she says. Like it's nothing."

"Oh, shut up, Joey."

"You gotta think of the baby."

She patted her round belly, all seven months of it. "Baby's fine. Now go back to your crap on TV."

"Crap, she calls it."

Virginia ignored him. Let him grumble. Let him groan. This was history in the making and she wasn't about to miss it.

"Ahhhh, whatever," Joey said, watching the UFC on the tube, totally oblivious to the rioting in the streets below. "Come on, Shane! Pound that fucker! Put him in the fucking morgue! Work him! Work him! *Watch that left! SHEEEEEIIIT! That's the stuff!*"

Virginia shook her head, watching the action below.

Two or three dozen men were mixing it up with the National Guard and some of the boys from the 49th Precinct. The men were throwing rocks at a couple APCs rolling down the street and over a bullhorn the cops were telling everyone to disband and go back to their homes.

Jesus, it looked like a scene from Palestine or Northern Ireland or one of those godawful places. Who'd think you could see this kind of stuff here in the Bronx?

The men were not disbanding.

They were lighting up Molotov cocktails and throwing them at the vehicles. Clouds of fire burst over the faces of the vehicles and the guy on the bullhorn was getting increasingly pissed off, telling them it was their last chance and their last warning.

A gunner in one of the APCs fired a few rounds over their heads from a mounted machine gun.

"Joey! Get over here! You gotta see this shit!"

"Hey, what? I'm doing nothing over here? I'm trying to watch the fights... hoo, shit, watchit, Shane! That's it! Drill him! Drill him! Bust his fucking teeth out!"

Virginia sighed. What an idiot.

The baby kicked, feeling her excitement and awe.

Now a couple of police cars came tearing up the street followed by a gray tactical van. The van squealed to a halt and two dozen cops in full riot gear pressed in, pushing the men back and scattering them. These guys weren't fucking around. Those that didn't move fast enough, the cops beat to the ground. More Molotovs were launched.

Five, six, seven of them.

The cordon of fire made the riot cops pull back and the men surged forward to reclaim their wounded and then the APCs opened up and cut down nearly half of the men in a single sweep. The others tried to run and they were cut down, too.

The cops were calling out over their bullhorns.

There were bodies in the street, pools of blood. Men screaming. Shattered glass and bullet-pocked cars at the curbs. Virginia just watched it with her jaw hanging open.

Joey came running over. "Hell's going on down there?"

"I told you! There's a fucking riot!"

"Jesus Christ," he said. "Why didn't you say so?"

# GAZA CITY, GAZA STRIP

## SHATI REFUGEE CAMP

**10:58 P.M. PALESTINE TIME**

By pale moonlight, the Israeli Defense Forces moved in. Although it was technically a biocontainment operation, to those who watched from ruined buildings and behind heaps of rubble it was a military strike: trucks and armored vehicles, ground troops charging forward, helicopter gunships circling overhead. And lights, lots of lights. Because the refugee camps were nothing if not dark as the pit by night.

So the IDF moved in.

Down narrow snaking streets crowded with cinder block houses and the rubble of neighborhoods blasted to wreckage, around the hulking debris of makeshift buildings that had been leveled by F-16 strikes, cutting down alleyways deep with refuse and trash and skittering rats. The flat, bullet-scarred faces of buildings and bomb-cratered streets were testament to the bloody clashes between Hamas and the Fatah and the intervention of the IDF. Open walls were crowded with the graffiti of Palestinian Islamic Jihad and peeling posters of suicide bombers, all glorifying the death of innocents.

The IDF soldiers wore bright orange biocon suits and carried IMI Tavor assault rifles which had now replaced the Uzi in the Israeli arsenal. Every third man had a flamethrower.

Cautiously, they moved deeper into the maze of the camp.

The lights behind them—headlights and spots, parabolic reflectors and beam projectors—turned night into a very surreal, shadow-crawling sort of twilight. Shapes were in constant motion. Everything was gliding, stealthy, and threatening. The carcass of a rusted minibus was a looming threat. Heaped bricks were enemy combatants.

The night was humid and the soldiers sweated in their suits.

They waited for what came next.

They operated with strict unit discipline and nobody spoke. There was no idle chatting, only the voices of commanders urging them forward. Backlit by the sweeping spots, gigantic shadows of the advancing troops played against ruins like immense filmy ghosts.

Something just ahead.

Nobody had to tell the troops that. No sergeants called out and no officers told them to stand ready. They knew it. They felt it, intuited it. It went up their spines and crawled down into their bellies.

People.

Thirty, then forty of them coming out of the shadows, sliding free like juicy, well-oiled maggots, pressing closer despite the warnings in Arabic from the IDF to stand back, to not approach the troops.

The people glided forward.

They were coming from every direction and the IDF troopers in front saw them quite clearly: shambling scarecrow shapes with eyes like black glass. They surged forward like paper dollies cut from a single sheet of vellum. But it was not paper that held them together; they were threaded by worms. Immense white worms running in glistening, pale, noodly loops mouth to ass and mouth to ass, horrific parasites that pushed their hosts forward. Some were not connected, some walked alone. But even these opened their mouths to reveal the pulpy white undulatory lengths of the things that owned them.

The IDF opened up.

Their original idea was to force the crowds back with small arms and suppressive fire from belt-fed .30 caliber machine guns. And when the crowd rushed forward, this was exactly what they did but there were far too many and the worms that piloted the human husks used the only tactic they seemed to understand: *flood the intruders, bury them in numbers, then we can convert them.*

This was no cognitive decision on the part of the flatworms, merely instinctive as all they did was instinctive even if, sometimes, the brains of their hosts seemed to translate the worms' desires, impulses, and appetites into thought and words.

The IDF dropped rank after rank of the worm-hosts, but they kept coming from all directions and soon the soldiers were fighting a pitched battle for survival. Assault rifles fired on full auto, machine guns tried to hit the crowd without hitting the soldiers, flame throwers threw out twenty-foot gouts of flame.

People were burning.

Worms were sizzling.

Aflame or not, the hosts rushed the IDF troops, burning and popping, cracking open from the heat, skins splitting and hair burning. But they were not to be denied. And as they fell into blackened heaps that let off rolling clouds of churning, sickening-smelling smoke, the worms came out of them like rats from sinking ships. They came out of mouths and asses. They burst from chests and stomachs and exploded from heads. They reached upward, trying to escape the fire like pale white rootlets seeking summer light.

As the IDF fought amongst them, were overwhelmed by them, and infested by them, the worms melted like tallow in the flames. But not all. No, not all. Many of them rose up, immense and steaming things the size of pythons, rippling with egg-fattened segments, unwinding their sinuous lengths and oozing a vile sweet-smelling slime that reached many soldiers right through their ventilator masks and brought them drunkenly to their knees. Made them strip off helmets and welcome the foul attentions of the writhing vermin.

Other soldiers tried to claw their way free of burning biosuits and those that were successful found themselves in far worse predicaments. Wound up, encased, buried in sliding pulpous-white forms, they fought valiantly as was their way, gloved hands slashing bodies of soft rot with knives, hooked fingers daggering into swollen pregnant proglottids only to release gushing swamps of jellied eggs. Slobbering mouths found their own, stinging spines and pheromonal worm-secretions took the fight from them and in the end there was acceptance, and the wisdom of the great white infesting worms: that men and women were but vessels to be invaded and leeched dry.

For the worm would come for all and the feasting would be grand.

As the trucks and armored vehicles tried desperately to retreat, worm-hosts by the thousands came sliding out of every hovel and tent, every shadowy tangle and sewer-ditch.

In the end, the worm feasted and feasted well.

The Shati Refugee camp was quite literally infested.

# CHICAGO, WEST RANDOLPH

## THE LOOP

**5:33 P.M.**

The thing that really amazed Shawna was the tenacity of the American shopper. Even the threat of martial law could not keep the buying public away from a really good deal on shoes at Payless or discount vitamins at GNC, a plate of bourbon chicken at New Orleans Kitchen or a noodle bowl at the Tokyo Lunch Box. As she took the pedway from building #1 to #2 at Illinois Center (reminding herself nearly continually not to turn around and make eye contact with Harry, who was shadowing her), the amount of people out and about was amazing. According to the news, martial law would be enacted at midnight and anybody who violated it was subject to arrest. On her way over, she saw several National Guard trucks prowling Michigan Avenue and a few groups of bored soldiers on the walks.

When she reached #2, she caught sight of Harry reflected in the plate glass, sighed, and moved deeper into the mall. The crowds weren't as heavy as usual and there was a noticeable lack of teenagers, other than that it was business as usual.

She walked around, window shopping, making eye contact with no one, looking about as casual as casual got. She saw a few men in suits coming out of restaurants but she didn't think they were feds. Most were either chatting on cellphones or distracted by newspapers. None that she saw paid her the slightest bit of attention save for one of them who gave her the hungry eyes but today that was perfectly all right.

She passed by Elegant Nails twice, not lingering but seeing if there was anyone around that did not belong. She saw nothing. As per their arrangement, after her third pass she found a bench and sat down while Harry reconnoitered the salon. After a time he walked past her and winked, meaning it was about as safe as they could hope for which, she knew, meant it was still chancy as all hell.

Shawna walked down there again and this time she did not hesitate: she walked right in the salon. There were two girls working in there, but she slipped past them and sat across from her mother.

"Oh, hello," said her mother. "Now how can I...Shawna?"

"Hey, Mom."

Her mother looked around suspiciously. "What are you up to?"

"Just do my nails, Mom. Pretend I'm any old customer. Give me the works."

Elaine Geddes sighed as always, realizing at that moment that she'd been sighing ever since Shawna came into the world. She examined Shawna's cuticles and then proceeded to remove the old polish with a cotton ball dipped in remover. "Anytime you want to begin, I'm ready to listen."

"What makes you think I'm up to anything?"

"Well, you never stop by. First red flag. And, second red flag, I've gotten several calls from men looking for you. And when they don't call, they stop by and try to impress upon me how very important it is that they get in contact with you."

Shawna felt a slight butterfly of panic in her belly. "And what do you tell these men?"

"What can I tell them? You don't answer my calls either. Sorry, Charlie."

Shawna smiled. *Sorry, Charlie.* Her mother's favorite catchphrase next to *Don't say I didn't tell you so* or *why ask me? What do I know? I'm only your mother.* Good old Mom. That's the one thing about parents she found very stabilizing: after they reached a certain age, psychologically, they were set in stone.

While Elaine buffed her nails, she said, "You have such beautiful hands, Shawna."

"I got them from you."

"From me. Ha. You got your hands from your Aunt Lorelei. She has grandma's beautiful hands, too. Me? Let's not talk about these stubby pig's knuckles."

Shawna watched her nails being buffed. "Mom," she said. "Why did you name me Shawna?"

Her mother stopped and looked at her. "Of all questions. Oh...your father found out he was like one-sixty-fifth Indian. Shawnee. I made your name up out of that." She shrugged. "Who knew you'd turn out this way?"

"Mom..."

"Who knew I'd have IRS men knocking at my door?" She stopped buffing. "How did you get in trouble with the IRS?"

"They're not IRS."

"Sure, they are. I know IRS men when I see them: those suits, those dead eyes. IRS for sure. How much do you owe?"

Shawna sighed herself. Her father—now long since passed—had an almost unnatural fear of the IRS when he ran his jewelry business and his wife had caught the bug as well. Shawna had no doubt that her dad cooked the books to squirm out of taxes and lived in fear of being caught.

"Mom, listen to me. Those guys are not with the IRS."

"Sorry, Charlie. What do I know?" Then she looked at her daughter and maybe saw the fear in her eyes. "Okay, then, who are they? The FBI? The Secret Service?"

"I don't know. But they're feds and they're after me."

Elaine Geddes sighed again and crossed herself. "Good Lord, what did you get into this time? Or should I say, who got into you?"

"Mom, really."

"I'm just saying is all."

"Just keep telling them you don't know where I am, and you haven't heard from me."

"That should be simple enough."

Shawna ran it through her mind, trying to figure out how much she should tell. "I videoed some men doing something—"

"This I don't want to hear."

"—something bad, Mom. They abducted another guy and took him away and it's all part of this thing that's going on now: the parasites, martial law. All of it. Those men work for the government. They think I know things which I really don't. I'd turn myself in and tell them that but I think if I do I'd never be seen again."

Elaine Geddes massaged oil into her daughter's fingers. "You could try the police. Tell them. Show 'em what you filmed."

"I think these guys are much bigger than the police, Mom."

"So why ask me? What do I know? I'm only your mother."

*God, here we go.*

"I'm not even going to ask you how you got involved in all this, Shawna. The fact is, I'm not surprised with that fast crowd you run with. Something like this was bound to happen. So don't say I didn't tell you so." Elaine shook her head slowly. "You fool with powerful men you make powerful enemies. You need to get out of all that, Shawna. Think of your father. Think how disappointed in you he would have been. But it's not too late. You're young. You have your looks. Come to church with me. It'll give you a new perspective on things."

"Mom, please..."

"I'm serious, baby. You know what? Danny Botcha still asks about you every time I see him at the market."

Shawna almost started laughing. *Danny Botcha.* Sure, a forty-year-old mama's boy. He had fish lips and bad skin, creepy dark eyes. He looked like he should be hanging around outside a playground with a raincoat on. *Brrrr.*

"Mom, this isn't about any of that," Shawna explained, remaining very calm. "This is not about my lifestyle or Danny Botcha or Dad or guilt or whatever else you're trying to lay on me, okay? This is life and death. I think those men will kill me. They might be watching us right now. No, don't look around." She grasped her mother's hands in her own. "I don't know if I'll see you again. I want you to know I love you. I'm on the run. I won't call you because your line is probably tapped. But I'll get word to you somehow."

Her mother's eyes misted up, the reality of the situation finally hitting home. "Shawna, please—"

"I have to leave now, Mom. I love you and I'm sorry I'm a disappointment to you."

"Oh, you're not. Never. I'm just a bitter old hag. I—"

"Bye, mom."

"Shawna..."

But her daughter did not hear. She left the salon without another look backward and she was right about one thing: it was the last time her mother would see her.

**5:54 P.M.**

Harry did not see Shawna come out of the salon because he spotted the two men waiting outside of Gallery Investments and knew they had her in their sights. He had a choice to make. He either turned his back right now like a coward or he helped this woman because never before in her life had she needed his help so badly. When she came out, she turned the corner fast and blended in with the other shoppers.

The two men started after her.

Harry closed the gap.

When Shawna saw him coming, she was wiping her eyes but she smiled. But the smile did not last very long when she saw the look on his face which was about as close to complete tragedy as he could manage. He blinked his eyes twice and she kept going. Again, prearranged. This was where he threw himself in harm's way and he saw no way to avoid it.

The two men came on.

They did not seem to recognize him which meant either he was a minor target or these two weren't exactly bright. They were both thick-necked athletic types sporting the same blonde crewcuts.

When they got close, Harry saw his opportunity.

All he needed was a few minutes so Shawna could fade.

He spotted a security guard.

He cut in front of the two men and pointed at them. "Hey! These two guys have guns! They've got fucking guns!"

That lit a nice little blaze under the security guard's ass. Such a blaze that he was joined by another and the two feds weren't going anywhere. The other shoppers had pulled back and away and some stormed away thinking there was going to be a shoot-out.

"That's Harry Niles," one of the feds said.

They both flashed their IDs at the rent-a-cops. "Homeland Security," one of them said and that was like flashing a Gestapo ID in Berlin the same time their haircuts were in vogue. The rent-a-cops backed off. The two feds took Harry and cuffed him right then. They were not as physical as they could have been.

"Nice one, Mr. Niles. You've got guts but it won't save her."

They dragged him off and everyone stood and gawked including a couple National Guard soldiers in for a smoothie. Harry did not fight; he kept an eye on the crowds and did not see Shawna anywhere. That was all that mattered at that moment. The only thing that really bothered him, other than his predicament, was that he had a nasty feeling he'd never kiss her lips again.

"Aren't I supposed to get a phone call?"

"For interfering with a federal officer in the performance of his duty?" Crewcut #1 laughed. "No, I'm afraid that's not what you're going to get at all."

**5:59 P.M.**

A man and a woman in demure business suits were tailing Shawna Geddes. And Stein was tailing them.

By now, Cave and the others must have figured out he wasn't coming back. He'd given McKenna the slip at the Clark and Lake CTA station because there was no doubt in his mind that he was up to something, probably wearing a wire for the Old Man and recording all their conversations. That was Stein's guess. And while McKenna was trying to find him—he'd be in deep shit for losing him—Stein caught the train over to the mall. Because that's where they were waiting for Shawna Geddes and he knew it.

But they weren't going to get her.

He'd already decided that.

As he'd already explained to Cave it was purely academic by this point and Cave agreed. So she'd videoed a few things? It meant nothing now because it was breaking everywhere. It was hardly secret by this point. But the Old Man insisted and you couldn't say no to the Old Man, now could you?

So S5 security units were watching her mother's house.

The nail salon her mother worked in.

Just about everywhere.

Sooner or later, she would surface with Harry Niles in tow. Except...now they had Niles and Stein had watched him run interference for the girl and he had to respect that. Real balls, that's what it was.

Stein bought a newspaper at a stand and continued on after the S5 people who were closing in on the Geddes woman like the jaws of a crocodile. As he closed in on them, he started thinking about the Old Man again. Just what was it with him? What was his fascination with Shawna Geddes? He was beginning to wonder if it was the girl at all.

What had Cave said?

*Harry Niles is trouble. You can bank on that. I've been through his file. He might be a tabloid hack now, but he sniffed around D.C. a lot in the old days. He had a way of finding out things. The Old Man is uncomfortable with that. He doesn't trust him. He think Niles might be the guy to shake the dirt from his rug.*

Sure, that was it.

The Old Man was scared.

Scared of a second-rate tabloid writer.

Wasn't that a riot?

Or maybe it wasn't so funny after all. The Old Man had survived as long as he had by knowing who his friends were and who his enemies were. To Stein, that made Niles more intriguing.

*Maybe there's more to that guy than I'm thinking.*

Not that it mattered. S5 had him now. The Old Man would pick his brains until there was nothing left but a few red scraps. Then Niles would end up in the river.

*Okay...*

*There.*

The S5 agents were making their move.

Shawna Geddes had just jumped into an elevator up to the parking garage and S5 had taken the one next to her. As they got in with about ten other people, Stein took the stairs. He vaulted up one flight after another. He had to get to her before they did. If for no other reason than to fuck up the Old Man's plans.

And from where he was standing, that was enough reason.

*Move!*


**6:04 P.M.**

It was all coming apart now. And the really ugly thing was that it was her fault, and she knew it. She had pushed Harry to see her mother even after he told her what a bad idea it was, what a risky venture it could indeed become. But she had pushed and now they probably had Harry and, dear God, they would have her soon, too. And what was she supposed to do without him? He had come to encompass her whole world in these past few days until it seemed like she was just a satellite caught in his orbit... and, honestly, wasn't that just fine and good? He'd been her friend and confidant for years and she turned him down again and again, not wanting to get romantically entangled (and mainly because she usually was already entangled) and now she had let that happen and it was good and she liked it and she was almost beginning to believe in crazy romance novel shit like star-crossed love and cosmic destinies... only now he was probably gone.

And it was her fault.

She was alone.

Terribly alone and, dammit, she was just no good at subterfuge. She didn't think like that (which is why the wives always seemed to find out).

*Hurry up for godsake, hurry up!*

The elevator was creeping up to the garage and Shawna's heart was pounding, perspiration making her shirt cling to her spine. She tapped her foot, swore under her breath, bunched her hands into fists.

Closer, but not there just yet.

She wondered what they would do to her when they caught her. If they'd even listen to what she had to say. Maybe they'd think she was holding back and torture her. Did they still do that? *Remember waterboarding, honey? What do you think they were doing with those Muslims? Holding their fucking hands?* Right, right. Only it wasn't called torture anymore, now it was known as *enhanced interrogation techniques*. At least to those doing it, but to the people receiving it, it was still fucking torture.

Bing.

The door opened.

A woman in a business suit was standing there. "Miss Geddes?" she said. "I'd like you to come with us."


**6:07 P.M.**

They had her and Stein saw it.

He stepped outside and waited for them. He slid the 9mm Beretta from inside his windbreaker and casually threaded the silencer onto it, facing the wall.

*Just what the hell do you think you're doing?*

But he didn't honestly know.

*What are you going to do with her once you grab her?*

Again, he didn't know but it seemed to be the right thing to do so he was going with it. God only knew there had been precious few moral and ethical decisions made in his life so this time he was doing what was right.

He could hear the Geddes woman sobbing.

They were coming.

He kept his back to them. A few other people in the parking garage were watching now. People passed in cars, staring. No doubt one of them would be calling the Metro boys on their cell. Not much time, but enough.

"Oh, please, please," Shawna Geddes was saying. "I haven't done anything...I really haven't."

They were ignoring her, showing no mercy as good little S5 cogs.

As they made to pass him, Stein said, "Excuse me."

When the man turned, Stein brought up the 9mm in one smooth practiced motion. The guy's eyes bulged and his hand tried to make it inside his coat, but a slug went through his forehead, scattering blood and brain matter to the concrete. He made it like three steps with a scarlet stream gushing from his head before he hit the ground. The woman, who had Shawna Geddes hooked by the elbow, let out a cry, released her and came at him with a very sloppy kick. Stein dodged it, cracked her in the face with the butt of the Beretta which elicited a sharp little scream from her as her nose snapped and blood fountained from the nostrils. Before she could hope to recover, he smashed her in the face with two quick left-handed jabs that dropped her to one knee.

Shawna Geddes stumbled back and tripped over the man's corpse.

The female S5 agent should have been done, but she launched herself, swinging at Stein. He dodged it, but not the kick she brought to his shin which threw him off balance. Then she kicked again. A perfect sidekick just like she'd been taught which caught him a glancing blow on the ribs and threw him up against the wall.

Her face webbed in blood, her eyes huge and crazy, she tried another move. Stein dropped the gun, dodged her kick, caught her arm and twisted it in the socket which made her cry out and fall forward...just in time for his knee to make contact with her nose, further mutilating the cartilage.

She went down and he kicked her in the ribs.

Then he stomped the back of her neck a little harder than he intended because he heard the vertebrae snap.

He grabbed up the gun and those precious few bystanders that had been thinking about intervening ran off.

But so had the girl.

"SHAWNA!" he called out as she ran through the garage. "I'M HERE TO HELP YOU! STOP! WAIT FOR ME!"

But of course, she didn't. Stein went running after her, ignoring his throbbing shin and closing in on her. She nearly made it to an exit ramp when a car raced out and struck her, throwing her up on the hood and rolling her off to the pavement.

*Shit! The dumb bitch!*

But as Stein ran to her aid, he saw that it was no accident, because the car slammed on its brakes and now it was revving to back up and finish the job. Stein put a round through the windshield and that threw off the driver's trajectory. The car—a maroon sedan—missed her and slammed into the cement barrier, tail lights shattering in shards of plastic.

And by then, Stein was at the car.

The driver looked at him once and Stein shot him through the head, spraying the inside of the sedan a brilliant red.


**6:12 P.M.**

*What?*

*What?*

*WHAT?*

Shawna heard a voice speaking her name, she was sure she heard a voice speaking her name, then hands taking hold of her—*ow, shit, that hurt, man, that hurt*—and carrying her. Like a child. Picking her up and carrying her away. Voices. Voices were screaming. Sirens in the distance. Somebody was shouting. A man shouted back, *FBI, FBI, FBI, stand clear...*

Her eyes opened and she was in a car.

Driving.

*Oh no, oh no, it was one of them. They had her. They had her. Shit—*

She reached for the door, but her limbs were rubbery and weak, she couldn't seem to coordinate them. But she had to get away. She had to find Harry. Get to Harry. There was safety with Harry.

A hand patted her shoulder.

What?

"Take it easy, just take it easy," the voice said. "I'm getting you out of here. I don't think anything's broken. Just keep your head down for now."

Well, that part was easy.

She felt herself drifting off even though she was aching. No. She couldn't drift off. She tried to sit up and that hand forced her down again.

"Sit still," the voice said.

"Fuck you," her own voice said. "Let me go."

"If I let you go, they'll kill you."

"Who the hell are you?"

"I'm a friend. Now take it easy."

It was pointless to fight against him or resist him in any way and she knew it. So, she sank down in the seat and it was warm and soft and nice. She thought about Harry and her eyes flickered open, then closed again. She felt herself drifting away.

"That's better," the voice said. "That's better now."

But by then Shawna was in dreamland.

# DETROIT, HOLY CROSS HOSPITAL

## THE MORGUE

**6:32 P.M.**

Cold, holy Jesus it was cold.

Colder than Rudolph's nuts.

This playing possum business was all and fine but Johnny Kopok had been at it for hours now, sleeping with the dead, and he knew he couldn't do it much longer. Good thing was, he figured, that when they brought him down into the morgue with the cold cuts there wasn't enough room to put him in a drawer so they stacked him up with the others. And it was only in the last hour or so that they'd begun the grim business of feeding the bodies into the incinerator.

"You don't want to go in, too," he whispered, "then you better do something."

"What do you got in mind?" said another voice.

Johnny jumped...as much as he could jump with the dead crowding him to either side on the floor...and looked around. *Did I hear that? Sometimes my brain ain't so good and I don't remember the last time I had a good taste, so maybe, just maybe—*

"Name's Bertie Panella," the voice said. A woman. Of all things.

Johnny sat up and introduced himself to the old woman down the way. "Pleased to know you, Bertie."

"Same here, Johnny."

"You ain't got a worm in you, do you?"

"Not yet," Bertie told him. "But some of these dead ones might."

Johnny explained his situation and Bertie responded in kind. She had been in the hospital to have a benign tumor removed from her throat—fifty-odd years of smoking will do that to you, she pointed out—and all went well. She was set to be sprung today...then the Martians came and what a mess it all was.

Johnny didn't know what all that Martian talk was until Bertie explained that sometimes when she had a good load on or hadn't had a taste of the old Mary Lou in a few days, she started seeing Martians.

"Sometimes they come right out of the walls," Bertie told him. "It's a helluva thing. Mostly I hear 'em whispering in the closet."

"Sorry to hear that," Johnny told her with all sincerity.

"I know they're in my head," Bertie explained. "But I don't like 'em none better."

Johnny could sympathize with that.

"Then when those people in the white suits and hoods came in, I was sure I was just imagining 'em. Martians. Goddamn Martians. But bigger and not green-faced. Then they stuck needles in me and I knew they was real."

"They're real, all right," Johnny told her. "Real as snot on a doorknob."

"So what's our plan?" Bertie said.

"We... ssshhh... they're coming."

"Martians?"

"Yep."

Johnny and Bertie curled up with the rest of the corpses and waited it out. A couple men in white containment suits bustled in and grabbed a few corpses and dragged them off. They loaded them on gurneys and wheeled them away, off to the incinerator.

When they were gone, Johnny said, "Okay, doll. We make our move now."

"I'm with you."

They worked themselves free of the corpses and stepped out of the cold room and threaded their way through the various autopsy rooms and then out into the hallway.

"Okay," Johnny said. "There's the elevator, down at the end."

"You think that's wise?"

"Maybe you're right. Let's make for the stairs."

Together, they went to the fire door and got through it just in time. As Johnny peaked through the window in the door, he saw four more soldiers in their suits—not so white anymore—come for more corpses. Being as quiet as they could, Johnny and Bertie climbed up the stairs, making for freedom...if there was such a thing left anymore.

# CHICAGO, RIVER NORTH

## THE WAREHOUSE

**6:51 P.M.**


Wake up.

You must.

Wake.

*Up...*

Harry felt his eyes open, then shut; open, then shut; open, then stay shut and nothing he could say or think or do could seem to change that. He knew he was dreaming. Even though it was all drugged and narcotic and surreal, he knew it was all a dream, it had to be a dream. He just needed to wake up because Shawna was in danger and he needed to help her.

It felt like he was laying on a table.

He drifted off and then almost came around but just couldn't open his eyes.

He could hear voices.

Voices he did not recognize.

One of them said: "Just how much did you give him?"

"The usual. Just enough to take the fight out of him."

The first voice laughed. "That's a lovely black eye you have."

"He got the jump on me."

"Ah, and you a professional. How perfectly amusing."

Who the hell were these people and why was he on this table? Not only that but strapped to it.

"Cut him loose," the first voice said.

"If he gets crazy again..."

"I have no fear of that. Besides, I have a professional like you to subdue him."

Harry's eyes flickered open.

He saw faces. He did not recognize them.
Dreaming, still dreaming. He must be dreaming.
"Mr. Niles," said the first voice. "Can you hear me?"
Harry opened his eyes. He licked his lips. "Where the hell am I?" he said.
"Yes," said a voice. "Where exactly?"

# GAZA CITY, GAZA STRIP

## SHATI REFUGEE CAMP

**1:13 A.M. PALESTINE TIME**

Meir Cohan listened to the things speaking in their hissing, whispering voices. He could not be sure if they were talking to one another or just to themselves. There was no way to know and he honestly did not want to know. They were things. They were men and women and children infested by grotesque parasitic worms and he had all he could do not to break down sobbing or vent his mind in one wild shrieking scream.

*You are a soldier,* he told himself, *in enemy territory. You must look at it no other way. If you were facing Hamas murderers, you would not shrink so. Do not shrink now.*

*You're maybe the last one left.*

*Dear God.*

But it was certainly possible. Laying there amongst the bodies and wreckage, his face blackened by soot and his orange biocon suit torn and burnt, his helmet gone, he knew he must keep his nerve. If they taught you nothing else in the IDF, it was to keep your nerve. To keep a cool head in a combat station.

Around him were literally dozens of IDF soldiers scattered and heaped and tangled together. A few were melted together from the fires. Several fires were still burning, throwing jumping orange-yellow illumination against the rubble and debris. The air stank of burning corpses, pungent clouds of smoke drifting about. Cohan was in a real situation here and he knew it. The bombed-out husks of block houses surrounded the little courtyard on three sides, the fourth being the serpentine alleyway that had brought the IDF here in the first place. Gathered in the mouth of the alley and along the walls, coveting pockets of crawling shadow, were the infected ones.

They were not human anymore.

He could not see them clearly...just glimpses of hunching things, slack things, flaccid and vermiform like that which infested them. Now and again, he would see one move with a hideous inching sort of motion that made him shudder, made his stomach feel almost watery.

The idea of trying to break out was ludicrous.

He'd never get past them. And the idea of going through them... no, absolutely not. He still had his knife. What a sweet relief it would bring drawn across his throat.

Better suicide than to become something like that.

What, then?

He did not know. Much like Johnny Kopok a world away, Cohan was doing his best to pretend he was a corpse. So far, he had fooled the hosts themselves who were little better than mindless shells under the dominion of their respective worms. But he knew he would not fool the worms. And they were active. Of the fifty or sixty bodies of the IDF and Palestinians cast about and heaped in ramparts, there were several Israelis that were still alive...if you wanted to call it that. They were infested now. When their hosts had been gunned down or blown apart or lit up by flamethrowers during the assault, their individual worms had burst free, many severely damaged, seeking new hosts, new bodies to infect and enslave.

Right now, there were an uncounted number of worms sliding amongst the bodies.

Cohan had seen one of them take a survivor not ten minutes before.

He was still shaking from the sight. The man had been Eli Stern, the lieutenant of Cohan's platoon. Stern had been grazed by friendly fire. Wounded, but nowhere near death. That's when the worm found him. It rose up amongst the bodies, a pallid ribbon that looked—if anything—like some mammoth inchworm considering a leaf to chew on. It arched itself and hung its head-bulb down low like a rattlesnake readying itself to strike.

Stern saw it hovering over him.

Cohan was certain of that. He saw it and he made a choked whimpering sound in his throat.

Cohan had never felt more of a coward than he did at that moment, knowing the lieutenant needed him but unable to move, to act, to do anything but hide there within the skin of his suit. Far too terrified and revolted by the worm to do anything else.

*I'm sorry, Stern. God knows how sorry I am. But I can't. I just can't. I'm afraid, you see, I'm afraid that if I so much as twitch it will come after me. And the idea of it touching me...the feel of it sliding over me... it's too much. Please forgive me but it's just too much...*

The worm's body, Cohan saw, was made of segments, each of them a pulpous, glistening white and oiled with an opaque slime that looked oddly like the jelly from a canned ham. The smell coming off it was sweet and repellent. It made Cohan's mind sink into a droning field of fuzz and made his stomach pull down low, bottoming out.

He gagged.

He felt bile squirt up the back of his throat.

He tried not to flinch. It took every ounce of willpower he had to avoid coughing or vomiting at that moment. He didn't think the worms could hear, but he had a feeling they could sense vibration, movement, maybe even body heat.

The worm drew its head-bulb over Stern's face and Stern was aware of it, oh yes, but he was drugged out, senseless like a junkie with an arm full of heroin. All he did was stare with shining, glazed eyes, his mouth hanging slack, a thread of drool coming from the corner of his lips. The worm kept bumping Stern's face with its head-bulb, Cohan saw, but what it was in fact doing (he soon realized) was jabbing him with the scarlet stinging spines that ringed its mouth…which was sort of like two dark slits intersecting in an X-shape.

Then the mouth opened.

It seemed to split the head-bulb wide and Cohan looked down the black maw of its throat and it was spiked with teeth. Maybe not true teeth, but barbed protrusions that looked oddly like the thorns of rose stems. And not just a single ring of them, but one ring after another and another, all crowded and overlapping. Then three pink squirming things came out like tongues, except they were more akin to the tentacles of a sea anemone.

They brushed over Stern's face, licking at his eyes and cheeks, exploring the cavities of his nostrils and sliding between his lips.

*Oh, dear God,* Cohan thought. *It's tasting him, it's goddamn well tasting him.*

But was it? Could the thing even taste? Maybe it was something else. Maybe there were chemoreceptors on the tongues. Maybe they were general sensory organs.

It was at this point, as he watched those pink tendrils looping over Stern's mad staring face, that Cohan lost control of his bladder. He felt hot piss run down his legs and drain inside his suit. And as he did so, biting down on his lip to keep from crying out, something happened. The smell of urine was more than obvious to Cohan himself who trembled in his shame… but the worm sensed it, too. Its split-open bulb-head rose and pointed in Cohan's direction, those pink tendrils waving in the air like fingers.

Then, thank God, it turned its attention back to Stern.

The abdomen of Stern's suit was ripped, and the worm saw this as a perfect invitation. It squeezed itself into the aperture and Stern began to convulse. There was a moist ripping sound and the worm's body began to contract like sinewy muscle, expanding and deflating, making the most horrible gulping and slobbering sounds. In the light of the fires, Cohan saw that its segments began to go from that phosphorescent white to dull pink as it fed. It didn't bother parasitizing Stern because he was wounded and of no use as a host.

Then it slid itself back out of him, its bulb-head pulling back with red strings of tissue, its mouth packed with fleshy ropes of undigested meat, filaments of ooze and bile hanging free.

It fed upon him with slurping noises for the next ten minutes until it was gorged with blood and pink as uncooked meat, then swam back amongst the bodies.

Trembling, Cohan waited his turn.

He heard slithering sounds. Two then three, then five, six, and seven more worms rose up amongst the bodies. Some were small, but others were huge like the one that fed on Stern. They rose up together and reached their head-bulbs skyward, seeming to move in tandem with some uncanny rhythm like deep-sea kelp in a current. Then they dove at the bodies, more of them rising by the moment, until the corpse heaps seemed to be covered in roping, noodly forms that suckered themselves to throats and bellies, ingesting blood and flesh, gorging themselves until their segments were bloated and glossy pink.

After a time, they retreated.

And, again, Cohan waited.

He figured he was mad by that point and even if he somehow managed to get out of this he would never be right again. Like his Great Uncle Sol who had survived the Auschwitz death camp...he had lived, but his mind was never right again, always seeing Nazis lurking in every shadow. Cohan figured that's how it would be with him. He would never stop seeing this night, he would never close his eyes without seeing the spiraling shapes of worms coming at him.

*You'll die every day for the rest of your life, or you can die quickly right now,* he told himself.

He moved then.

He reached down for his knife. Laying not too far away was an assault rifle, the Imi Tavor TAR-21. He would die tonight but he would inflict damage. Trying to move cautiously and quietly, he reached a hand over and gripped the rifle. He would charge. He would counterattack. He would blaze a trail right through those worm people that blocked his way. Maybe he would make it. Maybe he would live to find a life haunted by the memory of this night. And maybe he would escape only to be gunned down by Fedayeen youths.

No matter.

He would do this, he would—

*What is that? The worms?*

From the shadows something was coming and not just one thing but many. He could not see them; not yet. But they were coming and from all directions. Cohan pulled himself up into a firing stance. And that's when he saw—people. Things that had once been people. They undulated on their bellies, crawling sacs inching in his direction in imitation of their masters. They were creeping at him in waves. Too many. There couldn't be that many...they were clustered around him, snaking things with wide mouths and limbs dragging like vestigial appendages.

Something had happened here.

Some grim and monstrous mutation had taken place. These were not people: they were creeping, slavering horrors slithering at him to feed, to glut themselves on his blood.

When they got close enough that he could see their yellow faces and lidless eyes, their oval lamprey mouths, Cohan let out a scream and brought the TAR-21 up to deal death.

*Click.*

*Click-click.*

The rifle was empty. Wasn't it the final indignity in a night of the same? As those faces neared him, mouths opening and closing to reveal tiny hooked, grasping teeth, Cohan felt something warm and wet break inside him and he knew it was his sanity running like the yolk of an egg. He began to giggle uncontrollably.

When the worm-things were but inches away from him and he was giggling so loudly that it filled the night and drool hung from his grinning mouth, he pulled the knife and quickly, expertly slit his own throat. When they fell on him, he was still smiling. From two bloody sets of lips.

# CHICAGO, NORTH SHORE

## EN ROUTE

**7:32 P.M.**

As he made his way back into the city from Elmwood Park, Gabe Hebberman began to get a very bad feeling. Martial law would be in effect at midnight, yes, but that was hours away and he was amazed at the lack of traffic and commerce on the streets. It seemed since that morning that it had been cut in half. And was that because of the troops in the streets or general fear... or was it something more? The parasite outbreak? Some six people failed to show up for work that morning and he did not like it. These were omens and he read them as being bad ones.

But was the outbreak moving that fast?

He had no answers. The country had no answers. Every newspaper and news network were working overtime to get some facts so they could scoop their rivals, but facts were hard to come by. Facts weren't something that Gabe's publications obsessed over, of course. They were basically selling entertainment to the masses. But even tabloids needed something, some basic truths to exploit or distort completely out of shape.

*What exactly are these parasites? And how fast would they spread? What protection is there from them?*

That's what every journalist in the country wanted to know. There were plenty of rumors making the rounds and some were pretty good ones, they had plenty of meat on them, but Gabe knew he had to step very lightly. If he went for the throat like he wanted to—Harry Niles, God bless him, was so very good at that—then he raised the risk of pissing off the military government which were running everything now. News was being very carefully censored. And if he started printing some of the good juicy gossip out there, he'd probably get shut down. Inciting a riot or something. He'd already been warned by the Army PR guy.

But martial law or no martial law, didn't people have a right to some kind of information?

Thus far, Gabe's contacts were saying it was everything from cooties to crotch rot. The one making the rounds again and again was the story of worms. Parasitic worms. The reality of that was a horror beyond horrors, but for a tabloid...good Lord, it was manna. Even the Jews in the wilderness had not eaten so well as Gabe's publications would if he could just put out some worm stories. Oh, he could see it his mind: U.S. INVADED BY TERROR WORMS or WORM HORROR INFESTS THE NATION. *Gah!* So revolting it was perfection. Add to that government conspiracies and cover-ups... oh boy, it was heaven sent, it was truly heaven sent.

But as tasty as all that was, there was also the reality which was the sting at the heart of the beast: parasites. The military government had not declared that anyone should hide away or avoid contact with others—but it was coming, Gabe's sources said—but people were doing it anyway by the looks of the streets. Unless, it was not paranoia keeping them indoors but actually infestation and if that was the case—

*There it is again.*

There was a blue sedan following him and he had seen it two or three times that day. Not good. Had he broken some directive? Were they hoping he'd lead them to Harry and Shawna? Well, so sorry. He knew nothing.

*Shit!*

A truck came barreling out of a side street and crossed Grand Avenue going right through a stop sign. Gabe hit the brakes on his Lexus but it was too late. There was impact. The sound of his own cries. Shattering glass and blaring horns. The Lexus spun around, hopped the curb and came to a rest.

Gabe opened his eyes, blinking at the spider-webbing of shattered glass where his windshield had once been.

*Oh boy.*

He expected people to be surrounding the car as they always did in such situations, but it was no soap today. Gabe sighed, massaged the strain in his neck and popped the seatbelt. He was unbroken. That was the important thing. His door was jammed and he couldn't get it open. He crawled across the seat to the passenger side door... and the door was opened for him. Two thick-necked men were standing there. They were huge and bristling with matching crewcuts. They looked like NFL linemen squeezed into cheap suits.

"Thank God," he said as they helped him out.

"Are you all right?" one of the men asked.

"Yes... yes, I think so."

Gabe stood up, stretching his neck. That's when he saw the blue sedan parked at the curb. These were the men that had been following him. He knew better than to ask any questions about that. He would treat them as if they were just a couple of interested bystanders. As he looked around, he noticed that while there were a few people watching, they were doing it from a distance as if they dared not get too close. That was disturbing. It was also disturbing that the truck that hit him was also gone.

Just a hit and run.

But why was he finding that so hard to believe?

"You'd better come with us, Mr. Hebberman," said one of them. "We'll take you somewhere to get that neck looked at."

"Oh, it's not so bad. I think I'll wait for the police."

"I'm afraid I'll have to insist," the man said.

"Ah, it's like that, is it? You know my name, you follow me around all day... and now you want to take me to some undisclosed location?"

"Please, Mr. Hebberman. Don't make this harder than it has to be."

Gabe knew he was going. There was no earthly way he could elude these two men. And it wasn't just a matter of age but condition. These men were powerful, athletic, and probably dangerous... still, he knew he had to buy himself some time. Even in the desolation of the city, the police would show, sooner or later. "All right, all right," he told them. "But first, please show me some identification. If you're going to abduct me, then have the decency to explain to me why that is and by what authority you're doing it."

"We're doing it by authority of the Department of Homeland Security," the man said. He let Gabe see his ID card. "Now, Please, come with us."

"Is this about Harry Niles again?"

"I wouldn't know. I was only told to bring you in."

Gabe shook his head. "You know, this whole thing is amateurish. I hope you realize that, son. The truck hitting me and all that. You could have been a little more imaginative."

The man looked to his associate who emoted like a block of granite.

"Mr. Hebberman. We don't have time for this."

"Maybe you should make time."

"Not today." He hooked Gabe by the elbow and when Gabe fought against him, the other guy pulled out an injector gun and shot Gabe in the throat. Gabe went limp and they dragged him to their car. By the time the police arrived, they were long gone.

As they drove, the guy with the injector gun said, "I guess he's going to the Warehouse."

"Yes, he is."

"Too bad. Seemed like a nice old guy, too."

# CHICAGO

## WICKER PARK

**7:57 P.M.**

"So you kill people for a living."

Not a question nor an accusation really; just a statement. Stein had just finished laying out the skein of events that brought him to the mall where he had most assuredly pulled Shawna Geddes' fat out of the fire. He left nothing out. The country was moving closer to absolute anarchy day by day and he saw no reasons to be the keeper of dark truths and state secrets any longer. No sense in protecting the people that wanted him dead. After he got out of the mall, he had driven her to a safe house that was known to him and him only. It was a place to lay low until the heat cooled, if it ever did.

"I'm...was...a security consultant."

"Ah. I see. Not an assassin, a security consultant."

"That was my official title."

"That's like calling a whore a pleasure consultant."

Stein bristled even though he knew she was more or less correct. "Whether you agree with what I did for a living or not, Miss Geddes, the least you can do is accept the fact that I got you out. That I knew what I was doing was wrong and I exited. I don't expect you to fall to your knees and worship me, but the least you can fucking do is maybe be a little appreciative that I saved your life."

She nodded. "Call me Shawna please."

"Shawna."

"I'm not unappreciative, Mr. Stein. I just don't know what to believe or who to believe anymore. You say you pulled me out of there for purely altruistic reasons. If that's true, then you're a hero. You have my respect and loyalty," she explained, dragging off a cigarette slowly and purposefully. "But, you have to understand that who you are and what you do scares the shit out of me. Until a few days ago, I thought guys like you existed only in novels and movies. And the fact that you worked for Blackpool..."

There was always a stigma with that, he knew. It was the very reason Blackpool had changed its name to XI: to avoid certain associations with human rights violations, torture sessions, and assassinations carried out while it was a military contractor during the Iraq War. Not that changing the name could wash the blood from its hands or alter its particularly dark corporate image.

"I wasn't involved in any of that stuff."

"But you openly admit you murdered American veterans."

"Yes. They were infected. They had to be eradicated."

Jesus, he'd actually said it. *Eradicated*. It scared him that the Old Man was speaking through him. It was like he was channeling that fucking monster.

"I like that," Shawna said. "*Eradicated*. It's very neat and clean."

"Sarcasm duly noted and understood."

They sat in the living room of a little house on Campbell Avenue and listened to cars passing outside, just watching each other. Stein was beginning to wonder why he'd bothered with any of this. He'd didn't expect her to go down on her knees before him or anything like that, but he did expect a little gratitude. He couldn't imagine hiding out with her here in this place for an undisclosed period of time and having to fend off her accusations and contempt.

"So what happens now?" she asked him.

"That's up to you."

She didn't seem to believe that. "What if I just leave?"

"Then you leave. Walk out the door."

"And you'll let me?"

He shrugged. "Listen, lady. I saved your bacon. That's it. You want to throw your ass in harm's way again then please do so. You're not a prisoner." She kept staring at him with complete suspicion and mistrust. Then he got it. "I see, you think this is part of some ongoing conspiracy? That I brought you here to turn you over to them? Well, that's fucking foolish and if you use your brain for a minute and consider what happened at the mall I think you'll realize that." He stood up and stepped over to her, towering above her. "I killed two people to get you out of there and injured a third. You think the people I work for would sacrifice their own like that just to set you up so I could grab you when they already had you?"

For Shawna, ridding herself of the suspicion did not come easy. "I guess it doesn't make much sense."

"No, it doesn't. And while we're on the subject, Shawna, I think your attitude is bullshit. And the idea that I'm somehow holding you prisoner here is insulting. Leave, okay? Walk out the door. Do me a favor."

She stood up and walked past him, stormed past him actually like a brat that had just gotten a good, but much needed, scolding. He heard the front door open and close.

He sat back down.

She left her cigarettes, so he helped himself to one. He allowed himself one a day. No more, no less. As he sat there smoking, he figured this was the part in a sitcom where the character knows the person who just left was coming back and they count to five and they come right back through the door. He wouldn't have been surprised. For, really, where the hell was she going to go? She didn't strike him as the type that could go undercover and accept the deprivations of that sort of life. She was very attractive, had a way of using that via body language that she probably wasn't even aware of it was so ingrained in her. She was probably used to having men fawn over her. If he had to peg her, he would have said she was a rich man's toy: used to being handled gently and getting her way. Well, that wasn't going to happen here. He wasn't going to chase after her. He hoped she'd go and stay gone. Last thing he needed was to be watching out for a headstrong woman who considered him to be nothing but a lowlife killer.

*I don't need it*, he thought.

About the time he finished his cigarette, she came back through the doorway.

"I don't have anywhere to go."

"Figured as much."

"Can I stay?" Pouting now.

"Suit yourself. But get rid of the attitude. We're not going to get along if you don't."

She just nodded. "Where do you think they took Harry?"

"To the Warehouse." He explained all that to her and she knew the place. "I'm sure he's with the Old Man now."

"What will they do to him?"

He shrugged. "They could kill him. They might just lock him away until this is over then let him go. Then again…"

"What?"

"There's always personality reassignment."

Her eyes widened. "And what is that?"

"Brainwashing." He gave her the gist of a place called The Resort. What went on there. "If they do that, he's lost to you. He might as well be dead. They'll program him with a new life, a past history, likes and dislikes, fears and desires…everything."

"Is it that complete?"

He looked at her. "Shawna, when they're done even your own mother will have no memory of you. It's like the ultimate witness protection program."

"Then we have to go get him out."

He laughed. "Really? Just you and me?" He shook his head. "Not possible. They have security everywhere. They'd kill us."

"Then what?"

"Sorry to tell you, but nothing. We can't help him. You seem to think he's pretty smart, pretty crafty. Okay. That's good. Because if he's going to get out of there with his life and his mind intact, he'll need every bit of that because it's all in his hands now and there's not a damn thing we can do about it."

# CHICKASAW COUNTY, MISSISSIPPI

## POLE CREEK ROAD

**8:13 P.M.**

There was one thing for sure that everyone knew: Elmer Cassling hated children. He hated the sound of their voices, their laughter, their joy, their exuberance. But mostly, he hated their youth because at sixty-three years of age, his own was quickly abandoning him. And this was why he put up with zero shit from them. Whenever he caught them around the campground, he chased them off. He went out of his way to make it hard for them to enjoy themselves on his watch. The way he saw it, he was the manager and that was his job.

So that evening, when he heard the sound of their squealing voices, he saw red.

*Goddamn them!*

He knew right away it was probably the Bohannon kids or the Galligan twins from the farms up the road. They were usually the ones he had trouble with. They were thick as thieves. A rat pack of monsters that would become meth-heads and crack dealers given time. Their parents didn't give a shit, they were drunk and useless (Ritchie Bohannon), welfare cases (Rip Galligan), or whores (Kathy Bohannon). It was pointless to appeal to such people to keep their shitting brats in sight because the apple didn't fall too far from the tree.

Oh, Elmer had tried. After all the stop signs had been stolen from the campground, he'd gone straight over to the Bohannon place and confronted Kathy Bohannon (he made sure Ritchie wasn't there because he was one violent SOB). She had answered the door in a pair of shorts so tight her gee-gee was sticking out like a hungry clam, her nipples trying to poke through her T-shirt. She had refused to listen to him because her kids were not criminals.

This was the last straw.

This time he was going to straighten them out the way their parents should have. The campground was privately owned and they had no business hanging around, vandalizing things and raising hell. Elmer only needed to catch them in the act just the once, then he'd have something for the sheriff.

Nan, his wife, always told him to go easy because they were just kids. That's all, just kids doing what kids do. But she couldn't know. She couldn't understand that on some level, Elmer was certain that they played these pranks and fooled around just to belittle him and make him look ineffective at his job.

All the hooting and hollering was coming from the woods, the restricted area of the woods. This was the place where campers were not encouraged to go because it was where the sewage lagoon was located, the pit where the campground waste was collected and broken down naturally by bacterial action and evaporated by the wind and sun.

They wouldn't be there!

Who in the Christ would play around the shit pit? Even those goddamned inbred, dumb-assed Galligans and Bohannons would know better than that. At least, Elmer hoped so. The lagoon was fenced off, but he wouldn't put it past them to scale the fence so they could get near the sewage. It was only three feet deep, but it was dangerous. You could easily be overcome by the fumes and—

It took about twenty minutes to reach the lagoon if you followed the meandering path through the woods, but if you cut straight through, you could make it in five if you knew the way. Elmer charged through the brush, sticks scratching his hands and face, pickers sticking to his pants, mossy logs trying to trip him up. *Little bastards! God, when I get my hands on them! Evil monsters are probably throwing puppies into the shit pit!* By the time he reached the clear cut where the lagoon was located, he was bleeding and red-faced, ticks on his arms and skeeter bites dotting his neck and forehead.

There was a wide grassy verge around the lagoon fence so that the wind would not be impeded by heavy growth. He saw right away that the gate was wide open, something which was impossible because he kept it locked. He was warned again and again by the state inspector to never, ever leave the gate open because kids or animals could fall into the slew and drown.

But here it was, standing open.

Panting, sweating, pissed off and at the very end of his rope, Elmer caught his breath and approached the fence. The kids' voices were very loud now. And that's when he saw something that just could not be, something that made his stomach flip-flop and a weird terror build inside him.

The kids, all those damn kids, the Bohannon boys and the Galligan twins and half a dozen other shavers that he did not recognize...they were, they were—

*Can't be! I can't be seeing this! I can't !*

But he was. The children were not fooling around on the edge of the lagoon, they were *in* it. They were hip-deep in that foul, slopping sewage, playing in it like it was the local swimming hole.

"Get... get out of there!" Elmer cried in a hoarse voice. "You can't be in there!"

His mind was whirling around and around in his head. Part of that was from what he was seeing, something he found nearly impossible to process, but much of it was from the gagging, noxious odors of the lagoon itself which was all stirred up by these bat-shit crazy kids.

The children stopped leaping and splashing and dunking one another in the mire. They stood there, looking at him, brown with shit like they'd been crawling through mud. It was greased in their hair and splashed across their faces. Their eyes were wide and bright. In fact, they were bleached white like ping pong balls, no pupils, no anything. The glazed eyes of dead men.

"You kids..."

Elmer tried to speak as he stood there at the gate, but the words and what he was trying to convey with them got all tangled up in his head. His mouth felt numb, his mind foggy.

*Come in with us, Mister Cassling. It's warm and deep...*

That voice... did he hear it or imagine it? He couldn't be sure. He only knew one thing: these goddamn kids were insane. He needed to get help. He needed the sheriff out here and maybe county mental health to boot. They were beckoning to him, inviting him into their little game and he was tempted, God help him, but he was tempted because even as a boy the other kids had never invited him to play with them. He was ostracized. An outsider. The subject of derision.

*It's okay, Mister Cassling. We want you to play with us. We want to show you what fun it is to do those things you're not supposed to do. We want to show you what it's like to be a kid, to run wild and free.*

Crazy, that's what, they were all just crazy. Did they really believe that he would play with them now after they'd ignored him so long ago? Sure, part of him wanted to, maybe it *needed* to... but he wasn't about to join in. His hand was wrapped white-knuckled around the gatepost just to show them (and maybe himself) that he wasn't about to play with them. He was an adult, and he would rain hell down on them over this.

One of them, a girl, stepped up the bank, brown clumps of shit falling from her. She held out her hand and he saw the swollen, undulant mound of her belly.

*Come on, Mister Cassling. It's so dark and warm in the lagoon, so safe and protected. Like going back inside your mother. Take my hand and slide down here, down into the womb.*

Elmer shook his head frantically side to side. There was no damn way he'd wade in that...that stuff. If his voice wasn't lodged in his throat, he would have told her that, made her see. The grass was dry. It crunched under his boots.

Such a hot day. A nice little dip would be relaxing. But that wasn't going to happen because he was gripping the gatepost...but if that was true, then why were his hands reaching out to her? And why was the methane stench of human waste filling his head and making him giddy? And, dear God, why was he stepping down into the sewage lagoon, sliding down into its brown, fecal slime depths?

But it was too late.

He looked one last time up at the blue sky before the sewage covered his face. He coughed and gagged as it filled his mouth, then his throat and lungs and by then, they were pressing in from all sides...the children and the worms they carried.


## 8:33 P.M.

When Elmer didn't come back, Nan started to get worried because he was nothing if not punctual. She knew in many ways that he was flawed, neurotic and brooding over a basket of insecurities, but he was a good man when she was with him. She knew this and understood this even if many did not. His childhood had been hard. There had been no friends and an abusive father. And it was the child, as her mother had once said, that describes the man (or woman).

He said he was off to straighten out those darn kids again and she had told him to hurry because his supper had already been sitting for an hour.

But now he had not returned and was not answering his cell. She did not like it. She took a quick walk through the campground and saw no sign of him. His truck was parked over by the woods. The only thing there was the restricted path out to the sewage lagoon.

Was that where he was?

She approached the path, feeling uneasy. She was not certain why, but she had a sudden terrible feeling of approaching tragedy. The perfectly weird thing about that was she had not felt it, not to this degree, in years. Not since just before the hospital had called to inform her that her mother had died in her sleep.

Maybe it was nothing. With everything going on in the country these days, she was simply feeling the way everyone was feeling, she supposed.

Her heart heavy and thumping in her chest, she started up the path to the lagoon. It was a long walk. It would be dark by the time she got there...unless she took the short cut. Elmer had shown her the way once. She hesitated to take it now because she had a healthy fear of the woods, always afraid she might step on a copperhead or a water moccasin.

Damn.

Though her tracking skills were limited, it was easy to see that someone had just been through here. They had apparently charged through like a bull elephant. The grass was pushed down, branches broken and saplings bent aside. It must have been Elmer.

Nan called his name loudly two or three times, but there was no answer. About half way there, she heard shouting. She paused. The voices of children... and was that Elmer? She distinctly heard the voice of a man mixed in with them.

Had he caught them at something?

Was he yelling at them?

She hoped that's all it was. She moved faster now, snakes be damned. If Elmer had finally lost control, she needed to get there and stop him before he laid a hand on one of those children.

Bursting from the woods, just as red-faced and sweaty as Elmer had been, she didn't bother trying to catch her breath. She charged through the grass to the lagoon where the voices were coming from. She could already smell its high, evil odor. By the time she passed through the gate, everything had gone silent. She saw no children. She did not see Elmer. There was just the lagoon, that steaming swamp of brown rippling excreta. A few ripples passed over its surface as if something was swimming beneath it.

That bad, very bad feeling peaked in her again and she felt that she was very close to an episode of some kind. She felt dizzy, woozy, her chest tight, her throat constricted.

*It's the gases. Oh Lord, I'm being overcome by the gases.*

The ripples moved and scattered sluggishly, coming from several directions at the same time though there was no wind. Sweat beading her face, Nan watched them, fascinated by them as her head revolved on its axis like a planet. She began to feel calm. The fear and mounting apprehension lessened appreciably. The ripples were hypnotizing, moving to and fro with no pattern, much like her thoughts.

She heard a splashing.

She was not surprised in the least when one shit-slicked head rose from the slough followed by another and another and another. Here the children were! They had only been hiding the entire time, simply playing some harmless little game. They stood there, dripping with sewage, great white worms swimming in the muck, coiling around them, sliding in and out of their mouths. Great glistening clusters of pearls broke the surface. She knew they were eggs, millions of eggs like frog spawn, and that made them much more beautiful as they glimmered and winked. She longed to hold them in her hands, press them against her lips, fondle the white pulsing phallic length of a worm and let it slide between her breasts.

*The lagoon,* she heard a voice in her head say. *Don't you see? Don't you get it? It's a nursery! It is here that the worms brood their larva—in this great lagoon of excrement which is essentially like an artificial womb to them. It mimics the lower human digestive tract where they come to term*

This knowledge made her smile, made her feel beautifully free for the first time in her life, part of something much, much larger than herself. As she slid out of her clothes, drooling and sexually excited, she fondled her breasts and watched the children playing with their worms and shoving handfuls of shit into their mouths which they slurped down greedily, filling themselves with the filthy, disease-ridden dung that the larval worms so favored, creating a perfect biosphere for them.

The children had formed a circle and from the center of it now rose the form of Elmer—he was naked and erect, a pagan god of fertility draped with worms, molded from brown greasy clay and strung with webs of eggs that pulsed like the hearts of newborn birds.

When he called to her, Nan did not hesitate to sink into the sewage with him and let it become her.

# WASHINGTON D.C.

## MARYLAND AVENUE

**8:50 P.M.**

Through it all, the Vice President maintained his healthy appetite because with the way things were going at the moment, he figured he needed every bit of strength he could get. With rioting breaking out in major cities, clashes between armed bands and the military, the parasitic infestation sweeping the country (and the globe, if the latest NSC estimates could be believed), things were most assuredly going to hell in a handbasket. Beginning tomorrow, he and the President would no longer be in D.C. together. The President would stay in the White House while the VP was shuttled off to a secure military installation in the Midwest where there was a command-and-control center where the country could be run if something happened to the Commander-in-Chief.

Though he would have a private gourmet chef at his disposal, the Vice President decided he would have one last good meal in the city. He chose SteakZen because they were not only one of the most exclusive restaurants in D.C. that commonly catered to politicians and visiting dignitaries, but because they simply had the best food.

He ate alone in a private dining room.

No aides, no secretaries, just his entourage of Secret Service agents. His wife had already been flown off to the secure location and he would be on Air Force Two within a matter of hours to join her.

When the Vice President finished his spiced beef and scallops and polished off his cheesecake, he smoked a cigar and that's when a perfect meal was topped off by a digestif that was a perfect tragedy. A waiter had come and collected the VP's setting and as he made to step through the door, nodding to the Secret Service agent who opened it for him, he pulled something that looked like a stick of dynamite out of his sleeve and tossed it behind him. It was a concussion grenade. He dove through the door and as the Secret Service agent reached for him, it went off with a subtle popping noise...followed instantly by a flash of blinding light and a detonation of noise so loud that it incapacitated everyone in the room momentarily.

By then, four men armed with Uzi submachine guns fitted with long cylinder-shaped silencers stepped into the room. They opened up and killed all three Secret Service agents within seconds. The last Secret Service man, trying to shield the Vice President, had his head blasted into pink-and-red strands of confetti that sprayed over the VP along with a lot of blood.

"On your feet, Mr. Vice President," one of the men ordered.

Still reeling and dizzy, the Vice President pulled himself up, noticing in dismay that the white tablecloth was covered in a smear of red gore.

"Please," he gasped. "We can discuss this..."

But as the men stepped forward, he knew there would be no discussion. They opened up. Their Uzis made only light put-put-put sounds with the noise suppressors screwed onto their barrels. A devastating barrage of 9mm Parabellum rounds chewed through the VP. In a matter of seconds, he took over thirty rounds point-blank.

Satisfied that the job was done, the men left the building along with their confederates who had infiltrated the restaurant staff.

At 8:37 p.m. on August 27, the Vice President of the United States had been assassinated.

# DETROIT

## HOLY CROSS HOSPITAL DETOX WARD

**9:16 P.M.**

It was a battle zone and Johnny Kopok had been through it before so he figured he fit right in seamlessly. He and his new pal—Bertie Panella, a real sweet kid—were on a mission. Their original mission after escaping the morgue was to get out of the hospital, period. But that didn't work so good because it was under quarantine and every door and window was sealed. It was like trying to break out of Leavenworth or Sing Sing. No dice. Soldiers in white suits were crawling around the building like termites looking for a crack in a wall. So that mission was scrubbed. Johnny and Bertie decided that they needed a better plan.

They thought and scratched their heads for a while until Bertie gripped his hand in her own—made Johnny feel kind of fuzzy and warm inside, that did—and said, "Well, we sure as hell aren't getting out. So, if we can't get out and can't go down below..."

"Means we gotta go up above." Johnny tapped a finger to his temple. "You got some brains, sister. That'll make up for my lack of 'em."

They chuckled over that and found themselves staring at each other and it wasn't long before they had found a broom closet to hide in and were sharing stories of their lives like a couple school chums that hadn't seen each other nigh on twenty years. A lot of those memories were a bit yellowed, distorted, and half-ass topsy-turvy from all the alcohol they'd been bobbing in all these years, but it was good to tell them and especially to a set of ears that were generally interested.

"I figure if I'd given up them cigarettes thirty years ago, I wouldn't be here," Bertie admitted. "Problem was, I always did like a taste of the old medicine to calm my nerves. And when I had a taste, I had to have a smoke. After a while, that smoking and saucing, well, it was like they were married in July under the sour-apple tree and decided they wanted to spend their lives together. Every time I had a drink, I'd light up. Every time I'd light up, I'd have a drink. The damnedest thing, Johnny."

"I know how it is, I know how it is."

"If we get out of this mess, I'll buy you a round."

Johnny smiled in the darkness, thinking that the last time he'd been in a broom closet with a girl was back in the eighth grade at Our Lady of the Blessed Heart. That was in 1959, he was guessing. He'd got a couple kisses off Missy Pedulla and then she'd surprised him by pulling his hand up under her school uniform shirt. And that girl, Jeez, for fourteen she sure had a set on her. He did some exploring that afternoon. That was, until Sister Mary Patrice caught them—ratted out by Bobby Farlane, no doubt—and gave them both a good taste of the paddle.

Johnny realized at that moment, though his mind certainly had a bad habit of drifting like a stray leaf in the wind, that he was not in the second floor broom closet at Our Lady. He was at Holy Cross with Bertie and damned if she wasn't holding his hand.

He was glad there were no lights in there because he was blushing bright red and what a state that would have made of him with his purple nose where all the blood vessels had blown like soap bubbles from the sauce.

"I'll get you out of here, Bertie. Or I'll die trying. You got my word on that."

Bertie gave him a peck on the cheek and Johnny felt his toes tingle.

They left the broom closet and made for the stairs. No commandos in enemy territory were more stealthy, more secret, more silent than they. And sneaking about like that reminded Johnny of when he'd joined the Marine Corps back in '66 out of high school. He wanted bad to be a commando. When basic was finished, the drill sergeant gave them the pitch like they did with all boots, that the Department of the Navy was beefing up their special ops units, the SEALs and Marine Force Recon. Johnny jumped at the chance until he learned that Force Recon Marines had to jump out of airplanes (he hated heights), had to go through frogman training (almost drowned when he was six, hated water), and had to go through extensive demolitions schools (he'd blown part of his pinkie off when he was seven and hated firecrackers). That was how he went to infantry school instead. Still, creeping about like this, hell it was almost as good even though he was in his sixties leaning hard towards seventy.

When they reached the stairs, they moved up them slowly. Each set they climbed required something of a rest period afterwards because neither of them were exactly kids anymore.

On the third-floor landing, Bertie peered through the square of window and said it looked okay out there. Johnny went out first, then she followed. The corridors were empty. Some of the rooms were offices and some were for patients. But all deserted.

They came around a bend in the corridor and a voice called out, "Oh, help me, please somebody help me..."

"You hear that?" Bertie said.

"I sure did."

"Should we..."

"I think it might be proper."

They tracked the voice, which never stopped calling out, to a room across from a nurses' station. They went in and some woman, maybe thirty or so, was crouched in the corner by the bed.

"I don't know where I am," she told them. "I don't know what's going on."

"Well, you're lucky we found you and not the Martians," Bertie told her, giving her a hand to stand up and when she did, that's when they saw that they had waltzed into a trap. Hell, not even waltzed so much as did the old two-step right into the arms of death.

The woman seized Bertie. Her face was yellow, jaundiced-looking, her eyes like green moons riding in black gulfs. Right away she began to hitch and convulse as Bertie screamed and fought against her. Johnny waded in and gave her a couple devastating shots to the face that used to floor his opponents in the ring and that worked. The woman tossed Bertie aside and came right at him.

"That's it," Johnny told her, bringing his fists up. "Come and get yours."

The woman lunged and Johnny hit her two or three more times, knocking her back, but his hands were aching and his arms hurting and she was coming back for more.

Then Bertie got into it.

She snatched a fire extinguisher off the wall and brought it up over her head and brained the woman with it. That put her to one knee and she convulsed again and made gagging sounds, drool hanging from her mouth. That's when the worm came out. It slid out between her lips like a rat snake from a gopher hole.

About the time its head-bulb opened, Johnny had the fire extinguisher. He popped the pin and hosed the woman and her parasite down with Co2. The woman screamed and the worm retreated and Johnny kept at it until the room was a thick white fog.

Then they went back to the stairs.

"That was real team work we did in there," he said to Bertie.

"You saved my life, Johnny."

She hugged him and he hugged her back and it was funny, real funny, but he hadn't been sweet on anybody in years—not since Georgia McKane swallowed that quart of grain alcohol and got run over by the train—and now he was beginning to feel real sweet on Bertie. What a time and place for such a thing.

"C'mon, hon," Bertie said. "Let's get to that fourth floor."

Johnny was right next to her. He figured he belonged there.

# WASHINGTON D.C., BOLLING AFB

## DEFENSE INTELLIGENCE AGENCY

**9:34 P.M.**

Though he had suspected it for some time, it was now beginning to look like a near-certainty that Robert Pershing, Director of the CIA, was at best a subversive and at worse a traitor. This knowledge brought pain to Walter Sleshing not only as the Director of Defense Intelligence but as a combat veteran. His service to his country was long and distinguished, and although he would have been the first to admit that he had been involved in many black bag operations that left him cold, never could anyone label him as disloyal. He was a patriot.

*I have to go slow here. I can't jump to any conclusions. Bob Pershing is crafty. He's well-connected. He has many powerful friends.*

That was the voice of reason speaking and he tried to listen to it, knowing that the evidence he had was at best circumstantial... yet, he'd had a very bad feeling about Pershing for some time now and it was getting worse. He never liked the man, and it would be hard to find anyone within the intelligence community that really did. As a person, that was. At his job, Pershing was fairly well-respected because he was good at subterfuge, good at playing both sides against the middle, good at playing the game and schmoozing the right sort of people. His appointment as CIA Director was basically a political one, of course, but he had a long career in military intelligence (which was a shark tank on the best days).

Bob Pershing was a survivor.

He was good at it.

But he was also ruthless and ambitious, and now DDI Sleshing was wondering just how far that ambition went. He was not the only one, of course. DCI VanderMissen was suspicious of him and his "gang of confederates", as he called them—General Mason, the Chairman of the JCS and Admiral

Paulus, the Director of Naval Intelligence. To name but two. They had discussed many times now what those three might be up to, but never had there been any clear indication.

Even now there was no concrete evidence, but what Sleshing had made him extremely nervous. There were warning bells going off in his head and a very bad feeling in his gut.

Less than an hour before, Sleshing had received a call on the encrypted line from Gus Costello, the National Security Advisor. Sleshing had long felt that Costello was on the same page with him and Chuck VanderMissen. Apparently, Costello thought the same of them. "Walt?" Gus said. "Stay in your office. I'm sending someone over to see you. You know him. Just be waiting for him. It's vitally important, I think."

His visitor was Vice-Admiral Dahn of SOCOM, the Special Operations Command. He did not look pleased. In fact, he looked equal parts angry and frustrated. Sleshing knew Dahn fairly well. He was a career Naval officer, a highly decorated Navy SEAL, and a man with absolutely no sense of humor. He was built like a wire cable and at sixty he was in better physical condition than most sailors were at twenty.

"I don't like what I'm about to say or admit to, General," he started the conversation off by saying. He sat across from Sleshing dressed in street clothes as if to downplay his rank and position. "Treachery and duplicity are not things that come natural to me, yet in the intelligence field and spec ops, I've had to use them again and again. It has brought me no satisfaction."

"It never does," Sleshing told him. "It only brings guilt."

"And maybe this scenario more than most," he admitted.

By that point, of course, Sleshing was expecting the very worst. "Okay, Jack. Why don't you tell me what this is about so we can understand each other? Gus Costello considers it very important and that's good enough for me."

So Dahn told him what it was about.

Apparently, DNI Admiral Paulus had been making some discreet inquiries as to the possibility of the SEAL Teams being deployed domestically in counterterror operations considering the current climate of the country. Groups like Delta Force and the SEAL Teams were not allowed to conduct operations within the country. That was the jurisdiction of the FBI and other federal and state police agencies. Under martial law, it would only take a quick sweep of the pen to change that. As yet, the President had not signed that order. But it was coming and everyone in the intelligence community knew it. DNI Paulus' inquiries were not unusual. What was unusual was when he began making inquiries, not so much discreet as completely under the table, concerning the possibility that the SEAL Teams be placed under the executive command of the Office of Naval Intelligence. It raised red flags immediately when it was learned that General Mason was making the same inquiries concerning Delta Force as well as several crack Ranger battalions.

"Something smelled rotten about it all, General. We didn't like the feel of it at SOCOM. So we launched an investigation in conjunction with the ONI and the JCS."

Sleshing was amazed. Not concerning the collusion between Mason and Paulus, of course, but that within the ONI—Paulus' own group—and the JCS—Mason's—there were suspicions that warranted such an investigation. He knew that the ONI orchestrating a clandestine investigation of its own director was nearly unheard of, but according to Dahn they had clearance from "the highest possible levels". And that went for the JCS Chairman, General Mason, as well. Interesting...but dangerous. Mason and Paulus were both powerful. Their underlings going after them amounted to political and professional suicide if it was found out. On the other hand, if it bore fruit...

Either way it was dangerous.

Very Dangerous.

"We went so far as to bug his car," Dahn admitted and that's when he delivered a thumb drive to Sleshing along with an accompanying transcript.

And that's what was eating at Sleshing now. The very fact that SOCOM and the JCS were doing the very thing he had long considered doing himself. It was like a confirmation of his worst fears and anxieties, justification of his paranoia concerning Admiral Paulus and particularly, Robert Pershing. He looked down at the transcript and sighed once again.

*Pershing: Our chance is almost here... we just have to wait for it...(unintelligible)... events are coming around nicely. This country is about ten feet from hell and I plan on giving it the extra push.*

*Paulus: I just worry about repercussions.*

*Pershing: What repercussions? For there to be repercussions there has to be somebody left in power to initiate them...*

*Paulus: I suppose, but...*

*Pershing: No buts. No looking back. This country is going to hell and the man (unintelligible)... he's no leader. He's going to fall with the rest. That will create a vacuum of power. People in this country will be starving for leadership...strong, decisive leadership.*

*Paulus: You're right. You're absolutely right.*

*Pershing: Of course I am. Everything is moving in our direction. We couldn't have hoped for a better set of circumstances than BioGen going global. It plays into our hands and we'd be fools not to seize the opportunity.*

*Paulus: Mason said everything is nearly ready on his end.*

*Pershing: I'm working hard on mine. The list of prime targets (unintelligible)... now it's a matter of taking them out.*

*The confusion and panic will put us in the position we desire.
And we'll take it. God yes, we will...*


That was the gist of the recording. Sleshing hated to think about it, but it sounded very much like Pershing, Paulus, and Mason were considering a military coup of the country. A violent takeover. The problem was that there was nothing absolutely conclusive in the transcript. Regardless, it hinted at the worst possible things. Sleshing didn't like it and neither did Dahn or Gus Costello. He knew if he brought this to Pershing tomorrow, the CIA Director would not bat an eye. Being the slick professional liar and spin manager he was, he would say they were discussing the overthrow of some Third World country. After all, no names or positions of power were mentioned.

But what if it was true?

What if?

That was the scary thing. The "prime targets" Pershing had mentioned could very well be the chain of command of the United States: the President, Vice President, the Speaker of the House, the Senate President Pro Tempore, Secretaries of State, Treasury, and Defense...a coordinated series of assassinations could absolutely debilitate the country at any time but particularly during a state of crisis as they were facing now. It would leave an immense vacuum in command.

And who better to fill that vacuum than Pershing and his confederates? With their rank and status they could easily bring their respective services into play and that was an absolutely awesome force. And with Pershing having control over the CIA's Clandestine Service and SOG as well as XI, Mason with Delta Force and several Ranger battalions at his disposal, and Paulus bringing the Navy SEAL Teams in...they could easily vanquish any opposition or threats to their position of power. It sounded absolutely fantastic, but it was not beyond the realm of possibility. And if what Chuck VanderMissen suspected was true, then it was not just the three of them involved in this. Each had a web of co-conspirators.

And who could rightly say how many members of the Joint Chiefs of Staff were still loyal to the President?

It was disgusting and went against everything that Sleshing believed in and had spent his life protecting and upholding, but it certainly was not as far-fetched as it perhaps sounded, in fact—

In fact, he stopped himself right there.

What if Pershing and Paulus *were* talking about nothing more than some shithole banana republic in South America or Africa? What if they were purely speculating about such a place? Jesus, Sleshing did not know what to think. Doubt had a way of flowering into suspicion until it became full-blown paranoia and that was not a good thing. But he knew he couldn't sit on this. He had to bring Chuck VanderMissen in on it. For if it was true—dear God, he hoped not—then Pershing would see to it that all his adversaries were off the grid. And it wouldn't just be the President and his cabinet, it would be Chuck VanderMissen, Gus Costello, and Sleshing himself.

*You need to proceed carefully, old man. Very, very carefully. Now, here's what you do. You give Chuck a call and the both of you have a little sit-down, then you give Gus Costello a call in the morning, set up a meeting.*

Okay, now that was both reasonable and rational. It was good common sense at work. That's how it would be handled, one step at a—

His secure cell buzzed. "Sleshing," he said.

"Walt...oh Jesus Christ." It was Gus Costello. He was breathing hard. "We've got a situation here."

Sleshing sat forward. "What is it, Gus?"

More breathing as if he were trying to steady himself. "The Vice President was assassinated."

"Oh, dear God," Sleshing muttered.

# MANHATTAN

## TIMES SQUARE

**9:53 P.M.**

Tourists from around the world came to view the neon splendor of the Square by night and as the sun went down they got a very special treat. With martial law only a few hours away, they knew this might be their last chance for weeks, months, maybe longer. So unprecedented crowds flooded Times Square. The neon was bright, the billboards flashing, cops promenading on horseback, double-decker buses fighting for space amongst yellow cabs. And everywhere, tourists and exhibitionists and ticket-sellers, street vendors and hawkers. A wild funhouse of people and noise and bright lights.

It was as if people were saying goodbye to a way of life that would soon exist no more.

At some point during the festivities, people began to notice an odor that was at first vague and then overpowering. It was a sweet/sour/sickening smell that reminded many of the perfume of exotic hothouse orchids or the pungent sweetness of funeral lilies. But as it grew, fuming in the streets, it was not flowers, they decided, but rotting things tossed up on beaches. The moist damp decay beneath fallen trees. A septic stench of medical waste and drainage contained in a flowing hot honeyed sap that put many to their knees, gagging, and made the majority wander about drunkenly, eyes glazed, and mouths hanging open.

That, of course, caused the first of many tragedies that night.

Vinyl-eyed tourists with slack, drooling mouths stumbled into each other, fell over each other, shambling mindlessly out into the streets and were hit by cabs and dragged beneath buses and people screamed and sirens blew and vehicles smashed into one another or went careening into the crowds on the walks.

And it was amidst that chaos that the horror, the true horror, of the evening began. A chubby Portuguese tourist with a huge sack of knockoff Louis Vuitton handbags she'd bought from a street-corner vendor (and planned on hawking on eBay at a significant profit) bumped into a man with eyes like yellow waste and a foaming pink-white mouth. He licked his lips with a black-spotted tongue and the sweet sewer-stink that came off him nearly put the Portuguese lady to her dimpled knees. When he seized hold of her saying, *"I've brought something pretty just for you,"* and opened his mouth with an offering of a worm, said worm did not slide gently from his throat, it *exploded* out with the force of vomited ejecta. It forced itself into her mouth and filled her.

People saw it, of course.

It was hard not to... but at first, amongst the confusion and in a place where anything, absolutely anything goes, they paid little attention to the grubby man and the sizeable woman and the snapping elastic cord connecting their mouths. But when similar events began to break out in every quarter and in every crowd, they began to panic and scream and fight to be free. But the infected were amongst them. And everywhere, worms were revealing themselves. They were creeping from mouths, tangling like vines and sliding through the crowds like bleached snakes. Hosts spewed worm-sauce into faces, released adult forms and maggoty stews of larvae unto the unsuspecting.

Times Square became a sea of thrashing bodies, an ocean of pandemic parasitic infection. The worms were everywhere: undulant octopus tentacles seeking prey and squirming tubes of gut bursting from cleaved bellies, the tendrils of jellyfish snaring human fish and masses of living white hair and pallid rootlets wiring them up and infesting... and the tourists and soldiers and cops and peddlers were all caught up in it, sinking in that ebon slime-sea as more worms made themselves known, most erupting in appalling flesh-trains from the mouths and asses of their hosts, but others—larger gape-mouthed predatory varieties—rising from sewer gratings and subway ventilation shafts, spraying gouts of clear juice from their mouths that immobilized their victims with a gushing chemical euphoria until they stood around like stunned cows, drunken and grinning. The biochemical trickery of the worms' secretions made their own brains betray them in their hour of need, blocking neuroreceptors that signaled pain and panic, locking down instinctual drives of fear and self-preservation in tar pits of apathy, reducing them to hollow-eyed junkies and preyfood and fleshmeat tripping out on the unrestricted flow of endorphins from the drug stores of their own gray matter.

Their brains short-circuited and were hot-wired by the worms and they went happily down on their knees, open-mouthed, to receive white slithering worm-members between their lips and up asses and into vaginas, desecrated and violated, human shells and worm-hotels and dead-eyed host-vessels. The larger mutant predatory flatworms went on the offensive for the meat was free and the meat was easy. Their pink-skinned prey offered no resistance, they begged to be slavered and slobbered over, to be shredded and drained of sweet red juices. Prostrate before the roping, vile forms of their gods, the worms accepted them and turned those who were not already hosts into a slopping red sea of human chum. Glistening, pulsating worm ova overflowed its banks and mired those precious few that found themselves immune to the worms' neurochemical barrage.

Those that didn't lose their minds immediately, fought valiantly. One of them knocked hosts out of his path and had the audacity to take on a worm that was twenty feet from tip to tip, big around at its middle as a beer keg, its segments swollen like inner tubes inflated to the point of bursting with teeming egg clusters. Yet as loathsome and malignant as that worm indeed was, he threw himself at it, he tore into its flesh as its mouth fastened onto his neck and sucked out everything but the vertebrae itself. He went down with globs of running worm-meat clutched in his fingers and the worm itself was badly injured. It yawned its maw to the sky and its many pink tongues writhed and trembled with flying gouts of pink-pale ooze. It let out a shrieking, shrilling cry and then seemed to erupt from internal hydrostatic pressure and its attacker, quite dead by that point, was drowned in a swamp of pearly eggs as each proglottid burst in random succession. For the mother worm, it was not suicide, for each segment was a sac of eggs through which it could reproduce and regenerate itself thousands if not millions of times.

Others fought, too.

But most were swarmed by the original invasive hosts who forced them down, drowning them in a vomit-slush of immature worms that quickly invaded any available orifice. From above, it looked like they were sinking in slime-bogs of egg drop soup albumen.

The police and soldiers in the Square that were not inundated or over-whelmed and did not immediately retreat, drew their weapons and fired indiscriminately into the seething crowds, splitting open heads and puncturing torsos and splashing the throngs with cherry-red blood and scattershots of tissue and bone.

But it was quite pointless, for the worms owned this night.

And in the end, the worm conquered all.

# PROVIDENCE, RHODE ISLAND

## MARRIOTT HOTEL, CTHULICON

**10:13 P.M.**

When the lights went out, Kalen Morse was left in the dark with only half of her makeup applied and she was not too happy about it. The annual Prom-Nomicon was due to start in fifteen fucking minutes and the stupid power went out. As pissed as she was—and, boy, was she pissed—the imaginative side of her mind found it very atmospheric. Too bad there wasn't a storm to go with it. This was Providence, after all, H.P. Lovecraft's stomping grounds (or spawning grounds, if you prefer) and Cthulicon was the annual convention devoted entirely to the life and works of that notoriously reclusive horror author who died way back in 1937. He was considered to be the most influential horror writer of the twentieth century (sorry, Stephen King) and his ideas had been swiped by writers and movie makers ever since.

But a storm...now that would have been the balls, Kalen got to thinking. It would have been like Lovecraft's "The Haunter of the Dark" where Robert Blake meets up with old Nyarlathotep during an electrical storm.

*Ah, if life was only as simple as finding a banned book and calling up a monstrosity from beyond time and space*, she thought.

Regardless, Kalen knew that lights or no lights, the faithful would be meeting downstairs in Banquet Room C. In fact, the idea of doing it by candlelight would pack them in. With that in mind, she was not about to miss it. Being a former Girl Scout, Kalen was ready for any emergency and she dug a candle out of her bag, gave it some flame, and did her best with her makeup. When she was done, she slipped into her white tunic dress, twisted the gold serpent armband over her right bicep—no easy bit—slid a stack of fifty bracelets over her left wrist, and stepped into her sandals.

*Not bad*, she thought. *Not bad at all.*

The tunic fit her curves very nicely and the shining blue trapezohedron necklace captured the blue of her eyes and gave her that Cleopatra look she'd been going for. Stuffing her blonde hair up into a hair net, she pulled on a tripartite Hathor wig with long beaded locks and completed the look with a horned headpiece complete with solar disc and a *uraei-kalathos* cobra.

"Bling-bling! Tell me I'm not Queen Nitocris," she said to the mirror. "Tell me I will not wow those fanboys and leave them drooling all over their rubber tentacles, oh Nyarlathotep the Black Pharaoh."

This was going to work and she knew it. It was only really a matter of navigating her way down there now. Elevators would be out so she'd have to take the stairs and try not to trip over her sandals. It would not be an easy descent. She couldn't wait to get down there and feel all those eyes on her. She knew she would be absolutely devastating by candlelight. The only downside was Rube Keeler, the editor of the small-print rag *Tome of the Black Winds* which published Lovecraftian fiction, mostly fan-stuff. Rube would be sniffing around her all night and if she didn't pay any attention to him, he'd get miffed and start an argument.

Rube was good at that.

That morning in the dealer's room, Kalen had picked up an old Lin Carter paperback and Rube went after her right away. "How can you read such shat?" he asked her.

"Who said I read this stuff? I just like the covers."

That only exasperated him more. He got so worked up he had to hit his inhaler twice. "Lin Carter is tepid, repetitive, unimaginative imitation. Save for August Derleth himself, nobody spread more shit around than this guy."

"Do tell," Kalen said, deciding then and there she simply had to buy a Derleth book if she could find one. As Rube went on and on, she located the British Panther edition of Derleth's The Shuttered Room and made sure Rube saw it.

"That's a perfect example!" he steamed. "That's fucking Derleth again taking a fragment, a sentence Lovecraft wrote, and building a story off of it and claiming they collaborated. Collaborated, my ass. That's like me finishing the missing texts of The Dead Sea Scrolls and saying I collaborated with fucking God. Derleth and Carter were two completely talentless fuckwits cashing in on Lovecraft. That's all they were."

"Who's arguing?"

"Really," he said. "What's Lovecraft's greatest contribution?"

"Tentacles?"

"Cosmic horror. That's what it's about. The idea that there are things out there that consider the Earth and its inhabitants to be meaningless. Of no more significance than ants you step on. An immense, malignant cosmic horror that dwarfes the puny anthropocentric religions and races of this minor speck of dust. And that's exactly what Derleth and Carter missed—it's not about forbidden books and unpronounceable entities and all that tripe. That's window dressing. That's the look without the content."

He was right and she knew he was right. Just as he'd been right last year when he told the crowds that Lovecraft's novella *At the Mountains of Madness* was simply a metaphor for Lovecraft's own insecurities and intolerances. A class struggle. The Old Ones were the highly-cultured, refined, and intellectual WASPS of New England and the Shoggoths were the crude, boorish working classes and immigrants flooding Lovecraft's beloved countryside. He was right but, hey, you could also read it as a monster story.

Kalen knew that tonight Rube would be drinking and he'd be in rare form.

Leaving her room, she moved down the corridor via the emergency lights. She bumped into a guy festooned in green papier-mâché tentacles. "Nitocris! You look awesome!" he said.

"Wish I could say the same for you."

That stopped him. "What?"

"I'm teasing you, oh great Yog-Sothoth."

"I'm a Cthonian...can't you tell?"

"Whatever."

Kalen found the stairs, wondering why she came to these things sometimes. People were so cliquey and thin-skinned. The truth was that the fanboy's costume was mega-lame, but she wasn't going to hurt his little feelings. A lot of these people bruised so easily. And she was nothing if not kind and understanding. Okay, now and then she spoke her mind and pissed people off and that had cost her four boyfriends and two best friends, but fuck 'em if they couldn't take a joke. Kalen saw herself as a reasonable person. Others rarely agreed. She would have been surprised—and bruised—if she found out that on the fan circuit she was often referred to as *Cunt-thulu* or *The Black Bitch of Karneter*. She could never have conceived of such petty hatred and jealousy.

Down the stairs she went and aside from a few glowing red EXIT signs, it was very black in the stairwell. She passed no one. Saw no one. She wondered what caused the blackout as she felt herself being pulled deeper into the darkness, slowly engulfed. As she made her way slowly towards the first floor landing she became aware of a high, sweet stink that was as weird as it was intriguing...fruiting, fermenting, ripe and sharp... it made her feel like she was stoned and she wondered if somebody had been smoking some imported stuff in there.

When she felt hands take hold of her, all she could say was: "What?"

Then something was pressed into her hands and at first, she thought somebody had slid his willy into her palms...something that in her current state of mind wasn't quite as offensive as it might have been otherwise... and she gripped it. It slid across her fingers. Tactilely, the feel of the thing was exciting and somehow soothing. It was warm and throbbing and quite phallic, so soft and greasy. Without really giving it much thought, she decided it would feel exquisite against her tongue, so she sank to her knees and opened her mouth and let it slide on down as she gagged.

At the Prom-Nomicon, she was going to really wow them.

# CHICAGO, RIVER NORTH

## THE WAREHOUSE

**10:30 P.M.**

When they came in to untie him, Harry Niles figured they were only doing it because they were going to kill him. Because soon as he was taken to this place—when was that? Two hours ago? Three? Five? Six?—he knew one thing and one thing for sure: there were Spooks in this world and then there were *Spooks*. And this guy, the old one with the white beard and eyes like sapphires... he was the real deal. He was the apex predator in a world of shadow agencies, black budget ops, and clandestine spookery. He had been in to see Harry twice now and each time he said nothing, he just looked and nodded, studied Harry with his flat, predatory almost reptilian eyes.

Now he was back, and he had two thugs with him. Not the guys that had brought Harry in but a couple others. In his mind, they all blended together: mannequins, wooden dummies, marionettes worked by a dark and malefic puppet-master whom Harry suspected had a white beard and eyes like a snake.

The thugs untied him.

"Is that better, Mr. Niles?" the Old Man asked.

"In comparison to what?"

One of the thugs nearly smiled which proved no matter what kind of heavy he was, there was something remotely human in him. A weak, nearly extinguished candle of it, but something.

Harry sat there rubbing some feeling into his wrists. Time had gone somewhat fluid and elastic for him and he was not sure how long he had been here or where here was. When they had taken him out of the mall and to a waiting sedan, they had injected him with something. Some kind of tranquilizer. He remember getting real silly in the car, saying crazy shit, old jokes rolling from his lips: *What happened when Jesus went to Mount Olive? Popeye beat the shit out of him. Why did Mickey Mouse file for a divorce? Because Minnie was fucking Goofy. Three guys are walking down a road. They see a sheep with its ass up in the air. The first guy says, I wish that was Megan Fox. The second guy says, I wish that was Jessica Alba. The third guy says, I wish it was dark.* On and on and then waking in this place. With these people. He was in the shit and he knew it. Shit that was so deep he might drown in it, but not before its smell was shoved so far up his nose that it became a permanent part of him.

The Old Man watched him.

Harry watched the Old Man.

"Anytime you want to get around to it," Harry said. "I'm listening."

The Old Man pulled up a chair and sat down so very carefully and precisely that Harry thought maybe he had a sore ass. But that wasn't it at all and he knew it. This guy was not only precise, but meticulous, fastidious: everything he did was done with great care and absolute mental application.

"Do you know why you're here, Mr. Niles?"

"No, I don't. Are you guys Jehovah's Witnesses? Listen, I'm sorry I slammed the door in your faces."

"Hmm," the Old Man said. "About what I expected. From all I've heard of you, Mr. Niles, you seem to enjoy your flippant sense of humor."

"Why shouldn't I?"

"Because this is very serious."

"I figured that when your boys arrested me."

"You're not under arrest exactly, Mr. Niles. Let's just say you'll be confined for a time. If you play ball, you'll walk out the door. If you don't, well, you'll have to stay."

"That sounds pretty black-and-white."

"It is."

Harry looked at the thugs standing there. "Okay, before you have your goons break my fingers, let me tell you what I think this is all about. First off, you've linked me with Shawna Geddes. You've got that right. She's my friend and I am with her. So, you're good on that part. Now, what has your tit in the wringer is apparently that you think Shawna saw something she wasn't supposed to. She did. She saw an abduction and then, later, a secret biocontainment operation. And since then, she's been on the run and in fear of her life. The bottom line is: she doesn't know exactly what she saw. I'm guessing it was the earliest outbreaks of the mystery parasite. But now there's similar operations going on everywhere. So hunting her down is absolutely pointless. Don't you see that?"

The Old Man was considering it. "You have a reputation of nosing into things that don't concern you, Mr. Niles. You have to know you've made more than a few powerful enemies."

"Correction: I *had* a reputation for nosing into things. Now I'm a tabloid writer. Shawna was an assistant gardening editor. What possible danger are we to you now?"

"None."

*"What?"*

The Old Man studied his manicured nails. "At first, you were a security risk. But not so much now. The only problem, Mr. Niles, as I see it, is that I'm not entirely convinced that your tabloid career is not a cover."

"A cover?"

"Yes. A cover. And that maybe Shawna Geddes is working for you."

"That's ridiculous. I'm no Seymour Hersh. I have no interest in that shit anymore."

"Don't you?"

"No, I don't. So why don't you be reasonable and call off the heat on us already? We're no threat."

"Have you ever heard of something called Section Five?" the Old Man asked him.

"No."

"You're lying."

Harry shifted in his seat. "All right, I have heard of it. Years ago. A shadow agency. Scientific in nature. My sources in Washington said Section Five was fooling around with weird things. Fringe science for military/intelligence applications. Genetic engineering. Nanotechnology. Psychokinesis. Brainwashing. Things like that. But that was years ago when I was still active. I leave that to the young guys now."

The Old Man did not look convinced. "Tell me about Project BioGenesis."

"Never heard of it."

That was true even if the Old Man did not want to believe it. Harry knew about Section Five or The Group as it was known, S5. He knew it had connections to CBT and a certain alley cat named Elizabeth Toma. He also knew that it was run by a nameless man who was considered very powerful and very dangerous. And that was the scary part because Harry knew he was sitting across from him now. The guy who had helmed teams that had developed devastating bioweapons and implanted computer chips in the brains of soldiers...if the buzz was true.

"I don't believe you," the Old Man said. "But...no matter. It's of no interest by this point. As you say, it's out in the open now. What interests us most is where Shawna Geddes is."

"I don't know that. I ran some interference for her. Your boys grabbed me. I hoped she got away."

The Old Man nodded. "She did. But not in the way you think."

He explained to Harry that one of his employees went rogue. He went into hiding, more or less. They had Shawna tracked to the mall and were moving in on her. This rogue intervened, killed two people and badly injured a third, and made off with Shawna. Why? He did not know. He suspected many things, though, ranging from simple subterfuge to domestic terrorism.

Harry shook his head. "Shawna is hardly the militant-type."

"It's not the girl that concerns me. It's our rogue. You see, he had access to classified information. Information that could threaten the security of this nation. She's a journalist."

Ah, the Old Man thought the rogue was going to spill state secrets. With all that was going on, all this guy could care about was his collection of lies and dirty little deals. Amazing.

"So, what are you going to do about your rogue?"

"Nothing. Not yet. Not until later tonight. We know where he is and it's only a matter of collecting him."

"And Shawna?"

The Old Man shrugged. "She'll be collected, too."

And that was the exact word he used: *collected*. It had a chilling effect on Harry, but he refused to let the Old Man know it. "And what then?"

"Then we'll see," was all he would say.

# NEW YORK CITY, EAST BRONX

## PELHAM PARKWAY

**10:44 P.M.**

They were at the door now.

They were beating at it.

They wanted in.

Virginia Astato had locked herself in the bathroom after they'd come through the front door and overwhelmed Joey. There had been seven or eight of them and although they looked like people, they took him down like animals. Joey had fought to the last, screaming for her to get away. She was squatted on the floor now, holding her rosary, one arm wrapped around the mound of her belly. The baby was kicking, shifting around in there, growing tense as its mother grew tense.

*Joey... oh dear God Joey...*

As terrified as she was, Virginia knew she had to think of the baby and plan for the baby and do everything possible to protect the baby. That's what Joey had died fighting for—because he had to be dead—and she could not let any of that be in vain. But the sounds of them out there...God. They were scratching at the bathroom door, running their fingers over it, whispering and hissing and making slithery sort of sounds that human beings could not possibly make. And what was that smell? It was coming under the door. It was sweet and sickening like fruit rotted to pulp and running sap. It made her feverish and giddy.

And it was getting stronger. It made her mouth water. Her hands shake. Sweat broke out on her face and her stomach rolled over. She was trying to think, to reason, to make sense of things, but her mind was spinning, tripping over itself as the room was flooded with that sweetness and she felt herself drowning in it, sinking into its sugary depths and there seemed to be no way out. Water was running from her eyes and the baby was not just kicking now, but jumping in her belly and the nausea...*oh the fucking nausea...*

And outside the door, hissing, guttural cries. Virginia pressed her hands to her ears because one of them was Joey's voice, she was certain it was Joey's voice echoing out at her from sweet depths: *"Open the door, Virge. Please open the door and then everything will be all right..."*

And she lost consciousness for a moment and when she opened her eyes—

*Oh dear God no, no, no...*

It couldn't be.

It couldn't possibly be.

The door was standing open and faces were peering down at her. Faces like shiny plastic with pink blubbery lips that drooled and dark hollow eyes that looked artificial, painted-on eyes like the eyes of blowup fuck dolls and that was so appropriate because none of them were human anymore and they were reaching out for her and...

Virginia screamed.

Screamed because she knew.

She knew who had opened that fucking door.

*You did, you little idiot. You're the one to blame. They secreted that rich, feverish, almost creamy odor of sweetness and you lost your mind in its heat and when Joey told you to open the door, you did. And now they have you and they'll have the baby, too.*

She screamed again and it was not for herself or what they might do to her because she was a mother and like any mother, she cared not for herself but for her children or child, in this case. They would defile it. They would dirty and violate the perfect life she carried within her, they would peel it from its pink cocoon of purity, and make it like them with their plastic faces and drooling mouths and mannequin eyes.

"Virge," Joey said. "Look at me..."

So she did, God help her, but she did. She saw that he held a huge, undulant snake that was a bloodless, pale sort of color. Almost bleached-looking. Snakes terrified her. He knew that. Why did he torment her like this... but he told her it was no snake. It coiled in his hands as the others held her down, breathing their cloving hot breath in her face and then the worm made a mewling sound right before it slid between her lips, winding its way down her throat as she gagged and choked and then... then she felt her personality slowly subside. It was warm butter melting. And there was a peace in that. Contentment.

Five minutes after the worm invaded her, Virginia Astato was no more.

# PROVIDENCE, RHODE ISLAND

## MARRIOTT HOTEL, CTHULICON

**10:55 P.M.**

Although Chaz had to admit he was seriously digging the Prom-Nomicon by candlelight this year—man, it beat the tits off the fluorescent lights and you couldn't really see some of the shitty costumes, molded plastic furniture, and the armies of wannabes and posers—he had to admit from the bottom of his thumping black heart that it had been a real disappointment in so, so many ways. When the power hit the skids, there were candles, not much dancing because the juice was out, and the only music to be had was provided by the strolling minstrel players of Eldritch Ed and the Yuggoth Three—they did a pretty damn funny song called "Unnameably" to the tune of The Beatles' "Yesterday": *"Unnameably... there are tentacles growing out of me... my ass looks like Wilbur Whate-alee... oh I've become Unnamableee..."*—who were a lot better than the shit-basket grunge of the Insects from Shaggai the night before... but still, it lacked a certain something.

Bree, who had dressed up like Clark Ashton Smith's Tsathoggua (try saying *that* after a dozen Jager Bombs), summed it up pretty good when he said, "Man, this shit ain't the dope. This shit ain't freaking eldritch, unnamable, or even blasphemous... it sucks cyclopean dick."

Chaz had to agree on many points. The vibe of last year's C-Con just wasn't there. It had gotten more corporate than your average Comic Con fisting-fest. Maybe it was the shit going on in the country. And maybe it was the lack of power which meant the air-conditioning was out and he was sweating fucking balls in his Azathoth costume, and if that wasn't bad enough the All-U-Can Eat Dagon Buffet (which was basically sushi) was starting to smell bad in the heat (downright fucking *nameless*, truth be told). Like the sweat on Cthulhu's piles.

Freaking twenty scant minutes into the Prom and he was already getting pissy.

If he bumped into one more limp-wristed *Twilight* cutey-boy vampire, they were fucking going down, man. And that was another thing. God-damn C-Con had been invaded by the paranormal romance fagadrones and homo-morphs. You couldn't spit without hitting one of them. Half the author readings this year had been women with their lovey-dovey vampire romance queer-a-thons and wet-pussy gag-sagas. Half-way through the reading of some lesbo vampire hunter jizz-jerker, Chaz had cracked-off a deadly bean fart and the author—some fat Goth chick—had nearly cried her black eyeliner off. Chaz excused himself and took a healthy dump and lost himself in a good gut-ripper by Guy N. Smith.

"We need to heat this place up," he told Bree.

"I'm up for it."

"Think I'm going to show them what sort of asshole the old Primal Chaos can be."

"I'm with you," Bree said.

Chaz looked around until he saw some pony-assed Edward Cullen look-alike chatting with female fans who were ready to masturbate with fucking icicles they were so horned-up. Chaz was going to stumble into that greasy wet pecker, maybe put him face-first into Dagon's rotten sushi and slide a slimy tentacle up his well-buffed girly ass. *Excuse me ladies, while I stake this sissy-boy.* One *Twilight/True Blood/Vampire Diaries* made-to-order vampire puss-wad gobadroid in his crosshairs, Chaz went after him with considerable speed. He hit the soul-sucker like they were body bowling and hanging ten. Dracufag was launched into the rotten sushi and his makeup was ruined.

The vacuous Goth girls with him pressed black-lacquered nails to their mouths in shock. One of them squealed like Eddie Cullen had slid all two inches of his pearly-white dick up her backdoor. The wet-panty brigade was not amused.

Chaz just shrugged, peeling off his Azathoth costume while Dracufag's attendant soul-suckers started laying into him. "Sorry," he said.

"That asshole again," someone said and Chaz saw it was the lady who wrote the slick-finger female vamp-fag operas. He'd disrupted her breathless author reading earlier and she hadn't forgotten. Chaz couldn't remember what her vamp romance series was called... *Diana Dike, Vampire Killer* or was it *Leslie Lickslit, Vampire Hunter*? And did it matter? She was all dolled-up like one of the undead with her kinky black hair and white-face, bat choker at her fat throat. She looked like Countess Dracula...if Countess Dracula was corn-fed on hogslop with a body by Hostess.

"Somebody should throw him out of here!" she said.

Dracufag didn't look so glam-rock pretty anymore with futomaki hanging from his smeary face. It angered him. He gave Chaz a shove and Chaz hit the floor, slipping on that gut-greasy sushi. Meanwhile, Bree had been captured by one of the staffers and a tall black dude who wrote outhouse poetry about the Elder Gods and was duded-up as the Black Messenger. Bree was cool and easy, but he didn't like people grabbing him. He knocked the Black Messenger to his ass and gave the staffer's left juglet the Chinese tweak... and she let go real fast.

Dracufag was trying to menace Chaz, so Chaz (being pretty looped by that point), said, "Cock the hammer, it's time for action!" Then he slammed into Little Prince Fondleroy and gave him a couple quick shots to face that put some real blood on his lips. Lesbot security was all over Chaz by that point and it would have ended up with either a jail cell or ejection from C-Con... but something happened.

Something that not only stole the scene but owned it.

A tall woman dressed like Queen Nitocris, showing a nice flat belly and plenty of cleavage, walked right up to Dracufag and took hold of him.

Chaz just watched. This girl looked better than Gal Gadot dipped in Wesson oil. There was a weird sweet stink coming off her and it was making people woozy. A few of them dropped to their knees.

But it wasn't that that held everyone's attention: it was the long white worm that came spiraling out of her mouth and forced its way between Dracufag's lips. About then, people seemed to notice that she wasn't the only worm-carrier.

That's when things really heated up.

# WASHINGTON D.C.

## GEORGETOWN

**11:14 P.M.**

When he got off the phone with the President, Gus Costello needed two things: time to think and time to drink. He took two fingers of Oban's Scotch and followed that with two more fingers. The impulse to get good and stinking drunk was almost irresistible.

But he couldn't do that.

There were other considerations.

As he finished his drink, he told himself that there could have been many reasons why the Vice President was assassinated. The FBI and the Justice Department were all over the crime scene and maybe they'd turn up something. A man like the Vice President would have many enemies, both foreign and domestic.

But he kept thinking of the recording made of Robert Pershing and Admiral Paulus. It was particularly damning. The President agreed but advised caution. He would need to speak with the Attorney General in-depth before they went any farther with this and that wouldn't be until tomorrow morning as the AG was overseas.

Costello thought about the state the country was in.

Was Pershing so ambitious and unscrupulous that he would take advantage of something like that? Costello did not want to believe it but he was beginning to grow very suspicious.

It was about that time that he also grew very suspicious of the taste of his scotch. It always had such a warm, mellow, smoky flavor to it... now there was a bitter aftertaste.

Costello gripped his throat and went to his knees, gagging out white foam.

As he hit the floor, he realized he had been poisoned.

# PROVIDENCE, RHODE ISLAND

## MARRIOTT HOTEL, CTHULICON

**11:21 P.M.**

Of course, it had to happen on Donny Pilan's watch because fate had long ago decided that he was a born pooper-scooper who lived to clean up whatever mess was dumped on the floor. Nothing he hated worse than working these damn conventions with all the freakos and comic book nerds. Donny found it real hard to be nice to these types. He was often seized by the urge to shove them around like he had in high school.

Down in Banquet Room C, all hell was breaking loose.

Jesus, why not?

Now he had to go down there and break up the shit. He had no idea what it was about, but given the crowd, a couple of mama's boys probably got into it over how pointy Mr. Spock's ears were or the color of Aquaman's fucking tights. And most of them were grown men (and women). That was the real sad thing about it. That's the thing that got right under Donny's skin like mites.

Power was out, of course, and probably would be for hours. Donny was sweating and the air was stuffy and stale and the goddamn elevators were down. That meant the stairs and by the time he got down there he'd be pissing sweat and in one real mother of a foul mood. First little X-Men jack-off boy that looked at him the wrong way was getting his asshole cored with his own *Star Wars* fanzine.

"Christ almighty, what a night," he sighed.

What was making him even pissier was that Bob was supposed to be helping him tonight. But God only knew where he was. Probably taking a nap up on six or out back catching a cigarette. *I'd fire that old sonofabitch. I'm so sick of his old fucking bullshit stories I could pass a couple stones.* No matter. Donny went down the stairs, flight after flight, until he got to the ground floor. The EXIT lights were about as bright as dirty penlight bulbs. He turned on his flashlight and stormed over to Banquet Room C. The corridor was full of nerds tripping over each other in their costumes. What a fucking crew. Pansy Central.

"Get out of the way," Donny told them. "Get the hell out of my way."

He elbowed a couple of nerds clear and got into the thick of it. Most of the candles were gone, knocked over probably—fucking fire hazard, oh yes—and people were on the floor, some with flashlights, beams bobbing around. People were screaming and crying out and Donny bumped into a bunch of them and almost tripped over a few more on the floor. An emergency light was putting out a couple pale beams, but it wasn't worth a shit.

Donny played his light around. He saw people with what looked like white hoses coming out of their mouths. Some kinda sex thing or what? They seemed to be all around him and that bunch over there had a big python, probably rubber...except it was moving.

What kind of clusterfuck was this?

They all started bumping into him and some woman was sobbing and some guy was calling out for help. There were funny wet sounds like somebody was sucking noodles out of bowl and that smell...sweet like cider. Strong enough to ream out your nostrils at fifty paces.

"HELL IS THIS ALL ABOUT?" Donny shouted out to those forms circling around him and crawling past his legs. "WHAT'RE YOU PEOPLE DOING?"

So they showed him.

# CHICAGO, RIVER NORTH

## THE WAREHOUSE

**11:36 P.M.**

Harry told the Old Man that he really, honestly, and truly did not want to know what any of it was about and that was the gospel truth: he did not. Whatever curiosity had driven him when he was younger was sadly absent now. He no longer had any interest in risking his freedom for THE STORY. He'd had enough of that. For THE STORY had never failed to sink him in the shit and he didn't want that anymore. What he wanted, was to get out of this place and have the Old Man call off the dogs of war so Shawna and he could relax.

That didn't seem to be asking so much.

But the Old Man wasn't having it. He wanted to talk, he wanted to tell. And the old Harry Niles would have been in heaven, but the newer and aged Harry Niles was terrified of the implications of knowing things that could cost him his life.

So, when the Old Man said, "Do you want to see what Project BioGenesis is? The very nature of the parasitic infection that's bringing this country to its knees?"

Harry told him he'd rather not.

The Old Man seemed to find that amusing; he nearly smiled. "What's happened to your curiosity, Mr. Niles?"

"I decided some years ago it was better to be free and ignorant than dead and informed."

The Old Man shook his head. "Your life is in no danger."

"So you say, yet you want to show me state secrets. And you can't possibly let me walk away knowing these things. I have visions of torture chambers and dark prison cells dancing in my head."

The Old Man shook his head again. "You needn't fear those either. You have my word that you will leave in complete safety. That you and your friend—Miss Geddes or is it Ms.?—will be free to live your lives."

"But can I believe that?"

"Actually, you can. As I said, the man who liberated your friend is our primary concern. Not you. Not Miss Geddes."

Harry didn't believe any of it, of course, but he had little choice but to join the Old Man on his little impromptu tour of the Operations Center. He was shown the various containment areas, the labs, medical facilities, quarantine bunkers, even the incinerators where contaminated biological materials were burned. Harry didn't have the heart to ask exactly what comprised biological materials. Then the Old Man took him through a pressurized door that said:

**EXTREME CAUTION**

**BIOHAZARD**
**BIOSAFETY LEVEL 4**
**DO NOT ENTER**
**WITHOUT SPACE SUIT**

"I'd rather not go in there if you don't mind," Harry said.

"You'll be perfectly safe."

"But don't we need one of those suits?"

"No, we're only going into an observation cubicle."

Harry followed him, his throat feeling like beach sand. He was well aware of the fact that the others in the biohazard area were all wearing biocontainment suits or "space suits" as they were generally referred to. The Old Man led him down a few intersecting corridors—away from the main action of that place, thank God—and brought him into a little cubicle, as he promised. There was a window of thick reinforced Plexiglas. Harry knew that he was supposed to look in there, but he didn't want to. He did not want to see what horror awaited him beyond the glass.

"C'mon, Mr. Niles," the Old Man said. "Slake your curiosity."

Swallowing, at a complete loss for a witty comeback, Harry did.

What he saw was appalling. It made his skin crawl and his belly swim. There were two bodies. Except, they were not dead. Two people, a man and a woman, lying on the floor, some lingering nerve function making their limbs tremble from time to time. They were both bloodless-looking, mouths hanging open and dripping foam, eyes wide and unblinking. And with them was something that looked like an extremely large albino snake at first glance. But it was no reptile and as he realized this, Harry felt a warm nausea gushing in his belly. *A worm. A fucking giant worm.* That's what the thing was. It was easily twelve or fifteen feet in length, segmented, and starkly white like a ghost pipe growing from a rotted tree. Each segment was distended horribly, the flesh stretched and rubbery like the bulge in a tire that might burst at any moment. Each were set with a pair of gripping hooks that were either used for locomotion or to cling to prey. Its entire length was gleaming and greasy as if the worm were constantly secreting oils. It had a head, too. A great bulb-like protrusion that was near the size of a football. There were no eyes on it, just long brilliantly red spines and an X-shaped mouth that was hanging open, several pink squirming tubes hanging out like the entrails of an eviscerated man.

"Jesus," Harry said, sickened in ways he could not even express to himself. "This... this fucking worm is Project BioGenesis? These things are infecting the country?"

The Old Man corrected him by saying that this particular specimen was exceedingly large and most would be much smaller, but, yes, this was the end result of Project BioGenesis. "There are mutations occurring daily now," he explained. "The worms are parasitic in nature, but we've discovery that many are only using hosts until they've reached a larger size, then they become predatory."

Harry did not know what to say, what to think. The idea that these things were gestating in thousands, *millions*, of people was absolutely horrendous.

"Project BioGenesis was speculative at best, right from the beginning," the Old Man said. "It was used experimentally on a village in Iraq. The results were most unpleasant, as you can image. The village was sterilized by containment units. We thought it was over. A weapon so horrible that we could never ethically use it. Then... six years later, trouble started. Domestically. Veterans that had passed through that general area were somehow infected. Through a process we have yet to identify, the spawn infected them...then went dormant. Six years after, well, it activated. Your friend witnessed us trying to contain this thing. We were unsuccessful. And somehow, in the Middle East, certain terror cells harnessed the BioGenesis technology and they have spread it from one end of this country to another to bring us to our knees. That, Mr. Niles, is essentially where we are now."

Like any sane, compassionate individual, Harry was offended.

Offended that this entire mess was created by his own government. Maybe the terrorists had seeded it countrywide in some misguided, reckless attempt at revenge, but at the core of the thing was this: it was created as a weapon. It was created to do what it was in fact doing. American tax dollars had funded this monstrosity and millions of innocents were now paying the ultimate price. *We're right and sorry about the loss of your husband, ma'am, nothin' worse than having a worm burrowing in you. Sorry about your kids, too. You have to know we never meant this to be used on real Americans, just them God-dang A-rabs. Not real people. You have our deepest sympathies.* But what could he say? Really, what could he say? He wanted to grab the Old Man by the throat and throttle him, but what good would that do?

"So you see the situation we're in here, Mr. Niles. I'm sure you can appreciate that."

The worm, which had been happily coiling up the bodies on the floor, had abandoned them now. Maybe it didn't have eyes but it seemed to know there were people beyond the glass and it wanted them. It was climbing the glass like a caterpillar up the side of a jelly jar.

Harry had to turn away. "So what now?" he said.

"That's what we're all wondering. We're hoping to eradicate the menace, but only time can tell."

Harry had been waiting for this. "And until then?"

"Who can say?"

But that was hardly enough. Too many maybes and unknowns for his liking. If they were going to do something to him, he wanted to know about it. And if they were going to do something to Shawna, he had to know about it.

"And what about me?" Harry asked him when they were back in the room—essentially, a holding cell or interrogation room.

"You?"

"You've spilled state secrets to me, shown me a worm, told me about BioGenesis, and let me tramp all over this classified installation," Harry said. "Surely you're not going to just let me walk away."

"Oh, but we will," the Old Man assured him. "Of course, by that time, you won't remember a thing anyway..."

# PROVIDENCE, RHODE ISLAND

## MARRIOTT HOTEL, CTHULICON

**11:49 P.M.**

It was happening, by God, it was really happening. And no Hollywood CGI could match it. The feel of it. The smell. The sights. It was insane. Some shadowy strobe-show of cavorting bodies all tangled together, looped and knotted into a wiry and weird perpetual motion machine of faces and limbs and mouths...*and worms.* Where they had come from and what they were, Chaz did not know. He kept his eye to the Internet and he'd read plenty of those crazy tales making the rounds like the clap... but that was fantasy and conspiracy, minds going to sauce because the country was going toes up along with the rest of the goddamn world.

*But worms...fucking worms...*

"What are we going to do?" Bree whispered to him.

But Chaz just ignored him. They were stuffed under a table watching the show in the glow of the fog lights or whatever they were up on the wall. The worms were threading amongst the crowd, coming out of everywhere, sliding out of mouths and stringing those people up. They were white and bloated with ring-like segments, sliding around like maggots gushing from a dead poodle's asshole. And that sweet-sick stench. It was nauseating and thick, made Chaz want to paint the floor with his stomach contents.

Bree was shaking next to him. "How we gonna get out of here?" he asked.

But as Chaz saw a worm dangling down from the table, inches from his face, he said, "We ain't."

# CAMP PEARY, WILLIAMSBURG, VIRGINIA

## THE FARM

**11:59 P.M.**

The time to move was fast approaching and DCI Pershing was impressed with the results thus far. In a matter of hours, two targets had been removed and by morning the seat of power in the country would have dramatically shifted. But now was not the time to relax. The vigil must be increased, if anything. Admiral Paulus and General Mason were not as yet having second thoughts, but Paulus was definitely weakening and Pershing knew he had to keep the pressure on him. Mason had the Joint Chiefs of Staff in his pocket and tomorrow at this time, they'd have no problem—in fact, no choice—in accepting their new leader.

But that might prove to be a minor fly in the appointment.

For although it was never truly hashed out amongst the gang of conspirators as to who would be in charge, DCI Pershing automatically assumed it would be him for he was the guy who hatched this particular egg of treason. Paulus wouldn't want it...but General Mason. Hmm. This was a military overthrow for the most part and Mason might see himself as the man on the top. He had something of a history of a taking credit for the hard work of others.

Pershing made a note to himself to broach that very topic as subtly and diplomatically as possible. If Mason hinted at his own ascension to the throne of power, Pershing would merely agree with him. But when the time came, Mason would go too. Pershing was not about to share this glory with anyone.

# AUGUST 28

# CHICAGO, WEST TOWN

## WICKER PARK

**12:03 A.M.**

Though she knew she would never sleep, Shawna laid there in the narrow bed, the wheels of her mind looms endlessly spinning out the whole cloth of fear, uncertainty, and anxiety. She was afraid for Harry. She was afraid for herself. She was afraid for the whole damn country. Every time her paranoia level began to spike, making her heart pound and her breath barely come, she forced herself to relax, to unknot herself inch by inch until she could breathe again.

Her entire world was up in the air and she did not like it.

She did not know what to think.

What to feel.

It was not that many days ago when she was happy in her little mundane existence...okay, that was a lie and she knew it. She had never been exactly happy or even content but she'd accepted her lot as much as one could.

*Miserable*, she thought then. *That's what you were—miserable.*

And it was true, she supposed. She'd gone about playing the good little assistant gardening editor, telling herself it would lead to bigger and better things. But the bottom line was that she knew it wouldn't and her career path was hardly the prime motivator in her life. That was her romantic life—using her looks to trap one rich man after another. And when she drew them in, she gave them exactly what their wives didn't: compassion and understanding...and a hot romp with a pretty young thing.

*Sooner or later*, she always thought, *one of them will dump their wives for me and I'll have the lifestyle I want.*

That was her mantra.

But it hadn't happened.

One disastrous fling after another. She had become a professional, high-dollar slut: immoral, predatory, merciless in her conquests. Eager to hang another head on the wall, she stalked her prey like a big game hunter. She was good at it. Her campaigns were successful... but in the end, she always lost her trophy kill.

That wasn't exactly much of a life, Shawna admitted to herself. But, then again, it beat the hell out of her current situation.

Although she was free to leave anytime she chose, she still felt like a prisoner. Stein seemed all right and he had saved her ass from the goons that were trying to take her away, but that didn't mean she liked him. He had done her a good turn, but were his reasons altruistic or was this another game? Plot and counter-plot? She just didn't know. He would not talk about himself or reveal his background other than to tell her that he was a member of Blackpool and he was a paid assassin. Did that make him an evil man? Again, she didn't know. A week ago, certainly, but now? Unknown. Things had changed. They were different. Her frame of reference was askew. Her world was crooked. She did not know what to trust or who to trust.

That's why she kept the door locked, hoping Stein did not have a key.

The last thing she needed was for him to develop some twisted hero complex and decide that she needed to be more grateful. She *was* grateful, but not *that* grateful.

Because really, where was she now? Alive? Yes. Safe? Comparatively. But she was very far from being happily adjusted to any of this or content with the situation. Stein had been very accommodating to her. Absolutely nonthreatening. Still, she did not trust him or men like him. Subterfuge had always been her specialty, but this guy survived in a world she could not comprehend, a shadow world of assassinations and black budget operations. How could you trust someone like that? And she was his prisoner. Not literally, but figuratively at least.

She had nowhere to go.

No one she could trust.

She wasn't like Harry who knew seamy characters in the underworld that could hide you out places. She was not a survivor. She was used to being catered to, treated with kid's gloves. Her ass was sore from being kissed by men desperate to have her by their sides. But Stein was no more like that than Harry was. He did not give a shit what sort of deluded princess fantasy she had been living these past years. That kind of thing was window dressing for a guy like him. Because most people looked at the world and saw what they were supposed to see: little pink houses and white picket fences, blue skies and opportunity and parks for their children to play in; but Stein saw beyond all that, he saw the dirty machinery that kept that world running and the blood that oiled the cogs and gears, the greed and power plays and ruthless profiteering that fueled it all.

A pessimist? How could he not be? But Shawna figured if she asked him, he'd say he was not a pessimist, but a realist.

She wondered what Harry would do. How would he handle this situation? And thinking that and knowing she missed him terribly and was worried sick about him, she became more depressed than ever. For she knew where he was, but she could not get to him.

*If it was you in that awful place, he'd get to you. Somehow.*

And knowing this and feeling completely helpless, sleep had never been so far away.

# DETROIT

## HOLY CROSS HOSPITAL DETOX WARD

**12:19 A.M.**

"It's okay," Bertie said to Johnny, holding his hand as he shook with panic. "It's all going to be just fine."

Johnny nodded, knowing she was lying but more than happy to lose himself in the lie, to become part of it. The desire to perpetuate self-defeating bullshit had never been so strong. He smiled. He breathed. And, yes, he believed.

From the upper, abandoned floor of the hospital, he watched Army Humvees and APCs patrol the streets. It was insane. It looked like something from Northern Ireland or Chechnya. The sort of thing you saw on the news.

Bertie squeezed his hand tighter. "The world's still there, it's just changed now. We'll have to change with it."

It was good to have her there with him like this when his head started getting funny. He hadn't had a good taste in days now and his mind was acting up. It always did after a time when they dried him out. It started with a funny sort of humming between his ears and before he knew it, it was like a desert wind blowing low and lonely between his ears that blotted out everything else. Then he'd start hearing the voices from the past, all of them trying to out-shout one another for his attention—voices from his childhood, from the war, from last week or fifteen years ago.

"I'm okay," he heard his voice say. "I'm okay."

But he wasn't okay and he knew it, because he did not trust what he was seeing or what he thought was going on. The soldiers everywhere, the choppers in the sky with their scanning searchlights, police vans blaring out from their loudspeakers that curfew was in effect. Oh Christ, martial law. He knew what that meant. It was like being in Hue City again.

Oh Jesus, that humming. It opened his mind like a door and all the voices started talking to him again, telling him things and questioning where he was and what it was he thought he was doing.

"I'm Johnny Kopok," he said. "That's who I am, and the place is now goddammit."

God, if he could just have a taste. Just one taste—

He realized then that Bertie was no longer holding his hand. She was lying there on the floor and he couldn't be sure of anything. Had she really been holding his hand? Had she been talking to him? Or was he just out of his head again?

The knowledge of it made him sick. It made him weak inside with terror. *She's been sick for hours now, you idiot. You had to drag her up the last few flights of stairs. Don't you remember that? Don't you remember how sick she got?*

He went over to her, kneeling at her side. He didn't want to touch her, and, at the same time, there was nothing he wanted more. He whispered her name and held her hand. It was clammy and he did not like the feel of it.

She had the worm.

He knew she had the worm.

"Oh, Bertie not you," he sobbed. "Oh, for the love of Christ, not you. I looked my whole life for you and now that I've found you...not this, not this."

He put a hand to her swollen belly and he knew for certain. He could feel the sick, dirty heat coming from inside her, generated by the evil thing that owned her now.

*If she's got it, you should get away from her before it's too late.*

But there was no way in hell he was doing that. He would stay with her. He would hold her and protect her. She was the only rose he'd ever held, and he was not about to let go of it.

# WASHINGTON D.C.

## THE WHITE HOUSE

**12:43 A.M.**

"I've got people crawling up my ass any given hour of any given day, burying me alive in facts and figures and projections," the President of the United States said to Adam Tiggman, White House Counsel. "And now that I need intel and I need it right goddamn now, I've got nothing."

"Well, we've got what Chuck VanderMissen brought us. That's a beginning."

The President paced back and forth. "Which is general as hell." He shook his head. "Bob Pershing a traitor? I just find that a little hard to swallow. I've known him for years. If you had asked me yesterday what an example of a patriot was, I would have pointed to Bob. But this... I just don't know."

"It's a strong possibility, Mr. President," Charlie Goade, the FBI Director said. "Certainly worth pursuing. At this juncture, regardless of loyalties, we don't dare overlook anything."

The President nodded. "Still...Bob Pershing."

"Wouldn't be the first deception out of Langley," Tiggman said.

"Or the last," Goade put in.

"Okay, okay," the President said.

He, like everyone else in the room, was more than aware of the FBI Director's animosity concerning the CIA. Hell, it pretty much went with the job.

The President paced faster, wringing his hands. "Somebody's got their crosshairs drawn on this administration and I plan on finding out who. If it's Bob Pershing, then I'll hang his ass."

Secretary of State Arlene Rabin watched the three of them sparring through steepled fingers. "Point being, Mr. President, what Chuck Vander-Missen brought us is enough to raise more than a few eyebrows, I think.

There's also whispers at the JCS about General Mason and at NAV/INT and SOCOM concerning Admiral Paulus. Something's in the wind and it stinks."

She didn't push it any farther than that because she knew the President as well as any and if you pushed too hard—he pushed back. He was hurting. She knew that. Deep inside, he was hurting. There had been many, many threats to the country since its inception...but never from within. Not like this. Foreign enemies could be handled, but when you had to purge trusted friends, members of your own cabinet and agency heads, it became very complicated and genuinely disturbing. That in itself was bad, making a confident leader like the President unsure of himself and fearing reprisals from every direction, but both the Vice President and Gus Costello had been close personal friends. And right now, he needed the both of them like never before.

This sort of thing would have been a nightmare at any time, but with what the country was facing right now, it was an atrocity.

Tiggman cleared his throat. "It's easy in a situation like this to let our emotions rule the day, but let me caution you, Mr. President, that proceeding calmly and with a clear head is very important—"

"C'mon, Adam," Goade said, "somebody might be trying to take over this fucking country."

There it was said. It was put into words. No more dancing around the perimeter of the beast—a blade had been thrust into its guts.

SecState Rabin shook her head. "No, Charlie, Adam's right. We can't go off half-cocked rattling our sabers and pissing people off. Particularly powerful, connected, and well-placed people like Pershing, Mason, and Paulus. This country is facing a dire threat from the parasites. We've never been in such a terrible state. If the aforementioned are innocent, we can't afford to lose their support. We're going to need them."

"So what then?" Goade wanted to know.

"So we gather our intelligence and confirm our sources before we go off half-cocked. We must be judicious."

Goade uttered a cynical laugh. "We're talking treason here. We're talking a goddamn military overthrow of the country." He sighed. "Do you know what's going on out there? We've got armed uprisings, riots. The media is feeding off it and fanning the flames. The people out there are scared. Their faith in this administration is wavering. If they get wind of this...Jesus H. Christ. The time for action was yesterday. The country needs a strong man right now. Someone fearless. A leader."

"But not a despot," Tiggman said. "Not a dictator. Martial law has already been called. The country is holding its breath and the world is watching. What happens in the next few days is critical. We must proceed carefully or our enemies have already won."

Goade just sighed. The President looked angry. The shit was coming from every direction now. In a national emergency, the commander-in-chief was very reliant on his inner circle and now even that had been compromised.

Tiggman went on. "What I mean is that history will be made in the coming days. We need to be careful. The last thing we need is to further weaken the infrastructure of this country and the faith of its people by launching a series of purges."

He was talking common sense and they all knew it. This was a time for clear heads. The President considered everything, still pacing, still thinking, fighting against his own inner turmoil.

"All right then," he said. "We move on this quietly and covertly, but we move. I want every one of you to begin making some inquiries. Adam, I'm tasking you with digging as deep as you can with this. I want to know who's loyal and who is not. That's imperative. Right now I'm suspicious as hell about not only the CIA and NAV/INT but the NSA and the Joint Chiefs, maybe even SOCOM. Let's get on this, people, and head it off at the pass."

"Yes. Mr. President," Tiggman said.

"It won't take them long to realize they're in our sights," the SecState said.

"So be it," the President said. "If I find anyone that's taking advantage of this crisis for personal gain, any hint of duplicity or sedition, I'm going to make an example of them. And I don't give a good goddamn who's standing behind them."

Everyone in the room could read between the lines on that. There were power players in DC, corporate lobbyists and big money snakes that slithered in the darkness. The President was ready to drag them out into the light and expose them before the American people. It was unprecedented...and dangerous.

But long overdue.

# RICHMOND, VIRGINIA:

## CBT CORPORATE HEADQUARTERS

**12:59 A.M.**

*My God, they're really doing it.*

As the intelligence rolled in and the details of the Vice President's assassination and the death of Gus Costello piled up, Elizabeth Toma sat behind her desk in stunned silence. This was The Collective, she knew. This was how they played the game. They were grabbing the country via Pershing and his conspirators. It was no longer just talk; it was happening.

She thought of the President.

She thought of all that she knew.

She thought about what she should do as a loyal American and knew she didn't dare get involved. Not now. It had gone too far.

*And let's face it, you're bought and paid for.*

In her mind, she thought of Astrid who had been the only real friend, real confidant she'd had in many years. The Collective had taken Astrid from her. She would never forgive them for it. In the back of her mind, she entertained highly satisfying revenge fantasies that she knew she never would have the guts to turn into reality.

Regardless, something had to happen.

"Assholes," she said under her breath. "They need to pay for what they've done."

# CHICAGO, WEST TOWN

## WICKER PARK

**1:07 A.M.**

When the pizza guy knocked at the front door, Shawna didn't hesitate to open it. It was just a delivery guy, what harm could he possibly be? Which just proved that her paranoia wasn't as well-developed as it should have been.

"Nobody ordered a pizza," she said.

Stein came out of the bathroom and two men had her. A third had a gun in his hand with a silencer screwed onto the end. Before he could bring up his sidearm, it made two quick popping sounds and Stein went down, the holes in his head painting up the walls with grisly splotches of blood and skull matter.

"Oh my God," Shawna said.

The killer—the pizza guy—just stared at her. He was completely composed. Not so much as a twitch. He'd just killed a guy and to him it was of no more significance than taking out the garbage or sharpening a pencil. She was sick to her stomach, shocked, confused, many things... she went limp in the arms of the other two guys, then, just as quickly, went wild, kicking and clawing and screaming. The two men fought her to the floor.

"Gag her and cuff her," the pizza guy said. "Put her to sleep."

They did so efficiently and expertly. She kept struggling until the jet injector gun shot something into her neck, then she had no cares at all.

# CHICAGO

## LOGAN SQUARE

**1:23 A.M.**

McKenna was missing Stein something awful and he knew that agreeing to wear a wire and record him was just bad news. And he knew it was bad news because his new partner, Kessling, was probably doing the same thing to him now. And wasn't that just karma? Wasn't that poetic justice?

*Ah, you're just being paranoid.*

They had just come from a containment operation that had been no more and no less ugly than some of the others. Kessling handled himself pretty well. He had balls and a finely-tuned cruel streak, absolutely merciless—*those kids, those poor damn kids, I couldn't have done what he did*—but he had the personality of a mango. It was all, *yes sir, no sir, target is off the grid, sir, with him*. Teaming with him was like being back in Afghanistan with MARSOC again, hunting ragheads in caves. Stick-up-yer-ass leatherneck jarhead bullshit.

Not like Stein.

Stein had good stories. Stein always had a few good jokes. Stein looked at this whole operation with the absolute cynicism it deserved. He'd been critical of it from day one and that's what had rubbed Cave the wrong way and that led to McKenna wearing the wire and ratting on the only good friend he had left. Stein was right: it was time to get out. McKenna was thinking on joining him. Maybe getting to him before the other Blackpool hitters or ERT units closed in. Because they knew where he was and it was only a matter of time before they punched his ticket or sent him west to The Resort for some brain-scrubbing.

*Don't be so naïve, asshole: that's where you're going, too, sooner or later.*

That gave McKenna the cold sweats.

He pulled the car to a stop at the curb before a convenience store. "Why don't you run in and get us a couple cups? Gonna be a long night."

"Affirmative," Kessling said and McKenna wanted to strangle him. *Affirmative, my ass.* Once he was gone, McKenna stepped out of the car and had himself a smoke. He stood there, looking at the cars parked on the streets, the lights of the city. He exhaled a cloud of smoke. Yes, this was martial law. Full curfew was in effect.

*Like a fucking graveyard.*

But it was going to get worse, much worse. The stock market was dangerously volatile, seeing record losses day after day after day and with martial law, it was expected to crash like it hadn't since 1929. The ripples were being felt globally. People were running scared. They were losing their minds. Today, they were frightened. In a week, they would be desperate. In a month, dangerous. The glue that held the country together (cash) was evaporating. And what happened when the money ran out? When the police and the military were no longer being paid?

*Then the worms win. They conquer all.*

Kessling came strolling out with two cups of steaming coffee about three minutes later. He handed one of them off to McKenna over the roof of the car. McKenna accepted it without a word and took a sip, splashed some down the front of his windbreaker and dropped his cigarette.

"Shit," he said.

Stooping over to pick it up, he heard a hollow popping sound across the street and Kessling's head blew apart in a sloppy gruel of blood and brain matter. He slumped against the car. Dropped his coffee. Then slid down the quarter panel leaving a smear of gore that looked oddly like Heinz ketchup.

McKenna knew it was meant for him and rolled away just as another round sought him out and the driver's side mirror literally exploded. *Heavy caliber with a silencer. This is a pro.* He got behind the trunk and fired two three-round bursts from his Beretta in the direction he'd seen the muzzle flashes.

He heard feet running off in the distance.

Again, Stein had been right: the cleaners were being cleaned.


**1:28 A.M.**

*Getting old, that's what. Just getting fucking old.*

Tommy Quillan hopped a fence and jogged down the alley to where his car waited. A couple of teenage toughs were lurking about out on the sidewalk in defiance of the curfew. They saw the L96 sniper rifle Quillan was carrying and ran away. *Consider it your lucky day I don't take your bloody asses out.* Quillan hopped into his car and took off, putting some streets in between him and his targets.

Four blocks away, he pulled to the curb and broke down the L96 into its respective components and put them into their respective form-fitting compartments in a briefcase.

He checked his encrypted cellphone.

Two more messages from Pershing.

Oh, hell.

The first was a query concerning target attrition.

The second was to add another name to the roster.

Good old Pershing. Not only did he want the cleaners eliminated, he wanted the command and control structure of S5 to cease to exist. Getting this new name would mean an infiltration into the Warehouse compound itself. Intriguing. Quillan began to make plans in the back of his head.

Pershing was taking advantage of events as he always did. Behind all this was a grab for power. Whatever Pershing was doing—and with the full resources of the CIA behind him—you could be certain it had very little to do with national security and very much to do with some private agenda. That's what Quillan liked about the CIA Director: at heart, he was nothing but a cheap fucking mercenary. Quillan knew a brother when he saw one.

There was another text message, this time by one of his private assets. He clicked it up.

*Jsac: T, we got a positive on the Ratman. He's on the ground in Dearborn. Out of his skull. Waiting for it.*

Well, now that was good news. Quillan felt a tingle of excitement. The only reason he'd agreed to come Stateside and do some wet work for Pershing was that it played into his hands. He'd been tracking Sheikh Sa'ad al Khalafari half way across the fucking globe, from Syria into Iraq, through every Muslim shithole in Afghanistan. Word had it that Sheikh Sa'ad had escaped into Afghanistan with the assistance of some Paki militants who, in their spare time, were Inter-Services Intelligence operatives. Quillan liked that. Probably the same cunts who shielded Osama Bin Laden before the Yanks took him out. When rumor suggested that Sheikh Sa'ad had fled to the United States, Quillan was only too happy to go Stateside under the guise of hunting some enemies of The Company for Pershing.

Now he knew where he was.

He had confirmed target acquisition.

That meant that he had to catch a plane to Detroit immediately. This other business could wait. S5 wasn't going anywhere and neither were their cleaners. But he couldn't go out on some mad lark without Pershing's okay. He might anyway, but it might be complicated being hunted while he was trying to hunt. And with the subcutaneous biochip transponder injected in his shoulder, it was not like he could hide...Pershing's boys could watch every step he made via satellite.

He brought up Pershing's secure line. "It's me. We got a positive of our favorite raghead. He's in Detroit. Yeah, I know where. Approximately, mate.

Just approximately." Quillan listened. "All right. I can be in the air in an hour. This time, we tag him."

"I want him alive."

"What the hell for?"

"I have my reasons," Pershing said. "You are to capture him and bring him here. Do you understand?"

"If that's the way you want it."

"It is. I have uses for our friend. When you get here, I have another target for you. The most high profile you've ever attempted."

Quillan grinned. "Well, now you're talking."

# LOCATION UNKNOWN

## THE BIRD NEST, S5 BEHAVIORAL SCIENCES FACILITY

**1:45 A.M.**

Shawna's mind was not her own and she knew it. They had given her an injection and reality was getting fuzzy, it was beginning to fray around the edges.

*Am I even here?* she thought. *Am I even anywhere?*

The room was dim and the walls, even the ceiling, seemed to be made of smoky dark glass. Was such a thing possible? Did they make places entirely of glass? Entire buildings? She shook her head because nothing was making sense or maybe it made too much sense. She tried to concentrate, but her thoughts were filmy, they were wisps of smoke that dissipated in her mind's eye.

She was breathing in and out. Her eyes were seeing. Her ears were listening. She could feel the cool metal table beneath her hands. So, yes, she was tethered to reality, yet she felt wholly divorced from it. She was scared, too, because she had the most unnerving feeling that she was in a secret, secret place and dark mysteries and wild conspiracies were about to make themselves known to her.

*Soon you will know everything*, a voice said in the back of her head. *All there is worth knowing.*

"You should tell us about Harry Niles," a voice said.

Shawna let out a little cry because she was not alone in the room. A man sat across from her. He wore a dark suit. His face was white... in fact it was a bald, featureless white oblong. The only thing that distinguished it was its mouth through which it spoke.

"Who are you?" she asked him, her voice cracking in fear. "Where is your face? Where are your eyes?"

"You see only what I tell you you can see."

"I don't know where I am."

"Tell us about Harry Niles," he said and his voice was very loud in her head, echoing and reverberating, becoming not one voice but literally dozens, all asking the same question. Some of them whispered and others shouted and still others sobbed or screamed, but they all wanted to know the same thing.

"I don't know where he is," she admitted. "He was taken. At the mall, I think. He was arrested."

And, suddenly, in her mind, she could see it all: him running interference for her so she could get away, the men in suits arresting him. Yes, looking back now, she realized it was the most selfless thing anyone had ever done for her. She was not surprised. He had always been there when she needed someone.

"What are his connections to the underground press?"

"I don't know what that is."

"Think."

"I can't. I'm all doped up." She realized there was a water bottle in her hand and she sipped from it. "I don't... my brain isn't working."

Now the voices were asking questions again, only it wasn't dozens of voices but what sounded like hundreds and hundreds of them filling her head in a resounding cacophony until there was no room left for her own thoughts.

"STOP IT!" she cried.

"Tell us about Harry Niles," the faceless man asked. "Tell us about the underground press. Tell us about his connections to subversive organizations."

"He works for a tabloid!"

There was a tittering of laughter and she realized for the first time that there were two men in the room—one in a suit, another in a lab coat. Both were faceless.

"The tabloid is merely a cover for a deeply entrenched extremist network," the voice said. "We need to know how it operates. Where it receives its primary funding. We know that Gabe Hebberman is the number one man. Is Niles number two? And what is your function as a whore?"

"I'm not a whore!"

The faceless men looked at each other and chatted in squeaking voices like mice plotting to steal cheese at midnight.

"But you are a whore. Do you think we don't know about your various liaisons with certain prominent, wealthy businessmen? Come now: tell us. Are these men members of your network or are you just extorting them with sex?"

Shawna didn't know what to say—they had created an elaborate fiction from bits and pieces of her life. Fueled by paranoia, they had crafted a conspiracy that involved not only her but Harry and Gabe. It was insane. There was no network. No extortion. No covers.

When she got done denying it all, the man in the suit sighed and interlocked his long white fingers on the tabletop. "Now really, Miss Geddes, we don't have all day. You told us you would be cooperative. Is this your idea of cooperation? We want you to tell us things without us having to dig deep into your mind via other means. So, please, tell us what we need to know, and you'll be released."

There was a specimen jar on the table. In it was a worm. It wasn't moving, but she knew that if the jar was opened, it could become quite lively.

"Please, Miss Geddes," the voice said. "We have no wish to become invasive."

As he said this, she noticed that through the smoky glass wall behind him and his lab-coated associate, there was a building yellow sort of glow that was pulsating in rhythm to the beat of her heart. The supernal radiance grew brighter and brighter and she could see some immense abstract shape just beyond it. It was blazing like an alien sun and if she was drawn into the cosmic furnace at its marrow, she would melt into a puddle.

"Might I remind you that we had an agreement," the man said. His associate nodded.

"I don't... I can't remember," she mumbled.

"You agreed to cooperate and tell us what we needed to know," he said, "and we agreed not to steal your mind."

"You can't steal my mind!"

"How wrong you are," said the lab-coated man. "There is a book on the table. Pick it up."

Shawna blinked and, yes, there was a book on the table. It was... it was *Green Eggs and Ham* by Dr. Seuss. She held it in her hands. They shook terribly. "My favorite book... when I was little, this was my favorite book."

The lab-coated man nodded. "We know. You told us all about it."

"No, I didn't!"

"Yes, you did. The book is important. Very important."

The other man whispered something to him, and he nodded. "I'm so sorry, Shawna. You've left us no choice. We must begin..."

The pulsing light seemed to consume the entire room and she could feel its awful gravity pulling her in as she screamed and screamed. Now they would take something private and intimate from her, handle it with clumsy, crude fingers, then shove it back into her head, dirty and damaged.

*Sam-I-Am, oh please dear God, help me, Sam-I-Am...*

# WASHINGTON, D.C.

## WHITE HOUSE PRESS ROOM

**2:10 A.M.**

"So, I think, in essence you can see the insurmountable problems this administration is facing," Roger Thorogood said from the podium. "God knows I would like to stand here before you and tell you the situation is well in hand, but I'd be lying. This country is going to hell in a fucking handbasket and that's the name of that tune, ladies and germs. The Veep has been gunned down and the National Security Advisor died under...*dum-da-DUM*—mysterious circumstances. Who will be next? Only The Shadow fucking knows." He sighed, then shrugged. It was simply out of his hands. "My advice: keep your mouth shut and your asshole puckered. That is essentially the nature of our dilemma, ladies and gentlemen." He cleared his throat, sipped some water—*why, Jesus and the Saints, that's vodka and the good stuff, too!*—and adjusted his 18 karat yellow gold cufflinks, brushing his fingertips over their blue topaz faces. *Fancy, schmancy.* "Now, I'll be fielding questions if there are questions to be fielded in the field."

The Secretary of Defense checked the white gold Cartier Roadster on his wrist. Plenty of time. There was no hurry whatsoever. Just fine and dandy.

One of the reporters held up a hand. The others deferred to him. My, but they were a well-mannered and considerate crowd this evening. SecDef Thorogood listened to the question and sipped his vodka, *good shit*, feeling that funny burning in his throat. He'd felt it ever since he'd pricked himself on that needle left carelessly on his office chair. No matter. That burning seemed to be in his nostrils, too. Like pine cleaners and he wasn't even drinking gin.

*What?*

The journalist was shouting his question and the sound of his voice was at once maddening and at the same time hilarious. Why, his voice— *WHOP-WHOP, WHOP-WHOP-WHOP-WHOP*— sounded like the voices of the parents on the *Peanuts* cartoons. God, that was funny! Or... maybe it was disturbing. The SecDef could not make up his mind. He had watched a *Peanuts* cartoon with his granddaughter, Kaitlynn, last Halloween. The one about the Great Pumpkin. Hee-hee, that one was just as funny as this press conference. He wondered if Kaitlynn was watching him on TV. He knew she'd be impressed. He was wearing his Gianni Manzoni single-breasted charcoal pinstripe and he always cut a sharp figure in that. His wife told him so. Hadn't the President commented on it once? Or was that the British PM? Regardless, he was certain he looked dashing, absolutely dashing. With his silver hair and gold specs, he was a world beater, yes sir.

"But to your question," he said, clearing his throat and swallowing some more vodka. *Mmmm, good booze.* "The worms are the result of a highly classified black budget operation green-lighted by this administration...more or less. *Wink-wink, nudge-nudge.*" He set his vodka on the podium and took up a heavy, sealed folder. On its cover was printed PROJECT BIOGENESIS and beneath that, POTUS/EYES ONLY. "Yeah, okay, technically the Prez didn't know he was green-lighting this baby because it was vetted above top secret and it was strictly need-to-know. The worms were created using cutting-edge biogenetics and molecular biology. It's really quite technical and I can't say that I understand it that well myself. It involves transgenics, selective mutagens, genome transfer...crazy shit I can't begin to wrap my brain around. What it comes down to, brothers and sisters, is that the MAN has made hisself one motherfucker of a flatworm. And them bitches is everywhere and I do mean *everywhere*. Even in your underwear."

Another question was posed. "Ah yes," said the Defense Secretary, staring out at the rows of empty seats before him. "The project was called BioGenesis. It was but one op in a series of genetic engineering experiments with military applications. Don't get me going on *that!* Your tax dollars are paying for some seriously scary shit. Case in point: these fucking worms. What's that? Oh, it was all done under the umbrella of the Cee-Eye-Ay. Hush-hush shit, peoples. Ssshhh, ssshhh!" he said pressing a trembling finger to his lips.

His eyesight blurring, his head leaping with hallucinations, he sipped more vodka. "Okay, now where was I?" he asked. "Yes, I'll field a question from...hmm, let me see...yes, the leggy blonde from Fox News. And may I say, madam, that you have some seriously juicy-looking tits. What's that? The Worms? Who created them? Glad you asked, Miss Jugalicious."

Thorogood cleared his throat because this was important stuff here.

"They were engineered by a unit known as Section Five. Yes, that's correct, my bro-bros, Section Five. As in the section after four but preceding six. You got it. They are, of course, top secret and we do not openly acknowledge their existence. S5, as we spin doctors like to call them, reaches its dirty fingers right back to the early days of the Cold War. I believe it was known as SIG back then, Scientific Intelligence Group or Scientific Investigation Group. I forget. Serious *X Files* shit. No, I can't tell you who runs it. We call him the Old Man.

He has another name but if I told you I'd have to kill you. So, don't get me started!"

The SecDef finished his vodka.

*(Am I telling them too much? Am I going too far? Nah, I just have to keep it on the old up-and-up so I don't blab on about the Aurora stealth aircraft or those things on ice down at Area 51... did they move them? Ssshhh! State secrets! Be quiet! Next thing you know you'll be telling 'em about those things they thawed down in Antarctica... now there's a word that's hard to say when you're a little fucked up)*

Thorogood cleared his throat. Damn, but if he wasn't feeling funny.

"Next question. Yes, sir! You are correct, sir! CBT does have their filthy hands all over this. Very astute of you. Just keep that on the down low, if you dig. You know what they say on the hill, you piss off Liz Toma and you'll be shitting blood in forty-eight hours."

He blinked his eyes a moment and thought he saw no one out there as if he was talking to himself or something. Such an idea was preposterous, of course. He was Roger Thorogood. He was the Secretary of Defense and the fucking SecDef did not hallucinate and talk to himself like some crazy homeless fuck with turds in his pockets.

"Now, my fellow Americans, ladies and gennlemen of the Press Corpse... I mean *Corps,*" Thorogood said, his voice echoing. "Will there be any more questions? I'd like to wrap this up because it's martial law time."

Thorogood stood there, wishing he had a guitar so he could show them some of those moves from when he was a teenager. But that would have been unprofessional... the SecDef laying out some Hendrix for these peeps. No sir, must maintain the old dignity and the SecDef knew that. He began to sweat. His hands were shaking so badly he couldn't hold his papers still, even if there actually were papers in his hands which there were not.

Jesus, he felt like he was tripping his brains out here.

Had somebody drugged the vodka?

He was watching the faces of the Press Corps through bleary, watery eyes and they were changing. Each one of those happy/pretty/smiling/staring faces was beginning to stretch. Yes, they were swelling and making the rubbery sounds of inflated balloons. And why not? They were balloons. He watched the heads of the Press Corps drift free of their necks and then pop one after the other.

"Ladies and gentlemens," said the SecDef. "I want to thank you for coming and engaging in this most fascinating discussion with me. Unfortunately, I can answer no more questions as I have a very pressing engagement that requires my immediate attention." The sweat pouring off of him, his body shuddering with convulsions, he took a lock-blade knife out of his pocket and opened it up. Without further ado, he slashed both wrists until he got the arteries and bright red blood began to spurt over the podium, staining his Gianni

Manzoni, and spattering his face with crimson droplets. "Now...if there are no further questions...I will...exit stage left..."

Thorogood stumbled forward, crashing into the empty chairs and hitting the floor on his back, staring up at the lights above as the life drained out of him.

# CHICAGO, RIVER NORTH

## THE WAREHOUSE

**2:46 A.M.**

Harry woke up, shielding his face, trying to pull away from the hand that kept slapping him. A light was clicked on. It was directed into his face. Hands grabbed him and pulled him out of bed and he hit the floor with a thump. He looked up and a man was standing there. A man with a sharp blonde crewcut. He did not recognize him or the other guy with him. And then, the very scariest thing of all was that he could not remember where he was. He looked around and nothing registered. There were gray blobs at the edge of his memory when he tried to recall anything.

Crewcut grabbed him, hoisted him up, sat him on the end of the bed. "Easy," he said.

"Sure," said his friend. "We're not here to hurt you. We're here to liberate you."

Harry just looked at him, stunned, senseless, feeling very loopy and tired. "I...ah...I..."

Crewcut looked him in the eye. "You've been injected with a psychochemical. It's erased your memory temporarily. Certain areas of your hippocampus are still asleep, but we'll wake them up." He handed Harry two white pills. "Take those or it'll be hours before you remember who you are."

Harry just looked at him. *That's fucking crazy. Not remembering who I am.* But the ugly thing was he couldn't. He really couldn't remember anything. He didn't know who he was or when he was born or what day it was or what fucking city he was in. He sat up straight, panicking, his eyes darting around, head thrashing from side-to-side. Crewcut took hold of him. He patted his shoulder, calmed him.

"Take those fucking pills."

Harry swallowed them, slugged them down with water. What the fuck was this all about? Last thing he remembered he was…he was… hell, he had no idea. It was a blank. Just a darkness there. Nothing else.

"Your name is Harry Niles," Crewcut told him. "You're a journalist. You write for a tabloid. You live here in Chicago. This place is called the Warehouse. You were brought here and given a drug that erased your memory. It'll come back. Right now, you can't access it. Those pills will help. Now do exactly what I tell you or you'll end up a fucking robot."

Harry did not know who this guy was and if he should even trust him, but what choice did he have? A ray of light was a ray of light. His only fear was that these two guys would take him somewhere worse.

Crewcut said, "We got here just in time. In an about an hour, you would have been given another injection and some intensive hypnotherapy. That's a road to hell you don't want to walk, my friend," he explained. "But breathe easy, we're taking you away from all this."

Harry still did not know what any of this was about. Nothing was making sense.

Crewcut led him away down a cramped corridor whose floor was soft rubber and whose walls and ceiling were draped in plastic sheeting. A turn to the left, another turn to the right. Then a guy was stepping in their direction. He looked almost like Crewcut. He had the same flat, dead eyes. Something in Harry's mind was triggered by the sight of him.

"Taking away our prize Guinea pig?" the guy said.

"Yeah, orders is orders," Crewcut told him.

"The Old Man won't like it."

"Fuck him. These orders come from way above his pay grade."

They led Harry through a maze of corridors and out into a van waiting in the parking lot. When they drove off, none of the armed men at the gate even dared challenge them.

"What the hell is this about?" Harry asked him as they pulled away.

"You'll see," Crewcut said. "Until then, enjoy it. You won't like it when it all comes back to you."

# CAMP PEARY, WILLIAMSBURG, VIRGINIA

## THE FARM

**4:04 A.M.**

DCI Pershing knew he would never sleep this night because things were happening on every front and his phone was ringing off the hook. Thus far into the operation—which had no file except the file he kept in his head and no operational name save the one he had given it: COLDCASE—was proceeding like clockwork, exactly the way he had mapped it out originally. There would be snafus and he expected them, but by morning, as things worsened, there would be a decided shift of power in the nation. If not, then the situation would exist that would be advantageous to the same.

Thus far, three prime targets had been removed.

By morning, there would be six. Once that was accomplished, the leadership of the country would fall, through chain-of-command, to the Secretary of the Treasury. The President himself was not a target per se, simply because he was far too high profile and just getting someone in close enough to him would be near impossible. Especially now. But that didn't mean he'd be in any condition to run the country. Pershing would see to that. Who would allow an insane man to be Commander in Chief?

No one.

And that would leave the Secretary of the Treasury, Harlon Manning, and he would be no problem whatsoever because Pershing owned him. He just didn't know it yet. For many years, Pershing had been compiling files on would-be enemies, adversaries, and competitors. His file on Manning was especially juicy. Manning, though apparently happily married for some twenty-odd years, had a certain taste for young muscular men and had been videoed in action with several. When command fell to Manning, Pershing would release the dirt to some sixteen key media outlets. Of course, under martial law, the Internet would be shut down, but Pershing had enough pull to keep it going long enough to completely disgrace and discredit the man. The conservative minority—always the first to start screaming about anything—would be incensed. The moderate majority would be offended. Even the liberal left would be shaken up. The waves this would create following the deaths of cabinet members would be devastating. An already shaky leadership would be further weakened, creating an immense vacuum that Pershing would step in and fill.

He did not see it going that far, though.

He would personally present the information to the Secretary and he, of course, would immediately cede power to Pershing and his confederates. By then, the President would be in no shape to run anything, his public image would be destroyed. After Manning, command fell to David Constantine, the Attorney General. But the AG needed kidney dialysis three times a week and he would not survive his next treatment. The command after that was weak and no match for Pershing, Mason and the JCS, and Paulus with the might of the Navy and Marines firmly in his pocket.

Turmoil was the key.

Turmoil created opportunity.

Turmoil created disillusionment amongst the ranks and a strong hand on the wheel would be a welcome one.

What was needed of course were scapegoats. Pershing already had several even though they were, of course, not aware of it. There were three people of power that would cause trouble: DNI VanderMissen, General Sleshing of the DIA, and Secretary of the DHS, Maddie Hughes. And these would be the very people that the blame would fall on. The trio that had attempted to overthrow the United States of America. Pershing already had enough plausible, well-planted evidence to have them arrested. It was manufactured, of course, but by the time a Select Committee or a Congressional Investigatory body sorted out the loose threads, dead ends, and red herrings, it would be weeks if not months.

And by then, the party would be over.

The unknown quantity here was Gordon Parks of the NSA. He was very powerful. Every time Pershing spoke with him, he had the worst feeling that Parks knew something he didn't. That was unacceptable.

He would have to go.

Same went for Liza Toma of CBT. She knew too much and could name too many names.

Pershing could have seized the moment and presented the "evidence" to the President right now—it would be a great moment for that—but there was a problem there. Mainly, the President did not trust him. Pershing found it very easy to snow most of his cabinet, but the President was very shrewd. He did not trust Pershing. Nor did he trust General Mason. In time, the President would have forced Mason to step down as Chairman of the Joint Chiefs of

Staff. No, the direct approach would not work. Once the prime targets were removed, the "evidence" would be disseminated.

His secure cell beeped. Incoming from Matt Connelly, his Deputy Director. "What is it, Matt?"

"I have a few pictures I'd like to send you."

"Go ahead." They came as attachments over the encrypted net. DCI Pershing opened them and found himself looking at grisly crime scene photos of women that had been hacked up and disemboweled.

He got back on the line. "What the hell is this about?"

"These are courtesy of the Chicago Metro Police. Two of them thus far," Connelly explained. "I've gotten copies of the lab work through our field office. The DNA traces match that of Tommy Quillan."

Pershing sighed as the DD/CIA went into gruesome detail.

"Okay, I get the picture. He's at it again. He's on his way to Detroit right now to find Sheikh Sa'ad."

"Should I arrange a welcoming committee?"

"Absolutely not."

"But sir..."

"No, let him get the Egyptian first. I want that sonofabitch." *He'll be a wonderful propaganda tool for me.* "Keep an eye on him. His chip still operating?"

"It is."

"Good. Track him. Watch him. And when he bags our boy, shut him down. Get him to the clinic. He needs new programming for special targets."

"Will do."

Pershing broke the connection.

Yes, it was all going to work out just fine. Once they had Sheikh Sa'ad, it would only cement the evidence he had against VanderMissen, Sleshing, and Hughes into place. They were running an illegal black bag operation, trading bioweapons for information on Islamic militants that were attempting a nuclear strike against Israel. Unfortunately, extremists appropriated said bioweapons and used them against the United States. A tangled web from beginning to end.

"We were sold out by those we trusted with the security of our great nation," Pershing whispered under his breath.

How opportune.

The secure line rang again. It was Admiral Paulus of the ONI. "Ursa Major has retired," Paulus said and hung up.

Pershing grinned. Ursa Major was the code name for the Secretary of the Navy, an avid bear hunter. Now he was dead and Paulus would fill the vacancy.

# CHICAGO, CERMAK ROAD

## CHINATOWN

**6:58 A.M.**

Kathy Ling sat in the darkness, burning with fever.

She had been nauseous for days, but she never made a connection between what was in her belly and what was going on in her skull. Not until it was too late.

It had been a long night of pain and confusion. She'd watched through the window of Fong's Gourmet Noodle House many hours before as martial law became a reality and military vehicles and police cars patrolled the streets. It reminded her of her childhood in Hong Kong, the workers' riots of 1967 protesting British colonial rule. There was that same sense of danger in the air.

*But here in this country.* It was something she never thought she would live to see.

She was alone as she had been much of her life and it was funny how she got to thinking about that. *How alone I am and how alone I have always been.* But that's the way it was when you were a fixer like she was. You orchestrated and manipulated people, events, and outcomes, always tweaking things in a direction that was beneficial to yourself or your friends and business associates. When you worked the lives of others like a puppeteer, there was no time for your own.

She slid into a red leather booth, breathing fast, her heart rate rising and falling. She cried out as convulsions in her abdomen made her jerk and jump. Sweat that was thick, warm, and oily like petroleum jelly clung to her face. Her eyesight blurred and thoughts flashed through her head like chain lightning.

She gasped with dry heaves, then threw up a quantity of blood and bile. Her entire body was shaking.

*What the heck is this?*

*What the hell is wrong with me?*

It was a question that the majority of Americans had been asking themselves for days and weeks.

Something moved in her stomach. It was not simple muscular contraction, but the independent movement of something sliding through her guts. Thoughts passed through her mind but she could no longer make sense of them as she was manipulated from within.

She began to writhe wildly, falling from the booth and striking the floor where her body moved with an obscene boneless locomotion much like that which had parasitized her.

Pain blossomed in her head and for one moment as her eyes filled with blood, she knew what was happening to her. "Oh, God," she said and then said no more.

# CHICAGO

## NORTH MICHIGAN AVENUE

**8:26 A.M.**

When Harry finally, truly came out of it, when the blood stopped rushing in his head like a pumping jet, he sat up and gasped for breath.

"What the hell is this?" he asked.

He was in the back of a van. The man sitting next to him was a stranger... yet, he thought he'd seen him before somewhere. That hard mouth and crew-cut. The memory was misty and obscure. Another guy behind the wheel, dragging slowly off a cigarette, merged into a line of traffic.

"Where are we?" Harry managed. "Where are we going?"

The driver said, "We're here in this van."

Crewcut nodded. "It's okay. Just try and take it easy. You've been out for like four hours."

"Who the hell are you?"

"I'm Jerry and this is Frank. We got you out. We're your saviors. You remember any of that?"

"No... I can't seem to remember anything..."

And it was true. His memory was blank. He tried and tried to remember, but there was nothing. He began to panic right away. Shaking his head back and forth, trembling.

"Relax," Jerry said. "You were doped up. It'll take time to come out of it."

He was right because when he relaxed with some deep breathing, it began to come back in bits and pieces. Gradually, memories crowded his head. Shawna. The mall. The DHS goons. The Warehouse. The Old Man. S5. Project BioGenesis. The injections. Then these two getting him out of there.

But for what?

Harry breathed in and out slowly to calm himself. There were too many things to remember and too many things to do. He needed to get away. Yes, that had to be the first thing.

"Well, I appreciate your valiant efforts on my behalf, but—"

"Sit still," Jerry said.

"Ah, I see. I'm prisoner. And which agency of our beloved country do you represent?"

"The only one that matters," Jerry said.

Frank laughed at that.

"Which is?"

"Which is something you don't need to know," Frank told him. "Let's just say we represent a friendly corporate entity."

"You have to trust us," Jerry said. "Trust is very important between friends and we are your friends. You should thank us for getting you away from the Old Man. He can be a real sick SOB."

"Yes, I can just imagine."

"No, you can't. Trust me: you can't."

Harry sat there silently for a time. He hoped Shawna was okay. Right now, he was powerless to help her. The way things were looking, he was going to have his hands full just trying to help himself.

"Can you at least tell me where I'm being taken?"

Jerry sighed. "No. You'll be brought to a certain destination to meet a certain individual. And if that sounds spooky, sorry, but that's all I know. Somebody is very anxious to meet you. Someone important. Again, that's all I know. We're not gangsters. We're not hired guns. We're not feds. We're just escorts. So relax and enjoy the ride."

"Sure," Frank said. "We're like tour guides. We'll be at our destination soon. Just sit back and leave the driving to us. Clear your head."

Jerry smiled. "You'll need it."

# CHICAGO, RIVER NORTH

## THE WAREHOUSE

**8:44 A.M.**

The Old Man was beginning to feel something that he had not known in a long time: fear. Real terror, in fact. For so many decades now as an employee of CBT who contracted with S5, he had been on the cusp of every covert scientific operation and dirty black budget deal. And now he had the worst feeling that he was being marginalized. That there were games being played that he had no knowledge of, agendas he could not conceive of. And worse, that there were forces aligned against him and his usefulness was coming to an end.

*And you know what that means, don't you?*

Yes, he did. He very much did. Guys like him just didn't retire, they didn't step back, not with everything they knew and all the careers they could potentially destroy. No, they did not retire, they *were* retired.

He had felt it coming for some time, of course. The signs were all there. But now with the blowback from Project BioGenesis and the chaos it had created, he knew it was all coming to an end. The political puppet masters wanted to erase the entire operation, and anyone involved with it.

If he needed evidence of that, the fact that Harry Niles had been taken from the Warehouse by high-ranking operatives of CBT (presumably Third Eye heavies) and he had not even been consulted was very telling. As was the fact that S5 had the girl, Shawna Geddes, and he had not been called in. If he needed more, Elizabeth Toma was no longer answering his calls and Bob Pershing was treating him like a non-entity.

Yes, it was coming.

As the country trembled on its death bed, the Old Man knew his time was up. It was only a matter of time now before they came for him.

# LOCATION UNKNOWN

## THE BIRD NEST, S5 BEHAVIORAL SCIENCES FACILITY

**9:07 A.M.**

Shawna could still hear the funneling voices, but they seemed to be coming from some distant place, some shadowy and ghostly plane. They bounced around her, echoing in her head, moving within and without her. Sometimes she could see them—the reverberating sound waves moving like ripples around her. When she reached out her fingers, she could disturb them, send them oscillating in a dozen different directions.

*Can't be sound waves, must be a current. You must be underwater. Drowning in the deep dark blackness.*

But she didn't feel like she was drowning, there was no panic, just a sense of helplessness because she was floating in some thick, syrupy medium, drifting along, being pulled down and down like a soap bubble being sucked down a drain.

*You must fight now,* a voice that was not them told her. It was an inner voice and she had heard it before during times of great stress and mounting tension. *They have you just where they want you. You have something and they want it. They will take it by force, they will tear it from your head, pull it out by the bloody roots. That something is your mind. They are searching for it and you must not let them find it or it—and you—will never be the same again. They will change it, subvert it, reengineer it, and pervert it. They will make you into something awful, something that they can easily manipulate.*

*DON'T LET THEM!*

Yes, yes, yes, as she floated in that fluid medium—*warm, comforting, the womb, I must be in my mother's womb again*—she knew she must not let them, but that took willpower and hers seemed to be stripped away. She couldn't even remember what resistance really was. Her mind changed like the weather, her thoughts were fluffy white clouds that blew across an endless blue sky.

She could see herself.

That was the perfectly insane thing that scraped along the inside of her skull like claws and turned her thoughts to confetti. She was naked, floating along like a corpse in a river, limbs dangling, body shrunken. She looked somehow deflated like a cast-aside rubber love doll. Her head lolled, her mouth was agape, her eyes wide but glassy. Her hair floated around her face like deep-sea kelp. But she did have a voice and it was saying, *my name is Shawna Katherine Geddes and my mother is Eileen and my father is/was Rupert. I was a Girl Scout and I was in Key Club and my favorite book was Green Eggs and Ham and I had a dog named Sherbet and my best friend was Angela Meter and I was on the honor roll four years in high school and I went to Columbia and I had an affair with my Ethics professor who was twenty years older than me and I worked for one shitty newspaper after another where I was judged on my looks rather than my intellect and that was my card so I played it and became either a high-class whore, a rich man's toy, or a gold-digger and and and—*

She screamed because she was telling everything, letting them know her entire life story from kindergarten to losing her virginity to the men she slept with and the lives she had inadvertently ruined in the process. *No, no, no!* She reached out and clamped a hand over her mouth and her flesh was like cool muslin and her eyes were spinning glass balls. Her mouth continued to move, spilling all the dirty secrets of her life and she could not make it stop.

And then she was no longer floating. She landed with a terrible, jarring thud on a metal table and people with white lab coats were holding her down, fitting her arms and legs into restraints. Her head thrashed from side to side, but a rubber harness was fitted over it that held her mouth open in a wide, screaming O. A tube was shoved down her throat and needles inserted in her arms and some kind of viscous cold jelly was splashed over her, gluing her in place. And the entire time voices were speaking and telling her things that were not true and made no sense at all and, yet, made all the sense in the world. And she felt a pressure at her temple as they cut into her, opening her enough so that something could be inserted under her skin that would make it all so much easier.

And through it all, a terrible monotone voice kept speaking: "You will not remember this place or what happened here. To recall any of it will cause great pain and greater anxiety. Your name is Shawna Geddes and you have a special place in this world and a very special purpose..."

# DETROIT

## EAST DEARBORN

**9:19 A.M.**

Like a rat crawling on its belly through the filth.

This was the life of the man once known as Sheikh Sa'ad al Khalafari. He crawled through the sewers on his belly as the rats skittered about him and foul water seeped through his ragged clothing. Where once he had been a potent force in the jihadi and he commanded an army of militants and extremists whose mantra was the destruction of Israel and the liberation of Allah's people from the enslavement of the West, now he was vermin, filthy and stinking, scratching at insect bites and listening for the approach of the great white worm. His home was the tunnels that carried away the waste of the Motor City.

He crouched there.

He waited there.

In night-black arteries of crumbling brick, in flooded byways of gushing, stinking water afloat with rodent corpses, leaves, twigs, and the occasional putrefied dog or cat, he waited. He coveted the stigmata of sores that covered his body, smelling the sludge and filth in his beard, fighting against legions of rats and squishing the swarming dung beetles that nibbled on him as he slept, thinking, always thinking in the crowded cellar of his mind, that the beetles were the Americans who sullied his homeland, handled it and dirtied it with money-stinking fingers. *Infidels, yes, nothing but infidels, corpse-worms and dung beetles that have turned an oasis into a festering corruption where they can feel at home. For like the Israelis, filth is their natural element.* And being that he was Muslim, he knew he was far better than them. Here in his sewer-den of rot and dripping ooze, he felt superior.

But he was not alone.

No, never alone.

There were others and he had seen them in dank concrete corridors where the roots of trees reached through cracks like skeletal reaching fingers and mats of luminescent green mildew grew in profusion and toadstools plump and round felt like warm, pulsing flesh. Oh yes, they were here. Sheikh Sa'ad had seen them more than once, the burrowers, the things with faces like soft fruiting pulp. They beckoned to him with fingers webbed by fungi and grinned at him with faces like moist yellow straw. Once they had been nothing but crawling human vermin grown accustomed to the seeping darkness and clotted waters, but now they were something more, part of something bigger than themselves. They had found their god and they gave worship before it.

Their god had no name.

But Sheikh Sa'ad had seen it. In clammy hollows and slime-dripping vaults of congested waste where the dead things wash up and go to green mulch and bone matter, he had seen it. There where the women gathered, their faces swollen white like juicy subterranean mushrooms, collecting dead things to feed upon.

It had been among them.

The great white worm.

When Sheikh Sa'ad had first seen it, he had lost his nerve and whimpered like a child. It was immense. A great pulsating white worm that was easily twenty feet in length, each milky segment fat and ripened, its yawning mouth dripping a noxious slime. He had looked upon it and though it had no eyes, he knew it saw him for he could not only smell its toxic syrupy sweetness running like sap, but feel its sinister and polluted mind brush against his own. Its mouth was like a tunnel ringed by concentric rows of teeth that were licked by perfectly obscene rasping pink tongues. Its worshippers clung to its bloated, oily body, watching Sheikh Sa'ad and opening their own mouths in imitation of their god to show him the blossoming and succulent heads of their own parasitic worms.

*Even down here*, he had thought. *Even down here the worms have infested.*

But it was more than that and he knew it. For down here in the boggy and sluicing drainage of the dying city, something had happened. A ghastly mutation had taken place that could never have come to term beneath the eye of the sun. This worm, this great white worm, this progenitor worm and mother worm, had spawned and mutated into the horror he saw. It had infected the sewer-dwellers and disenfranchised, and now they held it in reverence, running pocked hands over each of its egg-bloated segments which must have held enough pulpous ova to inundate the entire city in squirming white larvae.

Knowing that he had brought it to being, that Allah had spurned him now for inadvertently creating this monstrous spawn, this freak of all that was holy and natural, Sheikh Sa'ad wept. His world was a prison, a narrow cage of his own making and he wept for the ruin of his life and its wasted potential.

For above he was hunted.

And below he would be prey.

No more would he know the tranquility of the prayer mat and the sweet music and comforting hand of a just and loving god—

*That sound. All that is holy, what was that sound?*

But he knew and knowing, went pale to his marrow. It was the sound of something colossal and undulant moving down the tunnel in his direction, its bulk sliding through thick, tepid water and over greasy decaying leaves, brushing the walls and moving ever closer. Like some gigantic jungle serpent slithering free of a green tropical pond in search of human prey.

But it was no snake.

It was the worm.

He heard it moving ever closer so that it might glut itself on his blood and meat. With a manic and hysterical cry, Sheikh Sa'ad jumped off the concrete shelf where he had been resting. He splashed through the standing water, slipping and sliding but never losing his forward momentum as the worm crept after him. The sound of its angry mewling filled the tunnel. No longer could Sheikh Sa'ad smell the slopping and noisome waters around him, for another odor had canceled this out: the cloying vinegary sweetness of the worm's juicing secretions. It was the sweetness of rot and death and perhaps something black and invasive beyond these things.

He screamed.

Screamed with pure atavistic dread.

The worm would have him now for the viscous stench of its sweetness was horridly strong, overpowering him, weakening his resolve and turning his legs to warm rubber. He was slowing. The worm would bury him beneath its coils, it would take him into the catacomb depths of its throat and peel his skin with those waiting rows of serrated teeth. He would be its food, its sacrifice.

But then—

Allah was good and gracious. For ahead, shining beams of God's sunlight reaching out to him, calling him free of the vaporous, stinking underworld. Sheikh Sa'ad ran for the light and saw that a manhole was open above. He looked back once and saw a rushing, titan blur of whiteness coming at him and then he climbed up and out, crawling over the pavement and screaming:

"THE WORM! THE WORM THAT FEASTS! THE WORM THAT TURNS! THE WORM THAT WAITS BELOW!"

And then he was on his feet, running through the sunlight, gibbering in Arabic, thoroughly insane, smelling and slicked with shit, crying out for the mercy of a just god.

One of the sewer workers standing nearby, gape-jawed, said, "Did he say *worm?*"

But the man with him just shook his head and pushed the manhole cover quickly back in place. With an involuntary shudder, he thought he saw something down there, something with an immense maw widening. But it couldn't have been, and he refused to mention it. There was a rumbling from below, but he told himself it was a nearby train. That's all it could have been.

# WASHINGTON D.C.

## WHITE HOUSE, OVAL OFFICE

**10:03 A.M.**

One of the things Maddie Hughes liked about visiting the President was that he always served good wine to his guests. It didn't matter if the meeting was trivial or critical, wine was served. And today it was an especially good vintage—a 2007 Liber Pater that was excellent.

She sipped from her glass and said, "What we have here is an abuse of power, Mr. President. This S5 business goes back to the late 1940s. According to what my people have been able to glean, S5 has been providing our military with exotic battlefield technologies since then. They were employed in the Korean War, Vietnam, and every conflict since."

"And under the nose of every president since Truman," the President said.

"Yes. But just try to find records of it."

"Bob Pershing would have them, I'm thinking."

"Yes, he's dead center of this mess with BioGenesis. That's a given. But he hardly stands alone and I think we both understand that," Maddie explained. "His accomplices are just about everywhere—on the hill, in the intelligence services, and the military-industrial complex. And I have no doubt, members of your own cabinet. S5 has strong connections with Congdon BioTech and dozens of other research enclaves in the private sector. To put it bluntly, Mr. President, Bob Pershing and S5 are well-connected, well-placed, and very powerful."

He thought over what she said.

She knew none of it could possibly have come as a surprise to him. Certainly he heard the rumors just as she did. She watched his eyes, wanting him to know that, without question, as secretary of the DHS she was one hundred percent loyal to his administration.

"This entire Bob Pershing thing bothers me greatly."

"It is disturbing, sir."

"I've known him for years. He's a spook and I know better than to trust his kind, yet... yet, I was always certain he had the country's best interests in mind."

"In his own twisted way, he may actually believe that. That what he is doing—alleged to be doing—is the only way to save this country."

The President sipped his wine, then slammed down the glass on his study desk. "I don't care for black budget programs. Never have. Never will. I'm a strong believer in not only accountability but transparency. When I learn about this bullshit going on in secret, being orchestrated by the very people I put in power, it sickens me. I think of the taxpayers. All their hard-earned taxes being used for this...this goddamned corruption."

Maddie cleared her throat. "Sometimes, I suppose, it's necessary for security of the nation."

He looked at her, his eyes blazing. "Don't hand me that old chestnut. I've had plenty of this nonsense cross my desk and I've okayed more than I'm comfortable with. But this...BioGenesis... it's disgusting. It makes me wonder how much of this special access crap is going on under the table."

"Sir, I think with people like Bob Pershing, this kind of thing is old hat. It's part of the game. They subvert funds and resources for their pet projects."

"Yes, yes, yes. But this is far worse and we both know it. This puts the country at risk. It puts the whole damn world at risk. The political pushback on this is going to be catastrophic. That's the only reason I okayed Yankee Alert—to save this country and the integrity of this office even if it is a sham."

Maddie let him stew a bit on that. She wasn't about to risk riling his temper, which was legendary. Let him compose himself before touching upon more sensitive issues.

After a time, he said, "Go ahead, Maddie. There's something you want to say, and I know it."

She swallowed. This had to be broached carefully. "The biggest problem here may not be Bob Pershing and his alleged circle of conspirators, but who stands behind them."

"You mean the aforementioned power players?"

She shook her head. "I don't want to sound like an alarmist or a conspiracist, Mr. President, but for many years there have been rumors of a group known as The Collective. Whether there is any truth to that is unknown."

"You're talking about the shadow group who orchestrate world affairs?" He sounded more than a little skeptical.

"Yes, more or less. A reputed clandestine executive branch." She held her hand up. "I understand your skepticism, sir, believe me I do. But if there's anything to this, we need to move on it. We need to find out who these people are and what their agenda might be. If all of this—from BioGenesis to the conspirators—have been engineered, we're dealing with omnipotent enemies with unbelievable amounts of power and persuasion. Bob Pershing and the rest might be nothing but puppets that they play."

The President stood up, walking back and forth across the room like a nervous, expectant father. Finally, he stopped. "If you would have come to me with this two weeks ago, I would have insisted you step down. But now with everything else going on, I'm just not sure. I'm not sure of anything." He cleared his throat as she had seen him do so many times at the podium. "The subject has been discussed in this office more than once. I've dismissed it as nonsense again and again. And simply because there is no quantifiable evidence for their existence."

"None," she said.

"And yet, I've heard of this for decades. When I was governor of Rhode Island. During my terms as a state senator. This bugaboo has been broached more than once by the House Intelligence Committee and tabled every time. Yet, the rumors persist." He shook his head. "Imagine: an illegal cabal with enormous amounts of public and private resources that lords over an ultra-secret empire of the most powerful people on the planet. Moving them like chess pieces, manipulating world events. It's frightening."

"And, all the while, to the general public across the world," Maddie said, "it's all a matter of coincidence, of chance."

He sat back down. "This is a dry hole, Maddie. Unless you've got something for me, finding these people would be like tracking down bigfoot."

She nodded. Now was the time for her gambit. The President would either take her seriously or he would call her a fool. "What I'm going to suggest is not an easy thing, but I believe we have enough evidence to bring in Bob Pershing. To sweat him a bit. You'd have to confer with your counsel, but if Adam Tiggman green lights this, it might be worth asking Mr. Pershing some hard questions. If he was given immunity from prosecution in the matter of treason and sedition, maybe he'd be willing to give up The Collective or at least point us in the right direction."

The President thought it over for some time, staring at his glass of Bordeaux. He sighed and then rubbed his eyes. He had slept very little in many days. "What you're asking me to do is to make myself look like a fool. To sit here with a bomb on my lap and hope it doesn't go off and scatter me to the four winds."

"It's a chance, sir. Nothing more."

"And a terrible risk. I'd be taunting a power structure that could destroy me."

"Yes, certainly. But if there's anything to this, if The Collective actually exists, then exposing them would tie-in nicely with Yankee Alert. This entire mess would be their doing."

He looked hard at her. "I've had quite a few people say these very things to me, usually after too many cocktails, but they've always seemed to lack one thing—conviction. You seem to have it. You seem to be sure The Collective is a living, breathing entity. Why is that?"

This was the question she had been waiting for. "Because certain names have come to my attention again and again since the BioGen fallout began. They've come from reliable sources and CIs. I believe they hold water. I believe I know who our enemies are, the puppets of The Collective."

"And would you like to share their names with me?"

Smiling and confident, Maddie did just that.

# DETROIT

## HOLY CROSS HOSPITAL DETOX WARD

**1:19 P.M.**

Sobbing, sobbing, sobbing.

Bertie was gone now. How briefly she had passed through his life. He had only known her a matter of hours and in that time, somehow and someway, Johnny honestly believed that he had fallen in love with her. Was that even possible? Could such a thing really be? He did not know. Romance was hardly something he had a lot of experience in so he figured anything was possible.

*It was a big, crazy sort of love*, he thought, wiping tears from his eyes. *A movie love. The kind you see on the screen but not in real life. That's how it was for us.*

Had he met her ten or twenty years before...hell, thirty years before... it would have made a big difference in his life. He would have done something important. Something big and impressive. He was sure of it. Her love would have... well, it would have lifted him up like the song said.

Poor old Bertie. She never woke once she went into her fugue. The worm was in her. It owned her. Johnny sat with her comatose form for hours... then when he slipped off to piss and grab some food for them, he'd seen the white-suited biocon teams sweeping around. He'd hidden in a closet. They'd taken Bertie away with them. He wanted to kill them for that, but he knew it was inevitable.

*Those stinking rotting sonsofbitches.*

Johnny jumped as something in his guts twisted like the dull blade of a knife. He knew what it meant. He'd been having them on and off for hours now and there was no denying what was causing it. Goddamn wonder it hadn't happened earlier. Entire hospital was infested.

He sat there, thinking, wondering, worrying. How long would it be until he wasn't able to do anything? Until the worm shut him down?

His stomach spasmed as if in answer.

He stood up. Well, if he was going to die anyway, he decided he would die in a big fashion. He'd discovered a couple dead soldiers in his travels. He went back to them now. They'd been gunned down by their own people. He pried the blood-spattered rifle from the cold, dead hands of one of the corpses. It wasn't an M-16 like he'd carried in 'Nam, but it was close enough. It was shorter, but the action looked the same. It felt good in his hands.

His plan, which wasn't much of a plan, was to fight his way outside. To get out into the air and sunshine one last time before cashing it in. It wasn't the greatest of ambitions, but he'd already decided he would not die staring up at sterile white walls and fluorescent lights.

He took the stairs, pausing several times when his stomach kicked and when he heard soldiers moving in the corridors. Third floor. Second floor. Not bad. Not bad at all. He was actually going to do this. Nobody was going to stop him.

Then two soldiers stepped into the stairwell from the first floor fire door. They looked up at Johnny through their plastic bubbles. He looked down at them. Before they could raise their weapons, Johnny wasted them.

And damn if that didn't feel good!

At least for a moment or two...but the sound of the automatic rifle in the stairwell was loud, jarring, echoing. Johnny's head began to feel funny again and Bertie wasn't there to talk him down. He was all by himself and everything got confused because—

*Because the goddamn Cong were running the perimeter!*

"Shit," Johnny said under his breath.

It was 1968. The fucking Tet. Christ, everything was confused. He had his rifle but where was the rest of his gear? No frags. No magazines. Jesus, where was that belt for the Sixty? Goddamn L-T was going to core his ass over that one. He was separated from the platoon. He jogged down the stairs and examined the enemy he had killed.

Hell was this?

VC in white uniforms and spaceman helmets? Fuck was that all about? Johnny had seen some crazy-ass shit in the 'Nam, but this beat all. And they were big for Viets, real big like Americans. Hell was going on in this war now?

He kicked them to see if they had any fight left in them, but no, they were toast, he'd greased both of them with the first volley. That's when he noticed they were both carrying American weapons. Well, didn't that beat all?

*Goddamn Charlie Cong! What's this about now?*

He took two magazines from them, but he didn't have time to do much else; he had to link up with the platoon. He went through the door and the goddamn VC were everywhere. Christ, a nest of them! He opened up on full auto, wasting three of them before they even got their AKs up.

The others began to return fire.

Johnny got behind a desk. Oh, what he wouldn't have given for a couple frags right then. He heard voices shouting. Since when did the gooks speak English? They were messing with him. Psychological warfare. He darted up, getting off a few rounds and driving the white-suited Cong back.

"LIUETENANT!" he cried out. "CHARLIE'S GOT ME BOXED IN! NEED BACKUP HERE!"

Where the fuck was Pete with that Sixty? Shit and shit. Only one thing to do now. Johnny ran out from behind the desk firing from the hip as rounds chewed up the real estate around. Oh yes, oh fucking yes, he could see the daylight! Get out of here! Hump it! He caught one in the shoulder and he drilled two more bubble-headed VC and then he was out the doors.

He ejected a magazine and saw a dozen Charlies bearing down on him. He began firing, counterattacking as per his Marine training. He jerked as bullets ripped through him, but he didn't stop until he'd emptied his mag and killed three more of those fucking Cong. Then his legs went out from under him and he rolled into the grass, blood gushing out of him, his entire body convulsing.

"Too late, too late," he muttered as the VC surrounded him, staring down at him from their bubbles. "You ain't got me... I'm KIA, you fucking slopes... I won and you lost and...and...and..."

Johnny smelled the fresh air and saw the blue sky one last time before the darkness took him. But it was okay, it was all okay, because he was going to a better place where those fish-stinking slopes could not follow.

As he died, it was the Tet Offensive of 1968 again and he had bought it there by the Perfume River, enemy dead scattered around him. And being that he had not really lived since that night so long ago, it was fitting. He had died like a Marine and he had never wanted anything more.

# RICHMOND, VIRGINIA

## CBT CORPORATE HEADQUARTERS

**2:10 P.M.**

As she listened to the voice of Gordon Parks ramble on and on and on, Elizabeth Toma contemplated the end of all things, the destruction of western civilization as she knew it, the termination of the dirty machine of democracy that had started as a pleasant dream and ended up as a corrupt nightmare.

*"Our ultimate goal, of course, is to realign, reengineer, and reimagine society. The body of the nation and that of the world in general has been contaminated by divisiveness and subversion. There is no going forward at this juncture. There is only a drunken stumbling from the right to the left and back again, miring ourselves in the waste products of so-called freedom, which inevitably leads to—"*

Sneering, Elizabeth shook her head. Here was one of The Collective's vanguards of the New World Order. A pompous, chatty, treacherous fool. Of all the unmitigated idiocy. Parks was so arrogant that he dared lay out the subjugation of the masses in a memo to himself. She could just imagine him pacing his spacious office in the hub of the NSA, listening to the rest of the world, never once considering that he might be listened to.

She was both surprised and disturbed that the nation's uber-spook was not even aware of the technology that CBT routinely employed—Skybox, an autonomous drone technology that could look down through any building and listen to any conversation, even that of a certain pretentious gas-bag who happened to be the director of the NSA in his supposedly secure lair.

*"...have learned that nearly any belief system can be implanted in the human animal following an injection of fear, anxiety, or unwanted excitement in their dull, compart-mentalized lives. Such shocks to the societal system of the sort following declaration of war, a terror attack or pandemic, create a void of uncertainty in the common man or woman. As anxiety spikes, so does the need to be reassured and coddled, leaving the population at large wide open to mass*

*suggestibility. They will willingly summit to the suspension of civil rights and due process of law if their leaders will only 'make it better' so that they can return to their simplistic, dumbed-down roles of workers, breeders, and mindless consumers. These are our livestock. They can be reimagined and refitted at our will—throwaway soldiers to tax payers, incited mobs to bovine animals, all drugged on self-indulgence, preservatives, and professional sports..."*

It would have been so easy to discredit him at this point, to report him to The Collective and watch with great amusement as they took him off at the knee, destroying his life and bleeding the hot air from him. There had been a time when such things were a major pastime with her, an addiction, a drug she craved...but not any longer. She was not sure what was important anymore.

She thought of Parks and his games.

She thought of Bob Pershing and his infantile little coup.

But mostly she thought of The Collective—their subterfuge, their betrayal, their disloyalty. It was the deceit that irked her. She had given up everything for them, performed the most vile, unethical, and, yes, even disgusting and treasonous acts for them. They had been like a religion to her. She even let Astrid go because that's what they wanted. She hadn't even dared to raise an eyebrow when they killed her.

And for that, for all of that, they include that pathetic dick-sucking frat boy Gordon Parks into the highest echelons of their agenda and disclude her? How dare they. It went far beyond insult. It was a personal attack on her intelligence and loyalty. They were kicking her like a sick dog.

Fuming, she listened.

*"...and with this radical, cutting edge EMF technology, the memory, consciousness, and instinctual drives of our livestock can be accessed, rewritten, and reengineered to benefit society's needs. Now imagine this marvelous electromagnetic tele-stimulation of the brain used in conjunction with an implant of sorts—an organic implant, if you will, a parasite that can be completely controlled by the aforementioned EMF transmissions. As said parasite is controlled, it controls its host. And that is the basis of what we have come to call MINDWORM, a triumph of experimental social engineering which will completely subvert and redirect the future of the race, bringing a calming, benign influence that will restore order and stimulate purpose, creating a unified world government out of chaos..."*

Mindworm.

Mindworm.

*Mindworm.*

Elizabeth had listened to the above a dozen times now and each time, it made her angrier. This was what they had let Gordon Parks in on and left her out of—the greatest manipulation of the masses ever conceived. There he sat, dictating out loud the basis of something that was leagues above top secret. The sort of thing that could easily destroy the military-industrial-political establishment of the country were it leaked to journalists and foreign nations.

"And you picked this buffoon over me," she said out loud, hoping that she was being listened to. "The man who sold the world."

She knew that The Collective had access to technology far beyond anything available to the NSA. Skybox was something they routinely employed. There was another shadow technology, she had heard, which could target and follow the unique bioelectrical brain frequency of anyone on the planet. There was even a rumor that information processed by minds could be decoded by evoking the potentials emitted.

*But I don't believe they can read my thoughts. Not yet. And if they can, then what I'm thinking will not only bring them to their knees but destroy their Machiavellian fantasies of world domination. No longer shall I be the fuck-ee, but the fuck-er. See how they like it.*

She knew exactly what she was going to do and it was not so much out of anger, but because of what they had done to Astrid. How they had dirtied her and tossed her into the trash. That was unforgivable and they would pay for it. One good fucking deserved another.

Her plan hatched in detail, now it was only a matter of waiting for the inevitable phone call.

But until then, until Mr. Brown called and arrangements could be made, she pulled the SD card from her laptop and inserted it into a MOTO prepaid phone, a burner, that she would throw away after using it. She sent a file to DCI Charles VanderMissen. She was certain he would enjoy it.

# OKLAHOMA CITY, BRICKTOWN

## ROLAND'S MEAT MARKET

**1:37 P.M.**

For days and days, Audrey laid in bed, on the floor, and, for a strange sojourn of hours, in the closet when the bright lights of daytime had threatened to burn her eyes from their sockets. And all that time, as her guts bucked and jumped and she vomited out a thin, watery gruel of bile, she had thought of food.

Particularly meat.

Though she was feverish, shaking and convulsing, and had lost complete control of her bodily functions, the parasite that dwelled within her desired nutrients, particularly protein. Fully in command of her limbic system by that point, it triggered her hypothalamus to release mega-doses of ghrelin in her stomach, the hormone that stimulates hunger.

By the time she made it out into the streets, hunched-over and delusional, her appetite had reached epic proportions. It cut her open from the inside like razor blades, making her hurt and cry out. People got out of her way and cars slammed on their brakes when she crossed their path.

Soon enough, she found others like her, and in a body, they shambled through the streets, seeking that very thing which would satisfy them. By the time they reached Roland's Meat Market, there were nearly twenty of them fixed on a single unified purpose: to feed.

As Audrey stumbled along with the others, panting and sweating, her eyes pink as fresh tenderloin, the hunger erupted inside her like a cluster bomb of biochemical compulsion. She needed food, she wanted to stuff the yawning hollow within, pack it with juicy red meat, marinate it in blood, and season it with salty nougat globs of yellow marrow.

*"Hungry,"* she grumbled, slime running down her chin. *"Am so hungry hungry hungreeeee…"*

With the knowledge that meat was near to hand, her appetite became a raging sugar-toothed monster of addiction. It understood only satiety. There was nothing else in the world and maybe there never had been.

Her hands morphed into ensanguined claws as she tore ruts in her jaundice-yellow face. Her teeth worried at her lips, tearing and gnawing the delicate tissue into pink bleeding strips that she ground to flesh mush beneath her molars, her greedy mouth sucking the blood from them.

It tasted...*delicious.*

Like the juice of plump cherries and succulent strawberries and dewy blood oranges. Pure ambrosia. Pure ecstasy that made her tremble right down to her piss-soaked loins. The others were pretty much doing the same—driven into a frenzy of hunger, they bit and chewed at themselves, eating their own lips and mouths, even biting their arms and nipping at their fingers.

Then they burst through the sliding glass doors of Roland's Meat Market, red-mouthed and blood-eyed, a monstrous throng that sent customers running. But not Rico Pedaris. This was his goddamn place and things were going to hell in the world, surely, but he was not about to surrender the market to these...these crazies. Absolutely fucking not. It was his bastion of safety and normality. He was not about to give that up.

"HEY!" he cried out. "GET THE FUCK OUT OF MY STORE! YOU HEAR ME? GET THE HELL OUT OR I'LL CALL THE COPS OR THE FUCKING ARMY!"

Although they were everywhere, he sighted in on the one closest to reach, which happened to be Audrey. She was going wild, scattering loafs of bread and buns in every which direction in her search for what her parasite demanded.

Rico grabbed her by the crook of the arm and pulled her away. She snarled at him, bared teeth on full display through the ragged hole of her mouth. She clawed at his face. He shoved her back, putting her right on her ass. Then another arm circled his throat. Rico pivoted and broke free. Another crazy was standing there, this one a man with red tears running from his eyes. Rico punched him right in the face two or three times, but he did not go down. No, in fact, he just stood there as if he could not understand the nature of being hit.

Rico shoved him out of the way and took hold of a woman who was tossing canned goods around. He cringed instantly because the flesh at the back of her neck sloughed free in a single moist sheet.

The good thing was that while most of his employees had bolted, some had stayed to fight the good fight. Margie Cantrell was one of them. She fought a valiant defensive action, trying to keep the crazies away from the meat cases. She had a broomstick in her hands, and she was whacking away at them like a Viking with a broadsword.

Audrey was unconcerned about what was happening to her associates. Like the others, she was completely selfish in the getting of food. As Margie

Cantrell fought side-by-side with Stevie Coombs, the stock boy, she took advantage of the situation and slipped right around the fighting, hissing mob, and climbed over the counter.

She found the meat.

*Mine*, she thought. *It's all mine.*

Ribeye and sirloin and porterhouse steaks, raw hamburger and chicken, pork chops and fresh sausages and linked wieners, roasts and shanks and filets. It was all hers. Inside, she surged with delight. She felt like a starving shark happening upon some disaster at sea—here was all the bloody chum she would ever need. She smacked what remained of her lips and licked pink foam from her mouth.

Without further ado, Audrey began to eat.

She lunged at the meat, not just biting it but striking it like a hungry piranha, ripping out juicy chunks and well-marbled strips and tender slivers, shoving more and more into her mouth until she gagged. She vomited out globs of half-chewed meat in a foamy gush, only to begin eating again, trying to fill the hollow within herself that could never be satisfied.

The other crazies overwhelmed Rico and his last two employees. They weren't interested in what was in the meat cases, that was purely pedestrian, but what was hanging in the back—the hams and beef shanks, turkeys and chickens. This was what they went after.

About that time, the police showed.

They were not in the best of moods. This martial law shit was strictly for the birds. It quadrupled their workload and every available body was pulling twelve hour shifts (and hoping that when the dust settled, they'd get paid for it). Three of them stepped through the door with riot guns in their hands. They were led by Sergeant McQueen. He was not amused by what he saw because he'd been seeing it all day. At times, it made his flesh crawl; at others, it sickened and angered him.

"YOU PEOPLE!" he called out. "I WANT YOU OUT OF THIS GOD-DAMN STORE RIGHT NOW!"

The other cops looked at him—*was this guy for real?* It was plain to see the sort of condition these *people* were in. They were infested. Trying to talk them out of the store was like trying to talk a mole off your arm or the nose off your face.

"Well, I tried," he said. "Okay, waste these shitbags."

The cops opened up. They dropped five or six of the crazies in the first volley, the remainder in the second.

It was a horrible sight.

The crazies—McQueen preferred to call them *wormies*—were so used and abused by their parasites, drained and degraded and broken, that they seemed to liquefy when the rounds chewed into them. Parts dropped off, fluids splashed and tissue spattered. They hit the floor in writhing tangles, quivering and convulsing, the parasites inside them making slurping and rending sounds as they exposed themselves—oily white worms slick with blood and bile, fattened on the juice of their hosts, exuding milky secretions like lactating tits. They burst from mouths and asses and soft, spongy bellies. The body pile continued to shudder and the worms continued to erupt in vermiform coils, suckering mouths opening and closing. They were like dozens of disease-swollen tongues licking the anatomical waste that had given them birth, leaving their shrunken hosts folded and pinched like origami, squeezed out like fleshy peaches in a gushing soup of human pulp, abandoned like deflated sex dolls.

Audrey oozed free of the central mass (the cops having fled in terror), crawling forward like a crushed spider, leaving a trail of slime and septic discharge in her wake. She moved with cracking, popping, slushy noises as the colossal parasite which had dislocated her jaws as it emerged pulled itself ever forward in search of food, its hooks scraping over the floor like cat's claws. The majority of it was still inside her and it dragged her carcass along behind it until it reached the refrigerator room in the back where all the immense shanks of meat hung by hooks. Only then did it discard her as it drilled into a juicy side of beef, clusters of eggs dropping from it as it tunneled ever deeper, glutting itself and awaiting a new host to complete its life cycle.

# LOCATION UNKNOWN

## THE BIRD NEST, S5 BEHAVIORAL SCIENCES FACILITY

**3:09 PM**

By that point, Shawna didn't know much of anything. She'd been shot up with drugs. Interrogated. Threatened. Locked in a cell. And—it had to be the drugs—abducted by aliens. All of it was scrambled in her head. She was not even truly sure what her captors wanted. Part of her—the part that was trying desperately to escape from the fog like a sabretooth tiger trying to claw free from a black sucking tar pit—told her that, yes, she had asked again and again, maybe until her throat was raw and dry but—

*(answer the fucking questions you whore you fucking whore or you'll be sorry we'll make you very fucking sorry)*

—she got no answers, only more rough treatment. She was tied to a table and now and again, the heavies that tormented her would be replaced by a couple nondescript, faceless—

*(were they really faceless?)*

—men in white lab coats who would examine her and mumble things to one another in some jumbled language she could not understand. She remembered being jabbed in the throat with needles and scalpels cutting into her head...or was that a dream? They seemed to believe that Harry and she were part of some greater conspiracy, some underground press movement aimed at bringing down those in power and exposing their dirty secrets.

*(whore you fucking whore we'll fix you)*

Swimming in and out of consciousness, she forced her brain to concentrate and her eyes to focus. But it was simply no good. Everything was murky and dim. It was as if she was suspended underwater, trying to look through darkening waters. She was choking. She could not breathe. Her lungs would not draw air...then she thrashed herself awake, gasping, and she was tied to a chair.

"Please," she managed. *"Please..."*

But then she pressed her lips shut. She would not beg or grovel or demean herself. *Let me go oh please let me go I'll do anything.* Her eyes opened and she realized she was alone. But when she blinked, her two tormentors were there. They were dressed in black. *The fabled Men in Black, how fitting.* They were just watching her, chatting, but their words were garbled and thick like they were speaking through mouths filled with molasses. Dear God, that was just a comparison, a simile, but... yes, she could smell it. Like brown sugar. It was heavy in the air. She could actually taste it on her tongue.

Now how could that be?

The Men in Black watched her. Their words were still unintelligible but they were getting clearer by the second and Shawna was picking up bits and pieces.

"...not too long...you...works...at first..."

Were they both speaking or just one of them? Shawna blinked her eyes and there was only one of them in the room. She blinked them again and she was alone. She squeezed her eyes shut and the two men with the lab coats were in the room with her. Their voices were clear when they spoke.

"She should be about ready."

"Let's get this done with then."

Shawna was looking at them, but it couldn't be real: their faces were gone again. It was a nightmare. It had to be a nightmare. She tried to focus...still, those faces were white blurs like somebody had erased their features. But it couldn't be a dream. God, she could smell their cologne, hear them breathing.

She licked her lips. "Where...where are your faces?"

"Just relax, Miss Geddes. What you are experiencing is a post-hypnotic suggestion reinforced by psychotropics. You cannot see our faces because we told you that you cannot."

*Don't let them. Get. Away. With. It. It's mind control. Just like the stories Harry writes in that weekly rag... remember that doozy about the Kennedy assassination? Psychotropic, mind-altering drugs were fed to the nation and the true memories of what happened on November 22, 1963, have been suppressed to this day. Only Harry could come up with something that unbelievably goddamn whacked-out. You laughed about it over chai tea. CIA BRAINWASHING BLITZKREIG. Harry did something similar with the Roswell/Area 51 thing. The soldiers were brainwashed. The guys who reported the crashed saucer and aliens later recanted because they were brainwashed, too. False memories were implanted. They believed it was bullshit because they were conditioned to believe it. That's what they're doing now. But it's real. They're trying to change you, strip away your personality, implant something else. Do not let them. DO. NOT. LET. THEMMM—*

"What? WHAT? WHAT DID YOU SAY?"

"No need to shout," said Faceless Man #1. He turned to Faceless Man #2. "Common symptomology following Post-H and DS-7. Temporary."

"She's resisting," said Faceless Man #2.

"Typical."

"Listen to my voice, dear. Listen very closely to what I say: *Do you like Green Eggs and Ham?*"

Shawna screamed, but it was no good because resistance was futile like in an old movie. Her mind was not her own and she could feel it slipping away from her. She could actually see it: a shapeless white blob. She tried to hold it in her hands, but it oozed between her fingers like soft dough. Other hands had it now and they were molding it, pressing it into an alien shape. She was losing. She was losing her mind. It was theirs now. *Oh dear God no, not that. Don't let them take my mind. Don't let them steal my memories.* She kept fighting, resisting, and that caused white slivers of pain to bisect her brain like cold piercing needles.

Fight! Fight! Fight!

*Make yourself see their faces.* Yes, yes, yes, that was how it had to be done. It was a simple mental exercise and she was good with things like that. She simply had to focus her mental energy and force it out of her head, drag it out of the locked trunk they had shut it in. Just...concentrate—

*(a face a face a face yes she could see a face like a TV screen in her mind a face in a storm of sawdust...grainy...obscure...indistinct...a round kind face with sad blue eyes the color of a late summer sky, bulbous nose, salt-and-pepper clocksprings of hair sticking out to either side of the head—that's Albert Einstein no it's Gabe Hebberman but why am I seeing his face why why?????)*

"You need to hear my voice, Miss Geddes. You need to listen to my words because they are the most important words you will ever hear. Remember: I told you you must obey and to not obey will be agony. Hear my words."

Shawna tried to fight against it but to deny it was agony. Each time she tried, there was less of her. It drained her. Emptied her mind. She had to listen because those words meant no pain and she did not want pain. So the voice spoke and she listened but the words were against everything she believed in. She would not listen, she would fight FIGHT FIGHT—

*(you better listen you fucking whore you better listen)*

*(but it's awful I don't want to be like that a monster nothing but a mindless monster)*

"...you'll be told. You will be told. You will be given a photograph and a name and a place. You will go to that place and seek that face and that name. When you find them, when you make positive identification, then you will do what is necessary for the guilty must be punished..."

"I WON'T! I WON'T DO THESE THINGS!"

"Yes, Miss Geddes. You will."

*(no no no no no nooooooo I will not won't not cannot I will not do these things Sam-I-Am, I will not eat Green eggs-and-ham Sam-I-Ammmm)*

"Would you, could you in the rain? Would you, could you on a train?" said Faceless Man #1.

Shawna's head was a radio receiver and it did not matter if she refused to listen, because it was inside her mind, those transmissions were coming in LOOOOOUUUUUD and clear and whenever she tried to think her own thoughts there was not pain, but a squelching buzzing static that swallowed everything up and her head became an empty drum of white noise. It was better to tune in and listen because that white noise would drive you crazy—

*(absolutely caaaaaa-rayzeeeee, I saaayyy)*

*(PUNISH the guilty PUNISH the guilty)*

*(yessss yessss I will do it in the rain I will do it on a train I will kill them in the dark I will kill them in a park)*

—so she was listening and what she was hearing, loud and oh-so clear, were not the voices of the Faceless Men but her own voice and it sounded very nice, very soft, very in control and that's how she knew she had bested them: "...I will find them here, there, and everywhere, said the girl in the chair. I'll find the guilty and fry 'em in a pan, this I'll do but only for you, Sam-I-Am..."

# WASHINGTON D.C.

## WHITE HOUSE, OVAL OFFICE

**3:46 P.M.**

Robert Pershing was not a man who liked to be maneuvered into a corner, but that's what he was getting today. He'd expected this meeting, but he did not expect such a brash display of bravado from the President and his inner circle. The commander-in-chief was known for his calm and civility, but that was giving way now. The stress was getting to him. He was beginning to crack.

*Well, this is going even better than I could have hoped for*, Pershing thought, inwardly grinning ear to ear.

As he was watched, he watched, and as he was studied, he studied. The President stood behind his desk, FDR's desk actually, glaring down at the CIA Director, Maddie Hughes and Adam Tiggman seated nearby. Everyone was tense, expectant. And why not? The country was falling.

On the desk was a transcript of his discussion with Admiral Paulus of ONI concerning the coup. There were some other documents there as well, but nothing concrete. They knew it. Pershing knew it. They were trying to make him sweat, but they were hopelessly out of their league.

"So, let me understand this, Mr. President," he said, studying the bottle of wine he had brought. It was uncorked on the desk, waiting. "You tasked Adam with investigating me? Am I understanding this?"

"You are."

Pershing nodded. "And, in the process, my car was bugged?"

Tiggman shook his head. "No, no, we did not authorize any wiretapping. We received this recording anonymously. The source is uncertain."

Pershing did his very best to appear grave, even though there was absolutely nothing they were going to say that he didn't already know about...courtesy of his own illegal wiretapping of the offices of Adam Tiggman and Maddie Hughes.

"That is you on the recording," the President said. "You're not going to sit here and deny that, are you?"

"Of course not. The conversation is between myself and Admiral Paulus, just as you already know. It was a privileged conversation not intended for scrutiny by untrained minds and careless ears."

It was a dig, but it bounced right off Tiggman. As an attorney, he was impervious to insults. Which was fine, because it wasn't directed at him but at Maddie. She had a temper and Pershing was an old hand at manipulating people like her.

True to form, she was incensed. Her dark eyes were narrowed, her lower lip trembling.

*Excellent*, Pershing thought.

"Would you like to tell us what you and Admiral Paulus were discussing, or should we tell you?"

He smiled thinly. "Mr. President, at this point I would like to file a formal complaint that I am not comfortable discussing the particulars of this matter with the DHS Secretary. I have nothing but great respect for Ms. Hughes, but I believe her knowledge of the inside workings of the international scene is lacking."

"Cut the shit," Maddie said, her cheeks reddening.

"Yes, Bob, let's do cut the shit."

All eyes were on him now. Pershing licked his lips and sighed. "What Admiral Paulus and I were discussing was a proposed—and I must emphasize *proposed*—political operation against the Islamic Republic of Mauritania. I'm sure the Admiral will gladly bear me out on this."

"Oh, come on," Maddie said. "You're flat-out lying."

"Am I missing something?"

"No, as usual, Bob, you're not missing a thing," she said. "The members of this cabinet are being systematically removed by someone who is taking advantage of the BioGen outbreak. That someone is you."

Pershing glared at her. "I'm offended by such an accusation."

"It's not an accusation, it's a fact."

"Then produce your evidence."

Maddie rolled her eyes. Tiggman just watched. And the President lost it. "Goddammit, Bob! Are you saying that you've had nothing whatsoever to do with what's been happening in this country? That you are not willingly plotting to overthrow this administration with a circle of confederates that include Admiral Paulus and General Mason of the JCS?"

"I categorically deny it, Mr. President."

"And do you deny the existence of a group known as The Collective?"

This one stopped Pershing cold. Where the hell was this coming from? But then he knew: Maddie Hughes. It was exactly the sort of conspiratorial thinking she was known for. "Sir, the existence of this so-called Collective has been debunked time and again. It's not worth bringing to the table."

"So, you're saying they do not exist?" Tiggman said.

"I am."

"Dammit, you're lying to us!" the President snapped. "I'll give you one more chance to tell the truth and if you don't, swear to God, I will demand your resignation!"

Pershing's demeanor did not change. He was cool, calm, and most assuredly collected. "Mr. President," he said after a lengthy silence. "Are you well?"

"I'm in complete command of my faculties, damn you!"

Tiggman tried to intercede. "Sir, please, if we could just—"

"Bullshit!" the President said, slamming his fist down on his desk. "This is no time for politically correct fuckwongling! Bob, you are treading on very thin ice and at a time when this country needs a unified front!"

Maddie was practically in love.

Pershing stood up. "If you are questioning my loyalty, then you, sir, with all due respect, are certainly not well. How dare you infer that I am a traitor. How dare you call me anything but a patriot. I have shed blood and tears for this country. I have suffered. I have put my needs last and unlike others in this room, the needs of this great nation have always come before those of lobbyists and political puppet masters."

"Enough," the President said. "I want your resignation by morning. Not a moment longer. I do not ask for it, sir, I demand it!"

Pershing looked to each set of eyes in the room. "Then you are making a horrendous mistake, Mr. President. You are putting conspiracy theories before facts and national security." He stepped towards the door, then stopped. "But, yes, you can certainly seek my resignation, but I categorically state that you will not get it under any circumstances."

The door closed.

"That sonofabitch," Maddie said under her breath.

The President slowly sat down. "If I don't have it by morning, Adam, I'll have no choice but to have Bob Pershing forcibly removed."

"Go easy, sir," Tiggman said. "This is politically volatile stuff."

"You should have fired him and thrown his ass into the street...Mr. President," Maddie said. From the look on her face she would have relished the very idea. "I say we drink a toast to getting rid of him."

The President, still visibly shaken, took a deep breath and appraised the bottle of wine that Pershing had brought as a gift. He always brought an expensive bottle and today was no exception. "A Chateau-Lafite Rothschild 1982...hell, we can't let this go to waste. Had Bob known what he was in for, he would have never brought this."

"I'll drink to that," Maddie said.

Glasses were poured and wine was sipped and enjoyed. Tiggman finished his glass and stepped over to the windows. He looked pensive.

"Is something bothering you, Adam?" the President finally asked.

"Maybe." Tiggman shrugged. "I have a very bad feeling, sir. I can't get past the notion that Bob *did* know what he was in for. Which begs the question—just what exactly are we in for?"

461

"Maybe." Tiggman shrugged. "I have a very bad feeling, sir. I can't get past the notion that Bob *did* know what he was in for. Which begs the question—just what exactly are we in for?"

# CHICAGO, CHINATOWN

## PING TOM MEMORIAL PARK

**5:15 P.M.**

Harry had spent all day being shuffled from one location to the other by his tour guides, Jerry and Frank. Apparently, whoever he was scheduled to meet was more than a little cautious and kept changing his or her mind as to where that should be. Finally, they took a water taxi to the park and Harry was left at the pagoda.

"This is where we say goodbye," Jerry told him. "You won't see us again."

"But—"

But they were already gone and he sat there, thinking, smoking, and worrying. There were more choppers in the air than usual and three times now in the past hour he had heard gunshots coming from across the river. Martial law. Things were getting worse all the time. The worms were infesting and the country was crumbling. It was a mess and he honestly didn't see what could possibly lift the nation from this horrendous onslaught and restore order.

He thought about Shawna.

He wondered if he'd ever see her again. He felt guilty about it all and mainly because he had slept with her. Had she really wanted that, or had he manipulated her into it? A typical middle-aged man desiring a younger, sexy, pretty woman? He wasn't sure. He really wasn't sure. He was so mixed up. Some of it was the drugs, yes, and much of it was the whirlwind of events in the past days, but more than a little of it was his own conflicted emotions. He desired her. He cared for her. But at the same time, he felt very protective and fatherly about her. The sex thing had felt perfectly right at the time and now it just felt wrong in every way. She was confused, naïve, and the last thing she needed was another swinging dick in her life.

*But it was consensual, wasn't it? She didn't do it just to appease me... did she?*

Oh hell, he hoped not. The idea made him feel dirty like he'd used her. But as he thought that, he reminded himself that he was not talking about some virginal prom queen here. Shawna, God bless her, was a gold digger who routinely used sex as leverage in her relationships with wealthy men, many of whom were married.

*You used each other and that's what it all boils down to. Don't worry about it. Your relationship with her has always been more than a little odd.*

That made him feel marginally better, but only until he began to wonder where she was and what sort of awful things might have been done to her, if she was even alive. Because there was a good chance that—

"Don't turn around," a voice said.

Harry froze there on the bench, a breath wedged in his throat, his heart racing. There was a hand on his shoulder. It was not menacing exactly, but more to keep him sitting and facing forward.

"If you're going to put a couple in my head," he said, "go ahead. I won't make a fuss. I'm too tired."

"It's nothing like that, I assure you. I set this meeting up at the behest of someone in a position of some power that wishes to remain anonymous. It's better if you do not see my face."

The voice was clear and calm, well-spoken. It belonged, Harry guessed, to a man of middle years who was educated, held a position of authority, and had grown up in New York City, judging by the lingering accent in certain words.

"Would I recognize you?"

The man sighed. "Possibly."

"Let's leave it at that then." Harry cleared his throat, lighting a cigarette with a hand that trembled despite all his efforts. "You arranged to get me out of the Warehouse and away from the Old Man?"

"I did."

"Then I thank you for that."

"Don't thank me yet. You are no longer wanted by S5, but what I am about to give you will make you a great deal of enemies. Very powerful, influential enemies. The person I represent believes you will do the right thing with it."

A yellow envelope was handed over his shoulder. He took it. There was something very small in it.

"A flash drive," the voice said.

"And?"

"What's on it is world-shaking. It's dynamite, as they say in the movies. It will ruin the careers of countless power players. You have been told, we all have been told, through selected media outlets that what is currently going on is the result of a bioterror attack by radical Islam. That is true and false. When you view what's on that drive, you'll see exactly the nature of the threat matrix, and you will learn that the BioGenesis outbreak is no accident, but only one step in a much greater and darker agenda."

"You're scaring me. I'm not too big of a man to admit that."

The man sighed again. "You should be scared. We should all be scared."

"And you want me to go public with this?"

"It is our hope. Everything you need to know along with a list of related black budget operations, names, places, abundant facts and figures. Altogether, Mr. Niles, what you hold in your hands is something that will make Watergate and Iran–Contra appear positively pedestrian. I cannot emphasize this enough. We hope you'll do the right thing with this, but, if not—and we can easily understand why you may want no part of it—see to it that it reaches the proper hands where it can be disseminated for the good of the taxpayers before it is too late."

"But why me?" Harry asked. "I'm a tabloid writer."

"Once you were something else, though, weren't you?"

"But—"

"I'm walking away now, Mr. Niles. Do the right thing."

"Wait... do you know where my friend is?"

"Your friend?"

"Shawna Geddes."

"Unfortunately, I do not. I wish you luck in finding her. If we can help, we will. Remember: the clock is ticking. Good day to you."

Harry sat there, the cigarette burned down to an ash in his hands. He tossed it away. He heard the footsteps of his mystery guest fade away. He relaxed slightly. But only for a moment. He opened the envelope and palmed the flash drive. He slipped it in his pocket. This was something he'd always dreamed of—a meeting with a real Deep Throat, someone who knew where all the bodies were buried. Why did he feel so disillusioned over it all?

*Because you're scared. You're middle-aged and comfortable with your meaningless little life. You don't want this kind of knowledge.*

Regardless, he had it. Now it was time to find out exactly what he had. It was time to roll over the rotting log of the country and see what squirmed in the darkness beneath.

Shaking, terrified, he walked off.

# LOCATION UNKNOWN

## THE BIRD NEST, S5 BEHAVIORAL SCIENCES FACILITY

**6:46 P.M.**

*There is something in her hand.*
*There is something in her brain.*
*Brain rhymes with train and pain.*
(connect connect the two)
*Will you? Won't you? Can you do it?*
(no please)
*She knows everything and she knows nothing. There is that thing in her hand and she must connect her mind to it until they are one, unified in a single dynamic purpose.*
(use it)
(use it)
(you must use it)
*Her entire body shakes and red dots explode in her head. She catches glimpses of faces and awful places, things she must never remember and those she does not dare forget.*
(can you will you near or far)
*In her hand there is a gun and her fingers are wrapped tightly around it, melded to it. It is her and she is it and even though something tells her there are reasons she cannot do the things asked of her, she knows she will because that Sam-I-Am has asked her to and she cannot refuse him.*
(can you will you won't you near or far)
(kill them kill them here they are)
*She hears Sam-I-Am's voice and it tells her what to do, how it must be accomplished and how simple it will all be. The gun is in her hand and she must now use it. That's the most important thing. To refuse is to know pain and suffer*

*horrible agonies, but to comply brings peace and joy and a wonderful, if secret, sense of accomplishment.*

(get them get them in the cell hurry hurry before they tell)

*She steps forward, seeing them and knowing how dangerous they are and only by eradicating the danger can she feel better, so she must do this thing, she must, she must...*

(do it do it do it now)

**6:51 P.M.**

Gabe Hebberman was not sure how long they had kept him there or how many beatings and horrible deprivations he had endured. He was not alone. There was another with him and his name was McKenna. It was not his real name. Gabe knew that. In this awful place, nothing was real.

"Someone's coming," McKenna said. "Listen."

Gabe tried to quiet his breathing and the steady boom-boom-boom of his heart as it threatened to explode in his chest. What more could they possibly want from him? He had told them all there was to tell; there was nothing else. The torture, the drugs they injected him with, the dark cell, the regression... it had brought forth no new details because he simply didn't know anything else.

The footsteps stopped.

He could hear a low breathing outside the cell. Oh God, what did this mean? What were they going to do to them now? The cell door was opened, and a figure stood there. It was a woman and her eyes were bright, terribly bright like incandescent bulbs. She looked at him and at McKenna, back and forth, back and forth. He allowed himself to smile with recognition, but the smile faded because she did not know him—her face was blank, her lips drawn into a cold and cruel line.

In Gabe's head, there were horrible flashes of the things they had done to him—the screaming, the darkness, the probing and cutting, the injecting and immersion, the red lights, dear God, the dreadful red lights that made your brain bake inside your skull—

"Shawna," he heard his voice say and it was old, weary, and broken.

The girl stood there, her head cocked to the side like an animal that was confused. She seemed to be silently forming words with her mouth.

"She's been programmed," McKenna said. "She's a Sigma. It's temporary, but it's deep. She doesn't remember you. They won't let her."

Gabe knew then that he was a fly trapped in a spider's web. He was entangled in the silk and there was no escape as the spider crept closer and closer still.

"Shawna," he said, his voice so terribly pathetic and weak. "Oh please look at me, Shawna. It's *me*. It's Gabe. Harry's friend. He works for me. Please, dear, please try to remember. You stayed at my house when you were in trouble... can't you remember?"

"It's pointless," McKenna said, fatalistic in his final hour as he had been every day of his life. "They've blanked her recall. She only knows what they tell her. Sigmas are temporarily programmed to carry out certain operations over a period of days. Then... then they forget."

"Shawna!" Gabe shouted with everything he had left.

She jerked as if she had been jolted. She shook her head back and forth. Then she screamed.

"Shawna!'

She was shaking and screaming now, her entire body quaking.

"SHAWNA!"

Then she stopped moving, stopped screaming, stopped everything. She was still and stiff as a corpse. Her mouth opened and closed rapidly. Her eyes blinked, focusing and unfocusing.

Wiping sweat from his face with a shaking hand, Gabe said, "Listen to me, Shawna. Hear my voice and remember it. I'm your friend. The ones that did this to you are your enemies."

"Do it, do it," she said in a loud voice. "Before they tell."

"Shawna! No!"

She stepped forward and brought the Glock 9mm up. Her eyes lit with that weird glow, that animal shine, she squeezed the trigger, painting up the wall of the cell with McKenna's blood and brains. He shook a moment and slumped over.

Then she aimed the gun at Gabe. "You must not ever, never tell. Sam said so."

"Please..."

The bullet went into Gabe's left eye socket, blowing out the back of his head in a wet spray of skull fragments and gray matter. He fell to the floor in a loose-limbed heap. Shawna stared at the gun for a moment or two, then dropped it. She turned and exited the cell. Thirty seconds later, she had no memory of what she had just done.

# CHICAGO, WEST MONTROSE AVENUE

## RAVENSWOOD

**7:15 P.M.**

It didn't take Harry long to realize that what he had on the flash drive was indeed dynamite, as his friend in Ping Tom Park had said. In fact, that didn't even begin to cover it. No, not dynamite but a freaking nuclear weapon. Because it was all here, all the answers to all the questions that anyone could possibly ask. The dirty agendas and dirty power players were finally, ultimately revealed.

It was a bombshell. Disturbing to say the least. In the old days he had lusted for full disclosure like this. But now that it was in his hands, he did not want it. It was too big. Too dangerous. Too damning. It would shake the country to its roots, tumble dynasties, expose all the crawly things in the big, filthy military-industrial complex...and in the process, probably destroy the infrastructure of the free world. People were going to be pissed. They were going to tear the political machine apart.

He didn't want that kind of power.

He had lost his edge through the years. This was for someone who still had the passion. He was too lazy now, too content in his ignorance. This needed someone who still had the fire. He wasn't about to throw the flash drive in a drawer and forget it, no, he would sent it to people who would know exactly what to do with it. Then from the sidelines, he would watch the death of the machine.

*But there's a time limit and you know it,* he thought with rising anxiety. *If you wait twenty-four hours, no one will care. In fact, they won't be able to care.*

The world would change forever...

# RICHMOND, VIRGINIA

## CBT CORPORATE HEADQUARTERS

**7:22 P.M.**

Liz Toma studied the projections on her desk and each one was more guarded and pessimistic than the last. The parasite infestation was spreading in every direction. There were major outbreaks in Canada and Mexico, Brazil and Argentina. The UK was sealing its boarders. All European flights were grounded. Asia and Africa were particularly hard hit, as were the republics of the former Soviet Union. BioGen had been unleashed as part of the agenda for global domination and now it had become a species-threatening event. At CBT, there was only a skeleton crew as everyone either had it or was afraid to leave their houses and apartments for fear of infection.

The world was now ruled by fear, just as The Collective had planned. This was the death blow to the old ways. A brave new world was poised to replace it.

She picked up her cell and called one of her 3Eye operatives. "Was the package delivered successfully?"

"It was."

"How did he take it?"

"Hard to say. I guess we'll have to rely on his journalistic instincts. I'll monitor the situation."

She broke the connection. Good. That much was done. That was the first step of her own little agenda. By the time they discovered the fly in their ointment, it would be far, far too late to do anything about it. This made her smile, but it didn't last long as she contemplated the small refrigerated box on her desk. This was it. It was in there. The very thing they would not suspect.

She checked the time.

Any minute now.

She had quit smoking ten years before, but she had bought a pack that morning. Although smoking was forbidden inside CBT, she took out a Marlboro Red and lit up. It wasn't as if anyone would dare question what she was doing. She took long, slow drags, the nicotine firing in her brain. As was the way with it, it felt like a cloud had been lifted and she could see clearly for the first time in years.

"What nasty, addictive stuff it indeed is," she said, contemplating her cigarette.

She waited.

She smoked.

She waited some more.

The phone rang. Just the sound of her ringtone—a simple chiming, no silly show tunes or pop culture sound bites—went right up her spine and made her belly roll over like a startled hedgehog. Her entire body went tense, it coiled like a spring. She wanted to run out the door and drive, drive, drive until she reached her secluded cabin on the Shenandoah River, a place she had not even been near since Astrid's death.

But there was no running, no hiding, there was only endgame.

She picked up the phone. "Yes?"

"Hello, Elizabeth," said Mr. Brown. "And how are you this day?"

"Quite fine, thank you. Much better than the country at large, I would say."

"Yes," he said, then giggled momentarily as if it was a joke. At to him, it probably was. "Yes, indeed. At any rate, we have considered your request for full disclosure and, quite unanimously, we've decided on complete inclusion in your case."

"I'm glad to hear that."

"This will be a big step for you, my dear, but I'm sure you can handle it. You're our kind of people and I have no doubt that our goals are the same. Will you be free at eleven tomorrow morning?"

Her heart pounding, she said, "Yes."

"You know the Piedmont Building in D.C.?"

"Of course."

"Good. Be there. You will be guided to our chambers. We will see you then."

That was it. She was either being brought in or groomed for murder. If it was the former, all the much better, but if it was the latter, she could count on Mr. Brown's arrogance: he would tell her face to face.

She lit another cigarette and took a photograph out of her desk. It was of Astrid and she at the cabin. A selfie she had never been able to let go of.

"Soon, darling," she whispered. "Very soon now."

# FORT BELVOIR

## EN ROUTE

**8:53 P.M.**

Oh, it had been a merry hunt, but it had to end sooner or later. And it was predestined who would come out on top. It could only be one man and that had to be Tommy Quillan. There could have been no other outcome.

For some hours now since capturing the elusive Sheikh Sa'ad al Khalafari, one of the most wanted men in the world, and getting him aboard an Army C-17 Globemaster, Quillan had been watching him, trying to ascertain what made this man a prophet of the jihad, someone that thousands would fawn over and kiss the feet of. Sa'ad was filthy, insane, and delusional. There was nothing special about him. For all intents and purposes, he was just another homeless man from the Motor City.

Pershing insisted that he wanted Sa'ad alive. He was to be used as a propaganda tool as were dozens of other martyrs arrested in the country to bolster the fiction of Yankee Alert. They would be paraded before the cameras, the architects of the BioGen outbreak. Enemies of the state that would either be executed outright under the auspices of martial law or held permanently in some dark dungeon at an undisclosed location. No one (hopefully) would ever learn who created the worms in the first place or that the CIA and other security organizations had allowed these men to enter the country or that they had freely supplied them with BioGen spawn so they would spread it coast to coast.

*To have the very effect it's having*, Quillan thought. *All part of their game to destabilize the country.*

In the mammoth cargo bay of the C-17, Quillan was alone with his prisoner. He had Sheikh Sa'ad tied to the bulkhead where he watched and watched and watched him. He had beaten him, tortured him, even urinated on him, but it did little good—he could not answers questions about his network or

Al-Qaeda sleeper cells in the United States or Pan-Islamic terrorism in general. He was too far gone. He didn't even seem to know who he was, what he was, or his purpose here on the planet.

It was disappointing. The hunt had ended with a lunatic.

*And here I brought a present half way around the world for you,* Quillan thought, staring down at the empty specimen jar at his feet. It had contained a worm. He had taken if off a dead cleric in Afghanistan, one of some seventy worms that had been smuggled into India, he had learned, and secreted into the water supply of Calcutta.

It was the last one of that particular shipment. The cleric had saved it for himself.

It had been two days now since Quillan had swallowed it. At first, there had really been nothing but a sense of nausea, something which might have been more psychological than physical. This was followed by a voracious hunger that was insatiable. And now in the past few hours, regular abdominal pains and an odd sort of crawling sensation in his head as if something was circumnavigating the inside of his skull.

*I must be infested.*

He giggled.

Sheikh Sa'ad fought against the wires that bound him to the bulkhead. He was shaking and straining and muttering in Arabic, his eyes bulging from his head.

*Shit, shit, and shit!*

Here came the pains again. They dug deep into Quillan's guts with white-hot fingers and he went down to his knees, shuddering and retching out a thin, yellow bile. He blacked out for a moment as the pain escalated. He could take more agony than most, but even he had his limits.

He could feel them not just in his belly, but in his head and behind his eyes. They were corkscrewing in him and the pain was unbelievable. He tried to think, to reason, to make sense of what was going on, but who and what he was was gradually fading. He was quickly becoming a non-entity, a host, a vessel. *Yes, yes! That's it! A vessel for the greater doom of the world!* Then even this was gone.

He stood up, hovering over Sheikh Sa'ad, a mindless thing, a worm zombie with no will of his own. He was only aware of the hunger that spiked in his belly. There was nothing else.

The skin of his face was pulsating, his belly quivering. He opened his mouth and screamed as his eyes blew from their sockets like rotten, slimy eggs and worms emerged, twisting hungrily in the air. Another, larger parasite emerged from his mouth like some immense, oily white phallus. All of them opened their mouths, mewling, demanding to be fed.

Quillan brought them in close to Sheikh Sa'ad's fear-distorted face. They were hungry and he let them eat.

# CHICAGO, RIVER NORTH

## THE WAREHOUSE

**9:31 P.M.**

The Old Man was not happy He was tense, nervous, possibly even frightened. Dr. Benheim had never seen him like that before and it scared him.

"We don't have the time for nonsense. Call everyone in. And I mean everyone. I want the entire Op Center shut down, sterilized, and packed up tonight."

Benheim shook his head. "That's not possible. It'll take twenty-four hours at the very least. We set it up in eight, but taking it apart is an entirely different matter. I think you know that."

"We don't have a choice."

"Maybe if you could tell me what this is about."

The Old Man shook his head. "The country is in chaos and this city is poised to become a war zone."

"But we're safe here. The compound is secure."

"I don't have time to debate this. Orders are orders and this one comes from the very top. This facility is to be dismantled today. I want all animals and specimens incinerated along with all samples and contaminated medical waste. I want all files backed up and computer work stations packed away. Equipment can left behind, but it must be sanitized and destroyed. Tomorrow will be too late. Do you understand?"

"Yes, I'll cut the order. I just wish I knew why. We were making significant progress in—"

The Old Man hooked Benheim by the elbow and towed him into his makeshift office. They had worked together many years in one project after another. He not only respected the man, but he liked him. He was one of the very few people he considered a friend. What he had to say could only be between the two of them. Problem was, he feared they were being listened to.

"Hell is this?" Benheim asked, not used to being handled like that.

The Old Man got in very close to his face, so close it looked like he wanted to kiss him. "Listen to me," he whispered. "According to latest estimates, this city has a seventy-four percent rate of infection. We're fighting a losing battle here. Unfortunately, our superiors are throwing in the towel. They're cutting their losses and that includes us."

Benheim swallowed. "And then what?"

The Old Man looked around. "That's what worries me."

"How so?"

"We're going to be shut down."

"Then we're shut down. So what?"

"Don't be so naïve. You know what kind of people we're dealing with here."

Benheim did. He did not like them and never had. But in the field of pure biological research, their resources were unlimited. He wouldn't have been the first scientist they wooed and won with handsome pay, benefits, and the opportunity to toy with things that were generally thought to be the province of science fiction. Technologies that were exotic and unbelievable.

"There are dozens of temporary Op Centers like this across the country. And every one of them is going to be shut down, erased, eradicated. The entire thing will be blamed on domestic terrorists. I got that through clandestine channels. Tomorrow an armed group will hit this place with everything they have. When they leave, they'll leave nothing left alive. They'll burn everything."

"They're going to kill us?" Benheim said. "Dear God, we just did what they asked. We were only following orders."

The Old Man nearly laughed. Such naiveté. How had this man survived in the business this long? He nearly felt sorry for him.

"We're nearly out of time."

"But can't you call your people at CBT—"

"They're not even answering my calls."

"There's no way out, is there?"

"I just don't know. It could happen tomorrow or ten minutes from now for all I know," the Old Man admitted.

Seconds later, the entire Op Center exploded and went up in a roaring fireball that spread burning wreckage for two square blocks.

# CHICAGO, RIVER NORTH

## SEDGWICK STREET

**9:45 P.M.**

Shawna looked up when she heard the explosion. It seemed to rock the world. Like the other stragglers out on the walks that evening, she wondered what had happened now. The world certainly was becoming a strange place. There was danger and disaster everywhere.

She watched as people scurried about. As police vehicles came screaming up the road, followed by several Humvees of the National Guard. High above, a helicopter swooped down, shining a spotlight down onto the dying city.

It was quite a night.

Shawna stood there, thinking. Whatever was in her mind passed quickly enough. She lit a cigarette and watched the smoke rising into the sky a few streets over.

She wondered where Harry was.

She had to find him.

It was the most important thing she would ever do.

# CHICAGO, BUCKTOWN

## ST. MARY'S

**10:20 P.M.**

Tonight, for the first time in many years, Elaine Geddes felt the power of the church. She felt the presence of Christ within her and without her as she prepared to commune with God and offer her soul unto him.

*And not just for me*, she thought, *but for Shawna. I need you, oh Lord, to watch over her and bring her back into the fold if you can.*

The church was nearly full tonight. The faithful had been called upon to this special emergency mass to pray for the country and the horrendous suffering on every front. Elaine watched as people received the host and she was certain that they felt the hand of God as she did. Some of them could barely walk afterwards—they were swept up in the mystery of faith, feeling what she had been feeling all day, that the holy spirit was reaching out to them.

She had not been this excited in church since she was a child! Oh, how she wished Shawna was there because she would have felt it, too, despite her terrible lifestyle and misguided atheism. This would have been the night that would have changed everything for her. She would have been recreated as the Lord God intended.

Now the usher was guiding Elaine's row up to the altar. No one was forgotten. It was all very orderly and respectful. That was even more important tonight as they asked Jesus Christ to intervene on behalf of the nation.

Elaine approached Father McHale. He did not look well. That was the first thing she noticed. He was pale, sallow, his eyes bloodshot. He was overdoing it again, sacrificing himself body and soul for his congregation. It wouldn't have been the first time.

He held a chalice in his left hand which was odd. But, then, tonight of all nights, it was not her place to question. She need only accept and her acceptance was acquiescence of God's plan.

Pressing her hands together in prayer, Elaine closed her eyes, opened her mouth and extended her tongue.

"The body of Christ," Father McHale said, placing the host upon her tongue.

Elaine gagged as she felt something squirming in her mouth. The ushers took hold of her as it slid down her throat. There was a moment of absolute terror and absolute repulsion as the worm invaded her...then, a state of grace. This was communion. This was the blood and body of the almighty living God. She understood as she had never understood before.

She was made one with Christ.

# CHICAGO, WEST MONTROSE AVENUE

## RAVENSWOOD

**11:45 P.M.**

Harry approached his building with more than a little trepidation. His mysterious benefactor at Ping Tom said that he was no longer wanted by S5, but he had a little trouble believing that. For all he knew, he had just been set up with an elaborately crafted trap that he was now waltzing right into. The problem was it was nearly curfew time. And if he was caught out in the streets, he would be detained, arrested, or even shot on sight. The latter seemed more likely given the rioting and burning that was going on in the city.

Warily, tense, he let himself into his building with his key card.

Okay. That was a beginning. At least he hadn't been gunned down out in the street. But that didn't mean they wouldn't be waiting in one of the corridors or in his apartment once he stepped through the door.

*He said I was no longer a target.*

*Sure. But do you believe that?*

He sighed. He'd been out of the game too long. He didn't know what to think. In the old days, he lived by his wits with a healthy sense of paranoia concerning everything and anyone. It had been second nature like breathing and pissing.

But now?

It just wasn't in his blood anymore and he was certain he was making mistakes, putting himself in terrible danger. He took the elevator to his floor and as he stepped out, someone was waiting for him. His heart jumped in his chest, but it was just Linda, the building super.

"Oh, Harry," she said. "I've been waiting for you."

And here his paranoia flared like an ulcer. He looked at her with a combination of fear and trepidation. *Oh Christ, not Linda. She can't be one of them.* He nearly laughed at himself for his naiveté—of course she could be one of them. The intelligence services hired people from every walk of life. The best cleaners were the ones that were the most nonthreatening, the ones nobody would suspect.

"Well, here I am."

"That friend of yours came by earlier. She said she needed to see you. She said it was important."

"What friend?"

"The girl. The pretty one."

He felt hope surge inside him. "Shawna?"

"Yes, I believe so. She stopped by, said it was important she talk with you. She gave me a number. I slid it under your door. I was going to put it into your mailbox, but then I thought, what if he doesn't check his mail?"

"Thanks, Linda."

"Is something wrong, Harry?"

"Oh no. Just worried like everyone else with what's going on."

"Hang tight," Linda said. "This, too, will pass."

Harry thanked her and went to his apartment. *This, too, will pass.* American optimism that in the end, everything would be okay. But she didn't know what was going on, what was about to happen. If she did, she would not sleep tonight. Much like the staff of the Washington *Post* would not be sleeping tonight with what he had sent them.

The corridors were empty. He fumbled his access code twice before getting it right. Then he was in. He shut the door and locked it, threw the dead bolt. He saw the slip of paper on the floor that Linda had spoken of. Okay. With trembling hands, he picked it up. He read the number on it three times, shaking his head.

It made no sense.

The number was for Abe's landline.

# AUGUST 29

# WASHINGTON D.C.

## WHITE HOUSE, OVAL OFFICE

**12:09 A.M.**

As the President stared at the empty wine bottle on his desk (as he had been doing on and off for many hours now because it was green, green, it was emerald like the city, *his* city), he remembered that it had been a gift from Bob Pershing, his Director of Central Intelligence, *Bobby Boy, Booby, bub-bub-bub boo-boo-boo*, the last loyal patriot in the country.

No!

NO! NO! NO! NOOOOOOO!!!!

Bob Pershing was a traitor. He was trying to take over the country. He was attempting to stage a military coup now that the nation was on its knees because of the worm outbreak. *Dirty stinking goddamned turncoat!* Memories of the meeting with Pershing flashed through the President's mind. But like so many other things, it was no longer making sense. He wavered between seeing things with a disturbing hallucinogenic clarity to seeing them as blurry, abstract ideas and half-formed possibilities.

"Damn, but that was good wine," he said.

"It was delicious," Maddie Hughes agreed, nodding her head. She was sprawled on the sofa across the room, using her finger like a paintbrush as she drew images in the air, trying desperately to describe the things she saw in her mind, which were at once silly *and* frightening.

Adam Tiggman, White House Counsel, was still there. He was standing before the doors leading to the Rose Garden and watching the world.

"How goes our great Union?" the President asked.

"I wonder if I stare out this window long enough if my image will be impressed upon the glass?" Tiggman said out loud, though he was certain he only thought it.

*Lemmings, lemmings, lemmings,* the President found himself thinking. *They're following me right off the cliff!*

There were a series of explosions that shook the White House. It was pure anarchy out there now and he wasn't really sure what was going on. Gunfire and explosions, shouting and screaming and dying, of course. Lots of dying. Lots and lots and lots of dying. His personal guard, Marine sentries, and Secret Service agents were firing at rioting crowds pressing up to the fence from Pennsylvania Avenue. Not that any of this was surprising in his tight, delusional world. The shit had definitely hit the fan. D.C. was a mess. The National Guard were fighting pitched battles with private militias and bodies were piling up in the streets, according to what was coming across his desk, none of which was good. Great sections of the city were burning now, and no one seemed interested in fighting the fires. Rioters were raiding from one neighborhood to the next. Sooner or later, they would reach the White House. That's what the President was told by what few advisors he still had left.

The majority of his staff was dead now.

With Maddie at his side, he had toured his domain from the West Wing to the East Wing, from the Press Briefing Room to the lobby, Map Room to the Presidential Library to the State Dining Room. What he saw was disturbing, horrible really, but in his current state of mind he was unable to process any of it correctly. Much of his staff had committed suicide, everyone from cooks to maids, secretaries to economic advisors to communications specialists to security personnel. They had hung themselves, slit their own throats and wrists, blew their brains out, swallowed poison...in fact, they had destroyed themselves to avoid what was taking the country. Even death was better than becoming a host. It was going on across the city and across the country, and maybe even the world.

The President didn't know because he was no longer taking international calls (or domestic ones for that matter). His security chief—who was out there battling crazies—had recommended that he leave the White House again and again. Marine Helicopter Squadron One was standing by to chopper him out of the city, but he wasn't having it. Let MHS1 stand the fuck down.

"A king does not abandon his castle when it's under siege," he told Maddie and she agreed completely.

In the Oval Office, he kept a tight eye on his kingdom, particularly the hub of the city, the central business district—7th Street to Pennsylvania Avenue to Mount Vernon Square and on and on—which was the most important part of D.C. in his opinion. He had live video feed from around his kingdom so he could watch the rioters surging down F Street, National Guard units firing at them, pitched battles between various military units, and people, what seemed hundreds of people, jumping off the roofs of tall buildings and splattering on the streets below, armored military and police vehicles rolling right over their remains.

Yes, it was quite a day, quite a day.

His last sane act of the day was to invoke the Insurrection Act of 1807 which gave him the power to deploy military units domestically to put down rebellion. Fort Bragg was standing by, as was Fort Stewart in Georgia, and the Marines at Camp Lejeune in North Carolina.

"THEY THINK I'M WEAK! THEY THINK I HAVE NO RESOLVE!" he shouted. "BUT THEY'LL SOON KNOW BETTER! I WILL DESTROY THIS COUNTRY BEFORE I HAND IT OVER TO TRAITORS!"

His voice echoed through the Oval Office and as he listened to it fade away, he began to laugh with a high, hysterical sound. Both Maddie and Tiggman looked at him with wide, glazed eyes as if they thought he was some kind of madman.

"What now, Mr. President?" Maddie asked.

There were a series of concussive booms that made the world shake and tremble. Something shattered down the corridor. The smell of smoke grew stronger.

"Airstrikes, sir. We've got quite a situation out there," she explained, studying her iPad. She seemed unconcerned that Adam Tiggman was relieving himself a few feet away. "There are terror bands seizing key locations in the city. We suspect they may be Blackpool and SOG units activated by Bob Pershing. SEAL Viper Teams and Delta Force Black Mambas are engaging them as we speak. I believe they just called in an airstrike on them."

"Excellent! I never trusted that bunch!"

That would show them that he would not bend nor sway in his dedication to the nation and the principles it stood for. He'd grind D.C. to rubble if he had to, but those bastards would not survive their treachery. Yes, yes, yes! It made him feel bigger than he had ever felt before in his life, omnipotent, a veritable god which clutched the destiny of the free world in his fist.

"THEY WILL NOT WIN! I WILL NOT ALLOW THEM TO WIN! THIS IS MY KINGDOM AND I RULE ABSOLUTELY!" he shouted. "IF I HAVE TO, I WILL CALL HELL DOWN ONTO THIS CITY TO PROTECT IT! THEY BETTER UNDERSTAND THAT!"

"Bravo, Mr. President," Maddie said. "No sacrifice is too great! If you have to level this city in a nuclear barrage, then so be it!"

"YES! THAT WILL MAKE THEM SEE HOW VERY POWERFUL I AM! HOW I STAND IN THE FACE OF ADVERSITY! THEY WILL KNOW WHO IS KING! WHO IS LORD GOD ALMIGHTY! WHO IS COMMANDER IN CHIEF! I'LL SACRIFICE MILLIONS IF I HAVE TO! I'LL WRITE HISTORY IN THEIR BLOOD!"

"But we must be prudent above all else," Tiggman said, shaking a few drops of urine from his penis. "If we kill everybody, who'll be left to vote for you?"

"TOUGH TITTY, SAID THE KITTY! LIFE AIN'T FAIR IN THE BIG BAD CITY! IT'S FULL OF PAIN AND AIN'T THAT A PITY?" said the President, remembering his mother saying the exact same thing to him before she gave him the strap. "THEY MUST UNDERSTAND WHO THE MASTER AND COMMANDER IS! I AM THE GREATEST MAN EVER TO LEAD THIS PROUD NATION! I AM THE GREATEST AMERICAN TO EVER HAVE LIVED! THERE CAN BE NO DOUBT THAT I AM THE MOST POPULAR PRESIDENT IN HISTORY!"

"Yes, *yes!*" Maddie cried, tears streaming down her face like some star-struck hormonal teenager who had finally met the popstar she fantasized over. "No one has ever been greater than you! You are the man the country has waited for! You are the one to lead! We worship you! We worship you!"

She fell to her knees and hugged his legs. She was his to command. Oh, if only he would let her prove her adoration! She wanted so badly to take his divine scepter into her mouth and swallow what he produced for the good of the nation.

Tiggman began laughing. He couldn't seem to stop. As he watched the President, the laughter filled him, bursting from every seam. He doubled over, tears rolling from his eyes. He was not certain what was so funny about his boss, but, man, it was hilarious.

Maddie was not about to put up with such disrespect. "Stop it. Do you hear me? *Stop it.*" But he only laughed louder. "You stop this right now!" She slapped him across the face and still he laughed. "You stop it, you fucking stupid little Jewboy! You goddamn kike! *Do you hear me, you motherfucking yid heeb hymie cocksucker!*"

By then, despite being slapped repeatedly, Tiggman was down on his knees, still laughing, out of his head with it.

The President did not seem to notice any of it. He strode back and forth with an exaggerated gait, his hand shoved inside his bedraggled suit like Napoleon. "OH, I WISH THAT FUCKING BOB PERSHING COULD SEE ME NOW!" he cried. "NOW I HAVE PURPOSE! NOW I HAVE DIRECTION! NOW I HAVE ABSO-FUCKING-LUTE MANIFEST DESTINY! *I* KNOW IT! *YOU* KNOW IT! THE ENTIRE GODDAMN COUNTRY KNOWS IT! THAT'S WHY I AM EVERYONE'S FAVORITE PRESIDENT!"

And out beyond the walls of Emerald City, there was sporadic gunfire and a distant explosion, a soundtrack to the final days of the office.

# WASHINGTON D.C.

## THE PENTAGON

**1:41 A.M.**

*Tick-tock, tick-tock, tick-tock.*

Time was running out and there was no one at the wheel of the country, no leader or guiding hand. Maybe all the mindless and easily manipulated taxpayers did not know it yet, but those in positions of power—like Arlene Rabin, Secretary of State—knew the awful truth that the flowers of this particular dog-and-pony show democracy had folded up and were withering at the roots.

She rose from her desk, something in the back of her mind telling her that she would soon be in line for the presidency, that it would fall into her lap and the idea terrified her. To be president was to be in the crosshairs and she did not want to be in the crosshairs.

A lurching, eye-watering stab of pain in her belly, the SecState rose from her desk, doubling over and spraying a scarlet, muddy vomit from her mouth. It went right down the front of her eight-hundred-dollar plaid jacket. She stumbled into the water cooler, wiping her mouth and leaving a bloody handprint on the wall just beneath a framed photo of the Prez himself.

*Tick-tock, tick-tock, tick-tock.*

Arlene considered herself a realist and even in this final hour, that did not change. She was infested and she knew it. There were worms in her. It was a horrible thing to have to admit and it had caused her more than a little anxiety and outright horror, but now she accepted it. It also helped that the parasites in her that were fighting for dominance amongst themselves were constantly juicing her with sporadic, conflicting bursts of neurotransmitters—specifically serotonin, dopamine, and norepinephrine—that pushed her psychologically up peaks only to kick her back down into valleys. Depression, anxiety, paranoia, hope, anger...her brain was a stew of chemicals and no mood seemed to last for more than a few minutes.

*This won't stop*, a voice informed her, *until you get those damn things out of you.*

Down on her knees now on the plush carpeting, she jabbed a finger down her throat and gagged. She knew how to induce vomiting. She had suffered from bulimia as a teenager and she had become a pro at it. Her belly rolled and heaved, bile shooting from her mouth in a hot stream.

Endorphins flooded her brain, making her emotionally content. Her guests wanted her to know that this was unnecessary. Only they could make her happy, only they could alleviate the crippling depression she'd known most of her adult life.

*But you are foreigners and infidels and invaders*, she thought. *You do not belong inside me.*

She crawled over the carpeting as her guts continued to spasm painfully. The worms offered her serotonin to inhibit the pain, making her feel better, then cutting her off so that she understood that deliverance could come only through their offices.

She clutched her stomach as they toyed with her, her eyes huge and glistening, threaded with brilliant red capillaries. *Fuck...you.* She shoved her finger down her throat again, searching for the elusive sweet spot as a sour bile squirted into her mouth. *That is their flavor, the taste of their secretions.* Knowing that she was on to them, they filled her mouth with sweetness...honey and sugar, chocolate and nougat and cherry fizz. They tried everything. Once they had tapped into her brain, nothing was beyond them. She was a machine to be driven and it was just a matter of learning how to handle her, how to turn corners and apply the accelerator, easing off on the brakes and clutch. She was a much tougher animal than most, but they would turn her into a thoroughbred.

She worked the finger in her throat and more bile came up. There was no time to disguise its unpleasant taste. The worms compensated, by tightening her esophagus and constricting her lungs. She gasped for air, falling face-first into the carpeting. It was plush and soft. Black dots popped in her head. She writhed, she fought, but the lack of oxygen took the fight out of her quickly enough as she felt sinuous forms sliding through her innards.

She could breathe again.

Of course, she could breathe again.

They weren't about to kill their beast of burden any more than a jockey knowingly rides his horse to death. Her wind back, Arlene threw herself into the fight with amazing vigor. She worked the sweet spot at the back of her throat while simultaneously punching herself in the stomach. It made her fold up, but she kept at it. It hurt her, yes, but it also hurt the worms. Bile and stomach acid spilled from her mouth as they tried to get their animal under control.

But she was not easily trained.

She lay there, gagging, contorting, her body contracting and releasing, contracting and releasing, as her eyes filled with blood and her bladder voided itself. Her mouth filled with a viscid, jellied slime that spurted from her nostrils with each rapid exhalation. She was winning and she knew it. The worms tried frantically to master her, but it was useless by that point—Arlene was doing the impossible and purging them. They fought frantically against her, but battle had been waged and now they were losing.

With one last immense contraction, she vomited out a slush of bloody tissue and two sixteen-inch worms came out with it, squirming in her waste products. White as a slug's belly, they twisted and mewled with a muted squeaking sound. She smashed them into a fleshy paste with her fists. Then she gagged again, a swollen mass coming up and ejecting with a greasy expectoration—a pulsating egg case that looked like it was breathing. She crushed it with a five-pound glass paperweight and it released a webby sludge of eggs, larval worms trying to escape into the carpeting.

Finally, filthy and blood-smeared, eyes bleeding and insane, she stepped over to the window and dove three stories to the pavement below.

She had won. *Tick-tock, tick-tock, tick-tock.*

# FORT MEADE, MARYLAND

## NATIONAL SECURITY AGENCY

**2:10 A.M.**

They were within hours of activation now and Gordon Parks could barely contain himself. He knew he should be getting some sleep because tomorrow was a big day—ha! It was the biggest day in history!—but there was no way in hell he was going to be able to shut his mind down. Just wouldn't happen.

*Imagine.*

*Just imagine*, he thought.

Within the next twenty-four hours history would not only be made but rewritten. That was the amazing thing. After activation, they could craft any fiction they so desired and wrap it up in a big, pretty bow and offer it up to John and Jane Q. Public and they would swallow it wholesale, without the slightest complaint or suspicion. Complaints of subterfuge and wrongdoing, corruption and graft, would all be things of the past.

Finally, ultimately, the powers that be (and Gordon was most certainly one of them) could begin leading this great nation to its ultimate destiny.

God bless America.

God bless us, one all.

# SUITLAND, MARYLAND

## NATIONAL MARITIME INTELLIGENCE CENTER

**3:30 A.M.**

*Bob, I'm so sorry,* Admiral Paulus thought with dismay and self-loathing, *but when the chips were down and it was time to seize the reins... I just didn't have the guts. I didn't have the initiative to see it through. I apologize for letting you down, for letting the country down, and, worse, for letting myself down... but in the end, I'm an old man and I'm so sick of it all and I'm so goddamned tired.*

Pershing had been calling for hours, but Paulus refused to answer any calls. He had hidden himself away and he wanted no one finding him, not until it was over with. He wanted them to remember him not as a conspirator but an honorable man, an officer and a gentleman.

His cell rang again. He shut it off and slid it into a drawer of his desk. It would hardly stop Bob Pershing. He had worked too hard and too long on this. He would not give in now. *He'll send people to find you. If you don't tell them what they want to hear and give them viable excuses for being incommunicado, they will kill you. It will look like a suicide.* He knew it was true. But not just a suicide. No, that wasn't Bob Pershing's way. Things would be doctored for dramatic effect. Some kiddie porn would be found on Paulus' phone or hard drive. Maybe drugs would be involved, human trafficking. Whatever it was, it would paint Paulus as a monster.

Oh yes, oh yes, oh yes.

He was only glad his wife was not around to see his disgrace. He swallowed a few fingers of whiskey, then began to type out a complete confession about the coup. He named names, dates, places. Everything he had been making notes of these past months went in there as well as all the dirt on Bob Pershing's dirty machine. When he was done, he duped the file to a flash drive and sent it to three different clouds. A copy also went to his lawyer and a certain congressman from Iowa who absolutely despised the CIA in general and Bob Pershing in particular.

There.

No more wet feet.

No going back.

No fucking retreat.

Feeling better than he had in some time, the Admiral finished his whiskey, thought of the old days, his wife, his parents, every one that had passed. Yes, it had been a good life, a meaningful life. But now it was over. He took out his service pistol and, quite calmly, inserted the barrel into his mouth and blew his brains out.

# WASHINGTON D.C.

## OVAL OFFICE PATIO

**3:53 A.M.**

The Eisenhower Executive Office Building was burning. Adam Tiggman stood there watching the flames shoot up into the night sky along with a storm of sparks which danced like fireflies high overhead. Black smoke blew across the White House grounds in great, churning clouds that made him cough and blackened his face.

*It's all coming apart now and there's nothing we can do about it. Nothing at all.*

The thought appeared in his mind and he wasn't sure if he had thought it at all. Then again, he wasn't sure about a lot of things anymore. He only knew he was paranoid and fearful and confused. He couldn't think or make sense of anything. He needed to run. To escape from Emerald City before the great Oz destroyed it with his hateful wrath.

He saw dark figures running around in the night, firing randomly at one another out on the South Lawn. On West Exec Avenue, he could see combatants illuminated by the fire, hiding in the rubble and shooting at each other.

It was time to get out.

# WASHINGTON D.C.

## THE ROSE GARDEN

**4:03 A.M.**

Hunched over with a carving knife in her hand, Maddie Hughes lifted her head up and released a screeching feral cry into the night. The fighting going on around her was invigorating and exciting. The staccato reports of automatic weapons, the smell of burning rubble and cordite, the screams of the dying... yes, yes, yes, that's what life was about. That's what it was really about. Forget those pretentious fictions about love and compassion, humanity and morality, life was about violence, about getting what you deserved, about striking before your enemy did, and lastly, seeking vengeance on those who betrayed you.

Betrayal in her mind took the form of Adam Tiggman. The President had trusted him and now he was running when that great man needed him most.

*It will not be allowed. The President anointed me as his war chief and I will not let him down.*

She ducked down as groups of figures passed within earshot. She did not know who they were, but she saw in the firelight that they wore the black fatigues of counterterrorist commandos.

*Move! Go now!*

She scampered away, drawing closer to the flaming hulk of the Eisenhower building. Someone was standing there, watching it burn, mesmerized by it. She moved in closer until her target was in view. There was no doubt by that point that it was Tiggman. He had made a fatal mistake in his betrayal—he had not run as fast and far away as he could have.

He let out a grunt when Maddie tackled him, driving him to the ground. He barely fought. That took a lot of the fun of it away. Not that it got him any sympathy. Maddie tussled with him for fifteen or twenty seconds, then slit his throat.

The President would be pleased. Another enemy of the state had been removed.

# WASHINGTON D.C., BOLLING AFB

## DEFENSE INTELLIGENCE AGENCY

**5:02 A.M.**

"It almost certainly came from Elizabeth Toma," DNI Charles VanderMissen said. "I can't imagine anyone else with this sort of information."

"I wonder what her agenda is," DDI Walter Sleshing mused. "I have a well-developed sense of paranoia when it comes to that woman. Any altruism from her is greatly suspect."

"And with good reason."

What she sent VanderMissen was, essentially, confirmation of what they had long suspected—that Bob Pershing of the CIA was indeed involved in a coup to overthrow the country. His co-conspirators were indeed Admiral Paulus and General Mason of the JCS. They figured that much. But what they hadn't known was that Pershing's plot was only the first step in something much larger, much more horrifying known as MINDWORM. Gordon Parks of the NSA seemed to be one of the architects of this. And if it wasn't stopped, the idea of a free society would no longer exist.

They'd been at it all night, trying to figure out how to handle this, who they could trust and who they could not. The information had to be gotten to the President, but he had sealed himself in the White House and refused to see anyone but his closest aides.

"There's something going on there," Sleshing said for not the first time. "He's no longer in control."

"But how to prove it."

"There's only one way—we have to get to him."

That was the problem. The White House Communications Agency was in complete disarray. And whether that was because of the heavy fighting around the White House and the Capitol Building or from the BioGenesis outbreak, it was anyone's guess.

"We should be hearing back from Charlie Goade any moment now," VanderMissen said.

He had never imagined the nation being in a situation like this. Everyone across the land wanted to know what was going on, but there was nothing coming out. Absolutely nothing. These were dire times and the nation waited to be reassured by their leaders, but, again, there was nothing. It had all been planned quite expertly by Bob Pershing and the conspirators. The Vice President was dead. The Speaker of the House and Senate President were missing. Secretary of State Rabin had committed suicide. Same for the Secretary of Defense. Key members of the President's cabinet had either been killed or had dropped out of sight. What it came down to was that the chain of command had been carefully eliminated. If—God help them—the President was dead, command was passed down the ladder to the Secretary of the Treasury.

And that was big trouble.

*And it's also exactly how fucking Pershing planned it*, VanderMissen knew.

The Treasury Secretary was Harold Manning, a former investment banker and an old friend of Bob Pershing. If the mantle fell to Manning, there was no doubt who would really be running the country.

Again, just as planned.

Which made getting to the President priority number one. They had to get this latest information to him one way or another. But getting there would mean going through some heavy fighting and landing right in the middle of a war zone. Neither VanderMissen or Sleshing wanted to use their resources at the SOCOM. There was every possibility that through Admiral Paulus they could no longer be trusted. The best bet was Charlie Goade at the FBI. He could get a chopper in there with a security detail of HRT counterterror operatives. It was going to be dicey as hell, but it was this or nothing.

It all depended on Charlie Goade now.

And the clock was ticking.

# THE WHITE HOUSE

## PENNSYLVANIA AVENUE

**6:06 A.M.**

As the sun came up, Maddie saw the bodies stretched across the avenue, hundreds of them, a veritable sea of corpses tangled together, heaped, piled, pressed into a great common whole.

She had never seen anything so beautiful in her life.

Although something buried deep in the back of her mind told her that it was an atrocity, she quickly shrugged that away because there was a greater significance to this endless charnel sculpture.

*They're here... they're here for me.*

The idea was exciting. Her drug-laced, super-charged ego told her that there was no doubt of it: she was, after all, the DHS Secretary, so was it really any wonder that they had taken their lives for her? Offered them up to she who walked in the shadows and breathed in the dark, the ultimate ghost of vengeance that hunted down the enemies of the nation and made sacrificial offerings of them, bathing in their blood to keep her youth?

The very idea made Maddie giggle like a little girl. *I sharpen my teeth on their bones and suck the blood from their throats. In the final analysis, I am Kali, I am the goddess of death and destruction, I seed doom unto the wind. I slay demons and devour the evil children of Islam. I am made eternal.*

She stood there for some time, swaying to unheard music, out of her mind, drooling and delusional. These were the bodies of spec ops soldiers and Blackpool terrorists, private militia extremists and protesters, government workers and journalists...a great seething pool of the dead. She watched crows and ravens and gulls picking at them. Stray dogs and rats gnawing upon throats and soft bellies.

Stark naked, she stepped into the sea of the burned, the shot, the dismembered, the slit and gutted and decomposing. Their blood was scarlet waters washing her feet, their flesh fine rare steak, tender and juicy. She delighted in what she saw and, more so, in what she felt—the glorious seeping, leaking, pulverized, oozing and slushy carpet of the dead. She was the DHS Goddess of Death and it was only fitting that she walk upon something like this, a soup of bloody discharge squirting up between her toes and coiled entrails petal-soft beneath her feet.

As she stepped lightly over the spongy, putrefying remains, she smiled down at reaching disarticulated limbs and decapitated heads. An eyeball with a length of veal-pink optic nerve pushed up between her toes, watching her. This was her moment. Her nipples erect, a lascivious grin on her blood-spattered features, she dropped to her knees, fingering her labia with pure, shuddering orgasmic joy.

When she came, she fell down amongst them, feeling countless bluing faces appraising her, bodies pressing hungrily against her own, countless hands embracing her. It was how a goddess should be adored. The head of a lovely blonde woman watched her and Maddie squealed with delight—it was News Team 4 anchor Erika McCauley. Maddie secretly crushed on Erika, even though Erika continually rode herd on her and the DHS, calling them on more than one occasion the American Gestapo. Now here she was.

*In the end, you worship at my feet, darling.*

Maddie, still tripping her brains out, clutched Erika's head in her hands, petting her lovely golden locks and pressing her bee-stung lips first to one breast and then to another. Glistening claret dripped from Erika's ears and one nostril.

There was something sexually exciting about this. Erika's hair knotted in her hand, Maddie began to kiss her exquisite face. The perfect jawline, the perky nose, the high cheekbones and crystal blue eyes. Shuddering, she forced her tongue into Erika's mouth, bucking with orgasm as she did so, her tongue penetrating deeper and deeper into the moist, velvety confines. Erika's tongue was cool and rubbery, but that only made it all that much more exciting.

Together they rolled through the mushy, sloshing depths of the corpse sea, Maddie's blood-greased weight forcing tongues from mouths and viscera from gashed-open bellies. She particularly liked being licked by the tongues and she was certain that Erika moaned, too. They swam through the carrion depths, twisting and turning, sliding free and surfacing from the human jelly, gasping for air.

All that meat, all that blood.

Erika whispered something to her and Maddie grinned ghoulishly. She was hungry. In fact, she didn't think she'd ever been hungrier.

They had all sacrificed themselves to her so that she might feast and fill herself with them. Like a shark in an ocean of bloody human chum, Maddie began to feed. The flesh of her worshippers was butter-soft, it was sweet and delicate in flavor. Her face splashed with blood red as burgundy, she began to greedily gnaw upon the corpses she was nearly buried in. She sought ruptured heads so that she could dip her fingers into the shattered fondue pots of their skulls, licking wet brain pulp from her fingertips that had the consistency of over-ripened fruit.

Now that the sun was rising, its warm rays were making the corpses bloat and fizz and steam with flies. Maddie continued to eat—licking, sucking, chewing, and swallowing. It did not seem like she could ever be full.

Unbeknownst to her, she had picked up a significant other that now resided in her belly and it could never, ever be satisfied. As she stuffed herself, Erika grinned down upon her from her perch atop a litter pile of the dead.

Maddie was the Goddess of Death and she had trained for it her entire life.

# CHICAGO, WEST MONTROSE AVENUE

## RAVENSWOOD

**6:40 A.M.**

Harry had called Gabe's number again and again throughout the night, trying to reach Shawna. She was out there somewhere and she was free. He knew that much now and it made his heart practically tap-dance with delight in his chest. She was hiding at Gabe's. Somehow, she had made her way back there. If it hadn't been for damn martial law, he would have went over there and found her.

And now, that's exactly what he was going to do.

He picked up his phone. One last try.

The phone was picked up on the second ring. "Harry?"

"Who else were you expecting?"

She giggled with a tinny, high-pitched sound. The sound of jangled nerves. "I'm so glad you called. Did your landlady tell you I stopped by?"

"Yes. I thought... I thought I'd never see you again."

"I'm sneaky," she said. "You learn that when you cat around with married men."

"I'm coming over. I have to see you. We need to talk. We have to get out of the city. I know a place we can lay low until the country gets back on its feet."

"No. Don't come here. I think I'm being watched. Meet me at Ping Tom at 10:30. The Fieldhouse."

Ping Tom again. He saw a connection, but he refused to consider it. "Okay."

She broke the connection. He was overjoyed and yet somehow disturbed. There was something different about her voice that he just couldn't place.

# THE WHITE HOUSE

## PENNSYLVANIA AVENUE

**7:07 A.M.**

The chopper was going down.

There was no doubt of it now. As it approached the White House, making for the helipad on the South Lawn, it was strafed by ground fire from not one but at least three different locations. The FBI Blackhawk pilot was an ex-Marine who had flown his Super Cobra into one shitstorm after another in Afghanistan and he was utterly fearless.

"A little ground flak," he said over the headset. "Nothing to worry about. We barely even felt it."

He seemed to be enjoying himself and then something big hit them, swatting the chopper like a fly. There was a tremendous, concussive explosion that tossed both Sleshing and VanderMissen in their seats. The cabin filled with smoke and heat. Fire was gushing outside the fuselage.

"What the hell is going on?" VanderMissen shouted over the headset as the chopper rocked back and forth.

"We're hit!" the pilot said. "Goddamn missile!'

"Set us down!"

Which the pilot was trying frantically to do, but the Blackhawk was not responding. It was banking to the left, nose dipping down, flying erratically like a wounded insect. The HRT members began to cry out because they knew what was coming next. The chopper skipped on the pavement, jumped up, glanced off a parked car, then came down again, flipping over.

Sleshing came to with a terrible pain in his arm, fighting with his harness. By luck or pluck, it released and he tumbled against a bulkhead. The cabin was filled with smoke and flames. He sought a square of brightness and crawled out of the cockpit, falling to the pavement.

"CHUCK!" he called, cradling his broken arm. "CHUCK!"

VanderMissen did not reply.

And then, even if he was alive but unconscious, it didn't really matter because the Blackhawk was engulfed in flames. A great whooshing fireball rolled into the sky, sucking the wind out of Sleshing's lungs and knocking him on his ass.

Like a dying animal he crawled away from the inferno, dragging himself ever forward. After a time, he collapsed. Maybe he blacked out again, because when he opened his eyes the chopper was burning in the distance. The White House was still a block away. But if he could get to his feet, he just might make it.

Using a street post for support, he pulled himself up. He was alone. God-damn alone in this fucking warzone. His arm was broken, his face burned, his back wrenched out of shape. And his left eye wouldn't quit filling with tears. He spit blood from his mouth and hobbled forward.

But into what?

What he saw all around him was not a warzone but a hell zone. Here in the capitol of the United States was absolute devastation. Buildings were burning, some having fallen right into the street. The blackened, mangled carcasses of cars, trucks, and military vehicles were scattered about, still smoldering from the night's combat. There were huge, blasted potholes in the streets. And bodies. God, they were cast in every direction, many cremated right down to skeletons. Others dismembered and sheared in half as if they'd been snipped by a giant pair of scissors. The smell of roasted flesh and spilled blood was positively nauseating.

Sleshing hobbled forward, grimacing with pain, breathing hard. The wreckage of civilization around him reminded him of one of those Goya painting he'd had to study in college, the Black Paintings, as they were known.

The closer he got to the White House, the more bodies were in the streets, hundreds now. In the distance, he saw a mad woman leaping and bounding amongst them, swinging a severed head by the hair.

The entire city was infested.

# RICHMOND, VIRGINIA

## CBT CORPORATE HEADQUARTERS

**8:12 A.M.**

It was the Washington *Post* that broke the story and within minutes, it seemed, it was all over the newswires and Internet, being disseminated worldwide at lightning speed. The puppet masters of martial law didn't dare try to censor or suppress the story in any way—it was too hot. They didn't dare touch it. Elizabeth Toma's phone began ringing immediately, of course, but she didn't bother answering it. Let them all crawl in the shit they had produced.

"It appears our Mr. Niles does not fuck around," she said under her breath. "He plays for keeps."

Good and good. This was exactly what she wanted. Gordon Parks was probably hiding under his desk. Bob Pershing and his conspirators were pointing fingers at each other. And The Collective...ah yes, The Collective had been exposed and if she had not lost her talent for spookery and subterfuge, then all trails would lead back to the NSA, painting poor, silly, stupid, under-handed Gordy Parks in a very ugly light.

"You see, Astrid? Karma. Everything is cyclical."

# FORT MEADE, MARYLAND

## NATIONAL SECURITY AGENCY

**8:27 A.M.**

So they were going to have themselves an old-fashioned lynching, were they? Gordon Parks giggled at the very idea. They did not understand that it was simply too late.

He hadn't come this far to stop now.

The Collective were trying to contact him. A Congressional investigation was in the offing. And all this as D.C. burned and the President lost his mind and the country reeled from insurrection and a parasitic outbreak that got worse by the day. And in the midst of this, the media were having him for lunch.

*Guess again, shitheads.*

*Guess again.*

He checked his watch. It was nearly time and nothing, absolutely nothing could stop him now.

*Tick, tick, tick.*

# THE WHITE HOUSE

## PENNSYLVANIA AVENUE

**8:45 A.M.**

Maddie Hughes—former DHS Secretary who swung her big balls with the best of them on the hill, and current death goddess—found that she (and her friend, Erika, the rotting head) was sinking deep into the maggoty carcass of the accumulated dead. Where before she saw them as individuals, she now knew the corpse field had become one seething mass of carrion. A putrescent beast, a graveyard whole made of hundreds of cadavers melting into one another, assimilated by the creature that was in fact a great creeping death entity.

And she was trapped in it.

As she drowned, she listened to the music of the flies, the buzzing, droning storm that covered her face, enveloped the dead around her and under her and became the melody of her personal dirge.

Where before she saw herself as the ruler of them all, now she was simply part of the beast, another wriggling vermicular shape that had communed with it. They were all moving now, and she was moving with them, inching along on her belly, dragging atrophied limbs behind her, joined to the others, welded to them, intertwined with them into a great slimy, sinuous mass. A monstrous writhing horror woven together from hundreds of pulsating, coiling worm people. Their eyes were red translucent bulbs running with pink sap, their mouths ejecting a foam of yellow vomit. Their voices squealed and shrieked. Their bodies slithered. Swollen licking tongues pushed out from puckered mouths along with snaking white flatworms whose pregnant segments palpitated with gray, snot-webbed ova.

Together, they had a purpose.

And a destination: the White House.

# LANGLEY, VIRGINIA

## CIA CRISIS CENTER

**9:39 A.M.**

DCI Pershing scowled.

*How dare they,* he thought. *How dare they conspire above and beyond me.*

Now that the chain of command had been decimated right down to the Treasury Secretary (whom he owned), he should have been a happy man. But he was not. And it wasn't just that the President was still alive—hopelessly goddamned insane—because that had been planned, too. No, according to what he read in the *Post*, there were accusations that Gordon Parks was involved in a high-scale black budget operation known as MINDWORM, which—if it was true—was the apex conspiracy theory of all time.

*It's no theory, goddammit. It has something to do with that fucking ECHO array up in Alaska. Maybe the article didn't name it specifically, but that's what this is about.*

And apparently Parks had been scheming with The Collective, if they did in fact exist.

"Shit," Pershing said. "And all this right under my fucking nose and right on my watch."

Okay, okay, he would not panic. He could spin this, too. The problem was that he was implicated in the coup. He was named in the article.

*And how am I going to fix that?*

But, of course, he knew. Gordon Parks. He was the scapegoat, he was the sacrificial lamb. The country in general didn't really trust the CIA, but they trusted them a hell of a lot more than they trusted the NSA, particularly following the Snowden revelations (politically motivated or not). Now old Gordy was involved in an insidious mind control plot? Tsk, tsk. Obviously (at least the way Pershing was going to spin it) was that old Gordy was in collusion with not only foreign extremists but with an ultra-powerful shadow group known as The Collective. Together they had hatched a plot with the blessing of certain unscrupulous industrialists, politicos, and high-ranking military personnel to take over the country. They had created a doomsday scenario with the genetically altered parasites and taken advantage of the chaos by systematically dispatching the nation's chain of command and were poised to activate a national mind control weapon that would make free will a thing of the past. It was all part of Gordy's insane lust for power and the institution of a New World Order.

Excellent.

He typed it up and sent it to Matt Connelly, his deputy director, for immediate disbursement. Thrust, counter-thrust. With martial law in effect, the *Post's* story would be yanked immediately and they might even be charged with treason...that was, if anyone dared.

No matter, it was out on the Internet now. There was no stopping it.

Let the bullshit fly.

Pershing studied the pile of reports on his desk. Chaos and trouble. Nothing but.

According to the latest CDC estimates, over seventy percent of the country was infected by the worms or would be by the end of the week. Millions were dead and dying. Hospitals were overloaded, most at quarantine stage. It was end times and the religious kooks out there were having a field day.

*Enjoy yourself, my friends. Spread your manure far and wide.*

Another disturbing little pearl had just come in an hour ago. The military was in a state of emergency due to parasite outbreaks. There were mass desertions across the country. National Guard units were abandoning their posts as their families fell ill, deciding that they were needed more on the home front than patrolling cities that were on their last legs.

Oh yes, it was certainly time for a change in leadership, particularly now that the President was completely mad, tripping his brains out on a military-grade classified psychotropic. It would be days before he came out of it and when he did, it would be a whole new world out there.

First things first.

He got Connelly on his sat phone. "Two things need to be handled immediately," he said. "First off, our NSA friend needs a long vacation and secondly, we need to find out about that ECHO array."

"First has already been arranged. I'll get on the second right now."

There. He could still make this work. *God, yes, I can. I will rule. In the end, only I will rule. Only I can drag the carcass of the Union from the ashes and breathe life into it.* Feeling somewhat better, he thumbed the intercom. He would have his secretary bring him a coffee. That would go down well.

There was no response.

"Doris! I need you," he called.

Nothing.

He tried the other secretaries. Still nothing. Dammit. What was going on? Frustrated, he thumbed the buttons for the office of the Associate Deputy Director. Nothing. The Chief of Staff. Nothing. General Counsel. Public Affairs. Inspector General. Operations Center. Foreign Intel. Nothing, nothing, and nothing.

*I can't be alone. That's not possible.*

Panicking, he raced to the door and threw it open...and screamed.

What stood there was a man... yet, it was not a man but a gory, crawling thing, a catastrophic anatomical meltdown that looked like a man that had been turned inside out, a nameless cosmic afterbirth threaded by dozens and dozens of long, creeping worms. It rippled and gushed and coiled, spilling blood and serum and seeping drainage to the floor. It reached out for him with a rawboned hand. And its face, like the pulp of crushed tomatoes, was infested with wriggling spawn, a seething, pulsating wormy yarn ball. Where its eyes should have been, bloated worms with sucking black mouths jutted forth like eyestalks.

But despite all that, as uber-spook DCI Robert Pershing felt his bowels let go and hot shit run down his legs, he knew it was Tommy Quillan.

"The President is expecting us," the horror said.

# CHICAGO, CHINATOWN

## PING TOM MEMORIAL PARK

**10:33 A.M.**

"Hello, Harry."

He turned and she was there, Shawna was right there, and his heart began to race because he had really, honestly, and painfully thought he would never see her again. It was like waking from some awful nightmare or coming out of a prolonged fever.

"My God," he said, "it's really you."

"Yes."

He scooped her into his arms, and she hugged him back. He kissed her mouth, and it was cold. That was the first thing he thought. Her mouth was cold, but her body felt very hot. He wasn't fool enough to believe that it had anything to do with any passion for him... this was something else. She was burning as if she had a terrible fever. He could only think of one thing that could cause it and it made him pull back in horror.

"Are you all right?"

"Of course, I'm all right."

He reached up a hand and pressed it against her brow. "You feel warm," he said, narrowing his eyes. "I mean, really warm."

"I've been running, Harry. I thought someone was after me, so I ran. It was probably just my paranoia." She smiled. "I'm pretty sure I don't have the worm."

"That's good."

"You don't sound relieved at all." She offered him a little girl pout. "And here I was hoping we could slip off into the bushes for a quickie."

That made him smile. At least momentarily. *She said that because she thought that's what I wanted to hear. She's trying to distract me from something else.* He stood there, staring at her, suspicious as hell. He should have been overjoyed to be with her... but he wasn't. Was he losing his mind, or did there seem to be something almost synthetic about her? Contrived? He shook his head. That was ridiculous. This was Shawna... and yet some part of him thought it wasn't Shawna at all.

He took her by the hand and led her over to a bench in the distance. It wasn't a matter of being alone. Today, there was no one in the park. A relaxing day of fun and sun was the farthest thing from anyone's mind.

"So, tell me what happened," he said to her, releasing her hand which, like the rest of her, was too warm, too...something.

She blinked three times, then smiled thinly. "Oh, it was a real mess, Harry. A guy named Stein rescued me from the mall. He was a killer, an assassin. He killed two of the goons that came for me and beat the hell out of the other one. I've never seen anything like it in my life. He took me to a house. He said it was a safe house. He told me about something called S5, which were part of the CIA or something."

"What happened to him?"

She sighed, rubbing her eyes. "He was killed. Some guy dressed as a pizza guy came to the front door and shot him down."

"And you?"

She blinked her eyes three times again. "I ran. I've been running since. I finally made it to Gabe's. But he's not there. I don't know where he is."

"So you've been hiding?"

"Yes."

She blinked her eyes again three times and it did not go unnoticed. There was something very off about her, but he honestly couldn't put his finger on what exactly it was. It was as if she was being imitated and the imitation was nearly perfect...but not completely. Her mannerisms weren't quite right. That strange blinking. Even her voice sounded off-timbre, her eyes glassy.

"Are you sure you're okay?" he asked.

For a moment there, something softened around her mouth and she trembled. Her eyes got watery. She nodded slowly. "I'm fine, really I am." Her voice lost that odd mechanical cadence. "I'm okay."

He held her, but she did not conform herself properly to him. Her body seemed nearly artificial as if he were hugging a mannequin. It sent a chill up his spine.

She pulled herself away. "I'm perfectly fine now that I've found you."

She smiled, but he didn't like it. It was a crooked smile, the left side of her mouth pulling up higher than the right. Shawna did not smile like that—like an old lady with a terrible secret. Her eyes seemed to go out of focus.

"Shawna? I want you to think and tell me what happened. Did they do something to you?"

She blinked her eyes three times again. "I ran. I've been running since. I finally made it to Gabe's. But he's not there. I don't know where he is," she said.

*Same words. Same exact intonation. They did something to her. Probably the same thing the Old Man was going to do to you if they hadn't gotten you out of the Warehouse.*

"Well, I'm just glad you're okay."

She stared into space. "What should we do?"

He stood up and took her by the hand, something he was not completely comfortable with. "We're going to a place where we can stop running. A place where we can rest and relax."

"Oh, I'd like that. It sounds nice."

She didn't even ask where that was. Yes, they had done something to her. She was traumatized at a very deep level. Whatever it was, it was bound to come out. And that's what scared him.

# WASHINGTON D.C.

## THE PIEDMONT BUILDING

**11:07 A.M.**

Of course they kept her waiting; Elizabeth expected that much. She was about to meet possibly the most powerful group of people in the world, the engineers of the New World Order. They controlled industries and politicians and world events. They were the puppet masters and there was not a single event of political or economic significance that they did not have their hand in. What was another trifling appointment to them?

*And never forget for one moment, Astrid,* she thought, *that they are probably not too happy with me. I forced this meeting and that will not go unpunished, my darling.*

Patiently, she waited, sipping her Kopi Luwak, exuding a regal poise in her ruby-red Victoria Beckham power dress. None of the suits and flunkies that passed through the lobby of the exclusive penthouse offices of Exceptional Futures, Ltd. would have suspected for a moment the hot, bubbling cauldron she was on the inside, the seam of pure hate running through her veins, or the need for vengeance that beat in her black heart.

No, she was calm, composed, a woman of substance and power. She often surprised even herself that the hotter her emotions ran beneath the surface, the cooler her exterior was. She had disarmed countless enemies with it. But today there would be no games. The playing field would be leveled—predator against predator.

"Ms. Toma? Mr. Brown will see you now."

Elizabeth swallowed, smiled slightly, her belly filled with a swarm of butterflies. *You are a soldier going into battle. Never forget that. Never weaken in your resolve.* She followed the well-dressed secretary down the corridor. My God, it was business as usual at Exceptional Futures, Ltd. (you had to love the name of their cover organization). You wouldn't have thought that the country was crashing on all fronts and the city was in chaos. But then, what was there to worry about when you already knew the outcome?

She was brought into a marvelous oak-paneled conference room with a massive cherry boardroom table. A distinguished man in a charcoal-gray suit that matched his watery eyes waited for her. No one had to tell her this was the mysterious Mr. Brown. His white hair was combed straight back from his forehead like Count Dracula.

*How fitting with the amount of blood he's sucked*, she thought.

"Ah, fair Elizabeth, we meet at last."

His handshake was limp and oily. He grinned with beautifully white teeth, a piranha in a business suit, his appetite for human flesh barely kept at bay.

He motioned to the others at the table. "This is Mr. White, Ms. Smith, Mr. Cho, Mr. Daniels, and Mr. Constadine."

They were quite a group. Mr. White had the pallor of a drowned man. Ms. Smith was dangerously cadaverous as if she might crumble to dust in direct sunlight. Mr. Cho's sniping dark eyes made you feel weak in the knee. Mr. Daniels, an African-American, had the long narrow teeth of a rodent. And Mr. Constadine had a widow's peak and thin black mustache that made him look like a comic book Satan.

"Pleased to meet each of you," Elizabeth said, with all due respect to their positions and power.

She sat down. Mr. Brown stared at her with dead eyes. She stared back with great intensity.

"Let's put our cards on the table, shall we?" he said. "I promised you full disclosure and that's what you shall have."

"I could ask for no more."

Ms. Smith said, "I am much-admiring your beautiful jade necklace. It's exquisite."

"Thank you. It's Cartier."

"Marvelous," said Mr. Constadine. "Absolutely marvelous."

Elizabeth smiled. It was definitely a one-of-a-kind piece. A large jadeite broach surrounded by smaller jade beads, all of a brilliant emerald color that instantly caught the eye. It was mounted in platinum, set with cut rubies and baguette diamonds. She touched it briefly, left it there outside her dress for them to admire.

"Now to business, Elizabeth," said Mr. Brown, dispensing with trivialities. "First off, might I say that was an excellent stratagem sending the details of our agenda to Charles VanderMissen and Harry Niles. Brilliant. The trail led perfectly to Gordon Parks. Outstanding work. I commend your subterfuge. Now the news has been disseminated to the four corners of the world. And our good Mr. Pershing, never one to miss exploiting an opportunity, has launched a propaganda blitz further discrediting the NSA."

Elizabeth smiled. "I'm glad you found it entertaining. Gordon Parks is and will always be an impotent little fool."

Mr. Brown raised an eyebrow. Perhaps he was expecting an apology or at the very least, a denial. It was clear that he had underestimated her. She was a woman who knew exactly what she was doing.

"True, very true, Elizabeth," he said, his eyes darkening. "But he was our fool to play and not yours."

"I see."

"Which brings us to our dilemma," said Mr. Cho.

Mr. Brown sighed. "What you did was reckless, Elizabeth. You've caused us great trouble and have possibly caused irreparable harm to the agenda. And we cannot tolerate that in any form. I think you understand that."

"I understand a great many things I didn't a week ago," was all she would say.

Several of The Collective muttered amongst themselves. This was endgame. Mr. Brown had her up against the wall and now he would deliver the death blow. They were all waiting for it. By God, they looked hungry for it as if they got off on things like this.

*Here it comes, Astrid. Stay tuned.*

"I've personally spent a lot of time cultivating you, Elizabeth. Guiding you, forming you into the executive you are today. We had high hopes for you. Ultimately, we saw you sitting at this table."

"Which is why you ran MINDWORM through Gordon Parks and not me?"

That was a slap in the face and Mr. Brown grimaced. He was a typical CEO in that he was not used to being told the truth. He was accustomed to being addressed with great fawning deference, having people tell him what he wanted to hear (which was usually something he'd already told them; like all supposedly great men, he liked to hear his subordinates propagating his ideas).

"I don't find your attitude at all becoming, Elizabeth. I dislike confrontational personalities."

She said nothing, even though she was raging under the skin. He was a pompous bag of hot air like all men in power. He wasn't used to people like her.

*I am the pin that will pop your ego and bleed the air from it.*

"I was hoping this meeting would go far differently," he said.

She shook her head. "Somehow, I doubt that, Mr. Brown. I'm willing to bet you had this planned out the same way you plan everything out. You consult your collection of toads here, but ultimately the decision is yours and being the meticulous creature you are, the result is a given. You don't like chance or coincidence. That's for the herds, isn't it? The human population out there whom you crush, contain, and kill depending on your whims?"

"I won't be talked to like that!" he snapped.

The Collective cringed. It was not a good idea to anger Mr. Brown. One word from him and the rich became poor, dynasties crumbled, and politicians were ruined.

*He'll play his hand out now, Astrid. He'll finally pull his thumb out of his ass and get to it.*

Offering her a sneering grin, he reached under the table and produced an aluminum case. He unsnapped it carefully and removed a vacuum-sealed jar from within. He set the jar on the table along with a forceps. There was a worm in the jar.

"Your future looks bleak, Elizabeth. I wish there was another way, but you've forced my hand." He slid the jar over to her. "Take the worm as punishment for your interference and insolence. That is not a request."

Did he expect her to beg for her life? If so, he was disappointed. Nothing he said or did was unexpected. She knew exactly what she was coming into and had prepared herself accordingly.

She shook her head. "I have to admit that the ultimate goal of MIND-WORM is lost on me. You'll have an entire country and, soon enough, an entire world parasitized. What good will that do you? How does that advance the agenda?"

Mr. Brown smiled. "Well, the worms will reduce the herds to what they should be—mindless drones. Once ECHO is activated, we will have a population of consumers and workers whose overriding desire will be to keep the wheels of industry spinning. Imagine what we can achieve once we're all on the same page!"

"It's doomed to failure."

"Why?"

"The human animal must have something to struggle against. Any second-year psych student could have told you that."

"Something other than himself, eh? No matter. Selective programming will take care of that. The herds will be servile and productive. And those few of us immune to the parasites, via a certain medication, will be their masters. We will think for them, make choices for them, control their destiny for the common good. Once they have a worm in them, Elizabeth, the ECHO technology can control them completely."

"I see."

He tittered. "Do you really, Elizabeth?"

She picked up the jar. "Ah, one of your children, Mr. Brown. How it resembles its father. Equally as soft and spineless." She looked over at him, fixing him with her dark eyes. She tucked her jade necklace into her dress where it rested between her breasts, making full contact with her skin. Already it was growing warm from her body heat.

"Do you remember Astrid, Mr. Brown?"

He looked at her first blankly, then with undisguised contempt. He said nothing.

Elizabeth looked at the others. "Astrid was Astrid Austin. She worked for the CDC. She was my best friend and lover. Mr. Brown did not care for our relationship, so he had her murdered. He probably doesn't remember because

I'm sure he's murdered thousands since like a good little sociopath, but I remember." She was glaring at him now. "I'll never fucking forget what you did to her, you worthless piece of shit."

"Enough!" he said. "There is your choice. The worm or you'll skydive off the roof. Choose. If you don't swallow the worm, you will not leave these offices alive."

Elizabeth could feel the necklace getting very hot between her breasts, almost painfully so now as if it was branding her. She could handle a few more moments of pain. "Oh, you silly, arrogant little twat—none of us will leave these offices alive."

She had their attention now, not that she lacked it. Mr. Brown stared at her with derision. The others looked frightened, but not him. He was a veteran game-player and he was obviously intrigued.

"Are you familiar with the process of co-crystallization, Mr. Brown? It's a concept from materials science wherein two materials are combined into a crystal architecture in order to create a single improved material," she explained. "It's something our people at CBT have taken an interest in for possible military applications. For example, the Army's standard explosive HMK can be combined with a new, much more powerful explosive called CL-20. This hybrid has the stability of the former with the awesome, devastating capabilities of the latter. It's a real breakthrough, as you can understand. This new crystalline material can be formed into just about anything...like a jade necklace for example."

Everyone, including Mr. Brown, stiffened. Their eyes were wide. They were eying the door and wondering how quickly they could get through it.

"Imagine that, eh?" Elizabeth said. "A necklace that is both beautiful and deadly. Equipped with a thermal trigger, it requires only body heat to activate it."

The necklace was burning now.

Mr. Brown waited for the punchline and when he didn't get it, he raced for the door with the others in tow. Elizabeth smiled. *We'll see them in hell, eh, Astrid?* By the time Mr. Brown got his hand on the doorknob, the necklace blazed between her breasts, scalding her. There was a rumbling and that was the last thing any of them heard as the fourteenth floor of the Piedmont Building was vaporized into a rolling mushroom cloud of fire and debris.

# CHICAGO, CHINATOWN

## PING TOM MEMORIAL PARK

**11:27 A.M.**

Harry worked it from every possible angle, but he still could not break through. Shawna seemed impervious. If she was indeed the victim of some sort of behavioral modification, then the control went deep. He didn't really think he'd be able to break her. She would need to be deprogrammed by professionals. Only that or some major trauma would snap her out of it.

But what might that be?

As they walked through the park, they chatted about what they were going to do next. Harry had a few plans and laid them out for her. Her responses seemed perfectly ordinary. She was happy to get out of the city, disturbed and frightened by what was happening to the country, and paranoid about the future. That was right, that was in line with rational, independent thinking.

But he wasn't satisfied.

Not in the least.

He kept working the subject back to what she had done when the pizza hit men had gotten Stein. And every time, she blinked her eyes three times and said, "I ran. I've been running since. I finally made it to Gabe's. But he's not there. I don't know where he is."

It made him scared for her. Scared because he was totally out of his league with this shit. If he could find the trigger, he might be able to switch her on and reveal her programming...and would that be a good thing or a bad thing?

About the fifth time he'd asked her the same question, something which should have annoyed the shit out of her, she suddenly stopped. She looked at him with glassy eyes. Then she reached into her purse and pulled out a slim book. *Green Eggs and Ham* by Dr. Seuss. She stared at the cover. She began to page through it with a silly little grin on her face.

She turned to him. "I need to do it before you tell," she said in an alarming monotone.

"Do what, Shawna? What are you supposed to do?"

"I have to do it before you tell."

He was getting the gist of it now and he began to sweat. "It's too late, Shawna. I already told. Everyone knows now. They know all about it."

That stopped her for a moment. Her eyes became very glazed and she said, "But you must not ever, never tell. Sam said so."

"Who's Sam, Shawna. Tell me who Sam is?"

"Sam-I-Am."

What the hell was this? Dr. Fucking Seuss? *Sam-I-Am, Sam-I-Am.* Was he hearing this right? The children's book was her trigger? But, sure, why not? They had pulled this out of her mind, out of her childhood. It must have meant a great deal to her, so they used this as the basis of her programming. It was the foundation and the trigger.

"That Sam-I-Am," she said. "That Sam-I-Am. He says you must not ever, never tell."

"Shawna..."

He knew what was coming next. He saw her reach in the bag and come out with the handgun. Then he grabbed her wrist and she screamed. On the ground, they fought for possession of the weapon as she shrieked like a madwoman, drooling and feral-eyed.

# FORT MEADE, MARYLAND

## NATIONAL SECURITY AGENCY

**11:43 A.M.**

They were coming for him and he knew it.

He did not know who to trust.

He did not know who to call.

Sitting at his desk, Gordon Parks tried to reach The Collective again and again, but there was nothing. Were they abandoning him now, too? Had they tossed him out into the cold to face the wrath of the country on his own? Would they dare?

But he knew.

Oh yes, he knew: they'd sacrifice him in a minute. The agenda was the thing, the careful engineering of the future—MINDWORM. That's all they cared about. How many times had they told them that nothing must stand in the way of the agenda?

Yes.

*Yes.*

And this could only be achieved through what was known as ECHO—Enhanced Cognitive High-Frequency Override. It was a miracle of cognitive science. Based upon research gleaned from MK-ULTRA and successive behavior modification programs, it was known that memory, consciousness, and self could be completely accessed and modified by electromagnetic means. Using remote tele-stimulation of the brain, existing personalities, drives, and desires could be erased and rewritten.

Which was the ultimate goal of ECHO.

First national, then global, control. The ultimate aim of The Collective right from the start.

Though it was whitewashed as an ionospheric heater for experimental communications, ECHO was in fact a binary electromagnetic weapons system, consisting of two highly classified experimental broadcasting arrays—one in Mexico and another in Alaska. Utilizing super-high frequency oscillations, its purpose was to create a neutral cavity between the ionosphere and the conducting layers of the Earth's surface, through which electrical impulses tuned to human brain wave frequencies could be broadcast for the purpose of mind control and mental disruption.

Once it went live, there would be no more resistance—the will of the few could be imposed on the many. Once programmed by ECHO, the human herds would not only accept it but actively seek it as a small child seeks its mother's approval.

Trembling, Parks knew he had to act now before the FBI came for him. Because they would come. It was only a matter of time.

He picked up his encrypted sat phone and called the number. It was preprogrammed. The line was answered immediately. Parks relayed the code words.

"Yes?" said the voice.

"Activate ECHO," he said, trying to sound calm. "Repeat: activate ECHO."

Which was his last command before the worms came for him, delivering him into a higher office.

# THE WHITE HOUSE

**11:51 A.M.**

Naked and deranged, the President of the United States crawled over the floor of the Oval Office, spasms making his entire body shudder with excruciating muscular convulsions. He vomited pale foam and curds of clotted blood.

*Inside*, he thought with rage and pure horror. *My enemies are not just outside looking in, but inside looking out. They are inside me, inside my guts, eating me from within, chewing and sucking and slavering...*

He went mad with the idea, rolling and quivering and kicking, tearing at his face and belly with his nails, trying to lay himself open, trying to make the evil within show itself, expose itself. He was an exorcist, and it was a demon possessing him. Blood ran from him. It oozed in droplets from his pores and spurted from open wounds, dripped from his mouth and even seeped from his ass.

*Oh, the monsters, the monsters, the monsters.*

He continued to convulse with jerking, spastic muscular contractions, screaming and spitting, hissing and shrieking like the lunatic he now was.

And then something began to happen.

He could feel it in his throat, something that made him gag and shudder and spit out loops of blood. It filled his throat, then his mouth. One last heave and it emerged—a coiling white worm. He pulled it free and threw it across the room where it wiggled obscenely, blind and helpless and essentially weak.

There was a pain down low in his abdomen and the President felt a marvelous sense of release. Another worm. This one hung from his ass and he pulled it out ring by juicy ring, first thinking it was his intestines, then realizing the gruesome truth. This one was much larger, nearly four feet in length. Like the other, it coiled and squirmed, a gelatinous slime exuding from its segments and running through his fingers like liquid soap.

He would destroy it.

He would crush it.

Let it know who the master was.

But at the last moment, he found that he could not. It threatened him in no way, it merely hung limp in his hands. It made an odd trilling sound as it vibrated subtly under his fingers, seeming to purr like a cat. Though something—some vague, as yet unsubmerged strand of humanity—in the back of his mind demanded that he kill the thing, smash it to paste...he found that he couldn't. It no longer stank of blood and waste. No, in fact it smelled sweetly. It smelled delicious. *Like honey*, the President thought. *Like Halloween treats. Like Christmas cookies and Easter baskets*. It brought with it the delight of childhood in those precious fragrances. It was moving now, sliding through his fingers and over his palm, its many segments juicing fatly with eggs.

This was not his enemy.

The President knew that.

No, this was his friend. The worm was a friend to all mankind if you thought about it in the right way. The worm could save the race from itself, open up new doors and close old ones, deliver humanity from itself and into a sparkling beautiful future where things like war and jealousy, hatred and discord were just bad dreams from the infancy of the race.

"You are good," the President said, holding the glistening worm up before his blood-spattered face, feeling sexually aroused from its continual phallic throbbing. "But together we are great."

Opening his mouth, he accepted the worm and was accepted by it.

# CHICAGO, CHINATOWN

## PING TOM MEMORIAL PARK

**12:15 P.M.**

*The sound, the sound, the sound, oh dear Christ, the sound—*

Harry and Shawna were no longer fighting for control of the gun. It was forgotten in the grass. They stared at each other with glassy, unseeing eyes, looking into each other and through each other.

A voice in the back of Harry's mind thought, *can you hear that? Can you? It's louder now, but you've heard it before...haven't you?*

Although his thoughts were scattering in his brain like rice at a wedding or, perhaps, dandelion fuzz blown by the four winds... he recognized the sound with some part of his reasoning mind which was failing rapidly now. *The humming.* It was so familiar, yet so exotic. But he knew, knew, that he had heard it before... at the very outer limit of audibility, it had always been there as a steady rumbling he could only hear in a silent room in the dead of night. Now it was gaining in strength until it filled his head with a building reverberation that became a cacophonous roaring... an irritating, delirious noise that made him want to scratch his skin off and gouge his eyes out. It was crawling over him in waves like millions of insects.

Shawna felt it, too. She was rocking back and forth in the grass, clutching her head, her eyes wide and wet, the pupils dilating and then shrinking to pinpoints, again and again and again.

Harry felt alone.

He felt not just afraid but terrified.

*This was not right... this was too loud...*

As the volume, at least his perception of it, increased, he stared up into the sky with gleaming eyes. My God, it was...*gigantic.* The sky was immense and endless, a titanic sea that was all of space and time, ever-widening, opening, becoming bluer than blue, a deep rich sapphire that was crystalline and geometrically complex, a world without end.

It was then as his mind began to empty, that he started to scream.

MINDWORM—NATIONWIDE

And all across the country, in cities and towns and villages, in fields and parks and streets and at crossroads, the infected stopped trying to spread their spawn and stuff raw meat into their mouths as something of a higher influence and complex order seized control of them with a stark, godless domination. Millions of them thronged and huddled together and looked up, up, and up into the sky that was bluer than blue, cerulean and sapphire and cobalt and blazing azure. They stared into it, transfixed by its immensity, hypnotized, compelled, and summoned by something much bigger than themselves. They looked up with translucent eyes as the worms within them answered the call of dominance that ECHO broadcast.

They were not human anymore.

They were not exactly worm forms.

They were a monstrous new hybrid that trembled beneath the electric indigo of the sky high above. They were a new generation that had just been born, a mass birthing of mindless drones and worker insects with no will of their own whose minds were hollow, empty...waiting, waiting to be filled. Millions and millions of mosquito larvae that had hatched simultaneously from the same black, stagnant pond to rise up into the mist, squirming grubs with no conception of their place in the order of things.

And slowly, subtly and with evil intent, the ECHO array instructed them on exactly what that was to be.

**12:17 P.M.**

At Ping Tom Park in Chicago, Shawna's carefully constructed conditioning eroded and collapsed and her psyche went with it. The intervention of ECHO rewrote who and what she was. In her mind, things crashed and shattered and were reduced to thousands of jagged tiny fragments that winked back the light of reason. She was aware that something was taking hold of her, some blind and hysterical compulsion that she could not deny.

"HAAAAAARRRRRYYYY!" she cried out with everything she had. "HARRY HELP ME OH HELP ME OH DEAR GOD HELP MEEEEEE!"

But he couldn't help her or make the booming noise in her mind just go away. He was stiff and fear-stricken, pure terror crawling in his eyes, reflecting his mind which was a cauldron of terror.

There was nothing left now.

With a lingering shred of free will, he knew it. This was MINDWORM. This was the absolute mindfuck, the mouse that roared, the thing from the pit, the house that Jack had built, and the horror bred by omnipotent men with too much money and too much power because it was never, ever enough—they always wanted more.

Now they were stealing the nation's minds, using ECHO technology to reduce the race to rats in a maze, shambling brain dead zombies, mindless drones serving the bloated, wicked queen of a corrupt and evil democracy—

With his last bit of strength, he picked up Shawna's gun as his mind ran inside his head like a runny finger-painting, dripping and mixing into a formless, colorless gray drainage.

She was face-down in the grass, shaking and sobbing as her mind was emptied.

*No, by God, I won't let you have her...I...will...not...allow...it...*

Trembling, he pressed the gun to the back of her head and jerked the trigger as something inside him screamed. By then, his ability to reason was gone. It was a light fading in the distance along with his life and any possibility of a free world of choice and intellect. The gun went in his mouth next.

Maybe he could no longer think, but his finger still knew how to pull the trigger.

And with what was coming, it was a blessing.

**12:21 P.M.**

At the White House, the human-worm mass flooded into the oval office, an undulating living carpet of wriggling bodies and coiling parasites, all knitted together, fused, welded into one, a squirming biological entity that flowed and oozed and rippled. A gurgling, hissing, steaming multiform profusion. Those parts of it which had once been human were naked and oily, contorting bonelessly, threaded like buttons by worms piercing their asses and hanging from their mouths, joining with other worms into a common whole of communal parasitism, an organic soup of flesh and worm and maggoty writhing.

The President—teeth chattering, sweating, and blood-slicked—watched this new horror enter his life. He stood there, numb and mindless, as the worm sea flooded forward and inundated him up to his hips. He should have gone stark raving mad, but since he was already there, there was nowhere to go but up.

*This...*

*This nightmare...*

*This abomination...*

*This grotesque aberration...*

*It has not come to eat me, but to seek my learned counsel...*

He spit. He stammered. Bile ran from his mouth. His own worm spiraled with great excitement inside him. *This*, it said to him without saying a word. *Yes, this, this, and this.*

The mass shivered around him, worms playing over his belly and hips. They were questing, greasy fingers that embraced him, imparting biochemical secretions into his skin where they were absorbed by ducts, translated by his own parasite which flooded him with pleasing, addicting endorphins which calmed him, pacified him, made him look out over the sea of worms and worm forms as he had once looked out over his constituents with a loving and just eye.

The entity seemed pleased. It throbbed and trembled, an immense sculpture of wriggling protoplasm formed into semi-human creeping appendages, crawling worms, millions of looping larva and gushing glossy eggs. It mewled and squeaked. It whispered with the tormented, enslaved voices of men, women, and children, and those mutant hybrid things that were all and neither.

The President grinned like the madman he was. "THIS IS EMERALD CITY," he cried, roared, and squealed as drool and an inky foulness ran from his mouth. "I AM OZ THE GREAT AND TERRIBLE...WHY DO YOU SEEK ME?"

The shivering, amorphous mass rippled, bubbled, then parted like the Red Sea to emit a great, evil, quivering mutation, a pulsating vermiculate monstrosity, a gigantic worm big around as a man's waist composed of swollen rings bursting with eggs and placental slime. And over its surface, melted into it and mingled with its own flabby tissue, was Maddie Hughes...or that which had once been Maddie Hughes. Her body was stretched over the worm like a hair shirt, overextended and elongated beyond the point of bursting, bones jutting in white staffs, anatomy knotted and disfigured. Her arms dangled as did her legs, still moving, still macabrely animate. Where her breasts should have been, there were five faces that he recognized—General Mason, chairman of the JCS, SecState Arlene Rabin, Bob Pershing of the CIA, Walt Sleshing of the DIA, and Gordon Parks of the NSA—pulled like taffy into exaggerated fright masks with gaping eye holes and yawning black mouths.

The President recognized his advisors, of course. Here, in this final hour, they had returned to him.

At the top of the worm, was Maddie's head. Like the others, her face was a rubber mask stretched out of proportion into a ghoulish visage that still lived, emoted, and breathed. Huge yellow eyes hot as neon rolled in their sockets, a distended slime-dripping worm licked her lips like a tongue, and a vast blubbery mouth spoke to him. *"We are here to serve thee, oh Great and Powerful Oz... tell us what it is you command..."*

So, the President told them about that most secret of secrets, the most highly guarded weapons system in the country that President after President mothered over like an egg they never, ever wanted to hatch. It was called the

Apex Ultimatum. It was the ultimate doomsday weapon that was so terrible no one dared even whisper its name. A linked system of experimental fusion weapons that were to be activated only if the country was overrun by invaders, held by the enemy in a death grip.

He only needed the codes to activate it.

But, of course, he knew them... the head of Gordon Parks whispered them to him because as the tribal chief of the NSA, he was the nation's ears and he heard everything. There was nothing his people had not tapped into, even the most classified codes in the country.

One by one, the President of the United States entered the codes and just before he fed in the last one, he went live coast to coast via satellite feed.

Suspended before the camera by a great viscid, undulatory worm, licked by the corkscrewing umbilicals of thousands of others, a gurgling worm puppet, he had one last message for the country:

"I AM ALPHA AND OMEGA! I AM THE BEGINNING AND THE END! I... I... I AM THE MAKER AND UNMAKER! CREATOR AND DESTROYER! I AM OZ THE GREAT AND TERRIBLE! AND I WILL SCATTER YOUR FLESH UPON THE MOUNTAINS AND FILL THE VALLEYS WITH YOUR HEAPED CORPSES AND THEIR WORMS! I WILL DROWN THE WORLD IN BLOOD AND PURIFY ITS SMOL-DERING BONES. NOW I AM BECOME DEATH THE DESTROYER OF WORLDS—"

And in went the final code.

And the sky turned to blood.

And the air became a yellow toxic haze.

And the sun became a burning red skull.

And the cities of men became graveyards blown by radioactive dust and a blazing, kiln-hot wind of crematory ash settled over them with an eternal darkness.

*In the end, the worm conquered all.*

# About the Author

Tim Curran is the author of *Skin Medicine, Hive, Dead Sea, The Devil Next Door, Blooding Night, Clownflesh,* and *Bad Girl in the Box,* among others. His short stories have been collected in *Alien Horrors, The Horrors of War,* and *The Brain Leeches.* His novellas include *The Underdwelling, The Corpse King, Puppet Graveyard, Worm,* and *The Sunken City.* His fiction has been translated into German, Russian, Japanese, Spanish, and Italian. Find him at facebook.com/tim.curran.77.

# THE END?

**Not if you want to dive into more of Crystal Lake Publishing's Tales from the Darkest Depths!**

Check out our amazing website and online store or download our latest catalog here.
https://geni.us/CLPCatalog

We always have great new projects and content on the website to dive into, as well as a newsletter, behind the scenes options, social media platforms, our own dark fiction shared-world series and our very own webstore. Our webstore even has categories specifically for KU books, non-fiction, anthologies, and of course more novels and novellas.

Readers...

Thank you for reading *Bioterror*.
We hope you enjoyed this novel.

If you have a moment, please review *Bioterror*
at the store where you bought it.

Help other readers by telling them why you enjoyed this book. No need to write an in-depth discussion. Even a single sentence will be greatly appreciated. Reviews go a long way to helping a book sell, and is great for an author's career. It'll also help us to continue publishing quality books.

Thank you again for taking the time to journey with Crystal Lake Publishing.

You will find links to all our social media platforms on our Linktree page.
https://linktr.ee/CrystalLakePublishing

Follow us on Amazon:

# MISSION STATEMENT

Since its founding in August 2012, Crystal Lake has quickly become one of the world's leading publishers of Dark Fiction and Horror books. In 2023, Crystal Lake officially transitioned into an entertainment company, joining several other divisions, genres, and imprints, including Torrid Waters, Crystal Lake Comics, Crystal Lake Games, Crystal Lake Kids, and many more.

While we strive to present only the highest quality fiction and entertainment, we also endeavour to support authors along their writing journey. We offer our time and experience in non-fiction projects, as well as author mentoring and services, at competitive prices.

With several Bram Stoker Award wins and many other wins and nominations (including the HWA's Specialty Press Award), Crystal Lake Publishing puts integrity, honor, and respect at the forefront of our publishing operations.

We strive for each book and outreach program we spearhead to not only entertain and touch or comment on issues that affect our readers, but also to strengthen and support the Dark Fiction field and its authors.

Not only do we find and publish authors we believe are destined for greatness, but we strive to work with men and women who endeavour to be decent human beings who care more for others than themselves, while still being hard working, driven, and passionate artists and storytellers.

Crystal Lake Publishing is and will always be a beacon of what passion and dedication, combined with overwhelming teamwork and respect, can accomplish. We endeavour to know each and every one of our readers, while building personal relationships with our authors, reviewers, bloggers, podcasters, bookstores, and libraries.

We will be as trustworthy, forthright, and transparent as any business can be, while also keeping most of the headaches away from our authors, since it's our job to solve the problems so they can stay in a creative mind. Which of course also means paying our authors.

We do not just publish books, we present to you worlds within your world, doors within your mind, from talented authors who sacrifice so much for a moment of your time.

There are some amazing small presses out there, and through collaboration and open forums we will continue to support other presses in the goal of helping authors and showing the world what quality small presses are capable of accomplishing. No one wins when a small press goes down, so we will always be there to support hardworking, legitimate presses and their authors. We don't see Crystal Lake as the best press out there, but we will always strive to be the best, strive to be the most interactive and grateful, and even blessed press around. No matter what happens over time, we will also take our mission very seriously while appreciating where we are and enjoying the journey.

What do we offer our authors that they can't do for themselves through self-publishing?

We are big supporters of self-publishing (especially hybrid publishing), if done with care, patience, and planning. However, not every author has the time or inclination to do market research, advertise, and set up book launch strategies. Although a lot of authors are successful in doing it all, strong small presses will always be there for the authors who just want to do what they do best: write.

What we offer is experience, industry knowledge, contacts and trust built up over years. And due to our strong brand and trusting fanbase, every Crystal Lake Publishing book comes with weight of respect. In time our fans begin to trust our judgment and will try a new author purely based on our support of said author.

With each launch we strive to fine-tune our approach, learn from our mistakes, and increase our reach. We continue to assure our authors that we're here for them and that we'll carry the weight of the launch and dealing with third parties while they focus on their strengths—be it writing, interviews, blogs, signings, etc.

We also offer several mentoring packages to authors that include knowledge and skills they can use in both traditional and self-publishing endeavours.

We look forward to launching many new careers.

This is what we believe in. What we stand for. This will be our legacy.

Welcome to Crystal Lake Publishing—Where Stories Come Alive!

www.ingramcontent.com/pod-product-compliance
Lightning Source LLC
Chambersburg PA
CBHW070400310726
48977CB00003B/504